PEKING

Books by Anthony Grey

PEKING

ANTHONY GREY

A Novel of China's Revolution
1921—1978

Little, Brown and Company
Boston   Toronto

FIRST U.S. EDITION

Except for any known historical figures and events, the characters and occurrences in this book are fictitious. Any similiarity to real persons, living or dead, is coincidental and not intended by the author.

The epigraph from *Doctor Zhivago*, by Boris Pasternak, translated by Max Hayward and Manya Harari, is reprinted by permission of Pantheon Books, a division of Random House, Inc. Copyright © 1957 by Giangiacomo Feltrinelli Editore, Milano, Italy; © 1958 in the English translation by Wm. Collins Sons and Co., Ltd., London, and Pantheon Books Inc., New York, NY.

Library of Congress Cataloging-in-Publication Data
Grey, Anthony.
    Peking: a novel of China's revolution, 1921-1978 / Anthony Grey.
    — 1st U.S. ed.
        p. cm.
    ISBN 0-316-32823-5
    1. China — History — 20th century — Fiction.   I. Title.
PR6057.R454P45 1988
823'.914 — dc19   88-565
                                                                            CIP

                    10 9 8 7 6 5 4 3 2 1

                                FG

                Published simultaneously in Canada
                by Little, Brown & Company (Canada) Limited

            PRINTED IN THE UNITED STATES OF AMERICA

Dedicated
with the greatest admiration
to

Alfred Bosshardt,

a true hero of our times,
who marched 2,500 miles as a prisoner
of China's Red Army in the 1930s
and survived through courage and faith that echo down the
years into the present

Art always serves beauty, and beauty is the joy of possessing form, and form is the key to all organic life since no living thing can exist without it, so every work of art, including tragedy, witnesses to the joy of existence.

— Boris Pasternak,
Doctor Zhivago

Contents

Author's Note

In this novel the romanized spelling of all Chinese terms and names is based on the Wade-Giles system. China and other countries commonly used the Wade-Giles from the nineteenth century until 1979. In that year the government in Peking introduced a system of romanization called *pinyin* into all its foreign-language publications, and other countries followed suit to avoid confusion. Since all the action of the novel takes place before 1979 and since the newer complexities of *pinyin* are still confusing for nonspecialists, the older system seemed more appropriate.

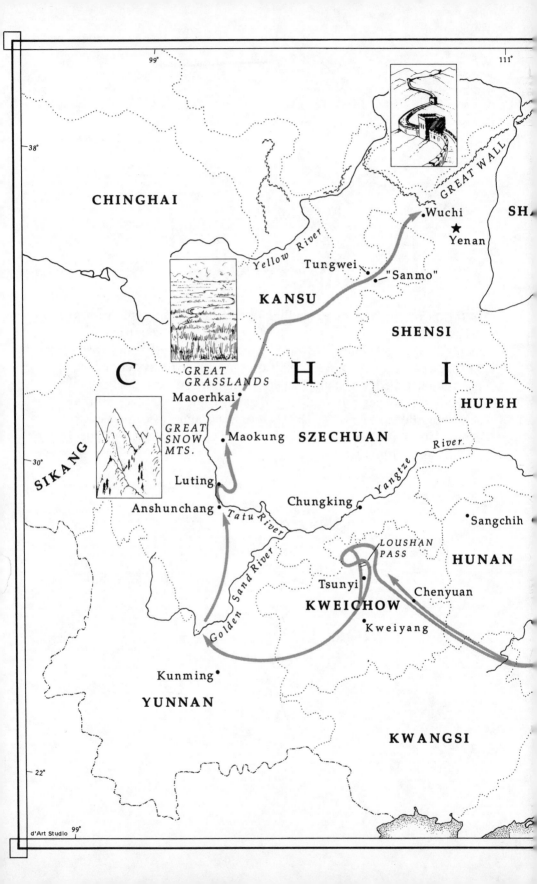

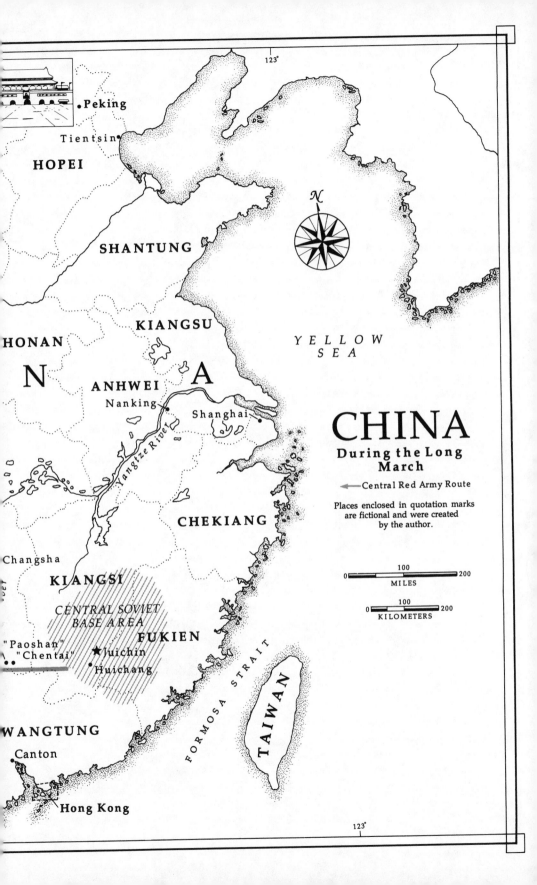

Peking

Tientsin

HOPEI

SHANTUNG

KIANGSU

123°

YELLOW
SEA

HONAN

ANHWEI

Nanking

Shanghai

CHINA

During the Long March

←— Central Red Army Route

Places enclosed in quotation marks
are fictional and were created
by the author.

Changsha

KIANGSI

CHEKIANG

CENTRAL SOVIET
BASE AREA

"Paoshan"
"Chentai"

FUKIEN

★ Juichin

Huichang

WANGTUNG

Canton

Hong Kong

Yangtze River

FORMOSA STRAIT

TAIWAN

0   100   200
MILES

0   100   200
KILOMETERS

PEKING

Prologue

"Because our eyes are blue, most Chinese believe we can see into the ground to a depth of three feet."

The sunburned features of the tall, quiet-spoken Lancashire missionary relaxed in an amused smile.

"They think we use that little trick to discover gold in China. But for some strange reason they're also convinced that we blue-eyed folk can't see through clear water."

The missionary's smile broadened; his teeth gleamed white in a lean, handsome face that had been burnished to the color of bronze by many years of Asian sun and wind, and the expression lent a temporary radiance to the drab church hall in which an audience of several hundred devout Mancunians were listening intently to his every word.

"They call us '*yang kuei tzu*' — 'foreign devils' — and they say we murder Chinese children in our missionary orphanages so that we can use their intestines to turn lead into silver! They say the high spires of the churches we're building in China are annihilating their spirits of the air . . . that the mine shafts and railways being constructed by British engineers are destroying the benevolent influence of terrestrial dragons coiled deep beneath the earth."

Near the back of the hall Jakob Kellner shifted suddenly on one of the hard wooden benches where he sat between his parents. Still-innocent blue eyes, inherited from his Swiss-born father, narrowed in concentration as he dragged his fascinated gaze away from the heroic figure of the missionary to stare fiercely at the coarse-grained planks of the floor. With all the force his ten-year-old mind could muster, he willed his sense of sight to penetrate the scuffed wood and enter the earth beneath.

Who could tell, thought Jakob excitedly, perhaps terrestrial English dragons, unknown to anyone, lay coiled in the earth beneath industrial Manchester? Perhaps it was their "benevolent influence" that had attracted the forest of cotton-mill chimneys to that region of northern England in the first place. Perhaps the thick black smoke that belched daily from the mill chimneys came in reality from these fire-breathing beasts! It was the mills and the industrial prosperity they promised which years before had lured his father westward across Europe from the impoverished canton of Zurich to seek work in the city as a textile engineer. Perhaps, thought Jakob, those same magic dragons had prompted the meeting between his father and his gentle, artistic English mother while she was teaching the new techniques of embroidering by machinery in the mills.

His father's big-boned hands, grimed permanently with oil in their creases, rested in his lap at the edge of Jakob's vision. He was a taciturn, mild-mannered man who had started attending the nonconformist church in a cobbled back street of Moss Side merely to please his wife. But now, like all the other rapt listeners around him, his faith had become a vital source of refreshment that helped him endure the hardships of life in the mean, dingy streets that had grown up around the mills. Notorious for its constant rain and raw fogs, Manchester was excelling its reputation even on that midsummer Sunday of 1921. Steady, soot-laden rain was drenching the cobbles outside the hall and a leaden sky pressed against the dirty windows. If only those invisible underground dragons could influence the weather, thought Jakob. If only the sun would burn down on Manchester as it obviously did on China to weather the pale, gaunt faces around him and make them resemble that of the tall, energetic missionary who was undertaking a short speaking tour during his first home leave in ten years.

"They call the new telegraph wires we have put up in the remote interior regions of China 'iron snakes.' When rainwater rusts on them and drips to the ground, they say it is the blood of the dying spirits of the air. If there is a famine or a drought they blame foreign missionaries and all our works, saying we have outraged those spirits. . . . So great efforts, you see, are still required to overcome this terrible ignorance and spread the word of God through the length and breadth of China!"

Jakob raised his eyes to find the missionary slipping on a wide-sleeved, embroidered Chinese long-gown. Smiling again, he held up a black satin cap with an artificial pigtail attached to the back, then pulled it into place to cover his steel-gray hair. Clasping his hands together within the sleeves, he inclined his head and shoulders in a mock bow, transforming himself instantly into the likeness of a Chinese mandarin.

"They say all Christians are cannibals — because we like to eat the body and drink the blood of our God! They sometimes draw pictures of our Lord on the cross as a crucified pig! All this stirs up hatred against missionaries, and it is no secret that many brave men and women have been martyred in China. So when you travel in the mountains it's sometimes wise to wear Chinese clothes like these. Then the bandits hiding on the mountaintops, with luck, will mistake you for a Chinese. If not, you might be robbed or kidnapped — or worse."

The missionary's face had become stern; now his voice deepened abruptly, taking on a commanding tone. "But whenever a missionary dies, another must be ready to step forward and take his place. Volunteers are needed to dedicate their lives to that vast, unfortunate country. Otherwise China will never be saved!"

Jakob stared fixedly at the exotically clad figure. As the missionary paused to survey his audience, the ten-year-old boy fancied that the steady blue gaze rested on him alone for a second or two before moving on. After removing the long-gown the missionary began speaking again, but this time Jakob neither heard the words nor saw his shabby surroundings. In his mind's eye he was surveying a distant land of towering mountain ranges thronged with writhing dragons and surging hordes of Chinese bandits armed to the teeth. Through the chaos and confusion he himself was striding, proud, straight-backed, and bronzed like the missionary by the merciless Asian sun. Braving all dangers, he was seeing into the ground to a depth of *six* feet on every side, he was finding gold everywhere without effort and turning lead into silver at will. Bandits and dragons retreated on all sides in whichever direction he advanced, powerless to prevent him from "saving" China virtually single-handed.

Jakob emerged from his daydream only when his father shook him gently by the shoulder. He looked up to find his mother smiling at him. The audience had begun rising from their seats and a wooden collecting box was being passed around. At its approach Jakob plunged his hand into his trouser pocket to pull out two copper pennies. Holding them on his palm, he looked questioningly at his mother.

"That's your tram fare home, Jakob," she chided gently.

"But can't I give it for China?" The boy shifted anxiously from foot to foot. "You could give your fares too — and we could walk home, couldn't we?"

"It's pouring with rain, lad," said his father. "And we've got nearly two miles to go."

"But Papa," he pleaded, "we should try to help save China, shouldn't we?"

His mother reached out and brushed the fringe of fair hair from his eyes. The expression in them was eager, endlessly hopeful. "Jakob's right," she said, opening her own purse and dropping three pennies into the collecting box. "Our need is not as great as China's."

On the way out of the mission hall they passed close to the animated group of people pressing around the missionary speaker. He was bending over a box, putting away the mandarin's gown and other Chinese curios that he had brought for display. Looking up unexpectedly, he caught Jakob staring at him and their eyes met; immediately the face of the missionary broke into a broad smile and one eye closed slowly in a conspiratorial wink.

Jakob grinned shyly in return and rushed into the street, tugging a flat cap from his pocket. Taking the hands of both his parents, he hurried across the slippery cobblestones between them, oblivious to the heavy rain. Inspired anew by the intimacy of the missionary's wink, in his mind he had already reentered the mysterious mountains and dragon lairs of China. During the long, drenching walk home he reveled in a giddy succession of blood-stirring adventures of the imagination, and by the time the family reached the door of their modest terraced house, without his realizing it, a fierce spark had been ignited inside Jakob. It would smolder on almost unnoticed for several years before being fanned into the bright blaze of a conscious ambition — and the pursuit of that ambition, fired in a drab, back-street mission hall, would ultimately shape his fate and determine the course of his adult life.

PART ONE

The Marchers Gather

1931

In 1931 China was politically dislocated and seething with unrest. Western nations were continuing to exercise a humiliating form of colonial rule over many "treaty port" areas that they had seized in the mid-nineteenth century, and an unfinished revolution had deteriorated after two confused decades into a Communist-Nationalist civil war. The revolution of 1911 had been sparked above all else by the ever-increasing intrusion into China by foreign powers. This had proved a particularly traumatic experience for a proud nation possessed of four thousand years of recorded history and a deep conviction of the inherent superiority of its civilization. China's very name, Chung Kuo — meaning "middle kingdom" or "central country" — reflected this ancient sense of authority, and its emperors had been accustomed since earliest times to receive annual tribute of silver and other gifts from neighboring Asian countries.

But neither the philosophies of China's great sages, the cultural refinements of its mandarin scholars, nor its large armies could provide any defense against those Western nations who burst forth from Europe during the nineteenth century, newly strengthened by the industrial revolution, to colonize much of the rest of the world. China's gold, jade, silk, and tea provided irresistible commercial bait — and its massive population of four hundred million, a quarter of mankind, constituted the biggest single potential market in the world. With their steel steamships, mass-manufactured weapons, railways, and telegraphs, the Europeans cowed backward nations on all continents, and by the end of the nineteenth century, exploitation of an enfeebled China had be-

come a mad scramble among the colonial powers. Britain, which
first forced China to open its ports to foreign trade after the
Opium War of 1840, had set up a colony proper in Hong Kong.
Shanghai, Canton, and Tientsin became the other major foreign-
ruled coastal enclaves where Europeans enjoyed the security and
protection of their own national laws and police forces: railway
and mining concessions and other trading privileges were also ex-
torted from China's helpless imperial governments. In addition,
the many treaties imposed on Peking forced the Chinese to grant
foreign evangelists wide-ranging rights. The number of missionaries entering the country increased rapidly in the wake of the co-
lonialist penetration, and churches, schools, orphanages, and
hospitals were set up both in the treaty ports and in many parts of
the interior. The numbers of Chinese converted to Christianity always remained small in comparison with the missionary effort
and the size of the population — but this did nothing to lessen
the fervor of the missionaries themselves. Even the antiforeign
Boxer Rebellion of 1900, which resulted in the ritual massacre of
many European missionaries and their wives and children along
with thousands of Chinese Christian converts, did not drive out
the foreign evangelists.

The overthrow of China's last emperor a few years later, in
1911, succeeded in ending more than two thousand years of imperial rule. However, this republican revolution, led by Dr. Sun
Yat-sen, was not able to restore China's pride and independence.
Instead it plunged the nation into a state of prolonged political
turmoil. Outside the foreign-ruled treaty ports, power passed immediately to the remnants of the imperial army, whose commanders became feared regional warlords. Reactionary mandarins
and feudal landowners as a result retained the same stranglehold
on the people throughout China that they had held under the emperors. Sun Yat-sen's Kuomintang, or Nationalist Party, which
had been founded in 1893, welcomed Communists into its ranks
as well as all other Nationalists, but it was unable to assert its
authority because it lacked effective military forces. Close links
were developed with Moscow, and in the early 1920s the Kuomintang began training its own armies. After the death of Sun
Yat-sen in 1925, however, his successor, Chiang Kai-shek, broke
with the Russian Bolsheviks, drove out the Communists, who had
founded their own party in 1921, and turned the Kuomintang into

a right-wing movement. In 1927 Chiang finalized the breach by staging a brutal massacre of thousands of Communist workers in Shanghai. The Kuomintang's own armies then swept northward to Peking, subduing or winning over the regional warlords one by one, and a triumphant proclamation was issued announcing that China had been unified under "Generalissimo" Chiang Kai-shek.

The authority of Chiang's government based in Nanking was not accepted, however, by the Communists; the bulk of them had already retreated deep into the mountainous rural regions of central and southern China to set up their own administrative areas, which they called soviets. About 80 percent of China's population were virtually landless peasants, and in their soviets the Communists were satisfying an age-old grievance by executing landlords and distributing their fields to those who toiled in them. As a result, peasant volunteers had begun flocking to their banners, and large-scale civil war developed when Chiang Kai-shek moved his Nationalist armies against these soviets. But the Communists, although inferior in numbers and arms, resisted stubbornly by means of skillful guerrilla war strategies. As 1931 dawned, none of today's perspectives was discernible amid the turmoil of the time. In particular, no hint of the strength and determination possessed by China's Communists had been allowed to filter to the outside world through the Nationalist military blockades. Consequently China's gigantic stew of complex causes and ambitions continued to lure many white Western adventurers into its midst. Fortune seekers of every kind thronged the relatively safe treaty ports, fascinated by the opportunities and excitements that a great and ancient country in ferment presented. The braver ones occasionally ventured beyond the international concession areas, and among those who did, none showed more courage than the men and women who traveled deep into the dangerous heartlands of China without protection — as missionaries.

1

Several hundred Pakhoi hogs imprisoned in willow-twig cages on the open afterdeck of the *Tomeko Maru* squealed with fright as the wind-lashed East China Sea buffeted the ten-thousand-ton Japanese freighter with gathering force. The ship was nearing the end of its seven-week voyage from Tilbury to Shanghai, and the cages had been stacked in layers five and six deep by coolies who had jog-trotted them to the wharves at Pakhoi, close to the Hainan Strait. Only narrow aisles had been left between the stacked cages, and ducks and barnyard fowl piled on top of them in smaller baskets were beginning to squawk anxiously in their turn as the wind rose.

The clamor increased when a young Chinese man and woman, attired in smart Western clothes, paused in their stroll around the deck and walked in among the cages to talk casually with the grimy deck coolie tending the animals. A sallow-faced European who had been walking in the opposite direction stopped when he noticed the incongruously dressed Asians conversing together. Moving quickly into the lee of a suspended lifeboat, he continued to watch the little group discreetly from a position where he could not be seen.

In his second-class cabin close beneath the stern, Jakob Kellner lay on his narrow bunk reading a Chinese language primer, trying to ignore the noise of the frightened hogs and the constant clatter and thump of the vessel's rudder that penetrated the cabin's bulk-heads. The boy whose imagination had been fired by a sunburned China missionary in a dismal church hall had grown into a tall, lean, serious-faced young man. At twenty, Jakob was now well over six feet tall — his long angular frame had yet to fill out but his shoulders were broad and straight. His face was determined and strong-jawed,

his short, neatly parted hair had retained the fairness inherited from
his Swiss father, and the eager impetuosity that had led him to do-
nate his tram fare to China ten years before was still evident in the
alertness of his expression. But the long voyage from Tilbury had
already made him restless, and as the ship began to roll more noticeably, his attention wandered from the book.

Beyond the porthole the dragon-backed coastline of Fukien was
faintly visible in the gathering twilight; the northbound freighter had
passed through the broad Formosa Strait and the sight of China's
jagged southeastern mountain ranges quickened the realization in
Jakob that soon he would at last set foot on Chinese soil. Landfall
in Shanghai was now less than twenty-four hours away, and as he
stared out through the porthole at the indistinct knuckles of land,
Jakob wondered for the thousandth time on the voyage what he
would encounter when he stepped ashore. At the thought that he
would know for certain next day, a fist of excitement tightened in
the pit of his stomach. Feeling an irresistible urge just to gaze at the
enigmatic coastline of which he had dreamed for so long, Jakob flung
the book aside, put on his jacket, and left the cramped cabin, heading
for the foot of the nearest companionway that led up to the afterdeck.

At that same moment the female figure detached itself from the
little group of Asians standing among the hog cages at the stern and
began to walk toward the top of the same companionway. The rising
wind plucked at her brimmed hat, forcing her to lift a slender arm
to hold it in place, and the long European skirt she wore beneath a
neatly tailored jacket pasted itself against her slim thighs as she
stepped carefully through the gaps between the cages. From the
shadow of one of the *Tomeko Maru*'s lifeboats, the eyes of the watching
European followed her closely but she passed his place of concealment without noticing his presence.

As Jakob mounted the narrow companionway leading to the afterdeck, the ship began to pitch and roll more sharply. He had to
clutch at the side rails at every step to prevent himself from falling,
and as he leaned his weight against the deck door, the ship rolled
suddenly to port, swinging it wide open. Thrown off-balance, he
almost cannoned into the Chinese girl, who had been reaching for
the door from outside. Before she recoiled, their faces almost touched,
and for a moment Jakob's vision seemed to fill with the golden glow
of her skin: startled Asiatic eyes grew momentarily round, raven-
dark hair shivered and swung to conceal a beguilingly curved cheek.

As she leaned instinctively away from him, stretching a hand toward a bulkhead to steady herself, the gusting wind lifted her hat free of her head and bowled it spinning toward the ship's rails. The same gust swirled out her long skirts, uncovering for an instant the full length of her slender legs from ankle to thigh; then Jakob lunged past her, bent double in pursuit of the hat.

He snatched it up when it flattened itself against the port rails and returned to find its owner waiting inside the closed door at the top of the companionway, her face composed and unsmiling.

"I'm very sorry." Jakob inclined his head apologetically. "It was all my fault. I almost knocked you over."

"Please don't apologize. We must blame China's rough seas."

She spoke her accented English carefully without any trace of self-consciousness, and her smile of response was no more than polite. Aged about twenty, she had a striking face, high-cheeked with dark, lustrous eyes. Her glossy black hair was cut in a fashionable long bob that curled softly to her shoulders, and her skirt and jacket of pale worsted matched the color of the now-battered hat that Jakob held before him . . .

"I'm afraid it's spoiled."

Jakob glanced awkwardly at the sorry object in his hands. It had become crumpled and dented, and the gray felt was wet and muddied from contact with the deck. He reshaped it as best he could and brushed away the mud with the sleeve of his jacket, preparing to hand it back — but he continued to cling to it illogically as he gazed at the Chinese girl.

"I'm Jakob Kellner. I'm traveling to Shanghai to take up a post with the Anglo-Chinese Mission."

"I hope your work is satisfying, Mr. Kellner."

The girl's tone was again formal, without real interest. She was graceful and self-possessed in her bearing, and as he looked at her Jakob realized he had seen her come aboard at Hong Kong with other new first-class passengers. Until then he had not had cause to pay her any attention, but the sudden intimacy of their near-collision had produced in him an instinctive desire to prolong the conversation.

"May I ask your name?" Jakob braced his legs against the ship's movement, holding the hat against his chest, unconsciously bargaining its return for her name.

"I am Lu Mei-ling."

"You speak English very well," said Jakob, groping uncertainly for words to justify his actions. "Have you been in England?"

"My brother and I have been studying in Europe for the past two years — he was in Paris and I attended the Royal College of Music in London."

"I've got sheet music in my cabin trunk — some hymns." Jakob rushed on impulsively, without pausing for thought. "There's a piano on the saloon deck. Perhaps you would like to play them this evening. It might help take all our minds off this storm."

Lu Mei-ling smiled politely again but this time she took firm hold of the companionway rail and held out her free hand. "My hat, Mr. Kellner. Thank you for saving it."

Jakob's face reddened in embarrassment. "Please forgive me. I had no right to assume you'd want to play Christian hymns."

"You need not apologize. I expect I already know them."

She took the hat from his hands and turned away down the companionway. Feeling both concerned for her safety and startled by the strength of his own reactions to her, Jakob watched the retreating figure of the beautiful Chinese girl until she went out of sight. But although the *Tomeko Maru* was wallowing in the troughs between waves and rearing over their crests, she descended the tilting steps quickly and confidently without looking back.

2

By the time Jakob stepped out onto the lurching afterdeck, he found the gathering darkness had almost obliterated the Fukien Mountains. The deck's only other visible human occupants were the hog keeper and the smartly dressed Chinese talking together among the cages in the stern, but as Jakob passed the lifeboat station a bulkhead light came on, illuminating the previously concealed figure of the European standing in the shadows. He wore a pale, double-breasted tropical suit and a white felt homburg, and Jakob had a fleeting impression of a gaunt, weather-beaten face and the glint of narrow eyes looking out watchfully from beneath its brim. Recovering from his surprise, Jakob nodded politely in greeting, but the man made no reply, and Jakob continued to the port rail and leaned against it, staring into the dusk in the direction of the Chinese coast.

The wind, driving up from the south with increasing force, was pushing a growing swell of water past the *Tomeko Maru*, steepening the inclines over which she rose and fell. Spume whipped from the wave tops stung his face, and in that moment a faint apprehension at the power of the storm began to mingle with the unfamiliar feeling of physical excitement which the encounter with Lu Mei-ling had produced in him. At twenty, he reflected as he stood at the rail, he was still innocent of all sexual experience by conscious choice: after leaving school at fifteen he had become an apprenticed engineer in a textile mill while he waited to enter the Anglo-Chinese Mission's training college. Because the ambition to become a missionary had developed early, he had gladly allowed the little chapel in Moss Side to dominate his young life and had followed its moral exhortations to the letter. Later, at college, he had conscientiously devoted all his energies to his studies with the distant goal of China in mind, allowing himself few distractions — but this fleeting review of his recent past provided no explanation for the surprising force of the attraction he had suddenly felt to the Chinese girl. In his mind's eye he could still see her startled almond-shaped eyes close before his face, almost feel the brush of her dark, glossy hair. Having come so near to her, he imagined he could still detect the presence of subtle fragrances which surrounded her, and these sensations persisted with an intensity he found faintly bewildering as he gazed at the white-topped waves mounting around the ship.

"Have you ever been in a typhoon before?"

The strange voice speaking close to his ear made Jakob start and he turned to find the European in the white homburg standing beside him. He had spoken with a pronounced French accent, raising his voice to make himself heard above the squawking and squealing of the livestock — but although he scanned the rising seas around them, Jakob noticed that the Frenchman's gaze returned repeatedly to the two Asian figures talking among the hog cages.

"Is it really going to be a typhoon?" asked Jakob at last, trying to keep his voice casual.

The Frenchman nodded. "I think it will reach its peak around midnight."

Jakob's feeling of anxiety mounted, tightening the muscles of his chest. "I've never been anywhere near a typhoon before — but I suppose I'll soon get used to things like this."

"Nobody ever gets used to typhoons. They're best avoided." The Frenchman eyed Jakob's serviceable suit of inexpensive brown worsted and the cheap brass tiepin which fastened the wings of his collar beneath his tie knot. "May I ask, monsieur, what it is that attracts a young Englishman like you to the Orient?"

"I'm a missionary. This is my first post." Jakob scanned the angry sea in the gathering gloom, making an effort to conceal his growing unease. "I've wanted to come to China ever since I can remember."

"And what do you hope to achieve in China?" The Frenchman's question had a perfunctory tone, as though he had little real interest in the answer, and as he spoke he shifted to a position in which he could keep the stern of the ship under constant scrutiny.

"A quarter of the entire human family lives here, many of them in the direst poverty. Confucianism, Buddhism, Taoism — all their own religions are weak and fatalistic. They do almost nothing to lighten the terrible burdens on the people. Millions die in famine and floods . . ." Jakob broke off, aware that he was repeating, parrot-fashion, the words of his mission college teachers; on that tiny ship in the midst of a rising storm, he wondered whether his words appeared foolish, and in an effort to retrieve the situation, he turned earnestly to face the Frenchman. "The people of China seem to be unable to save themselves, monsieur. I happen to believe the need to preach the Christian Gospel is greater in China than anywhere else in the world!"

"I've met Chinese military governors with very different views," said the Frenchman dryly. "They'll tell you there are far too many illiterate peasants and coolies. They positively welcome the droughts and the floods which kill their countrymen by the million — they see it as nature's way of solving China's problems."

Jakob found himself flinching inwardly at the callousness of the Frenchman's words but he did not allow his feelings to show. Instead he held out his hand in a formal gesture of greeting. "Everyone is entitled to their opinion — my name is Jakob Kellner, monsieur."

"Devraux." The Frenchman shook hands without enthusiasm. "Jacques Devraux."

"Do you know China well, Monsieur Devraux?"

"I know Indochina better — I served in the Infanterie Coloniale in Tongking. My home now is Saigon. I guide sportsmen who wish to hunt big game in the jungles of Annam." He waved a deprecating hand and stared distractedly toward the stern of the ship again. "I suspect you are better equipped than I am for China, Monsieur Kellner."

"My own qualifications are very slight," said Jakob tentatively. "I studied for two years at the Anglo-Chinese Mission training college in London before I left England — and I've only recently begun to learn Chinese . . ."

The Frenchman, who had given up all pretense of listening, was staring openly over Jakob's shoulder, and almost immediately the missionary heard the rapid sound of approaching footsteps. A moment later a Chinese in his late twenties passed them, walking briskly: he was wearing a well-tailored European suit and carrying a soft hat, and Jakob recognized him as the man who had been talking to the hog keeper. Devraux watched until he left the deck, and as soon as the companionway door closed behind him, he relaxed against the ship's rail and lit a cheroot.

"Did you pass an attractive Chinese girl on your way up to the deck, Monsieur Kellner?" he asked with studied casualness.

"Yes, I did."

"Do you know who she is?"

"I think her name is Lu Mei-ling. She and her brother have been studying in Europe."

"I thought as much." Devraux's eyes narrowed and he drew thoughtfully on his cheroot, staring in silence toward the stern. When Jakob turned to follow his gaze, he saw only the bent figure of the deck coolie, who was busying himself lashing the willow-twig hog cages together with lengths of rope.

"What makes you ask about the Chinese girl and her brother, Monsieur Devraux?" asked Jakob in a puzzled voice. "Do you know her family?"

The Frenchman turned back slowly to face Jakob, almost as if he had forgotten he was there. "Your missionary training college may have taught you a lot about China's ancient religions, Monsieur Kellner. But when you get into the interior you won't have to worry too much about the disciples of Confucius, the Taoist temples, or the Buddhists. They won't be your chief danger."

"What do you mean?"

"Didn't your training college tell you anything about China's Communists?"

"We were shown some newspaper stories. I think they said a few 'Red Bandits' were fighting in remote areas — but soldiers of the government were tracking them down and finishing them off."

A sardonic smile flitted across Jacques Devraux's face. "The Chinese Nationalists have flung a tight blockade around all the Red areas — that's true. But I'd be very surprised if they had 'finished off' the Communists."

"But Monsieur Devraux," said Jakob, mystified, "I don't understand what all this has to do with anyone on this ship."

The Frenchman put a hand on the rail to steady himself as the *Tomeko Maru* slid crabwise into a trench of foaming water. Turning to Jakob, he looked hard at him as though seeing him properly for the first time and spoke in a sarcastic tone. "Monsieur Kellner, the Communists in China — and in Indochina too — are mostly ignorant peasants. But the Asians who lead them and stir them up are often educated men and women. Many of them, unfortunately, have had the benefit of attending universities in England and France." He paused and his voice became heavy with irony. "You also ought to know that Chinese from wealthy families don't normally spend much of their time fraternizing with deck coolies."

Abruptly the Frenchman turned from the rail and hurried away toward the companionway, leaving Jakob staring at the angry waves. As he wrestled with the implications of what Devraux had said, the image of Lu Mei-ling's face returned unbidden to his mind once more: the dark, upswept eyes that made her face so hauntingly different from those of English girls seemed to swim again before him, and he realized with a slight feeling of shock that her physical beauty had quickly taken on a forbidden quality in his imagination. So startlingly unlike himself, she belonged to the country toward which he already felt a sacred obligation, and these new, disquieting feelings seemed out of keeping with his sense of duty.

On an impulse he closed his eyes and prayed briefly; when he opened them again he found himself looking toward the stern. The hog keeper was still binding the willow-twig cages with frayed ropes, working laboriously without raising his head, and Jakob stood and watched him. The coolie seemed totally absorbed in his task, and try as he might, Jakob could not fully understand the reasons for

Jacques Devraux's suspicions. Inside the cages, the frightened animals seemed to be taking little comfort from their keeper's efforts to make them secure. Sensing that the storm was worsening, they were becoming restless, and as Jakob hurried from the deck, heading back toward his cabin, their squeals increased, growing shriller and more fearful with each successive shriek of the wind.

3

As the *Tomeko Maru* headed into the teeth of the typhoon, the ship's diminutive Japanese captain, with many a deep bow, invited passengers of all classes into the aft saloon for their safety. By midevening a group of about thirty had assembled, among them Europeans, Chinese, Japanese, and Americans. Jakob had seated himself at a small table on his own and was trying to fix his attention on the ideograms in his Chinese language primer but the vessel was pitching and rolling violently, making concentration difficult.

Outside the saloon the night was filled with the roar of the wind and the cries of the badly frightened livestock on the afterdeck. Although few of the passengers had attempted to dine, because of the conditions, most of those traveling first-class had dressed as usual for dinner. Among them Jakob noted Jacques Devraux. Wearing a white smoking jacket and a black tie, the Frenchman had half buried himself behind an old newspaper in a corner of the saloon that, in the tradition of Japanese domestic interiors, was plain and unadorned. Two young Japanese women, in contrast, were arrayed in dazzling kimonos figured in gold, turquoise, and red, and Lu Meiling, who was sipping tea and conversing quietly with the smartly dressed Chinese whom Jakob had seen on deck, had chosen for the evening a high-throated, traditional Chinese gown of shimmering turquoise silk. Embroidered with flowers, clouds, and dragons, it fell from shoulder to ankle in a simple unbroken line, leaving her slender figure enigmatically undefined, and Jakob found he had to make a conscious effort not to stare in her direction. On the table before him lay several folios of piano music which he had rummaged from his cabin trunk in the hope that they might provide him with the opportunity of speaking to her, but a nagging anxiety that he might again appear clumsy and tongue-tied if he approached her had so far confined him to his seat.

Neither was he alone in feeling uneasy about the storm — without exception, the faces of all his fellow passengers were pale and apprehensive. Like him, they were doing their best to ignore the erratic movements of the ship, and white-jacketed Japanese stewards continued to move among them, serving drinks and light refreshments as unobtrusively as they had throughout the voyage. But flurries of salt spray lashed the windows every few seconds and tension rose whenever an unguarded glass fell from a table to smash noisily on the floor. Jakob was vaguely aware that the stewards were being summoned frequently to Jacques Devraux's table as the evening wore on but he was totally unprepared when, on looking up suddenly from his book, he found the Frenchman standing beside him, swaying slightly and clutching a large glass of brandy and soda.

"How good will you be, Monsieur Kellner, at gouging out the eyes of Chinese converts who die?" asked Devraux in a voice thickened by drink. "Will you be able to manage that?"

At that moment the *Tomeko Maru* tipped abruptly into another deep trough and Devraux dropped heavily into the empty chair beside Jakob. Some of the contents of his glass spilled down his jacket front and he cursed softly in his own language, dabbing perfunctorily at the stain with a handkerchief before lifting his gaze to Jakob again.

"I'm afraid I don't understand what you mean," said Jakob slowly, putting his book aside.

"No, I don't suppose you do." A humorless smile spread across Devraux's face. "But perhaps you're in luck. By chance I'm able to give you some vital information that every young missionary ought to have before he sets foot in China." The Frenchman took a cheaply printed booklet from an inside pocket of his smoking jacket and flourished it theatrically in Jakob's direction. "It's all in here."

Jakob could see Chinese characters on the flimsy cover but his knowledge of the language was not sufficient for him to translate them. "What exactly is that, Monsieur Devraux?" he asked uncertainly.

"It has a very quaint title. It's called 'Deal a Death Blow to a Corrupt Doctrine' — the 'corrupt doctrine' in question, of course, is Christianity." Devraux laughed unpleasantly. "Calling Christianity a corrupt doctrine is just about the nicest thing this book can find to say about the subject. That's why your college teachers didn't tell you about it."

"Perhaps the college has never heard of it." Jakob leaned forward to inspect the booklet and saw that scribbled translations into English were written in the margins. "Where does it come from?"

"They've heard of it, all right," said Devraux, pausing to raise his glass to his lips again. "It's a notorious publication. It was first printed fifty or sixty years ago, before the Boxer Rebellion — to turn the people against your predecessors."

"Then it's just ancient history."

Devraux shook his head exaggeratedly from side to side. "No, not at all. Freshly printed copies have been turning up all over Hunan and Kweichow in the last year or two."

"Who do you think has been circulating it?"

"Almost certainly the Reds, Monsieur Kellner. But whoever it is, rest assured they're no friends of yours."

Devraux drained his glass and wiped his mouth elaborately with the back of his hand; then he raised the book to read and leaned closer to Jakob again to make himself heard above the noise of the wind. "They say in the introduction that all Christian missionaries 'implement their evil designs by gouging out the eyes of dead converts, doing bodily injury to little boys and girls, and concealing the hair and nails of women under doormats.' "

He paused and leafed clumsily through several pages before reading again.

"Later they get into the more complimentary details. . . . They say that at the age of three months you give the male offspring of converts special treatment. 'Hollow tubes are inserted into their bodies to make them dilate. This helps to facilitate sodomy. . . . At the junction of spring and summer young boys procure and smear female menses on their faces before going to worship. Then fathers, sons, and brothers all join their vital forces and sodomize with one another. . . . Are the Christians not worse than beasts?' "

A feeling of revulsion rose in Jakob but he managed to conceal it. "Those are terrible, ugly lies, Monsieur Devraux," he said calmly.

If he heard Jakob's reply the Frenchman gave no sign. Instead he smiled crookedly and snapped his fingers peremptorily in the direction of a passing Japanese steward to order another drink. "It gets better as it goes on, Monsieur Kellner, so listen carefully." He flicked over several more pages and continued to read, laying exaggerated emphasis as before on the more lurid expressions. " 'Sunday services: the old, the young, males and females alike, all take part in these services. Invariably the proceedings end in mass copulation in which the whole congregation participate. . . .' "

Jakob drew away from Devraux and half rose from his seat, intending to move away — but the Frenchman reached out and placed a restraining hand on his arm. "Wait! That's not the worst of it. In case you're still in doubt about whether the Communists will make you welcome in China, I'll read you just one more extract." Again he flicked at the pages. "Ah yes, here we are . . . 'All Westerners regard the menstrual flow of women as the most precious gift of God. That is why they vie with one another to obtain and drink it. This accounts for the unbearable stench some of them have!' "

Jakob freed himself from the Frenchman's grip and stood up. The floor of the saloon was heaving, making balance difficult, and he had to hold on to a chair back to steady himself as he picked up his sheets of piano music from the low table. Devraux was already holding a fresh glass of brandy and soda which the steward had brought him and he watched Jakob over the brim, still smiling crookedly, as he drank.

"You must excuse me, Monsieur Devraux." Jakob gestured toward the folios in his hand. "I think some music might help pass the time for us more pleasantly."

Turning his back on Devraux, Jakob made his way unsteadily across the saloon. As he went, a long, low rumbling sound was heard from the direction of the afterdeck; this was followed by a series of grinding thuds and a new burst of squealing from the hogs. Jakob swung around to stare in alarm at the windows facing the stern and all the other passengers fell silent, following his gaze. But nothing could be seen in the howling blackness beyond the glass and, fighting down his apprehension, Jakob continued to pick his way among the tables until he reached the settee where Lu Mei-ling was seated.

"Good evening, Miss Lu," he said hesitantly, holding the folios toward her. "I've brought the music I told you about."

A small frown furrowed Mei-ling's brow and for a moment she did not reply. Then she turned and spoke in English to her companion. "This is Jakob Kellner. He's a missionary on his way to take up his first post in China."

"My name is Lu Chiao, Mr. Kellner! I'm Mei-ling's brother."

The Chinese who sprang up smiling to offer his hand was brisk and energetic. About six or seven years older than Jakob and almost as tall, he showed no outward sign of being afraid of the storm, and his direct manner bore no trace of the self-effacing humility traditionally cultivated by his educated countrymen. He had strong, regular features, wore a small modern moustache still rare among Chinese, and he seized Jakob's hand in a grip that was firm and confident.

"I'm very glad to know you," responded Jakob, warming to the friendly greeting. "Your sister told me earlier she knew some Christian hymns and I was hoping she might play for us." He turned and motioned toward a small upright piano at the end of the saloon. "I've brought some hymn music from my cabin. I thought we might all sing 'Eternal Father' — it might help us through the storm."

"Although Mei-ling and I had a missionary school education in Shanghai, we no longer believe in Christianity," said Chiao firmly, still smiling at Jakob. "But please sit down for a moment with us. I remember the hymn. It has a fine tune." He turned to his sister with a smile as he took his seat again. "Do you remember 'Eternal Father'?"

Mei-ling thought for a moment. "Yes, I think so."

Leaning forward eagerly in his chair, Jakob picked out the music and offered it to her. "Then will you consider playing it for us?"

Mei-ling reached out to take the music from him and began looking through it. Their eyes met for only an instant but again Jakob felt the same strange exhilaration he had experienced at the rail of the ship after their first encounter that afternoon. Although she held her head proudly, there seemed to be a faint shimmer of a smile in Mei-ling's expression and again the beguiling slant of her eyes and the soft ocher tint of her skin had an almost mesmerizing effect on him. He sensed suddenly that during that brief glance he had caught a fleeting glimpse of the very soul of the Chinese girl and that she in some indefinable way had shared in his awareness of a rare moment.

"If you wish it," said Mei-ling quietly without raising her eyes from the music, "I will play the hymn."

"It will give you more pleasure, I hope, Mr. Kellner, than your talk with the French passenger who seems suspicious even of his own shadow," said Chiao jocularly. "I couldn't help noticing that you weren't enjoying his company."

For a moment Jakob again felt confused and flustered: he wondered whether somehow his uncomfortable conversation with Devraux had been overheard. Then he realized it would have been impossible above the noise of the storm, and looking up, he found Chiao smiling at him good-humoredly.

"I would guess he is some kind of colonial policeman, am I right, Mr. Kellner? He spent a lot of time watching us have a casual talk with a deck coolie today. He seems to think nothing has an innocent explanation. He probably makes many remarks about the dangers of Communism in Asia. And believes his role is to rescue the whole continent from revolutionaries and the 'Red menace.' Am I correct?"

Jakob smiled and nodded in mystification. "I'm not sure — perhaps you are."

"And what about you, Mr. Kellner?" continued Chiao. "Why did you choose to come to China?"

"I've wanted to come to your country since I was ten years old," replied Jakob quietly. "I heard a missionary talking about China. I was fascinated and after that I never wanted to do anything else."

Two years at the training college in London had softened and blurred Jakob's northern accent without removing every trace of Lancashire from his speech — while his manner was not polished, he conducted himself with a natural courtesy that hinted at inner strength, and sensing this, Chiao sat forward in his seat, looking at him with greater interest.

"And are you from an old colonial family, Mr. Kellner?"

"No, nobody in my family has ever traveled outside Europe before. My father works in a cotton mill in the north of England. I was an apprentice at the same factory for three years while I was waiting to go to missionary college . . ."

Another ominous rumbling sound from the deck interrupted Jakob and again everyone in the saloon turned to stare out apprehensively into the night. As the passengers watched, the shadowy figure of the deck coolie became dimly visible, scrambling with difficulty across the pitching deck, clutching at loose hog cages. All the time the noise made by the frightened animals was continuing without letup and Jakob noticed that the faces of many of the passengers around him were growing more tense. Even Chiao's expression had grown serious as he peered out through the windows.

"You told me just now you no longer believed in Christianity," said Jakob, restarting the conversation to distract attention from the storm. "May I ask what made you change your mind?"

"China, unfortunately, is a very sick country, Mr. Kellner," replied Chiao, lowering his voice. "My father is among the lucky few. He owns several textile factories in Shanghai. That's why he sent me and my sister to a Christian missionary school. But I came to realize long ago that Christianity can't cure China's illness."

"What do you think can?"

A guarded look came into Chiao's eyes. "Great political changes are required, Mr. Kellner," he said shortly. "But this is not the place to discuss them." He glanced at his sister, who was still holding the piano music in her lap. "Perhaps it would be a good idea now to take up Mr. Kellner's suggestion to play the piano. That hymn has a rousing chorus, if I remember. Whether we're Christians or not, it would be good for everybody to sing and drown out the storm, wouldn't it?"

Chiao stood up and motioned them toward the piano. As Mei-ling got to her feet, the ship lurched sharply and Jakob reached out to steady her, placing one hand under her left elbow. Escorting her to the piano, he became keenly aware of the warmth of her flesh through the thin silk sleeve of her dress and he relinquished his hold reluctantly at the piano stool.

When Jakob announced to the saloon that the hymn was to be sung, most of the European and American men and women left their seats and crossed the tilting floor to join the little group around the piano. The rumbling noise from the afterdeck began again as the typhoon tore at the *Tomeko Maru* with renewed fury, but the moment Mei-ling played the stirring opening chords, the little group of singers launched spiritedly into the hymn.

> "*Eternal Father, strong to save,*
> *Whose arm doth bind the restless wave,*
> *Who bidd'st the mighty ocean deep,*
> *Its own appointed limits keep . . .*"

Mei-ling, to Jakob's surprise, struck the keys with all the force and slow deliberation that the sonorous seafaring hymn of praise demanded; although her hands were small and delicate, she seemed to sense intuitively in the mighty chords the hymn's deep feeling of yearning and supplication offered at the brink of awful calamity. Standing by her side, Jakob felt himself drawn to her anew — all sense of danger evaporated momentarily as his eyes took in her slim shoulders, the youthful curve of her neck, the sheen of the pale turquoise silk that concealed her small breasts. In her playing of the hymn, too, there was a passion which her rejection of its religious sentiments did nothing to diminish. In the core of the typhoon she was giving something vital of herself, and quite illogically, Jakob suddenly felt in his heart that he was the chief recipient of her gift. It seemed as if the tempestuous seas, the *Tomeko Maru*, and all sailing in her had been assembled and brought together just so that he might feel and know the intensity of this dizzying emotion. Beside him, Chiao was singing every line with great gusto and Jakob, feeling a joyousness well up within him, sang with all the power of his lungs, drowning out momentarily even the wind's roar and the terror of the hogs.

> *"O, hear us when we cry to Thee,*
> *For those in peril on the sea!"*

At the moment that Mei-ling lifted her hands to begin the next verse, the rumbling on the afterdeck grew louder. In quick succession two thunderous blows were struck against the outer bulkhead of the saloon. A flare of crimson blood splattered across one window and those passengers who turned their eyes toward the sound quickly enough saw a grotesquely distorted animal face flatten itself against the thick glass; it remained visible for only an instant before whirling away upward into the night, followed by a despairing banshee wail. The second willow-withe cage shattered on impact with the bulkhead and its squirming, shrieking hog scudded bloodily along the whole length of the saloon's windows before a great fist of wind plucked it up and hurled it into the boiling sea.

The noise from outside became a continuous roll of thunder as the mass of hog cages, which had broken free of their ropes, shifted and slid back and forth. Many cages were sucked intact over the rails: others broke open as they smashed together, releasing the imprisoned hogs for a few terrified moments of freedom on the slippery, wave-drenched mountainsides of the deck. The abrupt cessation of the hogs' agonized wails as they were swallowed one after another into the heaving seas chilled the human listeners in the aft saloon.

Mute with horror, the group that had been singing around the piano backed toward the one solid bulkhead, staring at the windows. They all flinched whenever the wind smashed another cage or its squealing occupant against the ship's superstructure, and they froze when they saw the deck coolie slide slowly into view. He was scrabbling desperately for a foothold on the seesawing deck, trapped amid a mass of fear-crazed hogs slithering back and forth in the slime that had been washed from the cages. A moment later he was struck by a moving wall of cages and a fierce gust of wind lifted him bodily into the air. The shuddering impact of his body against the saloon windows caused Mei-ling and some of the other passengers to cry out, and they could only watch helplessly as the coolie's grimy hands clawed futilely at the slippery glass. Mei-ling turned and buried her face in her brother's shoulder and Chiao's face drained of all color as he watched. A moment before the coolie disappeared, his mouth opened wide in a scream but the sound was lost among the shrieks of the dying hogs and the rush of water as he was swept away over the starboard rail with the shreds of the last cages.

Although he was pale and shaken, Jakob was the first to recover his composure when the terrible din ceased. After whispering to Mei-ling and her brother, he guided Mei-ling quickly back to the piano and propped another sheet of hymn music before her. She began shakily but Jakob led the singing of "O God Our Help in Ages Past" in a firm voice and one by one the rest of the frightened passengers joined the gathering. The *Tomeko Maru* was still lurching and shuddering violently under the impact of the screaming wind, but the group around the piano sang one hymn after another, their voices waxing stronger as the feeling grew among them that they were at least offering some resistance, no matter how puny, to the vast and dreadful elemental forces howling all around the ship.

4

One last shuddering groan from the rudder and the noisy clank of chains echoing through his little aft cabin marked the end for Jakob of the *Tomeko Maru*'s long voyage to China early the next afternoon. The anxieties aroused by the typhoon had largely subsided but a mixture of excitement and nervous anticipation made his fingers clumsy as he finished buckling his luggage and locking his cabin trunk. Already he could hear a clamor of shrill Shanghai voices growing louder as wooden-hulled sampans and lighters scraped and bumped along the freighter's sides. Boat hooks clattered against the rails, bare feet pattered across the deck above his head in flurries, and amid the shouting he heard the creak of hatches and lockers being levered open.

In his eagerness to savor every detail of his arrival, Jakob had been on deck at dawn to watch the Japanese freighter leave the East China Sea and enter the mouth of the mighty Yangtze River. The typhoon had blown itself out with surprising suddenness in the night and most of the exhausted passengers were then still sleeping. Although tired, Jakob had been unable to sleep and he had watched, fascinated, as the rocky islets and mountains of Chekiang's crenellated coastline gradually gave way to a low, blurred, featureless shore which bordered the estuary of Asia's greatest river.

Watching the waters grow dark and turbid, Jakob had felt a sense of awe steal over him — this giant stream, he knew from his missionary college lessons, was China's jugular. After rising among the snowy crests of the Asian continent in Tibet, it rushed down through steep mountain gorges, pumping life-giving water endlessly eastward along a winding, three-thousand-mile course through China's heartlands. In its benign moods it irrigated a vast bowl of rice plains and helped nourish half the nation; in its destructive phases it burst its banks to flood and devastate, claiming victims equally by the million. The Yellow River, to the north, and the Yangtze, he knew, were known as "China's twin sorrows" because of the regularity with which they inundated the land and its people, and as Jakob gazed into the wide river's muddy brown waves he sensed something of its enormous power.

The treeless banks of the estuary on which he could pick out gray-roofed villages and an occasional mud fort seemed drained of color in comparison. It was as though the river, while refreshing the earth, at the same time sucked something vital from it. The pale colors of the estuary's shores seemed to have been muted with dust and bleached by the sun, giving the land a fiercely austere appearance that was so different from the emerald green hills and woods of northern England. But although few figures moved through it at that hour, the bleak grandeur of the landscape immediately captivated him and this feeling grew steadily stronger the longer he stood by the rail.

When some sixty miles from the estuary mouth the bows of the *Tomeko Maru* swung to port to head into the Whangpoo River, Jakob understood fully for the first time why the two Chinese ideograms that made up the name "Shanghai" meant "above the sea." The winding tributary river that meandered away southward through the low-lying mud flats provided a natural refuge from the harsh sweep of the Yangtze's great union with the ocean. He could see also why the thousand-year-old walled settlement ten miles farther upstream had proved such an ideal site for the greatest of China's foreign-ruled treaty ports. Silk, rice, cotton, jade, gold, hides — all the exotic produce of China's inland provinces — had poured naturally down the Yangtze into Shanghai in the wake of the Opium War nearly a century before. Opium and other cargoes shipped across the world's oceans to China had obviously filled the same Shanghai warehouses just as conveniently on their journey inland to the world's most densely populated marketplace.

While thinking these thoughts and gazing at the tidal creeks veining the Whangpoo's banks, Jakob became aware suddenly that his preoccupation with these first inland vistas of China had led him to neglect his normal daily devotions. Each morning during the voyage he had set aside half an hour for prayer and Bible study; but his insatiable curiosity had on this special morning caused him to neglect his routine. He at once hurried below and began to pray for strength and guidance in all his tasks in China, and the intensity of these prayers confined him to his cabin right up to the moment when the *Tomeko Maru* at last dropped anchor opposite the congested Shanghai waterfront.

As soon as his baggage was finally secured, Jakob rushed eagerly up to the deck, and on emerging into the afternoon heat he was struck first by the frenzy of activity that met his eyes in all directions. Grunting, bare-chested coolies were already swarming over the ship, manhandling the surviving hold cargo into native lighters that reared beneath the stern. Beyond the rails at which he stood, the brown surface of the Whangpoo, stirred to turbulence by the inflowing tide, was covered with crowds of moored and moving craft. Along the whole length of the curving mile-long Bund, vessels of all sizes were plying back and forth, disgorging and taking on cargo, dropping or weighing anchor, mooring, casting off. Chinese junks with high, square sterns and dragon's eyes emblazoned on their wooden bows lumbered among the rust-caked freighters and tramp steamers from Europe; wallowing sampans and lighters weighed down with baled cotton, basketed vegetables, wine barrels, and livestock scurried back and forth between the cargo ships and the congested jetties. Among this seething, waterborne throng, pale, sleek warships from Europe and Japan lay ominously at rest as though silently reminding Shanghai's four million Chinese inhabitants that it was the twenty thousand foreigners among them who ruled the city.

Beneath the towering neo-Georgian frontages of the Bund's famous European trading houses, which had founded nineteenth-century Shanghai, Jakob could see dense crowds of Chinese mirroring the frenetic activity on the water. Long processions of ramshackle wooden carts and giant wheelbarrows drawn by oxen, buffalo, and perspiring coolies were hauling precariously stacked bales of goods to and from the wharves and waterfront warehouses. Trams built in England clanked noisily across rails set in the cobbled highway, wheezing trucks honked and hooted at the crowded pier heads, and rickshaws bearing white-clad Europeans and silk-jacketed Chinese threaded slowly through the confusion. Here and there Jakob noticed gleaming American and European limousines nosing among the crush with an almost stately dignity and it struck him that they were the land-borne equivalent of the dominating warships anchored in midstream.

"China itself is like the ocean, you'll find, Monsieur Kellner — it salts everything that's drawn into it."

Fragrant wisps of smoke from a cheroot drifted to Jakob with the words of Jacques Devraux and he turned to find the Frenchman standing beside him, looking across the river to the waterfront. "Those grand buildings might make it seem as though we've brought European civilization here — but when you know more, you'll discover all we've really done is adapt the corrupt and brutal ways of old China for our benefit."

Since the moment when the hog cages broke loose at the height of the typhoon, Jakob had noticed that Devraux's manner had been subdued. Although he had declined to join the group around the piano, he had not been immune to the horrors of the storm, and along with Jakob and the other passengers he had attended a short Buddhist funeral service for the drowned coolie that had been arranged by the Japanese captain on the freshly swabbed afterdeck soon after breakfast. He had stood silent and expressionless at Jakob's side, watching the Japanese crew members bow low and sprinkle incense before an improvised altar, and for the remaining hours of the voyage, like the rest of the passengers, he had remained wrapped in his own thoughts. Now as he peered across the harbor at the yellowish mass of humanity swarming along the Bund, his voice had a dull, resigned edge.

"Half of those poor wretches you can see, Monsieur Kellner, will die of disease or some natural calamity before they're thirty. In the countryside they're abused by corrupt mandarins and grasping landlords — that's why they flock to treaty ports like this in their millions. And here, even if our countrymen pay the Chinese compradors a fair rate for the coolies' labor, the comprador pays out only a paltry sum that barely keeps the coolie's family in rags. So the comprador grows rich on the coolie's sweat and in the interests of smooth trading we turn a blind eye."

"The Anglo-Chinese Mission doesn't turn a blind eye," said Jakob quietly. "Our missionaries represent many Christian denominations. They live among the people and try to help them in a lot of different ways."

Devraux shrugged. "Missionaries take European habits deep into the interior. You blaze new commercial trails for foreign goods wherever you go. Mission schools turn out a steady stream of Chinese translators and interpreters to run those trading offices over there. And where do you think all the donations come from to pay for your upkeep while you're saving a handful of Chinese souls?"

"I hope, Monsieur Devraux," said Jakob firmly, "that when I know as much about China as you, I won't be as cynical."

"It's quite likely, as I said before, that your knowledge of China is already superior to mine."

"But that can't be true," protested Jakob.

"Don't be too sure. There's an old saying that a foreigner understands China best on the day he arrives here. Then everything he's learned beforehand is clear in his mind. After a few years he becomes confused — and clings desperately to some of his early insights. But a man who's been in China a long time always comes to feel he understands nothing of this strange country where people eat their soup at the end of the meal instead of the beginning and call the compass the 'point-south needle' . . ."

Devraux broke off with another shrug as a cluster of canopied sampans that had put out from the nearest jetty began drawing alongside the *Tomeko Maru*. Groups of passengers had begun moving across the deck toward the gang ladder and several of them paused to shake Jakob warmly by the hand and wish him well. On catching sight of Lu Mei-ling and her brother, Jakob raised his broad-brimmed hat, smiled warmly at the Chinese girl, and wished her good afternoon. She was wearing a cool, full-skirted dress of blue and cream French muslin, and a ribboned sun hat of the same colors framed her face, heightening the beauty of her pale skin and lustrous hair. Although she merely acknowledged his greeting with a formal smile, Jakob turned involuntarily to follow her with his eyes all the way to the top of the gang ladder. No opportunity to speak with Mei-ling or her brother had arisen since the height of the typhoon; with the passing of danger he had been restricted once more to the ship's second-class areas and the sight of Mei-ling preparing to disembark produced a sudden sense of impending loss within him. Realizing he would have to hurry to disembark in the same sampan, he turned quickly and extended his hand in a farewell salutation to Jacques Devraux.

"Good-bye, Monsieur Devraux. You've made me appreciate that things won't be easy for me. But I hope God will give me the strength to do good work in China."

"I wish you *bonne chance*," said Devraux in a formal tone and stood aside to let a perspiring coolie shuffle by, bearing Jakob's heavy cabin trunk. The Chinese cleared his throat noisily and spat over the rail close to them as he went on his way, and the Frenchman raised a world-weary eyebrow in Jakob's direction.

"By the way, the Communists have a new slogan, Monsieur Kellner," said Devraux in an acid voice. "They say that if every Chinese could be persuaded to spit at the same moment, all the foreigners in China would drown."

5

Choppy waves slapped noisily at the steps of the stone jetty opposite the Cathay Hotel, where the first canopied sampan was trying to land its passengers. The clash between the inflowing tide and the fast, brown current of the Whangpoo was lifting the craft high one moment and dropping it the next. Seeing Lu Chiao rise from his seat to take his sister's arm, Jakob hurried impulsively ahead of them to the sampan's dancing stern and bounded across a gap of several feet onto the slimy steps. Turning quickly, he extended his right hand smilingly toward Mei-ling, offering to assist her ashore.

As the sampan lifted her, a pucker of uncertainty appeared fleetingly in Mei-ling's expression; then as she came level, she calmly stretched out a slender, white-gloved hand toward him and when he grasped her fingers she stepped confidently across the gap to the jetty.

"Thank you, Mr. Kellner." Her smile again carried a hint of warmth and her eyes held his as she spoke, but when they reached the top of the steps she withdrew her hand quickly from his.

"I haven't had the chance to thank you for playing the piano for us last night." Looking directly into her lovely face, Jakob felt his breath quicken. "I shall never forget the way you played."

Mei-ling gave him a puzzled smile. "But it was nothing. . . ."

At a loss for words, Jakob continued to stare at her. "Your dress, Miss Lu, is very charming . . . you must have bought it in Paris."

"My sister, Mr. Kellner, cares little for flattery or compliments." Lu Chiao strode confidently to the top of the steps, smiling broadly, but behind the smile Jakob noticed for the first time the hard, almost insolent intelligence of his gaze. "She's as determined as I am to change old Chinese habits. It's a thing of the past to regard young girls merely as ornamental flower jars." He held out his hand and shook Jakob's firmly. "Good-bye, Mr. Kellner."

"I hope we may meet again sometime." Jakob turned eagerly toward Mei-ling.

"Since you are a missionary, Mr. Kellner, our paths are not likely to cross. Good-bye."

Chiao guided his sister quickly away into the melee of yelling dock coolies and lightermen crowding the jetty and Jakob caught a glimpse of a gleaming limousine with a uniformed Chinese chauffeur at the wheel standing beyond the crush. Then he heard a voice call his name and he swung around to see a grinning white face approaching through the throng.

"Jakob Kellner? I'm Laurence Franklin. I've come to escort you to the mission house."

A pale, bespectacled Englishman in a dark suit and wide-brimmed hat offered his hand quickly; spotting Jakob's labeled trunk and baggage, he snapped his fingers in the direction of a group of hovering shoulder-pole coolies and, speaking sharply in staccato Shanghai dialect, barked orders at the first Chinese to scamper forward. Jostled by streams of stevedores sagging beneath pole-borne casks, canvas-wrapped boxes, and brimming vegetable baskets, Franklin led the way toward a phalanx of rickshaws. The pullers, bare-chested like the dock coolies, stood before the hooded vehicles, with the shafts jutting skyward over their shoulders, and when Franklin made a signal, half a dozen lunged toward them.

The pair who won the scramble dropped to their knees to hold the shafts firm against the cobblestones and Laurence Franklin lowered himself immediately into one of the cushioned seats, mopping his face with a snowy white handkerchief. Jakob, however, stood staring down at the bony, hollow-chested Chinese who knelt before him: the strip of cotton cloth wrapped turban-fashion around the aging man's head was streaked with sweat and grime and his puny shoulders sagged with fatigue. The expression of mute supplication that burned in his narrow eyes appalled Jakob and rooted him to the spot. In that moment he also became acutely aware of the throbbing, hundred-degree heat, the ceaseless surge of human energy all around him, and the raucous *"heh-ho, heh-ho, heh-ho"* chants of the trotting coolies which both cleared the way and gave rhythm to their breathing and their gait. An acrid, unfamiliar stench of body sweat rose sickeningly in his nostrils and he found that he was bracing his knees against the imaginary heave of the wharf induced in his senses by seven weeks at sea.

"Are you all right, old man?"

Jakob looked up to find Franklin watching him with concern. "Do we have to ride in these things?" he asked uneasily.

The bespectacled missionary laughed good-naturedly. "Ah, you've got a touch of 'rickshaw-itis'! A lot of new arrivals from Europe get it. It'll soon pass. You're just taking rice out of the coolie's mouth if you refuse the ride. Jump in. He can't make a living any other way."

Jakob obeyed reluctantly and as soon as he was seated, his coolie broke into a hobbling run, following in Franklin's wake. Coming out onto the crowded Bund they seemed to be carried along by the momentum of thousands of other iron-wheeled rickshaws; the shriek of tram sirens augmented the din, the feral reek of mules and buffalo hung heavy in the saturated air, and Jakob noticed with a start that the human draft animals hauling the giant platformed wheelbarrows rumbling all around him were often coolie women. With hempen ropes biting into their narrow shoulders they leaned low toward the road, staggering now and then with effort while their husbands strained and pushed the barrows from the rear. They never raised their heads and the unseen rickshaws swept past them like leaves on a millrace into the Nanking Road: there, thickets of brilliant hanging name banners splashed with golden Chinese characters drifted and rippled against every facade, dazzling Jakob's eyes.

The jumbled mass of carts, trucks, cars, and rickshaws ground to a standstill around the pedestal of a black-bearded Sikh policeman who was regulating the flow of traffic. As he waited, Jakob stared wide-eyed at the occupants of the rickshaws clustered around him — a wizened, obviously wealthy Chinese in a black long-gown and a mandarin's skullcap stared expressionlessly over the shoulder of his satin-jacketed puller; a palely powdered Chinese courtesan wearing a thigh-split cheongsam of mauve silk hid her face beneath a waxed-paper parasol; a corpulent, perspiring German abused his coolie in guttural pidgin English between pulls on a long cigar. On the congested pavements white-suited men from a dozen or more Western nations who enjoyed the protection of their own laws in Asia's largest city shouldered their way arrogantly through the milling crowds of Chinese, ignoring the ragged beggars and food hawkers stretching toward them from the gutters, stepping around the professional letter writers squatting at corners with ink and brushes, occasionally patronizing the Chinese bootblacks crouching before department store windows where British glass and wool, German leather, and French gowns were piled high beside Chinese silk and jade. The white men, Jakob noticed, greeted one another effusively and talked animatedly as they walked; but always they held themselves aloof from the swarm of yellow-brown humanity eddying all around them.

The rasp of the coolie's breath filled Jakob's ears again as the traffic blockage eased and the rickshaw jolted forward. The fierce sun, he saw, was basting the coolie's scarred back with films of sweat and the revulsion he had felt on the dockside at using a fellow human being as a personal beast of burden returned with a rush. Ahead of them the rickshaw of Laurence Franklin turned abruptly into a side lane and Jakob's coolie increased his pace to keep it in sight.

The moment the coolie's straw-sandaled feet struck the spine of ridge stones leading down the center of the cobbled alleyway, Jakob sat straighter in his cushioned seat. Rice-straw matting stretched across bamboo supports above his head blocked out the sun's glare and turned the narrow alley into a mysterious, subterranean tunnel: narrow-eyed faces poised above rice bowls and chopsticks peered from the gloom of open-fronted cookshops, intent craftsmen hammered and carved trinkets of jade, gold, and brass in dimly lit workrooms, and itinerant food peddlers sold noodles and rice cakes from little wheeled stoves. The whiff of hot spices, acrid oil smoke, and incense mingled with the reek from excrement handcarts in the stagnant air. Ragged, doll-faced children shrieked and giggled, pressing themselves against the walls to let the rickshaw pass; traveling barbers shaved the heads of old coolies in crumbling doorways; and from unseen wireless sets the discordant clamor of Chinese music rose hauntingly above the unceasing hubbub of excited voices echoing the length of the tunneled lane.

From that instant of entering the shadowy Shanghai alleyway Jakob in later life would date his true arrival in Asia. The sights, sounds, and odors which immediately excited his senses left an indelible impression in his brain. As the iron-wheeled rickshaw jangled along the cobbles, emotions began to stir which would never entirely leave him — a superficial fascination changed quickly to something much deeper.

As his eyes grew accustomed to the filtered light Jakob began to see the stark reality of what from the ship had seemed merely exotic and picturesque. Some of the shrieking children, he noticed, were calling warnings to files of blind beggars following them, hand to shoulder, through the gloom. One hunched figure clad in rags bumped against the rickshaw's hood and Jakob saw then that both sockets of his eyes were mutilated and empty. Many of the weary-faced women hobbled painfully on bound, stunted feet scarcely big enough to support small girls, and the pitted features of men and women alike betrayed the ravages of smallpox. Open sores were visible on many bodies, empty sleeves and trouser legs bore witness to the mutilations caused by China's many internal wars, and here and there the body of an adult or child lay motionless and lifeless at the foot of the walls. In the blank, sullen expressions of the people he saw on all sides, Jakob recognized despair and distrust, and soon he became aware that a dull, pervasive hopelessness existed beneath the surface commotion.

As they emerged from the narrow lane into a tiny, crowded market square, the tiring rickshaw coolie stumbled to a standstill. Looking down, Jakob saw that he had been forced to halt by a legless beggar who had propelled the trunk of his body across the cobbles into their path on a makeshift wooden trolley. Both the beggar's lower limbs had been severed at the hip, and to his horror Jakob saw that the unfortunate man had shaved his head and placed lighted incense sticks in a self-inflicted wound in his skull to solicit additional sympathy. Appalled by the sight, Jakob tugged money from his pocket and leaned out of the rickshaw to press a Chinese dollar into the beggar's outstretched claw. He murmured a prayer in English as he did so but the cripple turned his wooden-wheeled trolley around and rattled noisily away across the cobbles without uttering a word. When the rickshaw rolled forward again, Jakob noticed that sweat was coursing down his panting coolie's back like grease oozing from a spitted ox. The heat and the shock of what he was seeing all around him were making Jakob's own head swim and all his natural compassion focused itself with a sudden irrationality on the coolie.

"*Ting che!*" yelled Jakob. "Stop!"

The coolie looked around uncertainly, still trotting, and motioned queryingly with his chin toward the rickshaw of Laurence Franklin that was disappearing into the crowds a hundred yards ahead. Jakob shouted his command again and leapt out of the cushioned seat.

"Get in — please!" Jakob struggled with his rudimentary, training-college Chinese. "You're tired. I pull you now."

The coolie refused, protesting loudly, but seeing that a crowd was starting to gather, Jakob swung the astonished Chinese off his feet and lifted him bodily into his own vehicle. Seizing the shafts, he turned and set off at a fast run in pursuit of the other rickshaw.

The thick crowds impeding the stinking alleyway fell back against the walls on hearing the approaching commotion; as Jakob raced past them they gaped open-mouthed at the sight of a white European transporting a yelling Chinese coolie in his own rickshaw. Despite the heat which bathed him instantly in perspiration, Jakob felt a purifying exhilaration surge through his limbs. Restless after the weeks of inactivity at sea, his strong young body rejoiced in the act of running. Although the lane led up a slight gradient he increased his pace, lengthening his stride and throwing back his head. As he ran, the sustained exertion helped release the tensions growing within him: the perplexing feelings which Mei-ling had aroused, his other shipboard anxieties, and the new horrors of Shanghai's terrible poverty and disease all fused in his mind to produce, paradoxically, a sublime sense of elation. The magnitude of the task awaiting him in China was clearly greater than he had dared to imagine — but dashing through the densest throng of humanity he had ever encountered in his young life, he found himself welcoming the challenge with all his heart. It would provide a true and worthy test of his faith!

Rushing on past shabby *fan-tan* gambling dens and grimy teahouses that echoed with the clack of mah-jongg tiles, he saw Franklin's rickshaw turn into the gate of a walled compound in which the mission house evidently stood. From sheer exuberance he accelerated and ran faster now that his goal was in sight, swinging the rickshaw shafts out behind him to pass a swaying coolie cart piled high with gray roof tiles. Too late he saw another heavily laden barrow rolling down the lane in the opposite direction, and when his own coolie began to shriek a warning, he plunged toward the mission house gates with all his strength in an effort to get through the narrowing gap between the converging carts.

The approaching coolie's head was down, his eyes focused on the pitted surface ahead of him, and his own rhythmic trotting chant made him oblivious to the shouted warnings. He came on, his speed unchecked, and in swinging sharply from his path Jakob snagged the oilcloth hood of the rickshaw against the precariously stacked load of roof tiles. A rope snapped and the entire load cascaded from the cart, blocking the lane and overturning the oncoming barrow. One of the flying tiles struck Jakob a glancing blow on the temple and he sank to his knees on the cobbles, half-stunned. He heard soft-shod feet rush to surround the debris but the confused babble of Chinese voices remained muffled, as though reaching him through deep water. Feeling a gentle hand touch his shoulder he looked up: hazily, through a mist, he saw the pale face of a girl framed with soft brown hair.

"He's cut his forehead — but it's only a scratch."

The girl's voice bore a trace of soft American vowels which seemed to soothe Jakob's throbbing head, and as his vision cleared he saw wide gray eyes smiling sympathetically down at him. Then a man's face that was vaguely familiar appeared at the girl's shoulder. The weathered features had aged and his hair, previously steel gray, had turned white but when he spoke his voice too revived dim memories.

"You seem to have made an auspicious start in China, Mr. Kellner," said the man, smiling ironically. "Perhaps we'd better get you inside."

6

The gleaming, chauffeur-driven Buick limousine that had met the *Tomeko Maru* purred smoothly past the ornate Victorian grandstand that flanked the British racecourse on the Bubbling Well Road. It was heading toward the western edge of the International Settlement, where palatial mansions protected by wrought-iron gates and high walls stood apart from the turbulent sprawl of waterfront Shanghai. Its uniformed Chinese driver held himself formally erect at the wheel and in the luxuriously cushioned rear compartment, separated from the driver by a closed glass partition, Chiao and Mei-ling sat silently side by side, wrapped in their own thoughts.

As the car edged along the Bund and crawled into the congested streets adjoining the waterfront, Chiao had peered out at the dark, scrofulous alleyways and the wretched people emerging from them with a look of intense consternation on his face. Mei-ling too wore a troubled expression as she looked out of the window on her side, noticing the desperate contrasts between the poverty-stricken Chinese majority swarming the pavements and the minority of wealthy foreigners and Chinese merchants. Once or twice Chiao shook his head mutely as though in disbelief, but he did not break his silence until the limousine was clear of the dense throng and was moving more briskly through lighter traffic. Then he checked that the glass partition was fully closed before speaking in a low voice.

"Nothing has changed since we left," he said bitterly. "How can any Chinese who loves his heritage doubt that the Kung Ch'an Tang is necessary? Without the Communist Party how can we hope to win back our dignity and self-respect among all this?"

"Are you already rehearsing your arguments in your head, Ta ko, for the meeting with Father?" asked Mei-ling anxiously. "Are you having second thoughts?"

Although she looked at him with obvious affection, Mei-ling still used the formal mode of address — Elder Brother — when addressing Chiao. In his turn, Chiao habitually demonstrated his concern for his younger sister by the warmth of his expression and the extent to which he was prepared to confide in her. Often she read his inner thoughts accurately before he spoke but on this occasion he shook his head firmly, his features becoming set and determined.

"Shanghai isn't the Bois de Boulogne, I know, Mei-ling. Here we've got to do more than lie in the grass dreaming of how we might change the world. But I'm restless for some real activity. I can't wait to get down to the southern countryside. I'm longing to find out for myself what life is like in the new Central Soviet."

For a moment they both fell silent again, remembering the long summer afternoons in Paris when they had passionately debated the future with groups of young Russians and European Communists. Mei-ling had spent her vacations in France, and lolling in grassy hollows among the trees calling complete strangers "comrade" had induced feelings of exhilaration and hope in both of them: the existence of the Communist International forging a worldwide, seemingly unlimited brotherhood of youthful idealists had filled them with a great certainty that one day they would return home and help bring about sweeping, historic changes in their distant country. But now with the sickening reality of China's plight close before their eyes again, they faced the immediate prospect of an explosive confrontation with their father when they revealed their plans for the future.

"Wouldn't it be better to say nothing for a week or two?" suggested Mei-ling tentatively. "It would allow some time for us to readjust."

"No." Again Chiao shook his head firmly. "I'm sure Father will have arranged a homecoming banquet for us tonight. We must wait until that's over. But I shall tell him as soon as possible afterward." He paused and looked more closely at his sister, his voice softening. "You talk about waiting. Are you sure you still want me to speak for you as well? You don't have to come if you're not sure."

Color rose quickly in Mei-ling's cheeks. "Ta ko, if I stay I will be forced into an unbearable marriage with one of the Chang brothers or somebody like them. I would die of shame and humiliation!" Her dark eyes flashed angrily at the thought. "I'm coming with you."

Chiao smiled sympathetically. "I'm sorry for doubting your determination. I should have known better."

"What do you think Father will do?" asked Mei-ling in a quiet voice. "Will he understand, do you think?"

Chiao's face became very serious. "I will try to make him understand. I hope he will want to support us in some way. But I don't know . . ."

"Will you tell him you joined the Communists six years ago, before you went to Europe?"

"If he assumes it began in Europe, I won't say anything different . . ."

Chiao looked up warily as the limousine swung across a broad, tree-shaded avenue and glided into a willow-fringed drive that led to a cluster of single-storied pavilions ornamented with red pillars and blue upswept eaves. In contrast to the surrounding European villas and mansions, the residence had been built in the style of a traditional Chinese dwelling. Walled courtyards linked by circular moon gates and artificial gardens surrounded the pavilions; potted plum flowers and blooming shrubs abounded; water tinkled into quiet rock pools; and flickering lanterns and caged singing birds were suspended in the branches of small trees, giving the house an air of deep tranquillity and peace.

As the car sighed to a halt, their father's personal servant, Old Wang, an aged Chinese with a shaven head and the tight, strained features of a former court eunuch, hurried from the house to hold open the Buick's rear door. Smiling delightedly, he clasped his hands inside the sleeves of his black silk tunic and bowed low as Mei-ling and Chiao alighted. No other family member appeared to disturb the calm and they followed the old servant into the cool, silent house. In the corridors their eyes immediately fell on familiar ornaments of jade and ceramic, disposed with great precision on blackwood tables. Silk scroll paintings with which they had grown up hung alongside calligraphy banners bearing felicitous handwritten characters, and Chiao and Mei-ling both experienced a keen feeling of pleasure at returning to forgotten, familiar things. They glanced at one another, exchanging faint smiles, but each could see that the happiness the other felt was mingled with a growing apprehension about the reception they would get when they met their father.

7

House servants jacketed in red and gold bore a succession of rare culinary delicacies to the banqueting tables of Lu Peng three hours later to celebrate his son's return to China: sautéed tongues of wild duck and hummingbird, braised paws of bear, shark's fin, turtle with black mushrooms, ovaries of snow frog with ginseng. When the braised bears' paws were served, Lu rose to his feet and lifted high a slender-stemmed glass of Shao Hsing wine. A stocky, square-faced man with heavy brows and narrow, watchful eyes, he had an air of resolution and inner strength; only the pouches under his eyes testified to the fact that he was in his early sixties, and his otherwise unlined skin glowed with health. His hair was unrelievedly black and an unusual stillness in his manner had an ominous quality, so that the moment he stood up, his fifty invited guests gathered around several circular tables of polished teak fell silent.

"The bear was once the symbol of might in China. To eat the paws of the bear helps give a man the bear's strength. Today my son and heir has come home from abroad after two years of study . . . Now he will devote himself to our family business. To him, and to all those who offer him friendship and cooperation, I wish the strength of the mighty bear."

While the guests rose to drink the toast, Lu Peng's old manservant entered quietly carrying a scroll of calligraphy that bore verses inscribed by Lu in his own hand. Deferentially the servant placed it before his master and retired unnoticed.

"To mark this occasion," continued Lu, picking up the scroll, "I have penned a few unworthy lines of poetry in what was known as the 'old style' even in the time of the Tang emperors. Though undoubtedly quite worthless, these verses do perhaps convey the feelings of an old father's heart."

Lu, who wore an embroidered mandarin scholar's long-gown and a round, peakless cap of tight-fitting silk, turned toward his son, who sat at his right hand, and read from the scroll:

> "Like the ghosts and spirits
> Of our many illustrious ancestors
> A man is always happiest
> In the midst of his united family."

Chiao rose and bowed low to his father as the assembled company applauded; he too wore an embroidered Chinese jacket but was hatless. He offered his thanks confidently and elaborately, with much traditional self-deprecation, although Lu noticed that his son avoided looking directly at him. When the old manservant appeared at Chiao's side bearing a scroll inscribed with Chiao's own calligraphy, he took it and held it respectfully toward his father and read its complementary old-style verse aloud:

"One day in my father's house
Is far more precious to me
Than a thousand days
In lands beyond the sea."

Lu beamed with genuine pleasure and nodded his approval as he accepted his son's poem amid a further burst of applause. The banquet became more animated as other elderly male Chinese guests rose in turn to offer good wishes in the form of verse, epigram, or wordplay. When dishes of turtle shreds sautéed with bamboo fungus and black mushrooms were served, Lu rose again and looked toward Mei-ling, who was sitting opposite him. She wore a high-collared jacket of palest green silk decorated at the neck and across the sleeve ends with broad bands of pink satin; her jet black hair, lifted in a glossy chignon, gleamed in the candlelight, giving her a poised, detached air.

"My dear Mei-ling," said Lu, smiling affectionately, "this dish has been prepared as a thanksgiving to our ancestors for bringing you safely home through the storm at sea. A poetic interpretation of the characters denoting this delicacy might also be 'a golden willow bestrides a falling wave.' " He passed a decorated handwritten list of the dishes to her across the table. "I am very happy that my 'golden willow' has tamed the waves of the ocean and returned to glorify my garden once more . . . And of course I know that your return has made someone else happy too."

He directed his glance to the bespectacled young Chinese seated beside his daughter; a few years older than Mei-ling, he was already faintly proprietorial in his manner toward her and he smiled back with confidence at Lu.

"Now that you've finished your music studies, Mei-ling," added Lu, "we can begin to prepare for the joining of our family with the Changs. Not only have members of our two families been lifelong friends, since you've been away the Changs have become our closest business partners."

Mei-ling forced a smile as she murmured her thanks to her father, but she found herself unable to hold his gaze for long and she feigned shyness to avoid looking at the eldest son of the Chang family at her side. An excited buzz of conversation arose at the news that the two families were to be united, but as Lu sat down a small frown nagged at his brow. Before seeing his son and daughter he had asked his manservant how they seemed, and the old eunuch had replied that both were "more mature and self-confident." But in the brief meeting of welcome to which he had invited them in his study and now at the banquet in their honor, neither seemed willing to look him in the eye. He glanced toward his wife, who headed an adjoining table, but she seemed relaxed and at ease, unaware of any tension. At his side Chiao was bent over his chopsticks, seemingly preoccupied with eating, and he did not turn until his father addressed him directly.

"Soon, Chiao, we should decide when you will begin the task of learning how to take over the business from your aging parent." Lu spoke quietly so that nobody else overheard. "There's much for you to discover and there's no point in wasting more time."

Setting down his chopsticks, Chiao raised his head to find his father's eyes fixed on him but this time he did not flinch from returning his gaze. The striking stillness of body and mind that was so evident in his father's bearing had been achieved, Chiao knew, by strict adherence to a lifelong regime of self-discipline practiced rigorously in accordance with ancient Chinese teachings, and in an instant he was able to discern that the older man's dedication to his code had not diminished with age. The daily ritual over many years had never changed; although he had not observed him, Chiao knew that his father had arrived home from Shanghai's biggest textile factory at precisely the same time as on every other day and gone directly to his secluded garden studio without speaking to any member of the household. Assisted by his manservant he had dressed himself in a long-gown of high-quality gauze and seated himself cross-legged on the earthen bed in the center of the austere room. There for forty minutes he had practiced a combination of breath control and deep meditation exercises designed to still the mind. Focusing his consciousness in the imagined center of spiritual force in the lower abdomen, he had chafed and stroked his cheeks, his temples, his forehead, and the bare soles of his feet with the warmed palms of his hands until he felt waves of cosmic energy, which Taoist sages called *ch'i*, rising and coursing strongly through his whole body, expanding from the abdomen, flowing outward, growing and returning to build an inner reservoir of strength and energy at the core of his being. Then when he felt refreshed he had no doubt risen and taken up his brush to let the same vital energy guide his hand in the natural rhythms of calligraphy for the writing of the poem. Chiao knew all these things with such exactitude because his father had taught him to follow the same Taoist codes of self-discipline from an early age; Chiao had continued to meditate and perform the gentle T'ai Chi Ch'uan martial art exercises daily in France, and in the same moment that he recognized his father's continuing dedication, he knew that he himself would be coming under similar scrutiny.

"I've long looked forward to two things during my absence, Father," said Chiao at last, speaking calmly. "One is refreshing my eyes before the art treasures displayed in your private Chamber of Antiquities — and the other is discussing my future with you. May we combine those two things when the banquet is over?"

The quiet, direct demeanor of his son, with which he was more familiar, reassured Lu and he assented willingly to the request. A small group of Chinese musicians had entered and begun to play stringed instruments on a raised platform at the end of the room, a juggler was performing elaborate tricks beyond the tables, and father and son turned their attention to the entertainment along with their guests. When the festivities ended, Lu led the way through the house to a red lacquered door standing behind a security gate of iron bars. The old eunuch appeared silently from the shadows, holding a ring of keys, and he unlocked the gate and the door, closing them carefully behind the two men once they were safely inside. The large chamber, laid out as a private museum, contained many exquisite figures carved in jade and amber, bronzes from the Han and Chou dynasties, and bowls, vases, and wine jars of glazed porcelain wrought by Tang and Sung craftsmen. Occasionally father or son stopped to caress a piece of jade or inspect the colors and markings of a piece of porcelain, but for some minutes neither of them spoke: then at last Chiao broke the silence.

"Twenty years have passed since Old Wang served the last Son of Heaven in Peking," he said reflectively with his back to his father. "But China has known nothing but strife during that time." He picked up a slender-necked Tang ewer and traced the delicate curve of its spout which was fashioned in the form of a phoenix head. "It's wonderful to be home, Father, and see all these beautiful objects again. But I must admit I'm impatient to see a new China rise like this phoenix from the ashes of the past." He swung around to face his father, holding the ewer before him. "Surely, Father, you want to see China restored to greatness too, don't you?"

"China's greatness can still be seen clearly in every object in this room," said Lu crisply.

"But it isn't visible in the terrible sights of Shanghai and Canton and the other so-called treaty ports, where Europeans rule us. It isn't clear in Manchuria, where the Japanese are threatening to seize more of our territory."

Lu looked searchingly at his son. "Why do you talk this way, Chiao? Europe seems to have changed you. We came here to discuss how you might take over responsibility for the textile factories."

"Europe hasn't changed me, Father — it's helped me see things I've always felt much more clearly." Chiao paused, realizing he had meant to try to break the news of his intentions more gently, but now he found he could contain his pent-up feelings no longer. "I'm sorry, Father, but I can't spend the rest of my life looking after your factories. I have physical strength and a strong mind — you've given me those. And I want to use them for my country. If I stay in Shanghai and run your factories, I might make the Lu family and a few British traders more prosperous — but that's all."

Lu's face betrayed his feeling of shock for only a moment before he mastered it. "In enhancing the wealth of your own family, you would also be contributing to the well-being of your countrymen."

"But not enough of them, Father!"

As he registered the implications of his son's statement, Lu's eyes narrowed. "This must mean you've become a member of the Kung Ch'an Tang while you've been in Europe. The words of your poem were hollow — you've joined the ranks of the Marxists."

"Yes, Father, I am a member of the Kung Ch'an Tang," said Chiao quietly. "I believe only the Communist Party can make China great again. I intend to go to the soviet areas now and so does Mei-ling. She is too intelligent and creative to endure the torture of an arranged marriage with Chang or anybody else." Chiao paused again, his face growing tense as he searched desperately for the right words. "But my poem was not hollow. Mei-ling and I hoped you would understand, Father . . . The Kung Ch'an Tang needs the support of men of good standing. You could provide funds even if you did nothing else — nobody need know."

Lu stood straighter suddenly. His face had turned pale but the stillness of his expression betrayed that he was battling for inner control of his feelings. For a long time he neither moved nor spoke; then, without warning, he walked over to Chiao and removed the Tang ewer from his grasp. Replacing it carefully on its shelf, he gestured for his son to leave the chamber ahead of him. "Your decision will cut you off immediately from your family and everything dear to you," he said in an icy voice. "You and your sister have made a very grave choice."

Fully aware of the symbolic finality of the act, Lu ushered his son from the Chamber of Antiquities. Outside Chiao hesitated and turned back, half intending to make one last appeal for understanding. But he saw that his father's face was cold and stiff, and without any sign of emotion Lu closed the door firmly on the magnificent array of antique bronze, jade, and porcelain which he knew his son loved. Taking the key from the waiting manservant, Lu locked the door with slow deliberation. Then, turning his back on Chiao as though he no longer existed, he walked quietly away along the corridor toward his garden studio.

8

A strong gust of wind swept into the mission church as the notes of the last hymn died away. To Jakob's horror, the congregation of Chinese coolies and beggars began to writhe sensually in their pews as though stirred by the wind. Turning, he saw Mei-ling rising from her seat before the organ, the skirts of her dress billowing out from her body as they had done on the deck of the *Tomeko Maru*. But this time she made no effort to hold down the dress: her ankles, her calves, and then her slender amber thighs became visible in turn, her long, glossy hair swirled across her face, and she too began to sway languorously as she moved toward him.

The coolie men and women and the beggars had begun pulling off their clothing, moving in unison. Among them Jakob saw the legless cripple seated on his wheeled tray. Through the press of yellow-brown bodies moved the white-haired senior missionary who had come to Jakob's aid in the alley; still smiling benignly, he appeared to be encouraging and advising individuals in turn.

Mei-ling's dress was suddenly open from throat to hem as she came smiling toward him: she was near enough for him to see the play of muscles under her ribs, the curve of her belly, the gentle swell of her small breasts and their dark-nippled peaks. She began to stretch out her arms to him but he turned away to call frantically to the congregation, who now were grappling together in a naked, seething mass among the pews. He strained his throat and lungs — but no sound emerged. He felt cool hands touch his own shoulders and realized for the first time that he too was naked.

Standing apart, he saw, was the American girl with the brown bobbed curls. Dressed demurely in the same pale cotton frock that she had been wearing that afternoon when she bandaged his forehead, she had an expression of seraphic detachment on her face as though she was unable to see what was going on around her. Jakob tried to attract her attention — but she continued gazing distantly over his head, an unsullied and remote figure. Feeling delicate arms tighten around his naked chest, Jakob began to struggle and shout again. An animal warmth that was both pleasurable and frightening began to suffuse his body, making him struggle more wildly, and as he thrashed from side to side he woke himself from the nightmare.

Immediately the alien noises of Shanghai's alleyways reached into the darkened mission house bedroom where he lay breathing raggedly: the harsh cries of peddlers, the creak of their laden bamboo poles, the tinkling bells rung by the blind. Above all else he could hear the fast, staccato beat of Chinese voices raised in complaint and argument. When his breathing quieted Jakob raised a hand to his head and gingerly fingered the bandage bound around his brow. He remembered then the soothing voice of the American girl and the confident, capable way she had treated his injury. As she leaned close over him he had smelled the fragrance of the perfumed soap with which she must have washed herself, and he became tangibly aware of the aura of goodness and wholesomeness which she radiated.

He remembered too the calm, tactful presence of the older Englishman in the alleyway. His intervention had saved what might have been an ugly situation; in the midst of the angry crowd of Chinese he had unobtrusively handed out a few coins of compensation to the coolies whose loads had been spilled, and tempers had quickly cooled. It was he who had then suggested that Jakob get some rest immediately, although the graze on his forehead was not serious, and he had conducted Jakob to the bedroom himself.

The memory of that kindness, contrasting so brutally with the recollection of the senior missionary's imagined role in the nightmare, brought with it a feeling of shame and self-disgust. Stricken anew with the full horror of what he had dreamed, Jakob rose from the bed hurriedly and fell to his knees to pray. He had several times resorted to prayer in similar circumstances a few years earlier in resisting the teasing of earthy mill girls. Once they discovered the intended vocation of the apprentice engineer working among them, they had come to delight in taunting him and calling up his youthful blushes as he struggled to tend their machinery. Subduing the little-understood physical instincts of his healthy young body, therefore, had not been easy but the nightmare of sensualism he had just suffered had been unprecedented. Its shaming sacrilegious nature had obviously been inspired by the scurrilous anti-Christian propaganda read to him by Jacques Devraux on the *Tomeko Maru*, and for this reason he redoubled the intensity of his prayers, begging that all carnal thoughts in future be banished from his mind. He was still kneeling in this absorbed attitude when the bedroom door was opened quietly by the white-haired missionary. He waited patiently on the threshold until Jakob had finished praying and climbed back into bed, then advanced into the room, carrying a smoking oil lamp.

"Rome wasn't built in a day — and China can't be converted to Christianity overnight." The older man set the flickering lamp down on the bedside table, tapping the file of papers he carried tucked inside a big-character Chinese Bible. "I'm Matthew Barlow, and that's today's lesson for a novice missionary 'with boundless energy and enthusiasm for his calling.' I've been reading the report sent ahead from your training college; your arrival outside our gates certainly bears out that perceptive assessment."

In the lamplight, Jakob became fully aware for the first time of who Barlow was. In ten years the sunburned face that had seemed so heroic to a small boy in a back-street church hall had aged considerably — but it was still recognizably the face of the man who had inspired his boyhood fantasies of China. The name "Matthew Barlow" he recognized as belonging to the director-general in China of the entire Anglo-Chinese Mission, and this surprising realization left him momentarily at a loss for words.

"I'm very sorry about the accident, Mr. Barlow," he said hurriedly when at last he recovered himself. "I'm afraid I got carried away. Being pulled in the rickshaw seemed so humiliating — to the coolie *and* me."

"The Chinese, Jakob, have carried burdens as heavy as themselves for thousands of years. They think nothing of it. That's one of the many things you'll just have to accept."

Barlow smiled briefly but his manner was faintly resigned, and the expression was a pale shadow of the gleaming smile that had captivated Jakob in the Moss Side church hall. He could see that lines of fatigue were now etched deep around Barlow's eyes, his white hair was thinning and receding at the temples, and in his movements there was a hint of growing weariness. Jakob felt a vague stirring of disquiet at these changes — then he dismissed them as natural consequences of the passage of time.

"You've taught me an important lesson today, Mr. Barlow," said Jakob, smiling ruefully and rubbing his bandaged head lightly with one hand. "Thank you for coming to my rescue."

"Don't thank me, young man. You ought to thank Miss Felicity Pearson."

"Who is Miss Pearson?"

"Her parents were missionaries in Tientsin when she was small. They went home when she was eight years old. But as she grew up in America she found she couldn't forget China. She's just spent two years studying at a Bible institute in Connecticut and has come out with the Sino-American Missionary Society."

"Why was she here?"

"She'd been visiting me to discuss her application for language training. She saw you crash your chariot and came running to drag me into the fray."

"I must write a letter thanking her."

"You'll have an opportunity to thank her personally — both of you will be attending the same course in Peking at the new Joint Missionary Language School."

"When do I go to Peking?" asked Jakob in surprise.

"The day after tomorrow." Barlow glanced absently at his file. "We don't keep young men long in Shanghai doing nothing. You'll have time to get your land legs and buy a few essentials for traveling rough in China — a fiber mat, an oil sheet, some bedding. Then you'll be on your way. "

Despite the excitement he felt on learning he was to go to Peking, Jakob experienced a new sense of dismay. Barlow's manner seemed almost perfunctory, as though he felt little genuine interest in his task, and a silence fell between them, broken only by the distant gabble of Chinese voices and the discordant clanging of gongs and cymbals coming from the street outside. Perhaps a hint of Jakob's perplexity showed on his face, because the director-general sat down on the end of the bed, looking at him more closely. "When I came in, Jakob," he said quietly, "you were praying. Are you worried? Is there anything I can help you with?"

"No, thank you, not really . . ." Jakob avoided his gaze. "I had a bad dream, that's all."

"China always overwhelms new arrivals one way or another," said Barlow slowly. "This country teems with more people than any of us have ever seen before. Newcomers often feel as if they're drowning in an ocean of human bodies. It takes time for European nerves to adjust." He sighed and rubbed his eyes. "And I may as well warn you, Jakob, in China you have to be prepared to be crucified at least once a day. Here in Shanghai, for instance, the refuse carts pick up ten thousand corpses from the gutters every year . . ."

Barlow's voice trailed off with a shrug and a thin smile, and in the attitude of his sagging shoulders as he sat on the end of the bed, Jakob detected an unmistakable air of defeatism.

"But Shanghai isn't the whole of China, Mr. Barlow, is it?" he asked, injecting his question with a note of determination. "The Anglo-Chinese Mission is still making good progress in China generally, isn't it?"

"Yes, of course." As though suddenly aware that he had dwelled too much on negative thoughts, Barlow opened the Chinese Bible he carried and focused his gaze on the vertical lines of ideograms. "I've been working on a fresh translation of the Scriptures for some time. There's a great need, I believe, to preach in language ordinary people can understand."

"Is the number of converts growing?"

"I've been in China thirty-five years, Jakob. In that time almost fifteen thousand Chinese have become Christians through our mission — which isn't many out of four hundred million people. Cynics will tell you half of them are 'rice Christians,' who say they believe to make sure they have access to food supplies when the next famine arrives, and that another quarter of them are 'rice students,' who become converts to get a good education in our mission schools."

"But surely that's not entirely true, is it, Mr. Barlow?" Jakob, to his surprise, felt a faint sense of irritation with his superior. "How can it be with so many of our people working hard all over China?"

Barlow drew a long breath. "No, it's not entirely true, but we shouldn't delude ourselves. I suspect few adult Chinese ever become real converts. The Chinese tend to treat new religions like new business methods — they'll try them all in the hope that at least one might be right." Barlow paused and his face brightened a little as though in response to Jakob's enthusiasm. "But you're right. Many people are giving their best. We've got a hundred main stations and about five hundred outstations scattered across the country. There are about six hundred missionaries with twice that number of Chinese helpers. The core of converts still tends to be the missionaries' servants but we hope that there are as many 'silent Christians' as there are 'rice Christians.' "

"What are 'silent Christians,' Mr. Barlow?" asked Jakob.

"Officials who are believers of one sort or another — but can't admit it publicly because they'd lose face. We hope our influence is spreading unobtrusively in China through men like them. Some send their children quietly to the missionary Sunday schools. Those children carry our main hopes for the future."

Jakob's face grew thoughtful. "So it's likely to be a gradual, long-term process."

Barlow nodded. "In the end the Chinese themselves will have to evangelize China. We can only show them the way. I hoped that in my lifetime enough native Christians would have been trained to begin that task. But progress has been even slower than I'd expected . . ." Barlow's voice again faded away and his expression became abstracted. "One problem is that a lot of young men become missionaries through sheer wanderlust," he said distantly as though voicing an inner thought. "They're merely fascinated by distant places and strange peoples. Some never know the difference between that and the true missionary's spirit."

Appalled by the seeming implication that his own motives might be questionable, Jakob straightened indignantly against his pillows. "It was because of *you* that I came to China, Mr. Barlow!"

The older missionary frowned. "I don't follow you, Jakob . . . ?"

"You came to talk to my local church when you were on furlough. I was just a small boy. You told us the Chinese believed blue-eyed people could see into the ground to a depth of three feet. I have blue eyes, and I think that was when I decided I wanted to be a China missionary. You talked about dragons and gangs of bandits and discovering gold and I could think of nothing else for days . . ."

"Did I?" From his expression it was clear Barlow did not recall the occasion, but he rose from the end of the bed and patted Jakob on the shoulder in a friendly fashion. "Well done, young man. I'm sure you'll bring great credit to us all."

Jakob looked up at his superior expectantly. He thought that the director-general was going to suggest that they pray together but to his intense disappointment Barlow gathered up his papers and left the room without another word, closing the door quietly behind him. From the alleyway outside Jakob could still hear the muffled noise of cymbals and gongs and several Chinese voices raised in a shrill, angry dispute. The alien sounds reminded him just how far he was from home and everything familiar, and he closed his eyes where he lay and prayed again for the strength to carry out his new, daunting tasks.

9

From the moment he left Shanghai to travel to Peking by train, Jakob's spirits began to rise again. After the oppressive poverty of the Chinese sections of the sprawling port city, the vast, open plains of green terraced rice fields that soon spread out beyond his carriage windows were a refreshing sight to the young missionary. Stark gray mountains bordered the largely treeless plains and the rice fields teemed with bare-footed peasants turning the wheels of ancient irrigation systems, carrying earth for new dykes, hoeing, bending, lifting, wading, planting. Their lives in many ways were obviously as harsh and austere as those of Shanghai's coolies: from the train Jakob saw large groups of bent-backed figures hacking laboriously at the soil of dried-up fields with hand tools; ragged girls washed clothes in hollows where rain had gathered and men still pulled ancient wooden ploughs in the absence of beasts of burden. But nobody was suffering the cramped squalor of Shanghai's dark alleyways and the figures in the fields seemed to work with unflagging energy beneath the limitless sky.

Felicity Pearson traveled on the same train and when they met to take their meals in the ornate dining car, she and Jakob quickly found that the compassion they felt for China was equally intense. A strong sense of spiritual fellowship and common purpose grew up between them as together they watched the distinctive landscapes typical of central and southern China change to a very different picture in the north. Gradually, between the Yangtze and the Yellow River, the flooded paddy fields with their plodding water buffalo gave way to flat, dry fields sprouting wheat and *kaoliang*; giant loads borne by the unending caravans of pole-carrying coolies in the south were taken over in the north by camels, mules, and netted Peking carts; and eventually the vibrantly green land of rice fields and silver waterways was superseded entirely by a dusty brown, corn-growing zone with little grass and few trees.

On arrival in Peking, Jakob and Felicity settled quickly into the same class of the Joint Missionary Language School, which was housed in a European-style building to the northeast of the Forbidden City. Their fellow students included diplomats from the Legation Quarter and representatives of foreign commercial firms based in the old Chinese capital. Because of the similarity of their interests, Jakob and Felicity agreed to share the same Chinese tutor when the class broke each morning into groups of two or three for more intensive work. After the long hours of study were finished they also found themselves in the same gatherings, and they shared the pleasure and excitements of exploring the old imperial capital that had been fashioned in its lasting form by the emperors of the Ming dynasty more than five centuries earlier.

During the first weeks and months of their studies they eagerly visited every last corner of the rectangular walled enclosures — the Imperial City, the Tartar City, the Outer City — that surrounded the central Purple Forbidden City. They were enchanted by the simple grandeur of the Temple of Heaven in the southern reaches of the capital, where the emperors had once made regular ritual sacrifices, but they returned most frequently to the Forbidden City, the inner sanctum of China's emperors that had been named after the "Purple Luminous Constellation," because in ancient times the North Star was believed to have been the supreme center of heavenly power. At its heart, magnificently lacquered in vermilion and gold, stood the Hall of Supreme Harmony which the ancient Chinese had called "The Center of the World." Inside, a richly ornamented dais held the Dragon Throne, where until twenty years before the emperor had sat on ceremonial occasions. Neither Jakob nor Felicity ever tired of wandering through these awesome precincts, marveling at the magnificence of the shimmering marble balustrades, the guardian lions, the phoenixes, dragons, and other mythical beasts wrought in stone and gilded bronze. Each time they found new ornaments of ivory, jade, and porcelain to admire, new luxuriant furnishings of silk and brocade to wonder at, and as their language ability increased they whispered together with delight the beguiling Chinese names of countless gates, gardens, and halls: the Palace of Earthly Tranquillity, the Chamber of Beautiful Expectation, the Gate of Heavenly Purity, the Garden of Peace and Longevity.

Although Chiang Kai-shek had set up his modern capital to the south, in Nanking, and the remnants of the last emperor's family had been finally banished from the imperial enclosures, the splendor of the court and its precincts still cast an invisible spell over both foreign and Chinese residents in Peking. To Jakob's delight, the mission houses where he and Felicity were quartered stood inside the Imperial City itself. Traditional *ssu ho yuan*, the former homes of courtiers, both mission dwellings consisted of clusters of single-storied, gray-tiled pavilions built around shady courtyards adorned with rock gardens, lotus pools, and ancient fruit trees. Jakob slept on a clay-built *k'ang*, a bed that in winter could be heated from inside by a camel-dung fire, and the frames of the latticed paper windows through which the first rays of dawn filtered each day were lacquered in crimson and fading gilt. Often in half-waking reverie he tried to picture the mandarin noblemen who must have occupied the house in bygone days; he fancied he saw them worshiping in richly embroidered gowns before their ancestral tablets, bowing gravely to welcome high-ranking guests, composing scrolls of exquisite calligraphy, and smoking their water pipes in the shady courtyard while their caged birds sang melodiously in the branches of the fruit trees.

Under the influence of these many reminders of China's vivid history, Jakob quickly forgot the doubts and anxieties he had suffered on arrival in Shanghai. Almost daily he felt his mind expanding as never before. The lavish art and architectural treasures of the imperial palaces, and the stylized natural settings created in the surrounding lakes and garden terraces, induced in him a more intense awareness of beauty in both nature and art. Although he possessed no great natural language talent and had finished his formal education at fifteen, he found that by rising early to study before breakfast and working late at night he could at least keep in sight of the other students, who all came from superior academic backgrounds. There were a dozen or so mission churches of different denominations in the city where mixed congregations of Chinese and Europeans worshiped, and reciting the Lord's Prayer in Chinese at the services, sometimes at Felicity's side, never failed to inspire in Jakob's mind an exciting vision of his future self preaching the Gospel in Chinese in some remote walled township.

In the streets the courtly manners of the former imperial scholars and generals added an extra dimension of sophistication and refinement to the city which, it seemed to Jakob, he was also absorbing in some intangible way. In struggling with the rare problems of the written and spoken language under the guidance of a grave-faced Chinese tutor who was himself a former Board of Rites mandarin, Jakob felt that he was daily visiting other mysterious frontiers of the mind, and even his partial mastery of the difficulties proved highly satisfying.

All these new influences produced a heady sense of excitement in both Jakob and Felicity which rarely left them, and they worked energetically through the sweltering humidity of the long Peking summer without faltering. Their great enthusiasm for the beauty of the ancient capital communicated itself to their tutor, Mr. Li, and one day at the end of August the old scholar paused in the doorway of their classroom after a lesson and smilingly told them that they would soon discover that the approaching autumn was the most beautiful of all seasons in Peking.

"You're truly fortunate to be in the capital now," he said, stroking his wisp of beard reflectively. "The skies remain blue and without cloud all day. The air is crisp and invigorating and some say the dawn hour particularly has magical qualities."

"What kind of 'magical qualities'?" asked Jakob with a puzzled grin.

"To some extent that depends on the observer," said the wizened Chinese enigmatically. "We will meet soon for instruction at a place of special beauty — at sunrise. Then you will be able to judge for yourself."

10

A few mornings later the newly risen sun shining from an azure north China sky bathed the Pavilion of Eternal Spring with pure, clear light. Among the darker foliage of the age-toughened pines that had shaded the summit of Gorgeous Prospect Hill for six centuries, the glazed green tiles of its triple-tiered roof glittered like emeralds. Built at the exact center of Peking's walled inner city on its highest crest, the pavilion had been the crowning glory in the gardens of the Ming emperors: its open south side afforded a spectacular view of the imperial palaces built far below amid groves of cypress and acacia, and from their seats in the pavilion on either side of Mr. Li, Jakob and Felicity gazed down at the gilded porcelain rooftops in silent wonder.

"From here the palaces look like beautiful golden carp basking in a lake of green jade," breathed Felicity.

"No Chinese poet would disagree with you." Mr. Li smiled. "Anything is possible at the dawn hour."

On their way to meet their tutor in the hilltop pavilion, at his suggestion, Jakob and Felicity had passed along the willow-fringed moat outside the crenellated northern wall of the Forbidden City. To their surprise, for it was not yet six o'clock, they had found Chinese of all ages absorbed there in a variety of activities. All clearly shared a belief in the mystery of the dawn hour: boys played bamboo flutes or stringed lutes, following music fastened to the willow fronds; small girls paraded songbirds in little wicker cages; seated against the boles of trees or on the low moat wall young men and women pored over books or softly practiced a song; youths and scholarly-looking older men with beards rehearsed stylized swordplay with tasseled blades or moved rhythmically through the postures of T'ai Chi Ch'uan, the slow-motion, meditative martial art sometimes called "swimming in air." The lilt of the music on the still air and the silent, graceful movements of the different groups beneath the ancient palace ramparts lent an added enchantment to the crystal-bright autumn morning, and Jakob and Felicity took care not to intrude as they hurried on into the Ching Shan Park, which had once been a private garden of the imperial family.

"The purity of the dawn air also enhances the art of the calligrapher," said Mr. Li, drawing ink stick, stone, and brush from a satchel at his side. "We believe it helps beautify his script and brings greater distinction to the strokes of his brush."

Li, who wore a tight-fitting black cap and a robe of pale blue silk over white trousers, shook a few shimmering drops of dew from an acacia leaf onto his stone and ground the ink stick delicately in the moisture before beginning to fashion ancient pictograms, murmuring the names of shapes representing recognizably the sun, the moon, a fish, a horse.

"The character for happiness, *hsi*, for instance, is derived from a picture of a mother and child under a curved roof . . . 'grass' is simple upright strokes of the brush, 'brightness' is conveyed by placing the sun and moon side by side . . ."

The tutor outlined the characters skillfully in their antique and modern forms and Jakob and Felicity watched, fascinated, as the changing images retained their pictorial essence. Taking out brushes and ink sticks from their own pouches, they began inexpertly trying to imitate his fluid movements.

"If you are to understand China at all well, it is vital to know how deeply Chinese behavior is influenced by our written language." Li spoke softly, almost reverently, his brush flowing uninterruptedly across the paper. "Almost without our realizing, it reminds us subtly each day of our history, our customs, our traditions. It ensures that the experiences of our past play a full part in the thoughts and deeds of the present. And because those who can't memorize and write the characters have great respect for those who can, it confers authority on those who practice the art. In the beauty of our palaces and temples below us you can see similar principles at work."

Jakob looked down at the panorama of richly ornamented halls and pavilions spread out beyond the foot of the hill. They were separated by landscaped gardens, lakes, marble terraces, and walled courtyards, each large enough to shelter ten thousand imperial soldiers, and in the early light and shadow they had taken on an added air of mystery and majesty.

"The palace roofs were constructed around uniquely arranged beams that allowed their eaves to sweep upward — but they could equally have remained straight and rigid." The tutor illustrated his words by making a long, delicate, curving upstroke with his writing brush, then bisected it with a broad-slashed perpendicular. "The harmonizing of straight and curved lines, you see, lies at the heart of Chinese calligraphy. In combining the two in our script and in the design of our finest buildings, the qualities of strength and grace are intermingled and made visible for all to see in both."

"You write so beautifully, Mr. Li," said Felicity. "It's a pleasure to watch you on this lovely morning."

"*Hsiaochieh* is too kind. After many years of practice my accomplishment is slight." The old mandarin gestured toward Felicity's practice pad and smiled. "But *Hsiaochieh* is truly making good early progress."

"I lived in China until I was eight, Mr. Li. My parents were missionaries in Tientsin. I think perhaps that helps."

"*Hsiaochieh* is certainly making faster progress than me." Jakob laughed ruefully at his own comparatively clumsy efforts and made a pantomime of hiding his pad when Li turned to look.

For a moment the tutor peered intently at Felicity. It had not escaped his notice that she glanced frequently in Jakob's direction during their lessons and that there was always an eager brightness in her gaze in Jakob's presence. For his part Jakob was obviously enjoying her company, as usual, but the shrewd old mandarin decided that he was unaware of the special light in his companion's expression. When Felicity lifted her head from her pad to find the Chinese watching her, he smiled mysteriously and bent over his pad once more. "I will give you other examples . . . the character for grow, you see, is the pictogram for the earth placed beside a sprouting plant." He deftly drew the ancient and modern versions of the character, then turned to a fresh sheet of paper. "But perhaps most interesting of all is the character for love. Because it is an abstract idea it is composed of three roots: at the top is the character that can mean either 'a bird is on the wing' or 'quickened breath.' In the middle is the pictogram for the human heart and below that a character indicating a man walking with pride. When mingled together the poetic sense of each character helps define an important word with great beauty and subtlety."

The tutor smiled again at Felicity and held out the pad for her inspection — but she scarcely glanced at the newly written character, lowering her head instead to hide a faint flush that had sprung to her cheeks. When Li turned to show Jakob the pad, he peered good-humoredly at each part of the character, nodding his head vigorously in approval, unaware of Felicity's sensitivity.

"So I hope you have sensed something of the mystery of the dawn hour in Peking," said the tutor, packing his writing materials in his satchel and rising to his feet. "It is not advisable to linger too long on such rare occasions. The magic moments are fleeting." The Chinese tucked his hands into his sleeves and inclined his head to each of them in turn. "Until we meet again."

Jakob and Felicity watched in silence as the silk-robed figure of the Chinese scholar merged into the shadows of the gnarled pines and cypresses that bordered the narrow path along the ridge. The fluted trill of a songbird sounded from one of the four ornamented lodges that flanked the Pavilion of Eternal Spring and cicadas whirred softly in the nearer trees. Below, the lotus-spangled moat around the Forbidden City and the three lakes that the Manchu emperors had excavated outside its western wall sparkled silver-blue in the strengthening glow of the sun, providing a dramatic color contrast with the magenta walls of the palaces and their glazed roofs of fiery yellow.

"I think this is one of the most beautiful mornings of my life," murmured Felicity as she put away her writing materials. "I'm very glad, Jakob, that you were here to share it with me."

"I'm very glad too." Jakob filled his lungs appreciatively with the cool air and smiled happily at Felicity.

She was wearing a dress of peach gingham and low-heeled navy oxfords, and her hair, carefully parted at the side, was drawn back in a tidy knot at the nape of her neck. She was composed again and Jakob saw only the gentle, serious expression that had become so familiar to him during the past three months. They were still seated several feet apart on the long bench of carved teak and for some moments Felicity neither moved nor spoke; then she turned suddenly to face Jakob, her earnest gray eyes engaging his directly.

"You do understand, Jakob, don't you," she said with an edge of nervousness in her voice, "that I've surrendered my life completely to the Lord? I believe God called me to China for a reason which will be made clear in due course. Nothing can ever come before that loyalty."

"Yes, of course I understand," said Jakob, smiling uncertainly. "I've never thought otherwise for a minute."

The moment he had spoken Felicity half turned from him to stare down at the distant palaces. He saw at once that his casual answer had had a disturbing effect on her. Bright spots of color burned in her pale cheeks, betraying her inner disquiet, and Jakob realized then that she must have assumed wrongly that they shared deep feelings for one another. No intimacies had ever been exchanged or even hinted at between them, although a strong bond of friendship had begun to grow during the railway journey from Shanghai, and Jakob found himself at a loss for words.

"I think Mr. Li said it was advisable not to linger here too long," said Felicity awkwardly, picking up her satchel. "I ought to be going."

Jakob jumped to his feet, concerned that she should not be offended. "I'll come with you, Felicity. Let's go together."

"No, please, there's no need. I'd like to walk alone for a bit."

Felicity hurried away down the path, leaving Jakob staring after her. The sun was growing stronger and the pines brushed the curved eaves of the pavilion in the breeze, making a gentle rustling sound — but Jakob no longer saw the beauty of the morning. Feeling ill at ease, he sat down again on the bench, resting his chin thoughtfully on his hand, and watched Felicity until she disappeared from sight among the trees.

11

Over the next few days Peking's autumn skies remained a peerless blue but to Jakob's dismay Felicity avoided him outside of their study classes. At the end of each lesson she hurried away on one pretext or another and he found himself alone and sometimes lonely, with time on his hands. His own sense of discomfort grew as he realized how much distress and embarrassment Felicity must have suffered after inadvertently hinting at the depth of her feelings.

In class she now concentrated her attention on her work at all times, never once looking his way, and whenever he caught sight of her, she seemed more than ever to radiate simple piety and goodness. As the days went by he began to reflect how central a part Felicity had played in everything that had happened to him in China, and he was increasingly moved, too, by the memory of the words she had spoken so tentatively in the Pavilion of Eternal Spring. He began to castigate himself inwardly for having taken her friendship for granted and he made one or two attempts to apologize to her for this — but she politely brushed his approaches aside.

He slept poorly for the first time in his life and to his great dismay one night he suffered a recurrence of his Shanghai nightmare. It disturbed his sleep after he had dined out with a group of male classmates to celebrate one of their birthdays at a cheap eating house in the Outer City. Heavily rouged and powdered Chinese girls dressed in ornate costumes had entertained throughout the meal, singing shrilly on a small dais in the traditional style of Peking opera. Their pantomime acts of tragedy, joy, and sorrow performed to an often strident vocal accompaniment had left a vivid impression in his mind and later, while he slept, these supple-bodied girls rose up tauntingly naked amid the writhing congregation of his earlier nightmare.

As before, the beautiful image of Lu Mei-ling also appeared; but this time she was more provocative and sensuous than ever in her movements. Luridly rouged in the fashion of the singing girls, her naked body shimmered like liquid gold as she advanced and retreated before him, an alluring and forbidden figure in one and the same moment. Jakob felt her fingers tangle languorously in his hair, felt himself drawn helplessly toward her until her limbs dissolved slowly around him, and again a suffusion of heat engulfed his senses.

As in the previous manifestation of the dream, Felicity appeared too: detached and standing apart, her slight, angular body fully clothed in pale garments, she remained a symbol of unassailable virtue, rising above the seething scenes of carnality around her, and on waking in anguish, Jakob again prayed fiercely for deliverance from what he thought of as the darker side of his nature. This vivid recurrence of the nightmare left him profoundly troubled, and when he saw Felicity's calm, unsuspecting face in the classroom next morning, he felt a sudden sense of gratitude toward her. Over and above the warm companionship they had shared, she seemed more than ever before to personify near-saintly qualities which might help put the shame of his nightmares to flight, and he felt a greater sense of remorse than ever at having failed to respond positively to her in the pavilion on Gorgeous Prospect Hill. At the first opportunity that arose to speak to her alone, he begged her to join him on another visit to the Pavilion of Eternal Spring while the magical autumn sunshine lasted, and although she at first refused, he persisted until she agreed to meet him there at dawn the next day.

Rising very early, he hurried there ahead of her, arriving just as the sun rose, and he was waiting in front of the pavilion on the summit of the hill when she appeared. If anything, that dawn was more beautiful than the last; not even a faint breeze stirred the pines and the palace roofs below shimmered softly in a breathless silence. Almost horizontal shafts of brilliant sunlight were striking the pavilion from the east and as Felicity stopped, smiling shyly before him, her pretty face was lit softly by the dawn radiance. There was an awe-inspiring quality to the moment and Jakob at first found himself unable to summon words; Felicity too remained silent and they stood side by side without speaking, looking around them at the perfection of the morning. Then at last Jakob motioned her to sit beside him on the teak bench and he began speaking in a quiet voice, his gaze fixed on the palaces below.

"Since I've been in Peking, Felicity, I've felt joy grow inside me every day. The work is hard but the past seems to come to life so clearly here — I feel I'm really beginning to understand China. You've made all the discoveries with me and that fills my heart with a greater gladness." He stopped and turned to look at her. "When you said the last time we sat here that it was one of the most beautiful days of your life, I felt it too. But I was clumsy and thoughtless that day and I want to ask you to forgive me for that. I know now we felt the beauty keenly because we were together on this enchanted hill — and because both of us have decided to devote our lives to China."

Felicity looked startled for a moment; then she smiled uncertainly. "I don't really understand what you're trying to say, Jakob."

"Don't you? I'm sorry, let me try again." Jakob's expression became more animated. "At the time I left England the Anglo-Chinese Mission was seeking volunteers — young unmarried men — to itinerate alone in remote areas of southern China. I put my name forward. I was told that if I were chosen I'd help set up new outstations and I still want to do that more than anything in the world . . ."

"Of course, I understand," put in Felicity quickly, her expression defensive. "You were born to be an evangelist. You're strong and brave and filled with the spirit of adventure —"

"Yes, but I won't want to work alone forever," said Jakob impatiently, breaking in on her. "And perhaps we were meant to join our efforts, Felicity. We both love China. Perhaps I've been blind . . ."

Felicity's cheeks colored faintly and she half turned from him. "You sound as if you're talking about some kind of duty, Jakob."

"No, no, I didn't mean it that way." Jakob leaned closer to her, more anxious than ever to make amends. "I think I'm just being clumsy again . . . I've been too blind all along to recognize something wonderful even though it was staring me in the face."

Felicity kept her head turned from him. "I've been thinking and praying a lot recently, Jakob. I'm made of much frailer flesh than you. I'm probably best suited to a city mission school. When the designations are decided by our mission boards I'll probably find myself teaching here in Peking."

"If ever we were in danger together, I'd have strength enough for both of us," said Jakob earnestly. "I'd protect you always."

"I'm sure you would." Felicity hesitated again, struggling to preserve the air of detachment she had maintained since their last meeting on the hill. "But our wishes can't come before those of the Lord."

Jakob frowned perplexedly; then his face brightened. "Perhaps we'd best leave it to the Lord to decide for us. It's possible I won't be called to the south. Shall we wait and see whether the designations join our paths — or separate them?"

"Yes." Felicity stood up suddenly, still keeping her back to him, and started to walk away down the hill. "When the Lord is put second, you give only what's second best."

"Then I shall pray that our hearts will be set to work together!"

Jakob hurried after Felicity and placed a formal hand beneath her elbow to guide her down the path between the gnarled trees. The beauty of their surroundings struck them afresh and Jakob shook his head in wonder.

"On a morning such as this," he said softly, "I can't imagine an honest man's prayer could be refused."

For a moment they lingered, looking down on the old imperial palaces, reluctant to break the unique spell cast by the autumn dawn. The blue of the sky was deepening and the clear, sweet air of the early morning was soft against their cheeks. An almost tangible aura of timelessness seemed to envelop the old pavilions, and as Jakob gazed at their curved eaves, for an instant he felt an instinctive door of understanding open in his mind: perhaps at that very moment the imperial spirits of many dynasties were forgathering in the magnificent chambers below those ornate roofs to re-celebrate ancient ceremonies. Perhaps the immortal souls of many emperors returned in the autumn at that magical hour, just as the sun rose, to re-create fleetingly some of the great glories of China's past; perhaps it was in the radiance of these sublime moments that he and Felicity had unknowingly been privileged to share.

These intuitions remained elusive, hovering just beyond the shadowy borders of conscious thought, but as he descended the shaded hill, his hand lightly touching Felicity's bare arm, Jakob felt uplifted, light, exhilarated. Although the feeling did not become a coherent thought, he sensed that whatever lay ahead, the mysterious enchantment of that autumnal Peking dawn would remain vivid in his memory, dyed in fast colors, always indefinable but somehow deeply influential and important in his future life.

12

"The China that you're about to venture into," said Matthew Barlow in a hoarse voice, "is a leaking ship with a broken tiller drifting on an uncharted ocean. It's got no known or trusted leaders, and all the disciplines of the old social order that sustained the nation through centuries of upheavals have been swept away forever . . ."

A fit of coughing caused the director-general of the Anglo-Chinese Mission to break off and he sank back into the pillows propped behind his head. Gray-faced from a bout of bronchitis, he was resting beneath several thick quilts on a clay *k'ang* inside which a dung fire sputtered; outside the shuttered windows of the mission's *ssu ho yuan* a high wind was roaring down on Peking from the northwest, bearing great swirling clouds of Mongolian sand. As often happened during the days when winter turned to spring, the fierce wind had been blowing for several days without cease, blanketing the whole city with a film of grit that was as old as time itself. The wind's ferocity drove the sand in through door and window cracks, no matter how carefully sealed, and coarse grains squeaked under the soles of Jakob's shoes as he rose from his chair to pass Barlow a hot infusion of Chinese herbs and ginseng root that a Chinese servant had left on a lacquered table by the bed.

"What's more," he wheezed, "in the nine months or so since you arrived in China, Jakob, things outside your tranquil retreat here in Peking have gone from bad to worse."

Barlow had traveled to Peking from Shanghai to interview the half-dozen new missionaries in Jakob's language class and announce their designations. He had become unwell during the journey and had taken to his bed immediately on arrival. After two days of rest, he was still weak but had decided to conduct the interviews from his bedside to avoid further delay. Jakob was the last of the six to be called before him. When he entered, the director-general had invited him to kneel beside the bed while they prayed together at length, mentioning by name all the newly fledged missionaries and many men and women already serving with the Anglo-Chinese Mission in the field. In the course of the long-drawn-out prayer Jakob had to struggle to curb the impatience he felt rising within him — after the long, arduous months of study he felt he couldn't wait much longer to discover his fate, and when Barlow at last asked him to rise and turned to discussing a future post for him, Jakob had barely been able to stifle his sigh of relief.

"Because there's unrest and profound change . . . taking place throughout the length and breadth of China . . . the dangers for foreign missionaries are becoming greater all the time." Barlow spoke with tantalizing slowness, pausing to sip his tisane. "That's why I've spent much time in prayer before coming here . . . We've got to be sure you're aware of the dangers and are ready to face them . . . Some of our people, I should tell you, feel it would be best to confine all new activity to the big cities until more peaceful conditions return. . . ."

"But surely, sir," said Jakob, leaning anxiously toward the bed, "if the people of China are suffering new difficulties, their need to hear the Gospel must be greater than ever."

Barlow's gray features contracted in a frown and he studied the eager face of the young missionary before him for a long moment. Jakob's undisguised enthusiasm seemed to take him unawares, as though he had forgotten their earlier meeting, and he picked up Jakob's language-course file from the quilt before him with a look of puzzlement in his eyes. He read its contents in silence for several minutes before his expression gradually cleared.

"You've had a battle royal, I see, with your Chinese studies, Jakob. You just scraped through all your final examinations around the pass mark. You'll have to work hard over the next few years to finish your work on the language, you realize that, don't you?"

Jakob nodded, his anxiety deepening.

"But I see your teachers say that if there had been scores for spiritual merit, none would have been higher than yours. None of your fellow students was more ready to respond to the Lord's command to 'go and teach all nations.' "

"Thank you, sir," said Jakob quietly.

Barlow straightened himself on the pillows as though making an unaccustomed effort. "Before finally deciding on any designation, Jakob, I don't just pray for guidance, I also like to consult the man concerned. I have to know whether he has the burning determination that's needed." He gave Jakob a long, searching look. "Are you sure you still want to preach in the countryside in these turbulent times?"

"It's always been my dream to preach the Gospel in the remote regions of China, sir," said Jakob at once. "I would regard it as the greatest honor to win new territory for the Lord."

Barlow nodded and drew from a battered leather document case a linen-backed map. He paused for a moment, listening to the howl of the sand-laden wind outside, then spread the map before him on the padded quilt. "Only the Japanese, I'm afraid, seem to be winning much new territory at the moment," he said, tapping the map in the northeastern regions bordering Korea and the Soviet Union. "And nobody knows whether they'll be satisfied with occupying Manchuria. As it was so easy, they might be tempted to launch an all-out invasion of China — and if they do, all of our work here will come under threat."

"Do the Japanese show any signs of wanting to move farther into China, sir?"

"Not at the moment." Barlow coughed noisily. "But it's impossible to see what the future holds."

The Japanese had carried out their shock invasion of Manchuria only ten days or so after Jakob and Felicity had first experienced the magic of an early autumn dawn in the Pavilion of Eternal Spring. Tokyo had renamed the region Manchukuo, declared it independent, and installed as a puppet head of state P'u Yi, the last, infant emperor of China, whom they had made a virtual prisoner in his own palace. Chiang Kai-shek had withdrawn his Chinese divisions based in Manchuria to new positions below the Great Wall without offering resistance, contenting himself with a protest against Japan's aggression to the ineffectual League of Nations, and in a further flurry of related military activity, Japanese forces had attacked Chinese troops briefly at Shanghai in an effort to dislodge them from the Chinese-ruled parts of the city.

"There were some terrible outrages in Shanghai after China's Nineteenth Route Army was driven out," continued Barlow after he had recovered from another painful fit of coughing. "The Japanese soldiers strung up Chinese civilians in the streets to use them for bayonet practice. There was fighting all round the borders of the International Settlement — but Europeans went on dancing in their own nightclubs as usual as if it was nothing to do with them. It made me feel deeply ashamed."

Barlow sank back against the snowy pillows again, closing his eyes, and Jakob noticed just how lined his once-handsome face had become. His hair had whitened further since their last meeting and a deep weariness over and above that caused by his sickness was discernible in his sagging features. As he looked at Barlow, Jakob realized he had idealized the long-awaited designation meeting in his mind beforehand, and the reality was quite different. He had imagined Barlow would appear to him as a faltering Old Testament patriarch preparing to bless his young followers, and entrust to them his responsibilities and his hopes for the future. But now he sensed that the director-general's own faith had long since been undermined by his experiences, and to the awe and admiration he had once felt for him was added an overwhelming sense of sympathy and compassion.

"I'm telling you all this, Jakob, because the Japanese threat . . . has made us more aware of the new dangers all missionaries face in central and southern China." Barlow was speaking with his eyes closed and his voice was unsteady. "It's obvious that Chiang Kai-shek has not resisted the Japanese because he's more afraid of the Chinese Communists."

"Which areas are the Communists operating in, sir?"

Barlow opened his eyes and gestured toward the map. "They're reported to have two or three fixed base areas in Kwangtung, Kiangsi, and Fukien. They seem to have set up camps in the mountains in other areas. But their forces appear to be highly mobile."

"Have our missions there reported any trouble?"

Barlow shook his head. "So far there's been nothing. But China is a vast country, Jakob — big enough to lose whole armies in. One newspaper report said thousands of people were killed in Communist raids in Hupeh last year and many were taken hostage." Barlow raised his head from the map and looked at Jakob. "You know, don't you, that it's always been mission policy not to pay ransom money to secure the release of field missionaries captured by bandits?"

"No, I didn't know that, sir."

Barlow's expression grew thoughtful. "Now that you do and we've discussed all these things, does it make you want to change your mind about volunteering to itinerate in the interior?"

In the silence that followed, the noise of the wind outside seemed to grow louder; sand was being hurled against the paper-latticed windows with an ever-accelerating fury and for some moments Jakob sat rubbing a hand thoughtfully along his jaw. "It's obvious, sir," he said slowly, "that the difficulties you've spoken of are serious — but they don't put me off."

A spark of spontaneous admiration appeared in Barlow's expression. "I should tell you that several of your colleagues, Jakob, have chosen city designations. It would be no discredit for you to do the same."

"Your own example, I think you know, Mr. Barlow, brought me to China," replied Jakob unhesitatingly. "If you do decide to send me to the south, on every mountain track I hope that I shall remember that."

Barlow looked away quickly, busying himself with papers from his document case. When he picked up the map and jabbed a finger into the heartlands of southern China, his manner was suddenly brusque and impersonal. "Here at Pengshan, in southern Hunan, a married couple, the Carpenters, are about to begin a furlough in two months' time. They will be away six months. I would like you to take over from them. When they return you will be ready to carry out six months of itineration through this mountain region to the west. No missionary work has been attempted there before, but I've always wanted to open up the area." Barlow paused and tapped the map again. "You could set up a new station eventually . . . here at Chentai. Will you accept the designation?'

Jakob's face broke into a smile of relief. "I accept gladly. Thank you, sir."

He rose exultantly from his chair and moved closer to the bed to peer at the map. He was just able to make out "Chentai" printed in fine letters amid the dark brown mountain contours of southern Hunan. Still smiling, he stared hard at the obscure name, trying to imagine what the landscape around Chentai looked like, and when the older man smiled at him and offered his hand, Jakob shook it warmly. "Thank you, Mr. Barlow, for having faith in me. You won't regret granting me this opportunity."

As Jakob turned and hurried from the room, the shrieking of the wind outside rose higher but he neither heard it nor noticed the dust swirling in the air of the drafty corridor outside the bedroom door. Already in his mind's eye he was climbing a high southern pass, breathing the thin mountain air deep into his lungs, and singing a stirring hymn as he swung along toward the next ancient walled town where no white-skinned missionary had ever been seen before.

13

By noon next day the high winds from the northwest had blown themselves out. During the winter months a cloak of northern dust had as usual spread its drab folds over all Peking, coating without distinction the golden roofs of palaces and temples and the sea of single-storied, gray-tiled houses that spread out all around them. Wind-borne desert sand whirled hundreds of miles from the Gobi had dyed the cloak a deeper, more dramatic shade of red in recent days and as Jakob rode toward the Temple of Heaven in a hooded rickshaw to meet Felicity and hear news of her designation, he felt a sudden stab of regret at the prospect of leaving a city which in less than a full year had captivated him in all its many moods. The fierce, exciting heat of late summer and the sparkling clarity of autumn had given way to a winter which had often frozen the imperial lakes and sprinkled fine coverings of snow onto the spectacular palace roofs; and even the arid weeks of stinging dust storms that followed had seemed to Jakob to give the ancient capital a new dimension of austere grandeur.

Muffled beneath the fur helmet and the thick quilted Chinese robe of dark blue cotton in which he had withstood the sharp winter cold, Jakob felt at ease in the narrow *hut'ungs* through which he had directed his rickshaw coolie to take him en route to the southern district of the Outer City. The Chinese swarming in the narrow lanes of beaten earth wore bulky padded clothes of the same shade and scarcely glanced under the raised hood of his rickshaw. Gray walls reaching up to the eaves of the low buildings bordered the lanes on either side and whenever a gate stood ajar Jakob peered discreetly inside.

Such glimpses had long since made him aware that daily life for the ordinary Chinese in Peking was hard: inside the walled courts his eyes invariably fell on ragged clothes, pinched faces, wailing children playing in the dirt. The *hut'ungs* also had their share of beggars and cripples, and reeking handcarts of night soil trundled by frequently. But the visible poverty never seemed as coarse and harsh to Jakob as that he had seen in Shanghai. On the walls surrounding the Legation Quarter he could see foreign soldiers still patrolling thirty-two years after the Boxer uprising — but Peking, he reflected as he rode on, had never been forced to suffer the hu-

miliation of treaty-port status and perhaps for this reason had managed to retain its unique atmosphere of imperial dignity.

Despite the cold, barbers and dentists were plying their trade
busily at the curbside and food peddlers abounded in the crowds.
Their portable stoves, carried at the ends of bouncing shoulder poles,
spilled appetizing aromas into the cold air, and remembering that
within two days he would be leaving all these sights and smells
behind, Jakob stopped his rickshaw to buy a bag of *chiao tzu* — little
dumplings stuffed with spiced vegetables which had become a favorite during his stay. He munched on them hungrily in the rickshaw, acutely conscious that he might be enjoying them for the
last time, and simultaneously he felt a new tremor of excitement
at the thought that he would know within minutes whether Felicity might share with him the new adventure of life in the remote
south.

The rickshaw dropped Jakob at the Gate of the Western Sky,
and as he hurried into the walled enclosure of the Temple of Heaven
a fierce shower of rain, the first of the spring, drove down on the
long avenue of ancient cypress trees which led toward the Red
Stairway Bridge. In the past China's emperors had come to the
broad, wooded enclosure with great ceremony to sacrifice bulls
and sheep in porcelain furnaces before worshiping in the Hall of
Prayer for Good Harvests. The hall, a circular temple with a triple-
tiered roof of sky blue tiles set on a round terrace of dazzling white
marble, had impressed Jakob and Felicity deeply during their first
visit: both of them had been strongly attracted to the grandeur of
its simple lines soaring upward to the blue heavens from its pris-
tine setting in the midst of what was virtually a small forest of cypress trees. The southern wall of the enclosure was square and the
northern wall semicircular, in recognition of the ancient belief that
the earth was square and heaven was round; altars and halls designed for fasting, for the sacrificial killing of animals, and for other
ceremonial functions had been built with geometric precision throughout the enclosure, and Jakob and Felicity had often picnicked in
the shady woods during the summer in sight of these historic pavilions.

On this occasion they had arranged to meet at the Hall of Prayer
for Good Harvests, and because of his eagerness to hear news of
Felicity's posting, Jakob ignored the sudden deluge of April rain.

He ran the length of the quarter-mile-long avenue to the Red Stairway Bridge, a wide promenade linking the hall with the other major
sanctuaries, the Circular Altar Mound and the Imperial Vault of
Heaven. Seeing Felicity standing alone beneath the blue eaves of the
main temple, he continued running across the deserted enclosure
and leapt up the long flights of balustraded marble steps three at a
time to arrive panting at her side.

"What designation have you been given?"

Felicity's features were set in serious lines and Jakob asked the
question in a tense voice, watching anxiously for her answer. His
coat was drenched, his hat was askew, and strands of his fair hair
were plastered wetly across his damp face.

"Perhaps you'd better catch your breath, Jakob, before we talk.
Come inside out of the rain."

Felicity took him gently by the arm to lead him into the empty
temple and for a moment her face relaxed into a little smile at his
evident impatience. She wore over her long coat an embroidered,
wide-sleeved Chinese jacket of dark green silk decorated with phoenix
and plum blossom motifs, and her hair was tucked up inside a fur
hat with earflaps tied neatly across its crown. As usual she wore no
rouge on her cheeks or lips.

"I'm glad we came to this temple to talk, Jakob," she said in a
subdued voice. "It's always so peaceful. And today it seems especially
tranquil. Do you feel that too?"

"Yes, I do."

With his chest still heaving from the exertion of running, Jakob
gazed around the shadowy interior of the conical temple. Four central
"dragon well" pillars, carved from Yunnan trees of massive girth,
represented the four seasons, and there were two outer rings of twelve
wooden columns symbolizing the months of the year and the twelve
two-hour periods into which the ancient Chinese had divided each
day. Colored frescoes adorned the high roof a hundred feet above
their heads, while in the center of the stone-paved floor a circular
slab of marble was carved with the forms of a dragon and a phoenix,
the symbols for the emperor and his empress. Outside, the shower
had stopped as abruptly as it had begun and pale sunlight, filtering
through the wall partitions of latticework, was dappling the floor
and pillars with fragments of brightness. No sound penetrated to
the heart of the enclosure from the surrounding city, and when his

breathing returned to normal Jakob felt constrained by the deep, gentle silence to speak in a whisper.

"I've been assigned to the southern Hunan border, Felicity! I'm to help at an existing post at first — then set up a new station at an old walled town called Chentai." Jakob was unable to suppress the pleasure he felt and his eyes shone. "It's what I've always wanted."

"I'm very glad."

Jakob was gripped by a sudden apprehension. He stared hard at the American girl: her expression remained serious, almost grave, and although she had spoken very softly he had noticed a slight catch in her voice. "Don't keep me in suspense any longer, Felicity," he whispered urgently. "Please tell me your designation."

"I'm to go to Chenyuan — to teach in a school for Chinese children with three other women."

He stared in disbelief for a moment; then he seized both her hands joyously in his own. "But that's wonderful news! You'll be in Kwei-chow, the neighboring province."

"Yes." Felicity nodded quickly, but to Jakob's alarm glistening tears sprang into her eyes.

"Felicity, what's wrong? Why are you unhappy?"

The American girl shook her head quickly and tried to smile. "I'm not unhappy. It's just that I never expected to be sent to a remote inland station. My parents, you see, worked only in the city of Tientsin." She hesitated, biting her lip distractedly. "I can't really explain why, Jakob. I just suddenly feel afraid . . ."

"There's no need at all to be frightened!" Glancing down, he saw that they were standing on the dragon and phoenix symbols carved in the circular marble slab. "I'll cherish you, Felicity, as well as any emperor of China cherished his empress. You'll see. Come on!"

Smiling, he drew her out of the temple by the hand and led her at a run down the marble steps. The sun was shining more brightly and the heavy shower had washed the desert grit from the enclosure's cypress trees, turning them a sudden, thrilling green once more. Ignoring Felicity's protests he ran with her the length of the Red Stairway Bridge to the Imperial Vault of Heaven, a smaller temple with an umbrella-shaped roof topped by a gilded ball. At the sides of the promenade Jakob noticed that tiny shoots of paler green had suddenly become visible, as if by magic, on the flower-bearing shrubs and fruit trees; in the flower beds beneath the gnarled cypresses, too, fresh green shoots had been uncovered by the rain. Already the rose tints of the temple walls, the deep blue of their roofs, the milky white marble terraces, and the glossy trees had worked their special spell on Jakob's mind, and the sight of these tiny new specks of life heightened the sense of joy he felt welling up within him. As they ran he pointed them out to Felicity.

"Look, even the spring has chosen this morning to make a new start. The Lord has truly blessed us."

"Yes, it's beautiful — but where are you taking me?"

Felicity, her apprehensions blotted out for the moment by Jakob's exuberance, was laughing and panting for breath as she struggled along in his wake.

"To the Echo Wall, of course." Jakob slowed to a fast walk to lead her down the steps outside the entrance to the Imperial Vault of Heaven. "Come and stand by me on the San Yin Shih."

Jakob stopped by a hewn block known as the Triple Sound Stone, from which three separate steps had been carved. It faced a long curved wall of polished brick which had been constructed so that any whisper made close against its surface could be heard distinctly at any other point on the wall. On previous visits they had playfully tested one another's knowledge of difficult Chinese words with whispered echoes, but this time Jakob remained standing on the first step of the San Yin Shih and did not approach the wall. The stone had been artfully positioned so that the sound waves of words uttered from each of its three steps had to travel different distances to the wall's curved surface. The echoes consequently returned at different intervals, and from listening to Chinese children playing at the spot, Jakob knew that a call voiced from the first step returned once, a call from the second step, twice, while any call from the top step echoed three times. Drawing Felicity onto the first step beside him, Jakob held a finger theatrically to his lips, inviting silence, then turned to face the wall.

"Felicity . . . will . . . you . . . marry . . . me?" he called loudly, drawing the words out at length.

Felicity listened wide-eyed as the question rolled sonorously back to her from the curved rampart of polished bricks. At first the disembodied words seemed to overawe her and when she didn't reply, Jakob climbed to the second step and repeated the question with greater insistence. Felicity again remained silent on the first echo, but when after a brief silence the polished wall repeated the proposal with a seeming show of impatience, she hurried to the third step and made her reply in a soft, low voice.

Jakob moved to her side, his fingers intertwining tightly with hers as they waited for the echo. Then he smiled delightedly into her eyes as the centuries-old wall built by the Ming dynasty emperors sent her sibilant answer back to them. "Yes, Jakob, I will! . . . Yes, Jakob, I will! . . . Yes, Jakob, I will!"

PART TWO

The Long March Begins

1934

Japan's attempted conquest of mainland China, which began with the occupation of Manchuria in September 1931, had a profound effect on the subsequent course of the Chinese revolution. At the outset it caused Chiang Kai-shek to halt a massive offensive against the Communist Red Army just when he stood on the brink of a decisive victory; then, as time passed, his decision to continue fighting China's Communists instead of confronting the foreign invader alienated many Chinese and bedeviled his efforts to unite China under Nationalist rule. Japan's unopposed entry into Manchuria, which came as a galling climax to China's century of humiliation at the hands of European nations, was also to prove a historic turning point in the wider context of world history. It demonstrated that Japan had become powerful enough to challenge the supremacy of the white colonial powers and foreshadowed the end of their dominance in Asia during the Second World War. As weak as China was when aggressive European colonialists first appeared in Asia, Japan had deliberately turned its back on the traditional past and carried through a radical program of Westernization under its own emperors in the mid-nineteenth century. Within a few short decades the small island nation transformed and modernized itself. Deploying well-armed land and sea forces with great flair, Tokyo quickly built a new Asian empire, seizing Formosa from China, wresting the Manchurian seaport of Port Arthur from Czarist Russia, annexing Korea, and moving onto an equal footing with the European nations in China in 1919 by taking over Germany's concession areas.

On the day Tokyo moved into Manchuria, Chiang Kai-shek

was leading 300,000 Nationalist troops against Communist bases in the south in his third "encirclement and annihilation" campaign. Two previous offensives had failed, but his forces were then on the point of overwhelming 30,000 Red Army troops in the Central Soviet area in mountainous southern Kiangsi. Because of Japan's action, Chiang decided to postpone his offensive; the Communists were thereby given time to rest and recoup, and they succeeded in repulsing the fourth encirclement campaign, mounted in the winter of 1933. Increasingly frustrated, Chiang marshaled a vast army of seventy divisions — nearly a million troops — for the fifth campaign, which he launched toward the end of 1933. This time he was aided by German military advisers, who constructed ever-narrowing rings of concrete blockhouses linked by motor roads and barbed-wire entanglements to blockade the Kiangsi base area. Heavy casualties were inflicted on the main force of the Red Army as the Nationalists closed in; Communist desertions increased, and in the late summer of 1934 the Communist leaders realized they were trapped.

By coincidence, the Communists were also being guided by a German military adviser. Sent from Moscow by the Comintern on Stalin's orders, the German Marxist had insisted that the Red Army abandon its previous guerrilla tactics and defend the base area with well-tried positional warfare techniques: trenches and blockhouses. He was supported by two dozen youthful Chinese "Bolsheviks," who had been educated and trained in Moscow, and the young Chou En-lai. Among those continuing to advocate flexible guerrilla techniques was the still-unknown Mao Tse-tung, who had not yet gained a dominant position in the movement. But although no clear leader of the Communists had emerged and sharp differences existed among the contenders, on one thing they all ultimately agreed: with the Nationalist noose closing around them, the Kiangsi soviet base would have to be abandoned. A date for the breakout through enemy lines was set — October 16, 1934 — but none of those preparing to march knew then that this ignominious lunge for survival would turn into a historic fighting retreat across six thousand miles of some of the world's harshest terrain. In a year's nonstop marching at the rate of up to fifty miles a day, they would pass over eighteen mountain ranges, cross twenty-six rivers, and struggle finally through the desolate Great Grasslands of Szechuan before finding sanctuary in the northwest. None of the 85,000 soldiers and 15,000 civilians who set out that autumn could have guessed then that the small core of them destined to survive would form the nucleus of a people's army superior to all other armies in China's history. Their epic trek through China's remotest regions would later come to be known as the "Long March" — but while it lasted, it would go unobserved by the outside world. "Enemies" in the shape of landlords, Kuomintang sympathizers, and suspected spies, wherever they were encountered, would be taken prisoner to be dragged along with the baggage. Rough justice would be meted out to some, ransom would be sought for others — and among those prisoners would be a handful of foreigners whom fate placed in the path of the desperate marchers.

1

A flurry of rifle shots echoing across a distant valley caused Jakob to halt in midstride as he picked his way down a natural stairway of sharp rocks on a high mountainside in southern Hunan. Far below he could see a yellow stream rushing through gray stone outcrops, and on a little green plateau halfway down the cliff a small Chinese boy wearing animal skins and a felt skullcap was guarding a herd of scraggy sheep and goats. The boy had been playing a set of bamboo panpipes to which Jakob had been unconsciously listening as he descended but now the music had stopped; the little goatherd was obviously listening too for further sounds of shooting.

After a short interval of silence, more ragged bursts of rifle fire rang out, augmented this time by the faster, rhythmic stutter of automatic weapons. Although the early November afternoon was bright with sun and only a faint haze hung around the distant blue mountain peaks to the east, Jakob could see no sign of the men firing the guns. The narrow trail on which he stood snaked along the shoulders of the mountains high above the foaming stream, descending very gradually into a long, winding valley that spread out ahead of them as far as the eye could see. The lower hillsides were thick with trees, and the mud-walled hamlets that Jakob knew were nestling below remained invisible from the peaks. The sounds of firing, after rising quickly to a crescendo, died away just as abruptly and an enigmatic stillness took possession of the mountains once more.

"Who do you think is fighting down there, Ke Mu-shih?"

The short, wiry Chinese in his early thirties who had been following close on Jakob's heels breathed the question in an excited whisper. He had the dark, weathered face and permanently narrowed eyes of a mountain dweller and he carried his carefully balanced shoulder pole with its laden wicker baskets seemingly without effort. Behind him, two lowland coolies carrying heavy loads of provisions in shoulder sacks known as *paofu* halted with their knees calculatedly bent, their faces taut from the continuous effort of carrying.

"I don't know who it is, Hsiao Liang — but it sounds serious. Somebody is using machine guns as well as rifles."

"Could it be the Red Bandits, Ke Mu-shih?" A note of eagerness was detectable in Liang's voice although he was careful to use the respectful form of address: Ke, the Chinese character customarily used to denote the first syllable of Jakob's family name, followed by Mu-shih, meaning "Pastor."

"Possibly." Jakob, who spoke his conversational Chinese now with confidence, smiled and patted his cookboy affectionately on the shoulder. "The government troops wouldn't need to use machine guns against thieves or 'spirit soldiers,' would they?"

Jakob shaded his eyes with his hand to scan the distant crags and gullies. Rumors that Kuomintang forces had dislodged small groups of Communist bandits from mountain strongholds in neighboring Kiangsi had been circulating in the province for two or three weeks. On the narrow flagstoned trails that served as roads, Jakob in that time had encountered more patrols of government and provincial troops than he had ever seen before, but there had been no signs of fighting. In the two and a half years since leaving Peking, Jakob had become accustomed to facing the daily danger of attacks by armed gangs whenever he traveled on the remote tracks that wound across the hills and plains of Hunan, Kwangsi, and Kweichow. On longer journeys, district magistrates often provided small military escorts through areas where robber-bandits were notorious: a year before, when journeying without protection, Jakob had been surprised by a ragged group of sword-wielding brigands who ran yelling down a trailside scree to steal his money belt and all his coolie-borne supplies before lashing him with rope to a tree. He had offered his captors no physical resistance. As they tightened the bonds around him and his frightened coolies, he had urged them to give up their life of banditry and had tried to explain in a calm voice something of Christ's love for all men. But their wild, begrimed faces had registered nothing of what he said and as soon as they had secured all his belongings, they had raced off up the scree to disappear silently into the hills once more.

"Do you think we should go back the way we came, Ke Mu-shih?" Liang wagged his head back in the direction of the mountain pass over which they had just climbed. "It might be safer."

"No, we'll go on."

Jakob moved briskly away down the rocky path, waving and calling a cheery greeting to the little goatherd; without any hesitation Liang and the two coolies fell into step behind. As they climbed down past him, the goat boy stared curiously at the small group led by the tall man with a haze of strange yellow hair framing his face. But as soon as they had passed, the boy became totally absorbed again in coaxing from his pipes a haunting, plaintive melody that followed Jakob and his companions down the mountain.

From time to time Jakob stopped to peer ahead, straining his eyes for some sign of what they might find in the valley below. He was aware that his decision to continue the journey in the direction of the firing had possibly been hasty and made on impulse. He knew too that the sharp, spectacular peaks etched purple against the bright sky ahead had somehow helped influence him in making it. After more than two years in the field he had few illusions left about the practical difficulties of his calling: attempting to preach the Christian Gospel in wild rural areas among a largely illiterate peasant population nurtured on centuries of superstition and ancestor worship was, in reality, a slow, laborious task.

Often the frustrations had tested his resolve to the full — yet whenever he climbed alone to the high tracks and looked out over the rolling swell of rock peaks and fertile valleys stretching to the horizon, he experienced new feelings of exhilaration. Throughout this vast region of hill, valley, and plain which had changed little in the two millennia since Christ's birth, unseen millions of souls dwelled in total ignorance of the Gospel's message. At the thought Jakob rejoiced and gave thanks afresh for the magnitude of the responsibility which he bore. In such moments it was as though these great tracts of southern China and their people were in a way his very own. He felt keenly that God had entrusted them and their salvation to him alone, and the instinctive excitement at the prospect of adventuring in the mountains of China which had first gripped him as a ten-year-old boy again became a throbbing reality.

When first he had come south from Peking, Jakob could not believe that it was just the curiosity value of his "big" nose, blue eyes, and pale skin that drew dense crowds of silent, staring Chinese peasants around him whenever he entered a hamlet to preach in the dusty main street. Despite smiling warnings from senior missionaries at the central station in Changsha, he had continued for several months to harbor the private hope that the special power and fervor of his witness might be dramatically confirmed by a rapid rise in the number of baptized converts in the remote region around Chentai where no foreign missionary work had previously been attempted. But although he handed out hundreds of printed Chinese Scripture tracts during every itineration and diligently compiled long lists of "inquirers," a full year had passed before Jakob baptized his first convert on the banks of a mountain stream — and she had been an ailing widow of a village herbalist, who had been held spellbound in her suffering by his New Testament accounts of Christ healing the sick.

The elation he had felt at giving his first meticulously memorized sermon in Chinese had gradually given way to the realization that weary months and years of study still lay ahead before he could hope to handle intelligent questions and discussion about the Gospels in Chinese; and reluctantly, at last, he admitted to himself that the fascination of his European face for Chinese who had never seen a foreigner of any kind and even the sound of a phonograph or a small church organ were as responsible for drawing the peasant crowds as anything he was able to say about the power of Christianity.

This growing awareness of the true scale of the missionary's task in China, however, had not in any way undermined Jakob's deep sense of commitment. He had spent every spare moment poring over his language books, and after his marriage to Felicity eighteen months earlier, she had helped him improve his spoken Chinese in nightly lessons at home in the new mission they had set up together at Chentai. Getting married had also been inspirational in itself for him. Felicity's gentle, pious manner, which equipped her naturally to organize the daily routines of the Chentai station and its small Bible school, had served to complement his more forceful, physical brand of evangelism. Her quiet presence had in itself strengthened his conviction that they had somehow been destined to spread the message of the Gospels to every last hamlet in that remote corner of Hunan, and after the wedding he had ventured out on each journey with renewed zeal.

In addition, two years of striding the flagstoned trails had strengthened him physically: his long, lean frame had filled out and he had broadened noticeably in the chest and shoulders. The mountain winds and rain as well as the sun had roughened his features and given them a ruddy, weathered glow. He had fallen into the habit of wearing Chinese garments, marching the summer trails in straw sandals and a light long-gown and reverting in winter to the quilted, fur-lined robe and boots acquired in Peking. As a result, the fresh-faced, neatly barbered youth who had arrived in Shanghai more than three years before was no longer easily recognizable; his place had been taken by a rugged, confident-looking, tousle-haired man who had a ready smile in his blue eyes and who, on the brink of maturity, wore a full beard, thick on his cheeks, that was almost as pale as his blond hair.

Only a month earlier, the quiet contentment of his union with Felicity had acquired a new dimension of joy with the birth of a baby girl. The infant's imminent arrival had curtailed the number of journeys he had felt able to undertake during the summer months, and the expedition from which he was now returning had been a do-mestic errand to the nearest river port to collect stores and provisions shipped to them from Shanghai. The route of the two-day journey back to Chentai lay close to the long mountain valley into which they were now descending, and Jakob had decided to make a detour to one of its villages so that he could visit a serious inquirer family of peasant farmers to whom he had first preached nine months earlier.

In particular he had taken away from the village a vivid memory of how the eyes of a thirteen-year-old girl, a daughter of the farmer, had shone in the light of an oil lamp on hearing him read the story of the first Christmas from the New Testament. When he rose to leave, the girl's simple peasant face still wore a wistful, almost hungry expression, and because he had no Chinese Bibles left for sale, he had on an impulse given her his own. As the grassy slope beneath his feet began to level out and the first mud-walled houses of the village came into sight, Jakob realized that it must have been this dimly remembered image of the girl's spiritual hunger, left unfed by him for so long, that had ultimately drawn him back down that winding valley despite the disconcerting sounds of gunfire. The feel-ing that he had been neglectful of his duty nagged suddenly at his mind; the family's name was Hsiao, he remembered, the girl was called Lan-ko, and quite irrationally he began to quicken his pace, scouring his memory for the exact location of Lan-ko's home among the rows of straw-thatched houses.

"Wait, Ke Mu-shih! Something's wrong here."

The shouted warning from Liang stopped Jakob dead in his tracks. He had pulled ahead of the cookboy and the coolies and while he waited for them to catch up, he noticed for the first time that the dusty, unpaved street which ran the length of the straggling village was deserted. The doors of some of the houses stood open or swung slowly back and forth on creaking hinges in the afternoon wind. There was no sign of movement from the dark interiors — not even a dog, a pig, or a mule moved on the empty street.

"Where is everybody?" Jakob's voice sounded loud in the eerie silence.

"Maybe they have all run away into the hills — to get away from the fighting." Liang, panting to regain his breath, gazed up and down the street with watchful eyes.

They had stopped outside a slightly larger mud house that served as an inn for passing coolies where Jakob had spent a night during his first visit to the village. The curiosity of the village children had been so great that they had pressed into his darkened bedroom, surrounding him in ranks four and five deep to watch him eat his evening meal. Their eyes had sparkled with the wonder and excitement of seeing the first non-Chinese face of their young lives and they had giggled uproariously whenever he spoke to them in their own language. Next morning he had preached to a great crowd in the street outside before visiting several families in their homes. They had all made him welcome, offering him boiled peanuts and hot water to drink; all had listened politely to what he had to say. His recollection of the friendliness he had been shown on that occasion made the stillness of the deserted village suddenly seem all the more ominous, but he tried to set his growing apprehension aside.

"We can't be sure that the firing came from here, Hsiao Liang. Perhaps there's some other explanation." Jakob set off down the middle of the street, peering into the open doorways on either side as he went.

"Be careful, Ke Mu-shih! The soldiers could still be hiding somewhere."

Balancing the carrying pole expertly on his right shoulder, Liang trotted close behind Jakob, scanning the street protectively in all directions. Tough in mind and body, Liang was the second son of a mountain farmer who had lost all his land after falling badly into debt; before becoming a cook, Liang had served in the Chentai militia for a year or two. Jakob had hired him six months prior to marrying

Felicity and in that time Liang had frequently volunteered to accompany Jakob on his itinerations through the remote hills and valleys, carrying Bibles and tracts for him in his shoulder-pole panniers. Through spending many hours traveling the rough mountain tracks together, the two men had developed a bond of mutual respect that did not depend on spoken words. Liang had registered as an inquirer, as all mission employees tended to do, soon after taking up his job and had willingly received instruction. He had eventually been baptized in the river flowing under the walls of Chentai and Jakob had given him a fine, leather-bound Bible inscribed with a personal message to mark their friendship. Liang's devotion to Christianity, Jakob suspected, was more dutiful than inspired, an expedient pursued largely to protect his job at the mission, but he had developed an unusually strong sense of personal loyalty to Jakob which the missionary knew was instinctive and genuine.

"Look, Ke Mu-shih! Over there!" Liang called urgently to Jakob, pointing to a grain store set back from the street. Its doors were broken and outside split sacks of rice lay tumbled in profusion on the dusty ground. "There's been fighting here."

Drawing near, Jakob could see the crumpled bodies of several provincial soldiers sprawled among the spilled grain. Their distinctive blue cotton uniforms and gray puttees were spattered with blood and the lolling head of one man had been partially severed, apparently by a bayonet thrust. For a long moment Jakob stared aghast at the carnage: the bodies of these young Chinese troops were his first personal experience of violent death and he found it difficult to believe they were real corpses. Then he remembered the rudimentary medical training he had been given at his London missionary school and dropped to his knees beside one of the bodies, bending his head to the chest to listen for a heartbeat.

"I'm afraid they're all dead, Ke Mu-shih," said Liang quietly.

Jakob nodded in agreement and stood up, his face pale. After gathering himself, he lowered his head and murmured a short prayer. The eyes of the two coolies crowding behind Liang were round with fright. The cookboy, however, was absorbed, scrutinizing the bodies and the ground around them with great care.

"Their ammunition bandoliers have all been emptied. And their rifles have been taken. Look! There are cart tracks too. Whoever killed them has stolen rice from the granary."

Fresh wheel tracks made by narrow handcarts were visible in the dust outside the granary. They led away down the street which still lay quiet and empty in the bright afternoon sun.

"I think, Ke Mu-shih, it would be better not to stay long here." Liang spoke softly, nodding toward the smashed doors of the granary which hung open, revealing several neat rows of rice sacks stacked inside. "Whoever killed these soldiers may return for the rest of the grain."

"Before we go I must visit the house of the Hsiao family."

Jakob led the way quickly back to the street; searching left and right for some sign to jog his memory, he hurried through the length of the village. A pillared house with a loft stood apart, close to the edge of the terraced rice fields, and on catching sight of it Jakob immediately recalled the warmth of his previous visit there. But now the farmhouse stood as silent and apparently deserted as all the other dwellings. No animals or barnyard fowl scratched in the dirt outside and when he approached Jakob found its gates and doors were shut and barred.

It was while he was unfastening one of the coolie's packs of new Bibles, intending to leave a New Testament or two, that he heard a half-stifled sound of movement from inside. Motioning Liang and the coolies to silence he waited, listening intently, but there was no further noise. Seeing a ladder propped against one wall, Jakob climbed quietly to the loft, and pushing aside the rice straw covering its rough boards, he peered down into the earth-floored room below.

To his astonishment he found himself staring at a dense throng of silent Chinese. Many of the peasants crowded inside with their mules and other livestock were gazing up apprehensively toward the crack in the floorboards through which he was looking at them. In the gloom the whites of their eyes showed clearly and their faces seemed to glisten with fear. Men, women, and children were pressed close together in the half-darkness among the animals; although they made no conscious sound, Jakob could hear the anxiety of their breathing. After climbing down quickly, he returned to the front of the house and knocked softly on the main door.

"Mr. Hsiao, it's Pastor Ke from Chentai," he called softly. "It's quite safe. I've come to bring Bibles for you and your daughter Lan-ko."

Jakob thought he heard a flurry of whispers inside but no reply was made. Stepping back from the door he called again, more loudly — then reeled back in shock as a rifle shot rang out and a bullet whined close to his head. Hurrying to his side, Liang dragged

Jakob around the corner of the house and the coolies swiftly followed. They waited, crouched together against the mud wall, but no further shots were fired and the doors remained barred.

"We should go, Ke Mu-shih," breathed Liang. "These people have been badly frightened."

Jakob stared, mystified, at the mud walls that sheltered the dense, silent crowd of fearful humans and animals; then he nodded reluctantly and followed Liang and the coolies out of the village. Several times before they went out of sight of the house he turned to look back but no sound or sign of life emerged. When they had gone about a mile along the flagstoned track that led down through the rice terraces, Jakob heard a shrill cry from behind and turned to find the slender figure of Lan-ko racing after them. She was clutching his big-character New Testament to her chest as she ran and as soon as she reached them she thrust it into Jakob's hands.

"Take this, Ke Mu-shih," she gasped tearfully. "And please don't come back to our village ever again."

"But why?" Jakob bent to put an arm around the girl's shoulder, speaking soothingly to her in Chinese. "I thought you liked the stories."

"The Red Bandits came! They stole all our food! They killed the soldiers guarding us! They said many more Red Bandits would be coming soon."

"And did they tell you to stop reading this book?"

"They warned us, Ke Mu-shih, 'Do not tell the Kuomintang soldiers anything,' they said. 'Do not speak to foreign missionaries if they come here, they are spies.' " Lan-ko fought hard to hold back tears that were already trickling down her face. "They said anyone who talked to foreigners would be dealt with very severely. They said their orders are: 'Kill all foreigners! Kill all foreigners!' " Coming close to hysteria, the Chinese girl repeated the phrase "*Sha yang kuei tzu!*" several times, then tore herself from Jakob's grasp.

As Jakob watched her running blindly back toward the village, the chilling Communist order delivered in a piping voice continued to replay itself inside his head: "*Sha yang kuei tzu! Sha yang kuei tzu!*" Suddenly he remembered that Felicity and the baby were alone, unguarded, at the mission, and he turned and motioned quickly to Liang and the coolies.

"Come on! We must hurry back to Chentai."

2

When Jakob opened the gate in the high mud wall and stepped into the outer courtyard of the Chentai mission compound, the evening light was fading fast. The first things he noticed were the bunches of red peppers newly hung up to dry by Liang's wife. In the dying rays of the sun the peppers glowed like great scarlet blotches of blood on the dun-colored walls, and the sight of them at once reminded Jakob of the bleeding bodies of the soldiers sprawled limp in death outside the pillaged grain store. Then he noticed that the desks and chairs of the little Bible school which Felicity had set up above the prayer room in one of the two-storied outbuildings were strewn around the courtyard. Some were tipped haphazardly on their sides and as he stared at them in puzzlement, Jakob became aware how quiet it was inside the compound.

His anxious mind immediately equated this silence with the eerie stillness that had greeted them in the mountain village, and leaving the outer gate open for Liang and the two coolies, he dashed to the moon gate which led into the inner courtyard. The old dwelling which they had adapted for the use of the Anglo-Chinese Mission had once belonged to a wealthy Chentai landowner: its high, spacious halls were crisscrossed with intricately carved beams and the eaves and windows were decorated with classical three-color designs. The main door to their living quarters was made of polished teak, and when Jakob threw it open he found the central hall empty. The traditional Chinese furniture carved from dark, heavy wood normally gave the house an austere, spartan atmosphere but in the gloom of approaching nightfall the scene seemed suddenly to have taken on an ominous quality. There was no sign of Liang's wife or any of the other house servants in the downstairs rooms, no lamps had yet been lit, and no sound came from the upper floors.

Feeling his apprehensions grow, Jakob bounded up the shadowy staircase two steps at a time and rushed into one of the sleeping chambers that served as a nursery. From her seat beside the lace-covered crib Felicity turned to look at him with startled eyes; her face was pale and strained, and on seeing him she quickly raised a silencing finger to her lips. With a feeling of relief flooding through him, Jakob walked quietly to the crib and peered in. The sleeping face of his baby daughter was peaceful and composed. A few wisps of fair hair, as fine as silk, sprouted from the crown of her head and one hand was clenched in a tiny fist by her cheek. Felicity was rocking the crib gently to and fro, and Jakob, releasing a long, thankful sigh, dropped his hand affectionately on hers on the rim of the wickerwork crib.

"She's only just fallen asleep." Although Felicity spoke in a whisper, her voice was tight with anxiety. "The town's been full of soldiers today. There were hundreds of them."

"Were they government soldiers?" asked Jakob quickly.

Felicity nodded. "Yes, of course."

"And did they scatter the school desks all over the yard?"

"Yes. They arrived out of the blue early this morning. They commandeered quarters everywhere. They didn't ask me if they could use the school. They just marched in, threw out all the furniture, and turned it into a barracks. They were making a terrible noise. Abigail has been crying nearly all day."

"Where are the troops now?"

"This afternoon a bugle call suddenly sounded from the hill outside the town wall. They started to pack their equipment straightaway — and half an hour later they'd all gone. The town militia units marched out behind them."

"So Chentai has been left completely unguarded?"

The urgency of Jakob's question betrayed his inner concern and Felicity straightened warily in her seat. "Yes, I suppose so. Where do you think the soldiers were making for?"

"I don't know. I'll go and see the district magistrate to find out what's happening."

Jakob turned to leave the room but Felicity plucked nervously at his sleeve. "Why did you ask me if they were government soldiers? Who else could they have been?"

Looking down into Felicity's worried face, Jakob felt a sudden surge of compassion for her: although her cheeks were rounder and her slender body had become more voluptuously maternal in the month that she had been nursing their child, her wide gray eyes had often betrayed a sense of unease. For their wedding, in a Chinese garden at the central station compound in Changsha, she had worn a long, wide-sleeved dress of pure white Chinese silk and her hair had been crowned with a veil of fine Brussels lace. Her shy modesty had led her to avert her eyes while they exchanged their vows, but when at last she turned to smile at him her face was illuminated suddenly by a shining, once-in-a-lifetime radiance, and in that moment she had seemed truly beautiful. During an idyllic spring honeymoon at a hill station, they had strolled amid pines and foaming waterfalls, avidly discussing their future plans to make Christ's teachings known in the wild region around Chentai. But even then Jakob had fancied that he sometimes detected in her expression shadows of uncertainty about how she would face up to the hardships and dangers of life in a remote district without roads, hospitals, doctors, or proper communications. She had rarely given voice to her fears, but when she returned to Chentai with the baby she had borne in the Changsha missionary hospital, he sensed that her apprehensions had grown. Feeling increasingly responsible for having turned her radiant wedding-day smile into an anxious frown, he had undertaken no preaching journeys at all since the child's birth — but the sudden arrival in the walled town of large numbers of government troops during his absence on a domestic errand had obviously unnerved her further, and he realized he would have to tread very carefully in describing what he had seen and heard earlier in the day.

"On our way back we heard shooting in the valley ahead of us," said Jakob, making his voice sound casual. "It was twenty miles or so from here. When we got to the village some rice had been stolen. The villagers thought the thieves might have been Red Bandits — I'd better check with the district magistrate to see if he's heard anything."

Felicity stared at him, her expression of alarm deepening. "You mean they were Communists — and they might be coming here."

"It's just possible, yes." Jakob smiled and laid a comforting hand on her shoulder. "But there may have been only a handful of them. If there's the slightest hint we're in danger, I'll arrange for us to have military escorts. We'll go and stay at the central station till it's all blown over. There's no need to worry."

Dropping to his knees, he stroked her cheek gently until he coaxed an uncertain smile from her; then he hurried out into the darkening main street of Chentai and set out toward the *yamen*, where the district magistrate had his official residence.

3

"Although I am a humble man of deficient rank and too little learning, Pastor Ke, I can assure you the Red Bandits at present pose no threat to Chentai. Indeed, I am quite confident there is no significant number of Communist soldiers within three hundred *li* of our ancient town." The pouchy face of District Magistrate Yao creased into a practiced smile of elaborate politeness. "I understand your concern, Pastor, and might perhaps have been tempted to share it if I had not myself received the very same reassurance by telegraph in the last few hours."

Using a little pair of pointed wooden tongs, the Chinese official plucked a few wisps of black tobacco from a jade jar at his elbow and distributed them evenly in the bowl of a brass and porcelain water pipe placed before him on his lacquered desk.

"Then may one who has no real right to ask respectfully inquire why several hundred government soldiers were suddenly sent to garrison the town for most of the day?" Jakob, seated before the desk, spoke his Chinese slowly, taking care to match the magistrate's elaborate formal courtesy.

"The explanation, as a missionary of such high intellect as yourself will doubtless have anticipated, is quite simple. The bandit extermination campaigns of Generalissimo Chiang Kai-shek are on the brink of total success. An important bandit stronghold in Kiangsi has been overrun and captured. Surviving remnants of the Red Bandit forces are fleeing for their lives and it was thought yesterday a few stragglers might have begun heading toward Chentai. New information, however, shows that the doomed fugitives are panic-stricken and have been reduced to moving erratically in circles in a region nearly a hundred miles to the east. The force that garrisoned Chentai briefly today has therefore been ordered to advance rapidly to help in the final encirclement and destruction of what remains of the bandit armies."

The magistrate held a taper to the single flickering oil lamp that illuminated his private studio at the rear of the *yamen*. The only things visible in the resultant gloom were a number of gaudily painted miniature mud gods seated on wall niche thrones. Beneath each one a single joss stick smoldered in a tiny bowl, and having lit the pipe, the magistrate held the stem to his lips and inhaled with closed eyes before expelling a white cloud of water-cooled smoke.

"The information I'm about to speak of, Magistrate Yao, might already be in your possession," said Jakob slowly. "But even so I feel that in the interests of the people of Chentai I should tell you. . . . A village about sixty *li* from here was attacked this afternoon. I arrived there soon after the raid. Grain was stolen and all the government soldiers guarding the granary were killed. The village people are convinced the attackers were Red Bandits who intend to return in greater numbers."

The magistrate smoked his water pipe in silence, the insincere smile frozen on his fleshy face. He wore a close-fitting satin cap on the crown of his shaven head, which gave him an unpleasantly pugnacious air, and his wide-sleeved gown of dark blue silk did not quite conceal the swell of a glutton's paunch. Behind the oily self-deprecation of the magistrate's formal manner, Jakob felt he had long since detected a personal coldness and their contacts during his stay in Chentai, although perfectly correct, had been marked by reserve on both sides.

"Pastor Ke, as someone of your keen perception knows well enough, floods have again ruined the rice harvest in many parts of the region," said the magistrate at last. "Grain is scarce once more. Robbers and thieves who have preyed upon the people for many years are unfortunately only too ready to pose as Red Bandits to cover their tracks."

"I can see that's a possible explanation." Jakob nodded uncertainly. "But may I ask why the Chentai militia force has also left the town?"

"They have gone to assist the government forces in the final annihilation of the bandits." The magistrate rose from his seat, his smile fading from his face. "You can rest assured, Pastor Ke, that we've allowed our soldiers to leave the town only because we are quite satisfied that all danger has passed. There is no further need for you to worry."

"I'm not concerned for myself, Magistrate Yao — but my wife was very alarmed when the soldiers commandeered part of our mission for a barracks. We have a very young baby to think of."

"Unfortunately the soldiers arrived very suddenly. They began taking over billets before consulting me." The magistrate's formal smile flickered on and off again. "I hope you weren't unduly inconvenienced."

Jakob stood up suddenly, his mind made up. "If there are going to be food shortages and an increase in banditry it would perhaps be better if we traveled back to our central station at Changsha — and stayed there until the situation returns to normal."

The magistrate placed his hands inside the wide sleeves of his gown and bowed toward the missionary. "As you wish, Pastor Ke."

"I should like to leave Chentai tomorrow at dawn. Could a military escort be provided?"

Yao bowed low again. "Some men of the Chentai militia who stayed behind to guard the *yamen* will be put at your disposal. I shall send them to the mission compound at dawn."

"Thank you, Magistrate Yao! I shall go now to hire chair coolies."

A dark-robed servant appeared silently from the shadows and Jakob bowed low toward the magistrate in his turn before following the servant to the front gate of the *yamen*. Outside night had fallen, there was no moon, and the unlit main street was deserted. At the mud-walled inn, where traveling coolies rested, the evening ritual of boiling their meager rations of tea and rice over an open fire on the dirt floor would almost be finished. Soon, Jakob knew from experience, the coolies would be spreading out their bamboo mats around the fire and unpacking the opium pipes and lamps they carried with them, tied on top of their loads. The little thimblefuls of sticky amber fluid, on sale for ten cents, would be distributed by the inn-keeper and only when they had settled down to smoke would the coolies begin to forget the pain of the day's carrying. Once they started smoking they would care even less about finding work for the morning, and remembering this, Jakob set off at a fast run down the middle of the darkened street.

4

Farmer Hsiao's daughter Lan-ko awoke suddenly from an uneasy sleep just after midnight, imagining somebody was whispering urgently in her ear. More than twenty families and their animals were still pressed close around her in the pitch-blackness of her mountain village home and it was a moment or two before she realized her mistake; what she had taken for a whisper was the sibilant murmur of thousands of straw-sandaled feet marching rapidly through the soft gray dust outside the house. Suddenly frightened, the girl drew a sharp breath and turned to her father, intending to ask him what was happening, but his hand clamped itself tight over her mouth before she could speak.

Gently he guided her toward a crack in the door against which she had been sleeping and she pressed her eye to the opening. Although there was no moon, by the faint light of the stars she was able to make out the shadowy outline of a dense, endless column of men and pack animals passing within fifty yards of their hiding place. In near-silence the troops were marching swiftly up the narrow track heading for the mountain pass that led to the walled town of Chentai.

"The Red Bandits have come, Lan-ko," her father breathed close to her ear. "For two hours they have been moving through our village — and still there's no sign of the rear of the column."

Peering out through the slit in the door again, the girl strained her eyes, trying to see what the much-feared Red Bandits were really like. Although they were marching largely without lights, from time to time an isolated pathfinder passed, holding aloft a torch of burning bracken bound to a long stave. In the orange glare she saw that most of the Communist troops, in addition to their rifles, were carrying shoulder poles hung with boxes of ammunition, baskets of food, and kerosene cans. Mules and donkeys goaded onward by softly cursing muleteers were staggering under the weight of huge panniers bulging with weapons, tools, and machinery. Some of the soldiers wore cartwheel-sized hats made of layered bamboo and oiled paper to protect them from both sun and rain; others had distinctive jockey caps with long peaks pulled low over their eyes. Many carried sheathed swords at their belts, some were swathed in ammunition bandoliers, and all humped heavy backpacks as well as shoulder poles.

"They look more like a caravan of coolies with rifles than soldiers," murmured Lan-ko to her father. "And they're so quiet."

Whenever a baby whimpered or an animal bleated close to her, the watching girl stiffened with fright. Each time it happened, the offender was immediately hushed by the hidden villagers, but to Lan-ko's relief the fast-marching troops never showed any interest nor made any move to disturb the village's mud-and-thatch houses as they passed. Occasionally an officer rode by on a short-legged pony and once or twice she thought she saw among that great host of men an isolated woman or two, either riding on a mule or marching with the soldiers. She also saw several lines of dejected-looking prisoners roped together, their arms lashed behind their backs. They stood out among the brisk-stepping troops because they moved more slowly, stumbling now and then. There were soldiers in tattered Kuomintang uniforms and civilians in begrimed long-gowns but all, without exception, bent their heads in shame as they trudged up the mountain.

For perhaps an hour or more, Lan-ko kept her eye glued to the peephole but not once during that time did the flow of men and animals slacken. Then she began to notice that the column was moving more slowly and that more of the soldiers had wounds. Some had soiled and bloodied bandages wound around their heads; others who limped and hobbled had bandaged arms and legs. More severely injured men began to appear, lying on stretchers or being dragged in litters behind mules and donkeys. Their faces were all clenched and strained with pain and some were moaning softly as they passed.

Suddenly without understanding why she was doing it, Lan-ko began to cry quietly. Would this great silent mass of grim-faced men with their awful guns never stop marching through her village? Would she and her family and the other villagers have to stay hidden in the locked house forever? She didn't understand where the Red Bandits were going or where they had come from. She had never seen so many men marching together in her life and the sight of them, passing unendingly before the crack in her door, lit only by the orange-red glow of fiery torches, began to seem like a nightmare.

Were they human? Or were they really giant, shadowy demons of the night? The bloodied bandages of the wounded men and their agonized moans had made her feel cold and sad inside; and seeing the men with their arms bound tightly behind their backs had made her think of the friendly Outside Country pastor who had come to the village yesterday with new books for her. Why did they want to kill people like him? Why did the Red Bandits want to kill somebody with kind blue eyes and a happy smile who came to teach the village children songs and bring them books of stories about a white man who helped people? Singing his songs and reading the Yeh-su stories in big Chinese characters had made Lan-ko feel happy, and the thought that the great crowd of Red Bandits passing by outside wanted to kill the gentle Outside Country man suddenly made her break down and sob so loudly that her father had to reach out quickly and cover her mouth with his hand again.

5

By three o'clock in the morning the winding column of one hundred thousand marching men was slithering like a silent black serpent across the darkened rice plain below Chentai. All torches had been extinguished before the mountain pass was crossed so that no warning of their approach would be given to any sentries standing guard on the town walls. Orders to observe strict silence had been issued and the vanguard of the column had to pick its way carefully along the paved paths through the flooded rice fields by starlight.

This "caravan of coolies with rifles," which the frightened daughter of Farmer Hsiao had watched passing through her village, was in reality the First Front Red Army, also known as the Central Red Army, in the midst of a forced night march. Moving in disciplined columns, stepping quickly on soft-shod feet and following close behind one another without talking, the Communist troops were following a pattern that had quickly become a habit. In little more than three weeks since abandoning Juichin, the capital of their Kiangsi soviet, they had covered more than five hundred miles: sometimes they had marched only under cover of darkness to avoid the Kuomintang bombers and reconnaissance aircraft, sometimes they had broken into smaller groups, wheeling and feinting in different directions, and sometimes they had moved on continuously for seventy-two hours at a stretch, interspersing bursts of four hours on the march with four-hour periods of rest. A mobile diversionary force had been left behind in the heart of the Kiangsi soviet to fight a guerrilla rearguard action and confuse the Kuomintang armies. Because of the success of this maneuver and the rapid, undetected forced marches, these main units of the Central Red Army had broken through two lines of Nationalist encirclement after minor battles and skirmishes. Most important of all, ever since embarking on the breakout they had kept their enemies guessing about their intentions and their true whereabouts. The vital need for speed and secrecy if they were to survive had been repeatedly impressed on the troops by their leaders, and it was fear for their own lives that kept the men moving with such determination.

The plain which they were crossing so stealthily was some twenty miles wide and Chentai nestled on its western rim, guarding the lower slopes of another mountain range. By the time the slow-moving medical units at the end of the column straggled down onto the eastern edge of the plain the vanguard was already beginning to climb again into the western foothills, and a fleet-footed scouting party of two dozen Red Army men arrived before the locked gates of Chentai an hour before dawn. They threw ropes tipped with scaling hooks over the twenty-foot-high mud walls and climbed soundlessly into the town hand over hand. They quickly found and killed the sleeping gatekeeper and used his keys to swing open the creaking wooden gates. Running silently in their rice-straw sandals, they fanned out quickly through the narrow, deserted streets, reconnoitering and identifying the town *yamen*, the militia barracks, the grain stores, and the telegraph office. By the time the main units arrived at the open gates half an hour later the scouts were ready to lead assault parties to secure all the little town's key points.

One of the few lamps lit in Chentai at that early hour was burning in a window on the upper floor of the Anglo-Chinese Mission. Beside the crib in the nursery, Felicity, wearing only an open-fronted nightdress, was pressing her baby daughter against her naked breast. In recent days her growing anxiety had made the natural flow of her milk erratic and the infant had been crying intermittently through the night. As the Red Army men ran soundlessly down the street outside, however, Felicity at last succeeded in soothing the child, and she replaced her gently in the crib before returning to the bedroom, where Jakob lay asleep. She hesitated in the act of getting back into bed, her brow furrowing with worry; then she dressed herself quickly and shook Jakob's shoulder until he stirred.

"Please, Jakob, it's almost dawn! Will you go to the inn and try to rouse the chair coolies?"

Recognizing the quaver of fear in his wife's voice, Jakob rose at once and dressed, although it was still dark outside the window. All the preparations for their departure had been completed the night before. In the central hall below, clothes and food had been baled and stacked against a wall that was covered with a large framed oil painting of the birth of Christ in Bethlehem. After descending to check the bales, Jakob stood for a moment before the painting with his head bowed and murmured a short prayer. Then from the kitchen in the cellar he fetched the heavy bags of soybean-milk mixture that Liang and his wife had prepared for the baby. Because no other milk was available, the Chinese cookboy and his wife had worked late into the night crushing and mixing soybeans with calcium and sugar, which had been shipped to them from Shanghai.

When he had added the bags of soy mixture to the coolie loads, Jakob hurried out into the darkened courtyard, where he had already laid out for Felicity the mission's most comfortable *hwa gan*, a mountain chair slung between long, curved poles and covered with a waterproof oil-sheet awning. For extra speed he had hired four carrying coolies so that a free pair of them could run alongside the *hwa gan*, ready to take it directly onto their shoulders at each changeover without stopping or lowering it to the ground. After adjusting the seat cushions and checking the chair's ropes and its bamboo awning frame, Jakob unbarred the gate in the outer courtyard wall, intending to run to the inn to awaken the group of coolies he had hired — but before he had opened the gate the shooting began.

Only a few brief volleys were fired and Jakob immediately sensed that they had come from the direction of the town *yamen*. In themselves the isolated rifle shots did not at first seem alarming — more ominous was the swelling rumble of voices and running feet which followed. The noise grew quickly in volume and seemed to wash through the streets of the town with the speed of a flash flood. Coarse shouts began to ring out close to the mission compound and the crash of doors breaking and splintering reached Jakob's ears. Faint streaks of gray had begun to lighten the sky, and realizing that he could not risk fetching the coolies for fear of what might happen in his absence, Jakob quickly barred the compound gates once more and raced back into the house.

"It's too late, isn't it? The Communists have come."

Felicity's voice was hollow with resignation. She was standing like a statue at the top of the stairs, her face gray and stiff. In her arms she clutched their baby, swaddled in a woolen shawl.

"I don't know who they are — I'm going to the belfry to see what's happening."

Jakob raced past her up a short flight of unrailed stairs. A bell hung in a small turret whose sides were made of well-spaced wooden slats, and peering out between them, he was able to look down over the compound wall. In the growing light he could see that the main street was seething with armed soldiers. Using rifle butts and the hilts of their swords, the yelling men were smashing down the doors of the bigger houses and dragging out bewildered occupants in their nightclothes. Food, clothing, jewelry, and ornaments were being looted from the houses and some of the owners were being kicked and beaten by gangs of jeering troops.

Other groups were climbing walls and stringing white cotton banners across the streets or splashing slogans in fresh paint across the whitewashed walls of houses. From the unpaved square in front of the *yamen* he heard a great roar, and raising his gaze, Jakob saw a long banner being hoisted above the district magistrate's office. In giant red Chinese characters it proclaimed "Death to All Landlords and Capitalists!" A similar roar greeted a second banner raised a moment later which read "A Soviet Government Is China's Only Hope!"

Nearer at hand, at the entrance to the street leading to the mission, Jakob could see other soldiers daubing slogans on walls and shop fronts in black or red paint: "Refuse to Pay Debts to Rich Landlords!" . . . "Capture the Criminal Chiang Kai-shek Alive!" . . . "Support the Red Army!" A smaller group of soldiers slashing black brush strokes across a whitewashed end wall not far from the mission compound caught Jakob's eye and he recognized the characters *Chi tu chiao*, which had been widely adopted to represent "Christianity" or "the Christian religion." As the Communist soldiers added several more characters, Jakob held his breath, trying to anticipate the degree of hostility the slogan might convey. Although running tails of paint dribbled down the wall from the words, when the slogan was finished there was no mistaking its meaning. It was a paraphrased quotation from Karl Marx: "The Christian Religion Is the Opiate of the People!"

From the slogan's position on the wall facing the Anglo-Chinese Mission it seemed certain to Jakob that it had been painted there on specific orders. The location of the mission had obviously been discovered and it would only be a matter of time before the Communists came to invade the compound. This realization had only just begun to sink in when Jakob noticed that the commotion coming from the *yamen* was growing louder. Rifle shots rang out and hundreds of voices began chanting slogans in unison. Looking in the direction of the town square, he suddenly saw the reason: the dense, noisy crowd of soldiers was beginning to break up and many of them were surging out of the square toward the mouth of the street leading to the mission.

6

Felicity was still standing motionless at the top of the stairs when Jakob ran down from the belfry. On reaching her side he saw that the baby, lying quiet in her arms, was awake: her blue eyes, innocent of all expression, gazed blankly at him for a moment, then shifted away, as though listening abstractedly to the growing noise in the street outside. Felicity made no attempt to move but stared ahead unseeing, seemingly unable to speak.

"Remember we're in God's hands," said Jakob softly, encircling her shoulder with his arm and moving his face close to hers. "Our help is in the name of the Lord who made heaven and earth."

He ushered her gently down the stairs to the kitchen and ordered Liang to rouse all the mission servants. When they had dressed and assembled — Liang's wife, their two sons, aged eleven and thirteen, an elderly wash amah, the gate man, a gardener, and a goat boy — Jakob told them that if the Communist soldiers broke into the compound they were to do whatever they were asked and offer no physical resistance.

In the early dawn light filtering in through glass windows set at ground level, the simple faces of most of the Chinese servants before him reflected their puzzlement and apprehension. They gazed at Jakob and one another with uncomprehending eyes, lifting their heads every so often to listen to the growing pandemonium outside the compound walls. Only Liang's features were composed and intent as he tried to interpret the noises coming from the street. At his side, his two young sons, dark-skinned and alert like their father, struggled to reconcile the fear and excitement that warred inside them, sometimes biting their lips and sometimes giggling in mystification. Felicity sat a little apart from them on a kitchen chair, rocking herself gently from side to side and making soothing noises with her face bent close to the baby.

Speaking in a quiet, steady voice, Jakob told them he believed the

Communists would not harm ordinary Chinese people. He promised to do everything he could to ensure their safety, then asked them to bend their heads so that he could lead them in prayer. But almost as soon as he began to pray a thunderous hammering on the compound gate drowned his words. Without hurrying he finished the act of worship, although it went unheard, and beckoning to the gate man to follow him, he mounted the stone steps to the courtyard and motioned the Chinese forward to unbar the two heavy teak gates.

The hullabaloo of shouting and banging died away completely for an instant as the gates swung open. The sight of a blond-bearded European standing alone, seemingly fearless and unarmed, inside the empty compound, clearly surprised the Chinese troops crowding the gateway, clutching rifles with bayonets fixed.

"There are women and children inside," called Jakob ringingly in Chinese. "I ask you not to harm them."

The sound of Jakob's voice at once broke whatever spell had restrained the Red Army troops at the gate. On a shouted order from a tall, swarthy officer wielding a sword, a small group rushed forward into the compound and surrounded Jakob. Two men seized his arms, pinioning them behind him, while another bound his wrists with rope. The tall officer yelled further orders and two dozen or more men raced through the moon gate into the house.

"The Red Army arrests you as an imperialist spy!" yelled the officer in Jakob's face. "You have spied for Chiang Kai-shek. The penalty for spying is death!"

The crowd of soldiers outside the gates surged into the compound, echoing the officer's words, and pressed around Jakob and his captors. From the house behind him Jakob heard the sounds of splintering wood and breaking glass.

"I am not a spy!" Jakob, struggling to keep his feet in the crush, had to raise his voice to make himself heard above the din. "I serve only Jesus Christ!"

"You lie!"

The swarthy officer, whose coarse voice betrayed the distinctive peasant accents of Hunan, gesticulated toward the gate and shouted another order. The crowd parted and two young soldiers appeared, dragging the disheveled figure of the district magistrate between them. His torn and dirtied long-gown was bloodstained from a wound on the side of his head and his face was gray with fear.

"District Magistrate Yao has already told my guards how you spy for the Nationalists," yelled the Hunanese. Turning to Yao, he prodded him viciously with the tip of his sword. "And now he'll tell us again!"

Yao's eyes rolled with terror and his jowled face quivered as he tried to summon words that wouldn't come: then, after another prod from the sword of the Hunanese, who was clearly the commander of the guards, Yao began to gabble in a high-pitched tone. "This foreigner came to my *yamen* last night to report on the movements of what he called Red Army 'bandit' forces in a mountain village sixty *li* from here . . . I tried to ignore him but he said the 'bandits' had killed many government soldiers . . . He gave me the exact numbers of troops involved and the times of these events in the manner of an experienced spy . . . He said 'Red Bandits' had stolen many sacks of rice and carried them away on carts . . . He urged me to take measures to counterattack the Red Army and drive it away from Chentai . . . But again I ignored him . . ."

As Yao was speaking, the face of the Hunanese tightened slowly into a mask of loathing. Suddenly, without any warning, he held his left arm aloft in a silent signal. Two of his guards immediately lunged forward, their rifles held stiffly in front of them, and plunged their bayonets into the district magistrate's chest and abdomen, forcing them to the hilt. Yao's eyes bulged from his head but he did not cry out; his body sagged in the arms of his captors and he began to choke and retch. But even before he died, the Hunanese barked out another hoarse order and the guards dragged the body, jerking and twitching, out of the compound. Because the magistrate's shoes had been torn off, his bare feet left parallel tracks in the dust and Jakob stood gazing down in horror at the heel marks leading away through the gate.

"All enemies of the revolution should be executed like that, foreign spy!" The guard commander moved to stand directly in front of Jakob, his eyes bright with animosity. "But we are prepared to be lenient if your religious society pays a heavy fine. Come! You must write a letter for immediate dispatch."

The Hunanese turned and led the way through the moon gate into the house and Jakob's guards frog-marched him rapidly in his wake. Some Red Army soldiers were already running down the steps with sacks of rice and vegetables slung over their shoulders; others had ripped sheets and blankets from the beds and were sitting on the front steps tearing the material into strips to make crude cloth sandals for themselves. In the middle of the inner courtyard a trooper was pouring oil over a big heap of Bibles, and a loud cheer rang out when he dropped a lighted match and the books ignited with a hollow thump.

As he was hustled inside, Jakob caught sight of Felicity and the Chinese servants huddled fearfully in a corner of the central hall under the watchful eye of two armed guards. Felicity, who was clutching the baby convulsively in front of her, seemed to stare at him, round-eyed, without seeing him and he realized she must be close to hysteria. Several soldiers were ripping open the coolie loads of food and clothing that had been prepared for the journey to the central station and as Jakob entered, one of them thrust his sword into the oil painting of the first Christmas on the wall above and hacked it from its frame. Without even glancing at the picture, the soldier rolled up the big, practical piece of canvas and strapped it onto his pack for future use.

The Hunanese commander stood staring at Felicity and the baby for a moment, then ordered the guards to seat Jakob before a table and free his wrists. He sent one of the soldiers to search for writing materials, and when he returned the commander pushed a sheet of paper in front of Jakob and put a pen in his hand.

"Write a telegraph message to your headquarters!"

Jakob looked into the face of the Hunanese: his complexion was a muddy brown and beneath jutting brows his dark, narrow eyes were implacably cold and hostile. "What do you want me to tell my headquarters?"

"Tell them fines must be paid to compensate for your crimes of spying for the Nationalists!"

"How much are the 'fines'?"

"Fifty thousand Chinese dollars for each of you!"

Jakob glanced over his shoulder toward the corner where Felicity sat holding the baby, but she didn't appear to have heard what was being said. "How much are you demanding altogether?" he asked the Hunanese in a low voice.

"One hundred and fifty thousand dollars!"

Jakob drew a long breath and pushed the paper away. "My headquarters won't pay such a sum. We don't have that much money. And even if we did, I know it couldn't be used to pay a ransom."

The Hunanese stepped up beside the table. Lifting his sword, he used the tip to draw the sheet of paper gently back in front of Jakob.

"I command the Guards Battalion responsible for all prisoners," he said in a menacing tone. "I'm authorized to tell you that if the fine is not paid soon, your wife and baby will be executed."

7

The light was already fading and a steady drizzle had begun to fall by the time their Red Army captors forced Jakob and Felicity at gunpoint into the human river of marching soldiers that had begun flowing out of Chentai in the late afternoon. The whole column had rested in and around the walled town throughout the day, and during that time Jakob, Felicity, and the baby had been held prisoner in their own kitchen. Jakob's hands had been bound tightly behind his back all day and his booted feet slipped and slithered constantly on the slime-covered stones of the track as he struggled up the steep mountainside above the town.

His Communist guards in their straw sandals were more sure-footed and they cursed him roundly whenever he faltered. His gaze, however, remained fixed anxiously ahead of him on the broken-down horse which Felicity was riding, clutching their infant daughter. A yelling soldier was dragging at the halter of the unwilling animal and it too stumbled frequently on the slippery track. Through the gathering gloom the white blob of Felicity's frightened face became visible every few seconds as she turned in the saddle to look back at Jakob.

Once he fell to his knees and the soldier following him jabbed his rifle muzzle into his back. "*Heh pu chiao Yeh-su pang ni pa shan?*" he yelled jeeringly. "Why don't you ask Jesus to help you up this mountain?"

A roar of derisive laughter rose from the guard's comrades all around Jakob and he gritted his teeth in silence as he struggled back to his feet. In the gathering darkness the fertile green rice plain that lay below Chentai was becoming indistinguishable from the stony yellow mountainsides above and he realized then why the troops had torn down the long fence of split bamboo which had surrounded the mission vegetable garden. Each man carried a single stave and as the gloom thickened, these were being lit to make flaming torches.

Climbing higher, Jakob gradually became aware of the massive size of the marching column he had joined. The moving wake of flickering lights did not stretch back only into Chentai — other straggling units that had rested in the mountains on the plain's eastern edge were moving forward again to join up with the main body and the lights appeared to spill far across the broad floor of the valley beyond the town. On reaching the summit of the mountain, he found that the phalanx of flaming torches also extended far into the distance, zigzagging down into the next valley and flowing like a bright stream of lava up over the adjoining range of hills. The milling crowds of seemingly disorderly troops who had rampaged through Chentai during the day had merged themselves in an astonishingly short time into a well-disciplined column that was obviously tens of thousands strong.

By the light of the torches Jakob could also see endless strings of horses and pack mules laden with heavy equipment and weapons. Sewing machines, printing presses, machinery, and crates of documents were strapped to the backs of the animals and a few were dragging wheeled anti-aircraft guns. Suddenly he was seized by a new feeling of apprehension and awe at finding himself a helpless prisoner among such an enormous migration of men and animals. But mixed with these emotions, he felt too, to his surprise, a deep throb of elation.

Standing on that high mountain pass he found he could see neither the front of the column in the mountains ahead nor its end on the plains behind. Once again a fleeting memory of that thrill of childish excitement he had first felt listening to Matthew Barlow more than a dozen years ago in a Manchester church hall rushed back into his mind: he had always known that a great challenge and high adventure awaited him in China. Now he had become an isolated Christian captive of a truly mighty heathen force. The difficulties and frustrations of seeking converts day by day had been left behind. His faith would be put to the ultimate test — and he would not be found wanting. He had been selected, as he always hoped he would be, for great work and he relished the prospect of the ordeal. Above all it would enable him to bear witness to God's greater glory.

He stood staring out into the darkness for so long that his guard jabbed him viciously once more with the muzzle of his rifle; only then did his thoughts return to Felicity, who was already beginning to descend into the darkened valley below. With a stab of alarm he realized that the sight he had found so awe-inspiring must have struck her with equal force, intensifying her fears, and he lunged forward in her direction down the narrow mountain path. In his haste he shouldered aside the Chinese soldiers in his path, ignoring their angry shouts of surprise. His guards chased after him, yelling orders for him to halt, but he continued stumbling and sliding down the track until he came up panting beside Felicity's horse.

Her face was haggard from anxiety but the baby, cradled in her arms, seemed to be sleeping peacefully. When she turned and found Jakob unexpectedly at her side, the effort she had been making to conceal her fears faltered and her face began to crumple.

"What will they do with us, Jakob?" she sobbed. "There are so many of them. Where are they taking us?"

"Don't be afraid," said Jakob firmly. "The shield of our faith will protect us." He smiled encouragingly at her but his self-possession only seemed to unnerve her further.

"How can you take it so calmly? Abigail is only a month old. She could die on a journey like this!" Felicity's voice was frantic and she pressed the sleeping infant fearfully against her bosom.

Jakob moved close against the horse's shoulder, meaning to reassure her further, but at that moment his guards caught up with them and began yelling abuse at him for running on ahead. Again they jabbed their rifles into his ribs, causing him to wince, but he held himself determinedly erect.

"Trust me — and trust in God, Felicity!" He spoke loudly in Chinese this time so that the guards could hear him. "We must seize this chance to introduce as many of these strangers as possible to the way of our Lord."

The guard commander let out an unintelligible shout of contempt and pushed Jakob roughly on down the track, signaling the young soldier leading Felicity's horse to fall in behind. As they continued the descent, the troops carrying lighted torches began snuffing them out and Jakob heard urgent commands for silence passing down the line. From whispered conversations he learned that they were approaching a ridge above a village where a battalion of government troops was camped and an attempt was to be made to pass silently and unseen in the darkness.

Without waiting for orders from their company commanders, the troops closed ranks, each man placing his hand on the shoulder of the man in front: this enabled them to continue shuffling slowly down the mountain in what had suddenly become pitch-blackness. His guard quickly threaded a rope through Jakob's bound arms, and holding its free end, he ordered Jakob to walk on with his shoulder pressed against the horse's flank. Soon the torches along the whole length of the column were extinguished. The river of light that moments before had been surging noisily across the nighttime hills and plains of Hunan became invisible, and the column continued shifting almost soundlessly westward in the darkness with only the muted scuff of rice-straw sandals to mark its passage.

The drizzling rain began to fall more heavily and the stones of the track, polished smooth by the feet of coolies over many centuries, became more treacherous to negotiate. The ill-shod hooves of Felicity's tiring mare slipped constantly as the gradient steepened, and the animal whinnied in its distress. Rounding a rock it stumbled, then reared up in panic when its inexperienced handler dragged too hard on the halter. Felicity clutched wildly at its mane with one hand to stop herself from falling, but although she managed to save herself, the violent movement woke the baby, who at once began to wail.

The troops around them muttered angrily among themselves. Then, to Jakob's horror, one of them called out urgently, "*Pa na ko wa wa sha le!*" — "Kill the baby!"

Felicity began sobbing hysterically herself as her efforts to soothe the infant failed, and when the Hunanese guard commander appeared suddenly out of the rain, carrying a shaded hurricane lamp and an unsheathed sword, she tried to fling herself and the child bodily from the horse. But the Hunanese reached out and seized her by the arm.

"Give me the child!"

The Hunanese handed the hurricane lamp to the boy at the horse's head and dragged Felicity to the ground. With his free hand he grabbed at the thick shawl wrapped around the baby — but Felicity twisted away from him, shrieking in desperation. Other troops crowded around, struggling to wrest the baby from her grasp, but before they succeeded, Jakob forced himself between his wife and the Hunanese.

"Cut my bonds. I'll quiet the child!"

Jakob's loud demand, made confidently in Chinese, silenced the commotion. Although the baby began whimpering again almost at once, the guard commander had checked his raised sword. Seizing on his moment of indecision, Jakob turned quickly and offered his bound wrists to the guard commander's blade.

"Be quick if you wish us to remain undiscovered!"

After a moment's hesitation the Hunanese sliced through the ropes binding Jakob's wrists and watched him warily as he turned and took the baby from Felicity's arms. Sinking to his knees Jakob cradled the child against his chest and bent his head over her. Felicity watched with an anguished expression distorting her features. She saw his lips move as he murmured consoling sounds; then, almost at once, the child quieted.

Rising again, Jakob placed the baby gently in Felicity's arms. He helped her remount the horse and took its halter himself. Without looking back at the commander or waiting for his arms to be bound again, he set off down the steep mountain track, testing the footing ahead of the horse carefully as he went.

8

"Kneel, imperialist spy!"

The Hunanese commander glared at Jakob and pointed to the earth floor at the foot of the tethering post. "Do as I say — kneel. Now!"

Although he was shivering inside his sodden clothing and was weak with exhaustion, Jakob remained upright, looking levelly at the Hunanese and saying nothing. The stable in which they stood was illuminated by the flames from several braziers set up in the courtyard beyond the open door; by their light Jakob could see the guard commander's swarthy face flushing with anger as he continued to defy him.

"I kneel only to pray to God," said Jakob in a quiet voice. "It's an act of reverence I reserve solely for Him."

The officer's right hand dropped threateningly to the hilt of his sword which he carried thrust through his leather belt and Jakob heard Felicity gasp behind him. The young trooper in charge of the horse was in the act of tethering it to a wall ring, but sensing the rising tension between the two men, he paused and turned to watch.

Outside the stable door, their cookboy, Liang, and his two young sons, who had arrived only minutes before, shrank back apprehensively into the shadows.

"If you disobey my orders your wife and child will suffer!" The Hunanese took a menacing step in Felicity's direction before turning back to face Jakob. "Kneel! You are to be bound for the rest of the night."

Jakob looked at Felicity. She had just fed their baby daughter and settled her into a bed of rice straw in the horse's feeding trough. She was biting her lip and he saw a beseeching expression come into her eyes. For a moment he hesitated, then, pressing the palms of his hands together in front of his chest, he lowered himself slowly to his knees beside the tethering post, bowed his head, and began reciting the Lord's Prayer in Chinese in a firm voice.

"Bind him!"

The Hunanese barked the second command at the young trooper and seized Jakob's wrists, wrenching them behind his back on either side of the tethering post. After the youth had lashed them together, he ordered him to fasten a thicker rope around Jakob's chest and called three older soldiers to stand guard outside. As he was leaving, the Hunanese turned in the doorway and glared at the missionaries.

"The people have heard of your capture," he said brusquely. "They demand that you be put on trial at dawn in the town square."

"On what charges?" asked Jakob in surprise.

"Spying for the imperialists," rasped the Hunanese. "And the people themselves will be your judges, so be careful what you say. If you anger them, they will demand your execution — and the will of the people must be carried out!"

When they were left alone Felicity rushed to Jakob's side and fell on her knees. Flinging her arms about his neck, she buried her face against his chest and he felt her shoulders tremble with a fit of silent sobbing. Her dress and shawl clung wetly to her body and she shivered continually; around them the floor was dirty and the rank odors of horses' urine and droppings filled the air.

They had struggled more than twenty-five miles without rest over the rain-drenched mountains after a general command had been issued for the column to put as much distance as possible between itself and the Nationalist battalion they had encountered. It had been almost two A.M. before a brief halt was called at the market town of Paoshan. A prior warning had been issued that the march would resume again soon after first light, and the Red Army troops had at once begun looting the shops and houses of the township's wealthy landowners and mandarins.

The Hunanese commander had requisitioned the home of an affluent landlord to quarter his prisoners in the stables and granaries that opened onto a central courtyard. A noisy melee of soldiers, wearing their distinctive long-peaked khaki jockey caps, thronged the area around the blazing braziers, sorting and stacking bolts of cloth, sacks of rice, and endless boxes and baskets of food, clothing, shoes, and jewelry.

From time to time above the din, the cries of pain made by the owner of the house became audible. As they were hustled into the courtyard, Jakob and Felicity had seen the bewildered, potbellied Chinese dressed only in a rumpled nightgown being led away into one of the open-fronted granaries. A rope was hitched around one of his ankles and the other end thrown over a beam. Before they were pushed into their stable, they saw the Chinese jerked violently off his feet, and the next moment he was spinning and twisting upside down in the midst of the jeering throng of peasant soldiers. He had screamed and groaned constantly at first but gradually his agonized cries had grown fainter.

Hearing a new, long-drawn-out moan from the granary as she clung to her husband at the foot of the tethering post, Felicity stiffened with horror. "It's all like some terrible nightmare, Jakob," she breathed close to his ear. "I pray that we'll wake up soon."

"My own arms can't comfort you now," whispered Jakob. "But please don't lose faith. Arms that others can't see will protect us both."

A shadow fell across them and looking up, Felicity saw the figure of a Chinese silhouetted in the doorway against the light of the courtyard fires. With a little cry she sprang to her feet, dashed to the feeding trough, and swept her baby into her arms. But when she turned, she found Liang, the cookboy, advancing into the stable with his loaded shoulder pole. Grinning diffidently, he lowered the large twin baskets carefully to the floor and pointed into them.

"I bring you clothes for baby. I bring rice and soybean milk. I bring towels and quilts to make you and master dry and warm."

Liang glanced carefully over his shoulder into the courtyard every few seconds and his voice was uneasy as he spoke; although ordered by the guard commander in Chentai to accompany his employers and continue his domestic duties, he too was tense and fearful for his own safety.

"Hsiao Liang, you're very brave to have made the long journey in the dark. We're most grateful." Jakob grimaced and strained unsuccessfully against his bonds, trying to ease the growing stiffness in his limbs. "We shall thank you properly when we are all safely returned to Chentai."

Liang ducked his head shyly in acknowledgment, then busied himself rummaging in the panniers. He pulled out a small cooking pot, two bowls, chopsticks, some small bags of rice, and several packets of the soybean milk substitute and set them out on one of the upturned panniers. After handing Felicity towels and a wide-sleeved Chinese gown, he prepared a bed for her beside Jakob by spreading two rolled bamboo sleeping mats and a quilted coverlet on a mound of rice straw.

While he was doing this his two sons, who had accompanied him, watched from the doorway; when he called to them to run and find water and a place to boil rice they dashed off eagerly, racing one another to complete the task. Liang, after talking with the guards, went off and returned a few minutes later carrying an old metal bucket that contained a few glowing coals from one of the courtyard braziers. He had punched holes in its sides and after positioning this improvised fire close to Jakob so that it would warm him, he fixed a rope across the stable and motioned to Felicity to dry above the fire the wet clothes she had already removed.

After gazing at the second empty pannier for a moment, Liang stooped and filled it with clean straw, then set it beside the bed he had prepared for Felicity. Pointing to the baby whimpering fretfully in her mother's arms, Liang grinned and made a sleeping motion by pressing his joined hands against his own cheek. "The basket will make a fine crib for baby, no?"

Despite her anxiety, Felicity smiled for the first time since leaving Chentai, and kneeling beside the basket, she lowered the infant gently into the circular nest of straw. They watched anxiously for a moment or two; then a smile of delight lit Liang's face as the baby's eyes closed and she settled peacefully to sleep.

While Liang went off to cook the scraps of food he had brought, Felicity dried Jakob as best she could with the towels and wrapped a warm quilted coverlet about his shoulders. She folded another quilt, fixing it as a makeshift pillow between his head and the tethering post, and closed the door to the courtyard. With the damp night air excluded, the few coals inside the punctured bucket began to cast a comforting red glow around the stable, and when Liang returned with two steaming bowls of bean soup and glutinous rice, Felicity knelt beside Jakob in the straw and fed him.

Before leaving them, Liang tiptoed to the closed door to listen for the guards. When he was satisfied that they could not be overheard, he opened a tin of tea and rummaged among the black leaves. Extracting a tiny leather-bound volume, he held it toward Jakob. "I bring you 'Daily Light,' I know you like."

When Jakob saw the small, well-thumbed book of inspirational Scripture texts — each dated for use on a specific day of the year — a broad smile spread across his face. "Liang, you are a true Christian friend. This little book is as important as the food you brought — for the soul. Thank you."

Liang grinned delightedly and dipped his head once more in acknowledgment.

"Would you like to pray together with us now?"

An uneasy look replaced the grin on the face of the Chinese cookboy. "I will say prayers quietly later . . . on my own."

"I understand," said Jakob softly. "God will bless you, Hsiao Liang."

When the Chinese had closed the door to their stable prison behind him, Jakob smiled elatedly at Felicity. "You see, all is not lost. Faith is always rewarded in mysterious ways — even in the wild lands of China."

Felicity nodded and smiled sadly back at him.

"Will you read the verses for today aloud, please?"

Felicity nodded again and opened the book at that day's date. She held it toward the glow of the fire and in a quiet, reverent tone read the texts for the morning and the evening. In the damp and rank-smelling Chinese stable the hallowed words were immediately comforting and as Felicity continued reading, the gentle cadences of the verses brought them both a sudden sense of peace.

When at last she closed the book, Jakob smiled his thanks and motioned for her to lie down between him and the baby's temporary crib; with her head resting in his lap, they slept fitfully — until a clamor of raucous voices wakened them suddenly at first light. Felicity sat up and together they strained their ears to listen. A large crowd was moving nearer along the street outside, chanting raggedly in Chinese, and gradually it became clear that they were shouting the same words over and over again.

"Ti kuo chu i chou kou kai szu! . . . Ti kuo chu i chou kou kai szu! . . . Ti kuo chu i chou kou kai szu!"

As the meaning of the chants sank in, Felicity turned and stared at Jakob, aghast. Instinctively he shifted and tried to reach out his arms to her, but winced with pain as he realized again how stiff and numb his bound limbs had become. He tried unsuccessfully to smile, then shook his head in a little gesture of frustration and helplessness. Outside the chanting of the crowd grew steadily louder . . .

"The imperialist spies deserve to die! . . . The imperialist spies deserve to die!"

9

Barefoot and stripped to the waist, Jakob shivered in the chill gray dawn as his guards urged him down the muddy main street of Pao-shan at rifle point. His wrists were bound tight behind his back and a broad strip of blood red paper had been fixed around his neck on which black Chinese characters had been daubed, announcing "This Is an English Imperialist Spy!" Felicity walked unsteadily in front of him; her hands too were bound behind her back with rope, her feet were bare, and she wore the crumpled brown dress which Liang had dried for her over the fire.

Only a narrow passage in the middle of the street had been left open through the crowds of Red Army soldiers and townspeople, and as Jakob and Felicity passed, fists were waved angrily in their faces. Jeers and shouts of "Foreign Devils!" "Big Noses!" and "Hook Noses!" rang out from all sides as the onlookers craned their necks to catch a glimpse of them. A few paces behind, the potbellied landlord who had been tormented by soldiers all night in his own granary was being led by a rope fastened around his neck. His face was swollen and bruised and he stared sightlessly at the ground as he walked. A tall, pointed dunce cap had been placed on his head and paper labels around his neck denounced him as a "Local Tyrant." A group of captured Nationalist army officers brought up the rear under close guard; their labels described them simply as "Traitors!"

In the town square, three farm carts had been drawn up in front of the *yamen* to serve as a stage. Red paper banners strung above them proclaimed "Death to All Spies, Traitors, and Feudal Usurpers of Our Land!" Felicity and Jakob were pushed up onto the carts first, and the landlord and the Nationalist officers followed. Several thousand soldiers and townspeople had jammed into the square, and at the sight of the prisoners they broke into a storm of jeering and chanting.

A malevolent-looking Red Army officer wearing the arm band of a senior political commissar was already standing on one of the carts, preparing to harangue the crowd, and at his side a squat, swarthy southern Chinese was clutching a long, curved sword protected inside a scabbard of scuffed leather. As the first weak rays of the rising sun illuminated the square, the swordsman's narrow eyes seemed to Jakob to glitter with an unnatural brightness and he stared intently at each of the prisoners in turn as they mounted the carts.

"Today China is a semicolonial country," yelled the political commissar suddenly. "Foreign imperialists rule many of our great coastal cities — and treat the Chinese living in them like dogs. Big landlords in the countryside are the natural allies of those imperialists. They depend on them for their survival! And their political party is the treacherous Nationalist Party of Chiang Kai-shek." The commissar waved his arm contemptuously in the direction of the prisoners. "Today we have won great victories against all those enemies of the revolution! We have captured their representatives — and they've been brought here to receive punishment for their crimes!"

The Red Army soldiers in the crowd led a new storm of chanting and abuse as guards pushed Jakob and Felicity forward to stand alone, at the front of the cart. Jakob noticed that all color had drained from Felicity's cheeks; she swayed slightly on her feet and he feared that she might faint and topple into the crowd. "Try not to show that you're afraid," he whispered. "Trust in the Lord."

"Imperialist spies — tell the people of Paoshan who you are!" The commissar pointed scornfully at Jakob. "Tell them your name in English and spell it for them in full!"

Jakob looked around uncertainly at the sea of Asiatic faces so different from his own. The crowd quieted in anticipation and he drew himself up as straight as his bonds would allow. "My name is

Jakob Kellner," he said, and spelled it out letter by letter, speaking his English with slow emphasis. "I came to China from England to bring you the word of God . . ."

Without warning a wave of derisive laughter swept the square. Jakob, taken aback, stared at the crowd, mystified, and a moment or two passed before he understood fully: the people of Paoshan and the peasant soldiers, who had rarely seen a foreigner or heard one speak, were convulsed simply by the comic sound of his alien tongue. The commissar, who had obviously anticipated this effect, waved Jakob to silence and pointed a peremptory finger at Felicity.

"Now you!"

Felicity struggled for several seconds to find her voice. Then, summoning all her courage, she took a pace forward to the edge of the cart. "I am Felicity Kellner. I did not come here to spy for my country . . ." She spoke in little more than a whisper and perhaps because of this the crowd remained silent, listening intently. Felicity, as a result, became more confident and switched to Chinese. "I did not come to China for any selfish reason at all. I came for your sakes . . . to help tell you about the love that God has for all peoples of the world . . . to try to teach you to believe in Him so that you might be saved . . ."

"Kill the imperialists! Kill them now!"

An angry roar from a burly Red Army soldier in the middle of the crowd suddenly drowned Felicity's voice.

"Beat them — beat the imperialists! Drive them out of China!"

Jakob, from the corner of his eye, had seen the swordsman make a surreptitious signal in the direction of the burly soldier and hundreds of others immediately followed his lead. Felicity's gentle voice was overwhelmed and the commissar motioned to nearby guards to seize Felicity and Jakob by the arms. Stepping in front of them, he produced a sheet of paper from inside his jacket and began to read from it.

"From our investigations," he yelled, "it's quite clear that this man and this woman have been sent to China by the imperialistic government of Britain. They and others like them are trying to subjugate the masses of China by means of the so-called Christian religion. Their aim is to bring all the people of China under foreign control." He paused and glared around angrily at the crowd. "What fate should foreigners of this kind suffer?"

The same soldier in the heart of the crowd who had led the chanting before punched the air above his head with a clenched fist.

"Kill them! Kill all imperialists!"

He screamed the words wildly and the rest of the crowd joined in, shaking their fists at the two prisoners.

"Their readings from the Bible and their talk of 'God' are like opium! They use these lies to drug our people and subdue them — to prepare them for more widespread rule by foreigners. They use their 'religion' to mislead and deceive the people of China! What must be done with foreigners of this kind?"

This time the entire crowd erupted spontaneously with repeated roars of "Kill them!" and Jakob, who had been watching anxiously, realized that the yelling of the townspeople was becoming as frenzied as that of the soldiers. While they were walking in the main street the local people among the crowds had remained largely silent; their expressions then had been both curious and wary, and Jakob guessed that many had turned out to watch because the soldiers had told them to. The arrival of the Red Army had obviously been as much of a shock in Paoshan as in Chentai and at first its inhabitants, who had seen many armies pass through the town gates over several generations, reacted, as ever, by complying with its demands. But now the political emotion generated by the troops was becoming infectious. The hatred for the prisoners, sparked off deliberately by the swordsman and his accomplice in the crowd, was spreading to the people of Paoshan and they were starting to call for their execution as avidly as the troops.

"In truth these two 'missionaries' are both spies in disguise," yelled the political commissar, raising his voice to a higher note of complaint. "They have been sent here as advance guards for the imperialist armies that will surely follow. They want to partition China, to divide our country among the foreign powers. Along with others like them they have come to live deep in the interior of our country so that they can report the movements of the patriotic Red Army to our enemies —"

A spontaneous outburst of jeering interrupted the speaker and some of the troops in the front ranks of the crowd spat at the two prisoners. Holding up his hand for silence, the commissar folded his paper and put it away in his tunic. His face contorted into a new expression of loathing and he pointed again at Jakob and Felicity.

"On the march during the night, the imperialist spies became desperate after we had taken them captive. They made a great noise, trying to attract the help of traitorous Kuomintang troops camped close to our route. They did not succeed because our revolutionary soldiers were vigilant as always! But doesn't this show that they and their imperialist masters will stop at nothing to gain their evil ends?" The commissar paused for breath. Then, drawing his words out slowly for effect, he roared at the top of his voice: "What must we do *now* with such evil foreign imperialists and their allies?"

"Kill them! Kill them! Kill them!"

The crowd's baying rose to a crescendo and the front ranks began to surge toward the carts. In the same instant, the squat southerner armed with the curved sword stepped forward and seized Felicity by the arm. He pulled her roughly down the steps to the ground and, preceded by a group of guards, led the way to the nearest town gate. Jakob and the other prisoners were pushed and dragged in her wake; the crowd streamed after them, still shouting and jeering.

Among the milling throng Jakob caught sight of Liang. The cookboy was pushing through the onlookers, keeping abreast of him, and every few moments he turned to stare in Jakob's direction. His expression was pained but he was sensibly taking care not to come too close or reveal that he was associated in any way with the prisoners. Jakob saw with a start that Liang was not carrying his panniers and wondered desperately if that meant that his baby daughter was hidden still in the stable where they had left her. The chanting of the crowd in the courtyard at dawn had not wakened her, and moments before their guards opened the doors to drag them outside, Felicity had concealed the pannier basket behind several bales of rice straw in the stable's darkest corner. The commissar in charge of the trial had obviously overlooked the baby's absence but from Liang's worried expression it was impossible to tell whether he had yet found the child. Jakob longed to call out some instructions for the cookboy to retrieve her and care for her as best he could, but fearing a sign from him might turn the wrath of the mob on Liang himself, he remained silent.

Carried along by the rush of the crowd, Jakob lost sight of Liang before he could resolve the dilemma. The guards who had led the way through the gate in the city's yellow mud walls were heading up a grass-covered hillside where tall pines grew in clumps. Felicity stumbled and fell to her knees as she began the climb and Jakob felt his anger rise hotly inside him as the squat Chinese hauled her brutally to her feet. In the bedraggled brown dress and with her hands lashed behind her back, Felicity looked heartrendingly frail:

her hair had come loose from the combs in which she had dressed it and was trailing down her back. Her feet and legs were black with the mud of the street and her stumbling gait indicated that her strength, drained from her through fear, was almost at an end.

Halfway up the hillside there was a grassy knoll where several pines had been felled. The circle of surviving trees was silhouetted against the watery light of the rising sun, the black, angular boughs looking to Jakob as if they had been finger-painted on the brightening sky. The stumps of the felled trees had been left in the ground and in the moment that he realized they were to be their execution blocks, he became acutely aware of the sharp coldness of the dew on his bare feet. The thick grass was still white with moisture and in a remote part of his brain he found the sensation fiercely refreshing.

Soldiers and townspeople alike began running up the slope to form a ring around the tree stumps, and looking back, Jakob could see why the hillside had been chosen: the crowd that had filled the town square had spilled out onto the lower slopes and was staring expectantly upward. The whole of Paoshan, it was clear, was meant to have a clear view of the exemplary executions. Behind Jakob, the captive landlord was staggering at the end of the rope around his neck, his features contorted by his suffering, but the Nationalist officers held themselves expressionlessly erect, determined to endure their ordeal with as much pride as they could muster.

When the executioner drew his sword from its scabbard, the long, curved blade shimmered brightly in the light of the rising sun, and as though recognizing that a signal had been flashed to them, the crowd immediately fell silent. With two hands clasped around the sword's long hilt, the executioner stepped toward the pine stump beside which Felicity had been forced to kneel and positioned himself with his feet astride. Jakob had been halted by his guards some fifteen yards away, and in the moment that the executioner swung the sword aloft, Felicity raised her head and looked directly at him. Her mouth fell slackly open in mute supplication and an unbearable anguish burned in her eyes.

Jakob strained desperately against the stranglehold of his two guards and almost tore himself free; others, however, crowded around, holding him fast. Stretching his neck frantically to catch sight of her above their heads, he called out hoarsely: "God be with you, Felicity!"

A moment before the sword descended, her captors pressed her facedown against the stump — but she struggled hysterically and the blade failed to strike home. A terrible piercing squeal like that of a pig rang across the pine glade before the blade rose and fell a second time: yet still the executioner missed his mark. Only on the third stroke did he succeed and then an eerie hush returned abruptly to the execution ground.

Jakob sagged in the arms of his captors, his gaze fixed numbly on the ominous figure of the executioner. With calm detachment the Chinese leaned down and wiped the blade of the sword on his victim's shabby brown dress; then he looked across the glade in Jakob's direction. The dark, brutal peasant face with its narrowed eyes remained impassive as he made a beckoning motion with the sword tip — but Jakob's guards had taken only one pace forward with him when a long, high-pitched bugle blast split the silence of the hillside.

"The Nationalist forces from Chentai are approaching," yelled a Red Army officer who had raced up the hill. "Their vanguard is only two miles away. Prepare to march at once!"

The Communist soldiers immediately started to break away down the slope in disciplined files. The townspeople, panic-stricken at the prospect of being found near the scene of the execution, ran with them in a disorderly scramble. The guards turned and began dragging Jakob and the other prisoners back toward the town, and the executioner quickly sheathed his sword and followed them.

Halfway down the hill Jakob managed to twist his head and look back despairingly over his shoulder — but all he saw was a crumpled brown shadow lying abandoned in the grass among the black stumps of the pine trees.

10

In his mind's eye Matthew Barlow suddenly saw a vivid image of Jakob's face, determined and blue-eyed, his features alive with youthful zeal. The young missionary was wearing a bandage around his forehead as he had done during their first conversation on his arrival in Shanghai and despite his injuries, he was attempting a smile. Again, in a calm voice Barlow heard Jakob say: "It's obvious, sir, that the difficulties you've spoken of are serious — but they don't put me off."

Standing ill at ease at Barlow's elbow, Laurence Franklin saw the director-general's tired eyes close momentarily and his deeply lined face contract as though in response to a passing pain. Then he lifted a ribboned pince-nez in front of him and leaned close to an oil lamp to scrutinize for a second time the urgent telegraph letter that Franklin had just brought to his study. His hand shook slightly and he drew his breath in a long, slow sigh before beginning to read the message aloud for Franklin's benefit. Addressed from Chentai to the Shanghai headquarters of the Anglo-Chinese Mission, it said:

Dear Brethren —

At dawn today Communist soldiers of the Red Army launched a surprise attack on Chentai and overran the town. I have been taken captive along with my wife and child. We are accused of acting as foreign spies and they threaten to execute us all. But they say they are prepared to be "lenient" and demand one hundred and fifty thousand dollars for our release. I've told them I'm certain no ransom money will be paid for us — now or later. I asked them to release Felicity and our baby so that they might travel back to Shanghai with a letter for you. But they refused. Before the attack came we were preparing to leave. Coolies and mountain chairs had been arranged. But the attack came too quickly. They sacked our house and burned our Bibles. All our food and household stores are in their hands. They have taken all our personal monies and the money sent by you for famine relief work. We are to march along with the Red Army as their prisoners. . . .

Barlow's voice faded away to a whisper and his hand shook more noticeably. Then with an effort he gathered himself again to finish reading the rest of the message.

They said they would execute us if I refused to send this message and we have no reason to think this is an idle threat. The district magistrate was put to death in our courtyard before our eyes. In this time of trial, however, we're confident that the Lord will be our shield. We are fortified and strengthened by our faith. We also pray that God may grant you grace and wisdom in guiding your decisions. — Yours rejoicing in His salvation.

Jakob Kellner.

Barlow removed his pince-nez and stared into the coal fire that flickered fitfully in the grate at his feet. A raw November fog drifting in from the Whangpoo River cloaked the streets and alleys of Shanghai outside the mission headquarters and Barlow had flung a woolen shawl about his shoulders for extra warmth. Looking down at the ailing director-general, Franklin felt a stab of compassion. Scattered pages of handwritten Chinese characters on which Barlow had been working when he entered lay all around him on chairs, tables, and the floor. They represented the fruit of several years' work translating the New Testament and parts of the Old Testament into vernacular Chinese familiar to ordinary people, but even at a glance Franklin could see that Barlow's calligraphy was becoming ever more spidery and feeble-looking. His face, once weathered by sun and wind, had become pinched and pallid from the years spent hunched over Chinese dictionaries and Scripture reference books, and the shock of reading the telegraph message had driven all remaining trace of color from his cheeks.

"Shall I convene a meeting of the full council to discuss the ransom demand, Mr. Barlow?" Franklin asked the question gently while bending to pick up the telegraph message, which had slipped to the floor among the clutter of translation pages.

"No — find two volunteers from among our Chinese evangelists who are prepared to travel into the interior to try to help Jakob Kellner and his family."

The curt tone of Barlow's response startled Franklin and he straightened up, looking curiously at the old man. Like the rest of the headquarters mission staff, Franklin had long since accepted that Barlow's accelerating decline had gone hand in hand with the growing chaos in China in the past few years. Although nobody spoke of it openly, everyone was aware that the frustration and disappointment of seeing the Anglo-Chinese Mission's efforts foundering amid the destruction of a bloody civil war had progressively depleted both his strength and a once-legendary faith. Gradually, all the mission staff had become conscious of the fact that he had undertaken the scholarly burden of the long Bible translation in an attempt to compensate for his inner disappointments. As time passed, the task had obviously come to weigh more and more heavily on a nature once better suited to braving the physical rigors of China's remote regions in search of flesh-and-blood Christian converts, and Franklin and the others had watched helplessly as the forceful man they had previously looked to for leadership had faded to a blurred, ailing shadow. All the mission staff had long since agreed, outside his hearing, that something essential had gone out of Matthew Barlow — but whatever that something was, to Franklin's surprise a hint of it had reappeared unexpectedly in his voice as he spoke from his seat before the fire.

"But how can we hope to save Jakob, sir, without meeting their ransom demands?" asked Franklin in a puzzled tone.

"Perhaps I'll go myself to negotiate with the Communists."

"But sir, you're hardly fit enough to travel in the mountains of the south. In spirit you might be capable of tackling such a journey, but your legs would surely find it impossible."

"I feel a personal responsibility for Jakob Kellner." Although he spoke quietly, Barlow could not conceal the emotion in his voice. "As a boy he heard me talk of China when I was on furlough in England. My account of life in China's mountains fired a profound ambition in him." Barlow hesitated and Franklin saw his eyes moisten. "When he arrived here, there was something unusual about him. He seemed to have a deep spiritual certainty about his destiny. Perhaps I recognized something in Jakob that I'd once felt very strongly myself. He made me realize suddenly how much I'd compromised my ideals over the years. . . ." Barlow's voice faltered. "For a while, Franklin, I think Jakob rekindled something in me and I went back to my translations with a new heart. But sadly, it didn't last . . . and in that time I was responsible for sending him to the region where he and his family are now in danger."

"But sir, you must have designated dozens of young missionaries to difficult areas over the years. And all were well aware before they set out of the possible dangers they faced."

Barlow nodded absently. "Perhaps . . . but I think when I considered Jakob's designation I might have been guilty of trying to correct the failures of my own life through him. Possibly I was trying quite wrongly to renew my own flagging ambitions when I should have been thinking of what was best for Jakob Kellner. He's had to face up to a China that has changed very greatly since my youth."

Barlow's voice was trembling with the intensity of his regret and he paused to compose himself. For a long time he remained silent, staring into the fire; then he made an effort to sit straighter. "I may not be capable of walking far, Franklin, but I've got to try to do something. I'll go by steamer and motorcar as far as there are rivers and roads to carry me — then I'll take to a mountain chair. I'm not too senile to sit in a *hwa gan* for a few days. Just find two good Chinese volunteers to accompany me!"

"I will, at once." Franklin hesitated, then his face brightened. "But I'd like to go with you, too, sir."

"Thank you, Franklin," said Barlow with quiet sincerity. "I'd be glad to have your assistance."

The prospect of journeying once more into China's hinterland caused Barlow to fall into a reverie and Franklin had to move around the fireplace to face him. "Sir, may I ask what you think can be negotiated with the Communists? We don't have sufficient funds to meet even a tenth of their ransom demand."

Barlow nodded, still staring into the fire. "That's quite true. But you must send a reply at once to the Red Army via Chentai. Messengers must carry it from there on foot to Jakob's captors. Tell them mission representatives will set out immediately for Chentai to seek his release. Ask for a meeting with Communist representatives there . . ." Barlow lapsed into silence once more, a frown of concentration wrinkling his brow, and when at last he spoke, his voice was firmer. "You must also telegraph instructions to all stations throughout China to begin offering prayers tonight for the safety of Jakob and his family. And send a telegram to headquarters in England. A message must be sent to his parents, in Manchester."

"Of course. I'll do that right away." Franklin moved toward the door, then stopped, his face becoming puzzled. "If we should succeed in tracking down the Red Army units holding Jakob, sir, how will you go about securing his release?"

The director-general lifted his head and stared distractedly at the younger missionary as though taken unawares by the question. Then, suddenly, his scraggy jaw jutted forward. "I'll offer myself as a hostage, Franklin, if necessary — in exchange for Jakob's freedom."

11

As darkness gathered on the third evening after Felicity's execution, Liang staggered to a halt on a rocky hillside and eased the bamboo carrying pole from his shoulder. The cookboy's face and clothes were grimed with dust, and lines of exhaustion were etched deep into his face. He nevertheless lowered his two wicker panniers to the ground with infinite care, as though both were packed with thin-shelled eggs. For a moment he stood motionless, staring down at one of the panniers, his head cocked on one side in a listening attitude.

The lidless basket appeared to be full almost to the brim with unhusked rice, but Liang bent over it and gently lifted out the shallow tray fixed in the top which held only an inch or two of grain. He peered into the cavity beneath, holding his breath: the only sound on the hillside was the excited chatter of his two sons echoing from the mouth of a dark cave which they had run ahead to find on his instructions.

"Be quiet, both of you," called Liang in an urgent voice. "Try to find some wild chestnuts for us to eat. And gather sticks for a fire too."

Liang dipped into the second basket and pulled out a curved sickle. He hurried to a nearby grove of trees and began cutting sheaves of long grass to spread as makeshift bedding on the cave floor. From time to time as he worked he paused to peer back down the hillside, searching for signs of pursuit, but he saw nothing. When he had cut enough grass to cover the cave floor he carried the baskets inside and rolled boulders in a circle before the cave mouth to screen the fire from any eyes that might be watching from below.

"Now fetch water from the stream!" commanded Liang when his sons returned with armfuls of twigs and brush. At once they ran off with tin basins toward a shallow gorge at the foot of which foamed a narrow white ribbon of river.

Liang built a fire inside a small ring of stones, and when its glow began to relieve the darkness of the cave, he went to the basket he had placed against the rear wall and lifted out a small bundle. Squatting cross-legged on the hard rock floor, he pulled aside the burlap sack in which the bundle was wrapped. To his surprise the eyes of the white-skinned baby inside the sacking were open, and when he unfastened the zipper of the tiny sleeping bag in which she lay, the infant shifted her curious gaze around the flickering shadows on the cave walls, seeming to study each dark shape and pattern in turn with intense concentration.

"Is the Outside Country child awake?"

Liang's older son, Big Liang, breathed the question in an awed whisper, clutching a dripping basin of water on the edge of the circle of light cast by the fire. Stocky and already physically strong like his father, the thirteen-year-old Chinese boy could scarcely conceal the inner excitement he felt at being caught up in a real-life adventure. From behind him, his eleven-year-old brother, Little Liang, peered at the baby open-mouthed. Slighter and more scrawny than the older boy, Little Liang still had the wondering eyes of a child and he hopped from foot to foot, spilling some of the contents of his basin as he stared at the pale, foreign baby.

"Yes, the baby's awake. Heat both basins of water. She must be washed and fed at once."

Liang shaped a nest in the sweet-smelling grass, settled the infant comfortably in it, and stood up, watching anxiously to see if she would cry. But although she began to gnaw one tiny fist, she continued to gaze quietly around the fire-lit cave as though giving her latest home a careful inspection. Since leaving Paoshan she had cried very little; the jogging, swaying motion of the pannier at the rear end of Liang's gently bouncing bamboo pole had seemed to lull her easily to sleep, and after becoming accustomed to this new mode of transport, she had shown few signs of distress. What little fretful crying she had done had come at night in the caves and derelict houses in which the cookboy had chosen to hide. On these occasions Liang had done his best to soothe and comfort her, cradling her inexpertly in his arms and feeding her frequently with the crushed soybean milk.

Liang's square peasant face clenched with concentration as he grappled with the unfamiliar task of cleaning the baby with water warmed over the fire. As he worked, his two young sons watched in awed silence, obeying instantly their father's grunted commands to pass him pins or carry away soiled garments for washing in the stream. From time to time the baby whimpered fitfully in complaint but quieted again the moment Liang pinned a clean square of toweling in place and re-dressed her in the close-fitting bonnet and warm woolens which he had brought from Chentai in his carrying baskets.

He zipped her back into the sleeping bag for protection against the growing chill of the mountain night and ordered Big Liang to sit cross-legged by the fire so that he could place her comfortably in his lap.

While Liang busied himself setting the wild chestnuts to roast and mixing boiled water with the crushed soybean mixture, his younger son sat by, pulling comical faces at the baby in an effort to entertain her. When a tiny field mouse scuttled suddenly across the cave floor, Little Liang chased and cornered it, then carried it back to the fireside in a closed fist. He held up the tiny animal in his cupped hands before the baby's face, making soft, imitative squeaking noises, and he and his brother beamed delightedly when she grew still in response.

When the soybean milk had cooled, Liang poured it into the glass bottle he had found beside the baby in the Paoshan stable and settled down to feed her. His two sons huddled beside him, close to the fire, chewing hungrily on the wild chestnuts. Although occasionally the howl of a wolf rang in the black silence of the night beyond the cave mouth, the wild animals were obviously far away and Liang felt the tension and anxiety which had gripped him for the past two or three days begin to subside a little.

Despite the danger he might have faced if he had been seen to be connected with the prisoners in the highly charged atmosphere of the execution ground, Liang had courageously followed Jakob and Felicity up the hill outside Paoshan. From an unobtrusive position close to the front of the crowd he had watched the executioner raise his glittering sword, and though sick at heart on seeing his kindly mistress so unjustly struck down, he had retained his presence of mind sufficiently to push his way into the melee surrounding the surviving prisoners when the crowd surged away down the slope on the raising of the alarm.

Using all his strength, he had forced a passage through the panic-stricken townspeople until he found himself stumbling downhill at Jakob's shoulder. The young missionary's face was ashen with shock and at first he had not appeared to register Liang's desperate inquiry muttered in Chinese close to his ear. Only when Liang repeated the question beseechingly in English — "What must I do with baby, Pastor Ke?" — had Jakob turned his head and focused his pained gaze upon the cookboy. For an instant his expression had remained blank, as though he were suffering total loss of memory; then his features contorted with the pain of recollection and he had gasped

out an order in an agonized croak: "Bring me the baby, Liang! If
you can, bring her to me!"

Jakob's guards had rushed him away then and the rearguard companies of the Central Red Army had deployed themselves rapidly
in and around Paoshan to cover the departing column. Fighting had
begun as soon as the pursuing Nationalist battalion came in sight of
the town walls, and shooting had gone on intermittently all day. But
neither side had wished to turn the battle for the insignificant settlement into a major engagement and only long-range fire was exchanged after the government forces dug themselves in at a safe
distance from the town gates.

Liang, however, had not dared to return to the stables where Jakob
and Felicity had been held captive with the baby overnight, for the
Communist troops had continued to use that house and compound
as a command post. With his sons, Liang had taken shelter from the
flying bullets beneath the workbenches of a silversmith's open-fronted
shop in sight of the compound entrance. There he had spent the day
in an agony of suspense, watching troops dash in and out, waiting
for a chance to steal inside to search for the helpless infant.

Not until two hours after nightfall did the Red Army companies
begin to slip silently out of the town, the soldiers climbing the
western walls one by one in the darkness. As soon as he felt it was
safe, Liang had run with his heart in his mouth to the empty courtyard. When he entered the stable it had seemed dark and deserted,
but his baskets and carrying pole were still standing in one corner
where Felicity had left them, concealed behind bales of rice straw.
There was no sound in the stable and Liang feared the worst; only
when he shifted the baskets into the center of the floor did a faint
whimper come from one of them. He had reached inside and lifted
out the trembling infant to press it consolingly against his chest —
but just at that point it had begun to wail piteously.

For several minutes in the darkness of the stable Liang had tried
to comfort the child without success. Then he heard ominous new
sounds of shooting and commotion. The Nationalist soldiers, having
discovered they had been tricked, were pouring into the town, looting
in their turn as they came. Liang had raced back to the silversmith's
to collect his sons and together they followed the escape route taken
by the Red Army rear guard, climbing to the top of the town's mud
walls and lowering the carrying baskets to the ground outside on
ropes before slithering down behind them. They ran on blindly

through the darkness for an hour until they reached a derelict village, and there they washed, fed, and consoled the baby as best they could after her fifteen-hour ordeal in the stable.

For fear of encountering both Communist spies and pursuing Nationalist troops, they had continued to hide throughout the next day in the ruined granary where they had slept, emerging to hurry on westward only after darkness had fallen. Liang had found a small purse containing fifty silver Chinese dollars pinned inside the child's sleeping bag, presumably put there by Felicity before the dawn "trial," and he sent his sons to buy eggs and green peppers when they passed peasant farms, taking care to keep himself out of sight with their precious human cargo while they did so. Several times he had been tempted to stop and ask village women to help nurse and care for the child for an hour or two, but fear of discovery had decided him against taking the risk. By the second morning Liang was confident that the baby was sufficiently settled to risk traveling by day, hidden in one of the panniers beneath the artificial layer of unhusked rice which they had bought. The tracks of the massive marching column were easy enough to follow and they pressed on as fast as they could, covering more than thirty miles before exhaustion forced them to halt for the night at the cave on the rocky hillside.

"How much longer will it be, Papa, before we catch up with the marchers and give the baby back to Pastor Ke?" asked Little Liang in a whisper as his father laid aside the feeding bottle and settled the baby back in the nest of grass.

Liang shook his head perplexedly. "I don't know. The soldiers are moving very quickly. They could be a hundred and fifty *li* ahead by now."

"*Hao*," said Little Liang, grinning sleepily. "*Hen hao!*" — "Very good!"

"Why are you so pleased?" asked his father. "Do you like her as a playmate?"

"Yes." Little Liang nodded happily.

"Why?"

"She likes mice."

He opened up a crack in his clapsed hands and the mouse pushed its head out. Leaning toward the baby he again made soft squeaking noises and held the mouse in front of her face. But the baby didn't stir. Her eyes were closed, her breathing was even, and she was already fast asleep.

12

Ahead of Jakob the red flag of his Communist captors flapped noisily in a stiff breeze. A big black star emblazoned in the flag's center contained a white hammer-and-sickle motif, symbolizing Communism's belief in the supremacy of urban laborers and rural peasants, and the standard-bearer waved it high above his head to encourage the thousands of tiring marchers strung out along the floor of a narrow valley behind him. Jakob slipped and staggered on the slimy stones of the coolie trail, sometimes slithering helplessly into the waist-deep liquid mud which heavy rains had left on either side of the crude causeway. His wrists were still bound behind him and a rope had been looped around his shoulders in such a way as to leave a length of "rein" dangling down his back; this his guards used to restrain him or drag him back onto the trail whenever he fell.

His boots had not been returned to him after the execution and only shreds of his *ts'ao hsieh* — the plaited straw sandals he now wore in common with the soldiers and other prisoners — clung to his blistered, bleeding feet. Fiery pains brought on by ten days of non-stop forced marching burned in his ankles and knees, his head throbbed with a dizzy ache due to lack of food, and the inflamed bites of lice and other parasites infesting his clothes and hair added to his discomfort. The weather was growing colder and he often shivered as he marched. After the execution, to cover his bare chest he had been given a *ch'en shan*, a rough Chinese shirt with frog fastenings at the front, and over it he wore a long-gown of thin blue cotton that had been looted from a landlord's house. These garments, now discolored and stained with mud, gave him little protection against the chill of the mountain heights. A meager bundle of belongings assigned to him — a rolled bamboo sleeping mat, an oil sheet, a thin wadded coverlet, bowl and chopsticks — was carried each day on one of the guard's pack mules, and at each overnight stop, after his wrists were freed, it was flung down beside him for his use.

On three occasions the column had marched all day, all night, and all the following day as well without resting. Distances of twenty, thirty, and sometimes forty miles were being covered each day and Paoshan now lay more than three hundred miles behind them. Along the way there had been repeated skirmishes with government troops, but because the prisoners were being marched in the middle of a column several miles long, they had only heard the low rumble of artillery and the rattle of distant rifle fire as occasional palls of smoke rose ahead of them. Afterward they had sometimes found the trail littered with dead and wounded troops but the guard commanders always hurried the prisoners past the battle areas at a fast pace. Kuomintang biplanes carrying bombs slung beneath their wood-and-fabric fuselages had flown overhead on some days, and prisoners and guards alike, as well as the troops themselves, had been ordered to wear garlands made of leaves and branches from wayside trees to make themselves invisible to the eyes of the Nationalist aviators. On hearing an aircraft, the officers ordered all marchers to throw themselves flat on the trail, and they remained motionless as one man until the danger passed.

Beneath the mud that spattered every marcher, the varied colors of the Red Army's tattered clothing also helped camouflage the column. Field gray predominated but Jakob had noticed that new uniforms were constantly being made out of pillaged cloth of any shade. At each stopping place tailors, working with the sewing machines that the pack mules carried, set up workshops in the open as soon as a halt was called and quickly produced standard tunics and trousers. Within a single company he had seen troops wearing crudely made blue, purple, green, black, and even yellow uniforms with long-peaked caps or the broad, cone-shaped hats of layered bamboo which deflected both sun and rain. All wore red arm bands, all wound cloth puttees tightly around their legs, and most of them thrust their chopsticks into these bindings for safekeeping. In addition to a shoulder pole, a rifle, and a home-smelted broadsword thrust in his belt, each soldier carried a pack containing a quilt, a padded winter uniform, a drinking cup, spare straw sandals, and often a rolled umbrella of oiled paper. Rather than marching in the conventional military sense, the Red Army troops all around Jakob moved with the tireless, mincing, bent-kneed gait of the peasant coolie, which allowed them to continue moving forward relentlessly without any change of pace hour after hour.

This desperate feat of endurance which Jakob was being forced to undergo had helped dull the acute mental agony that had seized him at the moment of Felicity's execution. He had staggered out of Paoshan numb with grief and the first of the thirty-six-hour forced marches had passed in a daze of shock and pain. The flag borne by the Red Army standard-bearer was carried furled whenever the weather was wet and Jakob saw that the large first Christmas canvas cut from the picture frame in the public hall of his Chentai mission house had been fashioned into a waterproof cylinder to protect the banner against the elements. By chance the oil painting, which depicted the Nativity scene, formed the outer case and the silver Christmas star shimmering in the midnight blue heavens above the Bethlehem stable remained clearly visible near the top of the staff.

In Jakob's tortured mind the star quickly assumed a miraculous significance: as he struggled to come to terms with the horror of Felicity's death and the possible loss of his infant daughter too, his gaze fastened onto the furled Communist banner bobbing above the heads of the moving throng fifty yards in front of him. For hour after hour he marched with his eyes on the Bethlehem star, feeling a certainty grow within him that he had been given a sign. Although trudging in the wake of the Communist standard, he began to feel with deep conviction that in reality he was following the star of his own faith on a journey as important for him as the pursuit of the original star had been for the three sages of early Christendom. This feeling helped him pray for strength to endure the ordeal — and he prayed hard too that Abigail might survive his desertion of her in that Paoshan stable. From time to time as he struggled on over rising ground he turned to survey the human wake of marchers flowing along behind him, searching for some sign of Liang. But because of the pain which frequent disappointment caused him, he had learned to restrain himself from looking back too often.

"If your God is all-powerful, why did he let you fall into our hands?"

Jakob heard the jeering question while struggling to extricate himself from a quagmire of mud into which he had slipped at a bend in the trail. Despite his exhaustion, he recognized the harsh accents of the Hunanese guard commander, and as he started to drag himself upright he felt the rope dangling from his shoulders tauten. His feet lost their hold completely and he was dragged bodily out of the slime onto the flagstones at the guard commander's feet. Although he was covered in mud from head to toe and the effort of rising left him breathless, Jakob summoned up enough of his failing energy to stand straight before his tormentor.

"Perhaps God brought me amongst you quite deliberately," gasped

Jakob. "To give me the chance to bear witness before you that He is the living God."

The Hunanese stared back expressionlessly at the young mission-ary — then spun him by the shoulder and pushed him roughly on along the flagstoned track. For another hour Jakob plodded onward, wondering dazedly whether he would be able to carry on through the night again if no halt was called. He had given up trying to anticipate when rest would be taken. Often in the past ten days, shortly after a stop had been made at the end of the day, new orders to resume the march immediately had been issued without warning. On other occasions the whole column had been roused to begin marching in the middle of the night. But sometimes after only a short stage in the early morning, a long rest of half a day had followed on an open plain.

By noting the position of the sun at dawn and evening and the flow of mountain streams, Jakob calculated that they were often wheeling and changing direction and even occasionally doubling back on their tracks. He never knew what to expect and he sensed that the Communist leaders of the march had no set plan themselves: it seemed obvious that the most difficult, inaccessible routes over mountainous terrain were being chosen to avoid all contact with Chiang Kai-shek's superior divisions, which he knew were equipped with tanks and armored transport. The column had stayed well clear of the region's few motor roads and Jakob guessed that radio and scouting reports on enemy positions must be responsible for the many abrupt changes of plan adopted by the Red Army leaders.

All around him the Chinese prisoners shuffled forlornly onward, as bedraggled and exhausted as himself. Long files of Kuomintang soldiers, roped around the neck, were being dragged along behind Red Army officers mounted on bony horses. Larger numbers of Chinese civilians followed: terrified landowners, local Kuomintang party officials, the servants of the rich taken hostage for their absent masters, and many nondescript men, women, and boys accused of spying for the Nationalists — all stumbled forward in undisciplined groups, their hands bound, their heads bowed. The limbs of many were swollen and disfigured from the chains and bonds they wore, and because they were never allowed water with which to wash, many bore the bloody marks of past beatings by the guards. Some nursed wounds and injuries inflicted during their capture, a few ailing landlords were being borne on stretchers by their servants, and one litter contained a pregnant woman who moaned loudly at the jolting she received on the roughest parts of the tracks. All the prisoners obviously felt their humiliation at the hands of the peasant army keenly and their pale, haunted faces betrayed their fear of what lay ahead if the ransoms demanded for them were not delivered at the next stopping place.

In front of Jakob a thin, round-shouldered Kiangsi boy in his late teens sobbed incessantly with pain as he dragged himself through the long valley. Taken captive a week earlier in a small town, he had been repeatedly accused of spying for the Nationalists; night after night Jakob had heard him protest his innocence to the guards and he had always ended by shrieking hysterically for his mother to come and confirm his story. But nobody had appeared to pay the small ransom that had been set for his release. Close to despair, the boy had tried two days before to escape down a steep cliff beside the trail but had badly sprained or perhaps even broken an ankle. The damaged joint had swelled to alarming proportions, and ever since he had been limping badly, often falling to his knees in agony at the side of the track. Each time he fell he slowed the progress of the marching group of prisoners, and his furious guards often struck him savagely about the head and shoulders with their rifle butts before hauling him to his feet.

As the prisoners began to climb out of the valley, the Kiangsi boy slumped silently into the mud again at Jakob's feet. Despite yet another beating from several young guards, he failed this time to rise. Jakob, seeing that the guards were preparing to go at him once more with their rifle butts, stepped quickly between them and the fallen boy.

"Can't you see he has no strength left?" The missionary spoke quietly, barring their way with his own body. "He must be carried or given the chance to ride on a horse."

The young guards shouldered Jakob contemptuously aside and began to belabor the fallen boy again, but at that moment the Hunanese guard commander arrived. Pushing through the crowd of soldiers and prisoners that had quickly formed, the Hunanese stared down coldly at the crumpled figure. The youth's narrow chest heaved convulsively and his body was wracked continuously by a fit of silent sobbing. When the guard commander turned him over with his toe, he sprawled helplessly on his back with his eyes closed and the ring of onlookers saw that tears of pain were streaming down his cheeks.

"*Pa t'a pi la!*"

The guard commander spoke in a matter-of-fact voice as he moved away but his casual order — "Execute him!" — galvanized the guards and other soldiers standing close enough to hear. They crowded excitedly around the Hunanese, all shouting and calling at once.

"Let me do it!" . . . "I'll do it!" . . . "I want to do it, Comrade Commander!"

Turning impatiently, the Hunanese pointed to a fresh-faced youngster of about the prisoner's own age who had already drawn his broadsword and motioned him forward. He also singled out another soldier, who immediately plucked a short-handled hoe from one of the baskets of tools slung on his shoulder pole. Together the pair advanced on the prostrate boy and the soldier with the hoe bent down to drag him into a rough kneeling position. The weeping boy was so distracted with pain and exhaustion that he neither made any move to resist nor gave the faintest sign that he was aware of what was happening to him. His head, hanging low in dejection, presented an ideal target, and without ceremony the novice executioner swung his sword in a wide arc above his right shoulder.

By chance he severed the young prisoner's head with his first blow, and after wiping his sword on his victim's clothing, as he had seen his elders do, the soldier swung around to smirk in the direction of his fellow guards. Then he turned back to help tip the corpse into the shallow depression his helper had scratched out of the mire at the side of the flagstoned trail. Within seconds, slimy clods of mud hid the dead prisoner from view and the guards immediately began shouting and lashing out at the rest of the prisoners, urging them quickly up the rising trail out of the valley.

13

Lying exhausted on a straw-strewn wooden floor with only bricks for a pillow, Jakob tried to close his ears to the cries of Chinese prisoners quartered in an adjoining room. The thud of bamboo staves striking flesh and bone mingled intermittently with shouts of pain and despairing pleas for mercy. The exasperated voices of the guards yelling commands rose above the din from time to time and once, through the open door of his room, he saw two soldiers with drawn swords drag one of the terrified landowners away across the muddy courtyard.

They returned without him a minute or two later and from their uniformly blank expressions Jakob knew that the unfortunate prisoner had been put to death as casually as the Kiangsi boy a few hours earlier. On the march from Paoshan he had witnessed at least a dozen executions of both men and women. The younger guards clamoring eagerly to deal the fatal blow reminded him of excited lads killing rats in a stockyard and through the all-engulfing exhaustion which invaded every fiber of his body, he realized dully that he was becoming accustomed to the indifferent way in which his captors meted out death. This acceptance in its turn filled him with a sense of shame and unease and he dragged himself wearily to his knees to murmur a prayer for the departed souls of the murdered landlord and the lad from Kiangsi.

To Jakob's intense relief, that day's march had ended before darkness fell and all prisoners had been ushered quickly into the yard of a landowner's house in a small town of about a hundred families on the edge of a fertile rice plain. Half a dozen rooms opened off the yard house and, as was customary, the guards had segregated the prisoners for the night. Jakob, because he was the only foreigner, was quartered in strict isolation. The moment his wrists were untied and he was thrust into his room he sank to the floor and lay down. With its straw-covered wooden boards and brick pillows, this "cell" was an improvement on the succession of drafty stables and granaries with floors of cold stone or beaten earth in which he had shivered through previous nights on the march. Outside the open door the youth who had executed the Kiangsi boy took up guard, seating himself on a long bench with his rifle and sword at his side. Every few moments he turned to stare balefully at Jakob but otherwise he sat with his back turned, watching the bustle of activity in the busy yard, where pigs and ducks seized from a nearby farm were being noisily slaughtered and prepared for roasting over several fires.

The adjoining room housed what Jakob had heard the guards call "common criminals." This group of prisoners appeared to include all those accused of spying or informing for the Kuomintang. "Class enemies" — landlords, the wealthy, and local mandarins — he had noticed, were herded into separate rooms on the opposite side of the courtyard, and noncommissioned men and officers of the government forces were in their turn also allocated exclusive prisons. As he was hustled into his own quarters that evening, Jakob had been able to see through the open door into the adjoining room. The civilian prisoners inside filled all the available space, pressed close against one another in a dense mass on the floor. Their hands were manacled behind them and they were either lying motionless on their sides or sitting bolt upright. All were under strict orders not to talk or move. The brutal beatings which began later, he could tell from the guards' shouts, were being administered to those who had broken these harsh rules or were protesting at the conditions that left them stewing night after night in their own bodily wastes.

There was a core of perhaps two hundred prisoners in all, but at each stopping place the numbers rose and fell. Each night new victims were flung white-faced into the captive throngs at the same time that coolies hauling cash in pannier baskets hobbled into the camp after pursuing the column frantically from its previous resting place. From the loud arguments that often ensued Jakob had learned that as little as thirty Chinese dollars could secure the freedom of an unimportant prisoner, while the release of a landowner required anything up to three thousand dollars. The clink of money being counted at a trestle table set up outside the prison quarters had become a familiar nightly sound and on hearing the first torrent of coins spill out of a basket, Jakob dragged his aching body to a new position so that he could see the table through the open door.

A Communist civilian official who called himself the assistant magistrate was accepting and checking the cash delivered by the coolies. A tall, gaunt Cantonese with iron gray hair and hard eyes, he had come to Jakob's quarters a few nights before and introduced himself abruptly as Judge Yang. The legal system of the Central Soviet Base Area, he had declared in an officious tone, now extended to whatever territory came under the control of the Central Red Army, and it was his duty to see that it was administered correctly! Yang had made no reference to the public trial or Felicity's execution and Jakob guessed the magistrate had been given responsibility for the case after these events. For a long time Yang had merely stood glaring at him in silence. Then in a threatening tone he had said, "No reply has so far been received to the letter you sent to Shanghai." Jakob attempted to point out that the Anglo-Chinese Mission did not pay ransom, as a matter of policy, but Yang, becoming incensed, had cut him short. In an enraged voice he had ordered Jakob in future to refer only to "fines" which had been "legitimately imposed for flagrant crimes committed by the prisoners against soviet law!" and without a further word, the official had spun on his heel and stamped from the room.

As he watched the line of coolies dwindle before the magistrate's table, Jakob harbored no new expectation that any ransom payment would arrive from the Anglo-Chinese Mission. He remembered how Matthew Barlow had been at pains to spell out the mission's policy on ransom demands during his designation meeting and he could think of no reason why that policy should be changed on his account. As much as anything, he ran his gaze repeatedly up and down the waiting line of coolies in the hope that he might see Liang among them. Although it seemed unlikely that the cookboy would announce his arrival openly to the "magistrate," eyes that spent so much of each day desperately searching the landscape for a sign of Liang could not easily tear themselves away. It was while watching the coolies trot from the courtyard, followed dazedly by those prisoners whose release they had secured, that Jakob became aware just how regularly the daily patterns and routines of the march were now recurring.

By making lightning dashes again and again over long distances, the Red Army had obviously astonished the garrisons of many defended towns, arriving beneath their walls before it seemed humanly possible; the uniforms of the prisoners taken indicated that militia units and even Kuomintang detachments were repeatedly capitulating or fleeing in disarray. Despite their fatigue on arrival, the Communist propaganda squads quickly covered each successive town with revolutionary slogans, as they had done in Chentai. The homes of the wealthy were systematically looted for food, cash, and goods. Landlords judged "despotic" were executed at once and their lands allocated to the peasants who tilled them. Prisoners were taken; a ransom, or "fines," were levied; and the livestock of the rich was slaughtered for food. By observing exceptional discipline and driving itself hard day after day, the Red Army, Jakob realized, was cutting a rapid swath of change across southern China: feeding, clothing, and financing itself with ruthless efficiency as it went, this crusading force was also fomenting a social revolution all along its route. The terrorized faces of the new prisoners Jakob saw being dragged into the yard that night and those stumbling through the gates to freedom were those of men and women living through a waking nightmare, but as he watched them come and go, through the dark veil of all his grief and anxiety Jakob sensed for the first time the true extent of the determination and dedication of his Communist captors.

14

"Sit up and eat, foreign spy!"

Jakob awoke with a start from the exhausted doze into which he had fallen to find the young guard standing over him. On the floor by his head was a small basket of moldy rice and a washbasin filled with cabbage leaves which the guard was prodding contemptuously with his toe. He did not move away when Jakob dragged his aching body into a sitting position but stood looking down at him, his expression cold and hostile for no reason. Darkness had fallen outside and the only light came from the courtyard fires. The tantalizing aromas of roasting pig and duck drifted into the room but there was no sign of cooked meat in the basin of leaves. Nevertheless, Jakob knelt beside the meager meal and bent his head over his joined palms for a moment to murmur a short prayer of thanksgiving.

"What devil words are you speaking, foreign spy?" The guard kicked him roughly to interrupt the prayer and Jakob had to put his hands to the floor to stop himself from falling over sideways.

"I'm giving thanks to God for a meal tonight," replied Jakob quietly in Chinese, raising his head to look steadily at the youth.

"He can't be much of a 'God' if this is all he gets for you!" The guard laughed tauntingly and kicked the basket of rice so that some of the grains spilled onto the dusty boards.

Jakob sat quite still, fighting against a sudden anger that threatened to rise in him. Then very deliberately he pushed the spilled grains together with the sides of his hands and lifted them back into the basket. The guard's mud-spattered puttees were only an inch or two in front of his face and for a fleeting instant the image of him be-heading the sobbing Kiangsi youth flashed once more into Jakob's mind. With a great effort of will he dismissed it and, closing his eyes, repeated to himself a formula which he had devised a few days before to help him come to terms with the horrors happening all around him. "Christ loved all men and died for them all," he told himself fiercely. "He loved this man beside me as much as myself. So I must try to love him too." At once he felt the anger inside him begin to evaporate and he looked up into the guard's sneering face.

"Someday all men will have to account to the Lord for the evil things they do," he said quietly. "Unless they seek to repent."

"Enough devil words! Eat now."

The guard kicked the rice basket and basin roughly toward Jakob but despite the fierce pangs of hunger gnawing at his innards, the missionary continued to ignore the food.

"Perhaps you can help me understand your cause," said Jakob softly. "Why did you join the Red Army?"

"I was starving!" The youth spat out his reply with great vehemence, his eyes glittering in his dark face. "My father had only ten *mou* of rice fields — but the landowner demanded his taxes for thirty years ahead. At every harvest he confiscated all our crops and left us nothing to feed ourselves with. He cut off my brother's head for stealing a few pomelos from his orchard when he was only ten! My mother had to sell my sisters to him to serve as concubines. He made my cousins drag his produce carts like beasts of burden instead of the mules . . . in the end my father committed suicide out of shame."

Jakob, moved by the youth's indignation, looked away. "You've obviously suffered greatly. But does that give you the right to kill and rob anyone you choose?"

"Everyone in the Red Army has suffered in this way. It's the same all over China. Now we kill the oppressors!"

"How do you decide who is an oppressor in towns and villages where you are strangers?"

"If a man tills the soil himself he is safe. We take revenge only on those who get others to work their land for them. We take goods only from those who grow rich on the sweat of others. And those who help the oppressors by spying for them!" The guard aimed another angry kick at Jakob's basin of cabbage, overturning it, then turned and walked slowly back to his seat outside the door.

Jakob ate the sour rice and the uncooked cabbage slowly, squatting on the floor of the empty room. His diet until then had consisted largely of moldy rice captured from the Kuomintang and cold bean curd, although once when a cow had been killed he had been given a few slivers of stewed meat. The Chinese prisoners were being fed only rice gruel from big communal urns that he had seen guards carrying into their quarters morning and night, and even in the short time he had been marching with the column he had noticed that they were becoming thinner and more emaciated. The weather had been getting colder as November advanced and, because the room remained open to the night, Jakob rose to wrap a padded quilt around his shoulders. But before he could seat himself again beside the remains of the food, he heard the sound of rapid footsteps approaching.

"Judge Yang wishes to see the foreign prisoner at once."

A loud voice barked out the order; a moment later his guard and one of the assistant magistrate's staff appeared in the doorway. Without a word the guard seized Jakob by the arm and, pushing him ahead of himself, marched him across the courtyard and up a flight of wooden steps to a loft lit by a flickering hurricane lamp. The Cantonese official was seated at a rough plank table. As soon as Jakob entered, two other guards stepped forward to close the door and ranged themselves behind him. One, carrying a long, supple bamboo cane that was heavily notched at three- or four-inch intervals glanced threateningly at Jakob. The face of the assistant magistrate was dark with anger too, and he glowered at the missionary as the guard pushed him toward the table.

"The headquarters of your society has refused to pay the fines to secure your release," he shouted, rising from his seat. "You must have committed new crimes by concealing secret instructions to this effect in your letter!"

"It wasn't necessary for me to conceal such an instruction in my letter," replied Jakob firmly. "As I've tried to tell you before, the Anglo-Chinese Mission is responsible for the welfare of several hundred people scattered throughout China. If it agreed to meet even one ransom demand it would put all of them in danger."

The Cantonese stared venomously at Jakob, his fists clenched on the tabletop. Then he picked up a single sheet of paper. "Instead of sending money to pay the fines, Barlow, the head of your mission, is traveling to Chentai. He has asked to be allowed to take your place as our prisoner." He tossed the paper angrily onto the table. "What use is that to the Red Army? We need medicines, radios, guns. We have no use for a sentimental old man who wishes to become a hero late in his life."

Jakob's eyes widened in surprise as he absorbed the information. "I wouldn't agree to Mr. Barlow replacing me under any circumstances. His health wouldn't stand up to these conditions."

"You're quite correct." Yang spoke in a menacing tone and signaled to the two guards standing by the door to come forward. "Strip his clothes from him!"

The guard with the bamboo cane and his companion wrenched the cotton long-gown from Jakob's back and tore off his *ch'en shan*, leaving him naked to the waist. With a length of rope they lashed his wrists together and threw the loose end over a high rafter. They hauled on it together until Jakob's arms were stretched taut above his head, then fastened the rope, leaving him teetering painfully on the tips of his toes.

"You are an imperialist spy worthy of death, but we shall punish you now as the British punish poor Chinese people in Hong Kong." The Communist official motioned for the other guards to stand back before nodding to the man holding the bamboo flail. "Begin!"

Jakob heard the whistle of the bamboo through the air and the crack of it striking his back — yet the sharp, stinging sensation seemed to grow only gradually on his skin and a moment or two passed before a fine line across his flesh ignited in incandescent pain. By this time the second blow had landed and another fiery cut soon began to burn his skin, causing him to suck in his breath sharply. The guard wielding the bamboo applied it evenly and regularly, widening and deepening the trench of pain he was gouging across Jakob's shoulders, working with a calm deliberation born of long practice. The slender bamboo began to feel as sharp as a knife, cutting deeper with each stroke, but Jakob choked back the cries that rose in his throat and endured the punishment silently.

After two or three minutes the scowling Cantonese held up his hand and the guard let the cane fall to his side. "Guarantee that the fines will be paid soon and I will stop the punishment," he said gratingly.

"I'm dependent on the help of my friends at the mission," gasped Jakob, swaying helplessly on the rope. "I can't give you any guarantees."

"Then you will be scourged every day!" The Cantonese flourished his hand in Jakob's direction. "Strike him now in the face."

The guard moved around in front of him and lashed the bamboo several times across Jakob's face, raising angry red weals across one cheek. Jakob flinched with the force of the blows, which jerked his head back, but still he did not cry out.

"I've heard it said that your religion urges you not to resist if another man strikes you," said the Cantonese ominously. "You teach that Jesus Christ, when struck on the face, turned and presented his other cheek to his attacker. Is that true?"

Jakob lifted his head to gaze steadily at the Communist official. "Yes, it's true," he said quietly.

"Then if it is true, turn your cheek!"

Jakob looked at him in silence for a moment, then slowly moved his head so that his unmarked cheek was turned toward the guard with the flail.

"Strike him again," yelled the magistrate, and at once the guard lashed at Jakob, knocking his head back and raising another raw welt across his face.

"You're not laying it on hard enough." The magistrate rushed around the table and snatched the flail from the guard. Moving close, he delivered half a dozen full-blooded strokes to Jakob's face, leaning the full weight of his heavy, muscular frame into each one.

Jakob's head jerked back and forth under the blows but when he still made no sound, the Cantonese thrust the cane ill-temperedly into the guard's hand once more and returned to the table. Picking up a blank sheet of paper and a pen, he swung back to face Jakob.

"Afterward you will write a new letter to be carried to your director-general in Chentai. You will tell him that you have been punished in the same way as Chinese coolies are punished by your imperialist countrymen in Hong Kong — and that you will be punished like this every day until the fines are paid!"

The Cantonese motioned with his head toward the missionary and the guard moved back to take up position behind him. Again Jakob heard the whine and the crack of the cane before he felt the first stab of pain on his shoulder. But gradually the strokes blurred into one another and soon he was conscious only of the all-consuming fire that ravaged his bloodied flesh from shoulder to hip.

15

Chafing their cold hands together and blinking in the sudden glare of the gently hissing gaslights, a steady stream of worshipers stepped gratefully from the raw, foggy November night into the protection of the dingy church hall in Manchester's Moss Side. The cobbled streets outside glistened damply in the light filtering out through the windows and many men and women among the growing congregation coughed and snuffled and pressed handkerchiefs to their pinched, white faces. Few spoke and in the near-silence there was an almost tangible sense of anguish.

Each newcomer who stepped across the hall's threshold felt the atmosphere of crisis envelop him at once and all eyes on arrival flickered briefly to the straight-backed man and woman seated side by side in the front row. Staring fixedly ahead of themselves, straining to maintain a dignified composure, they were clearly the focus of the gathering crowd. Whenever a close friend bent over them to murmur a consoling greeting or wordlessly squeeze their hands, they acknowledged the gesture with stiff, silent nods, obviously afraid that a smile or any other relaxation of their self-control might burst the dam that held back the emotion inside them.

"The situation which has brought us here tonight could not be more grave," said a thin, bespectacled minister who mounted the polished pine dais when everyone was seated. "Two weeks ago we heard that a brave young man who grew up amongst us had been kidnapped in the wilds of China. Now we've learned with the greatest sorrow that his wife has been brutally murdered by his captors and both he and his baby daughter are missing in the wilderness. . . ."

Jakob's mother bit her lip and closed her eyes. Both she and her husband, who sat stiffly beside her, were white-haired now. Lines of age were deepening in their chalky faces and their drab, inexpensive clothes testified to the hard economic realities of their existence in northern industrial England. But despite their humble appearance, they held their heads erect, possessed of the same pride in their meager, hardworking achievements as those people gathered in sympathy around them. In her lap Jakob's mother clutched a sheaf of newspaper clippings, and as the minister spoke, her eye fell on them. Although she had read them many times before, in her agitation she continued to leaf through them again and again, as though she believed, against all odds, that there might be some chance of discovering hidden hope in their words.

"WIFE OF SEIZED MISSIONARY FOUND DEAD — NEWBORN BABE MISSING" declared the latest story clipped from a local newspaper, the *Daily Dispatch*. The report told how Felicity Kellner's headless body had been discovered outside the Paoshan city wall but added that there had been no trace of her month-old daughter or her husband. "Somewhere in China's dark interior," added the newspaper, "the young missionary who left Manchester three years ago is still held captive by bandits who threaten to execute him unless ransom, equivalent to almost twenty thousand pounds, is paid quickly. He is said by the Chinese authorities to have been captured by a band of 'rogues' — scarlet-clad banditry who infest the region around Chentai, where he was conducting work for the Anglo-Chinese Mission. . . ."

In her distress Jakob's mother was shuffling the news clippings rapidly as she reread them. Noticing that the sound was becoming audible in the quiet of the hall, Franz Kellner leaned across and removed them from her hands. He slipped them into a pocket of his jacket, then took his wife's hand in his own and gently drew her attention back to the white-collared minister addressing the hall.

". . . Although we're many thousands of miles away and we might feel helpless to assist Jakob in his suffering," continued the minister in a calm voice, "in coming together tonight we must remember that God is never defeated by distance. We must also remember that we're not alone in lending our strength. All over the world, friends of the Anglo-Chinese Mission are gathering to offer prayers for the safety of Jakob and his infant daughter, Abigail. Because the outlandish ransom demand can never be met, all of us must join together and pray that the threat to execute Jakob will not be carried out. And while mourning the tragic death of his wife, Felicity, with our sorrow we must mingle praise for the glory of her sacrifice. She was ready to lay down her life for what she sincerely believed, like all true Christians through the ages. . . ."

For some moments the minister allowed an unbroken silence to fall over the hall. When he sensed that the three hundred or so people present were joined and drawn together by their common bond of devotion, he led them in prayer. Seated and still, with their heads bowed, the congregation, which included men, women, and children of all ages, followed the minister's words with a silent intensity. Every plea and assertion of faith he made, they punctuated with the gentle explosions of their own responses; as the fog swirled outside, the murmured cadences of their prayers and later the sound of their hymns, sung with vigor, penetrated the closed windows. People passing by heard the vibration of their voices through the freezing dark and when the singing ceased, the quiet of the night around them was suddenly more dense.

Inside the hall, as the notes of the last hymn died away, the minister beckoned gently to Jakob's father and the big, gentle man stepped up onto the dais to face the gathering. In his hesitant voice the influences of his native Swiss tongue were still strong but he spoke with quiet determination.

"Thirteen years ago in this very place, Jakob gave his tram fare home to China, to help with missionary work in the country. He was a small boy but even then he was ready to give all he possessed for God's work in Asia. If I know my son, he still feels exactly the same today despite everything that's happened." The accented voice of the Swiss-born engineer faded and his callused hands tightened on the heavy family Bible he held before him. "From this hall, where he found his life's inspiration, we all have a special duty to help arm Jakob with the strength of our prayers. All of you have already been very generous and I want to thank you for giving us your help. My wife and I are deeply grateful to you all. . . ."

In her seat Jakob's mother gave way suddenly to a fit of silent weeping, and her husband stepped down to circle her shaking shoulders with one arm. After leading a final prayer, the minister brought the meeting to an end. Franz Kellner immediately rose and hurried his wife toward the door, but a studious-looking man carrying a notebook who had been sitting at the back of the hall hurried after him and touched his shoulder. "Mr. Kellner, I'm from the *Dispatch*. May I ask you what your hopes are for your son? Do you think there's a chance that he will be released unharmed?"

Franz Kellner turned in the doorway, still holding his wife's arm. His expression was pained but his manner remained polite. "Like Jakob," he said slowly, "I believe prayer has the power to change things. We shall have to wait and see."

16

A cold wind gusting across the hillside above Paoshan ruffled the spray of white lilies carried by Matthew Barlow and pressed his flapping black long-gown against his body. As he trudged uphill behind six coolies who bore a cheap coffin of unvarnished pine on their shoulders, his movements were slow and stiff but his face was determinedly clenched with the effort which climbing the hill was demanding of him. At his side, Laurence Franklin glanced solicitously at him every few seconds, placing a hand beneath his elbow to steady him whenever they crossed a patch of rough ground. Broken banks of leaden clouds were racing overhead, driven by the high wind, and through the gaps, occasional torrents of bright sunshine fell onto the stark mountain peaks beyond the town, changing the iron gray tints fleetingly to softer shades of blue and brown. In a green glade of firs close to the execution site a gash of red-brown earth lay open and waiting like a wound; when the coolies lowered the coffin onto wooden trestles set up beside the grave and removed the lid, Barlow bent with difficulty to place his spray of flowers reverently on the white shroud of cheap cotton in which Felicity's body had been wrapped.

"I am the resurrection and the life, saith the Lord: he that believeth in me, though he were dead, yet shall he live. And whosoever liveth and believeth in me shall never die. . . ."

The wind whipped wisps of thinning white hair across Barlow's eyes as he turned to address the knot of apprehensive Chinese who had followed him and Franklin up the hill. Composed mainly of those converts who had worked for Jakob and Felicity at the mission house in Chentai, the Chinese Christians glanced uneasily around the grassy glade as though fearful that some residual danger might still be lurking among the black tree stumps. As Barlow intoned the words of the funeral service, their gaze strayed repeatedly to the larger crowd of townspeople who had spilled out of the east gate of Paoshan to follow the coffin up the hill. The crowd, drawn on by morbid curiosity, had at first come to a diffident halt some fifty or so yards short of the burial area, but on hearing Barlow speak Chinese, they began edging closer little by little, trying to catch what he said.

Scooping up some earth, Barlow scattered a handful on the white cotton shroud in the shape of a crucifix; then, with head bowed, he stood aside. The six coolies fastened the lid in place and, using ropes, lowered the coffin into the ground. A moment later they began wielding spades, rapidly shoveling lumps of earth down upon the coffin lid.

"As it has pleased Almighty God to take unto himself the soul of our dear sister Felicity Kellner, we therefore commit her body to the ground," intoned Barlow, glancing toward the crowd of Chinese onlookers. "Earth to earth . . . ashes to ashes . . . dust to dust . . . in

sure and certain hope of the Resurrection to eternal life through our
Lord Jesus Christ. . . ."

Through a break in the dark cloud passing overhead, a pale shaft
of sunlight shone gently into the glade and the moan of the wind
and the scraping of shovels were the only sounds to be heard as the
coolies filled in the grave and banked a mound of earth above it.
Laurence Franklin saw Barlow lift his head; in the unexpected glow
of the sun the lines of sadness and anguish etched into the director-
general's sagging face seemed to soften.

"The violent and horrifying death of a brave young American girl
on this remote hillside in China might seem at first sight to be a
reason for us to feel the deepest sense of misery and despair," said
Barlow, raising his shaking voice so that it would carry to the crowd
of Paoshan townspeople beyond the little circle of mourners. "But
we mustn't fail to sense the glory of these tragic events. It's deeply
saddening to find how much evil and hatred can rest in the hearts
of men — but Jakob and Felicity both came to China because they
loved the Lord and the Chinese people. And although we perhaps
can't understand now why one of them should have been cut down
so brutally and the other borne off into the wilderness along with
their child, someday the meaning and purpose will probably become
clear to us all. . . ."

As he spoke, Barlow's voice was gradually gathering strength and
resonance and the large crowd of Chinese who had been milling and
shuffling beyond the ring of immediate mourners gradually quieted
in response. During the long journey from Shanghai by road and
river, Barlow's demeanor had been that of an ailing man girding
himself by will alone for an effort that he knew was beyond his
natural strength. After disembarking from the river steamer, he and
Franklin had taken to mountain chairs. Franklin had hired a team
of six coolies to carry Barlow and had alternated them frequently to
preserve their strength and help them provide a smoother ride. A
canvas-canopied chair rigged like a miniature covered wagon, with
a complex set of poles that allowed three men to bear it, had afforded
him maximum protection from the weather and Franklin's apprehensions that the jolting journey over the high trails to Chentai might
deplete Barlow's fading energies had proved unfounded. On the
contrary, the sharp, stinging winds blowing across the high passes,
far from proving debilitating to Barlow, had visibly invigorated him.
Frequently he had rolled his canopy back to expose his face to the

wind and sun, and by the time they reached Chentai, despite the dolorous reason for their journey, his eyes seemed clearer, his face ruddier and more animated, than in Shanghai.

On arrival in Chentai they found that the fearful Chinese converts had dispersed to their own homes. The sacked mission house still stood in the same chaotic state in which the Red Army soldiers had left it and Barlow had been moved to make a special effort to comfort and reassure the little group because of their evident loyalty to Jakob. He had succeeded to such an extent that most of them, including Liang's wife, had volunteered to accompany him to Paoshan. On finding there that Felicity's body had been courageously recovered and preserved by one of Paoshan's two Christian families, Barlow had decided to carry out burial immediately outside the town walls rather than risk sending her coffin back to Shanghai unaccompanied. Although the Chentai and Paoshan converts feared that Communist spies might still be mingling with the town's population, or even that the Communist troops might return again in strength, Barlow's presence obviously gave them new confidence, and Franklin was delighted to see that his superior was drawing inspiration from them in his turn.

"These terrible happenings will not frighten us nor deflect us from the purpose for which we came to China," continued Barlow in a firmer voice, looking again toward the Chinese crowd. "News of these events has already spread around the world. Young people in many lands are learning with awe of the deeds of these two brave missionaries who in their different ways have suffered and sacrificed themselves in fellowship with Jesus Christ. The world will also learn afresh an important lesson — that our enemies are unable to prevent the triumph of truth, even though they try to drown it in blood. Suffering saints have always been living seeds of the truth. From this spot in recent days great reserves of divine power and love have been set free. Nobody can measure the force of this new power — but in time I'm certain we shall see a glorious harvest reaped from this tragic hillside. . . . And then we shall watch it with wonder and thankfulness."

As Barlow finished speaking he closed his eyes and seemed to sway on his feet. Black clouds racing overhead had snuffed out the sunshine, blurring the light in the glade once more, and Laurence Franklin, seeing that the director-general's face had turned pale, moved protectively to his side, ready to support him. But Barlow, opening his eyes, smiled and motioned him aside. In a quieter tone he read the remaining formal prayers of the burial ceremony, his gaze fixed on the book in his hands. Then with his head bowed, he stood and faced the grave mound in silence, lost in his own private prayers. At last he turned slowly away and led the mourners back down the hill.

The watching crowd retreated at first before Barlow's little group of Christians; then its ranks opened to allow them passage along a path that led down to the east gate. As they approached the town wall, a ragged coolie wearing a blue Kwangsi turban around his head ran toward them, balancing a carrying pole on his left shoulder. In front of Barlow, the coolie stopped and lowered his baskets to the ground.

"Are you Director-General Matthew Barlow of the Anglo-Chinese Mission?"

A frown creased Barlow's face: the directness of the question, asked without any sign of a coolie's customary servility, surprised him. "Yes, I'm Matthew Barlow," he replied, studying the Chinese carefully.

"I have been to the mission house at Chentai — but they told me I would find you here. I have a communication from an assistant magistrate of the Central Soviet Government who is marching with the Chinese Workers' and Peasants' Red Army!"

The coolie unfastened one of the panniers, drew out a manila envelope, and handed it to Barlow. When he opened the envelope, the mission director found inside a single sheet of paper bearing a badly scrawled message in English. Taking his spectacles from a pocket of his long-gown, Barlow read the message through — then drew in his breath sharply.

"It's from Jakob," he said, turning to Franklin. "They're torturing him and he says they're going to continue it every day until we pay the ransom!"

Barlow handed the letter to the younger missionary, who ran his eye quickly over the uneven scrawl. "They're demanding medicines, radios, and anti-aircraft guns as part of the ransom," said Franklin incredulously.

Barlow nodded grimly and turned back to the coolie, who was standing by his baskets, watching them. He was young, not more than nineteen or twenty, Barlow guessed, and he had the intelligent face of a student rather than the rough features of a peasant coolie.

"Can you guide us back to the magistrate who sent you?" asked Barlow.

The youth nodded.

"What are you going to do?" asked Franklin in a low voice.

Barlow's features composed themselves into a more resolute expression than Franklin had seen for some years. "We've got no choice," he said slowly. "We've got to go and parley with the Red Army ourselves."

17

Running through a misty forest of thick-trunked trees, Liang could scarcely hear his own footfalls in the deep carpet of rotting leaf mold. The trees, which cloaked a long mountain ridge, grew so close together that sunlight rarely penetrated to the rank-smelling earth, and the half-light beneath their branches had a ghostly quality. Occasionally the sudden crash of a frightened animal fleeing from his path startled the cookboy and he caught a brief glimpse of a wild ox or a mountain boar dashing away into the gloom. Now and again Liang shouted loudly over his shoulder to encourage his two flagging, footsore sons; whenever he did so, his voice bounced and echoed back and forth so eerily among the great trunks of the ancient trees that they immediately spurted to catch up.

Far ahead of them the low grumble of artillery fire was faintly audible. Sometimes Liang stopped to cock his head and listen, trying to gauge their distance from the fighting, but the density of the trees always muffled the sound. However, he was in no doubt now that he was moving in the right direction: numerous paths tramped over only recently by many thousands of men, mules, and horses snaked through the previously virgin forest. In the clearings he could see traces of fires and the whiteness of the ashes gave him fresh heart. After pressing westward toward the Kwangsi border for two weeks, at long last he was really catching up with the marching columns of Communist soldiers!

The rumble of gunfire had begun in the distance early that morning and on hearing it for the first time, Liang had halted uneasily in his tracks. Then after a moment's thought he realized that he had no choice but to continue. If he was to carry out the wishes of Pastor Ke and return his infant daughter to him, the surest way to find the Red Army was to head toward the sound of fighting. Still clutching his carrying pole, he had run on faster than before, taking his bearings at every turn in the track from the sounds of firing.

Nestled into the bed of clean straw, which Liang renewed each morning in the rear pannier, his tiny human passenger remained obliviously asleep as he padded on silently through the mist-shrouded forest. On the remote tracks he always removed the false lid of the basket to leave it open to the fresh air, and to his immense relief as he jogged rapidly onward each day, the infant had fallen into the habit of sleeping most of the time, lulled seemingly by the rhythmic swaying and jigging of its makeshift cradle at the end of the bamboo yoke. Before passing through villages Liang disguised his burden with the false tray of unhusked rice that fitted into the basket top. Whimpers of distress from the baby had begun to greet this action after the first day or two, so to alleviate the darkness inside the basket Liang had cut slits in its sides beneath the tray. This allowed some light to filter in and gave the infant a limited view of her passing surroundings without betraying her presence to casual passersby.

Whenever the child awoke on the march, Little Liang and his brother were at hand to entertain her. Trotting close behind, they waved leaves and grasses plucked from the wayside, imitated bird-calls, pulled faces, cavorted, skipped and danced around the moving basket, competing to bring a smile to the baby's face. At night, wherever they bedded down, after Liang had washed and fed her, the two boys took it upon themselves to amuse and occupy her until she slept. So far Liang had managed to keep the child's presence in his pannier a complete secret, and although the hundred thousand marchers moving ahead of him were depleting the region's already meager food supplies like a great swarm of human locusts, he had nearly always been able to buy enough rice and vegetables from wayside peasant farms to feed himself and his sons. He had also eked out the soybean milk sufficiently to continue nourishing the baby.

"Look, Papa! Is that where the Red Bandits are fighting?"

The trail emerged abruptly from the trees beside a big spur of rock where the ground fell away precipitously, and at once the boom of the distant guns became louder in their ears. In front of them, stretching into the far distance, lay an unending chain of lower hills, crisscrossed with flagstoned trails, and following the direction of Big Liang's excitedly pointing finger, the cookboy saw gray-white puffs of smoke blossoming in clusters all along a dark ridge near the horizon. In the haze it was impossible to make out any detail but it was clear that a continuous artillery barrage was being laid down ten miles or so ahead.

"It looks like a big battle, doesn't it?" said Little Liang eagerly, shading his eyes with his hand.

"Come on!" demanded Liang. "Don't waste time. We must keep on until we find Pastor Ke."

He led his sons impatiently onto the steep path flanking the rocky spur and immediately found himself confronted by a hideously disfigured Kuomintang soldier hanging head downward above the trail. The soldier was already dead and his bloodied face, which had been partly shot away, was contorted in a soundless scream. One of the soldier's feet was trapped in a tangle of creepers growing across the face of a rock which overhung the track, and this accident had suspended him upside down with his arms hanging loose, as though he had been frozen in the moment of diving headlong down the mountain. Recoiling in horror, Liang looked around and saw the khaki-uniformed bodies of several other dead Kuomintang soldiers, some of them headless, tumbled in limp heaps where they had fallen on either side of the track.

"Keep moving!"

Turning back, Liang tried to use his own body to shield the hanging corpse from his sons' sight as he ushered them past. With only part of his mind he noticed that the white baby was lying silently awake in the uncovered rear pannier: her eyes were wide open and she was gazing up without curiosity at the dead soldier suspended above her. Twenty yards farther on, two or three more muddied corpses lay crumpled in death beside the track. The color of their uniforms was difficult to distinguish beneath the grime of many hundreds of miles' marching, and only the red stars on their caps marked them as Red Army troops.

Liang urged his sons onward with sharp, repeated cries, scarcely glancing at the bodies. During the long, wearying journey from Paoshan he had become accustomed to finding mutilated corpses lying beside the paved trails. Whether they were civilian prisoners, town militia, provincial troops, government soldiers, or Communists, it was often hard to tell — victims of skirmishes, bombing raids, executions, had all begun to seem the same to Liang. Most of the dead were so splashed and coated with mud and slime that from a distance they looked like life-size clay figurines that had been dumped haphazardly in the open fields or on the twisting mountain paths. All shared a chilling common identity, a cold, rigid stillness, and such gruesome sights never failed to spur the tiring cookboy forward with renewed vigor.

As usual, no weapons had been left lying around the dead troops. Ammunition pouches and cartridge bandoliers had also been wrenched from the lifeless bodies of both sides, almost certainly by the desperate Red Army men, and without looking, Liang knew that each man's ration bag would already have been emptied or removed. On one or two occasions when his sons had been weeping with hunger, he had steeled himself to search among fallen troops, but he had soon found that the marchers, despite their extreme haste, always scavenged every scrap of food and ammunition from dead comrades and enemies alike before moving on after an engagement.

Liang had tried to encourage his sons into the habit of ignoring any bodies they might encounter and to keep moving briskly, but to little avail. Both boys still became apprehensive at the sight of death and shied away from passing close to a corpse. He had to push them physically step by step down the steep, twisting track because they were fearful of what they might find around each turn; only when the ground began to level out did they fall into a rhythmic trot again.

At the foot of the ridge Liang saw that the rough-paved tracks through the foothills were coming alive with jogging files of straw-hatted peasants, all of them hurrying eastward away from the noise of battle. The cookboy stopped at once and covered the baby's basket with the tray of unhusked rice, warning the two boys, as always, to follow him closely at a fast pace. If necessary, he told them, they were to make enough noise to cover up the sound of the baby's crying. Many of the scurrying peasants were pushing handcarts or humping blackened cooking pots and other household belongings on their carrying poles. Their faces were taut with anxiety and as they ran they turned frequently to cast fearful glances over their shoulders.

Descending through the foothills, Liang and his sons passed many terraced fields in which the rice plants had long been cut. From the sparseness of the stubble Liang could tell the harvest had been poor. The sudden arrival of the voracious Red Army and its enemies in their midst must have alarmed the hungry people of the region greatly and the sudden boom of the guns early that morning had obviously triggered the panicky stampede eastward. Although they were the only travelers heading toward the roar of the artillery bombardment, few of the growing tide of people flowing in the opposite direction spared Liang and the two boys a second glance. The unseen baby girl in his rear pannier made no audible sound and Liang began to breathe more easily when he realized that the frightened peasant families jog-trotting all around them would have been far too distracted to notice, even if she had begun to wail.

As he ran on, Liang constantly scanned the trail in front of him, and whenever he saw what he thought might be a uniformed soldier he turned aside into the terraced rice fields or made a wide detour. In little more than an hour he covered five miles and was cantering through a deserted village of mud-walled houses, followed at a distance by his sons, when without warning, three armed Kuomintang infantrymen with bayonets fixed to their rifles stumbled out of a house a few yards in front of him. They were dragging a gray-haired peasant woman between them, tussling furiously with her over a small sack of rice which she was refusing to give up. The woman, tottering on bound feet, was shrieking defiance at the top of her voice while continuing to cling grimly to her rice sack.

The soldiers cursed the old woman loudly and kicked and struck her repeatedly with the stocks of their rifles, but Liang saw at once that they were clumsy in their movements and speech and he guessed they must be opium smokers who had deserted their units. Suddenly the sack at which they were all tugging split and its contents cascaded into the mud of the village street. The old woman unloosed a hysterical stream of abuse at the troops as they flung her roughly to the ground beside her puddle of spilled rice — then they forgot her the moment they looked up to find Liang with his two panniers turning to head back the way he had come.

"Stop — or we fire!" yelled one of the soldiers.

Liang increased his pace, bending low under the weight of his pole, straining to put distance between himself and the troops. But a ragged volley of shots kicked up spurts of mud around his feet, and fearing that his sons, who were just entering the village, might be hit, Liang slowed reluctantly and waited for the Kuomintang soldiers to approach.

"What have you got in the baskets?"

The first soldier's eyes were blurred and bloodshot and when he came close, pushing the tip of his bayonet against Liang's chest, the cookboy could smell the stale, sickly odor of the opium on his clothes.

"Just rice, as you see," said Liang, gesturing hesitantly to the rear pannier. "And some personal belongings in the other basket."

"Hand over the rice!"

The soldier fumbled with the rope, trying to detach the rear basket from the bamboo pole, but Liang pushed the bayonet aside with his arm and sprang forward to stop him.

"No! Please don't touch my rice!"

The other two soldiers pressed forward, pointing their rifles at Liang and eyeing the basket. They too reeked of opium.

"What's so special about unhusked rice?" muttered the stockiest of the three thickly.

He raised his rifle and thrust the bayonet tip into the shallow tray that formed the false top of the rear basket. A mystified expression immediately spread across his face. When he lifted the rifle tip, the tray of unhusked rice came away impaled on the bayonet. Craning forward, the three soldiers peered into the basket and saw the white baby. A streak of blood lay across one cheek where the point of the bayonet had nicked her and in that instant the child began shrieking with fright.

"Why are you hiding a foreign baby?" The first Kuomintang soldier rounded furiously on Liang, jabbing his bayonet repeatedly against the cookboy's chest. "Are you a foreign spy?"

Liang stared back, white-faced, at the soldier, saying nothing. He looked desperately around at his sons, who stood a few yards away: their faces too were pale with fright.

"Answer me!" The soldier jabbed his bayonet harder against Liang's chest but still the cookboy stared dumbly back at him.

"There's only one way to deal with this," muttered the second soldier; moving close to the basket, he lifted his rifle butt toward the sky, pointing the bayonet tip downward at the wailing baby's chest.

"No! No!" screamed Little Liang, darting forward.

In the same moment Big Liang threw himself bodily at the soldier, sending him sprawling in the mud. The rifle flew from his grasp and fell at Liang's feet. Snatching it up, Liang pointed the muzzle at the two soldiers who remained standing.

"Big Liang, take the baskets," he yelled. "Get them away from here."

The older boy quickly picked up the bamboo and heaved the heavy baskets clear of the ground: balancing them on his right shoulder as his father had taught him, he sprang away in the direction of the artillery barrage. Little Liang followed close behind him, running as fast as his legs would carry him.

The two soldiers facing the armed cookboy stared stupidly at him. Beside them their fallen comrade scrambled slowly to his feet, his face dark with anger. "Shoot him!" he hissed. "Shoot him!"

The two men started to raise their rifles but Liang did not flinch. Lifting his own weapon quickly into the firing position he had been taught to employ in his Chentai militia unit, he fired three quick shots at point-blank range and the Kuomintang deserters staggered back from him and collapsed. Liang did not wait to discover if they were dead; flinging the rifle aside, he turned and raced away down the street after his sons, calling loudly to them to keep running fast in the direction of the fighting.

18

In Jakob's ears the boom of the Red Army's artillery was like thunder. Half walking, half running amid a yelling, braying surge of men and animals spilling down a rain-swept hillside, he felt the ground beneath his feet throb every time the heavy guns and trench mortars unleashed a new broadside against the ridge that rose steeply above the next valley. The Communist guns had been sited in hastily dug fortifications half a mile to the east of the column's route, close enough for Jakob to see the orange tongues of flame spurting repeatedly from their muzzles. Smoke mushroomed from the improvised emplacements at each new detonation and swirled on the gusting wind toward the marchers, thickening the late afternoon murk closing in around them.

The high-pitched whine of enemy shells filled the air after each answering roar from the Kuomintang batteries. The guns of the government troops had been carefully dug in along the top of the distant ridge and as the Red Army marchers struggled down the rock-strewn slope they cocked their heads, trying to anticipate the direction of each successive salvo. Geysers of earth climbed skyward from the hillside all around them as the Kuomintang gunners searched methodically for the emplacements where the Communist guns were hidden. Two or three times Jakob saw a Red Army artillery piece rise up from the ground, spinning slowly end over end amid a black spout of mud and rock; on each occasion, the crews were left sprawling over the edges of their embrasures like lifeless rag dolls but replacement crews quickly appeared alongside the stretcher-bearing medics, hurrying forward to begin the task of reviving the firing position. Whenever shells exploded among the columns of marchers, the survivors rushed on in accordance with strict orders, leaving volunteer parties to carry away the dead and wounded on improvised stretchers made from the doors of village houses.

Like all the other prisoners pressed close about him, Jakob was sobbing and gasping for breath: his lungs ached from the fierce exertion and both his feet, protected by only a few remaining shreds of rice straw, were badly swollen and bleeding. Each time he set a foot to the ground he winced and groaned inwardly as an agonizing fire burned upward through his ankles and legs. His arms were still lashed together behind him and the pain this induced in his upper limbs had spread into his back and shoulders. As the downward slope steepened, he stumbled frequently and might have fallen if the other Chinese prisoners and their guards, mutely joined for once in the common desire to survive the artillery onslaught, had not been marching shoulder to shoulder. In their haste, the troops were breaking ranks to overtake slower men ahead, and the column was starting to spread across the hillside in an undisciplined scramble. On all sides amid the explosions, men were shouting angry orders and curses at one another in the accents of half a dozen provinces while the struggling pack mules and horses added their terrified braying and snorting to the din.

Every few minutes Jakob made a deliberate effort to raise his eyes to peer ahead into the driving rain. He could still see the furled Red Army standard being carried at the head of the guards' detachment and the sight of its waterproof canvas cover bearing the glimmering star of Bethlehem sustained him and revived his fading strength. The oils of the painting were beginning to crack and flake but the outline of the star, shining against the dark of the Christmas sky, remained comfortingly distinguishable.

The nonstop forced march had been ordered suddenly at dawn three days earlier without any prior warning or explanation. The entire column had been hurrying forward in a headlong rush ever since, marching four hours and resting four hours, around the clock. Sleep and a few mouthfuls of food had to be snatched wherever a halt was called — crouching by the flagstoned trails of the plains, squatting on precipitous mountainsides, or leaning against tree trunks in the dark, damp forests.

Through the pain and exhaustion, however, Jakob could see that the severe hardships of this stage of the march were being shared by prisoners, guards, and soldiers alike. During rest stops on the second day, many of the young Red Army soldiers sprawled on their backs near him had been weeping with the pain of their blistered and lacerated feet. Later he had overheard one of his guards telling another that there had been a sudden rise in the number of deserters. Muttered complaints were being exchanged openly by passing troops and an air of anxiety and uncertainty began spreading like wildfire through the column. The unit commanders had obviously reported these signs of failing morale to senior officers, for shortly after daylight that morning civilian cadres, wearing the badgeless tunics of political commissars, began galloping back and forth along the column on sturdy-legged ponies, yelling exhortations to the marchers to speed up.

"The forces of the Kwangsi warlords are attacking the flank of the rear guard!" they shouted again and again. "Keep moving! Keep moving — the column's bunching. If you don't speed up, your comrades in the Fifth Corps will be forced to stand and fight a pitched battle to protect your backs!"

Hour by hour the thunder of artillery and the rattle of machine-gun fire had grown, reverberating on the column's southern flank as well as ahead of the vanguard regiments leading them westward. From out of the mountain valleys and across the open plains other dense columns of Red Army men had appeared during the morning, moving with the same desperate haste. As they merged and flowed together Jakob realized that the Communist forces must have been pushing across some parts of southern Hunan in two or three parallel swaths, which were re-forming once more into a single massive body.

When the moving columns joined up, the roped lines of prisoners had been drawn aside to allow more important units and ordnance to move ahead. Standing dejectedly in the downpour, they had watched cartloads of wounded men with bandaged heads and limbs rumble past, drawn by oxen, donkeys, and horses. Long trains of mules followed, harnessed together, swaying under heavy boxes of captured arms and ammunition. Coarse-voiced muleteers, marching at their heads, whipped the straining animals constantly with thick bamboo flails to keep them moving through the mire. Fraying ropes parted and precious loads of food and weaponry spilled into the mud; exhausted animals fell and were shot or dragged reluctantly to their feet; axles snapped, carts overturned, coolie carriers stumbled, fell, and rose again, cursing volubly. But always they redistributed their burdens with the utmost care and moved on at a trot, screwing up their faces against a cold, drenching rain whose only virtue was that it was keeping the government air squadrons and their lethal bomb loads away from what had become a headlong retreat.

When the flow of marching men and animals eased, the prisoners moved on again, but they were halted repeatedly by their guards as yelling mounted commanders emerged from the curtains of rain to force a passage for their armed units through the growing confusion. The din of the artillery barrage became deafening as the column neared the ridge from which the Kuomintang guns were shelling the route. All around Jakob the faces of his fellow prisoners blanched with fear. The whistle of the shells grew more shrill, and during the helter-skelter dash down the exposed hillside, Jakob kept his gaze focused steadily on the canvas cover of the furled Red Army banner as it bobbed jerkily above the heads of the guards' detachment. At the foot of the slope the column wheeled sharply to the south, moving down beyond the range of the guns into a thick pine forest. Among the trees the noise of the artillery duel faded and the sight of the green fronds spreading above their heads soothed and reassured the frightened prisoners. After the terrifying dash across the bare hills, the protection of the pines seemed as comforting as a mother's embrace and all the captives instinctively slackened their pace, wishing to linger in the forest as long as possible. But again the guards harangued them with renewed threats and curses, and they struggled wearily onward.

Beyond the forest lay another rolling expanse of gray, empty hillsides and as Jakob and his fellow prisoners emerged from under the dripping branches of the pines, sudden orders to halt echoed loudly down the ranks. The marchers sank immediately to the muddy ground to rest. In the near-silence, the faint voices of political commissars addressing successive groups of troops reached their ears. Riding the lines at a gallop, the cadres were stopping every hundred yards or so and after a few minutes a stocky northerner reined in his horse in front of Jakob to address the guard units.

"Comrades," cried the cadre, raising himself high in his stirrups, "the Central Committee of the Chinese Communist Party regards you all as the backbone of the revolution. Because of you the future of the revolution is bright and glorious! But in the present all of us face great difficulties. We are all very tired. We've been marching nonstop for three days and you have a right to know why . . ."

The commissar lowered himself into his saddle and leaned forward on its pommel.

"The reason is this. The traitorous Chiang Kai-shek, instead of fighting the Japanese invaders of our country, has concentrated twenty of his divisions in this region and is deploying them to the north of us. Our scouts have spied on them secretly and they report that there are four hundred thousand well-armed men in those divisions. . . . They've been marching parallel with us for two weeks or more. They're making for the mighty Hsiang River, which lies forty *li* to the west. From the south, troops of the Kwangsi warlord clique are closing in all along our flank. In the rear, regiments of the Hunan and Kwangtung provincial governments are pursuing us closely. The enemy clearly intends to surround us on three sides and try to trap the whole of our Red Army against the banks of the Hsiang. Their plan is to wipe us out at one mighty stroke in the northeast corner of Kwangsi province. . . ."

The massed ranks of guards and infantrymen listened in a stunned silence to the commissar: despite their exhaustion they were sitting bolt upright, hanging on his every word. All around Jakob the troubled faces of the Chinese landlords and other prisoners reflected their confusion and bewilderment. Any elation they might have felt at hearing that government forces were close at hand and preparing to attack was counterbalanced by the terrifying prospect of being caught between the armies in the midst of a furious battle.

"In six weeks, comrades, we have marched two thousand *li* from Juichin. Our feet have victoriously trodden the soil of four provinces — Kiangsi, Kwangtung, Hunan, Kwangsi. Do you think we've come this far to die on the banks of the Hsiang River?"

The commissar paused and looked around the crowd of soldiers, but no voice from the ranks broke the silence.

"Didn't our assault engineers with their ingenious pole charges blast a way through the three fortified barbed-wire encirclements built around our Central Soviet Area? Haven't we fought off attacks every day since and captured all the food and ammunition we need from the enemy? Haven't we spread the revolution to every town and village we've passed through? Haven't we punished the evil landlords and divided the land among the poor peasants? And have we done all that, comrades, just to die on the muddy banks of the Hsiang?"

The commissar rose up in his stirrups, his head cocked in a theatrical listening attitude; then he lifted a clenched fist high in the rain, as though responding furiously to his own question.

"No, comrades, we haven't! We shall break through the enemy's encirclement at the Hsiang River just as we broke out of all his other traps!"

The soldiers, their emotions finally aroused by the fire of the cadre's words, raucously yelled their approval and punched the air above their heads. Sitting back in his saddle again, the cadre beamed with satisfaction as he swung his gaze back and forth among the throng. Then he lifted his hand once more, demanding silence.

"The Seventh Red Army Corps, comrades, will continue to protect our left flank, the Ninth Corps will protect our right. And as always the brave fighters of the Fifth Army Corps will continue to serve as our rear guard. Shielded by the strength of this invincible armed corridor, the leading comrades of the General Headquarters, the Revolutionary Military Commission; and the Central Committee of the Party will march across the turbulent waters of the Hsiang River to safety — and lead us on to victory. We shall survive to build glorious new soviet areas. We shall live on to fight the Japanese invader and drive him out of our country. Every man must fight to the last ounce of his strength at the Hsiang River. All of you who can do this and hold on steadfastly to the end will go down in history as heroes of our great revolution!"

The soldiers rose, yelling, to their feet and with a final flourish of his riding crop, the commissar wheeled his horse and galloped away down the line, followed by new gusts of cheering. Section by section, the column began to re-form itself and within minutes it had started forward again, moving with a renewed sense of urgency.

19

A few minutes later the rain eased, then stopped altogether for the first time in several hours. Although the leaden clouds did not break, the sky began to brighten and the light falling on the bleak hillside took on a harsh luminosity. From time to time as he marched, Jakob caught a distant glimpse of the Hsiang River flowing far below between steep cliffs. In the pewter glow of the sky the ruffled waters of the river seemed to shimmer with a metallic radiance and Jakob stopped to stare downward, straining his eyes for signs of troop concentrations.

"Show some respect, imperialist spy! Stand aside!"

The hoarse shout of the guard commander rang out a moment before a brutal blow between the shoulder blades sent Jakob sprawling facedown in the gray mud of the hillside. Struggling to his knees, he looked back the way he had come: the troops behind him had been quickly drawn aside and marshaled into two ranks on either side of the wide trail. A sudden hush had fallen and in the center of the slimy, rock-strewn avenue left between the silent marchers Jakob saw a silhouetted group of figures rise into view over on the crest of the hill. Some walked, some were riding, and three or four armed bodyguards were clustered around each horse. Following close behind came several strings of heavily laden pack animals, and as the group moved nearer, Jakob saw that the figures were as damp and bedraggled as all the other marchers. Something about the manner in which they carried themselves, however, set them apart: whether mounted or walking, they held themselves straight, and Jakob noticed that their eyes, wary and intelligent, rarely looked left or right.

Scrambling upright, the missionary took his place among the other prisoners as the leading figure in the group approached, walking with a quick, light stride. A lean, wirily built Chinese aged about fifty and of no more than average height, he had a strong, shrewd face as dark as the broad leather belt he wore around his waist. Good-natured humor lines were visible around his eyes, but his square, solid jaw and heavy brows hinted predominantly at an unusual physical strength. His sodden uniform of gray cotton bore no badges of rank; the four visible pockets on his tunic confirmed that he was a commissioned officer, but the red star on his shapeless peaked cap was his only insignia. As he passed the prisoners, his narrowed eyes flickered briefly over Jakob's pale, blond-bearded face — but they didn't linger.

"That's the commander in chief of the whole Red Army. He's as strong as an ox. He'd rather walk than ride — and he carries half a dozen rifles when his men get tired."

A yard or two away from Jakob, a Red Army infantryman who wore the arm band of a company-level political instructor was whispering in the ear of a fresh-faced comrade, who was gaping open-mouthed at the men of the General Headquarters striding past.

"So that's General Chu Teh?" breathed the young soldier. "I've really seen him now with my own eyes, have I?"

"Yes, comrade. And look! There's the head of the Communist Party. His name is Po Ku. He's the general secretary. He's been to Moscow to study revolution under our friends the Russians."

A bespectacled Chinese with the soft, round face of an intellectual jogged by on a pony. He was wearing a high-necked civilian tunic and a remote, disdainful expression. The four tall bodyguards pressing closely around him carried their rifles unslung, with bayonets fixed, and as they marched they constantly scanned the track ahead for signs of ambush.

"Who's the one with the bushy eyebrows?"

Jakob turned to see the young soldier gesturing toward a stocky, handsome Chinese with an open face and piercingly bright eyes who sat comfortably astride a bigger, high-stepping horse. He wore a red star on his peaked cap of soft gray cotton and there were red flashes on the collar of his high-necked Red Army tunic. Despite the rain and the mud he contrived to look neat and clean.

"That's Commissioner Chou En-lai. His father was a mandarin so he's brainy and knows how the minds of our enemies work. He's chairman of our Revolutionary Military Commission . . . And look, there are two more generals — Lin Piao, the commander of the First Army Corps . . . and Peng Teh-huai of the Third . . . The Outside Country comrade with the moustache and the yellow hair riding between them is the 'foreign expert' sent to us by our Russian comrades."

A group of Red Army generals engrossed in earnest conversation were jogging together side by side on short-legged ponies and Jakob picked out the pale-skinned face among them without difficulty. The German who had been sent to China as an adviser by the Communist International glanced Jakob's way by chance as they passed, and the missionary thought he saw a gleam of surprise appear fleetingly in his blue eyes. In that moment Jakob realized that almost three weeks had passed since he had seen a white face.

Against his will, this reflection triggered others, and new waves of misery swept through Jakob at the memory of Felicity's horrifying death. The physical agonies of the march often numbed his emotions for long periods, driving all coherent thought from his mind, but at least a dozen times each day the painful memories flooded back. He had given up looking for Liang, since the distance he had marched as a prisoner seemed to rule out any hope he might once have had of seeing his infant daughter again. He had struggled to keep his mind from dwelling on her, but fears about her likely fate suddenly pierced his heart afresh and his head fell forward on his chest in anguish.

"Is this anybody important?"

Jakob heard the boy whisper again as a stoop-shouldered figure hunched over the mane of an emaciated brown and white horse came into view. Riding alone down the desolate hillside well apart from the others, the man was huddled in a dripping blanket. He passed quite close to Jakob and the missionary could see the perspiration of a malarial fever standing out on the sallow dome of his brow. His thick black hair was matted and lank about his broad face, he was hollow-eyed from sickness, and he kept his eyes downcast, seeing nothing but the muddy, rock-strewn ground in front of his horse.

"I think that's Comrade Mao Tse-tung. He used to be chairman of the Central Soviet Government."

"What is he now?"

"Since there's no Central Soviet anymore I don't know whether he's anything. . . ."

Jakob continued to watch the hunched figure on the thin horse as he moved on unsteadily down the steep hillside, struck by some indefinable quality that compelled attention. When he turned back to look toward the crest again he was surprised to see silhouetted against the magnesium sky the slender figure of a woman. She was seated on a long-eared mule, her head draped in a cloth, and she appeared to be carrying a bundle in the crook of her arm. The mule and the woman remained unmoving on the hillcrest as Jakob watched, then the dark outline of a single male rose into view to take the animal's bridle and begin leading it down the slope.

Jakob stared transfixed as the mule and its rider drew near. He had previously seen no women among the vast columns of marching Chinese men and he wondered whether he might be suffering a hallucination. In the gentle attitude of the woman's head, bent over the shape of a child in her arms, he seemed to see a divine echo of the Madonna and his breath caught in his throat. Then as the mule approached the spot where he stood, Jakob saw that its rider was merely wrapped in a dripping blanket as protection against the rain, like some of the mounted men. In the moment of passing him, the figure on the mule's back turned in his direction and the movement caused the cowl-like blanket to slip.

In the luminous gray light, the unadorned beauty of the female Chinese face that was suddenly revealed took on the quality of a mirage for Jakob. The dark, almond-shaped eyes met his directly for the briefest instant, and he found himself gazing in disbelief at the golden Asiatic features that had once haunted his dreams. A breeze plucked a strand of black hair across her eyes, and the next instant she lifted the blanket from her shoulder to cover her head once more. As she turned to look forward again, quite involuntarily Jakob sprang forward toward the mule.

"Lu Mei-ling!"

He called the name softly, almost as though he didn't himself believe his eyes: but whether the mule's rider heard his cry he couldn't tell. She did not stop or turn her head and the mule continued to jolt on down the rocky hill at the same pace.

For a moment Jakob stood barefoot in the mud, staring helplessly after her. Incongruously, he had caught sight of the ugly butt of a Mauser machine pistol jutting from a leather holster, and the warring images of the Madonna and a female guerrilla fighter vied with one another in his mind's eye. The familiar face, beautiful and unsullied in its serenity, had moved him deeply but the fleeting glimpse of the masculine side arm, strapped around her slender waist, added an unfamiliar dimension to his remembered image of Mei-ling. This disturbed him and he stood rooted to the spot, watching her. One of his guards swore an angry oath but Jakob did not hear, and losing patience, the guard grabbed the rope dangling from the missionary's shoulders to drag him roughly back into the waiting group of prisoners.

Lower down the slope, the mule was slithering into a gully, its hindquarters jouncing and skittering in the mud. It seemed the animal must fall but somehow it succeeded in recovering its footing, and a moment later both the mule and its enigmatic rider disappeared abruptly from Jakob's sight, leaving him staring bemusedly down the barren gray hillside.

20

The flickering light given off by a cloth wick burning in a basin of melted lard shone softly on Lu Mei-ling's naked torso. A rough blanket was draped around her trim shoulders but her bare arms were free and her small, round breasts were deliberately exposed. The dark, purplish whorls of her nipples were distended from the recent attentions of the pale-skinned infant she cradled in her arms but the eyes of the baby were now closed and it slept fitfully with one cheek against the curve of her bosom.

Sitting straight-backed on the edge of a wooden bed in the shell of a derelict cottage that had been gutted by fire, the Chinese girl had an unself-conscious air that testified silently to her pride in her slender, amber body: her black hair, still cut in a long bob, curled down damply over her shoulders, providing a dark frame for her determined face, and even when the fragment of muddied sacking that covered the crumbling doorway was pulled aside to reveal an armed guard with cartridge bandoliers crisscrossed around his chest, Mei-ling made no move to cover herself. Instead she merely dropped a precautionary hand onto the butt of the Mauser machine pistol which protruded from its holster on the bed beside her and looked steadily at the guard.

"A comrade giving his name as Captain Lu Chiao wishes to visit you." The young General Headquarters guard flushed crimson with embarrassment the moment he realized he had made an untimely entrance, but he struggled to keep his gaze focused, unseeing, above Mei-ling's head. "The captain claims he is your brother."

Mei-ling nodded calmly. "Thank you, comrade, let him pass. And as you're new, try to memorize his face. Then you'll know him next time."

Half of the rotting thatch which served as a roof had been burned away, leaving the ruined cottage partly open to the night sky. Intermittent muzzle flashes from the Red Army's guns mounted high above the village were augmenting the feeble rays of the makeshift lamp and by its dim orange light, Mei-ling saw her brother pull the entrance sacking aside. Like the guard, Chiao was momentarily taken aback by his sister's nakedness and he stopped abruptly in midstride, his expression startled; then his face relaxed.

"Forgive me, Mei-ling, for staring." Chiao removed his red-starred cap and sank down wearily onto the end of the bed. "I'm still more used to seeing peasant women hobbling around on bound feet and hearing girls being dragged, weeping, to arranged marriages. I forget sometimes what a spirited daughter of the revolution my younger sister has become!"

Using one hand, Mei-ling rearranged the blanket around her shoulders, covering her nakedness without fuss. In the night outside, the roar of the Communist guns again merged with the enemy's and the din rumbled ponderously across the darkened heavens, swelling and diminishing like heavy surf pounding a rocky beach. Chiao lifted his head for a moment to listen, closing his eyes in concentration, and when he opened them again to look at her, Mei-ling searched her brother's face with an anxious expression.

"How is the battle going, Ta ko?"

"Very badly."

"What do you mean?"

"Defending a static corridor for the Party and government civilians to march through is turning us into sitting ducks. The Seventh Corps has been ordered to hold their positions south of here for three days at all costs. And they've lost ten thousand men already. The Ninth hasn't done much better to the north."

Chiao stood up and slapped his riding crop exasperatedly against the leather of his boot. Still listening to the artillery barrage, he began pacing back and forth across the earthen floor of the cottage. Despite the lines of fatigue in his face, his movements at the age of thirty were still those of the jaunty, self-confident student whom Jakob had encountered on the decks of the *Tomeko Maru* — but the three intervening years had wrought as dramatic a change in his outward appearance as they had in Jakob's. The dutiful son of Chinese tradition who had written and recited an old-style Tang poem at his homecoming banquet had disappeared forever: in his place stood a war-hardened officer of a revolutionary army who, after twelve months of study at the Red Military Academy at Juichin, had led troops in battle on countless occasions in and around the Kiangsi-Fukien soviet. An astute, quick-thinking company commander, he had soon attracted the attention of the leadership and after a year had been transferred to the Red Cadres Regiment, a force which protected the leaders of the Communist Party and the Central Soviet Government. All its fighting men were handpicked officers of company or platoon rank, and two distinctive red flashes on the collar tabs of their otherwise badgeless field uniform distinguished them as an elite force. Chiao's uniform was patched and begrimed with mud but he wore a broad leather belt and long riding boots which gave him a trim, military appearance. His face, however, once smooth and well fed, had changed most noticeably: now he had a hungry, weathered look and his experience in battle seemed to have given his once insolently intelligent expression a sharper, keener edge.

"Has a bridgehead been established across the Hsiang yet?" The tension in Mei-ling's voice showed that she half anticipated a discouraging answer and she displayed no emotion when her brother shook his head.

"Five assaults with sampans have been beaten back. The enemy has heavy machine guns everywhere on the far bank. Three attempts to swim across have failed. Most of our troops were killed in the water — the others were swept away and drowned."

"Can't a bridge be built?"

"The Hsiang is more than two hundred yards wide here. In the middle it's thirty feet deep. The engineer units have been trying to throw a floating bamboo pontoon across but the river's in flood and most of the rafts have been swept away. Those that weren't have been destroyed by the enemy artillery."

"Are they making another attempt?"

"The engineers have been under fire for two whole days. They've taken heavy casualties. Almost all their officers have been killed or wounded."

Mei-ling stared at her brother, aghast. "What's going to happen?"

Chiao stopped pacing back and forth and turned to face her. "I've been given command of the engineer companies. I'm making one last attempt to put a floating bamboo bridge across the river at midnight tonight. I came here to talk with Commander in Chief Chu Teh — he's just approved my plan. Two hundred men are cutting yellow bamboo in the forest at this minute. I've ordered them to make triple-tiered rafts that can be anchored to the riverbed. With luck the enemy won't be able to destroy those."

"What will happen if your attempt doesn't succeed?"

"The Seventh and the Ninth won't be able to hold out indefinitely — and the Kwangtung forces have started to break through the Fifth Corps' rear guard in several places." Chiao paused and drew a long, slow breath. "If we don't start to cross the river soon, we'll be trapped. The enemy will close in all around us . . ."

Mei-ling's eyes widened in alarm; then she gathered herself and set the sleeping baby aside in a makeshift crib of interwoven twigs and reeds.

"You look tired and hungry, Ta ko. You must eat before you return to the riverbank!"

She rose from the bed, pulling the blanket close around herself, and hurried to a blackened pot that bubbled on an improvised brick stove in one corner of the cottage. She ladled steaming rice gruel into a tin bowl and handed it to her brother, who lifted it straight to his lips. The baby, who had woken as soon as she put it down, began to cough and Mei-ling took it up in her arms again, wrapping it close to her body inside the blanket.

"Is the child ill?" asked Chiao gently, pausing as he supped the gruel.

She nodded and lifted a corner of the blanket to wipe away beads of perspiration gathering on the baby's pale brow. "He has a fever. It's getting worse."

"His father is going through difficult times, too, I expect you know," said Chiao. "He and Commissioner Chou En-lai devised the strategy for the river crossing. Now that things are going so badly and we are cut off from all contact with Moscow, many other leading comrades are questioning whether we should accept the leadership of a foreigner."

Mei-ling went on dabbing at the baby's brow and did not look up: her unchanging expression suggested she was aware of some of the tensions of which her brother spoke and was perhaps resigned to them.

"If we can break out of this trap there's certain to be a clash among the leadership," continued Chiao in a somber voice. "There's no means of telling how it will turn out. In some ways it's like the Warring States period of our history — they're all at one another's throats. Everyone is criticizing everybody else."

Chiao ate the gruel in silence for a while, his face creased in a pensive frown. Only when the bowl was empty did he lay it aside.

"The comrades who studied in Moscow, including Party Secretary Po Ku, are being labeled the "Twenty-eight Bolsheviks' by most of the other leading comrades. Mao Tse-tung will barely talk to any of them. He's so ill with malaria that he can scarcely speak anyway, but . . ." Chiao paused and his eyes narrowed as though he was wondering whether he should say what was on his lips; then he shrugged. "Well . . . the truth is, Mei-ling, whenever he does talk the others seem to listen — and mostly he blames the father of your child for directing a static, positional war with what should be a mobile army of guerrilla fighters."

"If we don't succeed in crossing the Hsiang safely, it won't matter who's to blame!"

The vehemence of his sister's words made Chiao look up sharply. Her expression hadn't changed — she was still gazing down at the baby in her arms — but he sensed a new tension in her. Ladling some gruel into another bowl he trod quietly across the earthen floor and stopped in front of her, a look of affection softening the hard lines of his tired, smoke-grimed face.

"Perhaps you should eat something too, Mei-ling," he said, putting down the steaming bowl beside her. "We'll need all our strength tonight. Our father is wrong about many things but we ought to be following the teachings of the Taoist sages he admires so much rather than the leadership of our 'foreign expert.' Now's the time to be soft and yielding, to 'use four ounces to deflect a weight of a thousand pounds.' We should be pliable reeds, moving and bending before the storm, but we've become just the reverse. We're rigid oaks planted firmly on the banks of the Hsiang. And we're in great danger of being uprooted or scythed down once and for all. . . ."

Mei-ling stood up suddenly. The baby had quieted and fallen asleep again and after setting him down, she slipped the blanket from her bare shoulders to fold it warmly around the child in the rough crib. Bound about her calves she already wore gray leggings into which she had folded her uniform trousers and turning her naked back to her brother, she slipped on her khaki cadre's tunic to complete the uniform. After fastening its buttons she buckled around her waist a leather belt and a pistol holster from which the butt of the Mauser automatic protruded. When she turned to face her brother again, Mei-ling stood transformed from a vulnerable nursing mother to an armed cadre of Commissioner Chou En-lai's personal staff who, like her male comrades, had also trained to serve as a revolutionary fighter of the General Headquarters guards regiment when it became necessary.

"I've never asked before why you became the mistress of our foreign expert," said Chiao slowly. "I assume you acted out of a sense of duty — of loyalty to the Party leadership."

"It wasn't only that." Mei-ling spoke with a calm dignity but a warning note in her voice indicated that she was not prepared to discuss her reasons, even with her brother.

"Romantic love outside of marriage is still a foreign concept in China, Mei-ling," persisted Chiao. "Do you 'love' our foreign expert?"

A sudden rise in the tempo of the artillery fire filled the derelict cottage with vivid flashes of orange light, and brother and sister lifted their heads to stare out through the roof rafters at the dark mountainside above. The uproar quickly became deafening, then just as suddenly died away, leaving the mountain eerily silent — but still Mei-ling made no reply.

"I ask the question because even if we escape across the Hsiang, I fear a break is coming between our Comintern comrade and the leadership." Chiao smiled sympathetically at his sister. "You may have to make a choice you didn't expect — between your country and the father of your half-foreign child."

"I don't love him — and the choice is easy. My first wish has always been to help carry the revolution through to victory." Mei-ling spoke quietly, her dark eyes suddenly alive and intense. "But whatever happens, I will do my duty as far as the baby is concerned."

Chiao nodded and moved toward the strip of sacking hanging over the doorway. "I understand. Be careful, though — it might be wise to begin to put a little distance between him and yourself."

Mei-ling gave no hint of her reaction to this suggestion but she followed her brother to the doorway, looking earnestly into his face. "Please be careful tonight, Chiao."

"Don't worry. We'll meet again soon — on the west bank of the Hsiang!"

Chiao turned to pull the sacking aside but Mei-ling plucked suddenly at his sleeve.

"Chiao, I've just remembered something strange. Today on the march, among the prisoners, I think I saw somebody we know . . ."

Her brother, anxious to be gone, frowned impatiently. "Who was it?"

"Do you remember the English missionary we met on the ship coming home? The one who led the hymn singing during the typhoon?"

Chiao's face clouded with the effort of remembering; then he nodded quickly, without interest. "Yes, I think so."

"He's one of the prisoners. I wasn't certain at first. . . . He was covered in mud like all the other poor devils. And he has a beard now."

"How can you be sure it was the missionary, then?"

"As I rode past I heard him call my name."

"Why are you thinking about an English prisoner at such a time as this?" asked Chiao.

Mei-ling dropped her eyes as if she suddenly realized she had spoken without thought. "He looked half-dead . . . his wrists were bound behind his back. His face was twisted as though he were in great pain . . ."

Chiao smiled. "Perhaps you should tell our foreign expert. He might be interested to know he's not the only 'foreign devil' marching with us after all."

The Red Army captain turned toward the doorway again only to find himself confronted by a tall, broad-chested European dressed in a crumpled gray uniform. Tufts of blond hair were visible beneath his red-starred cap and his blue eyes, surveying the room warily, shifted back and forth from Chiao to his sister.

"My Chinese is very poor," said the European, speaking English with a heavy German accent, "but I swear I heard you mention the 'foreign expert.' What is it he should know about?"

Mei-ling turned away, saying nothing, but Chiao grinned cordially and replied in English. "My sister has just told me she thinks there might be an English missionary among the prisoners — so perhaps,

Comrade Braun, you're not the only European among a hundred thousand Chinese after all."

Otto Braun looked hard at Chiao, searching his face for any hidden meaning in his words, then nodded abstractedly. "I think I may have seen the prisoner you speak of this afternoon. Good night, Comrade Chiao . . ."

Braun pointedly held the doorway sacking aside so that the Red Army captain could leave, and he and Mei-ling watched as Chiao strode to his horse, which was tied to a nearby tree. Along both edges of the street of the burned-out village, endless lines of mules were being tethered beside tumbled heaps of boxes and bales which the muleteers were unloading. The occasional artillery flashes emanating from the mountaintop batteries illuminated growing heaps of sewing machines, arsenal hardware, mint equipment, printing presses, document boxes, and baskets of silver dollars and bank notes which lay scattered in profusion along the muddy gutters. Improvised oil lamps burned in all the blitzed cottages above hunched groups of army commanders and civilian cadres; orderlies dashed back and forth between them and a constant stream of messengers galloped in and out of the street on lathered ponies, carrying messages to and from the battlefronts.

The surge of activity in the ruined street where the General Headquarters column had chosen to billet itself had a desperate, frenzied air, and Mei-ling and the German stood momentarily fascinated in the doorway, watching Chiao spur his horse away into the seething crowd. When at last the night swallowed him up, the German let the sacking fall back into place with an exasperated sigh. He lifted one hand wearily as if to touch Mei-ling's cheek but at that moment the baby awoke, coughing once more, and she turned away from him without a word and hurried back to the bed.

21

In a wooded hollow close to the sandy shore of the Hsiang River, Captain Lu Chiao strode swiftly back and forth among his squads of raft makers, carrying a shaded electric flashlight. The rising wind was whipping the surface of the rushing river into choppy waves and squalls of rain were blowing in among the trees, drenching the engineer companies and two battalions of the Red Cadres Regiment lying in hiding in an adjoining valley. Shaded hurricane lamps set in shallow holes in the ground cast a feeble circle of light around each working group and Chiao had to pick his way carefully among piles of bamboo, ropes, doors, and roof beams that had been dragged from cottages in the deserted villages along the riverbank.

By each squad Chiao stopped and shone his flashlight on the raft the troops had made, squatting on his haunches to question the squad leader and check that the three tiers of bamboo were being correctly interlaced and woven together to make them strong enough to withstand direct hits from the enemy artillery. Small, round boulders gathered from the shore were being lashed to anchoring cables to provide moorings for each raft, and men designated as oarsmen were cutting and shaping the longest, sturdiest bamboos so that they would be able to pole the sections of the floating pontoon into position.

The moonless night was black overhead, but to the east, north, and south along the riverbank there was a faint orange glow in the sky and the continuous rattle and rumble of mortar and machine-gun fire from all directions confirmed that the battles on three fronts were moving closer as midnight neared. Every few minutes the darkness above the hollow was illuminated by a star-burst of light from a chandelier flare fired across the river by one of the Kuomintang batteries dug in on a high bluff. A salvo of enemy shells inevitably followed, to be answered immediately by the Red Army guns; during each exchange the raft makers hugged the ground as the blast washed over them and tall plumes of water rose high above the river.

Chiao counted off the seconds between each star-shell, calculating how much time he might have to get the first rafts into the water to begin the hazardous two-hundred-yard crossing. The flares had been bursting at three- to four-minute intervals since dusk and the frequency showed little sign of varying. He had decided to send two platoons of the First Special Course Battalion assault force across the river on the first dozen pontoon sections to set up a small beachhead at the foot of the steep cliff that rose opposite them. These elite groups of specially trained troops, armed with stick grenades, broadswords, and light machine guns, would try to provide some covering fire for the engineers as they began anchoring and building out sections of the bridge from the far bank. At the same time a similar operation would begin on the eastern shore so that the bridge could be constructed rapidly with its two ends eventually joining up in midriver.

Thirty or forty completed rafts had already been moved in readiness to the mouth of the wooded hollow close to the beach and as the incandescence of another flare faded, plunging the river and the woods into darkness, Chiao decided on a sudden instinct that the time was ripe. Running forward, he rapped out orders to the vanguard raft parties and watched with bated breath as a dozen groups scurried forward, lugging the heavy bamboo caissons and their stone anchors across the dark sands of the flat beach. He also dispatched one of his messenger orderlies to send radio alerts to all mortar and heavy machine-gun units along the eastern shore to ensure that they would be ready to provide immediate covering fire. After he had done this, he stood staring up into the rain-swept darkness, counting the seconds quietly inside his head, waiting for the next flare to burst.

Nearly four minutes passed, and when the next shell bathed the river in its luminous glare, the twelve assault rafts were revealed twisting and spinning slowly in the strong, choppy currents just beyond midstream. Swollen by the heavy rain funneling down from the mountains, the engorged river was flowing at great speed, and some of the Special Course Battalion troops had slipped into the water and were swimming hard, helping the frantically poling engineers to propel the pontoon sections across the deepest parts of the river. Within seconds the Kuomintang guns opened up, raising plumes of spray all around the rafts, but the pole men and the swimmers kept them moving smoothly toward the far bank. Almost at once a direct hit lifted one raft high out of the water, tipping its screaming occupants into the fast-flowing river, and Chiao could only watch helplessly from the wooded hollow as the empty bridge section careered rapidly away downstream to be swallowed up in the rainy darkness.

In spite of the daunting odds, the little task force forged on under the withering bombardment, the assault troops courageously returning fire with their light machine guns from crouched positions on the exposed pontoons. They made slow headway and the Kuomintang barrage took a growing toll of casualties among both engineers and assault troops, toppling them one by one into the swollen river or crumpling them in lifeless heaps on the pontoons themselves. Another raft was swept away downstream when its pole man was killed, but to Chiao's great relief ten of the makeshift bamboo craft succeeded in grounding under the cliff on the far shore and the handful of surviving assault cadres leapt ashore to begin fortifying their precarious foothold.

The Red Army artillery batteries had begun to roar in reply the moment the first flare-shell burst and the earsplitting din of the artillery duel quickly filled the night. Machine-gun tracers criss-crossed in the weeping sky above the river, tall geysers of shell-burst flame gushed from the hills, and in mud-filled trenches on both banks fearful men of the Kuomintang and the Red Army alike crouched low, clutching their rifles as searing shards of metal smashed and maimed the bodies of comrades all around them.

On the near shore, the Red Army engineers quickly manhandled twenty or thirty more rafts into the river: although these also attracted a new hail of fire, the engineers immediately began the hazardous task of lashing them together and within minutes a short finger of latticed bamboo jutted into the flood, pointing the way toward the Kuomintang bank. A pair of supply sampans piled high with ropes and timbers was launched and maneuvered alongside the floating bamboo caissons — but these craft, manned by Chiao's deputy commanders, quickly became prime targets for the Kuomintang gunners. When one exploded in flames, Chiao dashed out from the cover of the wood and waded into the swirling water to supervise the bridge construction himself.

His engineers were working in the water stripped to the waist, their half-naked bodies glowing orange in the glare of the shell bursts, and Chiao wrenched off his own tunic to wade and swim from group to group. Ignoring the gunfire kicking up the water around the floating sections, he helped the men fix two sleepers between each triple-tiered bamboo raft and made sure that they lashed three or four crossbeams to them in every case, in accordance with his design. On top of these sturdy joists he ordered the engineers to spread the cottage doors, which were latticed with thin wooden slats. Some of the completed sections were repeatedly struck by artillery fire, but although they dipped and bucked in the water under the impact of the shells, Chiao was relieved to see that the interleaved bamboo structures always righted themselves and floated again in spite of being holed.

He had calculated that about one hundred sections would be required to bridge the river and by one o'clock in the morning, sixty or so were in place. Two further groups of Special Course Battalion troops succeeded in poling through the waves of the raging river under heavy fire to reinforce the tiny bridgehead, and a narrow bamboo peninsula of thirty or more pontoons expanded slowly from the far bank toward midstream. By two o'clock the gap between the converging sections had narrowed to twenty yards or so and Chiao allowed himself to hope that the floating bridge would soon open the way for a fully fledged infantry assault on the Kuomintang shore.

But in the middle of the river the swirling current flowed most swiftly, and two more rafts were swept away downstream before they could be anchored. Watching from the shore, where he had returned to hasten the construction of reserve rafts, Chiao saw a third pontoon spinning dangerously out of control and suddenly he realized that the whole of the delicate bamboo structure jigging on the angry surface of the river was at risk. His force of nearly five hundred engineers was already severely depleted: at the outset he had divided the men into separate detachments responsible for supply, raft making, bridge construction, and anchoring. He had created rescue and reserve sections and had watched with growing dismay as his rescuers carried dead and wounded comrades away from the riverside on stretchers made from doors. Barely half a dozen men remained in reserve and most of the bridge-building materials were exhausted. There had been little letup in the artillery bombardment and he could tell that the strain of working under fire for so long was beginning to affect the surviving engineers.

As he watched, one of the engineers detached himself from the crowd of troops thronging the unfinished bridge and raced back along the bucking pontoons toward him. When he halted, panting, in front of Chiao, the young peasant soldier, who had been a boatman before he joined the Red Army, was pale with anxiety.

"The stone anchors won't grip in midstream, Comrade Commander! The current is too strong and they're rolling along the bottom. None of the central pontoons will hold out there."

Chiao absorbed the information in silence, staring desperately toward the tantalizing gap that remained between the two arms of the floating bridge. In his ears the sounds of fighting all around the Red Army perimeter seemed to be growing louder by the minute, and out of the corner of his eye he saw a mounted messenger galloping full pelt along the riverbank from the direction of the General Headquarters.

"Weave two dozen baskets out of bamboo strips," ordered Chiao calmly. "And fill them with smaller stones from the beach. Push three sharpened pine stakes through each basket so they will stick in the riverbed. And hurry."

As the soldier ran off to carry out the orders, the General Headquarters messenger jumped from his horse and thrust a folded sheet of paper into Chiao's hands. When he opened it he saw by the beam of his flashlight that it bore the distinctive circular red stamp of the Revolutionary Military Commission. Above the signature of its chairman there were two brief lines of handwritten characters. The message read: "The Fifth and Ninth Corps must retreat soon or face wholesale slaughter. The bridge across the river has to be completed and ready for use within half an hour at all costs!"

The heavy rain began to blur the characters even before Chiao had finished reading the message. Returning it to the hands of the messenger, Chiao spoke slowly and clearly to make himself understood above the roar of the artillery. "Tell the leading comrades of the Revolutionary Military Commission that the floating bridge will be ready on time. They should begin moving the vanguard regiments toward the riverbank at once!"

The messenger nodded emphatically, sprang back into his saddle, and galloped off in the direction from which he had come. A moment after the horse and rider had disappeared into the rain, a Kuomintang shell scored a direct hit on the last remaining supply sampan, which was maneuvering between the two unfinished ends of the bridge. The craft was transformed instantly into a blazing pyre, bathing the river in its glare, and as the sampan drifted swiftly away downstream, the gap between the two heaving chains of unconnected pontoons seemed to yawn wider than before.

22

Crouching on the wildly seesawing end caisson at the head of the eastern span, Chiao watched anxiously as two new bamboo sections were poled toward the black stretch of swirling water that still separated the two outstretched arms of the bridge. Each bucking raft was crewed by a pole man and three other engineers, and the stone-filled baskets of woven bamboo that had been quickly made on Chiao's orders lay at their feet, ready to be thrown into the water the moment the caissons were in place. Chiao was holding his right hand aloft, restraining his men until the right moment, and the engineers responsible for the improvised anchors watched closely for his signal.

The current tugged and snatched at the rafts, twisting and spinning them in circles as they edged into the breach between the bridge ends, but Chiao controlled them without panic, directing a constant flow of calm orders to the men manning the poles. When the sections were a few yards short of their goals, he pulled down his arm abruptly and the engineers heaved the basket anchors into the swirling waters. Chiao held his breath while their ropes snaked swiftly over the sides. Then they snapped taut as the pinewood spikes jutting through the baskets dug into the sandy riverbed and the pontoons swung obediently into line. Gangs of waiting engineers carrying doors, sleepers, and crossbeams swarmed forward at once and began working feverishly to link up the new sections.

Three more rafts began to advance toward the linked pontoons and Chiao moved to a new position to direct them. The enemy artillery barrage that had waxed and waned during the past four or five hours intensified again suddenly, and long bursts of heavy machine-gun fire raked the water. Crouching lower, Chiao glanced at his watch with the aid of his flashlight and saw that it was almost a quarter to three. Little more than fifteen minutes remained before the deadline set by the Military Commission ran out, and five further pontoons were still needed to complete the bridge. The rafts lay ready on the beach and Chiao wondered why the group of engineers manning them had not yet launched the sections onto the river.

Straining his eyes, he peered beyond the rafts into the rain-lashed darkness that cloaked the eastern shore, trying to calculate the likely line of march of the approaching Red Army divisions. To his surprise he was able to see several glittering necklets of fast-moving light shimmering through the rain: spread across the face of the mountains that rose black and invisible above the river plain, the desperately outnumbered troops were obviously throwing caution to the winds. Despite the danger from the enemy artillery toward which they were advancing, whole regiments were holding blazing torches aloft to light their way, sacrificing the advantage of concealment to their urgent need for all-out speed.

Feeling his chest tighten with tension, Chiao closed his eyes and for several seconds he deliberately relaxed all the muscles and sinews of his body as his father had first taught him to do when he was a small boy: in an instant the tension evaporated and he felt new energy rise within him. Swinging around, he concentrated all his attention on directing the three rafts in midstream to their moorings, ignoring the chains of light flowing down the hills behind him. When the rafts were safely anchored, the unbridged gap had narrowed to ten yards, but on turning back to the shore again, Chiao saw that the five remaining bamboo pontoons required to complete the bridge still lay unlaunched on the sandy beach. Bending double in an effort to make himself a smaller target for the Kuomintang gunners, he ran back fast along the swaying wooden causeway, arriving beside the beached rafts at the same time as the young peasant boatman, who had been searching the wooded hollow for supplies.

"What's happening?" demanded Chiao sharply. "Why haven't the rafts been launched yet?"

"There's no more rope, Comrade Commander! I've searched everywhere." The young peasant's face was a mask of despair. "All our spare ropes were in that sampan that was sunk. We can't anchor the rafts."

Chiao saw that the basket anchors were piled uselessly on the decks of the pontoons without cables or ropes; around them the group of engineers stood disconsolate and at a loss.

"Launch the rafts at once — and give me your puttees!" Chiao pointed to the leggings of the startled boatman. "Be quick!"

Taking the muddied strips of cotton cloth that the peasant unwound from his legs, Chiao quickly knotted them and twisted them together. Holding the puttees up to the group, he stretched them tight to demonstrate their strength. "Every one of you is wearing puttees. Take them off to make ropes! Run to the assault battalions and get two hundred volunteers to give up their leggings for the future of the revolution!"

The frightened faces of the young engineers lit up with delight and they let out a cheer of relief as they bent to tug off the bands of cloth bound around their calves. While the last few pontoons were being launched, the remaining engineers frantically plaited the cotton anchor lines. As each line was finished it was carried at a run along the floating bridge and thrown aboard one of the unattached pontoons to be fastened to their anchors.

Four of the five bridge sections were steered successfully into position and secured with the makeshift lines made from leggings, but the last one spun out of control when a fusillade of machine-gun fire shattered the bamboo steering pole being wielded by the young boatman. The section changed direction in an instant and swung through the current, gathering speed, heading rapidly for the already completed bulk of the floating bridge. Realizing that the weight of the runaway pontoon would send it smashing through the fragile structure, Chiao snatched up a spare guiding pole and yelled to attract the attention of the boatman before hurling it like a javelin in the direction of the raft.

The pole bounced on the pontoon's deck and the boatman grabbed it with one hand as it flew past him. Bending low on tensed legs and jabbing the bamboo deep into the river, he gradually slowed the speed of the careering section. The Kuomintang gunners, aware that the bridge was nearing completion, had begun firing continuous clusters of flares to light the scene and now they poured a deluge of machine-gun fire at the engineers. Just as the young boatman brought the runaway section under control, a line of water spouts marking the passage of machine-gun shells jumped rhythmically across the flare-silvered surface of the river and cut him, screaming, from its deck. He sank below the waves and did not reappear, and again the pontoon raced away toward the almost completed bridge. Chiao, seeing there was no other choice, flung himself headlong into the waves and swam swiftly into the pontoon's path.

Although he reached out his arms to hold off the raft, the impact when it struck Chiao knocked the breath from him. Its momentum carried him back toward the floating bridge with dangerous speed but he kicked out furiously with his legs and managed to slow the raft's progress. A dozen other engineers, encouraged by his example, flung themselves into the water from the bridge and swam to help him. Between them, with bullets frothing the water all around, they manhandled the raft toward the remaining gap in the bridge. As he swam Chiao felt a sickening pain strike his right shoulder and in the minutes that followed he sensed his blood was thickening the water around him. Boat hooks grappled with the errant section, dragging it gradually into place, and when at last it closed the gap, Chiao yelled for the anchors to be dropped and for the sleepers to be lashed in place. Looking to the shore, he saw that the moving forests of torches were streaming down through the darkness in the direction of the beach. Under the ghostly light of the flares, a vast horde of

Red Army men was assembling all along the eastern bank and the vanguard battalions were already moving onto the beach around the bridge end.

One of his men bent over to pull Chiao from the river but the Red Army captain waved him away instead to help complete the plankway. The pain in Chiao's shoulder was turning to a numbness which seemed to affect his whole body; soon he was able to hang on to the rocking pontoon with only one arm. When the last door had been nailed in place, he ordered all his men to jump into the water, and they clung to the sides of the pontoons as he sent his orderly racing to the bank to announce that the bridge was finished.

Seconds later the flimsy bamboo structure began to rock and sway to the rhythmic beat of running, straw-sandaled feet. First onto the pontoons were men of the Special Course Battalion: trotting rapidly, three abreast, amid a thickening hail of gunfire, they passed close to Chiao's pain-contorted face in a moving blur. For a minute or two Chiao hung on, seeing as through a mist the dazzling silver flares, the glittering bayonet tips, the fearful expressions and pounding feet of his Red Army comrades. The artillery bombardment became a fearsome cacophony of shrieking shells and deafening explosions but in Chiao's ears these terrible sounds grew steadily fainter until only a ringing silence reigned inside his brain. Feeling his hands slip from their hold on the bamboo pontoon, he yielded consciously to the river's fierce current, but as it dragged him away, he struggled to hold his mouth above the waves. Still fighting inwardly to summon the instinctive disciplines that his father's early teaching had made second nature to him, he allowed the river to bear him rapidly away from the focus of the fighting and into the anonymous darkness.

23

Dawn was breaking by the time Jakob came in sight of the floating bridge of bamboo pontoons. The young missionary caught his first distant glimpse of it from a mountain pass a thousand feet above the river plain, and even the drifting rain and the gray morning light could not conceal the turmoil of the battle continuing around the bridge. The steep hillsides rising from the western bank were wreathed in drifting clouds of dark smoke from which lethal buds of red and orange fire blossomed every few seconds. The shriek of shells, the roar of exploding grenades, and the din of machine-gun and artillery fire were blending into one furious storm that made the mountainside shake beneath Jakob's feet. The bridge itself was swollen with men and animals inching across the flood, and from Jakob's high vantage point, they looked like an army of ants struggling to traverse a shivering puddle on a fragile stalk of grass.

Through holes in the smoke Jakob and his apprehensive fellow prisoners could see Red Army and Kuomintang troops swarming over the broken trenches and fieldworks that scarred the high parts of the far escarpment. Merging in repeated flurries of fierce hand-to-hand combat, both sides were advancing and retreating in waves, capturing and recapturing fortified hillocks and strongpoints in a desperate effort to control the winding tracks that led up from the riverside bridgehead. The sand-bagged emplacements through which the troops of both sides darted and ran were littered with the motionless dead of the night's battles and it was clear that with the coming of daylight, the Kuomintang infantry regiments were launching a massive counterattack to try to recapture the precarious fortified corridor which the Red Army vanguard had secured under cover of darkness.

While the battles raged, transport and baggage detachments were shifting steadily up the steep hillside. In their wake Jakob could see gun-making machines that required ten coolies to lift them edging across the bridge with painful slowness. Printing presses and other heavy equipment, mounted on pine-log shafts slung between pairs of mules, were also being moved toward the eastern end of the bridge, blocking the advance of the infantry. The natural funnel of land immediately below Jakob that led down through the pine woods to the beach was becoming more congested every minute with fighting units, and seeing this, the Hunanese guard commander ordered his detachment of prisoners off the track with an angry shout.

There had been countless delays throughout the night as the prisoners moved haltingly toward the river amid a growing multitude of soldiers and pack animals, and each new delay only served to add to the prisoners' unease. Jostled roughly by the guards, they cowered down now, squatting numbly on their haunches on a boulder-covered scree, their eyes dilated, their lips drawn back from their teeth as though already anticipating the dreadful agonies that might await them down in the river valley. As they watched, a Kuomintang biplane appeared from the north, winging low over the heaving surface of the river, its single engine inaudible beneath the noise of the guns. It dipped rapidly toward the makeshift bridge and released its clutch of twenty-pound bombs, which exploded instantly, throwing up tall columns of water all around the pontoons. A long train of squealing pack mules was hurled into the river and every single animal was quickly dragged under and drowned within moments by the heavy loads and tangled harness lines that joined them. Troops and muleteers tumbled from the bridge into the water in the confusion, and although the bamboo pontoons immediately settled back into place unscathed, the heads of the soldiers continued to bob frantically in the waves as the men fought to disentangle themselves from the melee of broken crates and thrashing animals.

All the Chinese prisoners stared transfixed at the horrifying scene below and only Jakob turned aside to sink to his knees in silent prayer. But when he opened his eyes again, he was taken aback to find himself staring at the curved blade of a broadsword held close before him. Still kneeling, he raised his head and found himself looking up into the face of the young peasant guard who had executed the Kiangsi boy so cold-bloodedly. The guard was holding the unsheathed sword pointedly in both hands, resting its tip on the muddy ground between his feet, and his face was as implacably hostile as ever.

"Turn around, imperialist spy!"

The guard rapped out the order in his usual peremptory tone and lifted the sword tip menacingly to emphasize his authority. Jakob, alarmed at the sudden appearance of the youth with a naked sword, hesitated, trying to read some hint of his intention in his expression.

"What do you intend to do?" asked the missionary slowly.

"Don't ask questions. Turn around!"

Reluctantly Jakob obeyed, turning on his knees to face the river. He steeled himself for a sudden blow from the sword and felt the hair on the nape of his neck tingle unpleasantly. But the press of the cold blade, when it came, was against his left wrist and Jakob felt the guard saw roughly back and forth with the weapon for a moment or two before stepping away from him.

"Now stand up!"

Again Jakob obeyed and he felt the rope binding his wrists drop to the ground. He stared down in surprise at the frayed ends of his bonds lying in the mud; it was the first time his wrists had been unbound on the march and he turned to face the guard with a puzzled frown.

"Why have you done this?"

"We've received orders from the Red Star column. From now on you are to be allowed to march with free hands. But it's not our wish." The youth glowered at Jakob and quickly slipped another length of rope around Jakob's shoulders in the familiar harness that left a free end dangling down his back like a restraining rein. "Although your hands are free, you must always remain close to your guard — close enough for him to take this rope in his hand if he wishes!"

Jakob eased his stiff, aching arms from behind his back and chafed his wrists to ease the fierce pain caused by the returning circulation. "What is the Red Star column?"

"There's no need for me to answer your questions. Just make sure you obey orders!"

The guard scowled and walked away, leaving Jakob staring after him in mystification. All of the Chinese prisoners were still bound and some of them looked at Jakob curiously — but they soon turned their frightened eyes back to the river again. When half an hour later the Hunanese commander gave the order to move on, Jakob noticed that the young guard instructed the comrade who had dug the Kiangsi boy's grave to walk close behind, while he himself moved away only a pace or two ahead.

Under their close escort Jakob was hurried down the mountainside behind the other prisoners, but although he still hobbled painfully on his torn and blistered feet, he rejoiced in the new sensation of being able to swing his arms freely on the move after being bound for nearly three weeks. Able also to hold his balance better, he slipped and fell less frequently and because he was less afraid of falling, he moved more quickly downhill. Despite the pain in his feet, he even began to run with confidence, glorying in a wider sense of freedom and wholeness that came with the unbinding of his arms. Because of all these things, although the fierce fighting on the far side of the river toward which they were rushing headlong had not slackened, Jakob illogically felt his spirits begin to rise.

The whole column was jog-trotting as they came down onto the river shore and a hundred yards ahead Jakob caught sight of the furled Red Army flag carried by the guards' company. Only its tip was showing but he could see that the canvas painting of the Nativity was still wrapped around it. As he watched, the standard-bearer reached the bridge and stepped up onto the first pontoon. The flag rose higher and turned in the bearer's hands so that the silver Christmas star which had previously been facing away from Jakob became visible, bobbing above the heads of the marchers. The Communist troops clustered close around it, bending low to begin the dash across the narrow bamboo causeway, and seeing this symbol of his faith being carried over the Hsiang sent a surge of exhilaration coursing through Jakob.

The renewed shriek of artillery shells filled the air, augmented by the dull, staccato roar of heavy machine-gun fire, but instead of shrinking from the bridge which lay across the first military battlefield that he had encountered in his young life, Jakob felt himself drawn forward irresistibly into the unholy vortex. The new sighting of the star symbol so soon after the unexpected freeing of his wrists had seemed to hint at the intervention of a divinity on his behalf, and together these two events produced in his mind a sense of euphoric certainty about his destiny. All the fears that had been gathering in him through the night suddenly evaporated and he ran forward faster, feeling light and buoyant, giving not the slightest thought to his life being in danger in the heart of the battle for the Hsiang crossing.

With part of his brain, however, Jakob also registered the stark horror of his surroundings: countless dead and mutilated men and animals lay sprawled in the gray slime of the shore on either side of him as he ran, the bloodied shards of their torn flesh washed a vivid red by the incessant rain. The mouths of soldiers and mules alike, agape in their fatal anguish, revealed the same screaming crescents of yellowed teeth; arms and hoofs, tangled and frozen in the paralysis of death, clawed equally vainly at the misty dawn air. Abandoned supplies and ammunition, broken open and soaked with blood, lay scattered wantonly among the corpses and the dying, all trace of the normal habits of careful husbandry having been abandoned in the mad scramble for survival. Screams of agony and shrieked pleas for help rang in Jakob's ears, but these terrible cries were ignored by the flood of still-surviving Red Army men which swept him on swiftly toward the bamboo bridge.

All around him the Chinese prisoners were stumbling and shouting, their eyes bulging, their mouths opened wide. As he moved up onto the bridge, Jakob was perhaps yelling too; he could not be sure. The gunfire became deafening and amid the frantic press of bodies on the swaying bamboo platforms men kicked and pushed one another, cursed obscenely, yelled, pleaded, and shouted orders which nobody heeded. In the middle of the bridge, Jakob saw that flotillas of rafts filled with armed troops were also battling toward the western bank farther downstream, followed by volleys of rifle and automatic-weapons fire. As he watched, two Kuomintang biplanes rose into view above a hill on the far bank and swung lazily down toward the water. One unleashed its bomb load directly above the raft flotillas and several of the flimsy craft rose spinning into the air, shrugging Red Army troops down into the water as a dog might shake fleas from its back.

Both planes flew on toward the bridge, where Jakob was trapped by the congestion of troops and baggage coolies ahead of him. But the leading plane released its bombs too late and they sailed low over the heads of the terrified troops to kick up harmless geysers of water upstream. The second plane swung westward before it reached the bridge and the leather-helmeted sergeant observer manning the rear cockpit swiveled a Lewis gun in the direction of the pontoons.

His first long burst of fire scythed down a dozen or more guards and prisoners all around Jakob. Some collapsed into the water over the unprotected sides of the pontoons, others slumped bleeding to the boardwalks made from the dismembered cottage doors. The panic-stricken survivors flung themselves into the river to begin swimming to the western bank or pushed forward blindly, stumbling and trampling over the fallen. Immediately in front of Jakob, the young guard who had so enthusiastically executed the Kiangsi youth spun around and fell to his knees, his eyes wide with shock. The left shoulder of his tunic was turning crimson with his blood and he clawed uselessly at it with his free hand. Pushed violently from behind by soldiers and prisoners desperate to pass, Jakob cannoned into the young guard, knocking him backward into the river. Frantic troops and the other prisoners rushed on heedlessly toward the western bank and as the peasant boy sank, his wild eyes registered his fright and disbelief.

"*Chiu ming! Chiu ming!*" he choked as the waves swirled over his head. "Help me! Please help me!"

Jakob watched the river sweep the young guard away for only a second or two before he flung himself into the water in a headlong dive. Because the current was strong it took him several minutes to reach the guard and drag him back to the bridge. The troops and coolies stampeding toward the far bank ignored his shouts for assistance as he clung to the side of a pontoon and Jakob had to struggle alone to haul himself out of the river, holding the collar of the now-unconscious guard. When he bent to lift him, Jakob was surprised at how little the scrawny youngster weighed; carrying him easily in both arms, he ran to the western shore among the panicking throng and started up the long, steep path that led to the top of the cliff.

Two companies of Kuomintang troops making a determined assault on the defended corridor halfway up the hill had partially overrun the outer Red Army defense trenches, and Jakob saw stick grenades wheeling end over end to explode among the marchers on the track above him. To his dismay the soldier carrying the canvas-covered Red Army standard went down suddenly in the middle of a group of guards and the flag fell to the ground. It slithered down the hillside until it came to rest against an outcrop of rock, and as he climbed, Jakob saw one of the Kuomintang soldiers detach himself from his unit and begin crawling down toward the fallen flag, intent on capturing it.

Hobbling faster, bent almost double under the growing weight of the unconscious guard, Jakob left the narrow track and struck out across the hillside toward the rocky outcrop. He reached it first, and hoisting the limp guard onto one shoulder, he bent to snatch up the Communist standard. As he straightened up with the furled flag in his left hand, Jakob saw the lone Kuomintang soldier slithering down the stony slope with his rifle held in front of him. For a moment they faced one another across twenty or thirty yards of barren hillside and the Kuomintang soldier's narrow eyes opened wide in an expression of amazement as he caught sight of Jakob's blond beard and white skin. Neither man moved but the soldier recovered quickly and, raising his rifle to his shoulder, fired three shots in quick succession at the young missionary.

In turning away, Jakob stumbled against a jagged stone and fell to his knees; the rifle shots passed over him and he managed to scramble behind a boulder, dragging the guard after him. The next instant a Red Army platoon advancing up the winding track came into view. Seeing the enemy soldier close before them, they opened fire at once with their own carbines. The Kuomintang soldier, hit low in the body, dropped his weapon and doubled over, grunting

PART THREE

The Marchers Change Step

1935

The five-day battle at the Hsiang River proved to be the biggest and bloodiest military confrontation of the entire Long March. The Communists, by their own admission, lost 50,000 men — half their strength. This near-disaster, however, became a turning point in the fortunes of the Red Army. After abandoning the encircled Central Soviet Area in Kiangsi, the Communists had marched about eight hundred miles in six weeks, but they were fleeing without a clearly defined political purpose, having no greater ambition than to link up with another Communist force of 30,000 troops, the Second Front Army, at the smaller soviet of Sangchih, in northwest Hunan. Chiang Kai-shek, however, deployed 200,000 men astride the northward route to the Hunan soviet, preventing the Central Red Army from attaining even that limited objective. The Moscow-oriented Communist leadership, known collectively as the Twenty-eight Bolsheviks, having brought the march to the brink of a debacle, was therefore compelled to admit its failures and bow to the more flexible military philosophies and guerrilla tactics of Mao Tse-tung.

The long-simmering antagonism between Mao and the "Bolsheviks," headed by the youthful Party general secretary, Po Ku, and the German Comintern adviser, Otto Braun, had been shaped by the Chinese Communist Party's history. Mao, with many others, had thrown himself eagerly into organizational work in the 1920s after helping to found the Party, but when Chiang Kai-shek began to massacre his Communist partners in the revolution in 1927, Mao followed the example of leaders of peasant rebellions throughout China's history and retreated alone to the mountainous countryside of eastern Hunan. The central Party leadership, guided by a Stalinist Comintern adviser on the spot, continued to operate from a secret headquarters in the French concession of Shanghai. Po Ku, like the other Bolsheviks, had gone to study in Moscow in his teens, before returning home to become general secretary in 1931 at the age of twenty-four, and while he and his young fellow leaders planned an orthodox proletarian revolution centered on cities and urban workers, an isolated Mao fought on in the rural wilderness, building and politicizing an army of peasant rebels. Chu Teh, an inspirational military leader, joined Mao, and together they created a fighting force that later founded the Central Soviet in Kiangsi, an area the size of France embracing a population of nine million peasants. By adopting a guerrilla strategy epitomized in the slogan "When the enemy advances, we retreat. . . . When the enemy retreats, we pursue. . . ." Mao and Chu Teh successfully preserved the Central Soviet against Chiang Kai-shek's first three encirclement and annihilation campaigns, in 1930–31.

But when the Communist Party moved its headquarters to the Kiangsi soviet in 1932, its Moscow-educated leaders were still obsessed with Russian orthodoxy, which demanded seizure of cities and urban uprisings. When Chiang launched his fifth encirclement campaign against the Central Soviet, the Bolsheviks, in line with this ideology, insisted on employing positional warfare strategies, building earthen walls to make the region "a bastion of iron" against the blockhouse siege methods of the Kuomintang. Mao, accused of betraying vital Communist principles by indulging in "timid guerrillaism," was removed from his post of chairman of the soviet government and took no direct part in the decision to abandon and dismantle the Central Soviet. Although nominally a member of the Military Commission, Mao remained outside the top leadership circle until the marchers reached the Hsiang River. By that time all direct contact with the Comintern and Stalin had been lost, and although he was suffering one of his periodic bouts of malaria, Mao succeeded in unseating the Bolsheviks by enlisting the support of dissatisfied Red Army generals to outvote them. He thus broke Moscow's stranglehold on the Chinese revolution, and the marching column was radically reorganized almost as soon as it had crossed the Hsiang River. Archive documents carried at the Bolsheviks' insistence were burned, cumbersome machinery and surplus weapons were hidden in remote mountain caves, and other unnecessary equipment was dropped into ravines. The surviving troops were transformed into a faster, more flexible force able to wheel, feint, and create diversions, and they pushed on rapidly across the craggy Yueh-cheng Mountains on the Kwangsi border and entered Kweichow's rugged Wumeng range. There they encountered the armies of the Kweichow warlords as well as the provincial government forces. Troops of the Central Government's army also continued in pursuit — but the Communists, by employing their new tactics, eluded them all.

Chiang, outwitted and outmaneuvered, temporarily abandoned the chase, allowing the Communists twelve days' respite in early January after they captured Tsunyi, Kweichow's northernmost town. It was at meetings in Tsunyi that the crucial leadership changes were formally confirmed: Mao Tse-tung became chairman of the Revolutionary Military Commission of the Party Central Committee, thereby wresting day-to-day control of the march from its previous chairman, Chou En-lai, and the German Comintern adviser. The young Po Ku, still only twenty-seven, was removed from office, and Mao from that time onward presided over meetings of the Party Politburo. Chou En-lai, who had long before espoused the Bolsheviks' cause, did a remarkable about-face and switched his support to Mao at Tsunyi, endorsing his new plan to swing northwest in a wide arc through lightly defended territory in an effort to link up with another small soviet set up on the Szechuan-Shensi border by the Communist Fourth Front Army. A vague, long-term aim to "go north to fight the Japanese invader" was also enunciated at Tsunyi by Mao to provide the toiling troops with a distant patriotic ideal, and all these complex factors of history and temperament played their part in defining the route the march was to take over the succeeding ten months. But as they pressed on through the mountains of Kweichow in the cold of late January 1935, none of the marchers could have suspected just how harsh an ordeal they would have to face on the trek that would take them even deeper than they suspected into China's wild heartlands.

1

The stony track leading north through the Taloushan Mountains toward the border of Szechuan was hard with frost beneath Jakob's callused feet, but as he climbed in the gathering dusk at the end of the line of prisoners, the faint, sweet fragrance of winter plum blossom unexpectedly teased his nostrils. In the gloom he could just see the outline of a grove of trees whose bare branches were speckled with the early blossom, and the perfume of the white flowers lifted his flagging spirits. Ahead of him the troops were lighting torches made from bunches of mountain bracken lashed to staves: they flared brightly in the half-darkness, casting a warm glow over the long, winding column of marching men, and spontaneously the soldiers began to sing as they climbed.

A silver crescent moon already lifting into sight above the peak of a distant mountain was spilling cold, pale light on its highest crags and in the dome of the darkening sky a few faint stars were beginning to twinkle. Against Jakob's cheeks the chill night air of the mountains was sharp but there was not a breath of wind and his body was warm inside the quilted long-gown his guards had given him at Tsunyi. He climbed more easily, since the foot lacerations he had suffered at the Hsiang crossing had been given a chance to heal during the twelve-day rest in the old walled city. The constant marching had also at last begun to toughen his feet, making the soles coarse and leathery. The grooves worn in his insteps by the bindings of plaited straw sandals had also ceased to chafe as calluses hardened to form a horny, protective hide inside the flimsy footwear.

As they marched in the stillness of the approaching night, the rough voices of the peasant troops raised in unison carried clearly along the winding tracks, echoing from the funneled walls of ravines and flowing invisibly up and down the bare hillsides of the Talou-shan. The singing, Jakob could sense, was binding the column to-gether, fusing the thousands of marchers into one serpentine body, imbuing each man with renewed vigor from a common well of en-ergy. Although he did not join in and the sentiments bellowed into the night were crudely exhortatory, in the deep silence of the moun-tains the songs in their essence took on the emotional force of hymns and Jakob felt himself strangely stirred by them.

Not for the first time, the cadences of the youthful voices inspired in him an illogical feeling of community with the multitude of troops marching all around him. He felt keenly the power of the common loyalty which bound them together; he felt the intense shared ex-citement of the challenge they faced, fleeing from a superior enemy into an unknown future, every man equal and carrying only the barest essentials for survival on his back — chopsticks, a rice bowl, a quilted blanket, an umbrella of oiled paper, a rifle. Jakob sensed that having survived the fiery slaughter of the Hsiang River, each man felt himself chosen to fight on for his fallen comrades as well as himself and faith in their cause seemed to ring from the soul of every man when they sang on the march. On such occasions the atmosphere of the column was that of a great spiritual crusade in which every individual gloried in the dangers and hardships still to be met. Jakob never forgot for an instant the deep hostility to his own faith that the Communists harbored and he still prayed fiercely each day for help to show them forgiveness for having so callously taken Felicity's life and robbed him of his daughter — but despite all these things, the strange sense of kinship with the soldiers con-stantly reasserted itself.

On other fine nights since leaving Tsunyi, when enemy regiments were known to be far off, the troops had also lit torches and sung as they marched beneath the starlit heavens. Often snow had dusted the Taloushan, etching its peaks on the sky in bold strokes of light and shadow, and the calm, silent beauty of these night landscapes had then, as now, induced a tangible sense of awe in the marching men. Their moving presence enhanced the scene when the torches they carried spread a rose-colored glow above their bobbing heads and from the heights, the entire column often became visible winding across the darkened highlands like the coils of a long, crimson dragon.

Amid the rough talk of the soldiers Jakob heard no direct reference to the awe-inspiring splendor of their surroundings. Something in their subdued demeanor, however, betrayed an instinctive respect. Whenever Jakob sensed that these unspoken feelings were becoming intense, the men around him invariably burst into their noisy, raucous propaganda songs, as though to prevent their minds from dwelling too deeply on the eerie majesty of the towering crags and black ravines which seemed to dwarf them into insignificance.

"Come, My Friend, We Must Avenge Our Parents' Deaths," they would roar into the darkness, or they would bellow "Let No Chinese Fight Chinese!" . . . "The Red Army Will Surely Be Victorious" . . . "Someday We Will Fight Our Way Back to Our Native Villages" . . . In one song after another of a repertoire that was becoming familiar to Jakob, accents of all the southern provinces — Kiangsi, Kwangtung, Fukien, Hunan, Kwangsi, Kweichow — blended in ragged chorus. But again and again the marching troops returned to one song above all others, "Till the Last Man," and as they climbed they brandished their torches above their heads both to rekindle the flames and to lend added emphasis to their strident rendering of the words:

> "The sacred earth and freedom
> Who dares to seize them from us?
> Our red political power,
> Who dares stand in our way?
> Our iron fists are ready
> To strike down the Kuomintang."

Many of the troops wounded at the Hsiang River still wore bandages on their heads and limbs: some had lost fingers, hands, or an eye, some had a bandaged cauterized stump in place of an arm, others limped and dragged a shattered leg or foot. Many heads had been shaved to the scalp to rid them of lice, many still suffered from boils and malaria, and dysentery had wasted other bodies and faces. But the wounded, diseased, and healthy alike shouted the songs with equal gusto, buoyed and supported by the intense camaraderie produced by shared suffering and survival against the odds. One company or battalion would take up a song, another would answer with its own version, yelled louder or more lustily, and the valleys and crags echoed and re-echoed with the choruses offered in fierce, friendly competition.

Now that most of the superfluous equipment had been dumped, the transport column marched separately, mainly at night. Even the heavy artillery weapons had been abandoned for lack of ammunition, and sometimes Jakob and the other prisoners walked in the wake of the less encumbered baggage mules, while sometimes they moved more quickly with the fighting columns. Under the new rules of march which had made wheeling and feinting commonplace, Jakob became used to seeing companies, battalions, and whole regiments overtaking the prisoners and their guards one day, then the next day countermarching rapidly in the opposite direction.

By watching and listening to the calls and banter that passed between the units, Jakob had come to realize that the vast majority of the troops who had survived the Hsiang River battle were young peasants, many of them in their late teens or early twenties. Most of them, he guessed, were illiterate, but from their visible self-confidence and their familiarity with their weapons it was obvious that a great number were experienced fighting men of several years' standing. To replenish the depleted ranks, new peasant volunteers were being recruited from the villages through which the column passed and Jakob also noticed that volunteers from among the captured Kuomintang prisoners of war were being readily welcomed into the fighting units. Apprehensive at first, these recruited prisoners, he saw, were quick to absorb the new ethos of the Red Army, which taught them to pay wayside peasants for any food they provided and to loot only from rich landlords and Kuomintang officials under the strict supervision of their officers.

Although no visible badges of rank were worn on their uniforms, the Red Army officers were readily identifiable: battalion commanders and above rode stocky horses while platoon and company commanders, often fresh-faced youths in their early twenties, were recognizable by their confident manner and the respect accorded them by the ordinary infantrymen. In conversations that Jakob overheard, the troops invariably referred to themselves and others as *chan shih*, a term meaning "fighter" or "warrior," and he noticed that they never used the expression *ping*, the faintly contemptuous Chinese word for the ill-famed looting, raping soldier of the warlord armies. As they marched and countermarched, they brandished gleaming, newly captured carbines, automatic rifles, and machine guns at one another, drawing attention to the visible British, German, and Amer-

ican markings on them. They laughed like children and called out
gleefully: "Look, comrades, Mr. Chiang, the Red Army's faithful
arms supplier, has made another fine delivery."

Any lingering suspicion Jakob might have had that the Red Army
was a force of reluctant, resentful soldiers press-ganged into service
had been finally dispelled in those early weeks of the year. Stories
habitually told by local Kuomintang officials in Chentai that the
Communists recruited their troops by surrounding a village and
cutting off the ears of any man who refused to join them finally lost
their last vestiges of credibility. With scarcely an exception, the
young Red Army men in Jakob's hearing chattered excitedly about
fighting for their homes and their land and ultimately defending their
country against Japan.

If further proof had been needed of the marchers' devotion to their
cause, it would have been provided by the ragged ten- and eleven-
year-old beggars and orphans who were recruited to serve as Young
Vanguards in every township through which the column passed.
Racing endlessly back and forth along the column, these scrawny,
grinning Chinese boys carried messages and medicines, fetched water
and fuel, and took down cottage doors to make beds for the soldiers
at overnight stops. Dressed in oversized caps and captured Kuomintang greatcoats reaching to their ankles, they did the work of
unpaid orderlies with unflagging energy and enthusiasm. They were
referred to affectionately by the troops as Little Red Devils and some
of the longer-serving boys bore their share of ugly wounds. Even
under fire Jakob had seen the Little Red Devils carrying out their
duties with the same roguish cheerfulness, striving to outdo in visible
displays of courage the troops who were only a few years their senior.
During the quiet marches after dark, their piping voices rose an
octave or two above those of the troops as they joined discordantly
in the songs, striding manfully alongside the units they served.
Whenever the march continued deep into the night, they stumbled
often with weariness and sometimes fell asleep in a heap at the side
of the route. On these occasions the troops would swing them up
onto their shoulders and carry them pickaback until the column
finally bivouacked.

As the way up the high mountainside steepened, half a dozen
Little Red Devils marching with the guards' unit began clutching at
the grass and bushes beside the track to make the climb easier. When
two mounted officers moved past them, several of the Little Red

Devils, with shouts of delight, seized the horses' tails and clung on, borrowing the animals' strength, with the good-humored approval of their riders, to haul themselves upward. But before long the rough track gave way to a bare rock face cut with steps waist-high to the Little Red Devils and they had to let go of the horses and scramble up the precipice on all fours. The rocky ascent became so steep that Jakob could see only the soles of the straw sandals of the prisoner ahead of him, and the singing died away as the troops began to grunt and gasp with the exertion of climbing.

Progress slowed to a crawl and delays became frequent as the steps grew narrower. Then one of the officer's horses stumbled above them, throwing its rider, and the animal's wildly thrashing body crashed back down the rock face, narrowly missing Jakob and his guards. It came to rest somewhere in the darkness far below and the agonized squealing of the dying horse rang eerily up the mountainside. Immediately orders echoed down the column telling the marchers to halt and sleep until first light. The weary men sank onto the narrow ledges of rock where they stood, wrapping the padded quilts from their packs about themselves. Jakob, who now carried his own sparse belongings in a bundle slung over his shoulder, followed suit, folding a blanket on the rock shelf and curling up on it with a thin quilt about his shoulders.

Within moments the steep mountainsides all around him were transformed. Every torch was extinguished and the fiery coils of the long military "dragon" melted without trace into the shadows of the slopes. Clouds drifting in front of the crescent moon cut off its feeble light and soon total darkness cloaked the Taloushan. But despite the cold, Jakob fell asleep immediately and slept fitfully until he was awakened by a long, chilling scream.

It rang hauntingly through the thin, frosty air of the mountains and Jakob sat bolt upright on the rock ledge, shivering and peering down into the blackness beneath him. In his mind's eye the terrible image of Felicity's last moments reappeared with great vividness: she was bent over the tree stump in her drab brown dress, her slender white neck bared beneath the falling broadsword of the executioner, and the scream seemed to be an awful echo of her dying cry. As he stared into the dark valley, the scream rang out again. It was shorter this time, ending abruptly, and Jakob wondered if the fallen horse had died among the rocks below and its last squeals of agony had wakened him.

Looking around he saw that up and down the precipitous path other men, awakened by the cold, had begun to light small fires. They squatted around these little tussocks of flame, murmuring to one another in low voices and looking up apprehensively at the ominous peaks towering over them. The black silence beyond the flickering globes of light seemed to thicken and press in around the marchers, and as though sensing this, they drew closer together around the fires.

Jakob squatted on his haunches on the narrow rock step, gazing at the comforting flames and longing for dawn to break. Once or twice his head fell forward for a moment as sleep overtook him but the memory of the scream that had awakened him so frighteningly jerked him back to consciousness again each time. When a tall Young Vanguard clad in pale, obviously looted cloth appeared at the top of the crag and began descending toward him past the spluttering fires, Jakob watched him idly, wondering what errand he might be making at that hour. As the boy came nearer, his flimsy clothing fluttered loosely about his slender body and it was then that Jakob saw that the firelight was reflecting on spotless, peach-colored gingham.

In the same moment he saw that the boy wore no cap, that his hair was not black and short but fell about his face in soft brown waves, and Felicity, when he recognized her, was not distraught and agonized as she had been at the moment of her death: she was smiling gently as she had done on that magical day in Peking when she had worn the peach gingham dress to visit the Pavilion of Eternal Spring with him at dawn. She came unhesitatingly down the stairway of rock, stepping lightly over the sharp stones until she stood before him, whole, pure, and aglow with the youthful inner radiance she had possessed when they had first met in Shanghai. Her face was calm, her expression faintly wistful but filled too with sympathy and concern. Her arms were bare, and her long, delicate hands hung relaxed at her sides, but she made no effort to reach out in his direction. Instead she stood motionless on the step above, smiling at him.

"Felicity!" Jakob breathed her name in an awed whisper, feeling elation surge through him. "Felicity!"

He wanted to stretch out and touch her but he found himself incapable of movement. For several seconds she stood and gazed down at him, her tender expression seeming wordlessly to say everything while saying nothing. Then, still smiling wistfully, she turned from him and was gone.

For an instant Jakob was engulfed by a sense of loss more devastating than he had felt at Paoshan; then this renewed feeling of grief gave way amost at once to an even greater sense of exhilaration. A tangible feeling of Felicity's presence remained which seemed to defy the finality of that gruesome execution at Paoshan and it was as though brilliant sunshine for a moment coursed through his veins, intoxicating him and making him heady with its warmth and purity. Not daring to move, he continued to crouch, spellbound, on the freezing mountainside, staring into the blackness of the valley. Inside his head he told himself again and again that he must have been dreaming, although he felt certain that he had been awake.

The small fires still burned up and down the stairway of hewn rock and the Red Army men's hushed voices carried clearly on the cold air. Beyond the spheres of light cast by the fires the dark, palpable silence of the mountains continued to hold them fast in its embrace, and when the rope that still hung down his back tightened suddenly, Jakob turned in surprise and looked up into the face of the young guard he had rescued from the Hsiang River. His left arm was still protected in a sling and although his face showed no flicker of sympathy, when he spoke, his voice had lost its former edge of malice.

"Come with me," he said curtly, jerking the rope and pulling Jakob to his feet. "I have orders to escort you to General Headquarters."

2

Crouched beside a charcoal brazier which only half illuminated the stone-floored inner room of a ruined mountaintop temple, Mei-ling opened a captured tin of first aid materials and took out a clean wad of cotton. Dipping it into a bowl of sugared water that she had warmed on the brazier, she held the cotton to her baby's mouth, so that he could suck the liquid from it. But the feverish infant struggled convulsively in her arms, wailing and coughing by turns, and Mei-ling unbuttoned her tunic and opened it to the waist. A bottle of honey stood on one of two plank beds set up beside the brazier, and seating herself, she took up the scrap of cotton again, dipped it in the opened bottle and smeared honey on her bared breasts to sweeten them.

When Mei-ling pressed the baby to her, he quieted to suck at the wild honey and she relaxed and closed her eyes, surrendering herself to the quiet exquisiteness of the sensation. But the infant remained content for only a minute or so: then he began to struggle again, wailing more loudly than before. His pallid skin glistened with perspiration and although she tried to hold him firmly, he thrashed his arms and legs repeatedly. She gazed perplexedly at the baby for a moment, then patiently picked up a new fragment of cotton and began to smear more honey onto her breasts. While she was doing this a General Headquarters bodyguard led Jakob into the inner room.

"The Outside Country prisoner has been brought here as Comrade Hua Fu commanded!"

"Comrade Hua Fu has been called away to a meeting."

Mei-ling spoke without looking up and there was a noticeable hardness in her tone when she uttered the Chinese fighting name for the German Comintern adviser. Turning her back on the men in the doorway, she dipped the cloth in the honey bottle again and resumed her task. When she had finished and the baby was nuzzled quietly against her, she looked up to find the tall, bearded figure of the young English missionary staring at her from the shadows. His hands were tied in front of him and in the half-darkness she saw only his pale, intent eyes and the glint of the fire on his fair hair.

"I know nothing of Comrade Hua Fu's orders," she said calmly. "What were they?"

"He commanded us to fetch the Outside Country prisoner without delay." The young bodyguard shifted uncomfortably at the missionary's shoulder and behind him Jakob's own guard hovered uncertainly in the doorway. "He said it was very urgent."

"Very well. Leave him here with me. You may wait outside."

The General Headquarters soldier motioned Jakob's guard ahead of him and together they left the inner room. Jakob, whose feet had also been hobbled with rope so that he could not run or move quickly, remained standing in the shadows, unable to take his eyes from Mei-ling. In the dull red glow of the brazier, her face and her naked shoulders shone with the soft luminescence of polished amber. Her hair hung undressed about her cheeks and beneath classically arched brows her almond-shaped eyes were as black as jet in the firelight. She looked steadily at him, her expression neither indifferent nor curious, and in the stillness of the ancient mountain temple he suddenly felt that he was gazing not just at the calm, oval face of Mei-ling but at the eternal, tantalizing image of Oriental beauty itself. The baby slumbered fretfully in her lap and her honeyed breasts were still partially visible inside her half-closed Red Army tunic, but she gave no sign that she was aware of her seminakedness. When the baby woke and began to wail once more, a woman orderly in cap and belted uniform appeared silently from another chamber of the temple and Mei-ling handed the child over to her without fuss.

"Is your baby ill?" Jakob spoke hesitantly in Chinese, watching Mei-ling refasten the buttons of her tunic and slip a broad leather belt about her waist.

"The baby's dying," replied Mei-ling in a resigned voice. "It's only a matter of time."

"That's very sad."

"Perhaps."

Mei-ling's manner was coolly impersonal but there was no sign of the kind of hostility Jakob was accustomed to receive from his guards. Her unemotional detachment about the child puzzled him but he assumed she must be hiding her feelings. "I'm sorry . . . that I've intruded here," he said haltingly. "I don't know why I've been summoned."

"There's no need to apologize. It will become clear when the child's father returns. He'll be here soon."

Mei-ling moved a blackened cooking pot onto the brazier and began to stir it. Close over the fire, her face became a copper-bronze color which to Jakob made her beauty seem unreal, something akin to the overemphatic, painted faces of the mud gods and goddesses that appeared to be watching and listening from shadowy niches ranged around the temple walls. Again the tranquillity of the ancient chamber gave him an uncanny feeling that he was living in a waking dream, on some plane raised above mundane reality: encountering the Chinese girl in the temple ruin among the peaks so soon after the inexplicable experience of seeing the half-waking vision of Felicity on the freezing mountainside seemed to imbue the encounter with an ethereal sense of fantasy.

"Have you forgotten that we met on a ship three years ago?" asked Jakob at last.

Mei-ling did not reply or look up, but although she ignored the question, her manner mutely confirmed her recollection of their meeting in 1931. Keeping her eyes averted, she went on stirring the pot on the charcoal brazier, concentrating all her attention on the movement of the ladle in her hand. When at last she did speak, her tone was neutral.

"How long have you been a prisoner?"

"I was taken at Chentai in early November. My mission house was looted. I was marched to Paoshan with my family." Jakob watched Mei-ling's face carefully but she showed no sign of having prior knowledge. "My wife was beheaded on the hillside outside Paoshan."

In speaking for the first time of the terrible events at Paoshan, Jakob's voice broke slightly and Mei-ling looked up in surprise. A hint of compassion showed fleetingly in her expression — then she turned away and a silence fell in the room, broken only by the occasional spluttering of the coals in the brazier.

"If you're cold, come nearer to the fire."

Jakob shuffled forward two or three paces, then stopped. "I was put on trial before a mob at Paoshan. They found me 'guilty' of spying on the Red Army. Aren't you frightened such an evil 'imperialist spy' might harm you?"

There was only a hint of irony in the inflections of his speech but she did not react to it. Instead she fetched a small bowl and a spoon and carried them to the brazier. "I've made ginseng stew. Eat some. It will keep out the cold."

She ladled steaming liquid into the bowl and turned to find Jakob had lifted his bound wrists in front of him. "You'll have to ask the guards if I'm allowed to eat."

Without a word she put down the bowl, took up a knife, and sawed through the plaited ropes that circled his wrists. In cutting his bonds she came close enough for him to smell the female musk of her body mingled with the faint, sweet aroma of honey, but when she put the ginseng stew in his hands she continued to avoid his eyes and moved away to seat herself on the plank bed again.

"I'm very grateful for your kindness," said Jakob quietly and he inhaled the pungent steam rising from the bowl for a moment before dipping his spoon hungrily into the stew. "This smells very good."

For some time he ate in silence, relishing the hot, tasty food after more than three months of harsh survival rations, and Mei-ling made no attempt to interrupt. When he had finished, she took the bowl from him and washed it in a wooden bucket in a corner of the room.

"Why were you spared?" she asked, speaking over her shoulder.

"It was an accident . . . my wife was taken first . . ." Jakob's voice faltered and died away. When he resumed, his tone was bitter. "A Kuomintang unit arrived in the nick of time — and afterward your comrades decided I was worth more alive than dead. The price for our freedom was set at one hundred and fifty thousand dollars. It's still the asking price for me. I think that's the real reason why I was taken captive in the first place — for money."

"That isn't true." Mei-ling's eyes grew bright although her manner remained calm and controlled. "Perhaps the action at Paoshan was hotheaded — but the Red Army takes missionaries prisoner only to show the world that China will no longer allow outsiders to bring foreign doctrines to our country."

She stood up and moved nearer to the charcoal brazier. Her eyes shone in the firelight and she stood close enough to Jakob for him to detect again the natural scents of her body. Instantly, memories of his fevered dreams of her tumbled through his mind and he took an instinctive pace toward her.

"Mei-ling, I dreamed of you many times after we met on the ship."

He spoke in a low tone, gazing wonderingly at her. The words had sprung to his lips involuntarily and he felt suddenly confused. The rush of elation which the waking-dream vision of Felicity had induced an hour earlier remained strong in him but suddenly he distrusted his still-tingling senses.

"And perhaps I'm still dreaming. I can't really tell."

Mei-ling, taken aback, stared at him in her turn, her expression puzzled and surprised.

"In the dreams you were always so real, but here reality seems like a dream. . . ."

His voice trailed off into a half-whisper and he looked up through the open rafters above one of the grinning god-idols. Against the starry predawn sky, the dark bulk of a neighboring crag reared over the temple. The thin crescent moon had reappeared to settle for the moment on the shoulder of the mountain and within the irregular frame of the roof rafters, nature seemed to have painted a picture of unearthly simplicity and power. Somewhere in the deep silence a brook was gurgling and Jakob fancied suddenly he could again smell the night scent of winter plum blossom on the still air.

Mei-ling was standing very still beside the charcoal brazier, watching him, and he saw a light in her eyes which sent his memory racing back to that moment at the height of the storm on board the *Tomeko Maru*. Then she had worn an embroidered silk dress which emphasized the delicacy of her high cheekbones and the soft tint of her skin; now, in the coarse, faded cotton uniform of the Red Army, burning revolutionary conviction gave her beauty a more elemental, passionate quality. But as before, the elusive shadow of a smile seemed to shimmer in her dark eyes and he was seized by the same instinctive feeling that something profound had been communicated between them.

On an impulse, Jakob shuffled forward suddenly toward the fire. Mei-ling, surprised, drew back a pace from him, but he stretched his hand past her to pluck a single live coal from the glowing brazier. He held it tight between his fingertips for two or three seconds, sucking in his breath fiercely between his teeth. Then he dropped the coal and held up his singed, blackened fingers for them both to see.

"This time, at least, Mei-ling," he said gently, "I know I'm not dreaming!"

3

Mei-ling stared at his burned fingers in consternation. She seemed puzzled by his action but some indefinable quality in her expression suggested to Jakob that she had an intuitive understanding of what had made him do it.

"I felt the same way when I saw you riding with the Red Army leaders above the Hsiang River," explained Jakob. "I didn't know then whether I could believe my eyes or not. Often my dreams of you have been just as vivid."

"I realized I knew you only when I heard my name called," said Mei-ling.

"Of course — you had no cause to remember me."

Mei-ling looked away into the fire, as if regretting immediately an indiscretion. During the silence that followed, the burning charcoal in the brazier shifted, releasing a little shower of sparks. In the sudden dance of firelight, Jakob could easily have imagined that the gaudily painted faces of the mud gods were stiffening and growing more intent in an effort to overhear what was being said by the flesh-and-blood occupants of their hall of worship.

"My wrists were freed the next day for the first time since I was taken captive. Were you responsible?"

"I told my brother I'd seen you. He's an officer in the Red Cadres Regiment — perhaps he gave the order."

"Please thank him for me."

"I can't — he was wounded at the Hsiang. He was swept downstream but luckily the current washed him ashore and a patrol found him."

"Where is he now?"

"He's traveling in one of the hospital carts in the transport column."

Mei-ling removed a pan of boiling water from the brazier to prepare a pot of fragrant yellow tea. After filling two small bowls, she handed one to Jakob and he sipped the liquid reflectively.

"A Frenchman was watching you talk to a deck coolie when we first met on board the *Tomeko Maru*," said Jakob. "He suspected you were Communists. Were you and your brother already revolutionaries then?"

Mei-ling gazed into the glowing brazier, holding her tea bowl in both hands. "I've been a revolutionary, I think, since I was nine years old."

"But I thought you said you came from a rich family."

"Yes, I do — that's why I became a revolutionary. Our family's wealth was first built up by my grandfather. He was a comprador for the British trading houses when they were building the foreign concession. British businessmen paid him large sums to hire wharf coolies but he imitated the capitalists and rewarded his laborers with a pittance. He recruited coolies for the Dutch colonists and shipped off thousands to die in the East Indies. He even joined the British in trafficking opium. He exploited the Chinese working people in every way he could to turn their sweat into wealth for his own family. But worst of all he dealt in *mu tsai* — that's what made me a revolutionary!"

"But surely *mu tsai* are family servants, aren't they?" asked Jakob with a frown.

"No, in truth they're slave girls — daughters of southern peasants too poor to bring them up. First they're sold to landlords to help pay extortionate land taxes and the landlords resell them as servants and concubines for the degenerate rich in Shanghai and Canton. In reality, their owners hold the power of life and death over them. All our household servants when I was young were *mu tsai* slaves — although my grandmother preferred to call them 'adopted daughters.' "

Mei-ling paused and sipped her tea, her beautiful face clouding with distaste at the memory.

"One of our servants had a daughter, Little Kwei, who without anyone's knowing became my playmate. Every afternoon we met secretly and played around the lotus pools in the southern courtyard, daydreaming of what we would do when we grew up. Then one day, to my horror, Little Kwei's face was powdered and painted and she was put up for sale by my grandmother along with ten other very young *mu tsai*. I hid in the room to watch and saw fat Chinese millionaires in flowing silk gowns drinking tea as they inspected their purchases. They made Little Kwei take down her trousers to show them her legs and her body. They prodded and touched her everywhere. They even scraped the powder from her face to inspect her skin. When an old man with a leering face asked her if she wanted to be his concubine, she nodded as she had been commanded, without looking at him, and burst into tears. She was still sobbing as he led her away. . . ."

A sad expression stole across Mei-ling's face and she sat quite still, immersed in her thoughts, until the faint sound of her baby crying in another part of the temple brought her back to the present.

"It wasn't until much later that I realized that even for women like me, life was little better than slavery. All the future held was an arranged marriage to the idle son of some Chinese millionaire of our class. There would be no right to work or inherit property. But most of all, it was the sight of Little Kwei sobbing that first sowed the seeds of revolution in me. I began to write childish stories of imaginary warriors who fought their way across the land to free all the unhappy little *mu tsai*. At the age of nine I began to want to change China. Now, because of the Red Army, those childhood fantasies are beginning to come true."

Deeply moved, Jakob drew a long breath, and for a minute or more neither of them spoke. "Perhaps we have something in common after all," he said at last. "I began to dream about 'saving' China when I was ten. I'd heard that Chinese people believed blue-eyed Englishmen could see three feet into the ground — and this helped them to discover gold. In my imagination I saw myself riding through China, discovering gold everywhere and fighting off great hordes of bandits so that I could give the gold to the poor people."

"And now the 'gold' you've come to give us is Christianity?"

"Perhaps that's one way of putting it."

"Christianity and all religions are fool's gold. The Red Army is the only real gold that can help the poor of China." Mei-ling glanced slowly around at the lurid mud idols placed in their niches in the hope they would promote fertility and good harvests in the region. "None of these gods has ever rescued the poor in the past."

"But killing people you hate won't change everything either," said Jakob softly. "Nothing will really change until the hearts of men are changed."

Mei-ling poured more tea into their bowls and seated herself with a quiet dignity beside the brazier once more. "Your Christian way would take too long — and it might never succeed. China needs to take its courage in its own hands now."

"You've shown great courage yourself in making this march with a sick child," said Jakob.

"I'm marching because I want to serve the revolution," said Mei-ling simply. "I work as an administrative cadre on the staff of Military Commissioner Chou En-lai. But there are other women who are much braver. Chu Teh's wife fights with her husband's units and the wife of Mao Tse-tung has just given birth to a baby on the march — although her body is full of shrapnel from a bomb blast."

"Is the foreign adviser *your* husband?"

Mei-ling looked up sharply. "No, he's not."

"Will you marry him later?"

Mei-ling held Jakob's gaze steadily. "No."

"What will you do if the baby survives?"

"There's almost no chance of that." In the firelight Mei-ling's face became regretful and sad. "Perhaps sometimes I've let my ideals blind me. The idea of other countries helping China to throw off its chains seemed more realistic in Paris and London than it does now."

"Why?"

"Here we're cut off from the outside world. No foreign help can reach us in this wilderness. We're fighting alone now for China's future . . ." Her voice sank to a whisper and her expression indicated clearly that she was equating her own personal experience with the wider plight of the marchers. "Perhaps it's only right that this child shouldn't survive."

The hint of a tear glistened in the firelight and Jakob could see in the set of Mei-ling's slender shoulders her female vulnerability as well as her determined strength, and he felt himself moved to compassion.

"There's another experience we perhaps share, Mei-ling," he said in a gentle voice. "I've already lost an infant daughter. On the morning my wife was killed we left our baby hidden in a stable in an effort to save her life. I was never able to return to fetch her. . . ."

Mei-ling absorbed the information without replying. She sat staring into the fire and a silence lengthened between them. When finally she spoke, her voice was pensive and she did not turn to face him. "How did I appear in your dreams? As a traditional daughter of feudal China? Dressed in a high-collared gown, embroidering silk tapestries, and writing exquisite characters on a scroll?"

"The dreams were always confused . . . and strange . . ." Jakob stumbled over his words, fearing she might somehow read in his manner something of the true nature of his dreams. "They were vivid — but bore very little relation to everyday reality."

"Why do you think I appeared in your dreams?"

"I don't know . . ." Jakob hesitated, groping for words to explain something he had neither understood himself nor allowed himself to think of too deeply. "When we met on the ship I could hardly take my eyes off you. . . . I'd never seen anybody as beautiful as you before. And you played the piano in the storm with such composure. For a time I think I hoped there might be things in life we could share. . . ."

"Perhaps now that you've seen the reality in a dirty uniform of the Red Army, your dreams will cease."

Framed by her smooth black hair, her face remained as beguiling as ever in the flickering firelight. "You're even more beautiful now," said Jakob involuntarily. "I'll never forget you . . ."

The wailing of the baby became faintly audible again and Mei-ling stood up. At the same moment the unfamiliar sound of booted feet on the flagstoned floors of the temple reached their ears and

Jakob turned to see a fair-haired European entering the inner room. He wore a faded, ill-fitting Red Army uniform of gray-blue cotton and a soft cap with a red star above its peak. The cheap uniform gave the man a coarse, clumsy look, and his pale Caucasian face seemed incongruous beneath a long peak that until then in Jakob's experience had always shaded yellow-brown Asiatic features. When he removed the cap, Jakob saw that the European's face was damp with malarial perspiration and he was shivering.

"This is the European prisoner you sent for," said Mei-ling in a formal voice. "I've freed his hands in order to give him some food."

Without waiting for a reply, she hurried from the inner room in the direction of the baby's wailing, leaving Jakob looking into the sickly white face of Otto Braun, the undercover Comintern revolutionist whom his Chinese comrades had named Hua Fu.

4

"You and I are the only two Europeans among fifty or sixty thousand Chinese, Herr Kellner," said Braun, speaking English in the hard, guttural accents of his native country. "That is why I've had you brought here."

The German was sitting hunched on one end of the plank bed nearest the brazier with a blanket pulled around his shoulders. Beads of sweat were visible on his cheeks and forehead but he was still shivering as he gulped down a bowl of the ginseng stew. Square-jawed, with small, watchful blue eyes, a ragged moustache, and big ears that lay flat against his cropped blond head, he was a physically self-confident man in his mid-thirties, but the malaria had given his skin a sallow, waxen appearance and his face was drawn inward in concentric lines that knitted his brows and bunched his lips in an ill-tempered expression.

"I also heard you speak and read Chinese, is that correct?"

Jakob, who still stood beside the brazier, nodded in confirmation. "To work as a missionary in China without practical knowledge of the language would be impossible."

"I've found the language difficult to master," said the German stiffly. "Therefore I work through interpreters."

"I'd agree that Chinese is very difficult to learn."

Jakob watched the man before him carefully as he spoke. He was still puzzled about why he should have been summoned to the General Headquarters in the middle of the night. In contrast to that of the guards and the assistant magistrate, the German's manner was not hostile, merely neutral, and speaking English for the first time in months suddenly seemed to Jakob to mark a turning point in the mental and physical siege he had endured since his capture. He began to hope that he might hear something about his likely release, and the German clearly detected signs of this in his expression.

"I haven't called you here to discuss your own case, Herr Kellner," Braun said flatly. "How the Communists of China administer justice in their country is no concern of mine. You are a prisoner of the Red Army but I would like to ask you as one European to another for some assistance." The German drew an already damp handkerchief from a pocket of his uniform and mopped his sweating face. Around his eyes Jakob could see lines of fatigue and strain, which gave him a gaunt look; despite his confident manner, he was not entirely able to conceal an air of embarrassment.

"I take it you are from Germany," said Jakob respectfully. "May I ask your name?"

"I am German, yes," snapped the Comintern agent. "In China, I'm known as Hua Fu — that is all you need to know. Are you prepared to help?"

"I try to bear witness to God's love for all men in my daily life whatever the circumstances," said Jakob quietly. "I'll help you if I can."

"*Gut, danke!*"

Braun lapsed into his own language in his pleasure at Jakob's acquiescence and smiled fixedly, obviously caring nothing for Jakob's reasons. Reaching inside his uniform tunic, he pulled out a sheaf of papers on which Jakob could see vertical lines of handwritten Chinese characters. Before scrutinizing them, the German rose from the plank bed and crossed to the narrow archway that led into the inner room. Peering into the darkness beyond, he looked this way and that until he was certain they were not being overheard, then he returned and lowered himself wearily onto the bed once more.

"You are to say nothing to your guards or anybody else about why I summoned you here, is that clear?" he said in an undertone. "This is something that will remain confidential between us. You must give me a solemn undertaking."

"I have no reason to defy your wishes."

Braun frowned at Jakob, as though mystified in some way by the simplicity of his answers. Then he dabbed distractedly at his perspiring face again. "How are your guards treating you now, Herr Kellner? Have things improved since we crossed the Hsiang River?"

"My hands were untied at the Hsiang. In Tsunyi I was given some of the provisions looted from the mission — fruit, eggs, milk, tinned tomatoes. The rest and better food helped me recover my strength." The German was leafing abstractedly through the papers on his knee, scarcely listening to his reply, and a sudden suspicion arose in Jakob's mind. "Why do you ask?"

"I overheard Comrade Lu Mei-ling tell her brother she had seen guards ill-treating an English missionary. I gave my opinion to the guard commanders that it might be wise to improve your conditions for the simple reason that a dead hostage has no value." Braun stopped shuffling the papers and lit a candle with a taper. Spreading some of the pages on the other plank bed, he placed the candle beside them and gestured for Jakob to seat himself. "And now one good turn deserves another, Herr Kellner, yes? You would like to translate some Chinese for me, perhaps?"

Comprehension dawned as Jakob took in the German's calculating smile, and he nodded and sat down on the second bed. Leaning close to the papers spread before him, he saw by the light of the candle that the two characters for the name "Hua Fu" had been ringed several times in red wherever they occurred.

"I will be straightforward to help you understand, Herr Kellner," said Braun in a confidential tone. "There were quarrels among the leadership at the meetings in Tsunyi. Very often I could not follow the proceedings because my Chinese interpreter refused to translate for me during heated debates. I was attacked and condemned for things I couldn't understand. Now I've obtained a draft of the minutes of the meetings. I'd like you to translate those passages in which my name is mentioned. Do you understand?"

Jakob nodded again. "I understand."

"First, please, this passage here which refers to the reasons for the Red Army's abandoning its base in the Central Soviet Area."

Jakob bent over the handwritten pages and read carefully through the first few sheets. Beside him Braun began to shake with the intensity of his growing fever and out of the corner of his eye Jakob saw him take out a bottle of quinine tablets and swallow two down. After reading the passages a second time, grappling with Chinese terminology quite different from the Christian Gospels with which he was accustomed to work, Jakob looked up, ready to begin.

"What does the resolution say?" asked the German impatiently, stretching himself on the plank beside the brazier and pulling a blanket up to his chin. "Read it aloud, every word of it!"

"It says that . . . 'in trying to defend the Central Soviet Area, the leadership under Party Secretary Po Ku and foreign adviser Hua Fu made many wholesale errors,' " reported Jakob, reading hesitantly from the text. " 'The Red Army was dispersed to resist attacks from all directions but in the end we were not strong enough to resist attacks from any direction. Hua Fu neglected the strategy of mobile warfare and because of his excessive fear . . . of the Kuomintang blockhouse encirclement . . . the Central Soviet had to be abandoned. . . .' "

Braun cursed softly as he shifted restlessly on his makeshift bed. "Go on, Herr Kellner, go on! What does it say next?"

"It says, 'Comrade Mao Tse-tung pointed out that if better military decisions had been taken, the Central Soviet could have been saved, the Fifth Encirclement could have been broken, and the strength of the Red Army could have been preserved. . . . In Comrade Hua Fu's mind our breakout from the siege was essentially a flight in panic, a house-removal operation, not a resolute fighting operation . . .' "

" 'A flight in panic'!" Braun sat bolt upright. "How dare they distort the truth with such lies? If it was a flight in panic, how is it that the key fighting units of the Red Army are still intact here in Kweichow, a thousand miles away? It's a tissue of lies cooked together to discredit me and the party secretary."

He glared furiously at Jakob as though the missionary himself were responsible, then sank slowly back onto the plank bed, mopping his brow and panting with exertion. Jakob noticed that Braun's eyes were becoming glazed with the fever, and he waited until the German's breathing quieted before resuming.

" 'Certain comrades, and in particular Comrade Hua Fu, displayed dictatorial tendencies and monopolized the work of the Revolutionary Military Commission. Differing views were unheeded or suppressed by all available means. Comrade Hua Fu exploited the authority vested in him by the Communist International and, using the material and technological superiority of Europe as an invisible weapon, abused his position to make a mockery of the Chinese Communist Party's principle of collective leadership. . . .' "

" 'Dictatorial tendencies,' Herr Kellner," whispered Braun hoarsely. "How could one European have developed dictatorial tendencies among a hundred thousand armed Chinese? How could one German adviser who has no formal power of command and no contact with the outside world single-handedly usurp the collective leadership of the Communist Party of China? How could one foreign adviser have done all that without speaking or understanding the Chinese language. . . ?" His head rolled from side to side in delirious anger. "Comrade Mao Tse-tung is trying to disgrace me and reject the help of the Comintern. *He* wants to be a dictator . . ."

The German's voice faded into an incoherent groan and he closed his eyes. A moment later Mei-ling appeared silently beside the plank bed. Bending over him, she mopped his brow with a cloth soaked in cold water. Jakob realized then that she must have been listening from the shadows and he tried to read a reaction in her face, but her features remained blank.

"You'd better leave now," she said quietly to Jakob, speaking over her shoulder. "If he needs you again, you can return when the fever has passed."

Before Jakob could reply she summoned the guards and they led him out of the temple. At the doorway Jakob turned to look back and saw Mei-ling standing motionless beside the prostrate German: a vibrant, glossy-haired figure in the fire-lit cave of darkness, she looked to Jakob like some beautiful spirit-goddess, sent to enchant anew the watching circle of painted mud gods. But from their expressions the Chinese deities seemed to have long since grown weary of the ways of the earthbound world and they gazed down from the niches unmoved and indifferent to her presence among them.

5

From his hiding place in a high gully overlooking a thickly wooded hillside on the Kweichow-Szechuan border, Big Liang watched weary units of the Central Red Army preparing a bivouac beside a rushing stream. A freezing drizzle was falling and the troops were obviously close to exhaustion after marching all day and skirmishing with advance units of Szechuan's most powerful warlord army, which was ranged against them along the southern bank of the Yangtze River. Newly wounded men groaning on stretchers or supported between their comrades were still struggling into the camp, medical orderlies with symbolic red crosses on their satchels were tending the worst afflicted, and many of the troops were treating each other's blistered feet.

Big Liang was crouching among a tall clump of rush grass on which the rain had frozen like slivers of glass, but the keen young eyes of the thirteen-year-old boy missed nothing. Some of the fitter soldiers and Young Vanguards were busy tying squares of looted cloth between the trees to form rough shelters and waterproofing them with strips of oiled paper; others were splitting bamboo to weave into coverings or peeling bark from pine trees to reinforce the roofs of the makeshift awnings. Those lighting fires were having difficulty because of the rain, and more smoke than fire was swirling across the hillside. Squads of Little Red Devils, Big Liang noticed, were also busying themselves digging channels around the bivouacs to drain away the rain.

The rattle and clank of iron cooking pots and pans rang up the hillside as cooks lowered their carrying poles to the ground and set about the task of building stoves, cutting fuel, and boiling water from the stream. One cook, who had staggered into the camp under the heaviest-laden pole, unloaded a small millstone, a sieve, and a winnower, and squatted patiently on the wet ground, grinding a small heap of unhusked rice. A group of Little Red Devils gathered around him, chattering excitedly and husking their own little heaps of the grain between broken shards of roof tiles that they carried in their packs. Some washed meager piles of wild vegetables and Big Liang could see that food supplies were running low.

As always, the activities of the Little Red Devils occupied more of his attention than was strictly necessary, because he found himself fascinated by the uniformed gangs of boys his own age who were always rushing back and forth on seemingly vital errands. Inside his jacket Big Liang carried a peaked Red Army cap with a five-pointed red star that he had picked up from the silent battlefield at the Hsiang River a few days after the fighting. He had occasionally worn the cap to pass himself off as a Young Vanguard when searching close to the column, and every time he spied on the camps he found himself envying their cheerful camaraderie.

The Chinese boy had become practiced at mentally noting all the details of the camps he observed so that he could report back accurately to his father each night. For some two weeks he and Little Liang had been searching anxiously among the different regiments and divisions of the Red Army as they maneuvered back and forth along the mountainous Kweichow-Szechuan border, seeking a way across the Yangtze and onward to the north to link up with troops of the Fourth Front Army. Day and night the two Chinese boys had strained their eyes for a glimpse of the tall, bearded, fair-skinned figure of Pastor Ke — but so far they had seen no sign of him among the tides of marching Chinese faces.

To the young sons of Jakob's cookboy there seemed to be no rhyme or reason to the constant feints, retreats, and forward rushes of the Central Red Army units. Often the boys and their father found themselves tracing and retracing their steps repeatedly as they shadowed the Communist troops through the mountains and valleys a hundred miles south of Chungking. Moving amid the confused manswarms on the ground, they had no way of knowing that Chiang Kai-shek was mustering a great array of anti-Communist forces for yet another new encirclement of the Central Red Army and had issued an edict proclaiming that "the fate of the nation and the Kuomintang depend on bottling up the Reds south of the Yangtze."

In Szechuan, civil war had raged unabated since the last emperor was overthrown, in 1911: half a dozen warlord armies had been fighting for control of the rich province, but Chiang had persuaded the strongest warlord, the provincial governor, to appoint two hundred Kuomintang officers to his regiments to help promote better discipline. These strengthened forces were now barring the Red Army's way north. All three southwestern provinces — Kweichow, Yunnan, and Szechuan — had remained independent fiefdoms, beyond the direct control of the Kuomintang government in Nanking, but their common interest in seeing the Communists defeated had encouraged them to cooperate with Chiang. While the Communists had been resting and hammering out new political and military strategies, the Kweichow provincial armies had regrouped to press northward toward Tsunyi, the Hunan army had begun moving westward again in pursuit, and provincial forces from Kwangsi had also moved, from the southeast, to begin tightening yet another noose around the Central Red Army.

Although they knew nothing of these strategic initiatives, the two sons of Jakob's cookboy were daily becoming more aware of their practical effects. The tempo of the Red Army's movements was increasing, a greater sense of urgency was evident in the actions of all the marchers, casualties were mounting, and signs of fatigue among the troops were again becoming visible. Liang's sons themselves were also growing leg-weary and footsore once more as they trudged long stretches day after day under their father's directions. They had rested after reaching Tsunyi, unable to gain any clue to Pastor Ke's whereabouts in the seething streets of the old town, where almost daily they saw batches of landlords tethered to execution posts and shot. This brief respite from their dogged shadowing of the Red Army had refreshed them physically, but now they were again beginning to feel the strain of hurrying on day after day through the mountains. Caught up once more in the tensions of the marching columns, they were searching with a growing sense of desperation for the tall figure of the English missionary, who had eluded them for so long.

Among the massed ranks of the Red Army men Big Liang had never once so far caught sight of a civilian prisoner. From time to time he had seen groups of captured Kuomintang troops in their distinctive khaki uniforms with shoulder flashes depicting a white sun on a square of blue sky. Sometimes they still wore their steel helmets and often they were roped together in long lines running behind a Red Army man's horse. Whenever he saw groups of military prisoners, Big Liang obeyed his father's strict instructions to follow the unit guarding them until he was sure there were no civilians attached, and it had been the sight of forty or fifty listless Kuomintang captives standing on the edge of the bivouac beneath him that had caused him to stop and hide in the high gully.

The prisoners of war stood dejected and ignored around a long string of pack mules to which they had been roped all day. They were still tied at the neck to one another and from his hiding place

Big Liang made himself inspect every one of the captured soldiers in turn, shifting his eyes slowly from man to man and scrutinizing every face minutely. A guard commander was moving among them and Big Liang heard him bark out orders, whereupon all the bound prisoners sank gratefully to the wet ground to rest. Again, to be doubly sure, Big Liang cast his gaze slowly over the seated men and when he was satisfied that there were no non-Chinese prisoners among them, he turned away on all fours, preparing to creep off down the gully without being seen.

It was in the moment of turning that he caught sight of a bedraggled group of half a dozen civilian figures; dressed mainly in black, brimless caps and the kind of padded ankle-length gowns habitually worn by landlords and mandarins, the first group of nonmilitary prisoners the boy had seen was standing behind the captured soldiers and had become visible only because the soldiers had been ordered to sit down. The clothing of all the civilians was worn and travel-stained, and most had their hands tied. Only one among them appeared to be unbound, although the boy could see that a long rope dangled down his back from a kind of shoulder harness. But it was not just the freedom of that prisoner's hands that attracted Big Liang's attention. The unbound man, who was taller than the average Chinese, was wearing a wide conical hat of woven bamboo to keep off the rain, and to Big Liang's great delight, when he removed the hat, he revealed himself to be the possessor of the same strange, straw-colored hair as Pastor Ke! Most of the man's face was concealed by a thick beard the same color as his hair and although his skin was obviously pale, from where he was hiding, Big Liang could not be sure he was really looking at Pastor Ke. But the resemblance was strong and the Chinese boy crawled back into the clump of tall grass with a fast-beating heart to keep the little group of civilian prisoners under close observation.

For some minutes the prisoners remained standing where they were, obviously awaiting orders. The Chinese civilians hung their heads, their shoulders sagged, and they eyed their captors apprehensively as they came and went around them. Only the European held himself upright on the banks of the stream, emanating a sense of calm dignity despite his disheveled appearance. When several guards divided up the group and herded the Chinese toward a separate bivouac, the European walked quietly ahead of his own two guards without any urging; even when one of his captors jerked roughly at the dangling rope to halt him beside a small shelter, he still managed to retain his composure. With coarse shouts and gestures the guards commanded their prisoner to enter the shelter and one guard squatted on a rock a few feet away, cradling his rifle on his knees, watching him with narrowed, intent eyes.

But the European did not obey immediately: instead he unslung the bundle of belongings from his shoulder and lowered himself to his knees beside the tattered awning. Pressing his palms together in front of his chest, he bent his head reverently to pray and in his place of concealment at the top of the ridge, Big Liang had to stop himself from leaping into the air with a loud whoop of triumph. Seeing the man with the straw-colored hair assume the attitude of prayer removed the last shadow of doubt from his mind. After many hundreds of weary miles their long search was finally over! Taking one last lingering look at the kneeling missionary to reassure himself, Big Liang bounded away up the wooded hillside in a crouching run, frantic to convey the good news to his father.

6

"I see you've got a foreign devil for a prisoner," said Big Liang, sidling alongside a pock-faced Young Vanguard boy dressed in an outsize Kuomintang greatcoat that overhung his hands and brushed the ground around his ankles. "What's he like?"

"He comes from a country forty thousand *li* away across the sea. All the people there have long noses and red or yellow hair like him." The Young Vanguard spoke without pausing in his task of gathering fallen pine branches for the campfires; his voice was partly contemptuous but also a little awestruck. "He says he has an invisible friend who looks after him all the time. That's who he prays to."

"Did he tell you that?"

"Yes. He calls his friend Yeh-su. He says Yeh-su used to make sick people well again just by touching them. I think he's cockeyed."

Big Liang stooped and added another branch to the growing bundle of wood in his own arms. His faded Red Army cap from the Hsiang River battlefield was pulled well forward over his face, and he spoke gruffly in an offhand manner as though his interest in the foreigner was only superficial. "Why is he a prisoner?"

"He's a spy for the Kuomintang traitors and the foreign armies who want to invade China. His crazy stories about his magician Yeh-su are just an excuse to travel deep into China to spy on us."

"Will he be killed?"

"I expect so. The Red Army has demanded a big payment for his freedom. But nobody will pay it." The pock-faced boy laughed jeeringly. "Not even his invisible friend Yeh-su, who's supposed to be the foreigners' Son of Heaven."

"I'm glad it's not me in the shoes of the Big Nose." Big Liang laughed in his turn, glancing toward the row of deserted mud-walled houses at the foot of the hill where he had seen the guards quartering their captives half an hour earlier. The fair-haired figure of Pastor Ke was visible, seated before the doorway of one cottage, resting from the day's march, and Big Liang's mind raced, trying to think how he might pass him the note written by his father that was burning a hole in a pocket of his wadded jacket. Since first spotting the missionary, he and his brother and father had been shadowing the group of civilian prisoners for two days, studying their movements and watching for a chance to try to make secret contact with him. When at the end of the second day his father had seen the Young Vanguard messboys, buglers, and messengers fanning out across the hill above the mountain village to gather firewood, he had urged his son to mingle among them and try to get into the camp. One of the Little Red Devils had asked which unit he was from, but Big Liang had mumbled and pointed over the hill toward another Central Red Army regiment camped nearby; to his relief, his reply had not been questioned.

"At least he's not a coward, like the landlords and local despots," said the boy as he turned back toward the village with his arms full of firewood. "He's been beaten with bamboo canes — a hundred stripes — and didn't cry out once. And he dived into the Hsiang to rescue one of his guards. Nothing seems to really frighten him. He says he's not afraid because he knows Yeh-su is always there beside him."

"Is his nose really very long?" asked Big Liang, turning deliberately down the hillside beside the boy, carrying his own bundle of sticks. "I've never seen a foreign devil close up."

"Yes — as big as this mountain." The Young Vanguard grinned mischievously and nodded toward the crest of the hill where a jagged outcrop of granite reared upward to a point. "And his eyes are really strange too — blue, just like the sky. Come on! I'll show you. He's sitting outside that cottage, look. We'll run past and I'll drop some of my sticks so you can get a good look at his nose."

Scarcely daring to breathe lest he should undo his good fortune, Big Liang broke into a trot behind the boy and followed him down to the village. The mud of the track between the cottages was rutted and frozen hard, and the patter of their feet seemed unnaturally loud in the late afternoon stillness. As they approached the doorway outside which Jakob was resting under the watchful eyes of a sentry, Liang hardly dared look ahead in case the missionary recognized him and called out. He had already decided what he would do, and when the Young Vanguard let a few sticks slip to the ground outside the cottage, Liang deliberately tripped over him, spilling the whole of his own armful of branches at Jakob's feet. As he scrambled up, Big Liang's face reddened naturally in his anxiety and he felt his heart race when he saw the missionary rise from his seat to help collect the fallen firewood. The Young Vanguard at his side, red-faced too, called his apologies to the guard, who started toward them, shouting and gesticulating. In the confusion Big Liang moved close to Jakob and tugged from his pocket the slip of paper that he had folded into a small square. In the act of reaching out to take the sticks that Jakob had retrieved, Liang pressed the square of paper surreptitiously into the missionary's right palm, then mumbled an apology and sped away, followed by the pock-faced boy.

"You clumsy turtle," hissed the Young Vanguard, "why didn't you look where you were going?"

"I'm sorry — I tripped!" gasped Big Liang, grinning widely in his relief. "But you were right. The nose of the foreign devil is truly enormous."

"I told you it was as big as the mountain, didn't I?" chuckled the Young Vanguard — then he burst out laughing and they ran on together down the frozen street, giggling uproariously.

Outside the mud-walled cottage Jakob stood clutching the folded scrap of paper in his right hand, watching mystified as the two Young Vanguards scampered away into the growing dusk. He had recognized one of the boys, the one with the pockmarked face. He remembered once trying to explain something of Christianity to him in answer to his questions when he had been working around his quarters. But the other, taller boy, who wore a large cap pulled down over his eyes, was strange to him. He knew he had not seen him around the camp or the marching column before, and yet he had felt some impression of familiarity when the boy came close. Giving up the puzzle, Jakob glanced about him to make sure none of the guards had noticed anything pass between himself and the anonymous boy. Then, turning his back on the sentry guarding him, he opened his palm and unfolded the square of cheap rice paper.

As soon as his eye fell on the handwritten note, Jakob recognized the clumsy Chinese characters. The hours he had spent trying to teach his illiterate cookboy to write at the Chentai mission had made him very familiar with the limitations of Liang's hand, and even before he absorbed the meaning of the words, a tremor of excitement ran through him. By the time he had deciphered the poorly made symbols, his pulse was racing.

"Pastor Ke, your baby daughter is safe," said the note. "We will wait with her at the top of the hill behind the big rock tonight. Try to escape. We will help you get away. Liang."

7

Lying on the floor of beaten earth in the mud-walled cottage, Jakob could see the granite crest of the hill clearly in the frosty moonlight. It was visible through the open door, looming over the shoulder of the guard who sat silhouetted on a bench in the doorway with a rifle at his side. Since nightfall, Jakob had gazed up at the crag hour after hour with a growing sense of desperation. He strained his eyes and ears constantly for the slightest sign of movement on the hilltop, but he could detect nothing and had to content himself with imagining his cookboy, Liang, crouched among the shadowy rocks, nursing as best he could the tiny baby that Jakob had long ago given up for dead.

It was already ten o'clock and the elation he had felt on learning that his infant daughter was alive and unharmed had turned into an agonizing ache that she was so near to him but still tantalizingly beyond his reach. Ever since he had read the note, thrust so unexpectedly into his hand just before dusk, he had cudgeled his brain for some way of diverting his guards' attention so that he might try to escape. But circumstances had been against him: because there was so little cover for the troops in the area, they had crowded into the village cottages. The cold earth floor around Jakob was covered with bedrolls, and a dozen or more Red Army soldiers were sprawled on them, some already asleep and snoring, others murmuring quietly to one another. The door had been removed from its hinges to make a plank bed and two other men had spread their padded quilts on a table in the corner of the simple room.

Outside the doorway the duty guard sat on the bench, swinging his legs back and forth and turning frequently to stare into the cottage. While feigning sleep himself, Jakob opened his eyes every few minutes to peer hopefully at the guard, but he showed no sign of dozing or leaving his post. While lying prone in the darkness, Jakob had several times prayed hard for help, but as the tense minutes ticked by nothing disturbed the calm order of the night. Then in the distance Jakob heard the faint sound of a bugle being blown. A minute or so later its high, clear tones were repeated from a nearer valley and the soldiers who were still awake stopped talking and sat up straight to listen. When, after a pause, another bugle sounded the same distinctive trill of notes from close by on their own hillside, the soldiers began grumbling and shaking their comrades into wakefulness.

"Roll up your blankets quickly if you want to take them with you," yelled the young guard, leaping up from his seat outside the door. "That's the signal to assemble and march."

As Jakob struggled wearily to his feet, his heart sank. The order to begin yet another forced night march seemed to have jeopardized any remaining chance he might have had of escaping. In the darkness and confusion all contact with Liang might be broken and his baby daughter would be lost to him again. As though to fulfill his gloomy expectations, the guard at that moment came into the cottage and seized the rope hanging from Jakob's shoulders to drag him outside.

All around the mud-brick houses the troops were hurriedly loading ammunition boxes onto the pack mules of the supply unit that was accompanying the prisoners. Within minutes the section of the column camped in the village had formed up and was marching toward a broad, level field at the foot of the hill. Other units were streaming down through the surrounding valleys to assemble there too, and the tramp of feet and hooves filled the night. Clouds were beginning to obscure the moon and Jakob looked about him desperately, seeking some avenue of escape. His young guard, however, as though reading his thoughts, held his shoulder rope firmly and gave him no opportunity to stray from the file of military and civilian prisoners. The shouted orders of officers echoed and re-echoed across the field as the troops were drawn up in massed ranks facing a mound of rising ground, and when the last companies arrived some ten thousand men stood assembled, ready to march.

On the rise, a group of mounted military commanders and political commissars had been watching the marshaling of the troops. As soon as the last units were in place, one of them spurred his horse forward a pace or two and stood up in the stirrups. The moon was breaking intermittently through the moving clouds and by its ghostly light Jakob recognized the lean figure of Chu Teh, the commander in chief of the Central Red Army, whom he had first seen striding through the mud and murk above the Hsiang River. His uniform and cap seemed even more faded and rumpled than before but his proud, upright posture in the saddle gave him a distinguished air.

"Comrades, the alarm to march was sounded thirty-five minutes ago," he shouted, making his voice carry far over the silent field. "It has taken you more than half an hour to form up and assemble. The time allowed for an emergency departure is twenty minutes. To-night's performance is unworthy of the Workers' and Peasants' Red Army of China!"

Chu's booming voice was fierce with disapproval and Jakob noticed the troops around him shift uncomfortably under the blunt criticism of their performance.

"At this moment, comrades, security units are searching your bivouacs, temporary barracks, and campsites. If they find so much as a rice bowl or a pair of chopsticks left behind, or a door that has not been rehung in the cottages of the people, the fighter responsible for the lapse will be punished. . . ."

As he listened, Jakob felt a new throb of hope pass through his body. From the Red Army commander's first remarks, it seemed almost certain that the marchers and prisoners were being put through a practice alert. Surprise exercises of this kind had been sprung on the troops during daylight hours in the past month to impress on them the extreme necessity for speed and efficiency in mobilizing the column. Such exercises had almost always ended with a march back to quarters, and Jakob turned his head to peer up at the granite crag where Liang had promised to wait with Abigail. Only the vaguest outline of the hilltop was visible in the feeble moonlight and he wondered desperately whether Liang, from his vantage point among the rocks, could see or hear enough of the proceedings at the foot of the hill to make him decide to remain in his hiding place.

"Since crossing the Chihshui River five days ago, comrades, we've encountered the warlord forces of Szechuan in growing strength," continued Chu Teh in a stern voice. "We know they're deployed to defend the banks of the Yangtze in large numbers — and we've just learned by radio that in northern Szechuan many divisions of the Kuomintang have begun attacking our own Fourth Front Army from across the Shensi border. So our comrades in the Fourth Front are at full stretch defending themselves against rear attacks! That means they will have no time to help us fight the Szechuan warlord armies here in the south. The provincial armies of Hunan, Kweichow, and Kwangsi are also pursuing us from all directions to our rear, and the fascist leadership of the Kuomintang has issued orders saying that the fate of China depends on bottling up the Central Red Army south of the Yangtze . . ."

Chu Teh paused, staring around the field. Even in the near-darkness his eyes seemed to search his men's faces individually and they gazed fixedly back at him, hanging on his every word.

"But China's fate, comrades, in reality depends on the Red Army *not* being bottled up. China's fate depends on the Central Red Army forcing a crossing of the mighty Yangtze and breaking through to set up a new soviet in the north with the Fourth Front Army! China's fate in the end, comrades, will depend on the Central Red Army driving through to the north to begin fighting the Japanese invaders — and forcing them out of China!"

Chu paused to lend emphasis to his words. When he resumed, he spoke with even greater vehemence.

"And those aims, comrades, will be achieved only if you hurry yourselves — and assemble in twenty minutes when there is an emergency, not half an hour!"

The Red Army commander swung his horse around abruptly, turning his back on his troops to underline his displeasure. Then slowly he walked the animal in a semicircle to rejoin the group of mounted leaders. The great assembly of soldiers, chastened by his harangue, hung their heads and shuffled their feet.

Among the group of horsemen, Jakob could see the distinctive, brooding figure of the man he had heard named as Mao Tse-tung when the leaders first passed him above the Hsiang River. Seated in a round-shouldered hunch on the same emaciated brown and white horse, he remained very still in the saddle, and only his head moved as he surveyed the serried ranks of Red Army fighters below him, seemingly calculating their capacity for further action and endurance. The neat, stocky figure of Chou En-lai straddled a bigger mount at his side. Chou's posture was watchful and wary and he wore a hat with fur earflaps tied across its crown and a neat-fitting overcoat, which even in the wilderness of the Szechuan mountains gave him a dapper air. When Chu Teh rejoined the other leaders, they nodded in approval at his words and continued to watch the soldiers closely as a senior political commissar urged his horse to the edge of the mound and began a fresh speech of exhortation. All the Chinese commanders, Jakob noticed, kept their faces turned away from the bulky European figure of Otto Braun, who sat morose and uncomfortable astride a clumsy, short-legged horse to one side of the group. His fever seemed to have abated, but nobody spoke to him and he offered no comments of his own.

A succession of commanders and commissars addressed the uneasy throng, emphasizing Chu Teh's message again and again. Then the gathering was abruptly dismissed to be marched back, company by company, to their camps and quarters. Jakob's battered wristwatch, which he had been allowed to keep, showed nearly one-thirty A.M. by the time he stretched out on his bedroll in the same mud-walled cottage and covered himself again with his padded quilt. The same crowd of soldiers bedded down around him and were soon snoring, but the guard was changed. At night fresh sentries were posted every four hours and Jakob saw that the youth whom he had saved from the Hsiang had taken over. In the moonlight he was pacing back and forth before the cottage doorway with a rifle slung across his back, but once or twice Jakob heard him yawn loudly.

The missionary realized then that perhaps the practice mobilization alert had worked in his favor. He had noticed that his individual guards slept in the period before their spell of duty, but the unexpected rousing of the whole column had deprived this young guard of his sleep. On hearing him yawn a third time, Jakob became determined to stay awake, and while pretending to sleep, he watched the guard constantly as he passed and repassed the doorway. During the next two hours the young peasant yawned often, but to Jakob's great frustration he remained on his feet, pacing relentlessly back and forth to keep himself awake.

At about four o'clock the guard stopped his pacing and entered the cottage. Stepping around the sleeping soldiers he moved quietly across the earthen floor until he stood beside Jakob. With a wildly beating heart the missionary struggled to imitate the regular breathing of the Chinese troops around him as the guard bent close to check if he too was asleep. After listening for a minute or more the guard went back outside, apparently satisfied, and lowered himself wearily onto the bench before the door.

For another half an hour he sat on the bench and swung his legs back and forth as the previous sentry had done, still yawning regularly. Then Jakob heard him drag a small table into position in front of him, and when he looked up, he saw the young guard had set his rifle down against the bench and was resting his elbows on the table. Still breathing rhythmically, Jakob continued to watch him through half-closed eyes, but although the guard's head fell forward once or twice, he shook himself awake each time. Along the row of cottages Jakob heard someone stirring and soon afterward the faint glow of a fire indicated that one of the cooks had risen and was beginning to prepare the early morning meal for the troops. Jakob realized then that dawn must be approaching and he clenched his fists tight at his sides in his frustration. Within minutes the guard would be changed and a newly awakened sentry would take over: the chance to escape for which he had watched and waited through the long, sleepless night would be gone!

It was while these desperate thoughts were flitting through his mind that Jakob heard the first burbling snore from the guard. Satisfied that the one prisoner he was guarding was not awake, he had obviously given in at last to his own intense desire to sleep. His next snore was longer and deeper and Jakob rose without hesitation to slip his feet into the woven cloth sandals he had placed beside his bedroll. He still wore the warm, padded long-gown but he did not pick up any belongings except his conical hat of woven bamboo, which he pulled low over his eyes. Instead he spread the contents of his bundle beneath his wadded quilt and tried to mold it into the approximate shape of his body to allay suspicion for as long as possible, then, stepping gingerly between the snoring Red Army men, he reached the door in four long strides. He held his breath as he squeezed sideways past the end of the bench on which the guard was sleeping; a louder snore jolted the guard's head and the missionary thought for a moment the youth must wake, but he settled again and his head remained sunk in his hands on the table. Once outside, Jakob turned quickly away from the fire that had been lit outside a cottage fifty yards away and hurried toward the hill, fighting down at every step the urge to run.

As soon as he could, he left the frozen ruts of the street and struck off up the trackless hillside. The frost on the grass was bitingly cold to his feet and his cloth sandals slipped off almost at once, but he picked them up and carried them in his mouth, leaving his hands free to clutch at bushes and trees on the way up the steep slope. Although the stones and rough ground cut his feet, walking and climbing alone after nearly four months in close captivity felt immediately strange and exhilarating. Every second that he climbed away from the village he expected to hear an outbreak of wild shouting behind him and his pounding heart seemed to swell until it filled his throat. Once or twice he stopped in the cover of trees and scrub to catch his breath and look anxiously backward, but in the darkness there was no sign of life along the village street apart from the red glow of the cook's fire.

Although he was tired, the frustration of the long, harrowing wait had fired him with a fierce energy and he pressed on rapidly up the hillside, reaching the crag in less than fifteen minutes. In that time the clouds thickened and obscured the moon completely, making the night darker than it had been at any earlier hour, and among the rocks he could detect no sign of life. Jakob walked around the summit twice, his lungs heaving, but saw nothing; he was beginning to fear he was too late when a dark shape rose up by his feet.

"Ke Mu-shih, it's me, Hsiao Liang." The voice of the cookboy speaking in Chinese was a barely audible whisper in the darkness and Jakob felt a hand take his in a strong grip.

"Hsiao Liang!" Jakob circled the cookboy's shoulders with his free arm in a fierce embrace of gratitude. "Is my daughter safe?"

"Yes. Look here!" Liang led him beneath an overhanging rock and pointed to his two wickerwork panniers, which stood on the ground in the most sheltered spot. A pale haze of moonlight was shining through a broken cloud and when Liang bent to remove the lid of one of them Jakob was able to see the face of his sleeping daughter. Tucked warmly into the zip-up bag and wearing a woolen bonnet, the child was serenely asleep and showed no signs of stirring.

"It's a miracle, Liang," breathed Jakob, leaning down to lift the child into his arms.

"Perhaps it would be better to wait, Ke Mu-shih." Liang laid a warning hand on Jakob's shoulder. "It's better not to risk disturbing the child. If she makes a noise it might attract the soldiers' attention."

Jakob nodded and continued to gaze down at the sleeping baby. Despite the meager nourishment she had received, the infant had grown noticeably since Jakob had last seen her and he fancied he could already see a hint of her mother's gentle prettiness in her features. He shivered suddenly, swept by a mixture of emotions in which joy and wonder predominated, but as he crouched by the basket, lost in the moment, a thin, keening note from a bugle split the silence cloaking the village below. There was a strident urgency in the bugler's call and Jakob knew at once it was not the regular reveille signal. In the act of reaching out to touch the baby's cheek he stopped and looked up in alarm at his cookboy.

"We must hurry, Ke Mu-shih. This way!"

Liang pushed past Jakob to replace the lid on the basket and quickly hoisted the bamboo carrying pole onto his right shoulder. His two sons appeared like silent genies from behind a rock and, followed closely by Jakob, dashed away down the far side of the hill in the wake of their father and his bouncing panniers.

Behind them the plaintive notes of the bugle quavered through the predawn darkness once more — and this time the wail of the alarm signal was punctuated by a ragged chorus of voices shouting orders to organize a pursuit.

8

Hobbling painfully on his lacerated feet and breathing raggedly, Jakob climbed the next hillside more slowly. Liang and his sons had to stop repeatedly to wait for him to catch up with them and each time the cookboy stared anxiously back into the darkness, watching and listening for signs of their pursuers. The track that had led them down from the crag overlooking the Red Army camp snaked upward again across the lower slopes of a bigger, partly wooded mountain and they had followed it until it petered out beyond the trees. Now they were scrambling over rocks and through patches of briar with the aim of getting as high as they could before dawn broke. Faint streaks of gray were already beginning to lighten the rim of the sky above the eastern hills and in the distance a growing cacophony was rising from the Red Army camp. Every bugle seemed to be blowing at once as though rousing the whole multitude of troops to action.

"I shall have to rest, Hsiao Liang," gasped Jakob, staggering to a halt. "Perhaps we should hide and watch to see what the soldiers do."

"No, Ke Mu-shih! Some of the officers have binoculars." He plucked urgently at Jakob's sleeve, drawing him forward. "We must try to get around the shoulder of this mountain. We need somewhere to hide before it gets light."

With an effort Jakob struggled on: although almost four months of marching had hardened him and increased his capacity to endure the stamina-sapping distances the Red Army covered each day, the poor food, his lacerated feet, and the strain of being frequently under fire had left him in no condition for running. The complete lack of sleep during the night and the excitement of finding himself unexpectedly beyond the clutches of his captors had also produced a strangely light-headed sensation in him. A feeling of unreality seized his mind as he clambered upward behind the swaying panniers on Liang's pole — he wondered suddenly if he were dreaming and began to fear he might wake soon and find himself lying once more on the floor of the mud-walled cottage.

He could scarcely believe that his daughter had survived the privations of Liang's dogged pursuit of the Red Army, and his overwhelming desire was to stop and open the cookboy's rear basket again. He wished above all else to hold the child in his arms, to soothe and comfort her and feel the reality of her against his own body — and yet drifting through all these tangled emotions like a thread of smoke was another, less tangible feeling of loss or deprivation. A vague, nostalgic ache seemed to gnaw at him without defining itself and he knew it was connected with the sense of dislocation he felt at having been torn suddenly from the unity of the marching columns of the Red Army.

Despite his maltreatment he had begun to feel an illogical empathy with the men among whom he had marched over many hundreds of miles; despite the brutality and harshness with which the Communists treated their enemies, the strength of their determination and their fierce camaraderie had a crusading, almost spiritual quality that he had never encountered among the Chinese before. The sense of outrage nursed by all the peasant soldiers as a result of the harsh lives they had led in their semifeudal villages had engaged his sympathy and compassion to a greater degree than he had previously realized. There was no denying the catalogue of injustices they and their families had suffered over many years, and finding himself unexpectedly outside their ranks again, he felt an irrational, barely understood sensation of regret.

"There's a temple, Ke Mu-shih." Liang pointed ahead through the blurred dawn light. "Perhaps we can hide there until nightfall."

Jakob, too breathless to speak or argue, nodded his agreement automatically and they hurried on, grateful for the jutting mass of rock that shielded them from the sight of their pursuers. The Taoist temple, an imposing, high-walled building with curved roofs of shimmering green tiles, had been built into the rock face overlooking a ravine. But when they reached it, they found all its doors barricaded against attack. As they searched around its thick stone walls for a means of entry, Jakob hung back, inclining his head beneath his wide conical hat as Liang had suggested, so that his features remained unseen. His weather-beaten face was now as brown as that of many Chinese, but there was no disguising his blond beard and blue eyes, and the sight of a foreign devil in a remote mountain area where few if any foreigners had ever been seen would, they knew, immediately cause alarm and prejudice any potential helper against them. However, nobody emerged to scrutinize the group and a complete search around the temple walls revealed no unbarricaded door. Liang, baffled, lowered his panniers to the ground and squatted on a rock outcrop to rest. Jakob seated himself beside the cookboy and gazed anxiously back down the track, watching for signs of pursuit. For the space of several minutes neither man spoke and silence surrounded them. Then instinct prompted Jakob to turn his head and he was surprised to find a Chinese of great age, dressed in a loose robe of the same color as the mountain stone, standing motionless against the rock face a few yards away. He was looking at them appraisingly, yet there was a hint of regret in his expression.

"It would be better for you to travel onward," said the old Taoist in a low voice. "The Red Army has come every day to search for landowners who try to hide in the temples."

Jakob could not see the priest's face without raising his own head and had to content himself with a glimpse of the old man's simple gray robe and a pair of wrinkled, shoeless feet. The priest stood absolutely still, holding his hands clasped gently in front of him: an aura of calm peacefulness seemed to radiate from him but the firm tone of his voice indicated his alertness and suggested he was unlikely to be swayed from his chosen course or be made easily to change his mind.

"We're not landowners — and we're in great danger," said Liang desperately, indicating Jakob and his sons with a sweep of his hand. "We must find somewhere to pass the day."

"If you stay here we shall all be in danger."

The priest looked pointedly at Jakob, eyeing his padded long-gown, which had been looted by the Communists from a landlord's house. Although he was unable to see the missionary's face below the wide bamboo hat, something about Jakob obviously conveyed an incongruous impression and the priest's demeanor seemed to suggest he knew everything about them without having to ask. In the distance the faint note of a bugle wailed again on the still dawn air; but the Taoist did not look up nor give any sign that he had heard it.

"The Red Army always comes to the temples first," he added, his tone suggesting he was as interested in warning Liang as he was in protecting his temple. "If we are found harboring fugitives, they treat all of us as enemies."

There was no hint of fear or self-pity in the Taoist's voice: his words were detached, matter-of-fact, unemotional. In uttering them he seemed himself to retain a neutral stance to what he was saying. During the silence that followed a faint but unmistakable whimper came from one of the wickerwork panniers that Liang had rested on the ground. The priest, although he had obviously heard it, again gave no outward sign and did not even look at the basket. Jakob moved anxiously toward the pannier but Liang raised a cautionary hand and the whimper ceased almost at once. When they turned back to look at the priest, they found he had disappeared. But a moment later he returned, holding a small bamboo basket containing cold rice, salted vegetables, and dough bread. He placed them in Liang's hands without comment and stood watching impassively as the cookboy gathered up his shoulder pole.

"The Red Army soldiers will probably try to march to the river to set a trap for you," said the priest quietly. "You will be able to see them on the plain below from the next height."

He pointed up the track to a knoll of rock amid a cluster of trees and stood aside, waiting for them to leave. Rising reluctantly to his feet, Jakob thanked the priest softly in Chinese. He no longer attempted to conceal his features but although the Taoist must have recognized Jakob's foreign voice at once, he showed no sign of surprise.

"I wish you a safe journey," said the priest, looking directly at Jakob. "If you encounter difficulties, remember that nature moves you — you do not move nature."

"I'm not sure I understand what you mean," said Jakob uncertainly.

"In the action of inaction you will one day find the truth," said the priest in the same gentle voice. "All human history until now has been winter — but spring is on its way."

In the steady gaze of the aged Chinese Jakob sensed a deep, serene knowingness that left him stilled and perfectly at ease. But he could not comprehend fully the meaning behind the priest's words, which were obviously meant to encourage them, and because he was unable to frame a coherent reply, Jakob thanked him again and hurried after Liang and his sons. The priest remained outside the temple, watching the four of them climb the steep track. In his rock-colored robe he was an impassive figure, tranquil and unmoving like the mountains behind him, and as they climbed higher toward the knoll, the priest seemed to merge gradually into the background, becoming almost invisible in the misty dawn light.

9

"The priest was right," breathed Liang as they paused among the pines growing around the rocky knoll. "They *are* running ahead to blockade the river and cut off our escape."

The cookboy pointed to a seemingly empty area of plain becoming visible below and Jakob, by following his finger, was just able to distinguish two groups of Red Army men jog-trotting fast toward the west.

"They will send men along every track behind us too," said Liang urgently. "We must find somewhere to hide quickly."

He led the way at a run over the peak and down the other side, but as they rounded a sharp turn in the track they almost collided with a wrinkled peasant woman carrying two buckets toward a well from a mountainside cottage. Jakob was nearest to her as they slithered to a halt and a look of terror spread across her aged features at the sight of his bearded face. Dropping her buckets, she turned and fled back to the house, cackling hysterically and peering around at him every few steps. Liang ran after her and Jakob saw a man come out of the door to talk to him. The man stared apprehensively over the cookboy's shoulder at Jakob and gesticulated repeatedly with his arms, waving Liang away until he returned disconsolately to the track.

"Everybody is frightened of you and the Reds, Ke Mu-shih. Nobody wants to help us."

"God will help us, Hsiao Liang, never fear."

Jakob smiled encouragingly in spite of his weariness and they set off together down the track that again led them in among trees. They descended for an hour through the forest, acutely conscious of the ever-brightening sun, which was rising above the eastern peaks. When they came to a village on the edge of the plain, Liang in desperation handed his carrying pole to his older son and ran ahead to the first big farmhouse, which stood apart from the other houses. Jakob watched him talk earnestly to the farmer, a swarthy, thickset peasant; then he ran back to them with a smile of triumph on his face.

"At last, Ke Mu-shih! He says we may rest in his grain store. If anybody comes he will say he didn't know we were there."

Jakob nodded his thanks and kept his head bowed as they hurried into the shadowy granary. The Szechuanese farmer stared hard at them from the edge of the yard, but when they had closed and barred the door and Liang was satisfied that they were no longer observed, he motioned to Jakob to settle himself on a heap of rice straw in the darkest corner. Opening one of his panniers, Liang gently lifted out the still-sleeping baby and carried her across to her father. Watching Liang, Jakob was struck by the extreme gentleness of the hardy mountain-bred man: he handled the child with such surprising tenderness that she settled into Jakob's arms without waking. Abigail continued to sleep peacefully as he held her and Jakob, deeply moved, sat motionless in the straw, gazing down at her with a rapturous expression lighting his face.

"I'll never be able to thank you enough, Hsiao Liang," said Jakob with a catch in his voice. "God blessed us when he gave my daughter into your charge."

"The child has a gentle, peaceful spirit," said Liang quietly, turning away in his embarrassment. "It hasn't been difficult to care for her."

The cookboy busied himself unpacking and setting out the food the Taoist priest had given them, but when he lifted the flask of soybean-milk powder from one basket it proved to be almost empty, and he turned a worried face toward Jakob.

"There's only enough soy milk to last a day or two more, Ke Mu-shih. I bought more soybean in Tsunyi — but it's almost run out. The money left in the baby's sleeping bag is nearly finished also."

Jakob continued gazing down at his infant daughter and the cookboy thought he had not heard. Then the missionary raised his head and Liang saw that although he was still smiling gently, his eyes were moist. Overcome with emotion, he could not master his voice and he spoke in a strangled whisper.

"Don't worry, Hsiao Liang. I'm sure the Lord will provide."

At that moment, the baby stirred and opened her eyes. She gazed blankly up at Jakob and he found himself holding his breath: Abigail, however, seemed to take no exception to the strangeness of his face and did not cry out. After a moment her uninterested gaze flickered away around the shadowy grain store, attracted by the narrow shafts of yellow sunlight infiltrating the gloom through crevices in the wooden walls. Liang and both his sons hovered beside Jakob, watching the child anxiously, and only when Liang was satisfied that she was going to remain quiet and calm did he hurry out to find water to boil. The two boys settled in the straw at Jakob's feet, whispering playfully to the baby girl, who smiled and chuckled at them in response, and when Liang returned, they watched proprietorially as Jakob held the feeding bottle to her lips.

"Thank you for being good playmates with my daughter," said Jakob softly, addressing both boys in Chinese. "I can see you've become friends."

"Yes, we have — and shall I tell you a secret, Ke Mu-shih?" asked Little Liang excitedly. "Your baby loves mice — we'll show you."

He and his brother scampered in among the rice straw piled against one wall, and after rummaging around for a minute or two Little Liang returned grinning broadly and clutching a brown mouse in his right fist. Holding the tiny animal so that its whiskered face was visible between his curled thumb and forefinger, he leaned over the baby and she immediately stopped feeding and smiled, kicking her arms and legs simultaneously in her pleasure at seeing the furry creature.

"You see, Ke Mu-shih?" Little Liang's face lit up with a smile and he settled down in the straw again to stroke the mouse and imitate its squeaks, to the baby's further delight. "If ever she cries we just find a mouse for her — and she's happy again."

Liang had bought eggs from the farmer with his last few cents and a new pair of woven cloth sandals for Jakob. When he had cooked the eggs and heated the rice and vegetables given to them by the priest, they all sat together in the straw on the earth floor and ate in silence. The baby, settled in one of the panniers, watched them contentedly for a few minutes before falling asleep again. When Jakob had finished eating he stretched himself full-length on a bed of straw Liang had prepared, and the cookboy took a wadded quilt from one of the panniers to cover him.

In the few moments before he fell into an exhausted sleep, Jakob felt a great sense of peace settle over him. With the baby daughter he had given up for lost sleeping safely nearby and faithful Liang and his two young sons themselves preparing to bed down around him in the clean-smelling straw, the physical pain in his body evaporated; the world seemed transformed and mellowed. During the rigors of the march he had rarely allowed himself to think of his home in England and the family and friends he had left behind. They seemed remote and unreal at that distance, but suddenly he found himself picturing the loyal prayer meetings they would undoubtedly be holding for him in the cobbled back streets of Moss Side and the image was immediately comforting. Unbidden, the memory of the beautiful, euphoric dawn he had spent with Felicity at the Pavilion of Eternal Spring in Peking also came back to him to augment his feeling of well-being, and as they mingled in his imagination, all these gentle, gladdening images gradually banished his fear of pursuit by the Red Army soldiers. Without his being consciously aware of it, the earthy aromas of the shadowy grain store soothed and reinvigorated some vital entity deep inside him, restoring his depleted energies, and within moments of stretching out in the rice straw, Jakob slipped into a blissful, dreamless sleep, feeling utterly safe and at ease.

10

Even before he awoke, the smell of dust tickled Jakob's nostrils. In a fleeting, confused dream he felt himself choking as he stumbled through one of Peking's winter sandstorms and on waking he discovered that in reality the air all around him was filling with clouds of dry dust. Night had already fallen, and although there was a faint luminosity of moonlight in the grain store he could see very little in the shadowy blackness. Only gradually did he become aware of the chants and yells that accompanied a violent hammering on all the wooden walls of the farmhouse. Sitting up in the straw he listened carefully and recognized for the first time that a chorus of wild Chinese voices massed outside was screaming "*Sha! Sha! Sha!*" — "Kill! Kill! Kill!"

He scrambled to his feet, coughing and groping blindly in the darkness toward the basket where he imagined his baby daughter still lay sleeping. He realized dimly that it was the deafening, rhythmic beating on the wooden walls and shuttered windows of the farmhouse that was raising the dust. He had assumed that the ringing blows were being struck with farm implements, but as the shouting and banging became wilder he wondered fearfully if weapons of some kind were being used. In the darkness he was unable to locate the wickerwork baskets, and a feeling of panic began to well up in him; then a hand clutched at his shoulder and he swung around in alarm.

"Climb up to the rafters quickly, Ke Mu-shih! I've taken the panniers up there."

Liang drew Jakob by the arm toward a ladder that leaned against a wall in one corner of the store and they scrambled up onto the heavy beams that supported the roof. Some of the beams had been boarded over and a few sacks of grain were stored on the planks. As his eyes grew accustomed to the darkness, Jakob was able to make out Liang's two sons crouching wide-eyed with fright among the sacks and he scrambled along the rafters to squat beside the twin panniers. He leaned close to the basket in which his infant daughter was lying, but although she was awake she made no sound, and he breathed a sigh of relief.

"What's happening, Liang?" gasped Jakob. "Surely it can't be the Red Army?"

"No, Ke Mu-shih, they must be *shen ping* — 'spirit soldiers'! They're armed with swords and spears."

Jakob listened tensely to the growing noise: the sudden splintering of wood in another part of the building was followed by a new outbreak of screaming and shouting, and some of the voices seemed to move into the house. Again yells of "*Sha! Sha! Sha!*" rang out and the hammering on the walls of the grain store intensified.

"We must try to get away, Hsiao Liang! They'll have no mercy on any of us if we're caught."

In his journeys through the mountain districts of southern China, Jakob had heard many tales of the armed bands of spirit soldiers whose members performed magical rites that they believed made them impervious to death. By day they were ordinary peasant farmers, but at night they gathered as secret societies to worship idols and take part in demonic rituals that ended in mass frenzy. The eating of special foods was thought to induce "spirits" to take possession of their bodies and make them immune to death by sword or bullet. Spirit soldiers were consequently fearless in the face of danger and Jakob knew that they hated outside military forces and were hostile toward all strangers who passed through their regions, believing them to be spies. Often they terrorized landlords who levied exorbitant taxes from them, but at dawn the ferocious spirit soldiers invariably hid their spears and swords and returned to work unobtrusively in the local fields. Jakob guessed that one such innocent-looking peasant must have seen the farmer offer Liang and himself sanctuary and then reported their presence to the local secret society leaders. While they slept, the local spirit soldiers had obviously been called together to perform one of their wild ceremonies before swooping on the farmhouse in a state of frenzy.

"The rafters stretch right through the house, Ke Mu-shih," whispered Liang urgently. "Follow me!"

There was a space under the eaves of the house which overhung the outer walls, and by stepping from rafter to rafter bent double, Jakob was able to follow Liang to a corner of the grain store where they could see down beyond the walls into the yard. By the faint light of the rising moon, Jakob saw a seething throng of peasants hacking fiercely at the front boards and window shutters with crudely smelted broadswords. At least one of them brandished an old rifle, all were yelling dementedly, and some of the attackers appeared to be frothing at the mouth. As they watched, a surge of men erupted through the smashed front door of the farmhouse, dragging the farmer and his wife and children in their wake. Their appearance provoked a new outbreak of crazed shouting, and more spirit soldiers rushed toward the grain store and rained heavier blows at the barred double doors with their swords.

"We must try the back of the house, Hsiao Liang — it's our only chance!"

Jakob spoke over his shoulder as he moved off along the rafters toward the rear wall, and Liang hurried to fetch the panniers and his two sons. When they reached the eaves above the back door of the farmhouse, Jakob held up his hand to halt them. Below by the light of the moon he could see a single Chinese peasant guarding the rear of the house: a burly, broad-shouldered man, he was swinging a sword around his head and shouting wildly in unison with the rest of the attackers, who swarmed around the front of the building. Beneath them Jakob heard the barred double doors of the grain store splinter with a loud crack and the screams of "*Sha! Sha! Sha!*" rose higher as the mob surged into the outbuilding. A single rifle shot, fired upward through the roof, rang out above the din; almost at once the mob became confused and angry at finding the grain store empty.

The burly peasant guarding the back of the house cocked his head, listening to the cries of anger and frustration. Then, unable any longer to resist joining in the attack, he raced away along the rear wall. The moment the peasant turned the corner toward the grain store, Jakob leapt outward from the rafter on which he stood and fell to the ground outside the wall. As he scrambled to his feet the contorted face of a spirit soldier appeared inside an open window of the farmhouse beside his head.

"*Sha! Sha!*" screamed the spirit soldier, brandishing his sword around his head.

"*Sha! Sha!*" yelled Jakob in an unthinking reflex response, hoping that in the near-darkness his conical hat and Chinese gown would deceive the attacker into thinking he too was a spirit soldier. In the same moment he seized the rope pulley, which held a single wooden shutter open above the unglazed window, and slammed it shut in the shrieking man's face.

"Quick, Liang, hand me the baskets!"

Jakob reached upward toward the eaves and caught each of the panniers lowered to him in turn by the cookboy. Liang jumped down, followed by his two sons, and they dashed after Jakob, who had hoisted the carrying pole and the baskets onto his own shoulder. A high bank that bordered a terraced rice field rose behind the house and Jakob scrambled up it, intending to drop quickly out of sight into the field — but he stumbled on the rough ground and fell to his knees as he neared the top of the bank. The rear basket hit the ground heavily and inside, Abigail, shocked into full wakefulness, began wailing loudly.

Liang hurried up the steep incline to help Jakob to his feet, scooping up the carrying pole at the same time. Each of his sons steadied a basket and the four of them slithered down onto the frozen ruts of the rice field. Once they reached flat ground they ran fast toward the far bank. The baby was still shrieking with fright and behind them they heard a dog begin barking loudly. Turning to look over his shoulder, Jakob saw the first group of spirit soldiers appear on top of the bank. Waving their swords and spears above their heads, they began yelling "Sha! Sha! Sha!" in chorus as they ran down into the field behind the barking dog.

A rocky trail led up the wooded mountainside on the far side of the field, but by the time Jakob reached it, all the spirit soldiers were pouring across the rutted ground in pursuit. Encumbered by the baskets, Liang had little chance of outdistancing their pursuers, and his sons were refusing to heed his repeated urgings to run ahead and hide. They clung doggedly to their father's heels as he ran up the forest trail and Jakob saw that they would have no hope of shaking off the spirit soldiers unless they broke away into the forest. Through the trees he caught a glimpse of reflected moonlight and increased his speed to clutch breathlessly at the cookboy's sleeve.

"Liang, the river! We must try to reach it."

Liang and his sons turned off obediently behind him as Jakob plunged in among the firs, and he led them between the dark trunks toward the rushing water. Some of the spirit soldiers ran on screaming up the trail but others, guided by the dog, followed through the trees, shouting and whooping frenziedly in anticipation of running down their quarry. When Jakob emerged suddenly from the forest he found himself on the brink of a high cliff with the river foaming seventy feet below at its foot. He turned south along the cliff, running desperately, the chants of the spirit soldiers growing louder in his ears, and when he saw the tangled tendrils of a gnarled vine trailing down the cliff he grasped it in his hands and swung his legs over the cliff edge. Calling for Liang to hand him the carrying pole, Jakob balanced it across his right shoulder and began lowering himself hand over hand toward the stony riverbank. With their pursuers approaching the cliff top, Jakob swung in toward the cliff under a ledge, scrabbling for a hold with his feet, and Liang and the boys followed suit. The pannier in which his daughter lay was suspended over the river, open to the darkened sky, but the baby, seemingly exhausted by her desperate wailing, had fallen quiet, and Jakob held his breath and said a silent prayer that she would not cry out again.

Hanging out of sight beneath the ledge, Jakob and Liang listened anxiously to the voices of the yelling spirit soldiers as they charged past. They faded quickly into the distance, but some instinct warned Jakob not to move, and he signaled to Liang to stay where he was. Before long, some of their pursuers came back to the same spot above their heads on the cliff top and stayed there, talking loudly among themselves. Jakob steadied Abigail's basket with one hand, rocking it gently to keep her from crying, and at last the voices moved slowly away.

After waiting a minute or two to be sure, Jakob called softly to Liang to follow him and slid down the rest of the hanging vine to the riverbank. As his feet touched the ground he felt a great sense of physical relief: then rough hands seized his shoulders, spinning him around, and he found himself staring into the narrow-eyed faces of men who wore eight-sided caps. Liang and his sons were grabbed in turn as they reached the ground and one of the soldiers prodded the rear pannier on the carrying pole with his bayonet. The baby immediately began to wail again and another soldier switched on a looted flashlight and shone it directly into the basket. In the glow of its beam the red, five-pointed stars on the caps of the Red Army troops crowding in all around them became clearly visible to Jakob and Liang.

11

"Keep going! Faster! Faster!"

The pock-faced Young Vanguard prodded the younger of the Liang boys between the shoulder blades with a sharpened stick, urging him up a steep bank toward the rattle of gunfire.

"Are you too cowardly to run toward the enemies of the Red Army, is that it?"

The boy hissed his words contemptuously in Little Liang's ear as he pushed him roughly from behind once more. "Or are you only good for helping imperialist spies escape from their captors?"

Little Liang stumbled and tried to climb faster but the thick rope loosely hobbling his ankles restricted his steps, and because his hands were tied behind his back he had difficulty keeping his balance. Ten yards ahead of him his older brother was clambering clumsily up the hillside, similarly hobbled and bound. From time to time he paused to glance around at Little Liang to check on his progress, then, gazing apprehensively ahead, resumed his climb alongside the fast-jogging column of Red Army troops moving purposefully toward the sounds of battle.

"I'm not frightened," sobbed Little Liang over his shoulders as he struggled over the rough ground. "If you'd untie my hands and feet I could run faster."

The Young Vanguard snorted derisively. "Oh, yes, of course I'll untie you. Then you can run screaming into the arms of your friends in Chiang Kai-shek's stinking army as soon as we get over the next hill."

"I wouldn't run away, I promise," gasped Little Liang. "I followed the Red Army with my brother for many weeks before we were taken prisoner. Whenever we watched you we wished we could join."

"Then why did you and your father act as running dogs to a foreign spy?"

"I don't understand about Pastor Ke being a spy. We were only doing what he told us to do — bringing his baby to him. My father was his cookboy in Chentai. He had to get a job when a greedy landlord robbed our grandfather of his land. Sometimes my father went with Pastor Ke when he made journeys to sell books about a man he calls Yeh-su — that's all I know."

The Young Vanguard snorted again but before he could reply, a flurry of explosions shook the hilltop above them and a shower of rock, broken tree branches, and other debris cascaded over the hillside, forcing the hurrying troops to fling themselves flat on the narrow track. The Young Vanguard grabbed Little Liang by the shoulder and threw him to the ground behind a hump of rock, calling loudly for Big Liang to crawl back to them. The moment the older boy reached their side, another shower of stick grenades arced in the air above the hill, thrown from hidden Kuomintang positions on an overhanging bluff, and the three youngsters buried their faces in the dirt as a further hailstorm of debris showered down around them.

"What's happened to my father, Comrade Mauser — please tell me!" As the dust settled, Little Liang rubbed the grime from his eyes and gazed pleadingly at the Young Vanguard at his side. "We haven't seen him for three weeks."

"Your father's scuttling at the heels of the foreign spy, carrying his belongings," growled the boy, raising his eyes cautiously to scan the hilltop. "That way they're both under the noses of the guards. The magistrate had the spy flogged for escaping . . . a hundred lashes. And his hands have been tied again."

Like all the other Little Red Devils serving as orderlies with the Red Army, the scrawny boy set to guard the Liang brothers was universally identified by a rough-humored nickname given him by the troops. In his case, the ravages of a childhood disease that had scarred his round cheeks with pockmarks had been likened through his nickname to the textured butts of the Mauser machine pistols which so many of the Communist troops had captured from the Kuomintang forces. Despite the outward scowls with which he greeted its use, Comrade Mauser, or Little Mauser, gloried secretly in this tough-sounding battle name. During their three weeks of captivity, Little Mauser had treated the sons of Jakob's cookboy with a fierce contempt, the more so on realizing that he personally had been a victim of Big Liang's deceit prior to Jakob's escape. But during that time both captives had come to recognize that the use of the nickname was pleasing to Little Mauser.

"And what about Pastor Ke's baby, comrade?" put in Big Liang quickly, taking advantage of the new confiding mood that seemed to be growing between them in the shared danger of being under fire. "Is she still alive?"

"You're not permitted to call me 'comrade,' and don't ask me questions about your fellow prisoners." Little Mauser spoke sharply, then fell silent, listening intently to the noise of the fighting. But during a lull in the shooting, his desire to air his knowledge seemed to get the better of his resolve not to communicate. "Don't go holding out any great hopes for the foreign spy's baby. The woman of the Comintern adviser who travels with the General Headquarters column had a child. But although they get the best food, it's already dying . . ."

All three boys buried their faces in the cold earth again as a new exchange of rifle fire broke out above them: it continued fiercely for a minute or more, then became intermittent. Eventually Little Liang risked turning his head to look beseechingly at their captor again. "Please, Comrade Mauser, will we ever be allowed to see our father again?"

"Just think yourself lucky your father's still alive!" A new edge of bitterness entered the Young Vanguard's voice, raised above the sound of the gunfire. "Kuomintang soldiers beheaded my father and fifty other poor peasants — just because one of them gave a little food to a Red Army patrol. So don't expect me to worry about when you might see *your* father."

Somewhere above them a bugle call rang out and the troops all around them rose up in a rush to hurl themselves over the crest of the hill. Little Mauser listened intently to the sounds of the skirmishing for several minutes — and once he was satisfied it was safe, he prodded the two Liang boys fiercely with his stick again and urged them upward. When they stumbled over the brow of the steep hill, the three boys looked ahead and saw high, sheer walls of dark rock towering above them. For several days the name of the famous Loushan Pass had been on the lips of everyone in the marching column as they hurried toward the massive screen of mountains protecting the Kweichow-Szechuan border. The noise of battle had grown louder hour by hour while they drew nearer and it was clear that a major engagement was being fought with great tenacity. But on finally catching sight of the pass itself, the youngsters found themselves awestruck by its grandeur. The unit with which they were marching, they realized, must have been delayed by an isolated pocket of Nationalist resistance which had at last collapsed, because dense phalanxes of Red Army infantry were already visible ahead, swarming through the great cleft in the mountains, using the dirt road that commanded the north-south route. After weeks of wheeling and feinting northward toward the Yangtze to confuse and sidetrack the numerically superior government and warlord forces, the Red Army had evidently concentrated its strength successfully once more to smash another encirclement and open up an escape route for itself to the south. Although all units were exhausted from repeated night marches, it was clear to Little Mauser and his two roped captives that the entire Red Army was now moving with new purpose once more. Reinvigorated by the first strategic victory of their entire trek, the troops were shouting and strutting with an unfamiliar sense of bravado.

"We've done it!" yelled the Young Vanguard. "We've broken through again!" In his excitement Little Mauser hurled his overlarge cap high into the air and danced a little jig. "There'll be no holding us now!" Turning to his young captives, he slapped them on the shoulders. "Now you know what a real army can do, don't you?"

The cookboy's sons looked at one another uncertainly. Although momentarily spellbound by the swirl of military activity among the spectacular crags of the Loushan Pass, Big Liang and his brother remained oblivious to the heady, celebratory atmosphere spreading rapidly along the marching columns of Communist troops. Gazing back the way they had come and forward in the direction of the crowded mountain pass, they scanned the seething mass of soldiery with anxious expressions — but nowhere could they catch a glimpse of their father with his bouncing pannier baskets moving in the wake of the manacled figure of Pastor Ke.

"Does this mean we might see our father again soon?" asked Little Liang plaintively.

"Forget about seeing your father," yelled Little Mauser. "Winning the battle of Loushan is far more important. Come on!" Poking them with his sharpened stick once again, the Young Vanguard urged them toward the pass at a run.

12

"I'm afraid the news from China about Jakob is not good," said the bespectacled Moss Side minister in a measured voice. "He escaped from captivity briefly last month, but was recaptured. His jailers now say they've put him on trial for the 'crime' of escaping, and the 'fine' they're demanding has been doubled, to three hundred thousand Chinese dollars. What's worse, they say unless the sum is paid very soon, they will execute Jakob as a spy . . ."

Weak shafts of pale March sunshine struggling through the grimed windows of the crowded Moss Side church hall illuminated two empty chairs in the front row close to the dais of polished pine from which the minister spoke. He glanced at the unoccupied places for a moment before surveying the gathering gravely over the rims of his spectacles. In their turn, the parishioners looked anxiously back at him, sitting still and upright in their seats.

Among them was a reporter from the *Daily Dispatch* who had attended the November meeting. He was seated near the door and on hearing the minister mention the threat of execution, he looked up sharply from the notebook in which he was writing.

"Please excuse my interruption, sir," he murmured apologetically, "but was any specific date mentioned?"

"Yes, next Monday, a week from today," said the minister quietly. "Jakob's captors demand that the ransom be paid to a go-between before then — if it isn't, they say they'll put him to death."

The reporter thanked the minister and scribbled a note on his pad, but the rest of the congregation received the news in a stunned silence.

"This of course isn't the first time that Jakob's persecutors have threatened to kill him," continued the minister. "Soon after his capture similar threats were made. Since the Anglo-Chinese Mission has a strict policy which does not permit the payment of ransom, an answer has been sent to the latest demand stating that the conditions for Jakob's release can't possibly be met. . . ."

The minister shuffled some papers before him on the small tabletop lectern and picked up a telegram. He scanned its contents briefly, then looked up again at the audience.

"Almost five months have passed since we first gathered here to pray for Jakob and his family. Since then we've never ceased to remember the Kellners in our prayers, but during that time we've received very little information about Jakob, and the harrowing effect of all this uncertainty, I'm sure, is responsible for the fact that Jakob's parents have not felt able to join us today."

The minister paused for a moment and looked significantly in the direction of the two empty chairs; then he lowered his eyes again to the lectern.

"But although the news is not good, it encourages us to think that our prayers so far have not been in vain. The communication from Jakob's captors giving this ultimatum to the headquarters of the Anglo-Chinese Mission, in Shanghai, at least confirms that Jakob is still alive. What's more, it revealed that his infant daughter, who was reported missing after the kidnap in November, has also quite miraculously survived. It seems she is being carried and cared for by one of Jakob's household servants."

A gasp of surprise and relief rose from the body of the hall, followed by an excited buzz of conversation. When it died away, the minister picked up a handwritten letter and glanced around the hall again.

"Also, you'll be glad to know that although it's impossible to pay the ransom, some steps are being taken in China to help Jakob. Mr. Matthew Barlow, the director-general of the Anglo-Chinese Mission, is himself traveling by mountain chair through the remote regions of southwest China in an effort to secure Jakob's release. Some of you may remember that Matthew Barlow came to this very hall to address us in person fourteen or fifteen years ago. He made a deep impression on us all with his enthusiasm and determination, and we must pray for the success of his efforts, because at great personal risk he is pursuing the armed force holding Jakob prisoner. He is carrying with him five hundred dollars' worth of medicines and a small amount of silver as an offering of goodwill to Jakob's captors. A rich Chinese Christian who wishes to remain anonymous has, I believe, donated the silver. It amounts to about ten thousand dollars. . . ."

Another buzz of comment rose from the audience, and the minister glanced down at the letter in his hand, his expression fleetingly indecisive. Then he squared his shoulders, having decided not to spare his audience the unpleasantness of the truth.

"Mr. Barlow has written an open letter to everybody here in Moss Side which has just reached us," said the minister gravely. "It is ten weeks old and does not make pleasant reading, but I think you should hear what it says in essence. Accompanied by another, younger missionary, Mr. Barlow has traveled in torrential rains, snow, and bitter cold, crossed swollen rivers and streams without number, and climbed mountains and hills almost daily, often without even a track to follow. His journey has also taken him to many scenes of dev-

astation and destruction. He reports seeing skeletons and headless
bodies hanging in the trees beside the tracks; he has passed through
many deserted, burned-out villages and seen many casualties of
bombing and other horrors of modern warfare. Famine conditions
caused by the presence of thousands of government and Red Army
soldiers on the march have made it difficult often to obtain food.
Traveling and carrying heavy loads on primitive tracks under these
conditions have been very trying. For a time, a Communist inter-
mediary was guiding them, but he disappeared unaccountably and
this has made their task even more difficult. But Mr. Barlow is still
doing his best, and his example is a great inspiration to us all in these
very worrisome circumstances."

Outside the hall, the pale sunlight of the cold spring day faded
suddenly behind a bank of clouds. Rain, quiet at first, began to drum
against the roof and windows and grew gradually heavier. The light
inside the hall became thick and gloomy but the gathering ignored
the weather, giving all their attention to the minister, who carefully
set aside the letter from which he had been reading and leaned
forward on the lectern.

"Many of you here, I know, would gladly cross those same swollen
rivers and climb those same mountains with Mr. Barlow to try to
help Jakob, if you could. That unfortunately isn't possible. But
because many of you have expressed a strong wish to do something
practical to help Jakob, it was decided two weeks ago to try and
raise petitions locally. The suggestion is that these petitions be sent
to our own government in London and to the Chinese government
to remind them of their duty to help restore Jakob's freedom. This
meeting, as you know, has been called to gather in those petitions,
and I now invite all those who have been collecting signatures to
bring them up."

The minister signaled to two men seated in the first row and they
moved forward to stand by a little table that had been set up below
the dais. In the body of the hall many men and women rose to their
feet, tugging well-thumbed sheets of paper from their pockets and
handbags, and one after another they filed quietly to the front. Most
of them placed a clinking bag of small copper coins on the table
beside their petition sheets, and the minister's two assistants jotted
figures in their notebooks after exchanging a few words with each
organizer. When all were seated again, the little table was piled high

with signature-covered petitions and bags of cash. After a whispered conversation with his assistants, the minister beamed around at his audience, visibly moved.

"To my astonishment, you've gathered the signatures of more than thirty thousand people. You've worked with great diligence. Through you, thirty thousand people of this city have shown their love and concern for one of their fellow men. And although nobody was asked to give money, many signatories offered a few coppers. Enough money has been donated, in fact, to allow representatives from here to travel personally to London to present the petition, if that is what you decide you want . . ."

A prolonged burst of spontaneous applause rose from the gathering and the minister waited patiently until it died away.

"Since last November," he said, raising his voice to make it heard above the noise of the rain, "an unseen battle between good and evil has been going on in China. We've offered our prayers regularly and now today we've learned that we are bolstered by the support of thousands of other people outside our church. But we mustn't falter in our devotions. Saint Paul reminds us that 'God hath not given us the spirit of fear; but of power, and of love, and of a sound mind.' Jakob, when he thinks of his home, will know we are concerned for his safety. He needs our prayers to sustain him, whether he realizes it or not. Many thousands of members of the Anglo-Chinese Mission and its supporters around the world have also been praying daily for Jakob — but we are his friends and neighbors and we have a special duty. So let us be sure we don't fail to use our spiritual strength to the full."

Bowing his head slightly, the minister invited the congregation to join him in prayers for Jakob and his daughter and at once the crowded hall fell silent. He led a succession of fervent supplications and then the broad-voweled voices of three hundred or so of Jakob's closest countrymen swelled in unison as they recited the Lord's Prayer together. The familiar words were immediately consoling and encouraging to the worshipers and for a few brief moments the sound of the prayer, recited with a heartfelt intensity, blotted out the noise of the spring storm raging in the cobbled streets outside.

13

A steady, day-long drizzle seeping from leaden skies had drenched the threadbare clothes of Lu Mei-ling, and as her mule carried her higher up an ancient mountain path beneath a vertical cliff of rock she felt her wet garments freezing slowly on her body. The mane of her mount was stiff with icicles and the tall grass brushing her knees in the darkness was already cloaked with ice.

Inside her tunic she hugged the body of her infant son fiercely against her breast, imagining that she could feel some occasional movement of his mouth. But several hours had passed since she had truly felt him twist and squirm in her grasp and despite the jolting movement of the mule on the rough track, she knew in her heart there was no longer any mistaking the stillness of his limbs.

Her head and shoulders were swathed in a blanket in which the moisture was also freezing and from time to time she still bent her head toward her chest in a listening attitude, as she had been doing for several days past. No reassuring whimper or even a fevered cough was any longer audible, but she continued to squeeze the tiny, frail body obsessively against the warmth of her own flesh as though she hoped that she could somehow sustain and revive the child by an act of will.

A few torches of split bamboo flared in the hands of guards escorting the General Headquarters column, and by their light she could make out the heavily built figure of Otto Braun hunched miserably on his mount, riding apart from the Chinese leaders of the Red Army. Through the fierce cold, which had reduced everyone to silence, men and animals alike were moving with a slow ponderousness. But although she registered these things, Mei-ling remained indifferent to what she saw: it was as if the unending marches had numbed her senses and the only reality she felt was the flesh-and-blood infant who had been dying in her arms for many days.

"Mei-ling, are you all right?"

Mei-ling recognized the voice of her brother immediately but she did not turn her head or reply. His right shoulder and arm, which had been wounded at the Hsiang River, were still swathed in a sling and it was only with difficulty that Chiao spurred his horse alongside her mule on the narrow path and repeated the question with greater concern. But still she made no answer.

"How is the baby?" he persisted. "Is he keeping warm enough?"

"Please, Ta ko, don't ask any more questions about the baby."

The sharpness of his sister's reply startled Chiao and he turned in the saddle to peer into her face. She had spoken in a hollow, remote voice, her gaze fixed determinedly ahead, and he looked at her closely in the flickering light of the burning torches, half expecting to find tears on her cheeks. But she was dry-eyed and her blank expression remained unchanging under his inspection. Glancing at the outline of the baby beneath the bulk of the blanket, he could detect no sign of movement, and he noticed then that there was something unnatural in the way his sister was clasping the child tight against herself.

"I will make any arrangements for you that are necessary," he said quietly. "It would be better not to mope too long."

"I will call you, Ta ko, when I need help!"

She spoke again in the same sharp, distant tone, holding herself straight in the saddle as though oblivious to the freezing cold. With only one hand on the reins she was paying little attention to controlling the mule, letting it find its own way up the mountain.

"Perhaps it's not entirely bad that this has happened," said Chiao gently. "Things will be better for you. You'll be able to devote yourself fully to your duties with the Military Commission again — and now that there's bad blood between Hua Fu and the rest of the leadership, it will be easier to distance yourself from him without the baby."

Mei-ling made no effort to reply. Somewhere ahead in the darkness rifle fire broke out and Chiao cocked his head to listen; but the firing remained sporadic and distant, and no order was given to extinguish the torches or cease conversation, as was usual when danger threatened.

"Mao Tse-tung's wife decided to give up her newborn baby last week," continued Chiao. "It was wrapped in a shawl and handed to a peasant family with twenty silver dollars. At least you've been spared that agony."

"All you've said is true," said Mei-ling in a low voice. "I know that well enough in my mind. But no matter how much she wants to change the world, a woman's heart doesn't concern itself only with revolution."

She tugged the stiffening blanket more tightly about herself and shuddered. Her eyes closed and in the same moment her face looked both determined and vulnerable. It was suddenly obvious to Chiao that the conflict between her loyalty to the revolutionary cause and her natural maternal instincts was causing her anguish, and he struggled to find words with which to comfort her.

"Is the child's father concerned?" he asked.

"He has shown little interest in the child since its birth," said Mei-ling wearily. "He broods only about his illness and how our leaders have turned against him."

They rode in silence for a while; then Chiao moved his horse closer to her. "I'll arrange for the burial," he said softly, resting his hand on her arm. "It will be better done without fuss."

To Chiao's surprise his sister steered her mule abruptly away from him, clutching the body of her dead child to her more closely than before. Her eyes opened very wide as she turned her head toward him and for the first time he saw the acuteness of her distress. "Say nothing to anybody. Just leave me alone."

Without waiting for his reply, she dug her heels into the mule and forced it ahead up the mountain track. Chiao stared after her in dismay: in silhouette against the flickering torches ahead of them, he watched his sister bend her head over the bundle in her arms, and although he could not be sure in the gloom, he thought he saw her shoulders begin to shake in a fit of weeping.

14

Higher up the ancient mountain path that imperial couriers had trodden over many centuries, the Red Army's prisoners had been herded into a series of low-ceilinged caves that were little more than shallow holes in the vertical cliff face. Alone on the floor of one of the smaller caves Jakob squatted, shivering on an oilcloth which Liang had been allowed to spread out for him. His rain-drenched padded gown was frozen stiff about his shaking body and because only a temporary halt had been called, his hands were still lashed tight behind his back.

Outside the mouth of the cave his guard had lit a small fire over which he was warming himself. The blaze, however, was too far away from Jakob to thaw out his clothing; only the smoke swirled into the hole in the rock, causing the missionary's eyes to smart. On the plain below the mountain during daylight the marchers had swung past fields of dark earth in which new shoots of green wheat and sorghum were sprouting. Despite the incessant drizzle, the early spring air had been warm and the abrupt drop in temperature as they climbed the mountain after dark had come as a shock, chilling their thin, underfed bodies to the bone.

Beyond the narrow cave mouth some infantry and medical units were continuing to climb the track and Jakob watched them fixedly, trying to forget the shuddering cold, the hunger pangs in his stomach, and the throbbing pain of his lacerated back. The hundred lashes of the bamboo lathe imposed by a scowling Judge Yang as punishment for his attempted escape had reopened the wounds of his earlier beatings. No medical treatment had been offered to him, but he had saved a few coarse lumps of salt given him with his meals and dissolved them in tea so that Liang could bathe the injuries. Nevertheless, some of the weals had healed poorly and were suppurating; sometimes when he fell along the march, he had felt the wounds reopen and begin to bleed again.

The cookboy had been ordered from the day of their recapture to march separately among the Chinese prisoners, carrying Jakob's few belongings and his baby daughter in his panniers. They met usually for only a few minutes each morning and evening, when Liang was allowed to serve Jakob what meager food he was given to prepare. At these meetings Jakob's guards insisted that they speak Chinese and stood close by to listen to what passed between them. Invariably Liang had been commanded to leave Abigail in his quarters and Jakob had not been allowed to see her since their recapture, despite repeated requests.

Liang's anxiety at being unable to care adequately for the small baby on his own was becoming increasingly evident in his expression and his voice whenever Jakob inquired about her. During the past two weeks, when the Red Army had been marching through regions where its presence had produced near-famine conditions, the cookboy had become openly agitated by the scarcity of nourishment available. The Red Army cooks were having to scour areas five to ten miles from the route to find food each day, and Liang had been reduced to feeding the baby thin rice gruel and sugared water.

Jakob could see that Liang always tried to sound reassuring in answering queries about the baby's health, yet often a laugh or a nervous smile betrayed his unease. Sometimes on the march Jakob had fancied he could hear the child wailing pitifully somewhere in the throng behind him, but the shouts and noise of the tramping columns made it impossible to be sure. Now his ears were pricked unconsciously all his waking hours for evidence of the infant's presence; even as he sat shivering in the freezing cave he constantly scanned the passing panoply of troops and animals in case Liang should pass with his panniers.

The skirmishing ahead, which became intermittently audible to Jakob, had slowed and finally halted parts of the column, and he noticed that mainly combat troops and ammunition bearers were moving past his cave. But then an abrupt change occurred in the atmosphere on the mountain track: the guard crouching over the fire leapt to his feet to stand to attention and even before he noticed their red collar flashes, Jakob recognized the unmistakable bearing of troops of the elite Red Cadres Regiment as they strode past, powerful arms swinging, their broad shoulders thrown back, and Mauser machine pistols jutting from holsters on their hips. From overheard gossip, Jakob knew that the regiment was composed of specially trained junior officers who stood permanent guard over the Red Army's top generals as well as the leadership of the Communist Party. They marched in double ranks, their eyes alert, commanded by mounted officers riding the tallest horses in the whole Red Army. In their midst, by the light of the cave fires Jakob saw for the second time the drab, travel-stained group of men who were leading the revolutionary migration which had ensnared him in its toils.

Almost at once he was able to pick out the distinctive European face of Otto Braun: his short-legged steed with its rolling, uneven gait threatened constantly to unseat him and he huddled morosely on its back, riding apart from the others. In the main group, the tall, long-haired figure of Mao Tse-tung was instantly recognizable: stooping in the saddle of his scrawny horse, he was talking intently to Chou En-lai, who rode at his side with a correct, soldierly bearing. Around them jogged other men Jakob had heard identified as generals of the First, Third, and Ninth Army groups, and as they passed his cave he could see that nothing had occurred to heal the breach between the Chinese leaders and their ailing Comintern adviser.

The memory of the circumstances in which he had last spoken

with Braun, in the smoky hilltop temple, caused Jakob to search quickly among the passing group until his gaze lighted on the sole female rider, who was traveling alone well to the rear. Mounted still on a plodding mule and with her head swathed as before in a blanket, Mei-ling was a slender, unmistakable figure. Past images, long absent, flooded back into his mind and he stared after her mule until at last the darkness closed around her. Only then did he realize that one of the riders had wheeled his horse through the protective ranks of the Red Cadres Regiment to dismount close by. Looking up, he found Judge Yang standing beside the fire with his booted feet astride. Behind him his personal bodyguard held his horse's head watchfully, one hand resting on the butt of his Mauser.

"I have to inform you, imperialist spy, that your masters place no value on your life!" rasped the assistant magistrate. "Shanghai has refused to pay three hundred thousand dollars to save you. We shall have no alternative but to carry out the ultimate penalty when your time runs out three days from now."

Jakob rose to his feet with difficulty. His limbs were stiff and cold, and because his hands were bound he had no way of chafing life into them. By the light of the flickering fire he could see that the face of the Communist official was set in its usual angry lines.

"The Anglo-Chinese Mission values the lives of all its missionaries equally — but it will never submit in the face of falsehoods."

"We do not lie!" exclaimed the magistrate, incensed by Jakob's calm demeanor. "You've been found guilty of spying on the Chinese people!"

"I'm not a spy."

"Then why did you try to escape?"

"Because my imprisonment among you is unjust. After my wife's death I instructed my cookboy to care for my child and bring her to me. I escaped when he caught up with us — to try to help my child."

"You failed to obey the laws of the Central Soviet Government," fumed the magistrate. "You must therefore take the consequences."

"You've already held me captive for almost five months," said Jakob calmly. "I've been bound, beaten, and starved without cause. If you choose to execute me, that will also be unjust. But I don't fear your threats of execution. I put my trust in God."

Yang let out a derisive snort. "All your talk of 'God' is a trick —

so that foreigners can exploit us. The Red Army, not your God, will save the people of China by liberating them. And one day revolution will liberate all the peoples of the world!"

The magistrate turned angrily away and swung up onto his waiting horse. But before he settled himself in the saddle Jakob stepped quickly forward.

"Judge Yang, I'd like to make one request."

Surprised by the missionary's earnest tone, the magistrate reined in his horse. "What is it?"

"I haven't seen my daughter since your soldiers brought me back. I fear she may be ill, suffering from cold and malnutrition. She needs a father's attention. I wish to see her, please."

The official stared hard at Jakob, then leaned down toward the guard and spoke quietly with him. Before spurring his horse away, he turned back to the missionary with an unpleasant expression on his face. "If your masters don't pay your fines, three days from now the child will have no father. Permission refused!"

Jakob lowered himself painfully to the oilcloth on the floor of the cave again, fighting a rising sense of desolation. The mountain cold seemed to numb his very bones and his shoulders and arms ached with cramp. Suddenly the certainty of his faith which had buoyed him up in the presence of the magistrate seemed to evaporate within him; feeling too downhearted even to pray, he sat with his eyes closed and his head bowed on his chest. He remained slumped in this attitude for several minutes until he heard a footstep and looked up to find Liang standing in the cave mouth holding an enamel dish of boiled rice. But when the guard untied his wrists, Jakob had difficulty straightening his arms and Liang had to massage them for several minutes. Then the returning circulation made his arms throb sickeningly and despite his hunger he found he was unable to eat.

"What were you able to feed my daughter with today, Liang?" asked Jakob in Chinese, seeing the guard hovering close beside them.

"Only rice gruel." The cookboy avoided Jakob's eyes altogether as he crouched miserably beside him on the cave floor.

"Is she all right?"

"Yes, the baby is fine, Ke Mu-shih."

Jakob studied his downcast expression. "Are you sure, Liang?"

"Yes, sure, sure," replied Liang hurriedly, rubbing the side of his face with his knuckles and staring at the floor.

The guard watched them with a bored expression for a moment longer, then, because of the extreme cold, turned away and moved back to the fire by the cave mouth.

"Baby need better food, Ke Mu-shih!" murmured the cookboy in English to ensure that the guard did not understand what was being said. "She very thin and cries a lot."

Jakob stared desperately at him. "They won't let me see her. I made a new request tonight."

"Natural milk would be the best for her, Ke Mu-shih."

Jakob nodded helplessly. "Yes, but what can we do?"

"I have idea." Liang glanced over his shoulder at the guard and leaned closer. "I've seen Chinese woman on march carrying baby. Maybe I ask her if she'll feed your daughter."

Jakob stared toward the cave mouth, checking that the guard's back was still turned toward them; in his mind's eye he saw again the image of Mei-ling on the mule, cradling an infant in her arms. "You mean the woman riding with the leaders?"

Liang nodded eagerly. "Yes, Ke Mu-shih. Is it all right I ask?"

Jakob hesitated for only an instant. "Yes, but be very careful. Try to ask her secretly if you can. Her name is Lu Mei-ling."

"Yes! Yes! I'll do it secretly, Ke Mu-shih. She often ride long way behind others." Liang nodded and backed away, grinning. "Please eat the rice now, Pastor Ke," he said loudly in Chinese for the benefit of the guard, and he ducked quickly out of the cave into the freezing night.

At the foot of the mountain, on its western slopes, Mei-ling was riding unseeing through the predawn darkness when Liang appeared silently beside her carrying his shoulder pole. He nudged the mule and called her name, but she ignored him and continued gazing straight ahead. Only when she registered the faint, continuous whimpering sound coming from the rear pannier did she turn in the saddle and look down at him with startled eyes.

"Comrade Lu Mei-ling, my name is Liang," said the cookboy, pitching his voice low so that it wouldn't carry to the nearest marchers. "I'm carrying the baby of the English prisoner, Pastor Ke. She's starving. She needs feeding. Could you please help?"

Mei-ling stared distractedly at him as though unable to comprehend what he was saying, so he repeated his request in a more imploring tone. "Please feed her — just a little. Nobody need know. It will save her life."

Mei-ling peered about in the darkness, trying to detect if anyone was watching them: seeing that the nearest torchbearer was thirty yards ahead and that they were not observed, she motioned Liang off the track into the shadow of a rock outcrop. She did not dismount but sat looking blankly at him from the saddle of the mule as she had done before. Then she gestured with her free hand toward the rear pannier.

"Show me the child!"

Liang lowered his pole to the ground and removed the lid of the rear basket. With great solicitude he bent and lifted the infant in his arms and held it up toward the mounted Chinese woman. Although there was no moon, the faint luminosity of the approaching dawn provided enough light for Mei-ling to make out the face of the six-month-old baby peering out apprehensively from its wadded zip-up sleeping bag. For a long time she sat motionless on the mule with her arms clasped tight about the body of her own dead child. Then to his surprise she closed her eyes as though suffering a sudden spasm of pain.

"I'll help you," she whispered. "But on one condition only."

"Yes, anything," said Liang quickly, "I will do anything."

"Then put this in your basket!"

Mei-ling unwound the ice-encrusted blanket from her shoulders and eased the swaddled body of her own lifeless baby out of her tunic. She thrust it down at Liang and he cradled it uncomprehendingly in one arm while raising himself on his toes so that she could take Jakob's daughter from him. As he turned away to place the bundle in a pannier, his hands detected its stiffness for the first time.

"I didn't realize your own child was so ill," he gasped, looking up at her with horrified eyes.

"Tell no one," said Mei-ling in a strained voice, unzipping the dark blue sleeping bag and handing it back to Liang. "Say it's the prisoner's — and bury it!"

She pressed the whimpering baby tenderly against her naked breast and wrapped her tunic and the blanket close about herself again. Without looking further at Liang, she turned the mule's head and applied her heels to its sides, urging it quickly back onto the track.

Almost at once she and Jakob's daughter disappeared from the cook-boy's sight, swallowed up by the near-darkness and the unending ranks of marching men and animals.

15

Narrowing his eyes against the glare of the setting sun, Matthew Barlow raised his head and watched an eagle circling high above him. With its broad wings spread taut, it was spiraling in wide, gentle arcs above the terraced mountains of western Kweichow and the director-general of the Anglo-Chinese Mission felt his own spirits rise within him at the sight of the great bird's grace in flight. In sharp contrast to the grunting and straining of the three coolies who were manhandling his cumbersome *hwa gan* with difficulty over the rough mountain trail, the eagle soared and wheeled in effortless silence in the high air, and as he watched it, Barlow gloried in the sight, envying both the eagle's legendary vision and its high vantage point that would have allowed it to see into the valleys and ravines that lay ahead.

Yunnan coolies back-hauling massive loads of dark rock salt east-ward through the mountains had described repeated sightings of Red Army units in the past week, and this had encouraged Barlow to press on rapidly. He and Laurence Franklin had jogged twelve or fourteen hours each day in their chairs, covering distances of up to ninety *li* at a stretch, followed by a dozen coolies carrying the "good-will offering" of ten thousand silver dollars hidden in sealed kerosene cans. But although Barlow and Franklin scanned the western horizon constantly, so far they had seen no sign of the Red Army's marching columns.

"It looks like another blank day, sir, I'm afraid." Franklin halted his chair coolies at Barlow's side and let out a long sigh of disappointment. "That only leaves us tomorrow if we're going to make contact before the deadline expires."

Barlow continued to watch the swirl of the eagle's flight above the terraced red earth, his eyes alight with appreciation of the scene's stark beauty; then he lowered his gaze and looked steadily at Franklin. "We must still hope and pray that the Lord will bless our journey with success, Laurence. If tomorrow is the last day at our disposal, we must use every minute we've been given to the best advantage."

In the almost horizontal rays of the setting sun Franklin saw just how dramatically Barlow's once-pallid face had been transformed by the long, arduous journey: weathered and roughened by many weeks of mountain winds, by cold, sleet, and rain, it was again as it had been in his earlier life, the face of a man thoroughly at home with the elements. But the change was more than physical. His previously blurred eyes were clear and bright now, reflecting a well of newfound spiritual energy which had carried him through each journey, despite the rigors of the harsh terrain. At the end of each day, when they found lodging in mud-walled inns or temples, to Franklin's surprise his superior almost always had sufficient reserves of strength to work on late into the night on his Scripture translations. Frequently he had found him at midnight, still poring over his dictionaries and papers by lamplight. These scholarly materials were always safely stowed in the coolie loads ready for departure at dawn, and the director-general had rarely flagged in his daylight tasks, questioning peasants, coolies, and *yamen* officials doggedly in the unending search for the Red Army regiments holding Jakob captive. Despite the repeated disappointments they had experienced and the dangers and horrors they had faced, Barlow had never shown any sign of wearying of their quest and Franklin could only marvel the more at his superior's indefatigability. In his turn, Franklin had felt his spirits gradually rise — out on the high trails he had shared the older man's growing feeling of inspiration and uplift without being able to define precisely why. But occasionally he worried that Barlow was driving himself on with an unnatural strength, and this feeling returned again as he looked into his face in the light of the setting sun.

"There are villages down ahead," said the younger missionary, motioning with one arm to the lower slopes, where straggling groups of mud cottages bordered the tree-rimmed rice plain. "Perhaps we could find lodging for the night at an inn and start again at dawn."

"It might be better to carry on without stopping," replied Barlow. He followed the direction of Franklin's pointing finger only briefly before lifting his eyes to scan again the distant mountains and valleys that were now falling into shadow.

"But you need rest, sir," protested Franklin, unable to hide his concern. "At least stop at an inn for an hour or two and have something to eat. That will give us a chance to speak to any coolies who've traveled from the west."

"All right, we'll go down." Barlow smiled in submission. "But I've never felt stronger, Laurence. I've never been more aware of God's comforting presence."

He spread both arms to embrace the mountains and forests that were beginning to merge in an infinite stillness with the crimsoning heavens. The dark crescent of the eagle, the only living thing visible in the vastness, was still dipping and soaring high above them in response to some unheard symphony, and they both watched it as though hypnotized.

"That eagle feels it too, don't you see?" said Barlow, speaking softly so as not to offend against the deep silence. "These mountains have the power to soothe and comfort us. They provide man with hope and optimism, a new perspective. And I sense, Laurence, that you feel it too. In a strange way, we both have Jakob to thank for this new awareness. On these heights, I've felt more clearly than ever before the strength and protection of God. With each pace we've taken and each prayer we've offered, I've felt the sense of communion with God deepen — and I've felt a certainty grow within me that our efforts to save Jakob will not be in vain."

Their assembled coolies, who had halted dutifully on the track beneath them, were watching for Barlow's signal and as soon as he waved his arm in their direction, they set off downhill toward the plain. Within half an hour the whole party was padding along the narrow main street of a village of single-story mud hovels, and a curious crowd of ragged, barefoot children quickly formed about them. The men of the village, gazing out from their doorways, were also barefoot and dressed in dirty, patched cotton rags. Their homes, little more than holes in the ground circled by mud walls, bore the same marks of poverty and disease that Barlow had seen in a thousand other Chinese villages: beds made from planks supported on old pots, beaten earth floors, filthy rag coverlets, and wash lines hung with other pitiful fragments of grimy cloth. Blindness, stunted limbs, open sores, and emaciated, unwashed bodies greeted their gaze wherever they looked and always the dark, unwavering eyes watched them with suspicion as they passed.

To their surprise they found a two-story inn with wooden-floored upper rooms opening onto a balcony that overlooked a muddy yard.

The growing crowd of children followed the missionary party into the yard and watched the coolies stacking the innocent-looking kerosene cans, under Franklin's supervision, alongside other loads. Through open doors some exhausted eastbound baggage coolies could be seen stretched out on straw mats on the earthen floors. Many were already oblivious to their surroundings, smoking opium pipes, while others watched the arrivals with guarded curiosity. In the middle of the yard, women and girls wearing wooden clogs and begrimed cloth bandages on their tiny bound feet cooked and washed amid the noisy clamor of playing children.

"It's a little more difficult to feel God's presence down here, sir," remarked Franklin with a sigh when he was standing beside Barlow on the railed balcony, looking at the squalor of the yard. "Disease and poverty make themselves more evident, as usual."

"If you look hard enough, Laurence, there's always a sign to be seen." Barlow, his features softened by compassion, nodded toward one corner of the yard where a tiny, mud-stained child was stumbling on unsteady legs in the wake of a mangy cur. The face of the child was alight with wonder and excitement as it chased the dog, and the animal, caught up in the game, gamboled playfully about the infant. But when Barlow turned to look at Franklin, he found the younger missionary's attention was elsewhere; following his gaze, Barlow saw two Yunnan coolies inspecting their stack of kerosene cans.

"I think I'll go and make sure nobody's trying to steal our 'fuel,' " said Franklin, hurrying toward the top of the steps. "I've ordered hot water and food, sir, to be brought up here to your room. It shouldn't be long. And I'll try to pump those coolies for some information while I'm down there . . ."

An hour passed before Franklin reappeared, but when he did he ran up the steps two at a time. After knocking eagerly on the director-general's door, he entered to find Barlow seated at a table, working on his translations by the light of an oil lamp. He had washed and eaten and put on a clean long-gown, and was so engrossed in his work that he did not look up.

"Half a dozen Yunnan coolies have just come in, sir," Franklin burst out excitedly. "They say they've seen many thousands of Red Army troops on the march this afternoon — about ten miles west of here. I've traced their route on our map. I think we could be very close to them!"

Barlow painstakingly penned a final line of Chinese characters without hurrying, and when he finally raised his head he was smiling in a knowing way. "That's perfect, Laurence. I've just drafted my last page. Seven years of work is virtually finished." He patted a pile of manuscript paper nearly a foot high with his right hand. "I'll just have time to check over the last few sheets in the chair after it gets light."

"Congratulations, sir," said Franklin warmly; then his own impatience intruded again. "When shall we start?"

"Call out the men straightaway, I'm almost ready."

The grumbling coolies reluctantly hauled themselves from their sleeping mats on Franklin's command and hung storm lanterns on their packs and carrying poles. Before half an hour had passed the dying fires outside the mud-walled houses were sinking into the darkness beneath them as Barlow led his party up the terraced hillside again under a clear, starry sky. In the hours that followed, the only sounds in the still night were the creak of the bamboo chairs, the scuff of the coolies' feet on the rough tracks, and their labored breathing. Lulled by the swaying motion of their *hwa gan*, Barlow and Franklin both dozed fitfully, and when, toward dawn, Barlow caught sight of a ribbon of tiny lights flickering across the folds of an unseen hillside far ahead of them, he thought for a while he was dreaming. But on waking fully he realized that the lights were still moving steadily onward in the distant darkness and he called urgently to Franklin.

"Laurence! I think we've found our quarry at last!"

Stopping their chairs on the ridge alongside the crowd of "kerosene" coolies, Barlow and Franklin gazed in silence at the spectacular river of burning torches that was lighting the way for a column of marching men tens of thousands strong.

"How far away are they, do you think, sir?" whispered Franklin.

"It's hard to say. Five miles, maybe ten." Barlow's voice was elated. "But with luck we'll overtake them before noon. If the Lord blesses our efforts, you'll be able to take Jakob *and* my finished manuscript back to Shanghai together."

The director-general called excitedly to the coolies to press on with all speed and soon they were jolting rapidly through the starlit darkness. As the sky behind them brightened the Red Army men extinguished their torches and for a time they became invisible to Barlow's party in the half-light; but when the sun rose fully the two missionaries were able to make out for the first time the tiny individual figures of men and pack animals climbing and descending together in a long, winding swath through the rumpled contours of the stark landscape.

The sight encouraged the chair and baggage coolies to adopt a faster pace and their rhythmic chants of *"heh-ho! heh-ho! heh-ho!"* increased in tempo. As they ran, Barlow bent his head intently over the bulging file of manuscript he had lodged on his knees in the *hwa gan* and, despite the chair's rolling motion, he continued checking his translation of the final verses of the New Testament. Only occasionally did he glance up to stare across the scrub-covered mountains and Franklin noticed then that his eyes shone with an inner excitement. It was as if his wish to complete his burdensome scholarly task before catching up with the marching Red Army column had become a race against time to be won at all costs, the last big challenge of a life dedicated to spreading the Christian Gospel in China.

As the coolies hurried them onward, Barlow became quite oblivious to his surroundings and he didn't lift his head even when the drum of horses' hooves sounded suddenly on a higher ridge. Franklin, however, turned in time to see half a dozen horsemen riding fast in the same direction as themselves. They were little more than silhouettes against the skyline and they disappeared from sight almost at once, but not before Franklin had recognized the ominous outlines of rifles and crossed bandoliers slung about the riders' shoulders. Even when the group of horsemen reappeared abruptly ahead of them, their mounts sliding in a storm of dust down the ridge, Barlow remained so absorbed in his task that he did not raise his eyes. He looked up only when his frightened chair coolies shuffled to a halt — but by then the horsemen were ranged in a small arc blocking the narrow track and they held rifles that pointed steadily at the center of his chest.

"Don't move!" The bandit leader, who had the dark skin and narrow eyes of a Kweichow mountain dweller, shouted the command in a harsh voice. "We're taking your silver!"

The rest of the bandits spurred their horses toward the terrified coolies, motioning with their rifles for them to turn back the way they had come. In that instant the scene in the inn yard flashed into Franklin's memory. He remembered how the Yunnan coolies had sidled around the kerosene cans, making sly conversation with the carriers, and he cursed his own lack of vigilance. Robber gangs that preyed on caravans and coolie trains carrying silk, opium, and silver were common in western Kweichow, he knew, and impoverished transport coolies who kept them informed could scarcely be blamed for wanting to augment the meager pittances they earned daily for backbreaking toil.

"Stop!"

Barlow's shouted command in Chinese was confident and authoritative and he rose out of his chair in the same moment, clutching the bulging file of translation manuscript against his chest.

"That silver is required to save a man's life. Leave it be! We are engaged in God's work!"

The bandit leader, taken aback by the forcefulness of Barlow's response, gaped at the old missionary uncertainly. The ill-clad men flanking him also seemed nonplussed and they looked uneasily back and forth from Barlow to Franklin. The coolies carrying the silver cowered behind Barlow, their faces taut with fright, but the director-general showed not the slightest sign of fear as he stepped down from his chair and moved slowly toward the bandits. One of them began to turn his horse's head and Franklin was sure all were about to take to their heels when a shot exploded from the bandit leader's rifle. The sight of Barlow staggering backward with a crimson stain blossoming on the front of his dusty long-gown shocked Franklin so deeply that he scarcely heard the sound of the second shot. His own shoulder was sticky with blood and he was lying prostrate on the stony track before he felt any pain. Through a snowstorm of manuscript pages plucked by the wind from Barlow's file, the sight of his superior tumbling slowly down the steep slope at the side of the track seemed like a hallucination. The coolies carrying the silver were being herded away across the ridge before the bandits' horses, and the rising wind was scattering individual sheaves of the manuscript far across the mountainside. By the time Franklin slithered down to where Barlow lay motionless at the foot of the scree, the chair coolies had fled too. With difficulty Franklin lifted the older man into a sitting position and began trying to pull aside the blood-soaked material of his long-gown. But when Barlow opened his eyes, he shook his head, motioning for Franklin to make him comfortable against a stunted tree. Pages of the Scripture translation from the file that had come to rest in a thorn bush were fluttering about their heads, and when he had settled Barlow to his satisfaction, Franklin clutched distractedly at some of the loose sheets.

"I'll gather up as many pages as I can, sir," he said in a desperate voice, although it was obvious that the wind was dispersing much of the manuscript beyond retrieval.

"Don't worry, Laurence . . . there's no need."

Barlow lifted one hand weakly in admonition: to Franklin's astonishment the old missionary's face was calm and composed and suddenly he smiled brilliantly as though he felt no pain from the lethal wound in his chest.

"It's a mistake to believe that the words of the Scriptures are all-important. . . ."

"But sir," protested Franklin, "all that wasted time and effort . . . it will come to nothing."

Barlow shook his head slowly. "It's not wasted work. . . . For seven years I've been blinded by too much doctrine. . . . I've been going through the motions. . . . The mountains have taught me a greater lesson. . . ."

"What's that, sir?"

"The lesson we learn early in our lives and too often forget . . . to listen to the word of God alive in our own souls. . . ."

Franklin noticed that Barlow was staring over his shoulder and he turned and looked up to see what he was watching: high above in the brightening dawn sky an eagle was again riding the wind with outstretched wings, drifting, rising, exulting in the birth of a new day.

"That eagle hasn't forgotten, Laurence," murmured Barlow. "And it's still trying to teach us. . . . If only we'd pay attention . . . nothing's more important than relearning that lesson. . . ."

Barlow's voice trailed off and they watched the eagle together in silence. Then Franklin instinctively turned his head and scanned the mountains to the southwest. It took him a moment or two to pick out the tail of the Red Army column — the marchers were moving swiftly, running or jog-trotting, and even as he watched, the rear guard began to disappear into a valley that still lay in deep shadow.

"Sometimes we mistake our great objectives," whispered Barlow hoarsely as though reading the younger man's thoughts. "We came to set Jakob free . . . but he's in God's hands. Instead what we've discovered . . . has set *us* free. . . . So our search hasn't been in vain. . . . Make sure you pass that on. . . ."

In the director-general's eyes a gleam of triumph had appeared, and comprehension lightened the feeling of sadness that Franklin felt welling up inside himself. The next moment Barlow shuddered and became still; on his face a hint of the smile remained and his eyes did not close but continued gazing up toward the eagle that was still soaring effortlessly above them in the clear dawn sky.

16

"Judge Yang summons the foreign prisoner. Follow me!"
The voice of the assistant magistrate's bodyguard was as harsh and hostile as ever but Jakob, deeply exhausted in body and spirit, heard it with a curious feeling of relief. Through his pain and despair he had been trying to prepare himself with prayer to face his executioners calmly. Three days had passed since Judge Yang had delivered his angry ultimatum and Jakob had begun to watch for the arrival of his bodyguard. When at last he heard the order, to his surprise it seemed almost welcome. After marching nonstop all night, the column had pushed on relentlessly throughout the day, and it was not until late afternoon that his guards had thrown him facedown on the beaten-earth floor of a small farmhouse on the Yunnan border. He had lain there unmoving ever since, shuddering with a fever, not knowing whether an hour or two had passed. His feet, on which his straw sandals had again shredded to nothing, were hugely swollen and festering, his back throbbed agonizingly, and he was wracked in turn by dizzying waves of nausea and stomach pain.

His hands were still bound behind his back and after making two attempts he found that he could not rise unaided. Impatiently, two of his own guards hauled him upright, cursing him loudly. But on seeing him sway between them, they seized his arms and frog-marched him bodily out of the farmhouse in the wake of the judge's bodyguard.

During the long day's trek, as his fever had grown, he had fallen often and one of the guards, perhaps suspecting he was feigning illness, had torn a branch from a tree and flogged him whenever he stumbled. Nationalist aircraft had spotted the column in midafternoon and showered it twice with bombs, forcing the marchers to fling themselves into roadside ditches. After each attack, torn and mutilated bodies of soldiers and prisoners alike were left scattered across their route and these sights had increased the sense of hope-lessness that had been growing steadily inside Jakob since his recapture.

Because of the pain in his feet and legs, Jakob was hobbling bent almost double between his two captors, and when the magistrate's bodyguard noticed this, his face darkened with anger.

"Walk upright," he yelled furiously. "You must appear respectful before the judge!"

One of the two men holding the missionary struck him hard in the chest, forcing him to straighten his back as they marched him out of the yard in front of the farm. The moment his head was forced up, Jakob saw the figure of Liang bending beside his panniers in a field of sprouting sorghum. It was a moment or two before the missionary noticed the short spade in the cookboy's hand; then as he was marched nearer, he saw that Liang had already dug a small hole in the damp black earth. Judge Yang was standing with a group of guards fifteen yards away and before Jakob reached them, the judge made a signal. At once Liang bent obediently over one of the panniers.

The cookboy kept his head bowed as he lifted the little blue zip bag from the basket. But for the briefest instant he looked agitatedly in Jakob's direction before kneeling beside the hole in the earth. At that moment Jakob saw that the sleeping bag was tightly closed, and with a moan of anguish he stumbled forward to the rim of the grave, dragging his guards with him.

"Liang, what happened?"

Liang looked uncertainly toward the Cantonese judge. Seeing that the official was watching him without expression, Liang avoided the missionary's eyes. "The baby died, Ke Mu-shih," he muttered in Chinese, placing his burden carefully in the bottom of the grave. "There was nothing I could do."

"But how, Liang?"

"I don't know."

Liang spoke so quietly that Jakob was scarcely able to hear his reply and he could only watch in horror as the cookboy busied himself covering the zip bag with clods of wet earth.

"Why didn't you tell me, Liang?" asked Jakob in a broken voice.

"I'm sorry, Ke Mu-shih. I informed the judge. He ordered me only to prepare the burial."

Liang continued filling in the hole and flattened a little mound of earth above it with the back of the spade. When he had finished, he retreated along with the guards, leaving Jakob standing alone. For a long time the missionary remained motionless at the graveside, his hands bound behind his back, his head bowed in abject sorrow. Then Liang, the guards, and the judge's party saw his lips begin to move in prayer. When he had finished praying he swung around and stumbled toward the judge, his eyes wide with grief.

"Kill me now!" he yelled, his voice a croak of desperation. "Kill me and be done with it. And may God have mercy on you!"

The judge's face remained impassive. "When you've had sufficient time by the grave," said the official quietly, "your guards will escort you back to the farm."

Jakob's face sagged uncomprehendingly and he stared at the official in bafflement. "Why do you go on torturing me?" he asked in a hoarse whisper. "Why have you changed your mind?"

For a moment Judge Yang remained silent and Jakob thought he detected a faint trace of embarrassment in his expression. "Your execution has been postponed." The magistrate turned away and signaled impatiently to the guards. "That is all. Take the foreign prisoner away!"

PART FOUR

The Marchers
Triumph

SUMMER 1935

Bottled up successfully south of the Yangtze by its Kuomintang enemies, the fleeing Red Army continued to trace corkscrew-shaped tracks across the map of southwest China during the early months of 1935. To escape the clutches of the 750,000 Nationalist and provincial soldiers ringing them at a distance, the 30,000 Communists split repeatedly under Mao Tse-tung's guileful orders and marched north, south, east, and west in a succession of bewildering maneuvers that the Red Army men themselves scarcely understood. Chiang Kai-shek, interpreting these erratic movements as proof that his outnumbered enemy was close to defeat, flew from Chungking to Kweiyang, the capital of Kweichow province, to assume direct command. To Chiang's alarm, however, Mao immediately sent attack columns hurrying toward the city, and in response the Nationalist leader called in forces from neighboring Yunnan to defend Kweiyang. This delighted the Communists, since Mao had predicted that the Red Army would succeed in breaking out northward across the Yangtze if enemy divisions could be lured out of Yunnan. As soon as the Yunnan troops were moved to Kweichow, the Central Red Army swung west and raced into unguarded Yunnan province in three flying columns. They crossed the upper Yangtze where it is known as the River of Golden Sand after a crack vanguard unit disguised as Nationalist troops made a phenomenal forced march of eighty miles in thirty-six hours to secure by subterfuge one of the few ferry crossings. This enabled the whole of the Central Red Army to be ferried across into Szechuan in a handful of small boats during the first nine days of May. Although the river crashes rapidly through deep rock-walled ravines in this wild region, not a single man was lost, and when the Nationalist forces arrived two days later, they could only stare hopelessly across the turbulent river: all the boats had been destroyed and the next crossing point lay two hundred *li* distant.

Therefore, seven months after setting out from their Central Soviet base in Kiangsi, the Communists succeeded spectacularly in separating themselves at last from a pursuing force hundreds of thousands strong — at least for a time. They were able to rest for a few days, but when they pushed on northward again, they encountered a new danger in the form of a fierce tribe of non-Chinese aborigines known as the Lolos, who inhabited the dense forests and mountains close to Tibet. In Kweichow and Yunnan the Communists had already encountered the Miao and Shan minority tribes, who were less warlike; some had even joined the Red Army's ranks. The Lolos of Szechuan were different: they harbored a fierce hatred for all Han Chinese, and, armed with spears, knives, axes, and shotguns, they massed ominously above the mountain trails along which the Red Army was marching. Few Chinese armies had ever passed through the territory of the Lolos without suffering severe losses, and this knowledge encouraged the Communists to negotiate rather than fight. The Red Army leaders explained that, like the Lolos, they too were enemies of the Kuomintang government and offered the surprised tribesmen rifles and ammunition, which they gratefully accepted. To cement friendly relations further, one Red Army general swore blood brotherhood with a high chieftain by drinking the blood of a rooster in a tribal ceremony. In the thick, primal forests, while marching among the Lolos, the Red Army also gained another advantage — for a long spell they became invisible to reconnaissance aircraft of the Kuomintang.

But frustrating though this was to Chiang Kai-shek, he knew that at the end of the Red Army's trek through tribal territory one last chance would present itself to trap the Communists against another great natural barrier, the Tatu. A thunderous, nonnavigable tributary of the Yangtze that rushed foaming southeastward beneath precipitous cliffs, the Tatu barred the Central Red Army's way to union with the 80,000-strong Fourth Front Army of Chang Kuo-tao in northern Szechuan and another Communist force of 10,000 men occupying a small soviet farther north in

Shensi. If they could not cross the Tatu, the Central Red Army and its leaders faced the prospect of wasting away in the wilderness on the fringes of the high Tibetan plateau, where food and opportunities to expand their cause were equally scarce. Knowing that Chiang Kai-shek would be preparing another blockade on the river, the Communists employed Lolo trackers to lead them swiftly over secret trails to the banks of the Tatu, and they arrived at its best crossing point, in the town of Anshunchang, days before it seemed humanly possible. A sleepy regiment of provincial troops awaiting reinforcements was attacked and put to flight and one Communist division was ferried across to the northern bank. But the river, swollen by floods and melting snow, was in its most savage mood: each crossing was slow and hazardous, and a dangerous bottleneck built up. All the Red Army's flanking columns, its transport units, and even the rear guard crowded into Anshunchang, while Kuomintang aircraft, having spotted this growing concentration of troops, began to bomb the area. With Chiang's land forces converging rapidly from the north and the southeast, the specter of total disaster rose once more before the eyes of the Red Army, and in the little town perched above the turbulent river, a crisis meeting of its top leaders was hurriedly summoned.

1

"Because of the speed of the current, the last boat we sent over had to start two hundred yards upstream," said Lu Chiao, raising his voice to make it heard above the roar of the river. "It took four hours to get across and two of the eighty fighters were swept overboard. In three days we have ferried over only the First Division . . ."

Chiao glanced around at the circle of Red Army leaders seated at trestle tables before him in a bare, whitewashed room: their faces were grim and intent and some were jotting notes on slips of paper resting before them on the rough planks.

"If we continue at this rate," continued Chiao, turning toward a map he had pinned on one of the walls, "it will take us several weeks to complete the crossing with all our animals and supplies . . ."

"Is it impossible to throw a bridge across, Commander Lu, as you did so heroically at the Hsiang River?"

The question was asked in a soft Hunanese accent and Chiao knew without looking around that it was the chairman of the Revolutionary Military Commission himself who had spoken from the center of the main table. Picking up a wooden pointer in his left hand, Chiao drew it along the twisting course of the Tatu as it snaked through An-shunchang.

"The flow of the river along all this stretch, Commissar Mao, is four or five yards per second. It is too fast even to attempt to drive a stake into the riverbed. In my opinion, putting a bridge across is out of the question."

Chiao paused and looked around quickly over his shoulder at the rest of his listeners, checking for signs of impatience on their faces. At a glance he saw that Military Commissioner Chou En-lai's dark brows were knitted in concentration at Mao's right shoulder and the piercing gaze of Commander in Chief Chu Teh on his left was fixed attentively on him; the other Red Army leaders, aware of his vital role in the Hsiang crossing, were also sitting motionless in their seats, content, it seemed, to hear him out in respectful silence. The meeting had been called in one of the small stone-walled houses that stood in two rows on either side of the neat, tree-lined main street of Anshunchang, and behind Chiao, through the open door, the boiling surface of the Tatu was visible at the foot of the steep bluff on which the town stood. Angry plumes of spray were leaping high in the air as racing waves crashed over rocky reefs and whirlpools sucked at the single visible ferryboat wallowing with a full load of troops and horses in midstream.

"There are only two boats and the search for others has proved fruitless. Each boat requires eight men to control it — so there wouldn't be enough experienced local boatmen to man other ferryboats, even if we could find any. Two enemy regiments approaching from the southeast are reported to be only sixty *li* downstream and marching quickly. Another division, the Szechuan warlord forces coming from the north, has only eighty *li* to cover. . . ."

Chiao paused and drew from a top pocket of his tunic a crumpled sheet of yellowish paper. It bore several lines of large, crudely formed Chinese characters that had obviously been printed with haste. He held the paper in front of him and scanned his audience again, preparing to read.

"The enemy planes that started bombing us yesterday are now dropping leaflets like these as well. They say: 'The end is near for the Red Army — surrender right away! Leave your traitorous leaders to their fate and your lives will be spared! Later there will be no mercy. You are all doomed to the same fate as Prince Shih Ta-kai!' "

With some difficulty Chiao tucked the propaganda leaflet back into a tunic pocket, using only his left hand: his awkwardness emphasized the stiff, unnatural way in which he still held his wounded right arm and shoulder, although he had dispensed with a sling. For a few seconds the angry roar of the river filled the room without challenge, seeming to daunt the men gathered there with its fierce, elemental energy — then the same Hunanese voice broke the spell.

"We shall not repeat the mistakes of Shih Ta-kai."

Although the assertion was not made loudly, the words were uttered with a whip-crack sharpness that carried the conviction of a shout. As he spoke, the chairman of the Revolutionary Military Commission raised his head to gaze searchingly around at the generals and political commissars crowded into the tiny room.

"The Workers' and Peasants' Red Army of China has not marched fifteen thousand *li* to make the same errors as yesterday's tragic heroes. We've already changed history. We'll never let the past return —"

"Who was Prince Shih Ta-kai, if I may ask?"

The bespectacled interpreter seated beside Otto Braun voiced the question in Chinese with evident reluctance, following a rumble of German from the Comintern adviser. At once a new tension became evident in the room and Chiao saw barely concealed expressions of irritation appear simultaneously on the faces of several Chinese leaders, including Commissar Mao's.

"Prince Shih Ta-kai was an unfortunate general of the Taiping Heavenly Kingdom. He led an army of a hundred thousand peasants to the banks of the Tatu in 1863. They were in revolt against the feudal rule of the Manchu emperors." The patient voice of Chou En-lai, intervening smoothly, calmed the atmosphere, and the German began nodding quickly as he bent his head toward his interpreter to concentrate on the translation. "Prince Shih's forces were trapped against the Tatu by the imperial armies and massacred. The river ran red with their blood. In the ancient past other armies have perished here. Read *San Kuo Yen I* — 'The Romance of the Three Kingdoms' — and you will understand. Local people say the tormented spirits of dead Taiping soldiers and Three Kingdoms' warriors still scream in agony along the river on dark nights . . ."

"Prince Shih surrendered and was sliced to death in Chengtu — you've heard of 'death by a thousand cuts,' comrade?" Chu Teh's broad Szechuanese voice was brusque and impatient and he stared belligerently at the European as he spoke. "If we're captured here the Kuomintang will do the same to us. Now let's get on!"

Mao Tse-tung pushed back his chair noisily and strode toward the map, motioning Chiao aside. Tall and gaunt in a crumpled, badgeless uniform of field gray, he bent forward at the waist to peer intently at the twisting strand of ink that represented the Tatu. His hair was unkempt, his eyes hollow and overlarge in his pale face, but even when he stood motionless, Chiao noticed, his body seemed vibrant with energy. Suddenly Mao jabbed a finger at the map and turned to look at the other men in the room.

"Luting! That's where we must cross. There's a bridge at Luting. What's your opinion, Commander Lu?"

Chiao shook his head dubiously. "Luting is three hundred and twenty *li* from here, Commissar Mao — that's three days' march over normal terrain. Local people say two regiments are already guarding the bridge. Several brigades of reinforcements must be on their way there too."

"What is the trail like on this side of the river?"

"Almost impossible, Commissar Mao. The normal route north is along the eastern bank on the far side. This side, the trail sometimes runs through waist-deep mud at the level of the river; at others it climbs thousands of feet to the tops of the ravines. . . ." Chiao hesitated. "Also, the bridge at Luting is made only of chains and planks. It stretches across a gorge a hundred yards wide — and the people of Anshunchang say the Kuomintang have machine-gun emplacements in blockhouses at either end. . . ."

"Thank you, Commander Lu." Mao turned his back to the map and faced the room. "We have no choice, comrades. Prince Shih delayed three days at Anshunchang to celebrate his wife's delivery of a son. The delay cost him everything. We must not delay. We must march on Luting at once."

Mao spoke with a quiet forcefulness, searching the faces of the men before him one by one as though challenging each in turn to disagree: when none dissented he swung around quickly to Chiao again.

"Commander Lu, are you recovered sufficiently from your wounds to undertake a hard forced march?"

"My shoulder is still stiff, Commissar Mao, but I can march well enough."

"The assault group for the bridge must all be volunteers. Choose the men from the Fourth Regiment of the First Army Group. If you are well enough, why not march with them and take personal command yourself?"

The chairman of the Military Commission looked hard at him, his eyes dark and unwavering.

"It would be a great honor, Commissar Mao."

"Good. Then waste no time. We must cross within three days!"

Without speaking further Mao strode out of the doorway and, turning his back firmly on the savage river, climbed away up the bluff toward his quarters. The set of his broad shoulders and his quick, sure stride confirmed wordlessly that his mind had been emphatically and irrevocably made up. Watching him go, Chiao realized that under the almost hypnotic power of his gaze, he had accepted the dangerous mission to seize the bridge at Luting without giving the consequences any thought at all.

2

Thunder crashed through the blackness overhead, drowning momentarily the roar of the Tatu, and a new deluge of rain drenched the slippery boulders to which Liang clung as he edged along the narrow riverside trail. The hundred-foot drop to the river on his right was sheer, with only the outline of an occasional stunted tree jutting from the rock face against the paleness of the foaming water. The storm had turned the path to slime and his feet, shod now with steel-tipped straw sandals, slithered alarmingly at almost every step. Above Liang on his left, a sheer cliff rose perpendicularly, and torrents of rainwater rushing down its gullies buffeted him roughly every few yards as they passed.

"The Fourth Regiment has a glorious battle record!" yelled a voice suddenly in the darkness ahead of him. "Our new mission is difficult — but we're determined to maintain our good name!"

"We'll outdo the First Regiment, which captured Anshunchang," roared another voice in response. "We'll capture the Luting bridge in three days!"

Liang, encouraged by the reassuring vigor and confidence of the shouts, peered ahead into the rain, searching for a hint of the white towel which each soldier in the Fourth Regiment had been ordered to drape across the back of his pack to make himself more visible. Seeing a patch of paleness begin bobbing rhythmically in the inky blackness, the former cookboy let go of the slippery boulder he was clutching and broke into a run again along the twisting trail.

As he ran, he pulled the long peak of his eight-sided cap lower over his eyes to keep out the stinging rain and eased the webbing straps of his backpack and rifle to more comfortable positions on his chest. In the pack he carried a ration bag of five pounds of cold boiled rice issued at Anshunchang, a metal drinking cup, chopsticks, a quilt, and two spare pairs of straw sandals. If the three hundred *li* separating Anshunchang and Luting were to be covered in three days, there would be no time for cooking, the Fourth Regiment's political commissars had announced in their departure briefings at dawn. In the eighteen hours that had passed since, only two halts had been called, to bolt down a few handfuls of the rice and drink a cup or two of rainwater.

"If you hear the Taiping water devils wailing from the river, don't listen," yelled another voice which Liang recognized as belonging to the Third Company's political instructor. "Forget the tragic fate of Shih Ta-kai. We will change history! We are the Chinese Workers' and Peasants' Red Army!"

"We are the Chinese Workers' and Peasants' Red Army!" chanted a chorus of voices, and Liang joined in eagerly as the shouted response was repeated over and over again in time with the jog-trotting pace of the troops.

A flash of lightning rent the darkness and for an instant Liang saw most of the men of the Third Company zigzagging upward along the narrow path, running in single file toward a high bluff that overhung the river. The white towels hanging from their packs shimmered in the glare, and among the infantrymen, Liang spotted a mounted officer battling to control a horse that had become terrified by the storm. The lightning also reflected for a fleeting moment on the steel helmets of half a dozen enemy troops crouching behind a sandbagged rampart near the top of the bluff. Before the darkness swallowed them again, Liang saw two or three of them rise up, swinging their arms stiffly above their heads in the familiar bowling action of trained Kuomintang grenade throwers.

"Watch out — grenades!"

Liang yelled his frantic warning, unslung his rifle, and dived for the cover of a shoulder of rock jutting from the cliff. Because they were closer beneath the overhanging bluff, the company vanguard had not seen the enemy strongpoint in the darkness and they were caught unawares as the grenades exploded among them. Violent orange flashes lit the night and the shouts of the wounded and dying rose above the terrified neighing of a horse and the rattle of machine-gun fire that followed.

When a new lightning flash illuminated the top of the bluff, Liang raised his rifle and fired twice at the Kuomintang machine gunner. But the range was too great and in the next interval of darkness he slipped out from behind the boulder, fixed his bayonet, and raced forward, bent double, up the slippery track, holding his rifle in front of him. The body of the officer's dead horse lying across the path brought him crashing to his knees; its rider, who was still trapped beneath it, let out a grunt of pain as Liang fell heavily against him. Struggling to his feet, Liang pulled the officer clear of the dead animal and together they flattened themselves against the foot of the rock. Thunder continued to crash through the heavens overhead and with each flash of lightning the machine gunner on the bluff swept the track with a fresh burst of fire.

"Are you hurt, Commander?" asked Liang, his chest heaving.

"I don't think so, comrade." Lu Chiao massaged his right thigh furiously as they lay side by side in the mud, their heads pressed to the ground. "But my right leg's numb from the weight of that brute."

"Somebody's got to climb the cliff and get around behind the machine gun, Commander," said Liang, screwing up his eyes against the driving rain. "I'm willing to try."

Chiao raised his head: scrub and brambles jutted from crevices in the sheer cliff face above them and the wet rock gleamed black in the glare of the lightning. "You'll have to climb like a mountain goat, comrade!" Chiao waited for the next flash of lightning to pass, then slapped Liang on the shoulder. "Go, now!"

Liang leapt to his feet and began hauling himself upward by his hands, seizing the bushes and searching blindly with his feet for foothold crevices in the rock. When the next fork of lightning split the sky, Chiao was surprised to see that Liang had scrambled fifty or sixty feet up the cliff and had begun edging toward the top of the bluff. The Kuomintang machine gunner noticed him in the same moment and began raking the cliff with long bursts of fire.

Unable to see Liang in the intervals of darkness, Chiao held his breath. Another flash of light on the mountainside picked out the former cookboy moving in a crouch along the top of the ridge; his rifle hung loose in his left hand while with his right he unfastened the pouches on his belt. Then Chiao heard two grenades explode inside the sandbagged emplacement in quick succession and the stutter of the machine gun died away. In another blaze of lightning, Liang leapt onto what was left of the parapet, thrusting his naked bayonet threateningly downward, and when Chiao scrambled up to the strongpoint, he found Liang still pointing his rifle at two prisoners who were stretched out facedown in the mud. The bodies of four other Nationalist soldiers lay still among the twisted metal of the wrecked machine gun, and after checking that they were dead, Chiao called up two other men of his company to bind the prisoners and take them away. Then he picked up a flickering hurricane lamp from a niche in the sandbags and turned back to the cookboy.

"What's your family name, comrade?"

"Liang, Commander."

"You're a brave fighter, Comrade Liang. You acted with great courage. How long have you served in the Red Army?"

"Eight weeks, Commander."

"But you have the speech of a man of Hunan."

"Yes, Commander. Before I was cookboy to your foreign prisoner. I carried his infant daughter in my baskets. I followed the Red Army all the way from Chentai to Kweichow. During that time I saw many Kuomintang prisoners change sides and put on your uniform . . ." Liang hesitated, dropping his eyes for a moment. "After the foreign prisoner's baby died I volunteered to join the Red Army. My two sons who came with me have become Hung Hsiao Kuei — 'Little Red Devils.' "

In the glow of the hurricane lamp, Chiao looked hard at Liang's strong peasant face: he had lost his cap in action and the rain had plastered his hair flat against his skull. Despite the arduousness of his climb and the exertion of the single-handed attack on the strongpoint, he had already regained his breath. His manner was respectful but he looked calmly back at Chiao with steady eyes.

"You may have been a cookboy, Comrade Liang, but you've learned to fight somewhere."

Liang nodded. "I served two years in the Chentai militia."

"And what made you want to join the Red Army?"

"I've seen you confiscate land many times from the *t'u hao*, and return it to the families they stole it from," answered Liang quietly, using the Communist term of abuse for despotic landlords. "The *t'u hao* stole my family's land. One day I hope the Red Army will help me get it back."

"The Red Army will confiscate the land of the *t'u hao* everywhere one day, Comrade Liang. All land will eventually be restored to its rightful owners, even in Chentai. But now we're fighting for our lives. We need thirty brave volunteers to seize the Luting bridge. It will be very hazardous. Do you wish to volunteer?"

"Yes, Commander," said Liang without hesitation. "I'll volunteer."

The sudden drum of hooves on the cliff path made both men turn and they watched a messenger from the Army Group Headquarters rein in a big black horse covered in lather. Jumping from the saddle, he pulled a sealed envelope from a leather satchel at his waist and hurried over to Chiao.

"I bring new orders from the Revolutionary Military Commission, Commander," said the messenger and thrust the package into Chiao's hands. Without waiting for a response, he ran back to his horse, swung up into the saddle, and spurred the animal back down the track the way he had come.

Chiao lifted the hurricane lamp to read the order, then looked at Liang again. "Our mission has become even more hazardous, comrade. Enemy forces are racing up from the south along the far bank of the river. We must double our speed and attack the bridge at dawn thirty hours from now." He smiled ruefully. "We still have two hundred forty *li* to go. We must cover two days' march in one."

3

Strung out over many miles along the forested heights above the Tatu, the Central Red Army rushed headlong toward Luting throughout the second night of their forced march, stopping neither to eat nor sleep. Ambulance carts, baggage animals, mortars, and other heavy weapons were left trundling far behind in the care of slow-moving caretaker platoons, while troops in the vanguard companies, faced with the task of covering eighty miles in twenty-four hours, dumped their packs and their ration bags at the side of the mountain trail and ran on more rapidly, carrying only rifles and ammunition pouches. The news that invisible Kuomintang regiments were racing northward somewhere on the far bank dropped a blanket of silence over the marchers, and only the tortured breathing of men and animals sounded in the smoky darkness as they pressed on rapidly over the precipitous trails, carrying a few blazing reed torches to light their way.

In the middle of the serpentine column the army and Party leaders had also dismounted to hurry forward on foot in front of the bodyguards who were leading their horses; to the rear of the General Headquarters column Lu Mei-ling was hastening ahead of her own mule, turning frequently to cast an anxious glance at the animal and her female orderly who was leading it. In the slippery mud of the narrow track the mule stumbled frequently, its hooves sometimes sending a shower of stones scudding noisily down the sheer drop into the river. Whenever the pannier basket on its back was jolted or shaken, a whimpering sound came from inside, but the woman orderly, without turning, made consoling noises over her shoulder as she plodded on.

"Although you're no longer Hua Fu's close companion, comrade, you don't seem to stray far on the march from the child you bore him."

Mei-ling recognized the friendly voice of Chou En-lai even before she made out his shadowy features; standing in the gloom with his back to the cliff, he had been staring across the river into the darkness on the far bank and as she passed he fell into step beside her.

"Am I right?"

Although there was no mistaking the warmth of Chou's interest, the directness of his question took her aback. Bending her head, she fixed her eyes on the muddy track before her as she struggled to frame her reply.

"There's no need to think of him as the child's father any longer, Commissioner Chou," she said at last, speaking with quiet deliberation. "A woman's emotions can sometimes lead her in the wrong direction for a time — but I want you to know that my enthusiasm for the revolution still comes first."

"Your loyalty to the revolution has never been in question, Mei-ling," said Chou reassuringly. "Perhaps in some ways you've even been too dutiful."

"Leading a mule through the western mountains with such an infant on its back is a major revolution in itself — for someone from a privileged world of arranged marriages and self-sacrificing wives. But I didn't plan things this way, Comrade Commissioner."

Chou, born himself of a privileged mandarin family, grunted in a way that indicated his sympathy. While marching beside her he had been scanning the far cliff top intently: now he looked at her again and smiled. "You're right. You already have much to be proud of. Giving women more freedom is an important part of breaking

the chains of the past. You're among a handful of pathfinders. . . .
Your work for me and the Military Commission has already shown
great imagination and dedication. . . ."

"I might have been more farsighted," said Mei-ling ruefully.

"You gave up a life of ease and you've endured the hardships of
the soviet areas and this march with courage as great as any man's.
No one woman can break through all the barriers overnight."

"Perhaps the trouble is that women in China have suffered too
long from bound minds as well as bound feet. I think the bindings
will have to be unraveled with great care. Many old traditions need
to be discarded — but traditions should not be confused with those
aspects of a woman's nature that are eternal and precious."

Chou looked hard at her. "You express your feelings well, comrade. Perhaps you should write down your thoughts for the benefit
of others. There will be a great need to help explain the sweeping
changes taking place in China."

"I keep a journal almost every day when we stop to rest." Mei-
ling smiled for the first time. "I intend one day to write something
of all I've seen and experienced . . ."

The commissioner nodded distractedly. He had halted suddenly
in the middle of the track and Mei-ling saw that he was staring again
into the darkness across the river. The Tatu was narrowing between
its high rock cliffs, and following his gaze she caught sight of a line
of flaming torches on the far bank, closing toward the ravine edge.

"They can't possibly be men of our First Division," whispered
Mei-ling. "We had radio messages from the First two hours ago,
remember, Commissioner? They've been blocked forty _li_ down-
river."

"Then that must be one of the Kuomintang regiments racing us
to Luting," said Chou grimly.

Mei-ling glanced ahead and saw that the course of the Tatu continued to narrow. Although the river foamed some three hundred
feet beneath them at the foot of the gorge, the trails along the cliff
tops on either bank were converging to within a hundred yards of
each other: soon the two armies would be close enough to be able
to hail one another — or open fire.

"If a battle develops here it might be impossible for us to reach
Luting in time," said Chou in an anxious tone. "They'll be close
enough to identify us soon."

"Bring up some Szechuan prisoners," suggested Mei-ling quickly. "I'll make the bugler identify us as their own men."

"An excellent idea." Chou instructed a messenger to hurry down the line to where the prisoners were marching and bring up several Szechuanese captives, including a company bugle boy. His hurried orders to march in total silence were passed along the entire column and while she strode on beside Chou En-lai, Mei-ling watched the moving lights on the far bank grow steadily brighter.

More and more torches appeared in a lengthening chain as the troops marched closer to the rim of the ravine, and soon it was obvious that at least a regiment was on the move, marching rapidly toward Luting. The Kuomintang units had clearly assumed that the few torches they could see on the western bank belonged to allies, since they made no attempt at concealment. The sound of ragged singing became faintly audible, then a bugle sounded, its clear, high notes echoing across the gorge: a moment later a hoarse Szechuanese shout rang out.

"Which units are you, fellow footsloggers?"

Three Szechuanese prisoners who had been captured on the march from Anshunchang had been hustled up the track to Mei-ling's side — two had their arms bound behind them and a third, a young bugler, had one arm free.

"Tell him to sound the answering call," ordered Mei-ling and the guard commander jabbed his Mauser into the ribs of the bugler, holding it there until the unfamiliar call floated out across the river. Turning to one of the bound prisoners, Mei-ling spoke quietly beside his ear. "Shout the name of your own unit — and make it natural."

"We are the Fourth Division of General Liu Wen-hui," yelled the prisoner, feeling the Mauser pushed sharply against his back. "We're heading for Luting to kill Red Bandits!"

After a brief pause the bugle on the far bank repeated its call in acknowledgment and the voice shouted back cheerily, "Good luck, Fourth Division — but leave some Red Bandits for us to kill!"

As the twin lines of troops hurried north side by side, Mei-ling looked down and saw the double row of torches glowing red in the turbulent waters of the Tatu below. For two hours the dancing reflections of the torchlight vied with one another on the surface of the river; then around midnight another storm broke. Lightning flashed and thunder rolled as new squalls of rain drove down onto the marchers. The storm gave way to heavy, persistent rain and across the river Mei-ling saw the line of fiery lights come to a halt.

"The enemy are making camp to rest," she whispered urgently to Chou En-lai, who was still marching at her side. "This is our chance!"

Chou nodded; in a crisp voice he issued fresh orders to move on faster. The messengers at once set off up and down the column and the pace was stepped up. As the marchers hurried past her, Mei-ling took the bridle of her mule from the female orderly and checked and tightened the girths of the saddle pannier. When she was satisfied that the basket was secure, she turned and bent her slender shoulders once more to the task of dragging the mule on more quickly through the downpour toward Luting.

Running with the spearhead companies of the Second Division, who had pressed forward for a whole day and a night without rest, Liang felt himself growing light-headed with fatigue during the hours before dawn. Time and again on the narrow mountain tracks he stumbled into men more exhausted than himself who were falling asleep on their feet. "Keep going, comrade," he yelled each time, pushing them hard from behind to waken them; then he ran on, searching in the darkness for the white towel on the next backpack ahead.

Once he saw a young soldier in front of him stagger like a sleep-walker for a few yards and pitch headlong over the edge of the track: he disappeared soundlessly into the darkness and only a faint splash in the Tatu far below marked his disappearance. Seeking out Chiao, the horrified Liang suggested that every man should unwind the puttees from his legs, join them, and tie himself to his comrades in front and behind. Chiao gave the order at once and the vanguard troops hurried on, linked together in a long chain that helped those who faltered and jerked back to wakefulness any man among them who fell asleep.

Often the leading troops had to hack new paths through the thick underbrush of the forested mountainsides. Detours were forced when it was found that the trail had collapsed into the river on sheer cliff faces, and twice bridges over fast-rushing tributaries of the Tatu that the enemy had destroyed were rapidly rebuilt by engineer companies with trees felled from the forests. By the time the first pale signs of dawn relieved the darkness, the rains had stopped and thick mist wreathed the high trails. Moving quietly like insubstantial ghosts in the half-light, the Red Army men jogged down through a sleeping mountain hamlet where terraced potato fields blanketed with white flowers surrounded neat stone-walled houses: in the orchards the fruit trees were heavy with pink blossoms and through gaps in the mist the troops saw a massive range of snow-capped mountains rearing to the west. Then they plunged into a deep forest again and climbed a long, steep path to the top of a pine-covered crag. As they reached the crest the first low rays of the sun penetrated the mist and Liang caught a glimpse between the trees of the black iron chains of Luting far below. Strung in one giant skein between two ancient towers that flanked the gorge, they were swaying slowly in the wind, high above the river. In an awed silence the men of all the leading companies stopped and gazed down at the centuries-old bridge, their exhaustion momentarily forgotten.

"They've removed the floor planks," said Chiao in a tense voice as he surveyed the bridge through binoculars. "That means we've got to fight our way across the gorge on the bare chains!"

4

Liang stared apprehensively into the reddish brown waters of the Tatu. Fingers of white spume flung high by jagged reefs groped toward the chain bridge as though trying to rip it from its pillars, and the river's roar drowned even the whine of mortar shells being fired from concealed Kuomintang batteries sited on the eastern bank.

"Never look down, comrades, once you get on the chains," shouted Chiao. "Keep your eyes on the opposite bank — that's the most important thing to remember."

Lying spread-eagled behind a low stone parapet on the hillside overlooking the western end of the bridge, Chiao and twenty-two volunteers had a bird's-eye view of their objective and the walled town of Luting nestling against the yellow mountainside beyond it. Thirteen chains in all swayed in the windy void above the river, each link as thick as a man's arm; embedded in the rock and stonework of the fortified towers at either end, nine of the chains formed the floor of the bridge while two identical chains at either side provided hand supports. A distance of about a hundred and twenty yards separated the two towers and from where they lay, the volunteers could see that the planks that normally served as footboards had been torn up across more than two thirds of its width. Only a few boards remained in place at the far side, approaching the tower which was one of the town's main gates.

"Machine guns have been set up in the bridge house at the eastern end," shouted Chiao, inspecting the ornate towers through his binoculars: the upswept eaves of the vermilion-tiled roof, the red-lacquered wooden pillars, and the enamel frieze decorations provided an incongruous imperial setting for the ugly muzzles of the Kuomintang weapons he could see poking out through sandbagged embrasures. "Your first task, comrades, will be to silence those machine guns. Nobody else will be able to cross until that job is done."

Liang waited until the dust thrown up by an exploding mortar shell settled in front of the parapet, then raised his head to look over it. Never in his life had he seen such a structure — swaying and clanking in the rising wind, the black iron chains were suspended in a shallow curve between the towers, a precarious passage over the river even in normal times. Through slits in the ocher walls of the stone tower, Liang imagined he could see the heads of Kuomintang gunners moving as they oiled, loaded, and sighted along the chains in readiness to repel the Red Army assault. Suddenly the hundred-and-twenty-yard stretch the shock force would have to cover crawling on the chains seemed more like twenty *li*!

Liang's body, like those of his twenty-one comrades, bristled with weapons: twelve stick grenades hung at his waist, a gleaming, long-handled broadsword was thrust through his belt; and a captured Thompson submachine gun with a circular magazine was strapped tight to his shoulder. Some of the men carried a Mauser machine pistol and others had long knives thrust into their puttees for close fighting. Half an hour earlier in a forest hollow, Liang and the other members of the group had ravenously consumed a catty of fat pork and a basin of boiled rice and cabbage. After choosing them from among two hundred volunteers, Chiao had told the little force that he believed men fought better on a full stomach; soon afterward the well-stocked larders of a landlord's house in the foothills had been gleefully broken open on his orders by the men who had run hungrily through the night to Luting. While Chiao and a group of battalion and company officers reconnoitered and planned the assault, Liang and the other shock troops had snatched a few hours' sleep, stretched out like dead men on the ground in the same wooded hollow where they had eaten. It was afternoon before they were roused, and by then a strong wind was gusting through the gorge.

"We estimate the enemy has two regiments inside the town," shouted Chiao, pointing across the river toward the sprawl of houses built within the protection of the twenty-foot wall. "We've sent a battalion down our side of the river to prevent enemy reinforcements moving on the eastern bank. The path we can see along the river is the only one they could use. Our First Division, which crossed at Anshunchang, is marching up that bank too, but they've been delayed by heavy fighting . . ."

Glancing around over his shoulder, Liang saw squads of engineers dragging logs down the hillside from the forest. The few deserted stone cottages clustered around the western end of the bridge had already been ransacked for doors and floorboards and the logs were being added to the stacks of timber piled up behind them. In the shadow of these buildings two other platoons of volunteers were standing by, ready to advance behind the first assault group and lay down planks and timbers that would make the crossing easier for the rest of the army. Along the length of a ridge higher up the hillside, half a dozen heavy machine-gun companies and several hundred riflemen, handpicked for their sharpshooting skills, had already been deployed to provide covering fire when the attack began. Liang had watched them creeping out of the forest earlier to take up their positions, hidden from the enemy by the contours of the hillside; they remained invisible now, waiting for the order to fire, and Liang also knew that all the other units which had dashed north from Anshunchang were bivouacked out of sight behind the crag above them. He imagined the thousands of tense Red Army men waiting there, watching and listening to discover whether the way beyond Luting was to be opened to them or whether they had run into their final trap on the Tatu, as Prince Shih Ta-kai had done. The thought filled him with renewed determination and he checked all his weapons carefully one last time.

"Comrades, the lives of thirty thousand Red Army men depend on you! The future of our revolution could be decided here on these chains!" Chiao looked toward the stone cottage behind which all the company buglers of the Fourth Regiment were gathered together, watching him. When he raised his arm the buglers, many of them Little Red Devils, lifted their instruments obediently to their lips.

"The moment you hear the bugles, remember you're the finest soldiers in the Red Army. Where the warriors of history have failed, the Chinese workers and peasants of the twentieth century will show the way to victory!"

Chiao snapped his arm downward and a liquid shaft of sound split the skies above the gorge as a dozen bugles blasted out "Charge!" in unison. A wall of noise erupted from the top of the ridge, the heavy machine guns and rifles opening up simultaneously at the far bank, and Liang and the rest of the assault force rose up as one man, yelling at the top of their voices, to sprint frantically downhill toward the bridge. Chiao ran with them, brandishing a pistol above his head and shouting encouragement to each man by name as he went. Liang, running behind him, felt nothing until he flung himself full-length onto the heaving chains of the bridge. Fear and elation, rising like fire through his body, had fused inside his head with the thrilling blasts of the massed bugles: loping easily behind Chiao, he had barely noticed the weight of weaponry he carried and seemed almost to fly over the ground. Only when Chiao ducked aside by the western tower to continue directing the operation did he hear the roar of the Kuomintang heavy machine guns.

A dozen of his comrades were moving ahead of him, hauling themselves forward on their bellies at great speed with both hands. Under the impact of the men's weight the nine chains were beginning to writhe and shake like living serpents — waves rippled toward Liang through the jangling iron links, which lifted him violently, dropped him again, threatened to roll him sideways into the void. The whole bridge was swaying in the wind and the chains beneath him parted whenever he moved carelessly, revealing sickening glimpses of the surging waves far below. Remembering Chiao's prime exhortation not to look down, he raised his head to stare toward the far bank and saw showers of sparks fly from the iron in front of his face as machine-gun bullets from the far tower gate ricocheted past him.

The man immediately in front of Liang was the first to fall. Hit in the chest, he slipped between the chains to hang head downward for a second or two with his foot twisted in the links: then the movement of the bridge shook him free and he plunged like a stone to disappear among the wave-lashed reefs. Gripping more tightly with his knees and arms, Liang tried to keep several chains bunched beneath him and inched forward, hugging them to his body. To

avoid the deadly frontal fire of the machine guns in the tower, half
a dozen of the volunteers lowered themselves deliberately through
the chains and swung along on rapidly pumping arms, dangling
vertically beneath the bridge. But the strong wind whirled two of
them away into the raging torrent like winged sycamore seeds, and
a machine gun dugout at the foot of the cliff cut the others down
from below before they reached the middle of the river.

With bugles still blowing at their backs, Liang and the surviving
volunteers scrambled onward, struggling in the chains like flies in
an iron-mesh spider's web. Several Kuomintang aircraft appeared,
winging down the gorge one behind the other, their engines only
intermittently audible above the roar of battle. Making a belated
attempt to destroy the bridge, they swooped low to attack and Liang
watched a cluster of finned bombs arc gently through the air toward
him as the aircraft rose above the chains at the last minute. Some of
the bombs flew over his head, others passed beneath him, all emitting
an eerie whistling sound. But the bridge of chains was a difficult
target, and new, explosive pillars of spray erupted from the river
below when the bombs burst harmlessly among the reefs.

Watching from the shelter of the tower on the western bank, Chiao
stood rooted to the spot; the second assault group, armed with planks
and logs, had moved up behind the tower and was waiting anxiously
for his order to move onto the chains. Regimental and battalion
commanders who were ready to bring their reinforcements down
from the forest watched and waited beside him too in an agony of
suspense. Each time one of the volunteers fell or was shot from the
bridge Chiao winced and added to the mental tally he was keeping
inside his head. His gaze was fixed hopefully on five or six of the
leading figures, who had struggled to their knees and were hauling
themselves along the hand chains on one side, firing their big Mauser
machine pistols at the tower with their free hand. Nearing the middle
of the bridge, they were attracting the concentrated fire of the Kuomintang machine gunners in the tower and one by one they collapsed
to lie entangled in the chains like lifeless rag dolls.

"Fourteen! . . . fifteen! . . . sixteen!"

Chiao in his anxiety began counting aloud without realizing it,
gluing his binoculars to his eyes to watch the half-dozen survivors
of the squad, who were still slithering forward in the belly of the
bridge. Only twenty yards or so separated them from the nearest

foot planks but they were having to crawl over the bodies of the fallen volunteers; seeing Liang pause beside one motionless figure, Chiao cupped his hands to his mouth.

"Keep going, Liang! Others will help the wounded. Go for the planks and charge!"

Over a field telephone Chiao issued fresh orders to the heavy machine-gun companies and another sustained roar rose from the hillside behind him. He signaled to the regimental buglers too and immediately a renewed clarion call echoed across the ravine. Shards of tile, timber, and stone flew from the far tower under the new Red Army machine-gun onslaught, but the redoubt survived and the Kuomintang gunners continued to pour fire toward the dwindling shock force. Through his glasses Chiao saw Kuomintang soldiers run suddenly from the base of the tower carrying heavy cans. They sent liquid cascading along the planks toward the center of the bridge and one dropped a lighted rag before they sped back into the protection of the tower. The orange wall of kerosene flame that raced along the planking in the direction of the shock force moved faster than a man could run and Liang started up on his knees among the chains, staring fearfully at the flames moving toward him.

"Charge now! The fate of the Red Army is at stake!" shouted Chiao desperately through his hands again, and the other officers and men around him took up the chant. "Charge now, comrades! Charge!"

Clouds of thick black smoke swirled in the gusting wind, obscuring the bridge, and in its midst Liang rose unsteadily to his feet. To his dismay his tommy gun had slipped from his shoulder and he watched helplessly as it spiraled down into the river. Then the heat from the wall of fire rushing at him struck his face like a blow and the crackle of the flames mingled in his ears with the shouts of exhortation coming from behind him. Looking around, he found four other young faces at his shoulder staring in terror at the burning planks; the sight of their fear increased his own, but on hearing Chiao's yelled commands, he drew his broadsword and flourished it above his head.

"Forward, comrades!" he yelled at the top of his voice. "Forward to victory!"

Stumbling off-balance along the last few feet of slippery chains, Liang launched himself into the fire and felt his feet touch solid wood. His cap caught fire at once but the wind plucked it from his head and tossed it, flaming, into the river. As he dashed deeper into the fire he suddenly heard his own voice repeating long-forgotten foreign words. "O Lord God, in my hour of need, please forgive and protect me! . . . O Lord God, in my hour of need, please forgive and protect me!" Swerving through the smoke and flames and stepping where he could on unburned boards, the former cookboy realized he was unconsciously repeating a short prayer Pastor Ke had taught him after his baptism.

Behind him he heard the frenzied drum of other feet, then abruptly out of the smoke reared the ancient yellow stone tower. A machine-gun barrel was spurting flame from an embrasure just above his head, and dodging beneath it, Liang smashed at it with his sword, knocking it askew; snatching one of his stick grenades from his belt, he tossed it through the sandbagged viewing slit above the weapon. As the grenade exploded, Liang flung himself to the ground and rolled frantically back and forth on the stone terrace of the tower, trying to put out his burning cotton uniform. Through a mist of searing pain he saw the remaining survivors dash out of the flames with their own clothes smoldering, firing their tommy guns and hurling grenades at other enemy machine-gun emplacements around the base of the tower. Dimly he noticed that the khaki-uniformed defenders were fleeing in panic, and soon the Red Army men had swung the muzzles of the weapons around and were firing on other Nationalist strongpoints along the shore.

Looking back across the swaying bridge, Liang saw men of the two support platoons rushing forward, fixing logs and planks across the bare chains. Engineers came on, beating out the flames, and from beyond them Liang heard a storm of cheering rise from around the eastern tower. Cries of "Long live the Red Army!" and "Long live the revolution!" rang out from hundreds of throats as reinforcement units began flooding across the bridge.

The pain of the burns on his face and limbs grew more intense and Liang began to lose consciousness as he lay on the ground at the foot of the tower. The sounds of battle spreading through the walled town behind him grew fainter in his ears, and when stretcher bearers arrived fifteen minutes later his eyes were closed. As they bent to lift him he murmured "O Lord God, in my hour of need, please forgive and protect me," but the English words meant nothing to the Red Army medical orderlies, and they paid no heed as they ran with him as fast as they could to a makeshift casualty station.

5

Beyond Luting the June sun blazed down on rich, fertile Sze-chuanese valleys dotted with pear, apple, and cherry orchards. Shady green forests swallowed them up, then gave way to field after field of tomatoes, potatoes, and pumpkins. Cloudless blue skies framed the stark beauty of the snow-covered Ta Hsueh Shan mountain peaks that every hour grew larger on the northern horizon. Finding them-selves elated by these great vistas and their resounding victory at Luting, the Communist soldiers marching around the dejected figure of Jakob joked boisterously among themselves and sang one of their favorite songs over and over again.

> *"Red Army sharpshooters are we,*
> *With each bullet we fell another enemy!"*

The battle in the walled town of Luting had lasted only two hours. The two defending Kuomintang regiments, astonished and disheart-ened by the speed and daring of the lightning strike across the bare chains, had quickly broken and fled. The First Division, which had crossed at Anshunchang, had marched up the eastern bank in time to put other Nationalist reinforcements to flight and all the remaining men, weapons, and pack animals of the entire Central Red Army had poured jubilantly across the swaying bridge during the next two days.

Stumbling in their midst, Jakob had given little more attention to the spectacular bridge than he had to the dramatic Yangtze gorges or the great primeval forests of Lololand through which he had been marched under close guard. Since watching Liang carry out the burial in Yunnan, his feelings of despair had deepened and he seemed to live with only half his conscious mind in the pain-wracked reality of the daily forced marches. Some part of him, rebelling against the mute hostility which surrounded him, had lingered, sorrowing, be-side the earth mound which the cookboy had heaped over the closed zipper bag in the black sorghum field.

An uneasy sense of shame at begging for death himself beside the tiny grave also haunted his memory and at other times he reexpe-rienced the helpless agony of that pine-clad hillside outside Paoshan where he had last glimpsed the dislocated shadow of Felicity lying among the tree stumps. Feeding on one another, these bleak images replayed themselves in his imagination, numbing his reactions to his own suffering until he marched often like a sleepwalker, unconsciously blotting out the sights and sounds around him. Even the sight of the Red Army standard and the canvas bearing the Christmas star failed to inspire him when it appeared above the marching column, and without realizing it he began to pray less often and with less conviction. Only when the Hunanese guard commander jeeringly asked if his God had deserted him because he no longer said prayers openly over each meager bowl of food did he become aware how far his faith had been undermined.

He had attempted at once to rededicate himself to a new discipline of regular worship but two days later, Judge Yang had appeared scowling beside him on his horse as they marched through Lolo territory. He announced baldly that Matthew Barlow had been killed by bandits on the Yunnan-Kweichow border. "They say a 'goodwill offering' of ten thousand dollars in silver was stolen by the bandits," he barked contemptuously. "That would not have been sufficient in any event to secure your release." The judge had flourished a paper and demanded angrily that Jakob sign what amounted to a prewritten letter of confession that he was a spy and that the full three-hundred-thousand-dollar fine was therefore justified. The letter also invited him to admit that he had further incriminated himself by trying to escape from the Red Army's custody — but Jakob, appalled by the news of Barlow's death, turned away in a daze without responding and trudged on, ignoring the judge's shouts. Whenever the Communist official approached him during rest stops, Jakob remained mute, immersed in his grief at the violent death of the heroic figure who had long ago inspired him to come to China.

His faith in prayer faltered again and over the weeks that followed his sense of desolation grew. The loss of Abigail so soon after rediscovering her and his separation from Liang and his sons left him feeling more acutely isolated than before among the marching horde of Communist soldiery. Liang had ceased to serve him immediately after the burial in the sorghum field; the cookboy had not come to see him again and no explanation had been offered by his guards, who resumed their practice of giving him his food wordlessly.

Then, a few days later, Jakob had caught sight of Liang in the distance. He still wore his faded blue cotton jacket and trousers at that time but his carrying pole was gone from his shoulder, gray puttees were wound around his calves, and he had tucked a broad-

sword through his belt. When Jakob saw him the next time, he had
added a gray cap with a red star to his garb, and within a fortnight
Liang was fully outfitted in a gray cotton uniform, ammunition
bandoliers, a bedroll, pack, and rifle. Soon afterward, among the
Hung Hsiao Kuei, the Little Red Devils, Jakob recognized Liang's
sons. Big Liang was toting a satchel of posters and a bucket of paste,
racing around behind the propaganda squads, who still plastered
every village they passed with slogans; Little Liang was assisting a
medical orderly, carrying a box with a red cross on its side and doling
out iodine and cotton bandages to lightly wounded troops. The
cookboy and his sons never looked toward the group of prisoners
nor attempted to acknowledge Jakob; whenever he spotted them,
they were going eagerly about their tasks as though no thought of
the past remained in their minds.

Despite his distractedness, Jakob could not fail to notice that the
impoverished peasants of the western provinces greeted the Red
Army with the same eagerness and enthusiasm he had witnessed
earlier — in each village they cheered as the troops and Little Red
Devils painted and pasted up slogans announcing that the Red Army
was the fighting force of the poor and oppressed. They lined up
eagerly to receive grain and clothes confiscated from the houses of
the rich and poured bitter recriminations on those officials and landowners marched away as prisoners. Stirred by the fiery speeches of
political commissars who urged them to rise against the exploitation
by the "local tyrants," young volunteers flocked to replenish the Red
Army's depleted ranks in many villages along the route. Nationalist
troops taken prisoner were also donning the Red Army uniform in
increasing numbers and the cheerful courage with which veterans
and newcomers alike endured battle wounds and the hardships of
the march impressed Jakob anew. Although there were some desertions, the infectious spirit of the columns spread to most of the young
soldiers, bearing them onward in a mood of high optimism, and the
realization that his Christian missionary work in China had never
inspired such a dramatic response dispirited Jakob further.

The furious pace of the trek along the ravines above the Tatu also
took a fresh toll on his fading strength. He was still suffering intermittent bouts of fever and his swollen, callused feet, protected only
by cloth and straw sandals, suffered fresh lacerations with each new
march. The raw wounds of his back also pained him greatly, and
because his hands were bound, he fell frequently. As his guards

hustled him down the hill toward the Luting crossing, Jakob had realized with a fresh stab of shame that almost his first thought on catching sight of the bridge was how easily he might seek release from his suffering by hurling himself over the low side chains into the surging river. But his guards, conscious of the dangers on the unsteady crossing, seized the rope harness that still hung at his back and frog-marched him in close order across to the eastern bank.

Stories of the Luting bridge assault had spread quickly along the marching columns as they headed more slowly through the fertile highlands of western Szechuan, free at last from close pursuit by the Kuomintang. Jakob's guards had taken perverse pleasure in informing him that his former servant had fought heroically in the battle, and he had endured their taunts in silence. Liang's espousal of the Red Army cause had not in fact come as a great shock to Jakob: the peasant cookboy, he understood, had much in common with the soldiers of the Red Army. Yet the readiness of a man who had lived with Christian missionaries to risk his life for a new, alien cause seemed to Jakob in his misery to cast even greater doubt on the value of his Christian teaching in China.

As they marched on through the strengthening summer sunshine, Jakob scanned the valley and forest tracks in front and behind for a glimpse of Liang but he did not catch sight of him until two weeks after the Luting battle, when he appeared before a rally of thousands of troops on a hillside in sight of the dazzling peaks of the Ta Hsueh Shan — the Great Snow Mountains. The assembled regiments sitting on the grass roared their approval as the Red Army's commander in chief, Chu Teh, presented new caps, new cotton tunics, enamel eating bowls, and chopsticks to the survivors of the Luting crossing. To Jakob's dismay Liang, like several of his fellows, still wore heavy bandages about his head and on one arm; his face had obviously been burned and he walked with difficulty onto a makeshift platform to receive his honor from Chu Teh. It was announced that special Gold Star medals for valor would be presented to the Luting heroes at a later date and renewed cheering greeted this news.

"Heroism is an ancient concept, comrades," shouted Chu Teh when the cheering had died away and Liang and the other Tatu heroes had retreated to the side of the platform. "In our past history heroes rose from among the ordinary people. They became generals and emperors and often came to despise the masses. Sometimes they tried to enslave the mass of the people. But today the Red Army is creating a new concept of heroism. We are creating mass heroes of the revolution who have no selfish interests, who are willing to die for the revolution if necessary, but who above all wish to live and fight until the mass of the people is liberated!"

Chu Teh swung one of his big hands in the direction of Liang and his group. "These few brave fighters survived the heroic struggle to seize the Luting bridge. Equally brave comrades met their deaths in the flames and the raging waters of the river. Others who survived were too severely wounded to be here today. For a few minutes the fate of the Red Army rested with them and they triumphed over great odds. For that we honor all of them — and to the survivors we offer both medals and gifts suitable to the Chinese Workers' and Peasants' Army — a new food bowl, chopsticks, a new battle tunic!"

A fresh roar of approval arose from the great throng covering the hillside, interspersed with chants of "Long live the heroes of Tatu Ho!" but before it died away Chu Teh lifted his right hand to point toward the snow-decked peaks shimmering above the hillside to the north.

"But now, comrades, ahead of us lies a route that is even more difficult than the one behind us. A route for new heroes. If we are to join up with our comrades in the Fourth Front Army in northern Szechuan and achieve our objective to fight and defeat the Japanese invaders, we must cross some of the highest mountains in the world, mountains bristling with glaciers and covered in eternal snow. We may have to break our own trails, comrades, and many of us are lowlanders who have never seen snow and never experienced extreme cold. . . ."

The massed regiments seated on the hillside grew quiet and turned their heads as one man to look up at the towering peaks of the Great Snow Mountains. Jagged and glittering like a forest of silver spear tips, the mountains stretched ominously into the far distance; glaciers sparkled like mirrors on the crags and deep chasms that divided the range shone with fresh snow.

"Szechaunese people will tell you those mountains are so high that birds can't fly over them, comrades! They call them the magic mountains. They'll tell you that the gods of the mountain will strangle you if you speak on the high passes — because the air is so rarefied. They'll tell you that only immortals can fly over them . . . but the Workers' and Peasants' Red Army of China will march over them, comrades — by making careful preparations! The enemy might expect us to detour to the east or the west and that's where they'll be looking for us with their bombers. But we shall do the unexpected as we've always done, comrades, and march straight over the top . . ."

Chu Teh raised his eyes toward the sun: burning out of an azure blue sky, it was bathing the hillside in a fierce warmth. Even in their thin cotton uniforms the men sweated whenever they moved.

"But although it's high summer down here, comrades, don't be misled. Commissar Mao instructs you to gather as many hot chilies and as much root ginger as you can. Boil them and fortify yourself well with the liquid before each day's climb. In the Great Snow Mountains it will be colder than any winter you've ever known. But the sun will still glare down — so take strips of cloth to tie around your eyes to ward off snow blindness. Take enough food and fuel in your ration bags for ten days, wrap rags around your feet, walk steadily without pausing, and never stop or speak on the heights —"

The commander in chief paused and his face relaxed into its famous simian grin, which creased his features with countless concentric lines. "I wish you luck crossing the magic mountains, comrades! Long live the Chinese Workers' and Peasants' Red Army!"

Jakob's guards hauled him to his feet and turned him to face the glittering peaks. Within minutes the whole of the Central Red Army was moving toward the icy mass of rock and snow that reared up along the borderlands between China and Tibet.

6

"Don't sit down to rest! If you do, you may never get up again!"

The quavering voice of one of the guards regiment's political instructors echoed along the sheer ice walls of a snow gully close beneath the first peak in the Great Snow Mountain range. The path leading up to the pass was solid, frozen snow which Jakob's rag-bound feet could not grip and often he fell to his knees and continued scrambling upward on all fours. The intense cold close to the sixteen-thousand-foot summit had rimed the beard around his mouth with white icicles and turned his lips and hands blue. As the column climbed higher, the jaws of an invisible vise seemed to be tightening slowly around his chest, constricting his lungs: from time to time

his hearing seemed blurred and faint and his breath had begun to
rasp noisily in his throat. The lack of oxygen was also making him
dizzy, and the billowing sea of snowy peaks stretching endlessly
westward into Tibet swam before his eyes whenever he turned his
head in its direction.

"Don't try to talk . . . Just keep moving!"

The voice of the political instructor was faltering badly from exertion and even he could not entirely conceal the sense of shock
which had spread rapidly through the ranks of all the regiments as
they struggled against the fierce, strength-sapping extremes of the
mountain heights. Starting the climb at dawn on a clear morning
after a day of rest, the whole Central Red Army had begun singing
lustily as it wound in single file up the narrow goat tracks leading
toward the snow line. The staves carried by every man rang on the
stony trails as the columns moved smartly out of the green valleys
into the barren foothills, but hour after hour of arduous climbing
seemed to move them no nearer to the shining passes high above
them. Soon the laborious effort of dragging their feet through the
deep drifts of the lower snowfields had begun to take its toll on their
morale, and all singing quickly died away.

Before they had ascended to halfway, the first storm had blown
up with frightening suddenness — dark clouds scudded across the
mountain face and furious winds began to whip the ground snow
into blinding flurries all around the marchers, blotting out the sun.
Among the shouts of alarm and the neighing of terrified horses, Jakob
heard the screams of a squad marching just ahead of him as they
plunged into a deep chasm beside the track. The guards had halted
the prisoners while attempts were made to lower ropes into the chasm
but heavy snow had begun to fall; driven by the rising wind, it
swirled in drifts around the rescuers, and orders were quickly given
to abandon the rescue attempt and resume the climb.

Many troops, shivering in thin cotton uniforms, had tied blankets
and padded bedroll quilts about their bodies in an effort to keep the
cold at bay and whole companies joined hands to climb the sheer
paths in footholds hacked from the ice by pathfinder units. During
one of the early rest halts below the snow line, Chu Teh himself
had appeared, moving quickly through the units, weighing each
man's pack in his hands to check that none was too heavy. When he
came to the prisoners — only about a hundred Kuomintang troops
and half a dozen dejected landowners remained under guard besides

Jakob — the commander in chief had paid as much attention to them as he had done to the Red Army men.

Jakob's guards had tied a food pouch made from cloth about his shoulders which contained buckwheat, two or three red peppers, some root ginger, and a cake made of *chingko*, a form of highland barley. His hands, however, unlike those of the civilian landowners and officials, remained lashed together behind his back, and when he saw this, Chu Teh had gestured smilingly toward the Hunanese guard commander for him to have one of his men unfasten them.

"If the foreign spy wished to escape in this wilderness, he would be very welcome, wouldn't he?" Chu had chuckled, but on glancing down at Jakob's swollen feet and the cloth and straw sandals he had been allowed to plait for himself, his face had grown serious. "You'd better give him a stout staff and find him some rags to bind around his toes as well — or he won't even be able to keep up with our slowest mule."

When the storm struck, Jakob had found the staff invaluable. Often the blinding blizzard blotted out the track ahead and he prodded drifts and rocks cautiously with the staff before proceeding. Once he knocked snow from a ledge onto which his guard was urging him to step and withdrew in time to watch tons of snow and rocks cascade downward into a yawning gulf. Back on the correct route, they found that the track led up cliff faces where footholds cut by others became virtual ladders in the frozen snow; Jakob climbed these clinging to the staff of the guard above while hauling up the guard below on his own. No words were exchanged but gradually Jakob became aware that the hostile atmosphere which normally surrounded him had given way for the first time to something different: battling side by side in the most extreme conditions they had faced, captors and captives were suddenly united by their common desire to survive.

After an hour the winds eased, the snow ceased to fall, and the dark clouds that had cloaked the mountain during the blizzard faded to haze and mist — but the marchers' alarm increased when they found how many of their comrades were succumbing to the combined effects of severe cold and lack of oxygen. Those enfeebled by dysentery and fever fell quickly, but hardier men respected for their physical strength and stamina were unaccountably dying in their tracks too: crouched or curled up in the drifts beside the path, they made no response when others seized their frozen hands and tried to haul them upright. Jakob, coming on a scrawny soldier of the guards regiment half-buried in deep snow, knelt to lift him to his feet, but the youth's head lolled loosely backward, his eyes frozen open, his body already chilled and stiff in the missionary's arms. Jakob recognized the features of the guard who had so eagerly carried out the brutal execution of the young Kiangsi prisoner in the early days of the march, the same guard he had rescued from the Hsiang River, and he automatically murmured a prayer and began trying to scoop out a shallow grave in the snowdrift. But the exertion made his head swim and another guard, coming up from behind, pulled Jakob to his feet and gesticulated silently for him to leave the corpse and hurry onward.

Before long, clear signs of panic began to show in the faces of the soldiers and guards marching around Jakob. The vague sense of awe which snow-covered mountains had always inspired in China's peasants had become a palpable fear and they stared up at the massive ice walls towering around them with frightened eyes. The suddenness with which their comrades were falling dead in the snow also made the surviving troops realize how weak and debilitated they had become after eight months of nonstop marching and fighting. Noticing this reaction, the political instructors made new efforts to reinspire them as they neared the pass straddling the summit.

"Just keep walking steadily, comrades," called the guards regiment chief commissar hoarsely, as they pushed on. "Loosen your tunics and your belts a little to help your breathing. Chew some ginger — but don't stop to eat or relieve yourself. It could be fatal."

Jakob unslung his food pouch from his shoulder and tried to eat some ginger as he continued the climb, but in his exhausted condition the pungency of the root made him cough and retch and he could not swallow it. His head felt heavy and his legs seemed to lose their strength for no reason. Seeing the bodies of Red Army soldiers scattered like chaff beside the track, he began to wonder whether he too was close to death: the rags which the guards had found for him to bind around his feet on Chu Teh's instructions were sodden and worn through already, his feet were numb with cold, and he shivered constantly inside his sodden gown which hung torn and threadbare about his limbs. When the sun came out to shine blindingly on the snow again, he found he could not focus his gaze and he began to sway from side to side on the narrow track. Beneath him the icy mass of the mountainside seemed to heave like the deck of a ship in a storm, and despite the repeated warnings of the political instructor, he had to stop frequently to control his ragged breathing.

"Please try to keep moving, Ke Mu-shih — if you don't you'll die!"

Among the turmoil of prisoners, soldiers, and pack animals pressing anxiously past him toward the crest of the mountain, Jakob could not at first be sure who had whispered the pleading words of encouragement. His own guard, who had slipped on the ice twenty yards away, was still scrambling to catch up, and only when he looked down at his side did the missionary recognize the round, cheerful face of Little Liang beneath a rime-covered Red Army cap several times too large for him.

"Please drink this." The Little Red Devil thrust a metal cup containing yellow liquid up at the missionary. "My brother and I boiled red peppers to make it this morning."

Little Liang replaced the stopper in a small vacuum bottle and put it away in the medical box he carried slung around his narrow shoulders. Both Jakob and the boy glanced inquiringly at the guard as he caught up with them, and when he nodded his approval, Jakob took the proffered cup and drank the hot peppery liquid straight down. It made him cough but it warmed him, and leaning heavily on his staff, Jakob began pushing himself up the steep incline once more with Little Liang trudging beside him.

"I've been marching with the medical corps, looking after my father," whispered Little Liang, nodding toward the rear of the column, which was visible snaking up the mountainside behind them. "He noticed you were staggering and sent me to help." The boy's face took on an anxious expression. "Are you all right, Ke Mu-shih?"

Jakob nodded, concentrating all his strength on climbing.

"My father hopes you don't think badly of him for joining the army holding you prisoner, Ke Mu-shih. He says for China it's a good army — it helps the poor!" Little Liang glanced around over his shoulder to see if the guard was listening and moved closer to Jakob. "My father says the Red Army isn't like the warlord armies. There's no looting or stealing from ordinary people. All food is paid for — except when it's confiscated from rich landlords! Officers and men eat and live together and the officers aren't ever allowed to beat the soldiers. Soldiers can even criticize their officers at meetings after the fighting! One day we hope the Red Army will get our land back for us — that's what my father told me to say."

"You can tell your father I understand," gasped Jakob. "But don't talk. Save your energy."

"It doesn't tire me, Ke Mu-shih," whispered the boy, climbing without difficulty at the missionary's side. "And I have something else to tell you from my father . . ."

Fifty or sixty feet above them Jakob could see that propaganda squads had planted a cluster of red flags on the pass to mark it; beneath them political instructors were waving and shouting encouragement to units as they neared the top. Gripping his staff with both hands to steady himself, Jakob levered himself up the slope, keeping his eyes fixed on the flags streaming in the wind.

"He was sorry he couldn't talk to you that day in the field when he buried the baby," whispered Little Liang, checking over his shoulder again to make sure they weren't overheard by the guard. "But he thought it best to say nothing in front of the judge. It was Comrade Lu Mei-ling who ordered him to say nothing, you see."

Distracted by the arduousness of the climb Jakob continued jabbing his staff into the compacted ice of the track, hauling himself upward yard by yard with painful slowness. He had climbed to within a few feet of the summit before Little Liang's words registered — but when they did, he stopped and stared down at the Little Red Devil, his chest heaving.

"What do you mean, Comrade Lu Mei-ling ordered him to say nothing? About what, Little Liang?"

"About your baby girl, Ke Mu-shih."

"Did your father talk to Lu Mei-ling about her?"

The boy nodded quickly. "Yes, she agreed to look after your baby."

"Then why did she die?"

"She didn't die, Ke Mu-shih!"

Jakob stared at Little Liang in disbelief. "But your father buried her in front of me in the field in Yunnan!"

"No, no, Ke Mu-shih. He buried Comrade Lu Mei-ling's baby. She took your daughter. But she said it had to be kept secret . . ."

The propaganda squads, seeing Jakob and the boy standing at the crest of the pass, began shouting and waving, urging them not to rest where the air was thin. Coming up behind, Jakob's guard propelled him forward sharply with his hands and as he crossed the summit, the missionary caught sight of the long, serpentine coils of men and animals winding down between ice-covered crags as pre-

cipitous as those on the ascent. He started in their wake, scanning
the thin lines of dark, antlike figures, trying to pick out the General
Headquarters column and the long-legged brown mule on which he
had seen Mei-ling ride. But a new wave of dizziness struck him
suddenly and the scene began to swim and dissolve before his eyes.
His staff skidded on the frozen ruts of the pass and he almost fell;
then, seeing others sinking to the ground, he followed suit and began
slithering down the mountain on his back.

7

For the next three days Jakob's eyes never ceased to search the
column ahead as he toiled over two more soaring ridges of the Great
Snow Mountains. Once, as the marchers spread out along a high ice
plateau above him, he felt certain he saw the silhouetted figure of
Mei-ling riding on her mule and the thought that the baby daughter
he had believed dead might be alive in the arms of the beautiful
Chinese girl gave him enough strength to keep moving.

But in his enfeebled state Jakob had found he could not eat the
coarse buckwheat and *chingko* barley cakes in his ration pouch: the
only nourishment he was able to swallow was the hot chili soup
which Little Liang brought to him two or three times each day on
the march. Because of the extreme cold he had also found it impossible to sleep when they bivouacked on the lower slopes after crossing
the first peak, and each passing hour found him climbing more slowly
and clinging more desperately to his staff. To his dismay, other men
and pack animals continued to die on the heights all around him.
Pole carriers transporting ammunition chests and cooks bearing heavy
loads of food and cooking utensils fell dead on the narrow passes, a
train of exhausted pack mules and horses dragged their handlers over
a precipice, and a young gunner shouldering his heavy mortar barrel
sank lifeless into the snow almost at Jakob's feet. To deepen the Red
Army's misery, violent hailstorms assailed the column on the third
day. The skies turned black and fusillades of fist-sized hailstones
drove down from the heavens, stunning the marchers and forcing
them to shelter under metal cooking bowls and tarpaulins. In the
afternoon Kuomintang biplanes appeared, spiraling up from below

to bomb the head of the column in the narrow ice defiles. To Jakob's relief the General Headquarters units escaped unscathed but although the planes were unable to fly high enough to attack on the passes, their bombs set off a series of avalanches which buried some vanguard units and swept others from a trail that wound along a narrow ledge.

The avalanches blocked the track, bringing the whole column to a standstill, and rescuers spent several hours digging out survivors. During the long wait Jakob huddled, shivering, against an ice-covered cliff with the other prisoners, and the bitter cold seemed to seep into the marrow of his bones. The blur of snow and ice all around him stretched endlessly into the distance and the conviction began to grow in him that his wasted body could not survive much longer in the towering canyons of snow and ice. When at last the order to move forward was given, his numbed limbs responded sluggishly. His strength seemed to ebb rapidly on the last section of a steep climb to another high pass, and he fell more frequently than before.

Soon after the prisoners had crossed the pass, a shrieking wind began to dash blinding flurries of fresh snow against the downward slopes, and a halt was called for the night in a bleak, forbidding amphitheater of jagged rocks. There the wind howled eerily about them as the soldiers fumbled with frozen hands to erect bivouacs, stretching tarpaulins over tent poles or wedging canvas shelters into the crevices between the massive blocks of stone. Many of the troops simply huddled together against the rocky walls, wrapped in their quilts, sheltering beneath the waxed-paper umbrellas they carried in their packs. As dusk fell, Jakob crouched, exhausted, beneath a bamboo shelter put up by his guards, watching dully as the General Headquarters units pitched their camp in a cluster of abandoned tribal yurts sited along a ledge at the foot of the rock valley. Only a few tattered strips of black yak wool fluttered on the bare poles but orderlies quickly lashed extra canvas sheets around them to keep out the weather. Before the whirling snow and thickening darkness obscured his vision Jakob saw an orderly tether the long-legged mule outside the last yurt at the far end of the ledge and carry the two large panniers from its back into the tent. It was in that moment that he knew what he must do before the last spark of life within him was snuffed out by the bitter cold.

Because water could not be boiled quickly at that altitude, the gruel of half-cooked buckwheat offered him by his guards was tepid, and he could not get a single spoonful past his lips. He drank only a mouthful or two of melted snow, then pulled a tattered palm-fiber rain cape closer about his shoulders and squatted, shivering, inside the shelter, staring at the snow whirling in the orange glow of the fire. A young guard lay down on an oilcloth at the rear of the shelter, wrapping his bedroll about himself, and within minutes had fallen into an exhausted sleep. Seeing this, Jakob reached over to his pack and picked up the red-starred cap that lay on it.

Besieged by the snowstorm in the high mountain rock basin, the exhausted men and animals were huddling together like corpses around their flimsy bivouacs, and from inside his shelter Jakob watched their fires guttering and dying, losing the battle with the thickening snow. Deep within his own body he felt the chilling cold spreading like poison, and fearing he would lose the power of his limbs if he waited any longer, he put on the guard's cap, pulled it down over his eyes, and stood up. Stepping out unsteadily into the whirling snow, he picked his way between the spluttering campfires toward the eastern wall of the high valley, holding the palm-fiber cape up around his ears to hide his face. Within moments the snow swallowed him up, making him invisible to anyone watching from the guard shelters, and when he reached the foot of the wall he turned south and began stumbling down the valley toward the yurts of the General Head-quarters units.

8

J akob fell several times in waist-deep drifts before he reached the foot of the ledge where the black yurts were pitched. Crouching in the swirling snow, he waited for the patrolling guard of the Red Cadres Regiment to pass before he scrambled up the slippery rocks and ducked behind the end yurt. To his surprise he found no mule tied up outside and for a moment he thought he had made a mistake. But, moving closer, he peered in through a gap in the canvas and saw that the animal was tethered inside, standing motionless against one wall. A fire crackled in the stone-ringed fireplace in the center of the floor and by its flickering light Jakob saw Mei-ling: seated on a bed of animal skins strewn around the fire, she was in the act of drawing one of the mule's panniers toward her.

He held his breath as she lifted a blanket-wrapped bundle in her arms. Turning it against herself, she drew back the coarse cloth and in the glow of the fire Jakob saw the peaceful, sleeping face of his daughter. For a moment Mei-ling also sat looking down at the child in her arms, her own face as still and composed as that of the eight-month-old infant. The wind shrilled across the icy rock face at Jakob's back, hurling furious gusts of snow against the yurt walls, but the beautiful Chinese girl and the pale-skinned European baby remained quiet and unmoving inside the fire-lit shelter. When a stick crackled and sparked inside the ring of stones, Abigail opened her eyes to look up at Mei-ling. The Chinese girl murmured a greeting and the face of the baby appeared to crinkle into a smile. Deeply moved, Jakob sank to his knees in the snow beside the yurt and bent his head over his clasped hands in a silent prayer of thanks. When he opened his eyes again Mei-ling was unfastening her tunic and moving closer to the fire. The expression on her face was intent but in the same moment serene and at peace as she uncovered her breasts.

Huddled in the storm outside, Jakob felt tears sting his eyes. Conflicting emotions of grief and gratitude engulfed him, and rising blindly from his knees, he turned to start back for his own bivouac. But his foot caught in one of the yurt's supports and he fell heavily against the wall of the shelter.

"Who's there?"

Mei-ling's voice was low but firm and Jakob, struggling to his feet, parted the flaps and stumbled inside, tugging off his cap.

"I'm sorry . . . I didn't mean to frighten you."

Jakob swayed on his feet, looking down uncertainly at the seated Chinese girl; then he sank slowly to his knees in front of her. He gazed wonderingly at his daughter, who had turned her head and was looking at him with wide, unblinking eyes.

"I thought she was dead . . . I found out only a few days ago that you'd taken her. . . . Thank you!"

Mei-ling stared in consternation at the disheveled missionary: snow lay thick on the shoulders of the palm-fiber cape and his beard was streaked with white. Exhaustion had etched deep lines into his haggard features and she could see the light of despair in his eyes. "Your daughter's doing as well as anyone could hope in these terrible conditions," said Mei-ling softly. "She lacks many things and I have to keep her swaddled more than is good for her — but despite everything there's a very strong will to live inside that little body . . ."

"Perhaps it's meant to be," gasped Jakob. He closed his eyes and his chin sank onto his chest. "Perhaps I am meant to die . . . Perhaps God wills it . . ."

Again the Chinese girl searched his face. "Do your guards know you've come?"

Jakob shook his head. "I slipped away in the blizzard . . . I wanted one last glimpse of her."

Lifting his head, he looked at the Chinese girl: her dark eyes, steady on him, were filled with compassion and in the glow of the fire the emphatic Asian beauty of her face was ethereal, almost painful to look at. Unaccountably, in the sudden warmth of the yurt he began to shiver more violently.

"I didn't mean to disturb you. . . . I was going back to my shelter when I fell."

"You're worn out. You need food."

Mei-ling wrapped the blanket around the baby again and sat her on a bed of animal skins beside the fire. In the months since Jakob had seen her, Abigail had grown noticeably. She was able to sit upright now without support and although her movements were clumsy and uncertain she gazed curiously about, gurgling occasionally and clutching at the tufts of fur on the skins. A blackened pot was simmering on a hob of stones and Mei-ling smilingly moved it beyond the child's reach, picking up a ladle and a tin dish at the same time.

"I'm unable to eat . . ." Jakob reached out impulsively with one arm to restrain her, and feeling his hand on her shoulder she turned back to him, a faint expression of surprise showing in her face. They remained motionless on their knees, their eyes on one another, and despite his exhaustion Jakob felt himself deeply stirred by her closeness.

"I must go back at once," he said shakily, "before my guards begin looking for me."

Mei-ling looked searchingly at him. It was clear he had little strength to drag himself out into the snow again and he made no attempt to move. Behind her in the shadows the tethered mule snorted quietly and shifted its feet in the straw. The fire in the hearth of stones spluttered and cracked while outside the wind howled to a higher note, rocking the yurt walls. The baby had grown still, and seeing her eyes close, Mei-ling settled her more comfortably among the skins and drew closer to the fire, adding a few sticks to the flames. "Stay here."

Her voice was quiet and firm and when he failed to reply, she came closer to him and removed the palm-fiber cape. She shook off the snow and laid it aside, then unwound the sodden quilt from his shoulders. The tattered long-gown beneath the quilt was wet too and she motioned for him to move nearer to the flames. Taking up a cloth, she knelt beside him and wiped the melted snow from his face and hair. He was still shivering but the flames were warming him and his eyes began to lose their defeated look. Mei-ling's tunic, unbuttoned to suckle the baby, still hung open, and when she had finished she laid the cloth aside and shifted her position to face him. For a long time she knelt in front of him without speaking. Then, reaching toward him, she cradled his shivering body in her arms and drew his face gently toward her naked breasts.

Still shuddering, Jakob closed his eyes: in his throat the sweet, life-giving liquid that he drew from her body was warm and comforting. Gradually, the noise of the storm seemed to fade and he became conscious only of the sweetness on his tongue and the soft warmth of Mei-ling's body against him. Pulling him gently down beside the fire, she lifted the animal skins to cover them both. As the minutes passed, Jakob's shuddering slowly diminished and soon he fell into an exhausted sleep.

When he opened his eyes again the embers of the fire were casting a dull red glow on the roof and walls of the yurt. Wrapped in the animal skins, they lay close against one another and he could feel the warmth of Mei-ling's unclothed body along the whole length of his own. Only a few hours had passed but he had slept deeply and he felt stronger in mind and body than he had for many days. Although the wind continued to howl outside, in the protected gloom of the yurt there was a profound feeling of stillness and peace, and gradually a new spark of hope rekindled itself within him. At his side Mei-ling seemed to be sleeping quietly and he was surprised on glancing down to find that her eyes were open. She was lying on her side, watching him with an unusual intentness, and she did not turn away when he shifted to face her.

Neither of them spoke; for some time they lay looking at one another with only the moan of the wind in their ears. In the end it was as if something outside of themselves drew them closer and when her slender arms tightened convulsively around him, Jakob clung fiercely to her. In the glow of the dying fire he saw her almond-shaped eyes grow bright with emotion as she looked at him — but she remained silent, saying nothing. As in his dreams, her limbs seemed to dissolve with an agonizing slowness around him and when at last their bodies joined, he gave himself joyously to the fierce animal heat of their embrace. In Jakob's mind a brilliant point of radiance began to expand with great force, flaring brighter as it grew: then a long rush of fire burned furiously through his heart and he cried out and crushed her tenderly against himself.

Outside, the wind buffeting the jagged peaks of the Great Snow Mountains rose to a piercing howl. The shelter shook and the restless mule snuffled and stamped its feet, but a foot or two away beside the hearth, the baby continued to sleep peacefully, wrapped in the skins and the rough wool blanket.

9

The straggling lines of famished, rag-clad men who descended unsteadily from the freezing heights of the Ta Hsueh Shan several days later looked more like fugitives from a natural calamity than soldiers. Suffering from frostbite and snow blindness, they shivered in their patched and tattered cotton uniforms. Some clutched sodden blankets or discolored sheepskins about themselves, huddling under tattered paper umbrellas, and as many wore round coolie hats of plaited bamboo as army caps to protect themselves from the steady rain drifting down onto the meadows and valleys of the desolate plateau that separated China proper from the mountainous highlands of Tibet. A lot of the exhausted troops had lost their rifles after scrambling through the unfamiliar ice and snow barriers and most of those who still carried arms wore bandoliers that no longer held cartridges. Lice-ridden and covered in scabies, thousands of the southerners accustomed to a rice diet were also suffering from bleeding dysentery brought on by having to ingest hard, half-cooked grains on the mountain heights and they were managing to stagger onward only with the support of their comrades.

By a special order of the General Headquarters, all political instructors and Communist Party cadres who fell sick or became wounded
were being carried on litters. Many infantrymen, transformed into
unwilling stretcher-bearers, trudged miserably through the rain and
mud with bowed heads and rounded backs, giving the depleted
fighting units a raggle-taggle, disorderly appearance. Unnerved by
the emptiness of the highlands ten thousand feet above sea level, the
survivors surveyed the cold, misty meadows with eyes that were
both hopeful and fearful in turn. The prospect of joining up soon
with friendly troops of Chang Kuo-tao's Fourth Front Army was
being spoken of with increasing frequency by the political commissars but as the ragged columns shuffled down from the mountain,
each successive valley revealed only eerily deserted yurt settlements
from which all the Tibetan tribespeople had fled. Fearing the approach of traditionally hostile Han Chinese, they had driven their
cattle away and hidden their grain. But invisible tribal horns echoed
hauntingly along the valleys and several times boulders had crashed
down steep cliffs into the midst of isolated units, killing and maiming
more soldiers.

"The men are desperately in need of a long rest," said Lu Chiao
wearily when he reported to Commissioner Chou En-lai at dusk in
an abandoned yurt village at the head of the steep-sided Maokung
River valley. "Hardly any are fit to fight. Lin Piao's First Corps is
down to three thousand men and Peng Teh-huai has about the same
in the Third. The Twelfth Corps has only a few hundred! With the
General Headquarters units, that makes fewer than ten thousand all
told. The giant army that left Kiangsi has become a skeleton without
muscles."

In the light of a kerosene lantern hanging from the crossed poles
of the yurt, Chiao could see that Chou's pale, sickly face was covered
in a film of feverish perspiration. Seated on an upturned ammunition
box before a rough desk made of pine planks, the commissioner was
sorting through a sheaf of radio signals. "How much ammunition
do the men have?" he asked, smothering a cough.

"Not more than five rounds each on average. Many have no bullets
at all."

"And the machine-gun units?"

"Almost no ammunition left. And only eight mortars got over the
mountains with a few crates of shells." Chiao placed a written report

on the desk before Chou. "We must hope that we join up with the Fourth Front very soon."

"If we're as weak as you say, meeting up with the Fourth Front Army may not be such a simple pleasure." Chou coughed painfully again: his face was strained, his features sunken, and the stubble on his unshaven cheeks was becoming an untidy beard. "Our radio contacts suggest they may be much stronger than us."

"How many troops do they have?"

"Nobody knows for sure. Between fifty and a hundred thousand, we think. They're all fresh, well armed, and well fed — and they've done very little fighting recently."

"But surely that's all to the good," protested Chiao. "They're our allies. Didn't General Chang Kuo-tao help found the Kung Ch'an Tang with Commissar Mao in Shanghai in 1921? He's been a member of the Central Committee and the Politburo ever since."

"Precisely. He's a strong, ambitious leader — but he's a very different man from Commissar Mao. He's the son of a rich landlord and he spent three years studying in Moscow. He sees the Kung Ch'an Tang with different eyes. Unlike Commissar Mao, who's always stayed close to China's peasants, General Chang has organized workers in the cities. But most important of all, General Chang is now in command of a strong, loyal army of his own. He's set up successful soviet areas in Hupeh, Honan, and Anhwei and now he's moved into Szechuan — so he's used to giving orders, not taking them. . . ."

"But do you think cooperation is impossible?"

Chou passed a hand shakily across his face. "Many emergency decisions have been taken without General Chang's knowledge while the Central Committee has been on the march. At Tsunyi, at Hweili . . ." Another fit of coughing wracked Chou and he broke off to mop his perspiring face. "There's been no contact with the Fourth Front Army for a very long time. We have a new leadership, and Hua Fu and Moscow have been excluded from our inner councils since Tsunyi. Commissar Mao is concerned that there might be strong disagreements about these matters with General Chang. A contest for the leadership between them is inevitable."

"But should disagreements among fellow Communists be settled by fighting?" asked Chiao in a disbelieving voice. His face too was gaunt with strain, and his uniform was as muddied and disheveled as those of the men passing outside the yurt. "Surely any differences can be resolved by discussion."

Chou drew a long breath. "We're outnumbered by eight or ten to one. General Chang's troops are well equipped and ready for combat. Ours are starving, ill clad, with, as you say, only five bullets apiece. It would be foolish to ignore the possibility . . ." Chou's voice trailed off into another bout of coughing.

"I can't believe we could march twenty thousand *li*, fighting the Kuomintang every day, to wage another civil war with the Fourth Front." Chiao shook his head in bewilderment. "And just for the sake of the selfish ambitions of two leaders."

Chou looked sharply at Chiao, his eyes carrying a silent warning to be circumspect. "It's more than a matter of personal ambition, Comrade Lu. The future course of the revolution is at stake. We must hope we can avoid conflict, but as a precaution Commissar Mao has ordered that we disperse all units except the General Head-quarters guard battalions before we meet the Fourth. We shall settle them in farms and villages over a wide area for a rest. That way it will be more difficult for General Chang to gauge our numbers, and surprise attack will be virtually impossible." Chou glanced down at the written report Chiao had handed him, rereading it quickly, and when he spoke again his voice carried a warning note. "Keep our real strength a close secret, Comrade Lu. We must always talk in terms of thirty thousand men at least. Don't mention our lack of ammunition until we've replenished our supplies from the Fourth Front."

"Very well, Comrade Commissioner."

From outside, the steady scuff of marching feet and the tap of staves were audible. Many of the troops were barefoot or wearing only tattered *ts'ao hsieh* — straw sandals — that clung in wisps about their ankles. Although they were glad to have survived the highest of the ridges in the Great Snow Mountain range, they were too exhausted to sing or shout and they continued to shuffle down the valley through the steady rain in near-silence, leaning heavily on one another.

"I see that you report the death of Judge Yang on the first ridge," said Chou without raising his head. "And request guidance regarding the remaining prisoners."

Chiao nodded. "None of Judge Yang's assistants survived the crossing. The guards are asking whom to turn to for instructions.

Another three captives died today — that leaves only two, a Luting landlord and the foreign missionary. I recommend that the landlord be turned loose."

"Agreed." Chou nodded. "And the foreigner?"

"Judge Yang was still negotiating with the Shanghai headquarters of the mission for his release. The judge's orderly had kept a file of papers — I have it in my saddlebags outside. It seemed best to refer the matter to you for a decision, Comrade Commissioner."

"Why did you reach that conclusion?"

"The missionary had been sentenced to death for spying before Judge Yang took over the case. The judge was originally demanding fines from Shanghai of one hundred and fifty thousand dollars to commute the death sentence. Later he asked for medicines, radios, and weapons. There were many changes of plan — perhaps because of the confusion of the march. The missionary escaped once and Judge Yang imposed a new fine for breaking the laws of the Central Soviet. He threatened to carry out the death sentence unless the mission headquarters paid a total fine of three hundred thousand dollars. The British ambassador in Peking has made appeals to the governors of Kweichow and Yunnan for help. There have been reports in all the newspapers. Some of the clippings are in the file."

"How have the headquarters of the mission in Shanghai reacted?"

"They've refused to pay the fine. But they say they sent their director-general to negotiate. They say he was killed by robber-bandits on the Kweichow border. He was bringing ten thousand dollars in silver as a goodwill payment . . ."

"When was the missionary captured?"

"In Hunan in early November — in the town of Chentai, with his wife and child . . ."

Chou looked up sharply. "Then he has been marching with us for eight months?"

"Yes."

"What's his condition?"

"He's very weak. His guards thought he would die on the Ta Hsueh Shan. But it seems he has a very strong will." Chiao frowned. "It's just possible the missionary is known to me. My family met many missionary families in Shanghai. My sister, Mei-ling, saw him marching among the other prisoners in Kweichow and told me she thought she recognized him as someone we had once met."

Chou nodded. "What happened to his wife?"

"She was executed after a public trial at Paoshan. They were both sentenced to death but the execution was interrupted by Nationalist forces."

Chou coughed and mopped his brow again. "Bring the papers for me to look at, please."

Chiao hurried outside to his horse and returned a moment later with a crumpled file. He placed it on the plank desk before Chou and the commissioner leafed quickly through the pages of notes, reports, and yellowed news clippings from provincial Chinese newspapers. He paused now and again to read more closely, then he closed the file and looked up at Chiao once more. "I see one of the guards reports that Comrade Hua Fu summoned the prisoner to his quarters one night in Kweichow. Why was that?"

"I don't know, Commissioner. It would be necessary to ask him."

Chou frowned and looked absently at the file again. "Do you know who pronounced the original death sentence for spying?"

"The trial was organized by a political commissar who was killed at the Hsiang crossing. His report says the people demanded the death of the missionaries and some local *t'u hao* — by acclamation."

"Did anyone plant agitators in the crowd?"

"The file has no information on that. Many such trials were held in Hunan and Kweichow."

Chou lapsed into silence, staring thoughtfully at Chiao. "I shall review the case. Slanderous newspaper reports constantly depict us as common bandits, so it's important that we're seen to act on principle in the case of the foreigner. If the executioner is still alive, find him and put him under close arrest and have him interrogated."

"Yes, Comrade Commissioner."

As Chiao turned to leave the yurt, a youthful messenger breathless from a hard ride burst in, his tunic black with rain. His face was alight with excitement and he didn't wait to be invited to speak.

"Commissioner! There's good news! Our vanguard scouts have made contact with a company of the Fourth Front Army — about forty *li* down the valley. Shots were exchanged at first before they recognized one another — but both sides blew their bugles and they all ran to embrace!"

Chou looked searchingly at the messenger, his haggard face expressionless. Then he forced a smile. "Thank you, comrade. Go and tell Commissar Mao — but make your announcement quietly."

10

On a rain-drenched afternoon in late June, bedraggled Central Red Army troops standing shoulder to shoulder along both sides of a banner-decked village street stared enviously at the columns of fit, well-equipped soldiers of the Fourth Front Army who were marching jauntily into the village between them. The bandoliers and cartridge belts of the Fourth Front men gleamed with ammunition, their ration bags bulged, and the uniforms and red-starred caps they wore were cut from strong new cloth. Strings of donkeys, mules, and horses swayed under the weight of crated munitions and stores, and the smiling, confident faces of all the marching men, unlike those of the roadside sentries, were round and well fed.

Above their heads, blood red banners strung between the mud-brick houses had been emblazoned with white characters proclaiming "Long Live the Unity of the Fourth Front and First Front Armies!" and "March North Together to Fight the Japanese Invaders!" Similar slogans had been painted on the walls of the houses and in a field adjoining the road a platform of farm carts had been decorated with banners so that short speeches could be made to mark the historic joining of the two forces. Beneath a temporary tarpaulin shelter erected at the roadside nearby, Mao Tse-tung and Chu Teh waited tensely, darting glances from time to time at the advancing troops of the Fourth Front Army who were streaming down the road toward them from the north. Around the shelter were clustered about a hundred Party and Central Red Army leaders, and among them stood Lu Chiao and his sister, Mei-ling.

"If you wanted proof of the friction that's building up between us and the Fourth Front, there it is," said Chiao quietly to his sister, nodding in the direction of a bobbing red banner being carried into the village by the marching troops.

Mei-ling followed his gaze. The banner said "Let Us Together Expand the Revolutionary Northwest Federation of Szechuan and Sikang."

"We're saying we must all hurry north to fight the Japanese — but General Chang Kuo-tao wants to take us all farther west into the wilderness to build his 'Northwest Federation.' "

"Why does he want to do that?"

"He thinks the vast spaces of the Tibetan-Chinese borderlands are the best place to set up a new soviet. He wants to build up our military strength here. Three quarters of his troops are Szechuanese — and they'd rather stay in their home province. But nobody who has marched fifteen thousand *li* from Kiangsi wants to hide on this high plateau. It looks more and more like an occupied zone than a liberated area. We've discovered that the Kuomintang has spread lying propaganda saying the Chinese Communists were coming to kill the tribespeople and eat their children. So it's not surprising they've all fled from their villages and hidden their cattle and grain."

Mei-ling screwed up her eyes and peered northward into the rain. She had pinned her hair beneath her uniform cap and she wore the Mauser machine pistol in her belt. "Is General Chang keeping us waiting so that we can have a good long look at his well turned out battle formations?"

"Probably."

The Fourth Front battalions were continuing to march into Fupien, a small village a mile or two north of the town of Lianghokou where the Central Red Army had set up its temporary headquarters. Two weeks had passed since scouts of the two armies had first met after the crossing of the Great Snow Mountains and some units had already held festive gatherings in villages along the route. Food confiscated from landowners by the Fourth Front had been shared at modest banquets and there had been singing, dancing, and theater shows put on by troops of both armies. But as the Central Red Army leaders continued to move northward and the Fourth Front command headquarters shifted south to meet them, communication between their top leaders had been confined to formal radio messages. The ceremonial reunion between Mao Tse-tung and Chang Kuo-tao, who had not met since the Third Congress of the Chinese Communist Party, in 1923, had been arranged by agreement to take place finally in Fupien — but the appointed time had come and gone and still there was no sign of the Fourth Front's commanders. Beneath the tarpaulin shelter, the waiting Central Red Army leaders were becoming increasingly restive and Chiao could see that the faces of Mao and Chu Teh were growing more taut as the minutes ticked by.

"I see no sign of Hua Fu," said Chiao, speaking softly, close to his sister's ear, as he scanned the crowd. "Do you know why he's missing?"

"He volunteered weeks ago to serve with the headquarters of the First Army Corps." Mei-ling's quiet response was matter-of-fact. "There's no reason for us to meet anymore."

"Do you happen to know why he summoned the foreign prisoner to his quarters in Kweichow?"

Mei-ling looked sharply at her brother. "He asked him to translate the Tsunyi resolutions — why do you ask that?"

"Commissioner Chou is reviewing the prisoner's case. I said I would try to find out."

"Why is his case being reviewed?"

Mei-ling asked the question with an unguarded urgency, her eyes suddenly bright and intent.

"Because Judge Yang, who was in charge of the prisoners, died in the Great Snow Mountains." Chiao looked hard at his sister. "May I ask why you're so interested in the foreign prisoner?"

Mei-ling turned away, feeling a sudden warmth flood into her cheeks. "The night he was summoned to our quarters I spoke with him. I discovered then he *was* the missionary we met on the voyage to Shanghai."

"So he really is the Englishman who persuaded the frightened passengers to sing hymns in the typhoon?"

Mei-ling nodded but did not look at her brother. "Yes."

"Then it's not surprising he's borne his suffering so bravely," said Chiao reflectively.

"What do you mean?"

"I've read the file Judge Yang compiled. Jakob Kellner is a man of considerable courage and stamina. He rescued one of his guards from the Hsiang River — and retrieved the Red Army standard under fire." Chiao paused, watching his sister's face. "The record says his wife was executed and his child died in Yunnan but he's endured many hardships in captivity without complaint —"

"His child didn't die in Yunnan. . . ."

Mei-ling spoke in a whisper and Chiao saw tears start in her eyes.

"But Judge Yang's notes show that the prisoner's infant daughter was buried in his presence," persisted Chiao. "How do you explain that?"

"It was my child who died! I've been caring for the prisoner's child ever since."

Fearing they might be overheard, Chiao glanced anxiously about —

but at that moment an expectant buzz of comment ran through the gathering and Chiao saw an impressive array of horsemen emerging from the rain. A big red standard, emblazoned with a black star and a hammer and sickle motif, flapped above them and in their midst on a tall white stallion jogged an upright, broad-shouldered figure holding a drawn sword in an attitude of ceremonial salute. Although the group was still some way off, it was obvious to Chiao that General Chang Kuo-tao was at last arriving, surrounded by a mounted body-guard of thirty or forty cavalrymen.

"You must have known, Ta ko," whispered Mei-ling.

"Yes, I suspected as much," replied Chiao in an undertone. "But I wanted you to tell me yourself. How did you arrange it?"

When Mei-ling lifted her head, rain was mingling with the tears on her cheeks. "His cookboy came to me secretly. He asked me to feed the child. I gave him my dead son — and took Jakob Kellner's baby in return." She blinked away her tears and a fierce expression of pride appeared in her eyes. "I acted on instinct. Among so much killing and suffering I wanted to give life . . ."

Looking up, Chiao saw that the mounted commanders of the Fourth Front Army were drawing near and the closer they trotted, the more daunting their appearance became. All the horses were tall and sleek: some were brown, some black, and biggest of all was the handsome white mount of the general himself. The metal of their bridles and stirrups gleamed in the dull afternoon light and the leather saddles had a polished look even in the rain. The riders, commanders and bodyguards alike, looked strong and vigorous. They sat straight in their saddles, their eyes flicking disdainfully along the rows of shab-bily clad Central Red Army soldiers at the roadsides.

"Please promise that you won't reveal my secret, Ta ko," said Mei-ling. "Please say nothing about it."

Chiao smiled affectionately and nodded. "I shall say nothing."

"Have you heard how Jakob Kellner is?" Mei-ling asked the question in a tense voice, her eyes fixed on the horses of the Fourth Front leaders, which were slowing to a walk as they approached the shelter where Mao and Chu Teh were waiting.

"While his case is under review, Commissioner Chou has ordered that he be given better treatment. He had become very weak. His guards have instructions to let him ride a horse for part of each day so that he can recover his strength."

Mei-ling absorbed the information in silence, still watching the horses. Then she moved closer to her brother. "Do you think he will be released soon?"

Instead of replying, Chiao lifted his hand in a warning gesture: the mounted escort flanking the white stallion had halted and General Chang was walking his horse forward alone toward the tarpaulin shelter. A sudden hush fell and the hiss of the falling rain was the only sound in the muddy street. Chang Kuo-tao reined in his mount and sheathed his sword as the effective leader of China's Communist Party and the commander in chief of its Central Army stepped out of the shelter side by side.

For a moment the three men stared at one another and the on-lookers saw that the contrast between them was startling. Hollow-cheeked, and grimy in their badgeless, threadbare uniforms, Mao and Chu looked more like weary railway workers than soldiers. Mao's lank hair, dampened by the rain, clung to his head and beside his tall, hunched figure the shorter Chu Teh seemed to have shrunk to something less than his full size.

In comparison, the man gazing down at them from the saddle of the white horse looked patrician and stately. Sitting astride the splendid animal in a new, well-cut uniform, Chang Kuo-tao was a composed, urbane figure. His cheeks were full and ruddy from comfortable living and his body well fleshed. There was also a hint of hauteur in his bearing and Chiao was reminded suddenly of a rich man visiting poor relatives.

Separated by a distance of no more than a dozen yards, the leaders looked at one another without speaking or moving. Mao had stepped slightly ahead of Chu Teh and was standing with his hands hanging empty at his side; his head was thrust forward in a challenging attitude and a furious, quivering pride drew him at last to his full height. Chang Kuo-tao too had unconsciously straightened in the saddle and as their eyes met, Chiao realized instinctively that the two men were equally afraid of one another. But both of them, he could see, were determined to put on a brave face to deceive their watching soldiers.

The Fourth Front battalions who had marched into the village were drawn up inside the field where the platform had been erected. Like the watching Central Red Army troops, they seemed oblivious to the antagonisms that divided their two leaders and they watched in silence as Chang Kuo-tao swung down from his horse and turned to face Mao.

Neither seemed inclined to take the first step toward the other, and with the seconds ticking away Chiao held his breath: then Mao stepped forward a few jerky paces. Chang advanced immediately in his turn as though in relief, their arms went around one another in a theatrical embrace, and a storm of cheering broke from the throats of all the assembled soldiers. The cheering released the tension in Chiao and he exhaled slowly, aware that he had witnessed a moment of electric confrontation that had been temporarily contained. With their arms about one another's shoulders the two leaders were moving awkwardly into the field toward the bunting-decked platform, determined despite the rain to make their brief speeches of greeting. Their entourages followed and Chiao and Mei-ling fell into step behind them.

"You didn't answer my question, Ta ko," said Mei-ling in a reproachful half-whisper as they walked among the crowd. "Do you think he will be released?"

Chiao had his eyes fixed on the two leaders, who were climbing onto the carts, and at first he thought her question referred to one of them. Then he remembered their interrupted conversation. "Unless Commissar Mao and General Chang resolve their differences quickly," he said quietly, "all of us might soon be prisoners — or worse."

11

The unsteady gait of the aged roan mare carrying Jakob northward beyond Lianghokou gradually jolted him out of a fitful doze into full wakefulness. Released from the pain and exhaustion of ceaseless marching, he had fallen quickly into the habit of sleeping in the saddle, one hand tangled in the horse's mane, the other grasping the crupper which passed beneath its tail. He awoke whenever the going became rough but although he may have dozed for only a few brief minutes, each time he reopened his eyes he felt refreshed and a little stronger.

Looking around he saw that the rear of the General Headquarters column, to which he had been transferred, was traversing a rolling expanse of rough moorland. His horse was following the faint tracks that had been made by goat and yak herds as they wandered across the high plateau, cropping the short, sour grass, but now not a single goat or yak was to be seen. With every passing hour the region into which the marchers were heading was growing more desolate and deserted. Every farm and village they encountered had been abandoned under the threat of Kuomintang reprisals and all food and livestock had been removed to hiding places in the mountains.

Even the homes of wealthy landlords had been stripped of everything of value and the marchers, growing daily more anxious about food supplies, had begun sending out requisition squads to hunt down straying cattle. Other groups scoured the countryside for wild herbs, edible fungus, and tree bark, which the cooks ground to a fine powder before it was eaten, and whenever they found a field of half-ripened barley or sorghum, the marchers fell to with scythes and later roasted the green, unmilled grain.

Jakob had once or twice been allowed to join the harvesters. After so many painful months marching with his hands tied behind his back, he had found an unexpected pleasure in the slow, rhythmic work of swinging the scythe. Although they offered no explanation as to why he was being shown greater consideration, his guards no longer displayed needless hostility in their dealings with him, and for their neutral expressions and their matter-of-fact instructions he felt an illogical gratitude.

Riding the horse each day had gradually allowed his feet to heal and as his strength returned, he discovered that his capacity to think and feel was also reviving. With the discovery came a sense of astonishment at how completely divorced he had become from his surroundings; jogging along on the back of the roan mare, Jakob felt as though he were awakening slowly from a deep, paralyzing sleep which had lasted for many months. Above all else he was surprised how little he remembered other than the unending physical pain in his legs, his feet, and his back. The limitless forests and the snow-capped mountains had become no more than a blur in his memory against which he had learned first of Barlow's death, then of the survival in Mei-ling's care of his infant daughter.

Because his guards were more relaxed in his presence and because his own senses had sharpened, Jakob had become aware of the worsening conflict between the leaders of the First Front and Fourth

Front armies. Although an order had been issued adopting a new name, the United Red Army, Jakob had heard guards and soldiers retailing rumors that armed clashes had already occurred between some units of the two forces. It was common knowledge that long meetings of Party and army leaders at Lianghokou had brought antagonisms to a head without resolving them; those guards who discussed the matter in Jakob's hearing seemed to believe that a compromise decision to march northward in separate columns had been agreed to until further discussions could be held. There was uneasy talk too that Kuomintang armies were slowly but surely regrouping to the north, south, and east to begin another attempted encirclement and it was this fear that lent urgency to the need to gather food and keep moving.

From the same soldiers Jakob also heard the first fearful references to the Ta Ts'ao Ti — the Great Grasslands which lay astride their route to the north. A vast, uninhabited tundra of oozing swamps and head-high grasses, according to those who knew the region, the Great Grasslands had struck terror into the hearts of all who had tried to cross them for centuries. They barred the route into Kansu province, constituting a fearsome natural obstacle, and every Red Army soldier around the missionary was hoping fervently that they would be spared the ordeal of marching across them.

But none of these fears diminished Jakob's new feelings of hope which had grown out of his clandestine visit to Mei-ling's shelter on the Great Snow Mountain ridge. As he rode each day, his mind filled with images of the fire-lit yurt: again and again he relived the moment of joy when first he saw his tiny daughter alive and safe in Mei-ling's arms, and he savored too the memory of her insistent instruction for him to stay by the fire, the lightness of her touch as she wiped the snow from his face, the warmth and softness of her unclothed body pressed against his beneath the animal skins.

The time when they lay clenched in passion burned on in his mind as some of the purest moments of his life. It was then that he had experienced the first fierce sense of renewal — something physical and spiritual in each of them had merged and blended, he was sure, in the gentle explosion of ecstasy they had shared. They had seemed to settle deeply into one another like the snow drifting and banking around the yurt and they had lain for a long time in one another's arms, quiet and unmoving. Neither of them had felt any need for words; something almost holy in their wordless union on that harsh mountainside had overawed them both, leaving them feeling content and at peace. Much later Mei-ling had helped him dress, touching his naked body wonderingly with her hands as she did so, but they had exchanged no further words before he left to climb back, undiscovered, through the thickening snow to his own shelter.

As the days passed and his strength grew, however, he had once or twice been troubled by the thought that perhaps in his weakened condition he had deceived himself and had merely given in to a lustful temptation. Memories of the sensual dreams of Mei-ling that had afflicted his sleep years before returned, and once he had felt constrained to ask God's forgiveness for his actions in a prayer. Then almost at once an equally strong conviction welled up in him that by praying for forgiveness he had offended and betrayed his own deepest emotions, and he had quickly pushed all such guilty thoughts from his mind. In keeping with his sense of revival, he tried to pray as he had been accustomed to before he was captured but was surprised to find that the doubts which had begun to undermine his faith in his task earlier in the march still continued to nag somewhere deep inside him. Was the Christian Gospel really relevant to the great suffering mass of China's people? Weren't the Communists doing much more than foreign Christians could ever hope to do to help the poor and poverty-stricken? Was it right for European religious missions to follow their imperial flags and try to convert to their own beliefs a foreign nation like China, with its own ancient and separate traditions?

More significant, he had not forgotten that during the most trying and despairing days of the march his agonized mind had begun to turn numbly from the very basis of his beliefs and his trust in God. In his mood of renewed optimism he tried to convince himself that this had been a fleeting lapse under almost intolerable strain, but a part of him knew that the profound certainties that had previously guided his young life had been replaced by a disquieting sense of confusion: on successive days he seemed capable of doubting and believing almost everything on which his faith was based.

The harshness and hostility of the landscape through which they passed also helped shape Jakob's thoughts as June ended and July began. The bleak moors and dense virgin forests gave way to rushing rivers plunging through rocky beds, which had to be forded with great care. Their route wound up and down the mountain ridges and over ice-bound passes above the snow line. Although it was summer in the valleys, the temperature dropped near to freezing every night and it became increasingly evident that the region was geographically part of Tibet rather than China — the Han Chinese villages grew fewer, giving way to tribal Tibetan settlements of clay and yak-dung dwellings, flat-roofed stone houses, or thatched huts.

All eerily deserted, these remote settlements displayed a greater concern with religion than Jakob had seen elsewhere in China — white pennants hoisted on tall poles flew outside most of the dwellings and he learned from one of his guards that the tribespeople believed these fluttering flags helped their prayers rise more easily to heaven. Luridly painted, life-size figures of wood and stone with fierce gargoyle faces stood guard at the approaches to many of the deserted encampments to ward off evil spirits and whenever the marchers encountered an abandoned lamasery, weird effigies of Buddha were to be seen grimacing in the gloom of the deserted shrines. All these macabre sights in a landscape scoured clean of all its natural human population seemed suddenly in Jakob's eyes to bear witness to the overwhelming role that superstition and fear played in religious thought. He found himself wondering each day how important disguised superstition had been in forming his own beliefs, and although he continued to pray through force of habit, these reflections strengthened the dark cloud of uncertainty that had settled over his mind. Reluctantly he accepted that his newfound desire to survive along with his baby daughter was at base narrow and selfish; this realization shocked him but he seemed to have lost the will to revive his faith. He found he wanted only to devote himself to the simple, short-term struggle of staying alive on that harsh plateau close to the roof of the world. If he could endure, he told himself, perhaps something could be salvaged later from the horrors of the long, harrowing trek. Perhaps it would be easier to resolve his innermost doubts when he was free of the strain of captivity and the restrictions his marching jailers imposed on him.

Uneasy thoughts of this kind were still drifting through Jakob's mind on a twilit evening in the first week of July as the men and animals of the General Headquarters column toiled down from another high, snow-covered pass and he saw with amazement ahead of them a vast and ancient stone fortress. A spectacular, multitiered tower adorned with columned balconies and curved roofs rose above it and the fading rays of the sun illuminated the clusters of wooden pillars lacquered in red, black, and gold. Precious gems seemed to sparkle around the bases of the pillars and as they drew nearer, Jakob saw that the great stone bulk of the fortress, built at the foot of a tall crag, was about four stories high. Its high walls were crenellated to provide emplacements for cannon and there were slits in the stonework through which defenders of long ago had been able to fire arrows. Mounted messengers trotting back along the column called out excitedly to the soldiers, telling them of the treasures that lay in the great tower of Chokechi, which for centuries had been the *yamen* and fortress of the great Tibetan chieftain of the region.

"The tower has seven stories — all with shrines to Buddha ornamented in gold and silver and jade! . . . There are silken couches on every balcony! . . . Fifteen marble reception rooms have huge woven tapestries covering the walls . . . A library contains ten thousand Chinese and Tibetan books and scrolls . . ."

As it drew nearer, the marching column began to buzz with other scraps of information: the stone chambers and courts of the fortress were big enough to house six thousand men, and bonfires were being lit, so there would be warm, dry quarters for all. Streams that flowed beneath its walls formed a moat of crystal-clear drinking water; massive storehouses for grain, flour, salt, spices, sugar, beans, and oil took up two stories; the stables could house several hundred horses. There were ten slaughterhouses and twenty pits for roasting whole carcasses of sheep, goats, and yak. The resident chieftain had fled hurriedly on Kuomintang instructions, taking away as many supplies as he could carry — but there was food, enough for a night or two for most of the troops!

By the time Jakob's guards led his roan mare into the main courtyard beneath the tower, darkness had fallen and the ancient stonework was bathed in the orange glow of many bonfires. Red Army men milled in crowds around two glowing pits over which dripping carcasses of yak were turning on spits. As Jakob was about to dismount, the throng parted to allow a small group of armed guards to approach; they were led by an energetic, quick-striding officer who reached out and took the bridle of Jakob's mare. When the officer raised his head to address Jakob, the missionary found himself looking into a familiar face. It was leaner, four years older, and much roughened by exposure to all weathers, but the brisk, confident gaze, the strong features, and the neatly clipped moustache without doubt belonged to the young Chinese he had met with Mei-ling at the end of his voyage on the *Tomeko Maru*.

"Jakob Kellner," said the officer crisply. "I am Regimental Commander Lu Chiao. Please dismount."

Chiao, who had spoken in English, studied the missionary carefully as he got down from the horse. His long-gown was torn and muddied beneath his fraying palm-fiber cape and he wore only *ts'ao-hsieh* on his still-swollen feet; his blond hair and beard were matted and uncombed, and the marks of his ordeal were plainly visible in his gaunt, strained face. But in his eyes there remained a calm, self-possessed expression reminiscent of the eager novice missionary who had led the hymn singing during the typhoon.

"I think perhaps we met once, Commander Lu," said Jakob slowly. "On board a ship."

Chiao nodded formally. "Yes, I believe that is so. For the present, Commissioner Chou En-lai has asked me to inform you that a review of your case is being undertaken. Please follow me."

Flanked by the escort, Jakob followed Chiao across the courtyard toward a third roasting pit that was surrounded by a dense crowd. There Jakob was shocked to see that instead of a skinned yak carcass, the writhing body of a Chinese man, stripped to the waist, had been suspended horizontally by ropes from the framework of beams above the pit. A few glowing coals cast a red glow on the underside of the man's body but his life was more immediately threatened by two long prayer-pennant poles which had been embedded in the pit bottom, their tips shaved to a needle sharpness. One spike touched the man's chest an inch from his heart and the other brushed his groin. By straining his muscles, the sweating victim was holding himself clear of the spikes, but his own weight threatened constantly to impale him on them.

"It's possible you may recognize this man," said Chiao quietly and motioned Jakob forward to the head of the pit.

One of the guards seized the suspended man by the hair and jerked back his head. This exposed his face, and although it was contorted with fear and pain, the sight of the man's brutal peasant features transported Jakob in an instant to the hillside outside the walled town of Paoshan. The missionary had last looked into those narrowed eyes as the squat southern executioner casually wiped the blood-stained blade of his long sword on Felicity's shabby dress; then he had beckoned with the sword tip for Jakob's guard to march him over to the execution block. Those same dark eyes, now dilated with fear, held Jakob's gaze for a chilling moment, until the missionary felt a sudden furious surge of anger tighten his chest. His breathing quickened as he struggled to reconcile the agony of the confrontation at Paoshan with the sight of the man hanging helplessly before him over the wickedly pointed stakes.

"You recognize him then, Mr. Kellner?"

Chiao's voice made the missionary start. The turmoil of emotions he was experiencing showed clearly in Jakob's face and he nodded mutely in the officer's direction.

"You're perhaps surprised to find your wife's executioner in this position," said Chiao quietly. "So I should explain that our investigations have led us to believe that this man is a Kuomintang spy. He tricked his way into our ranks on the road to Paoshan and endeavored to ingratiate himself by his readiness to carry out executions. We believe he deliberately planted agitators in the crowd at Paoshan to lead demands for the death sentence, so that he might prove his spurious 'loyalty'! It's not our habit to inflict this kind of treatment on prisoners but we believe this man tortured many Communist suspects for the Kuomintang in precisely this fashion. Stretching men under interrogation over growing bamboo spikes is one of China's oldest methods of torment. This is merely an approximation. . . ."

Jakob turned to look at Felicity's executioner again. He had been suspended facedown over the pit with great precision: ropes tied to his wrists and ankles left his trembling body resting lightly against the lethal points of the stakes and the rope ends had been fastened in notched pulleys that allowed the guards to lower him inch by inch at will. His shuddering body was bathed in perspiration from the effort he was making to hold himself clear of the spikes, but his chest had already been grazed and a small trickle of blood was running down the freshly whittled point of the pennant pole pointing at his heart.

"This new information emerged in our review of your case, Mr. Kellner. As there's reason to doubt the legality of the sentence of death passed on you, further consideration will be given to showing leniency and imposing a more appropriate penalty. In escaping from our custody you broke the laws of the Central Soviet — but if your headquarters show themselves willing to pay a reduced fine it might become possible to recommend that you be released at a later date . . ."

Jakob tried to concentrate on Chiao's words, wondering how much truth there was in them, but he found himself unable to take his eyes from the man hanging above the pit.

". . . Meantime we offer you the opportunity to give us your opinion on what fate you think would be appropriate for 'Executioner Wang.' No final decision has been reached yet — but if you wished to sever the ropes holding him so that the spikes can do their work, we shall have no objection. . . ."

Looking around, Jakob saw that one of the guards had drawn a broadsword and was holding it toward him. The breath of the executioner was rasping noisily in his throat as he struggled to hold himself clear of the spikes, and hearing this, Jakob made up his mind. Snatching the sword from the guard's hand, he advanced quickly to the rim of the pit. The executioner swiveled his head fearfully when Jakob swung the sword in an arc, and the missionary saw the southerner's eyes close. The next moment both wooden spikes, severed near the base by the same stroke, flew free into the darkness and Jakob used the sword to hack quickly through each of the four ropes binding the executioner's wrists and ankles. Supporting him beneath the shoulders, he helped lower the trembling man to the ground, where he collapsed into an exhausted crouch. All around the pit the crowd of soldiers had fallen silent; they watched without moving as Jakob returned the sword wordlessly to its owner.

"Why do you choose to free the man who beheaded your wife?" asked Chiao.

"I've seen too many terrible acts committed for reasons of hatred since I became your prisoner." Jakob spoke in an unsteady voice, struggling to control his own breathing. "I came to China to proclaim the truth that God loves all men. Nothing lasting will be achieved by hatred and killing. Whatever the facts are behind all this, we must learn to forgive one another."

He glanced down at the executioner, who remained hunched on the ground by the roasting pit: in the light of the fires his eyes were still glazed with shock and he was shuddering uncontrollably. Clasping his hands in front of him, Jakob bent his head and said a silent prayer. When he looked up again, guards were pulling the executioner to his feet and Chiao was standing at his side. "Please deal leniently with him," said Jakob firmly, "no matter what he's done."

From above a sharp cry of command rang out, and Jakob saw that colored glass lanterns had been lit on some of the terraces rising above the fortress. Against the starlit blackness of the heavens the softly illuminated tower of Chokechi, with its lacquered pillars and richly decorated pediments, looked like a historical fantasy conjured from the pages of an ancient adventure story. On one of the higher balconies the figure of a tall man was visible in silhouette, looking down into the courtyard, and as Jakob and Chiao watched, he leaned over the balustrade and beckoned. Chiao immediately took Jakob by the arm and guided him away from the roasting pit.

"Commissar Mao wishes to speak with you," said the Chinese officer, hurrying Jakob through the crowd of soldiers toward the tower's first terrace. "You must be prepared to explain your actions."

12

"The real missionaries in China today are the men all around you with red stars in their caps. They are the real prophets."

In the flickering light of a rapeseed-oil lamp the long, gaunt face of Mao Tse-tung glowed like the brass visage of a Buddha that Jakob had glimpsed in a shrine on one of the tower's lower balconies. Although the lofty sleeping chamber was richly furnished with a huge bed of polished teak as its centerpiece, a frayed hammock had been slung between two *lim*-wood pillars and Mao lay motionless in it, his hands clasped on his chest.

"In nine months we've marched through Kiangsi, Kwangtung, Hunan, Kwangsi, Kweichow, Yunnan, Sikang, and Szechuan. More than two hundred million Chinese live in those provinces. Most of them are poor, landless peasants. Most of them are illiterate. In every village we've passed we have taught three characters: *Fen T'ien Ti* — 'Divide Up Land'! That is our simple scripture, and those three characters are changing the lives of all who learn to read and write them."

High in the tower Jakob had been surprised to find that the noises from the courtyard were no more than a distant murmur. Colored glass windows decorated with filigree divided the chamber from the balcony, and although the soft, rounded consonants of Mao's southern accent gave his speech a sibilant quality, Jakob had no difficulty in following what he said. Having conducted Jakob into Mao's presence, Lu Chiao had unobtrusively retired: outside the door an armed bodyguard with a Mauser machine pistol in his belt remained visibly on watch, but otherwise nobody disturbed the peaceful quiet of the sumptuous sleeping chamber.

"What have foreign missions achieved in comparison? Eight thousand missionaries have been working in China for the last hundred years. They now lay claim to eight hundred thousand converts to Christianity — that's only one convert per missionary per year. And you know that most of those are rice Christians, who pretend to believe in order to ensure that their bellies are filled. Doesn't that prove the futility of your task?"

Mao turned his head an inch or two to look at the missionary. It was the first movement he had made and Jakob became suddenly aware of the quiet, still force in the man before him. The oil lamp sputtering on a lacquered antique desk beside the hammock illuminated a high scholar's brow, a shock of tousled hair, still blue-black although Mao was in his early forties, and intent eyes that looked overlarge in dark, hollowed sockets. He was unshaven and his faded tunic of crumpled gray cotton was unbuttoned at the neck, but despite his disheveled appearance, the reclining Chinese radiated an aura of vitality and inner strength. The desk beside him, on which a field telephone was rigged, was covered with reports and radio messages. Scattered on the teak bed and carved tables placed around the room were meager belongings similar to those carried by ordinary soldiers: two rough blankets, an oilcloth, a cotton sheet, a worn overcoat and cap, a broken umbrella. A knapsack divided into half a dozen compartments had fallen from a stool and from it spilled maps, faded yellow newspapers, and a few books, among them the Chinese classics *The Water Margin* and *The Romance of the Three Kingdoms*.

"We've always known our task in China would not be completed quickly or easily," said Jakob hesitantly. "That doesn't dismay us. We hope to sow seeds that will one day grow into a strong Christian church quite independent of foreign missionaries."

Mao's coal black eyes narrowed as he subjected Jakob to closer scrutiny. "You've marched a long way with the Red Army. You've seen who really champions the poor and the exploited. They can't wait forever."

"I've marched a long way and seen a great many poor men killed," replied Jakob, "in the Red Army and among the Kuomintang forces."

"Making a revolution isn't like a dinner party — it can't be refined and delicate. It's an act of violence: one class is rising up to overthrow another!" The voice that had been soft and sibilant at first had taken on resonance and depth, and Mao's big eyes grew suddenly brighter. "Some deaths are unavoidable — a surgeon sometimes has to amputate a man's limb in order to save his life!"

"It will never be enough just to change external things." Jakob, seated in an elaborately carved chair beside the desk, looked steadily back at the Chinese leader. "You may redistribute the land to the poor and needy but your Communist revolution fosters hatred. Even if it succeeds, men will remain selfish and deceitful. To live in harmony and peace, the hearts of men must change within them. Truth, freedom, and justice can't exist without divine salvation — that's why European missionaries have come to China."

Mao sank thoughtfully back into the hammock, peering toward the ceiling. Fumbling in a pocket of his jacket he withdrew a bent, handmade cigarette, lit it, and inhaled noisily. When he spoke, his tone had become quiet and reflective once more. "Missionaries have always followed the imperialist armies — that is the truth of the matter. In China people know that missionaries always arrive after military defeats. They set themselves up in grand houses with many servants, like rich landlords, which makes the people suspicious of them. Holy men according to Chinese traditions are always very poor and own nothing — if they are genuine. You missionaries also set up schools but most of the students you attract are opportunists who wish to exploit the system for their own ends." Mao paused, sucked noisily on the crumpled cigarette once more, then laughed. "Even Commissioner Chou En-lai, who is reviewing your case, was fortunate enough to be educated in a foreign missionary school. The Communist Party of China is very grateful."

Swinging his legs to the floor, he stood up. On his feet, he wore black cotton slippers, and walking softly to the window, he stared down into the fire-lit courtyard, his face serious again. In silhouette against the glass his burly shoulders and big peasant hands gave him a powerful physical appearance but Jakob noticed with surprise that his gestures in lifting the cigarette to and from his mouth were exaggeratedly graceful, almost feminine.

"Where will all this marching end?" asked Jakob quietly, watching the reflected glow of the bonfires playing on the motionless features of the man before him.

"In Shensi!" Mao rapped the words out with an abrupt ferocity before falling silent. For a minute or more he smoked the cigarette rapidly, his eyes fixed on something unseen in the courtyard below: then he continued in a lower tone. "There are disputes about our goal but you will see — we shall join forces with comrades who have set up a small soviet area in northern Shensi. Two years ago we resolved to fight the Japanese with or without the help of the Kuomintang armies. In the northwest we shall be ready to give battle. We don't want to fight a civil war while the Japanese invaders are swallowing our country — but Kuomintang armies have attacked us constantly and we have had to defend ourselves."

"Aren't you afraid of losing? You have no airplanes, no tanks or motorized transport."

"We're not afraid of losing because we won't lose!" Mao stubbed out his cigarette with unnecessary force and raised his clenched hands above his head in a passionate gesture. His small, pursed mouth had suddenly become a grimly determined line and all trace of femininity in his movements disappeared in an instant. "If necessary we will fight the Japanese *and* the Kuomintang with our bare hands and feet!"

Turning from the window, he walked back to the red lacquered desk and rummaged among its papers. Again his mood had changed abruptly, and leaning close to the oil lamp, he scanned several documents in silence. Absorbed in his reading, Mao behaved as though he were alone in the room: then he spoke in his soft voice again without lifting his eyes from a sheet of paper he held before him. "In the courtyard you showed pity to the executioner. Is that what your Christian teaching demands?"

"Yes," said Jakob simply. "It is."

"If *we* pity *our* enemies we shall be lost. . . . There's no room for compassion in a class war."

"Your doctrine seems right to you now. You make the soldiers marching with you feel they are part of a patriotic crusade. But in the end man will always feel a need to turn to God." As he spoke Jakob found himself surprised by the conviction he was able to muster. Confronted unexpectedly with the leader of his captors, he had expressed himself with unfamiliar force, as though he had not suffered any of the agonizing doubts of recent weeks and months. He wondered whether anything of his inner turmoil was discernible in his manner and he looked up to find the Chinese watching him intently.

"I have heard you like most of all to take to the mountains and visit villages where no missionary has ever been before, is that correct?"

Jakob nodded. "Yes."

"I've written a poem about the mountains of China. I write on horseback. There's plenty of time then to test meter and rhymes."

Mao picked up a sheet of paper on which Jakob could see that several lines of Chinese characters had been fashioned with a writing brush. Holding it before him in the theatrical manner of a Chinese scholar, Mao slowly read the verses aloud in a singsong falsetto, and as he did so, Jakob felt profoundly moved by the depth of passion in the words and the voice of the man reading them.

> *"Mountains!*
> *Faster I whip my speeding horse, never leaving the saddle;*
> *I start as I turn my head,*
> *For the sky is only three feet above me!*
>
> *Mountains!*
> *Like surging, heaving seas with your billows rolling,*
> *Like myriad horses,*
> *Roaring and plunging away in the thick of battle.*
>
> *Mountains!*
> *Piercing the blue of the heavens, your barbs unblunted!*
> *The sky would fall*
> *But for your strength supporting."*

Turning from the lamp, Mao handed the sheet of paper to Jakob. "Take it if you like. When you read it you will remember how you marched fifteen thousand *li* across the mountains of China with the Red Army." Lost in thought suddenly, Mao wandered over to the window and stood with his back to the missionary, staring down again at the roasting pits in the courtyard below.

"Is it your intention to order my release soon?" asked Jakob after a long interval of silence.

"If the headquarters of your mission agree to Commissioner Chou's proposal," replied Mao without turning around, "it might become possible in due course."

Behind Jakob the door opened softly and Chiao appeared. Taking Jakob by the arm, he led him toward the balcony.

"Meantime, eat plenty of yak meat tonight," called Mao over his shoulder, still looking down at the roasting animals. "There will be very little food to be found in the marshes of the Great Grasslands — and you will need all the strength you can muster there."

13

Holding a long bamboo pole crosswise in both hands, Jakob trod gingerly from one thick grass tussock to the next, fighting the feeling of panic that rose in him as each of his feet in turn sank down out of sight into the fetid black swamp water. The moment he stepped onto a new tussock, the one behind, freed of his weight, rose slowly above the surface once more, releasing his mud-blackened foot with a loud squelching noise. With each step the earth beneath him seemed to billow like the sea, threatening to dissolve to nothing; each new tussock seemed less substantial than the last, each step more fraught with danger. The constant fear, hour after hour, day after day, that he might at any moment slip down into the bottomless mire had produced a nightmarish sensation in Jakob's mind — time and distance had begun to lose their meaning and he moved like an automaton, his limbs tense, his head unnaturally stiff on his shoulders, his eyes wide with apprehension.

All around him rank, shoulder-high grass waved in the wind beneath leaden clouds. As far as the eye could see no trees, hills, or buildings broke the flat skyline above the gray-green desert of grass: only the heads and shoulders of Red Army men in front and behind were visible as Jakob and his guards trudged deeper into the silent, uninhabited wilderness. Although they had been marching for five days through the Great Grasslands, no landmark ever appeared by which they could measure their progress; after dragging themselves across the terrifying steppe throughout the daylight hours, buffeted by rain, snow, and hailstorms, there was never any way of telling how far they had traveled. The sun, on the rare occasions that it had been seen through the dense clouds, hung mistily in the sky above them, as pale and silver as the moon, and at night dense fogs cloaked the evil-smelling marshes. Jakob's straw sandals had long since rotted away in the water and his bare feet and ankles, beneath the sticky black mud that coated them, were again swollen and covered in sores. Across his shoulder he carried a long sausage-shaped food bag made of oxhide. Before the marchers entered the grasslands the bag had been filled with grain, pinecones, and edible fungus, but now it was nearly empty.

Coming to a sluggish stream that wound through the grass, Jakob tested the depth with his pole, then waded across, soaking his gown to the waist. On the other side the grass was thick and tangled and he had to feel his way forward a yard or two at a time. In the act of stepping across a mudhole, he stopped suddenly. Beneath the slime, the sole of his bare foot had come into contact with something softer than the spiky grass — it gave mushily beneath his weight, causing Jakob to recoil instinctively. Looking down, he saw he had trodden on the bloated face of a dead Red Army soldier. The lips of the dead man were drawn back from his teeth in the agonized rictus of death and black, foul-smelling swamp water filled his open throat. No other part of his body was visible and as Jakob stared down in horror, the head turned and slipped slowly out of sight again beneath the slime. He called a hoarse warning over his shoulder and one of his guards, edging along twenty yards behind him, automatically nodded his thanks. Stepping over the spot where the dead soldier had sunk from view, Jakob tested the next tussock carefully with both his bamboo staff and his foot before he moved forward again.

Scanning the winding file of marchers that stretched across the green wasteland into the far distance, Jakob wondered desperately how Mei-ling was faring with the baby. There were very few baggage animals to be seen any longer among the marchers: many horses and oxen had been slaughtered before the army entered the grasslands and the meat had at first been carried on the baggage mules. But the men, famished from their exertions each day, had consumed these rations rapidly and soon the missionary noticed that the few remaining baggage animals themselves were gradually being killed and eaten. It seemed likely to Jakob that by this time Mei-ling herself might be trudging on foot through the treacherous swamps, carrying Abigail in her arms, and anxiety mounted within him whenever he tried to imagine how she would be negotiating the terrifying bogs and mudholes with the additional burden of the eleven-month-old infant.

Jakob had not seen Mei-ling since their meeting in the Great Snow Mountains. After leaving Chokechi, the United Red Army had moved north to the larger Tibetan settlement of Maoerhkai, a town of several hundred stone dwellings, standing close to the grasslands. Over a three-week period in Maoerhkai, the army and Party leaders had tried to thrash out their differences at a series of heated meetings while the rank-and-file soldiers rested, sewed sheepskin garments, and plaited sandals of straw and oxhide for themselves. Each man had gathered and roasted about ten pounds of dry rations — green wheat or *chingko* — to fill his ration bag and Jakob had been allowed to join the troops in these preparations for crossing the Great Grasslands. He had been quartered in a stone house on the outer edge of the town and with the exception of a message from Lu Chiao saying that Commissioner Chou En-lai had become too ill to work or attend meetings, he had received no further information.

When news reached Maoerhkai in the third week of August that growing Kuomintang forces were breaking through the southern rear guard in strength, orders had been issued for the entire Communist force to move northward and strike through the grasslands into southern Kansu. Because the deep antagonism between Mao Tse-tung and Chang Kuo-tao remained unresolved, the United Red Army was split into two groups, the Left Column, headed by Chang, and the Right Column, headed by Mao. These groups marched out of Maoerhkai along parallel routes several miles apart with units of the original First Front Army and the Fourth Front Army mixed in each of them. Lin Piao's First Army Corps and Peng Teh-huai's Third Army Corps marched as before with Mao, while Chu Teh, appointed commander in chief of the whole army, marched at the head of the Left Column alongside Chang Kuo-tao. Behind him, the Fifth and Ninth corps of the First Front mingled with a majority of Fourth Front Army units. The ailing Chou En-lai was being borne on a stretcher among leaders of the Right Column, and in their wake Jakob marched with a squad of four new guards, youths younger than himself who had been recruited along the route in Kwangsi and Kweichow.

Having toiled up the flanks of the spectacular mountain ranges

that formed the high continental divide between the gigantic basins
of the Yangtze and the Yellow River, the marchers at a height of
twelve thousand feet had come suddenly upon an astonishing plain
of gently waving grass that stretched endlessly before them into the
northern distance. Its fringes were dotted with dazzling clusters of
yellow, violet, and blue flowers and many soldiers exclaimed aloud
at its beauty. Twisting tracks beaten by local flocks led into the tall
grass and Jakob's guards joked and laughed in relief.

"How lush and welcoming it looks," shouted a Kwangsi youth of
around twenty whose name was Hsu. "There must be people living
on this plain."

"Perhaps rice is grown up here," grinned one of the Kweichow
guards in reply. "It's not going to be so bad after all."

They had hurried eagerly onto the trodden tracks, following mark-
ers staked out by a vanguard regiment that had hired a knowledgeable
old Tibetan *hsiang tao* to guide them. The Tibetan, who was paid
well in silver, had insisted on being carried by half a dozen soldiers
on a wooden mountain chair, and in addition to marker stakes planted
at intervals, the vanguard soldiers under his directions had laid a
coarse rope of goat hair alongside the paths of spongy turf for their
comrades to follow. But within two hours the seemingly benign
mountain plain had changed to a dark, howling swamp. The warm
sunshine that had bathed the plateau at noon was suddenly blotted
out by black clouds that appeared from nowhere, and fierce, shrieking
winds rose to whip rain, sleet, then a blinding blizzard of snow into
the faces of Jakob and the other marchers. After wading across a
broad, freezing river that drenched their thin cotton uniforms and
left them gasping with cold, they found themselves in semidarkness,
stepping for the first time on the fragile crust of tussocks and tangled
roots that covered the viscous mire of oozing black quicksand. Within
minutes the snow obliterated the goat-hair rope and the tracks, leaving the Red Army columns stumbling by blind instinct along the
unknown ways.

Jakob and his guards had lost touch with the unit in front and
strayed off the pathway. Almost at once the Kweichow guard who
had hoped to find rice growing on the grasslands slipped from the
firm ground with a terrible cry. Jakob and Hsu, the Kwangsi youth,
who were walking ahead, turned to see him struggling chest-deep
in a morass of green and black slime, his face contorted in terror.

They hurriedly retraced their steps but he slipped swiftly downward, clawing at the firm grass in a helpless frenzy, and before they could reach him, the gurgling ooze closed over his head.

Numb with shock, Jakob and the other three guards stared helplessly at the surface of the swamp: then Jakob shouted loudly into the deepening gloom and when he heard answering shouts he led the young guards carefully back toward the main path. On joining up with the marching column they found that other men had begun to disappear abruptly into the quagmire. A few had been pulled out by their comrades but many dragged those who tried to rescue them to their deaths. A tangible sense of fear spread like wildfire through the marching regiments and it increased when darkness fell, leaving the marchers stranded on tiny tussocks of grass.

All soldiers had been issued with bamboo poles and most succeeded in pitching makeshift tents, using their quilted sheets. But the fierce winds blew many of them away and some companies spent their first night on the grasslands kneeling or crouching in the open. Others had to sleep as best they could standing upright, leaning back to back with four or five comrades. Jakob and his three guards were among the fortunate ones — they were able to rig a stable tent on a firm tussock, using poles and wadded quilts, and they knotted long clusters of growing grass above it as additional protection. Huddling with their backs together in this rough shelter, they slept fitfully until dawn.

To ward off the bitter cold the marchers kept fires going beside their shelters all night, although they knew this would quickly exhaust the supply of firewood that each man had been instructed to gather and carry in a bundle on his back. On the second day the clouds never lifted and freezing rain poured down on them throughout the gray daylight hours. Men fell frequently, covering themselves in mud until they looked more like shambling figures of clay. On the treeless, waterlogged tundra there was no fresh firewood to be found and by the third day, instead of boiling their roasted wheat and *chingko*, Jakob and his guards, like the rest of the troops, were having to eat them cold. The harshness of the rough grains and the effects of the black, brackish water they were forced to drink unboiled produced dysentery and fierce stomach cramps among many of the soldiers and as the numbers of stragglers increased, the pace slowed. The track itself, a firm pathway when the vanguard and their Tibetan *hsiang tao* marked it, became, under the tramp of thousands of feet, a flooded trench in which it was easy to take a false step.

As they grew hungrier, the troops marching around Jakob began to search for edible herbs and wild vegetables: they dug up aqueous globes as big as pumpkins and eagerly devoured the white, turniplike flesh. They gave Jakob a slice but he found it bitter and spat it out. Within hours some of those who had eaten the wild vegetable were retching; some stumbled and fell and were unable to get to their feet again. Jakob had eaten his dry rations sparingly after hearing political commissars tell the troops at the outset that the crossing might take a week or more, and on the fifth morning he had begun sharing his reserve with his three remaining guards, who already were carrying empty ration bags. As darkness closed in that night on the grasslands, the wind was freshening, whirling flurries of rain and sleet across the quagmire, and Jakob and the guards hurriedly erected their tent on a bank of dry ground beside the track. Jakob again knotted clusters of shoulder-high grasses in a cone above them and Hsu lit a tiny rapeseed-oil lamp which he placed on the dry rushes the others had spread inside the tent. Crowding inside on their knees, the three guards placed their tin bowls around the lamp and watched with anxious eyes as Jakob reached a fist into his ration bag and dropped a few charred grains of *chingko* into each bowl in turn. From habit he bent his head in a moment of prayer, and when he opened his eyes again, he found Hsu staring at him in puzzlement.

"Why do you want to share your precious food with men who are holding you captive?" he asked wonderingly.

Jakob looked at the young Kwangsi guard: his previously round face had become strangely bloated and the multiple effects of hunger, fear, and exhaustion had lent a dark, greenish hue to his features. He was shivering and sweating at the same time and although he chewed the hard, blackened barley grains determinedly, Jakob could see he was having difficulty swallowing.

"I'm a Christian," replied Jakob slowly. "Our Scriptures teach us to love God and to love our neighbors like brothers, whoever they may be. If men did this everywhere, it would be possible to end all strife."

"Why do you close your eyes over the food and move your lips?" Hsu's sweating face was tense as he waited for an answer.

"Every Christian has an unseen friend and helper in Jesus Christ. We pray through Him for strength and guidance. Tonight I was giving thanks to our Heavenly Father for the food we're eating."

"Does your 'praying' really help you? Is that why you have survived so many dangers?"

Jakob hesitated: the guard's naive question had reminded him all too forcibly of his turmoil of inner doubts and he was suddenly aware that he was incapable of clarifying his thoughts, even to himself. "If you have enough faith your prayers will always be answered," he said at last, repeating in a subdued tone the answer he would once have given with great zest.

"If Keng had been a Christian and said prayers, would he be alive now?"

A note of desperation crept into Hsu's voice as he spoke the name of his Kweichow comrade who had slipped to his death in the swamp and Jakob saw suddenly that his nerve was breaking.

"It's difficult to say. Perhaps — if he had truly believed."

The wind slammed against the makeshift shelter, rocking it violently. Not far away the long-drawn-out howling of wolves became audible and Hsu's eyes widened in fright. "Will you say a prayer for me tonight, please?"

"Of course, if you wish."

Taken by surprise, Jakob forced a smile and patted Hsu on the shoulder. Then he turned to the other two guards: they too were gaunt and hollow-cheeked and their jaws moved rhythmically as they chewed their few kernels of roasted grain.

"Would you like me to include you in the prayer too?" he asked in a quiet voice.

For a moment the two guards looked at one another — then the older of the pair shook his head. "We believe in the Chinese Workers' and Peasants' Red Army," he said defiantly. "We don't need your prayers."

Turning to Hsu, Jakob bent his head over his joined hands. Speaking aloud in Chinese, he prayed first for protection for all those who found themselves stranded in the desolate wilderness of the Great Grasslands; next he spoke Hsu's name in a prayer of supplication, asking that he be granted strength and courage to endure the ordeal. When the prayer was finished Hsu thanked Jakob quietly. His expression was calmer and he was less pale. After wishing one another good night, the missionary and his three guards turned and propped themselves together, sitting back to back, and covered themselves as best they could with wadded quilts. In the damp, confined space they drew warmth and comfort from contact with each other's bodies and gradually their heads fell forward one by one.

Jakob slept intermittently, conscious sometimes in his waking moments of Hsu shivering against him. Throughout the night the wind and sleet continued to lash the tent and from time to time he heard again the cry of wolves in the distance. In his confused, fitful dreams the quavering howls of the wild animals sounded like the wailing of human souls in torment and more than once they startled him into a fearful wakefulness. When the first streaks of gray light penetrated the dawn fog to rouse them, finally, Jakob found Hsu lying quiet and relaxed against his shoulder. But as the missionary shifted to chafe his own cold, aching limbs the young Kwangsi guard flopped soundlessly onto his back, his open eyes staring vacantly upward at the roof of the tent. Jakob touched his face with his fingers, then recoiled. The flesh of his swollen face was already cold and stiff: he had clearly been dead for some time.

14

By the seventh day the grasslands were taking a harsher toll of the Red Army marchers than even the Great Snow Mountains had done. Storms of freezing rain, sleet, and snow continued to obliterate the sun and without this sole navigational aid, even the old Tibetan *hsiang tao* lost his bearings. The trudging columns had to retrace their steps repeatedly, some units lost touch with one another, and confusion and disillusionment deepened. As men around Jakob became hungrier and weaker they fell more frequently into the swamps, and often their exhausted companions lacked the strength or the will to pull them out. Each man, intent on his own survival, walked with his eyes fixed on the next treacherous tussock before him, and many, Jakob noticed, closed their ears to the despairing cries for help unless they came from their closest comrades.

The medical orderlies had run out of medicines, and since the carrying of litters was fraught with additional dangers, the fallen were mostly abandoned where they lay. Several times Jakob stopped to try to help stricken soldiers but their eyes were wild and staring in their ravaged faces, and all strength had left their legs. Unable to walk, they clutched frantically at the missionary like drowning men, and only with the greatest difficulty was he able to disentangle himself. Feeling sick at heart, Jakob pressed on through the quagmire, and like those around him, he began to ignore the dying men crumpled beside the muddy trail.

The vanguard units had carried bamboo screens with them to build shelters for those who followed, but the sight of these temporary hutments among the waving grass, instead of giving cause for rejoicing, came to have a sinister significance. Inside each one the survivors began to find growing huddles of dead bodies: men who had crawled inside seeking protection from the ferocity of the cold, the wind, and the snow were dying in increasing numbers. Often a few grains of *chingko* lay beside them, left by their comrades in the vain hope they might revive, and anticipating this, the starving marchers began shamefacedly racing one another to each newly sighted shelter to gather up the charred and blackened grain for themselves.

In their desperation for nourishment, they broke up the bamboo screens to build fires, and after scooping up bowls of the acrid swamp water they boiled and ate their leather belts, their oxhide sandals, and the harnesses of their already dead horses. They also boiled grasses and drank the bitter broth, since they found this more nourishing than water alone, and on that seventh day Jakob for the first time saw men stooping along the trail to pick grains of undigested *chingko* from the feces of their comrades and the dung of the few remaining pack animals. They washed and reboiled the grains before wolfing them down and as they squatted beside the fires in the fog, their eyes glazed, their jaws working rhythmically, to Jakob they looked more like fear-stricken animals than men.

Jakob himself had eaten almost nothing since the guard Hsu died. He still had a few loose grains in the bottom of his oxhide ration bag but he fought down the impulse to eat them every time hunger pangs gnawed. Once when Little Liang passed him, hurrying forward with a message, he had given the Little Red Devil a handful or two of the grain to pass on to Mei-ling, but he had not seen the boy again. His own cold-blooded determination to survive had not in any way been diminished by the new hardships he faced, and after Hsu's sudden death he had made up his mind to hold out as long as possible before consuming the last of his dry rations. In any event, the sight of the desperate marchers tearing down the bamboo charnel houses for fuel and grubbing for barley grains among the trackside dung had left him without appetite; although he was weak, his fierce will helped sustain him and he contented himself with chewing the roots of dried grasses that he gathered as he walked.

In the early afternoon a ragged cheer rippled along the moving columns after news spread that the pursuing Kuomintang units had turned back after penetrating only a mile or two into the grasslands. In an effort to heighten morale further, political commissars read out the full text of a radio message from rearguard units, but Jakob could see that this did little to disperse growing fears that the trackless wastes of the grasslands and the region's ferocious climate might eventually succeed where the Kuomintang had failed and destroy every last one of them. Jakob heard men around him muttering enviously about the Kuomintang units as they eyed fresh banks of dark clouds bearing down on them from the north. Pressed close to the earth by a freshening northwester, the cloud banks threatened any moment to unleash another energy-sapping deluge of rain and they were already snuffing out the fading afternoon light with alarming speed. On the rising wind a faint commotion of shouting from up ahead also carried to Jakob's ears, which from experience he knew meant that more unfortunate men and animals were again struggling for their lives in the quagmire. In the deepening gloom he saw a diminutive figure splashing back along the column, but in the poor light he did not recognize Little Liang until he arrived gasping for breath in front of him. His pinched face was taut with anxiety, and because of his exertions, he had difficulty getting his words out.

"Ke Mu-shih, Ke Mu-shih! Something terrible has happened," he stammered at last. "Comrade Mei-ling's mule trod on a snake and bolted. She's fallen into a mudhole."

Jakob stared at the Chinese boy, aghast. "Is the baby with her?"

"Yes. They've managed to get a rope around the mule's neck but they can't pull them out."

Little Liang was tugging agitatedly at Jakob's arm, trying to drag him in the direction of the commotion, and without turning to look at his guards the missionary lunged forward, jumping rashly from one cluster of grass to another without waiting to test them with his bamboo pole. He slipped and slithered, feeling the unstable clumps swaying sickeningly beneath him, but his momentum carried him forward headlong in the wake of the nimble boy and within a few minutes he was pushing his way frantically through the dense crowd of men that had gathered on the fringes of a viscous pool of black mud.

Even before he could see what was happening, Jakob heard the terrified whinnying of the mule and, to his relief, mingled with it, the high-pitched wail of an infant. But when he broke through to the front of the crowd he saw to his horror that only the neck and head of the struggling animal were visible above the heaving surface of the mudhole. The rope that had been looped around its neck had drawn tight and the whites of the crazed animal's eyes showed in fear as it thrashed helplessly in the morass. The writhing female figure clinging desperately to its back was not immediately recognizable as Mei-ling. Her clothes, her face, and her hair were all covered in a uniform film of black slime and in the crook of one arm she clutched a struggling, mud-drenched creature which Jakob realized with a shock must be his daughter. The child, grown stronger in the weeks since he had last seen her, was jerking her arms and legs furiously as she struggled in Mei-ling's grip, but despite her obvious distress, Jakob felt a wave of relief sweep over him — at least she was still alive!

Yet even as he watched, the rope, looped around several men who were bracing themselves on a clump of firm ground, pulled taut and snapped. For a moment the mule, freed from the tension of the rope, ceased to struggle and lay exhausted and motionless, half-submerged in the encroaching mud. Because they lay still, animal and rider no longer sank so rapidly and the watching crowd clearly began to hope that the hooves of the mule had found a firm foundation beneath the ooze. But little by little they settled deeper and the mule stretched its neck toward the lowering clouds in one last feeble effort to hold its mouth clear of the swamp. At that moment torrential rain began to beat down, driven slantingly by the fierce wind, and it stung the faces of the men crowding helplessly around the mudhole. Jakob saw that only the smallest clumps of grass dotted the broad expanse of slime, none large enough to support a man's weight, and Mei-ling and the mule were obviously beyond the reach of anybody who might stretch out with a bamboo pole.

Spread-eagled along the length of the mule's back, Mei-ling lay horizontally in the mire, trying to hold the kicking baby above the surface with one arm. Her other hand clutched the mule's mane in an effort to control its head, and her mud-spattered face was a mask of concentration as she tried to prevent herself and the child from sinking farther; but she could see that her efforts were futile and Jakob heard a little moan of despair escape her lips.

"Quickly, gather up some quilts and as many rifles as you can from the men," shouted Jakob to Little Liang, who had pushed through the throng to his side. "I'm going to try to reach them!"

Slipping his pack from his shoulders, Jakob unfastened it, took out his own quilt, and flung it out over the edge of the mudhole. While it settled across the mud and sparse clumps of grass, he snatched two rifles from the soldiers nearest to him and bent to place them on top of it in the form of a diagonal cross. Then he crawled out onto them and called to Little Liang to pass him more bedding and weapons. The Young Vanguard did as he was told and in quick succession Jakob spread three more quilts ahead of himself and placed crossed rifles in the center of each one. As he inched forward on his hands and knees he felt the quilts slipping down into the mire and he knew that within a short space of time his flimsy raft would be swallowed up — but crawling forward steadily, he pushed this thought from his mind and kept his gaze fixed on Mei-ling and her precious burden.

In succumbing to the swamp, the mule thrashed wildly as its head went under, heaving the girl clear of its back. Feeling nothing but the liquid mud beneath her, Mei-ling showed her first real signs of panic: her mud-blackened face contorted suddenly as the lower part of her body sank rapidly downward and her mouth opened to release an involuntary cry of terror. She was trying to lift the wailing baby clear of the surface but her frantic movements were accelerating the rate at which she was sinking. Seeing this, Jakob threw himself forward in a desperate dive to clutch at the collar of her tunic with one hand. He felt himself begin to sink as he tried to drag her closer to himself — then strong hands circled his ankles and he realized somebody had crawled onto the sinking quilts and was beginning to draw him toward the firm ground. He managed to slip his other hand under Mei-ling's arm, and twisting with all that remained of his fading strength, he lifted her toward the flimsy pontoon on which he lay.

The momentum of her body rising jerkily from the mire turned Jakob's head and shoulders far enough for him to glimpse fleetingly the face of the man who had risked his life by venturing onto the quilts behind him. Even though his deep-set eyes were almost closed with the effort of trying to drag the combined weight of two bodies from the slime, there was no mistaking the swarthy, southern features of Felicity's executioner — but in the instant that Jakob registered the identity of his helper, gasps of dismay rose from the throats of the men crowding the bank of the mudhole. Turning his head again, Jakob saw to his horror that the act of snatching Mei-ling from the ooze had torn the baby from her arms: wailing and struggling, Abigail was sinking into the mud again a few feet beyond his reach. With his strength gone and Mei-ling clinging blindly to him, Jakob realized he was helpless to intervene.

A sudden weight on his own back pressed Jakob deeper as a blurred figure trod on him, using his back as a stepping-stone. For a second or two the slime before Jakob's eyes churned in a great turmoil; then a blackened head and powerful shoulders heaved themselves clear of the surface in the middle of the morass. Jakob heard a choking grunt of exertion as the tiny, muddied figure of his daughter was hurled in the direction of the bank, and he turned his head in time to see a soldier gather her up.

Other helping hands closed around Jakob's ankles again, starting to drag him toward the firm ground, and he locked his own arms tighter about Mei-ling's slender shoulders. He felt the suction of the swamp pulling at her and she clutched at him wildly, fearing she would slip from his grasp. On his own he was not capable of lifting her free but he continued to cling to her with all his fading strength, and slowly the Red Army soldiers hauled them both to safety.

Beyond anybody's reach, Abigail's rescuer was sinking deeper into the center of the mudhole. From where he lay exhausted on the bank beside Mei-ling, Jakob could only watch helplessly as the face of Executioner Wang tightened into a mask of horror. His eyes were blinded by the foul liquid and his mouth gaped despairingly for a last breath as the mire rose around his neck. But in the instant of submission to death, the mask of horror suddenly faded and the brutal features relaxed into a blank expression devoid of all emotion. No cry of protest or fear escaped his lips, and in the moment that the swamp claimed him in the baby's place, he lay motionless in its slimy embrace, passively accepting his fate.

15

"It has been decided," said Lu Chiao slowly, "that you will be released tomorrow morning."

Jakob looked down at the seated Red Army officer in silence. The words that he had wanted to hear more than any others for almost a year did not set his pulse racing wildly: standing between his guards in the ground-floor chamber of a watchtower at Tungwei, in southeastern Kansu, he felt only a dull sense of relief that he was still alive and had survived long enough to hear them.

"You will leave the column tonight with two guards. We've arranged for you to rest in an ordinary peasant household outside Tungwei. At dawn the guards will leave you there. Half an hour after their departure you'll be free to go."

"Free to go where?" asked Jakob wearily.

"You'll be provided with a mule to ride and five silver dollars with which to buy food." Chiao paused and pointed to a map of northern China spread before him on a trestle table. "The money should meet your needs until you reach the foreign mission here at Sanmo, where you will be expected. It's a half-day's journey."

"Does this mean that the Anglo-Chinese Mission has agreed to pay the ransom you demanded?" asked Jakob in a surprised voice.

"We're no longer seeking payment of fines." Chiao kept his eyes on the map, avoiding Jakob's mystified gaze. "Since Commissioner Chou En-lai recovered his health we've had the opportunity to undertake a thorough, final review of your case. We've decided from now on to treat all foreigners on their individual merits."

"And what are my merits?"

"We note from your file that your father was born in Switzerland and that you possess dual Anglo-Swiss nationality. We've taken full account of the fact that Switzerland is not an imperialist country. It hasn't forced unequal treaties on China or set up concession areas as the imperialist nations have done — that's why we have decided to set you free."

"Does that mean all charges against me have been withdrawn?" asked Jakob, still puzzled.

"No. The review showed that you broke our soviet laws and we've drawn up conditions for your release." Chiao picked up a piece of paper and scanned it. "You've been guilty on your own admission of preaching the Christian Gospel and escaping from the custody of the Central Soviet authorities. Therefore you are released on the condition that you don't break our laws again."

"But it's not against the law to preach the Gospel in China," protested Jakob.

"In our soviet areas the Communist Party reserves the right to ban the propagation of all religious ideas," replied Chiao firmly. "You and others of your calling should remember that. That is the second condition."

"And if I refuse to promise not to preach the Gospel?" asked Jakob in a hardening voice. "What happens then?"

"You're not being asked for any undertakings," replied Chiao quietly. "We're informing you of the conditions of your release. Commissioner Chou further asks you to bear in mind when speaking of the Red Army that we always act on principle and are not the common bandits depicted in your press. He also hopes you will not forget to relate how we help the poor of China and punish only tyrants who oppress the poor. . . ."

"I'd like to ask you a question, Commander Lu," said Jakob, "about Comrade Lu Mei-ling. . . ."

Chiao lifted one hand to silence Jakob and glanced at the missionary's two guards. Standing at his shoulder, they were listening intently to the exchanges, and after a moment's reflection Chiao motioned for them to leave. "Go and prepare the mules, comrades — for the prisoner and yourselves. Be ready to leave in half an hour."

Still holding up his hand warningly in Jakob's direction, Chiao watched the guards march out of the watchtower into the dusty street, which was swarming with Red Army men hurrying to a rally in the town's central square. Through the open door a distant platform decked with red bunting was visible and regimental commanders and political commissars were already marshaling their troops around it in closely packed ranks. It was the last day of September

and the starving, mud-drenched skeletons who had staggered out of
the Great Grasslands a month before had largely recovered their
strength. On catching sight of hills and the first hutted villages beyond the swamps, the men had danced and sung in relief; seeing
stones in their path again after treading fearfully through the black,
bottomless quagmire for days on end, they had picked them up and
kissed them joyfully; encountering friendly Han Chinese peasants
again in Kansu province after many weeks in the hostile Tibetan
tribal areas, the Red Army soldiers had embraced the startled strangers
and wept.

With thousands of their comrades lying dead in the swamps behind
them, their numbers had been further depleted when the conflict
between Mao Tse-tung and Chang Kuo-tao reached a sudden flash
point in the first week of September. Chang, apparently fearing
defeat at the hands of Kuomintang divisions in Kansu, had abruptly
radioed orders to his Thirtieth Army Corps and his Fourth Army
Corps marching with Mao to turn back to Maoerhkai. He had first
tried to order the unconditional retreat of the Right Column but
Mao, convinced that his opponent was plotting to seize control of
the entire Red Army, had broken away in the dead of night with
his loyal First and Third Army Corps, under Lin Piao and Peng
Teh-huai.

Jakob had been taken with them, and he had noticed the soldiers'
spirits revive as they marched across the more hospitable counties
of Kansu province, moving again among friendly Han Chinese peasants who sold them feasts of pork, chicken, and beef. Although
reduced to a force of fewer than six thousand men, this remnant of
the Central Red Army had broken through a ring of several Kuomintang regiments after a sharp encounter at the Latzu Pass, in the
Min Mountains. Fighting off a series of running attacks by the Kuomintang's Moslem cavalrymen, they had rushed headlong toward
the Shensi border and their final goal — the small, stable Shensi-
Kansu soviet which had first been set up by local Communist guerrilla fighters four years earlier. In every town along their route the
political commissars began to organize inspirational rallies once more
and the propaganda teams put on their political theater shows for a
populace that had never heard of the Central Red Army. On arrival
in Tungwei, a walled town lying southwest of the Shensi-Kansu
soviet, a big evening rally had been planned to precede an early dawn
departure next day, and from his seat beside the watchtower's open

door, Chiao watched the preparations in thoughtful silence before turning his attention back to Jakob.

"Before I try to answer any questions you might have," said Chiao, speaking very softly, "I've got something further to say. So far I've conveyed to you the decisions of Commissioner Chou and the Revolutionary Military Commission — but now I wish to say something on my own behalf. I don't wish you to misunderstand. This is purely a private matter between the two of us."

Jakob studied the officer's face carefully. Like all the other surviving marchers, Chiao still bore the marks of his ordeal in the grasslands. The sharpness of his intelligence was still evident in his quick, bright gaze, and the moustache he wore was trim and neatly clipped again — but the sallowness of his tightly drawn skin testified to the extremes of hunger and endurance that he and the rest of the other Red Army men had so recently experienced. Jakob could see also that a hint of uneasiness had crept into his expression because of what he was about to say.

"The courage you displayed in the grasslands when you saved my sister, Mei-ling, was greatly to your credit. She's a valued aide to Commissioner Chou En-lai and your actions may have helped the comrade commissioner decide to order your release without payment of fines . . ." Chiao hesitated, twisting his fingers together on the trestle table before him. "But because my sister has confided in me, I also know that perhaps you had a motive which others are not aware of — I'm aware that her own child died in Yunnan and that for several months she has been secretly caring for your own infant daughter in its place. . . ."

Jakob stiffened. "I didn't know she'd told anyone."

"I don't fully understand my sister's motives," said Chiao, "but I respect them. And whatever your reasons were for going to her rescue, I'm grateful that you did."

To Jakob's surprise Chiao rose from his seat and moved around the table. Reaching out, he grasped Jakob's right hand and shook it warmly with both his own. For a moment they stood looking at one another in silence: then Chiao turned away, speaking over his shoulder. "I've informed my sister of your impending release and she's asked me to pass you a message. She suggests you travel slowly when you leave your quarters in the peasant's house at dawn tomorrow. Your daughter, she says, will be brought to you in secret by her orderly —"

At that moment a storm of cheering broke out in the town square, and looking out through the watchtower doorway, Jakob and Chiao saw the tall, gaunt figure of Mao Tse-tung mount the rostrum and approach the microphone. Through loudspeakers the soft Hunanese vowel sounds familiar to Jakob from Chokechi sounded harsher and more high-pitched.

"Comrade Commanders and fighters of the Chinese Workers' and Peasants' Red Army, I salute you," yelled Mao above a fresh storm of cheering. "You've displayed great bravery and fighting spirit in journeying nearly twenty thousand *li* across China on foot from Kiangsi to Kansu. This 'Long March' of yours will go down in history as a unique achievement, the first of its kind . . ."

Mao laid great emphasis on the words *Ch'ang Ch'eng*, meaning "Long March," and he drew the words out sonorously so that they echoed and re-echoed on the quiet evening air.

"Soon this great Long March will end in triumph," he continued, stressing the words heavily again and raising a tightly clenched fist above his head. "Soon we shall unite with our comrades in the Shensi soviet and begin the great task of fighting the Japanese occupiers of our country. . . . Soon the Long March will proclaim to the world that the Red Army is an army of heroes who encountered untold difficulties and obstacles in sweeping across the length and breadth of eleven provinces. . . ."

Mao shook both fists above his head, drawing another surge of cheering from his troops. They too began to punch the air, in imitation, and chants of *"Ch'ang Ch'eng! Ch'ang Ch'eng!"* began to resound rhythmically from all parts of the crowd.

"Soon the world will know that the Long March has spread enlightenment to the broad masses of China," continued Mao, raising his voice to a higher pitch. "It has propagated great ideas that will sprout, grow leaves, blossom into flowers, bear fruit, and finally yield a great crop in the future!"

Standing side by side inside the watchtower, Jakob and Chiao listened to the cheers rolling across the square. The townspeople of Tungwei, stirred by the speech, were hurrying to join the troops and Jakob noticed that they too were getting caught up in the excitement and were beginning to cheer.

"I would like to speak privately with your sister before I leave, if that's possible," said Jakob, turning to Chiao. "I would like to thank her for what she's done."

"That won't be possible," replied Chiao without taking his eyes from the distant platform. "She's working with Commissioner Chou at present — and it's important that you leave at once if you are to reach your resting place before dark."

Jakob felt a stab of acute disappointment strike through him. "Then perhaps you'll thank her for me."

"I will, of course . . ." Chiao nodded quickly and pointed through the open door. "Look, here are the mules."

The guards had appeared, leading three black mules. On one of them Jakob could see his bedroll and pack already strapped behind the saddle. When the guard halted the animal, Chiao helped Jakob swing up onto its back. Taking its head, he led the animal toward the main gate of the town and the two guards mounted up and followed. Above the clop of the mules' hooves on the cobblestoned surface of the street Jakob could hear the voice of Mao Tse-tung still ringing out above the crowd in the square.

". . . For almost twelve months we've been under daily reconnaissance and bombing from the air by scores of planes. . . . On the ground we were encircled and pursued, obstructed and intercepted by a big force never smaller than several hundred thousand men — but by keeping our feet going every day and every night we swept across a great distance to reach safety here in the northwest. . . . Our great Long March, in fact, has bankrupted the pursuit and encirclement campaigns attempted by the imperialists and Chiang Kai-shek!"

At the gate Jakob turned in the saddle to look back: another great cheer was bursting from the throats of the soldiers in the square and they were waving their caps deliriously above their heads. Mao Tse-tung, motionless on the platform, raked one hand through his long hair as he gazed out over the throng, waiting for the noise to subside. For the briefest moment he seemed by chance to turn his head to look in Jakob's direction; then he leaned close to the microphone again.

"To sum up, Comrade Commanders and fighters, our historic Long March is ending in a great victory for us — and utter defeat for all our enemies!"

At Jakob's side Chiao reached up to offer a last handshake and spoke several words in parting. But the Chinese officer's words were drowned in a final crescendo of cheers. Beside Chiao, another officer had appeared and was studying Jakob intently. He was small but stocky and confident-looking, and despite the fact that he was very pale and thin, apparently from illness, his eyes possessed an inner light of rare intelligence. An unkempt black beard curled on his cheeks and he wore frayed cloth sandals with his soiled uniform of field gray cotton.

"This is Commissioner Chou En-lai," said Chiao when the cheering had died down. "It was his decision that brought about your release."

The newcomer stepped up beside Jakob's mount and to his surprise offered his hand in farewell. "Good luck, Mr. Kellner," he said with the hint of a smile, speaking in English. "We hope you will tell the outside world that the Red Army is not composed entirely of barbaric ruffians, as the Kuomintang press insists. We wish you a safe journey."

"Thank you, Commissioner." Jakob shook the proffered hand, taken aback by Chou's friendliness. "I'm grateful for the help you've given me."

For an uncertain moment the two men continued to look at one another; then, realizing there was nothing more to be said, Jakob swung the head of his mule impatiently toward the open gate. Flanked by his two escorts, the missionary turned his back on the Red Army, which had held him captive for nearly a year, and moved slowly out into the dusk settling over the low line of hills beyond the town walls.

16

The red rim of the sun's disk, lifting above the weirdly distorted loess hills of eastern Kansu, sent an avalanche of light flooding down the dark, silent valley along which Jakob was riding alone. Feeling the sun's warmth strike his face, the missionary took off the tattered palm-fiber cape he had wrapped around his shoulders against the predawn chill and in that hushed moment he felt fully free for the first time. For a few brief seconds the strangely shaped hills of yellow loam that had been blown south from the Gobi Desert centuries before glowed with the brilliance of fire, and the fast-running stream, which he was following southward, shone like silver in the shadows below. He closed his eyes, fearing suddenly that he might be dreaming, but when he opened them again the dawn-rouged valley still lay empty and deserted before him.

Coming to a shimmering pool of clear water in a basin of rocks, he stopped to allow his mule to drink and caught sight of his reflection — his beard was thick and tousled, his hair long and unkempt, yet he felt a curious satisfaction at seeing his own image for the first time in conditions of freedom. Turning in a full circle, he gazed around in all directions, glorying in the space and emptiness of the stark landscape: a flock of small, dark birds rose up and sped across the shimmering hilltops but he was the only human figure in that enchanted vale. With narrowed eyes he searched the trails criss-crossing the slopes, looking for signs of the promised Red Army orderly bearing his daughter, but he could see no sign of movement.

Long before dawn his two guards, who were strangers to him, had left the loft of the mud-walled farmhouse where they had slept at his side. They had taken no farewell of him and he had feigned sleep until they were clear of the house. As soon as they had gone, Jakob had slipped silently down to the stable and saddled his mule. He had given a silver dollar to the sleepy-eyed farmer who had been their host, led his mule out of the yard in the half-light, and set off down the valley, walking slowly, as he had been instructed, in a southeasterly direction. At first he had glanced repeatedly over his shoulder, fearful that at any moment Red Army hordes would reappear and take him captive once more — but he saw no living soul on the remote track. To his surprise he quickly began to find the sensation of being alone unnerving. The rearing loess hills seemed suddenly ominous and even the distant cries of birds startled him. Before long his earlier exhilaration left him; he began to feel tired and weak and he had to mount the mule and ride. On emerging from the grasslands the day after helping to rescue Mei-ling, he had collapsed from fatigue and had to be carried on a litter for a day or two. Over the next four weeks he had ridden a mule for part of each day because the swamp sores contracted in the grasslands had made marching difficult for him. The harsh starvation diet of the grasslands had weakend the majority of the marchers and Jakob, like the others, had found in the succeeding weeks that he had to be careful to conserve his strength.

As he jogged along on the mule he began to consider what danger he might face, in his weakened state, from common Chinese bandits out to rob and pillage unwary travelers. He fell into the habit of scanning ahead for likely hiding places on hills overlooking the trail, and when two riders appeared suddenly, breasting a pass between the hills, he feared he might have been singled out for attack. But as they trotted down a winding path in his direction, he felt a sudden surge of elation. Both were slender, obviously female figures and almost at once Jakob recognized Mei-ling on the leading mule. She and her orderly, to disguise themselves in Kuomintang territory, had forsaken their Red Army uniforms for blue peasant cottons and as they drew near he saw that his daughter was traveling in a basket seat rigged on a pack mule trotting in their wake.

Waiting on his mount beside the stream, Jakob felt his heart begin to beat faster: Mei-ling was capless and her long hair blew loose about her face in the fresh mountain breeze. Although she too was thinner from the privations of the march, the soft, bright color of her face was enhanced by the dawn light, and amid the dramatic sweep of the loess hills he found that her beauty moved him more deeply than ever before. When they were only twenty yards away, Mei-ling motioned to her orderly to wait on the far bank and splashed across the shallow stream alone, leading the pack mule. As she approached he saw that a little frown of anxiety was crinkling her smooth brow, and her face was set in serious lines when she reined in beside him.

"I thought I'd never see you again," Jakob's voice broke, betraying the hidden intensity of his feelings. "I was told to expect only your orderly."

"I decided to come myself — at the last minute."

"How's my daughter?" Jakob peered anxiously over Mei-ling's shoulder at Abigail, who was strapped comfortably into the basket seat on the pack mule. Little of her face was visible inside a hood of padded cotton, but he could see that her eyes were closed.

"Don't worry, she's asleep. The motion of the mule is very soothing for her. But you shouldn't waste any time getting her to your mission. She needs proper care."

"I'll never be able to thank you enough for what you've done."

Mei-ling looked steadily back at him, sitting straight in her saddle. Her face was expressionless but in her dark eyes he saw a depth of emotion which raised a sudden, frantic hope in him.

"Now that you've come this far," he said in a tense voice, "won't you stay with me?"

Although Jakob was astonished by his own abrupt invitation, Mei-ling's face betrayed no sense of shock or surprise: looking at her, he knew suddenly that she had already considered the question, but she made no attempt to reply.

"Our meeting in the Great Snow Mountains was very beautiful, Mei-ling. You saved my life. It felt as if God approved and shared the love we found there. Didn't you feel that too?"

Mei-ling's demeanor didn't change but the quiet expression in her eyes showed that she understood the force of his passion — and he felt a sudden certainty that she shared his strong feelings. For a long moment they sat astride their mules, looking at one another; then she turned away and gazed up the valley toward the dragon-backed spikes of loess that glowed like dull gold in the strengthening light.

"I've committed my life to the revolution, Jakob. It's impossible for me to turn my back on it — as impossible as it would be for you to deny your faith."

"We've both suffered," said Jakob desperately. "We're weary and exhausted. When all this is over we might find there's some way for us."

Mei-ling lifted her hand to brush an errant strand of hair from her face. "You saved *my* life — and risked your own in doing it. Caring for your daughter in a time of great hardship has brought comfort to both of us — these bonds will always join us."

"But there could be much more than that."

"Sometimes during the ride here this morning I wondered too. But I know now there can be nothing more."

Jakob searched her face with despairing eyes. "But why did you come if you didn't feel some hope for the future?"

"I came to say thank you," said Mei-ling softly, dropping her gaze. "For coming to our aid in the grasslands."

"I didn't do it only for Abigail."

"I know."

Jakob drew in his breath slowly. "Mei-ling, when we first met on the ship, I had a curious feeling. And every time you looked at me that feeling grew stronger. There was something wonderful in your expression — it was as though *both* of us knew inside ourselves that our lives would lead along a single path."

"Perhaps you imagine that was so after all that's happened."

"No, I dreamed often of you. They were tortured dreams. But after the Great Snow Mountains I think I understand. My dreams were strange reflections of the love I felt for you right from the beginning." He hesitated, then leaned impulsively toward her. "We could be married — it would make everything right."

Mei-ling looked directly at him again, her expression becoming suddenly uneasy. "So much is in turmoil in China, Jakob. Everything is new . . . I'm frightened of love — it seems like a drug that numbs the senses —"

The sound of whimpering broke in on their conversation and they looked around to find that Abigail had wakened. At once Mei-ling swung down from her mount and hurried to the pack mule. Reaching into the saddle basket, she stroked the infant girl's face tenderly with her hand until the whimpering ceased. At almost a year old, Abigail was thin and pale, but now that she was awake she sat upright in the seat, straining against her straps, and there was a lively expression in her blue eyes. For a moment Mei-ling stood looking at her, biting her lip; then Abigail smiled and reached out for her with both arms. Jakob felt a lump come into his throat as he watched Mei-ling embrace his daughter, speaking a few soothing words to her as she did so. Abigail responded at once with a little torrent of excited, unintelligible Chinese sounds and Jakob noticed then that Mei-ling became very still, taking care to keep her back turned to him.

"There's water and goat's milk in the other basket," she said at last, speaking over her shoulder in a muffled voice. "But you must get her to the mission at Sanmo as soon as possible."

When she handed him the leading rein of the pack mule, Mei-ling's manner was cool and impersonal and she hurried back to her own mule to remount in silence. From the saddle she looked down at Jakob, her eyes glistening with tears. He thought she would speak again but instead she tossed her head suddenly and urged the mule down the bank into the stream. Jakob watched her splash back to the far bank, fighting down the urge to run after her. Riding very straight in the saddle, she rejoined her orderly and they jogged quickly away up the steep track leading north. Jakob watched until they became minute silhouettes on the high ridge, but Mei-ling faded gradually from his sight among the misshapen towers of yellow loess without once looking back.

During his ride to Sanmo, Jakob saw few people. Curious, dark-faced children ran out of the cave dwellings hewn from the hard loess hillsides whenever he passed through a village, and peasants in the terraced fields raised their turbaned heads to stare at the unfamiliar sight of a white European traveling alone with a baby on a mule. But fearing that his strength might give out before he reached the mission, Jakob spoke to nobody and stopped only once, around midmorning. In the shade of some rocks he unstrapped his daughter and lifted her from the mule to feed her with the goat's milk. But although holding Abigail in his arms moved him silently to tears, she cried in his unfamiliar embrace and he did not linger long.

In the early afternoon he led the pack mule over a high ridge to find the walled town of Sanmo nestling in the bend of a gray river far below. Half an hour later, as he neared its gates, he saw a crowd of long-robed men and women gathered before a compound of whitewashed buildings outside the battlemented walls. On seeing him approach, the people began swarming along the dusty road in his direction, shouting and waving joyfully. One bewhiskered European leading several others was familiar and as the crowd converged around his mules, Laurence Franklin, smiling hugely in his relief, reached up with both arms to help Jakob down from the saddle.

"The Lord be praised!" cried Franklin, flinging both arms ecstatically around Jakob. "The Lord be praised!"

Jakob sagged in Franklin's embrace, his strength suddenly gone. Pointing to the saddle basket on the pack mule, he explained weakly that his daughter needed attention and he watched a gray-haired Englishwoman lift the infant tenderly from the basket.

"You've both been preserved — it's a miracle!" said Franklin in astonishment, guiding Jakob toward a sedan chair carried by two coolies. "Matthew Barlow was right!"

Sinking gratefully into the chair, Jakob allowed himself to be carried to the mission compound among the excited group of European and Chinese Christians.

"The Lord be praised," exclaimed Franklin again, unable to suppress the joy welling up in him.

"The Lord be praised," echoed Jakob in a weak voice. "The Lord be praised."

PART FIVE

The Marchers Falter

1957

ended a year later, in the autumn of 1936, the survivors there to-
taled no more than 30,000. Chang Kuo-tao, who had come so
close to unseating Mao as leader in the summer of 1935, had lost
large sections of his Fourth Front Army: only a thousand or so of
his troops eventually reached the safety of Shensi, and after facing disciplinary charges on his arrival, Chang defected to the
Kuomintang. The Second Front Army, under Ho Lung, made its
own Long March northward from its Hunan base, covering a similar route to Mao's — but only 10,000 out of 35,000 of these
troops survived the hardships.

These setbacks prompted Mao Tse-tung to seek a new united
front with Chiang Kai-shek's Nationalists, and Chiang agreed to
join forces with the Communists after being sensationally kidnapped by procoalition warlord forces in the famous Sian Incident of December 1936. Thereafter the Long March survivors
donned Nationalist uniforms and were reorganized as the Eighth
Route Army under overall Kuomintang command. This truce,
however, was never more than fragile, and Japan's armies swept
across the map, capturing the major cities and strategic coastal
areas by the end of 1938. In the face of these swift offensives,
Chiang Kai-shek retreated deep into China's vast interior, moving
his seat of government from Nanking to Chungking, in the southwest, and gradually the war against the invaders developed into a
stalemate. Mao Tse-tung and the Communist leadership in their
turn made themselves comfortable in cave houses amid the loess
hills of Shensi at Yenan. In this remote and romantic rebel capital
close to the burial site of China's founding emperor, they set up a
revolutionary university, which attracted idealistic and patriotic
youths from all China's great cities. For the next eleven years
Yenan became the cradle of China's revolution. Under the protection of the united front with the Nationalists, the Communists
rapidly built up their strength, employing skillful patriotic propaganda to recruit the northern peasants. Guileful guerrilla strategies
were used to harass the Japanese without risking big losses, and
consequently the Eighth Route Army mushroomed in size from
45,000 men in 1937 to 150,000 the next year. By the time the
Second World War ended seven years later, it embraced more
than half a million men, and when Japan surrendered after the
American bombing of Hiroshima and Nagasaki, Mao's Communist divisions controlled two hundred thousand square miles of

territory and a population of nearly twenty million people. By contrast, political and military corruption had become common-place on the Kuomintang side: lack of action had further under-mined the morale of the four million men under arms, and when the civil war burst into life again in 1946, China's disgruntled peasants continued to flock to Mao's banners. By 1948 the Red Army matched the American-aided Kuomintang forces with four million soldiers, and guerrilla strategies gave way to mobile posi-tional warfare. The Communists quickly won Manchuria and most of northern China; in early 1949 Peking was surrendered peacefully to preserve its ancient treasures; and the Red Army swept triumphantly south to cross the Yangtze and seize the other major cities one by one. Chiang Kai-shek, supported by the United States, retreated with half a million troops to the offshore island of Taiwan, then called Formosa, and set up his Nationalist government there.

On October 1, 1949, in a historic speech from Peking's Gate of Heavenly Peace, Mao Tse-tung proclaimed the founding of the People's Republic of China, and over the next seven or eight years Mao and his comrades of the Long March changed the old China beyond recognition. Heading a strict Communist govern-ment that pretended to be a coalition of various patriotic parties, Mao succeeded in imposing a purposeful nationwide discipline. Vast peasant work forces were successfully mobilized to over-come the ancient scourges of flood and famine: dikes, dams, and reservoirs were rapidly built to restrain the great rivers and con-serve water against drought. A sweeping land reform program abolished all private farming and introduced a collective system of agricultural cooperatives under which households pooled their labor, land, tools, and animals. Internationally China's prestige and self-confidence were boosted when her forces fought the armies of the United States and other Western nations to a draw in the Korean War, which broke out in 1950. Allied diplomati-cally and ideologically with the Soviet Union, the People's Re-public also received vital technical assistance from the Russians in laying new industrial foundations. Some sections of China's population of six hundred million, however, suffered grievously during this period — several hundred thousand rural landlords were murdered during early stages of the land reform program, and many small capitalists who stayed to help build the economy were victimized when the state eventually took over their businesses. But overall the new rulers in Peking enjoyed a period of widespread popular support during the early fifties. After harrowing decades of invasion, civil war, famine, corruption, poverty, and disease, the Communist regime had substantially improved the living conditions of the vast majority.

This honeymoon period, however, was to prove a brief one: invisible conflicts that would eventually plunge the country into a great new tragedy were already at work among the Party leaders, and in 1957 the first signs of the chaos to come began to surface. They grew out of the denunciation of Joseph Stalin by the new Soviet leader Nikita Khrushchev at a Party congress in Moscow in January 1956. This sparked popular revolts against the Communist regimes in Hungary and Poland, and the speed with which the Hungarian party collapsed following criticisms by intellectuals horrified Mao Tse-tung. Not long afterward Mao made a landmark speech inviting Chinese academics, students, and members of the other coalition parties to give free voice to any criticisms they had of Communist policy. His intent, it seems, was to uncover and defuse any latent Hungarian-style resentment by open discussion, and he employed a classical Chinese quotation to make his point. "Let a Hundred Flowers bloom!" he proclaimed. "Let a Hundred Schools of Thought contend!" The avalanche of criticism that this invitation unleashed shocked the Peking leadership deeply, and in mid-1957 they launched a ruthless "rectification campaign," during which many intellectuals were arrested and sent to labor camps. But news of these dramatic events filtered through to the West only in disjointed fragments. Few non-Communist visitors had been allowed across China's borders since 1949, and for information of what was happening to a quarter of all mankind, the outside world depended largely on the efforts of a community of "China watchers" — journalists, diplomats, writers — based in Hong Kong, the British crown colony perched on China's southern coast. As the little-understood Hundred Flowers campaign unfolded, every broadcast from China's many radio stations, every tattered provincial newspaper smuggled over the border, and every refugee struggling out through the "Bamboo Curtain" was being examined minutely in that tiny British enclave on the rim of the old Celestial Kingdom.

1

Abigail Kellner caught her first adult glimpse of China through a port window of a BOAC Constellation 749 as it circled downward out of high clouds a few miles west of Hong Kong Island. The serpentine coastline and a range of rolling hills writhing away to the northwest were only faintly visible beyond the New Territories in the afternoon haze, but Abigail's gaze remained riveted on the distant landscape until the Constellation's nose swung south again. Then, as the airliner flew lower and began its run in toward Kai Tak Airport, densely packed shack colonies housing the latest refugees from Communism caught her eye on both sides of the spectacular jade green harbor. The crowded waterway itself was alive with vast numbers of junks, sampans, and ferries as well as ocean-going ships; great wedges of moored craft rafted together seemed to choke bays and inlets; boats and buildings alike were bedecked with fluttering lines of tattered washing; and even before she saw any people, Abigail had an impression of the Crown Colony of Hong Kong as a seething, jam-packed, overcrowded community.

All along the waterfronts, modern buildings were springing up, and as the airliner drew abreast of Victoria Peak, Abigail saw that clusters of tall radio-receiving aerials jutted from the rocky summit. Among those aerials, she guessed, would be one or two erected by her father to serve the research organization he had founded in the colony seven years earlier. Straining toward the Communist mainland, they were almost certainly at that very moment plucking invisible Chinese broadcasts from the shimmering air for the Kellner Research Institute.

From her father's infrequent letters she knew that a team of his

Chinese translators would be crouching over high-powered radio receivers in work huts close to the foot of the masts, recording and monitoring around the clock every word picked up from Peking and each of Communist China's provincial capitals. Written transcripts of these broadcasts, he had told her, were translated into English and pored over by his small staff of analysts before being collated with translations of every significant newspaper report they were able to lay their hands on from inside China. Interviews with refugees were transcribed and analyzed with equal meticulousness to help the Kellner Institute build up a day-by-day, week-by-week picture of life behind the Bamboo Curtain. The products of these researches — daily, weekly, and monthly bulletins — were eagerly sought after, both in Hong Kong and far beyond its borders, by journalists, diplomats, academic Sinologists, and other subscribers anxious to keep track of what was happening to the world's biggest and most isolated nation.

This thought made Abigail lift her eyes again in the direction of the bare, haze-shrouded mountains that she was able to see intermittently through gaps in the hills that rose behind Kowloon in the New Territories. In the misty heat, the outer ramparts of China's vast landmass seemed to her to possess a mysterious, brooding quality, and sitting beside the round window of the airliner she felt suddenly very small and insignificant. Although she knew without doubt that she had been born in that strange and enigmatic country twenty-three years earlier, her first conscious sight of it left her feeling incredulous. Had she really come close to death almost daily in this remote part of the world during the first, unknowing year of her life? Could she have traveled thousands of miles across this alien landscape concealed in a peasant's shoulder basket? How could a defenseless infant have survived in all that wildness below the Constellation's glittering propellers when armies were swarming across a strife-torn land, killing, looting, and burning in a bloody civil war?

Confronted at last by the intimidating physical majesty of China, she felt that the sketchy accounts of her miraculous survival that she had been given were more than ever the stuff of dreams. Because she had been brought up by her grandparents at their home in Manchester's Moss Side, she had known nothing at all of her early adventures until she was eleven. She had retained few memories of her father during that period, due to his prolonged absence on active service during the Second World War, and in a well-meaning attempt to spare a young girl's feelings, her grandparents had told her merely that her mother had died in China soon after she was born. They had also said that before returning to England, her father had been forced to make a long journey with her across China to escape the effects of the civil war. But fearing further details might distress her, they had avoided all mention of his capture by the Communists and the trials and sufferings which she had unknowingly shared.

By chance Abigail had uncovered the real story for herself one day shortly after her eleventh birthday and the impact on her had been traumatic. While tidying up the attic during her grandmother's absence, she had happened upon a forgotten scrapbook of yellowing newspaper clippings. Sitting alone among the jumble of broken chairs, discarded ornaments, and dusty piles of magazines, she had learned with a deep sense of shock that her mother had been cruelly beheaded by the Communists. As she read through the news reports, intense feelings of desolation and sadness had seized her. The details themselves were horrifying enough, but the fact that they had been kept from her deliberately increased a nagging sense of uncertainty about her identity that she had nursed within herself for as long as she could remember. The complete absence of her mother, who had died mysteriously abroad, and the infrequent appearances of her barely remembered father had long before created a void in her young life that the care and affection of her grandparents had not been able to fill. From her earliest days at school she had always felt different from her playmates, sensing vaguely that she had been abandoned in Moss Side and that she did not really belong there.

While waiting for her grandmother to return to the house that day, Abigail had ached to know more about the tragic events which seemed to hold the key to her unhappiness; but when she found on her return that the old lady knew little more about the terrible adventure than she herself had been able to read in the newspaper clippings, Abigail had burst into tears and sobbed inconsolably. Her father had never shown much inclination to discuss the details of his ordeal, her grandmother had explained apologetically, and this revelation too had somehow deepened the sense of bewilderment which the discovery of the scrapbook had produced in her. As time passed, in her tortured adolescent mind she had begun to wonder whether some fault in herself was the cause of her father's reluctance to speak out, and this thought had further compounded her misery.

Staring out of the window of the descending airplane, Abigail remembered again the terrible intensity of those feelings of loneliness and abandonment that she had experienced twelve years earlier. For a time she had lived in hope that Jakob might someday help satisfy her curiosity, but after his demobilization from the army he had brushed aside all her questions with a baffling evasiveness and before long had returned alone to the Far East, leaving her to finish her education in England. The illogical suspicion that she had been left behind through some fault of her own had increased; on those few occasions when she had seen him during his rare visits to England, he had shown the same curious disinclination to discuss the past. Once, in response to her persistent questions about how she had survived as a small baby in such terrible circumstances, he had revealed that a Chinese woman had secretly helped his cookboy care for her. But although this had whetted Abigail's curiosity, whenever she tried to question Jakob further, he had been as reluctant as ever to turn his mind back to the past.

In his absence she had gone on to win a scholarship to Oxford, taking one of the first postwar places granted to candidates from northern grammar schools. She had been eager to read a subject related to Asia and China, hoping that this might help bring her closer to her father, but to her dismay he had gone to great lengths to dissuade her from such a course. Instead, he had guided her toward a modern-languages degree and at Somerville Abigail had read German and French, then stayed an extra year to learn Spanish. But far from diminishing her interest in China and her own early life, the contrasting nature of her studies, centered on Europe, had only served to heighten the feeling of fascination. Also, despite his unwillingness to discuss the past, Jakob had himself paradoxically fostered her underlying interest in China by bringing her Oriental gifts whenever he returned on a visit. She treasured the brocade jackets, the jade jewelry, and lacquered boxes he had given her more than any other possession because she had sensed intuitively that in bringing her such gifts he was attempting to express emotions to which he could not otherwise give voice. In brief notes accompanying the presents he always penned formal declarations of fatherly affection, but outside these intimacies he had still remained curiously remote. If she made any new attempt to break down his reserve, Jakob seemed to draw back further into an invisible shell, and in the end these inexplicable emotional barriers had forced all her past feelings of grievance frustratingly to the surface again, leaving her hurt and angry.

For a time Abigail had even allowed the intensity of this resentment to undermine her normal good judgment. In her first term at Oxford she had drifted almost defiantly into an unwise affair with a married don much older than herself. She had extricated herself in response to urgings by close undergraduate friends but had continued to neglect her studies for the rest of her first year. Careless, passionate involvements with several older students had followed until an eventually unfounded fear that she was pregnant made her realize that she had been in danger of sacrificing her future in a foolish search for a substitute for her father's love and understanding.

This experience had shocked her deeply and at the same time inspired her to apply herself more devotedly to her studies. But she had not been able to dismiss entirely from her mind the many unanswered questions about her father and his feelings toward her. Instinctively Abigail knew she was more likely to bridge the gulf that separated them if she could obtain some understanding of Jakob's past at first hand. She also reasoned that her efforts to come to terms with him would have more chance of success if she presented herself to him as an accomplished, well-qualified young woman rather than a pathetic victim of emotional misjudgments. While she applied herself with renewed energy to her degree course, a long-term plan to visit her father in Hong Kong had gradually taken shape in her mind.

Entwined with all these personal uncertainties, her curiosity about the people who had once held the power of life and death over her as a helpless infant had continued to grow. What were the Chinese among whom she had lived so briefly at the beginning of her life really like? Were they so very different from Europeans? Who were the men and women who had comforted and nurtured the baby she had been — and why were they so different from those who had brutally murdered her mother? More important, would understanding them help her in any way to understand her father and the motives which drove him? Questions like these had gnawed at her over several years and once her mind was firmly made up, she had begun to save every penny earned from vacation jobs to pay for this first-ever trip to Hong Kong.

She had told her father in a letter sent only recently that she intended to pay a prolonged holiday visit to the colony and he had acknowledged her note briefly. From the surprised tone of his reply she had not been sure whether he would genuinely welcome her, and several times during her flight she had taken the envelope from her handbag and reread his few lines of handwriting in a vain search for some clue to his real reaction. On hearing the undercarriage rumble out from beneath the Constellation's wings, Abigail realized that she would find out before very long. The plane banked steeply to the right, turning just when it seemed it must crash into the hills behind Kowloon, and soon the tops of many blocks of flats built close together appeared beneath the aircraft. In some ways, she reflected as she peered down out of the window, her father remained as much a mystery to her as the haze-shrouded land flanking the congested British colony, and the thought daunted her a little.

As the Constellation lost height and its engines quieted, Abigail reached for the small, envelope-style handbag of navy blue leather that matched her high-heeled court shoes. Taking out a powder compact, she freshened the lightly applied makeup on a face that was striking enough to have turned the heads of many of the male Europeans on board during the flight from London. In the little mirror she looked into calm, wide eyes as blue as her father's; thick yellow hair that caught the afternoon light slanting into the cabin reached to her shoulders, framing a broad, fresh-complexioned face that was given a hint of sensuality by her full, wide mouth. She wore a simple, inexpensive shirtwaist dress of turquoise green cotton that reached to midcalf, and around her neck hung a single strand of imitation pearls given to her by her grandmother upon graduation. A white duster coat with large patch pockets, folded neatly in the rack above her head, completed her outfit, and she decided to carry it over her arm when, after landing, she encountered the early June humidity outside the fuselage of the Constellation.

In spite of the long, tiring journey from England she felt a quickening of her pulse as she followed the other passengers into the customs shed. The chief officers were tall, hefty, pink-skinned Britishers dressed in tropical white shirts and shorts, and Abigail was struck immediately by the contrasting appearance of their slighter Chinese subordinates, who outnumbered them. Dark, narrow eyes, watchful in their yellow-brown faces, regarded her on all sides, and the movements of the smaller men were quick and efficient as they checked each passenger through. The sight of her British passport produced a polite deference; but in the unfamiliar faces of the Chinese men there was an implacable reserve, an unspoken declaration, she felt, of the racial no-man's-land that separated her from them. She noticed in herself a faint tendency to nervousness as she answered their routine questions phrased in sibilant, accented English; her unease was too slight to show but she wondered inwardly whether her subconscious memory might be reacting to her first contact for many years with the kind of faces that must have filled her vision constantly before her first birthday.

Distracted by these reflections, she failed to notice that her father was not among the crowd of Europeans gathered to greet passengers outside the arrivals hall — until a stoop-shouldered, graying Chinese wearing a pale short-sleeved shirt and dark slacks stepped into her path and ducked his head in a little bow of greeting.

"Excuse me, please. You are Miss Abigail Kellner?"

Taken aback, Abigail quickly scanned the group of waiting Europeans beyond the barrier. There was no sign of a familiar face and she experienced an intense disappointment. That her father should fail to meet her after a journey halfway across the world seemed to bode ill for her visit, but she managed to conceal her reaction and smiled at the bowing Chinese. "Yes, I'm Miss Kellner. Did my father send you?"

The Chinese giggled in relief and nodded eagerly. "Yes, Missy. Your father ask me to apologize. He very busy — can't leave office. You hear about the Hundred Flowers in Red China, I expect. Today many new developments." The Chinese signaled to the porter carrying Abigail's cases to follow them. "Come this way, please. I have car waiting."

The Chinese led the way to a battered Austin saloon, and after stowing her cases in the trunk, he drove Abigail out into the noisy, crowded streets of Kowloon. From the rear seat she stared out at the colonnaded shops emblazoned with torrents of Chinese ideograms painted in red, white, and gold. Vertical and horizontal banners jutted over the narrow lanes through which swarmed dense crowds of Chinese. Women and men alike were dressed in black pajamalike cottons, the tunics of the women buttoned high at the throat, those of the men often flapping open over scrawny chests. Wire-wheeled rickshaws drawn by barefoot Chinese wearing ragged shorts and small conical rattan hats weaved among the British automobiles, carrying wealthy-looking Chinese and complacent Europeans.

"The government in Peking getting very tough all of sudden with Hundred Flowers people who criticize it, Miss Kellner," said the Chinese driver over his shoulder as he steered the car carefully through the milling throng. "Many arrested and sent to do forced labor. Much trouble."

"I see."

Abigail acknowledged the information distractedly. With half her mind she was still trying to come to terms with the fact that her father had not troubled to come to the airport himself, but her conscious gaze was riveted on the streams of Chinese flowing past the car. Here and there she spotted slender Chinese girls wearing the long, sheathlike cheongsam, a high-collared, side-split dress that occasionally revealed startling glimpses of thigh. Distinguished-looking Chinese men were also moving through the shade of the colonnades, in traditional long-gowns and brimless caps, their faces impassive and unreadable. Although the majority of the working Chinese were clad in black calico, some, she noticed, wore Western-style clothes. Thin, often gaunt, but bristling with vitality, the men hurried eagerly along the packed pavements, giving the impression that urgent business was always about to be transacted nearby.

Never before had Abigail found herself surrounded by such a floodtide of humanity, and she soon began to feel overwhelmed. The rapidly changing kaleidoscope of Asian faces in the narrow streets was producing a dizzying effect after the long flight, and she had to make a conscious effort to tell herself that these were the same kind of people among whom she had lived without injury during the first year of her life. The unease that she had felt over her father's absence at the airport, however, would not leave her and she began to wonder apprehensively once more whether her meeting with him could possibly turn out well. Suddenly, also, she was unable to dismiss from her mind the thought that it was men with faces like those swarming around her who must have murdered her mother twenty-three years earlier, and she had to fight down an irrational surge of fear. In that moment everything about Hong Kong seemed disturbing and unsettling — yet instinctively she knew that it had been right for her to come. All her senses were excited by the exotic sights unfolding around her and, despite the misgivings, deep within herself she felt glad she had found the courage to make the journey.

2

Jakob Kellner frowned unconsciously as he ran his eye over the top sheet of a new sheaf of radio transmission texts handed to him by a bald, bespectacled Chinese translator. Seated behind a desk in a small, untidy, glass-partitioned office, he wore no tie, his shirt-sleeves were rolled halfway up his forearms, and as he read, he occasionally ran a distracted hand through his neatly trimmed fair hair, which was beginning to turn gray above the temples in his forty-sixth year.

"Anything special in this batch, Mr. Wu?" asked Jakob in a tense voice as he continued to scan the English translations. "Any new evidence that a crackdown has begun?"

"Shanghai Radio is using a new term of abuse to condemn critics of the government — *yu p'ai fen tzu*," said the translator, blinking owlishly behind his wire-rimmed spectacles. "I've shown that as 'right-wing elements.' The broadcast also attacks 'bourgeois rightists' and accuses them of misusing the Hundred Flowers movement to try to turn back the clock and overthrow the Communist Party, the proletariat, and the socialist cause."

The translator leaned over the desk and pulled the sheet to which he was referring from the pile. While Jakob studied the Chinese text, the older man continued to wait respectfully beside his chair.

"On the next page the radio quotes some examples of 'bourgeois rightist' criticism," added the translator as Jakob finished reading. "In particular they quote opinions expressed by a Peking university lecturer."

Jakob turned the page and read again. Then, raising his eyebrows in astonishment, he began quoting aloud from the translation. " 'Every Communist in the country deserves to be hanged or otherwise re-duced to impotence for all the harm they have brought upon us! China belongs to all its six hundred million people, not the Com-munist Party alone. . . . If the Communists do not carry on satis-factorily, the masses may knock them down, kill them and overthrow them . . .' " Jakob looked up at his chief translator and smiled grimly. "I shouldn't like to be in the shoes of that particular lecturer right now, Mr. Wu."

The Chinese, himself a schoolteacher who had fled to Hong Kong from Shanghai in 1949, shook his head sadly. "No, Mr. Kellner.

Further on there are references for the first time to an 'anti-rightist rectification campaign' to reeducate the critics — and at the bottom of the pile there is the transcript of an interview with a refugee who has just arrived from Kwangtung. He says some academics and officials have already begun disappearing from their posts in the province. Local people think they're being sent to labor camps."

Jakob rifled quickly through the pages, shaking his head in dismay as he read; then he glanced out through the glass partition at the clock on the wall of the adjoining room. It stood at a little after five-thirty and half a dozen other Chinese translators were bent busily over their desks, preparing material for the stenciled bulletin that the Kellner Institute produced promptly each evening at six o'clock for distribution by hand in the colony and by airmail abroad.

"Shall I tell the deputy editor you'd like him to write the commentary to go with today's translations, Mr. Kellner?" asked the translator, motioning politely in the direction of another tiny glass-walled office off the main room where a young Englishman was visible working behind a cluttered desk. "I warned him to stand by after you told me your daughter was arriving today."

"There was no need for you to do that," replied Jakob with an unusual brusqueness. "Finalize the stencils of your own translation texts now — but don't start running off the rest of the bulletin until I give you my analysis."

Jakob pulled a portable typewriter across the desk toward him and inserted a blank sheet of paper. For a moment he stared at the retreating back of his senior translator with a perplexed expression on his face. Then he turned his attention to his work and began to type rapidly, referring every now and then to the translated pages on the desk beside him. While he was writing, a Chinese messenger entered with an envelope and placed it on the desk. Jakob thanked him without looking up and continued composing his commentary, but during a pause for reflection, his eye fell on the envelope and he noticed with a start that it bore a special-delivery label as well as a Peking postmark and stamps issued in the People's Republic of China. Overcome with curiosity, he broke off from his writing to open it and found inside a stiff, embossed card headed in English "The Chinese Committee for World Peace." Beneath his own name and the address of the Kellner Research Institute, the printed text of a formal invitation read: "The Chinese Committee for World Peace cordially invites you to attend the Eighth National Day celebration

of the founding of the People's Republic of China in Peking on
1 October 1957." Below was appended the signature of the chairman
of the committee and a request to reply personally if the invitation
were to be accepted. Jakob sat staring at the card in astonishment
for several seconds — then, remembering the urgency of his task,
laid it aside and continued typing.

After he had finished his commentary Jakob pushed a buzzer
beside his desk to summon Wu, and when the bespectacled Chinese
reappeared he handed him the typewritten pages. As he turned to
go Jakob called him back and handed him the printed invitation to
Peking. "Mr. Wu, what do you think I should make of this?"

The Chinese stared myopically at the embossed card, then lifted
his head to look at Jakob, his eyes wide with surprise. "It is very
interesting, Mr. Kellner. Will you accept?"

"Probably not." Jakob's forehead crinkled in a frown. "It's more
than twenty years since I set foot on the Chinese mainland. And I
wasn't exactly made welcome by the Communists during my last
year there."

He grinned ruefully to soften the grim jest and the Chinese smiled
sagely in response. "I don't think you need fear a repetition of your
unpleasant experience, Mr. Kellner. The Chinese Committee for
World Peace would hardly allow one of its National Day guests to
be arrested."

"But they know I'm no fellow traveler like most of the people in
the Western peace movement. Why should they invite me?"

"Perhaps they've read *China's New Age*," said the Chinese, nodding
deferentially to a stack of newly printed books that bore Jakob's
name on their spines. "If so, they've already seen how fair you've
been in summing up the progress made by the Communists in their
first years in power."

Jakob stared hard at the translator, turning over in his mind what
he had said. The book had been published only six weeks earlier
and Jakob realized there was a certain logic in his speculation that
the invitation was linked with it in some way.

"But whether that's true or not, Mr. Kellner, I think I should
hurry now to cut the stencil of your commentary." Wu gestured
with Jakob's typescript toward the outer office. "Or the bulletin will
be very late."

As he turned and hurried through the open door, he almost collided with a tall, broad-shouldered man who entered, carrying a

copy of *China's New Age* under one arm. Stepping aside to allow the Chinese to pass, the newcomer smiled at Jakob in greeting.

"I called at the front counter, Jake, to pick up a copy of your daily bulletin — but it doesn't seem to come out on time the way it used to when I lived here."

"Joseph Sherman!" Jakob rose eagerly from his desk and advanced with an outstretched hand to welcome the smiling American. "What brings you back to Hong Kong?"

"I came just to buy this, of course." The American banteringly held up a copy of Jakob's new book. "The word's got around that it's the best appraisal of Mao's first seven years money can buy right now. My students can't be denied."

The two men shook hands warmly and Jakob waved Sherman to a chair in front of the desk. "It's good to see you again, Joseph. Are you still teaching Far Eastern studies at Cornell?"

"I'm on my way back to Ithaca right now to pick up the threads," said Sherman. "I've been in Saigon for six months."

"Back to your old stamping ground? Were you lecturing or writing?"

"Neither." The smile faded slowly from Sherman's face. "I've been with the Michigan State Group. You've probably heard that forty or fifty U.S. professors went up there as advisers to help draft a constitution and set up a civil service for President Diem. Well, sad to say, I discovered most of it was cover for Washington intelligence types who're channeling arms to a fairly unpleasant secret police outfit — so I resigned."

Jakob shook his head in sympathy. "And how long are you staying here?"

"Not long, unfortunately. But like any other red-blooded Sinologist, I'm utterly intrigued by this quaintly named Hundred Flowers campaign. So I thought I'd grab a couple of days in Hong Kong on the way home and get the latest dope from the horse's mouth — or the Kellner Institute, as it's locally known."

Jakob's pleasure at seeing a good friend from the past showed in his broad smile and he glanced quickly at his watch. "Today's bulletin will be ready in a few minutes. If you can wait, you'll be able to catch up on the latest chapter and verse from there."

"The Kellner daily bulletin was always worth its weight in gold when I was here for the *Gazette*," grinned Sherman, leaning back relaxedly in his chair. "So I'll wait if I'm welcome."

Jakob inclined his head in theatrical acknowledgment of the compliment; then his brow creased into a querying frown of recollection. "You disappeared from the colony without much warning, Joseph. About three years ago, if I remember correctly — just after Dien Bien Phu. No farewell parties, nothing. Why was your departure so abrupt?"

Sherman's face became serious and he studied the fingernails of one hand intently before he spoke. "I'd covered the civil war in China — and Korea after that, remember? I was in and out of Dien Bien Phu a couple of times and I think for me that was the last straw. Most of all I wanted to get away from the sight of grown men butchering one another — so I wasn't in the mood for farewell parties. The groves of academe beckoned and they seemed a very attractive prospect in comparison. . . ." Sherman looked up at Jakob and shrugged dismissively. "If I'm really going to level with an old friend, Jake, I'd have to say there were some personal reasons too. But they don't bear too close a scrutiny — even now."

"Did you and Tempe ever get back together?" asked Jakob in a quiet voice. "There were rumors that all wasn't well between you about the time you left."

"No, we got divorced." Sherman studied his fingernails again. "Tempe's just got herself married to a Pentagon colonel and seems very happy. We're still friends — of a sort. We meet from time to time when we visit our two boys at school."

"A lot of people missed you both after you left," said Jakob awkwardly. "Please remember me to Tempe when you see her."

"I certainly will." Sherman nodded quickly, feeling awkward in his turn.

"Have you remarried in the meantime, Joseph?"

"No — I haven't felt brave enough yet to venture out onto thin ice again." The American smiled humorlessly. "But what about yourself, Jake? We always figured at the foreign correspondents' club you were the kind of dark horse who might surprise us all one day by taking a dazzling Chinese beauty for your bride. Has it all happened behind my back?"

"No, it hasn't." Jakob half turned to look out through the window behind his desk. The office was on the top floor of a commercial block in the island's central business district and he gazed pensively at the saddle-backed heights of Victoria Peak, dramatically visible above them. "I suppose I'm married to my work, Joseph — as I've always been since I came to the colony. No wife in her right mind would tolerate the hours I put in here."

"Being married to China is certainly a full-time job, I can see that." Sherman grinned and rose to inspect a small framed page of Chinese calligraphy hanging on the wall. The cheap paper on which the characters had been written in a distinctive hand was a little discolored and the ink had faded in places, but the vigor and dash of the writer were still evident at a glance. "I suppose we should think of this rare relic as your marriage certificate, Jake, should we?"

Jakob glanced toward the short poem about China's mountains given to him by Mao Tse-tung at Chokechi more than twenty years earlier and smiled at his friend's affectionate irony.

"I hope it's well insured anyway," added the American. "You must know it's become one of Hong Kong's most famous landmarks among the China-watching community worldwide. I tell all my students at Cornell about it. It's nice to know it's still in place. . . ."

An uncertain knock on the frosted glass door of the office interrupted them and Jakob rose hurriedly from his seat when he saw the driver he had sent to Kai Tak Airport opening the door to usher in the tall, blond figure of his daughter.

"Abigail! Welcome to Hong Kong!"

He hurried across the office and embraced his daughter briefly. Then he held her at arm's length, smiling apologetically. "I'm sorry I couldn't get to the airport to meet you myself. It's been frantic here and I've been chained to this desk all afternoon . . ."

As he spoke the door opened again and the senior translator appeared, holding out three or four copies of the evening bulletin, hot from the duplicating machine. Jakob took them from him, thanking him profusely, and in the same movement turned and thrust one into Sherman's hands.

"That's my lastest installment on what's happening behind the Bamboo Curtain, Joseph — and this is my daughter, Abigail, who's just flown in from London." He slipped an arm around her shoulders as she offered the American her hand. "Joseph Sherman is an old friend of mine, Abigail. He used to write for the *Washington Gazette* from here. He's just turned up too. We haven't seen each other for at least three years."

"We have something in common then, Mr. Sherman," said Abigail smilingly. "I haven't seen my father since he visited me during my first term at Oxford — which is even more than three years ago, isn't it, Daddy?"

The remark came out more pointedly than Abigail had intended, and when she looked at her father she saw that a guarded, defensive look had come into his eyes. For an instant there was a brittle silence between them which she feared the American might notice, but he gave no sign.

"We seem to have achieved a historic three-way reunion by co-incidence," interjected Sherman smoothly, inclining his head in Abigail's direction. "I take it I'm enjoying the rare privilege of meeting the celebrated young lady who made that famous trek halfway across China with her father before her first birthday."

"That's what I've been led to believe. Unfortunately I don't have any clear recollections of my own."

She smiled as she spoke but again an uneasy expression showed fleetingly on Jakob's face. This time the American saw it clearly and moved off at once toward the door. "I'm sure you two have a lot to catch up on." He grinned broadly and flourished the bulletin in his hand. "And so have I. I'm going back to my hotel to devour the latest installment of *The Mystery of the Hundred Flowers* . . ."

"No, Joseph, wait!" Jakob laid a restraining hand on Sherman's sleeve. "We must all have dinner together to celebrate this unique occasion. I've still got a few things to tidy up here but my driver will take Abigail and her luggage on to my flat. He can drop you at your hotel on the way." Jakob opened the door and called orders to the driver, then turned, smiling, back to Abigail. "My cookboy will look after you — show you your room and prepare a bath for you. Just relax and make yourself comfortable, I'll be home within the hour." Turning to Sherman again, he slapped him affectionately on the shoulder. "I'll book a table for three at that Aberdeen floating restaurant where we used to eat — will that suit you?"

"That's fine by me." Sherman smiled tactfully. "If you're both sure I won't be intruding on your family get-together . . ."

"We're positive you won't be intruding." Without looking at Abigail, Jakob moved quickly back to his desk and picked up the telephone to call the restaurant. Abigail could see that her father's jollity was slightly forced and as she watched him dial, she felt a certainty grow within her that, whether he realized it himself or not, he was doing everything he could to avoid being left alone with her. "We'll meet there at eight o'clock," he said, addressing the American over his shoulder. "We can't waste this golden opportunity, can we? It may be years before we have another like it."

3

Sitting across the table from her father in the waterborne restaurant three hours later, Abigail wondered sadly whether in the end she would have to admit defeat and resign herself to accepting the enigma he represented for her. In the soft glow of colored Chinese lanterns that decorated the traditional triple-decked floating "palace," she had watched and listened as he talked animatedly with Joseph Sherman about the arcane politics of Communist China and Asia at large, marveling inwardly at his articulate grasp of the complex issues. Although she had little appetite after her fatiguing journey, he had also explained to her with great relish the origin and history of each mouth-watering Chinese dish as it was set before them: steamed *garoupa* fish, fried quail, green pilchard, stewed pigeons' eggs, shark's fin soup. Joseph Sherman too had treated her with an elaborate gallantry, toasting her repeatedly with little glasses of Chinese rice wine, and she suspected that the American was making a special effort to be convivial, having sensed that an underlying tension existed between her and her father. Sherman had spoken at length, sometimes lightly, sometimes seriously, about the people of Vietnam and Indochina, among whom he had spent much time, and despite her tiredness she had found the table talk of both men fascinating.

But in the midst of the starlit bay, with lantern-decked water taxis gliding like fireflies through the darkness all around them, she often had a discomfiting feeling that she was listening to the impersonal voices of total strangers. Abigail had hoped that seeing her father's home might help her understand him better, but his flat, in a modern block near the Botanical Gardens, had been a disappointment. Although spacious and airy, with a balcony facing the spectacular harbor, it was curiously lacking in identifiable character. Instead of the Oriental furnishings and curios that she had half expected to discover, the flat was equipped with simple, good-quality European

carpets and furniture but was otherwise bare of all superfluous adornment. Standing alone on a polished table in a study lined with books
about China and Asia, she had found a single, silver-framed photograph of herself as a shyly smiling schoolgirl. But no other photographs were visible anywhere else in the flat and with the exception
of a few calligraphy scrolls, which decorated the sitting-room walls,
there was a complete absence of pictures or ornaments which would
have allowed some judgment to be made of the tastes and preferences
of the flat's occupant. An aged Chinese cookboy had greeted her
politely and seen to her needs, but his retiring manner was in keeping
with the neutral atmosphere that pervaded all the rooms and Abigail
was left with a baffling feeling that the flat too, like her father, was
determined to hold her at arm's length and deny her any glimpse of
intimacy.

By the time Jakob returned from his office, she was dressed and
waiting for him, and he had showered quickly before driving them
to the pier closest to the floating restaurant. Their exchanges during
the journey had been confined to her flight, landmarks they passed,
and the health of his aging parents, and while they dined, he seemed
to Abigail to be taking infinite pains to confine the conversation to
impersonal topics. When, in the course of a discussion of *China's
New Age*, Joseph Sherman remarked casually that he was disap-
pointed to find no reference in it to Jakob's experiences on the Long
March, she noticed her father's expression grow suddenly wary.

"I'm impressed by your British sense of fair play," said the American with a smile. "You give the Communist regime a lot of credit
in the book — but does this mean you're never going to write anything about that terrible period in the thirties?"

Jakob hesitated and Abigail felt silently grateful to Sherman for
his persistence. She knew that if she had asked her father such a
question he would have found a way of hedging; she gauged from
his expression that he would have preferred not to answer his friend,
but Sherman was waiting affably for a reply, and Jakob was clearly
being forced to consider his response with care.

"For the average Chinese, life has improved vastly since the revolution succeeded," said Jakob earnestly. "I think that's what needs
emphasizing in the outside world right now. I'm not sure that what
happened to me in the thirties has relevance anymore."

"It probably has some oblique relevance for those unfortunate
Chinese intellectuals you wrote about in your bulletin tonight, doesn't

it," said Sherman grimly. "All those who responded to Mao's invitation to let a 'Hundred Flowers' of criticism bloom are now being shipped off to labor camps for their pains. It may not be a precise parallel with your own case but it's the other, darker side of the coin — the revolution's recurring tendency to dole out ruthless punishments arbitrarily to its innocent victims. Surely there's room for some of that in the whole story of contemporary China."

"It may sound strange to you, Joseph, but I've never felt able to put a final evaluation on what happened to me." Jakob toyed with his chopsticks, his eyes fixed on the tablecloth before him. To Abigail, his expression looked suddenly vulnerable, and for the first time, to her surprise, the feelings of resentment and mystification which her father's secretiveness habitually provoked were modified by a twinge of compassion. "Perhaps even now it's too tied up with personal feelings — which I'm not very good at disentangling. Perhaps that's why I've avoided writing about it."

"Do you mean matters of faith?" asked Sherman quietly.

"Partly, I suppose. My time as a prisoner on the Long March did make some fundamental change in me." Jakob continued to study the tablecloth. "I've never been able to define my feelings to my own satisfaction. But there are other things too . . ."

Jakob hesitated and Abigail straightened in her seat, wondering what he was about to say. But to her intense disappointment, he remained silent and Sherman, sensing her interest, smiled and winked exaggeratedly at her.

"Perhaps the pair of you ought to put your heads together someday and write a definitive joint account."

"I'm afraid I'm almost as much in the dark as you are, Joseph," said Abigail. "Daddy hasn't ever told me much about it either. But I haven't given up all hope of getting at least some of his secrets out of him."

Jakob looked at his daughter with a strange expression, as if he had almost forgotten her presence. Then he smiled and reached across the table for a moment to pat her hand in an uncertain gesture of affection. Again he seemed to be on the point of saying something further, but instead he reached into an inside pocket of his jacket and turned toward Sherman once more.

"It's curious, Joseph, that you should bring this subject up," he said, pulling from his pocket the envelope he had received that afternoon. "I'd always thought of China as a closed book for me personally — then this came today." He paused and turned to Abigail. "It's the first contact of any kind I've had with the Communists since 1935." He drew out the peace committee's invitation card, held it out briefly for her to read, then pushed it across the table to Sherman.

"Very strange." The American let out a low whistle. "It looks as though you're being courted."

"Will you accept?" asked Abigail.

Jakob hesitated a moment. "I haven't got over my surprise yet."

"When you do," said Sherman slowly, "I think you'll probably find the siren call of Peking irresistible."

"My first reaction, Joseph, is to say no." Jakob studied his friend's face. "Why do you think I ought to go?"

"I didn't say you *ought* to go. I said I thought you would in the end." Sherman returned the invitation to Jakob and stood up, smiling broadly at his friend. He had already settled the bill, and moving to the rail, he waved a sampan taxi alongside to take them back to the pierhead. When all three of them were settled in the wicker chairs beneath the canopy of the wallowing craft, he leaned toward Jakob and patted him gently on the shoulder. "If you do decide to return to Peking, make sure you're ready to face up to ghosts from the past," he said gently. "Take it from me, they have a habit of turning up when you make a sentimental journey."

On the jetty the two men took effusive leave of one another and the American kissed Abigail's hand extravagantly in wishing her well. But once Jakob was settled at the wheel of the car beside his daughter, he fell silent again, apparently preoccupied with his own inner reflections. Abigail had hoped that she might question him about the hesitant references he had made to the past over dinner, but she felt rebuffed again by his silence. On arrival home Jakob said she looked worn out from her long journey and insisted that she go to bed without delay. In the forbidding, impersonal atmosphere of the flat, the emotional gulf seemed suddenly to yawn wide and unbridgeable between them again. As he turned away toward his own room, Abigail saw an unmistakable expression of relief cross her father's face, and the moment she got into bed and closed her eyes, this image of him filled her mind, nagging at the old wounds of hurt and resentment that never seemed inclined to heal.

4

"**W**hen I was growing up I often used to wake in the morning feeling very sad but without really knowing why. Sometimes I dreamed about my mother. It was always the same dream. I was very small and running desperately through a big crowd of unfriendly Chinese. I kept calling out and searching for her but I never found her. In my child's mind there was a dreadful certainty that something terrible had happened. And I knew I was never going to find her . . ."

Jakob stared aghast at his daughter but Abigail kept her face turned from him, gazing out through the window of the little tramcar crawling slowly up the flank of Victoria Peak. Below them, the narrow strait that separated Hong Kong Island from Kowloon and the great hinterland of China shimmered like translucent jade in the morning sun; a moment before, Jakob had been pointing out landmarks and places of interest to her but he had not noticed that her manner was abstracted and her sudden vehement outburst nonplussed him.

"I used to be terrified sometimes before I fell asleep," she continued, still speaking in the same low, fierce voice. "I thought I might actually see her Chinese executioners chopping off her head in my dreams. Luckily it never got as bad as that. But it always came back to the same terrible, hopeless feeling that something awful had happened and I could never hope to find her again. . . ."

They were seated side by side on a double seat and when Abigail turned from the window to look at her father, she saw from his expression that her unexpected display of emotion had shocked him. Her face was pale too, she was breathing unevenly, and for a long moment they looked at one another in a strained silence. Then Abigail shook her head in a little gesture of apology.

"I'm sorry. I don't know why it suddenly all came out like that." She looked away out of the window again. The morning was bright but hazy and as the little funicular tramcar climbed higher, the island and its harbor were spreading out like a patchwork quilt below them. "Perhaps it's something to do with being here among all these Chinese people for the first time. I'm grateful for you bringing me up here, Daddy, but I can't pretend to think about sight-seeing with things like this on my mind."

"Abigail, I'm sorry . . ." Jakob stumbled over his words. "It's me that should be doing the apologizing. I had no idea you'd been affected this way. You've never told me about your dreams before."

"You never gave me the chance, Daddy. All these things have been bottled up inside me for so long. You didn't seem to want to talk about personal things at all when you came home." Abigail's voice had lost its explosive edge but deep-buried feelings of grievance were still evident in her tone. "It seemed as if you didn't want to understand how I felt. That's why I was never able to say things like this in England."

The tramcar was almost empty at midmorning and nobody was sitting near enough in the adjoining seats to overhear the conversation. Beyond the windows the hillsides of the Peak were covered in thick, trackless greenery from which banana trees sprouted at curious angles due to the steepness of the slope. To Abigail the vegetation seemed to shudder and dance as the tramcar rumbled up toward the summit and most of the wayside stations at which they stopped were deserted.

"I should have realized," Jakob's voice broke a little and he moved closer to his daughter and covered one of her hands hesitantly with his own. "I suppose I always thought the least said, the soonest mended. I never wanted to drag up the past for fear of upsetting you. Unconsciously, perhaps, I was trying to protect you."

Abigail turned to face him again. She had put on a yellow cotton blouse, a white linen skirt, and low-heeled shoes for the spectacular trip up the Peak. A square of green silk covered her blond hair and in her fresh, unself-conscious beauty Jakob suddenly saw an unmistakable echo of Felicity as she had been when he met her for the first time in Shanghai.

"Is that why you were so determined to keep me away from China studies at Oxford? Was that another attempt to 'protect' me?"

Jakob's expression indicated that he was probably considering his reasons seriously for the first time and he frowned uncertainly. "I don't really know. It was an instinctive reaction. I suppose I wanted to try to guide you into some area different from my own — that's all."

"But you seemed to want to cut me off completely from your life in Asia, Daddy. You've hardly ever told me anything about the past. It was as if you wanted to keep me in the dark about it all." She turned away again and her voice quieted. "When I was younger I could never understand why you didn't want me with you — why

I was always left with my grandparents. I never felt as though I belonged there or anywhere else. It just didn't seem right. I didn't understand and sometimes I felt very unhappy."

"I took you home to my parents in Moss Side as soon as we were released by the Chinese," said Jakob soothingly. "It was the only thing to do. You needed a good home and I was in poor health for a time after the Long March."

"Yes, but later you seemed to care so little about me."

"That's not true at all," protested Jakob. "I've always cared very deeply. Perhaps I haven't been very good at showing it."

Abigail looked at her father quizzically. "Talking with Joseph Sherman last night, you said your time as a prisoner changed you. But you didn't really explain how . . . I'd like to try to understand what you meant. I think it might help.'

Jakob took a deep breath. "After we got back from China I worked for the Anglo-Chinese Mission in England for a while. I traveled in Europe and America, giving seminars on field missionary work — but as I said last night, something had changed. Deep down my heart wasn't really in missionary work anymore."

"Do you mean you lost your faith in Christianity on the Long March?"

"No, not really." Jakob hesitated, searching with difficulty for the right words. "But nothing ever seemed as simple as it had before. As a young man I had a burning conviction that I could help bring salvation to chaotic old China by preaching the Gospel. But afterward I found myself questioning everything. I suppose my experience made me feel Christianity was irrelevant for China. Communism obviously commanded a much greater loyalty among the Chinese. It served the oppressed and raised them to sublime acts of sacrifice — but it brutalized them to a horrifying degree as well. None of this was very helpful in sorting out the sense of confusion in my personal beliefs. And that's never really left me. I didn't lose my faith entirely — but it was as if a hard inner shell grew around it."

"I can hardly remember anything about you at that time," said Abigail distractedly. "Except for that photograph of you in uniform that stood on the shelf beside the wireless set. It was as if you didn't exist beyond that."

"You were barely five when the war came, remember, and every able-bodied man had to go off and fight. . . ." Again Jakob's tone was gently placatory but he continued to struggle to find words that would comfort her. "In some ways, because of the confusion I felt, I was quite glad to volunteer for the infantry. It was uncomplicated, at least, and I was fulfilling a duty which transcended other things. . . . I was whisked off first to Africa, then later to Burma and India. I was as surprised as anybody to finish up as a captain. . . . But that's why you never saw me again until the war was over."

"Why didn't you stay in England when you came back?" asked Abigail, an undertone of reproach audible again in her voice. "That was the time when I'd just found out what had really happened in China. I was desperate to hear more about it from you, but you didn't have time to talk."

Jakob shifted uncomfortably on the seat. "This is probably difficult for you to understand, Abigail, but when I came home after the war I felt a bit like an outsider in Moss Side too. It wasn't that unusual. A lot of men had trouble readjusting. But I thought you seemed so well settled in your school and in your home life with your grandparents. In some ways I felt as if I was intruding and upsetting things by staying — and I was concerned that I'd already caused you enough trouble earlier in your life."

"But why did you come back to Asia?"

"Being in Burma and India gave me a strong desire to study all the religions of the East, so I decided to come back — just for a short while, originally. I lived a kind of hand-to-mouth existence, doing all kinds of strange jobs. I managed to study in some outlandish spots: at a lamasery in Tibet, with a Tamil community in Ceylon, and in a Moslem seminary in Iran. I traveled to Japan too and these experiences gave me a great respect for all the ancient traditions, whether they were Buddhist, Hindu, Islamic, Taoist — or Christian. It made me realize they all had an equal validity."

"What was it that made you settle here in Hong Kong?"

"At the end of all that, perhaps as a reaction, I felt a need to apply myself to something practical — not least to provide for you back home in England." He leaned toward his daughter, his expression earnest. "That's always been uppermost in my mind, Abigail. My savings had run out by then, it was 1949, and I found myself here. The Communists had just taken over in Peking, the Bamboo Curtain was going up all around the mainland, and I fell into some translation work for foreign journalists that paid well. I realized then I wasn't cut out to do much else and that's how the Kellner Research Institute

was born. Since then it's grown and provided us with a good live-
lihood, so I'm still here . . ."

Jakob's voice tailed off and for a while they rode in silence in the
rocking tramcar, wrapped in their separate thoughts. In the harbor
below, toy-sized Chinese junks and seagoing freighters carved creamy
wakes across the glistening water and new concrete housing blocks
sprouted like identical fingers from the populated areas of Victoria
and Kowloon. When the little vehicle finally shuddered to a halt at
the Peak terminal, Jakob guided his daughter out into the warm
breeze and they walked a few paces in the direction of the Kellner
Institute's radio monitoring station, which he had promised to show
her. But the breathtaking bird's-eye view of one of the world's great
natural harbors spread out below made them stop and they stood
side by side admiring the spectacle. Feeling herself moved by the
effort her father had been making to explain his past, Abigail stepped
closer to him and slipped her arm through his.

"I've often wondered, Daddy, why you've never married again,"
she said gently. "You weren't much older than I am now when my
mother died. You must have been lonely sometimes."

Jakob scanned the harbor minutely as though searching for something specific and when he spoke his voice was firmly controlled. "I
can't deny I've been lonely at times — but I've got used to it."

"Have you never wanted to marry anyone else?"

A strong mental picture of Lu Mei-ling, seated astride her mule
in the yellow loess valley where he had last seen her, flashed into
Jakob's mind the instant his daughter asked the question. The swirl
of long hair about her face and the direct gaze of her dark eyes in
the early dawn light returned with a vividness that seemed almost
tangible, and he found he dared not look at Abigail in case she sensed
something of this powerful internal image.

"I've never fallen in love with anyone here," said Jakob, choosing
his words carefully. "I've made some good friends. I haven't always
lived a monkish life. But nobody in Hong Kong has ever become
that important to me — I suppose that's the real reason I haven't
married again."

He felt Abigail's eyes on him, and fearing that she might become
aware of the ambivalence in his reply if she was allowed to dwell
on it, he lifted his arm and pointed across the harbor toward the
ridge of mountains that rose behind Kowloon.

"Look, the border between the Crown Colony and China lies

beyond those mountains. When we go to the New Territories you'll still be able to see what the rural China of old was like on our side. The farms are small, the villages still have their ancestral temples; some even have their old protective walls and watchtowers. For me, going there is a bit like stepping back into the thirties. Across the Shum Chun River, the communal rice paddies of the People's Republic are much larger now. You'll be able to see how abruptly it all changes . . ."

Shading her eyes with her hand, Abigail stared toward the mountains that hid the Chinese mainland from their sight and at her side Jakob relaxed. But when she turned to look at him again the intensity of her expression surprised him. "Daddy, do you remember a long time ago that you told me a young Chinese woman looked after me during part of the Long March? You never said much about her — what was she like?"

Abigail's eyes searched his face as she waited for him to answer and Jakob suddenly had an uneasy feeling that something in his manner had revealed his innermost thoughts. Haunted by the possibility that he might inadvertently betray some hint of the passionate feelings he had shared with Mei-ling so soon after Felicity's tragic death, he looked away.

"Why do you ask about her?" he asked, trying to keep his voice light. "I'd forgotten I'd told you."

"Perhaps it's because we're standing here together so close to China. It feels very strange for me to realize that someone's living up there beyond those mountains who was a mother to me all those years ago — if she's still alive." Abigail turned to her father again. "Do you think she'd still be alive?"

"I'm sure she is."

"How can you be certain? Have you had some contact with her?"

"No, of course not."

"Then how can you be so sure?"

"I have a file on her in the office."

Abigail looked startled. "Why do you keep a file on her?"

Jakob took his daughter by the arm and steered her toward a narrow path leading up to the institute's monitoring station. "She's become one of Communist China's best-known writers. Her name is occasionally mentioned in the newspapers and on the radio. The file is a routine part of the institute's reference library."

Abigail absorbed the information in silence as they walked. "I'd always assumed she was just somebody anonymous," she said at last in a puzzled tone. "What's her name?"

Again Jakob checked himself to guard against any inflection that might betray his feelings. "She's called Lu Mei-ling."

Abigail repeated the name slowly to herself, then looked searchingly at her father. "What's she like? What sort of things does she write?"

"If you're really interested, perhaps the best thing would be for you to look at the file when we get back to the office," he said dismissively. "Meanwhile, I've brought you up here to see our monitoring station, so let's go and introduce you to the staff."

Jakob dropped his hand from her arm, walking quickly ahead along the narrow path toward the cluster of radio masts, and Abigail followed more slowly, dismayed that the fragile mood of confidence that had been growing between them had evaporated so abruptly.

5

"Her translated stories have a strange quality," said Abigail, glancing up from the file of papers and booklets through which she was sifting at the small side desk in Jakob's office. "They're hard going a lot of the time because they seem to be obsessively concerned with the sufferings of the poorest peasants — and yet her descriptions of their feelings in the volume called *Women of the Revolution* are sometimes so poignant they make me want to cry."

"You have to remember that all published writing in the People's Republic of China has to serve socialism," said Jakob quietly without looking up from the sheaf of translations spread across his own desk. "Mao laid the law down on that in the early 1940s at Yenan. All fiction since then has extolled the workers and peasants with a heavy propaganda bias."

"And yet sensitivity does shine through in a lot of places," said Abigail, bending over the file again. "It can't be easy to write under those conditions."

Jakob looked up from his work and watched his daughter turn the pages of an old literary magazine published in Peking. She was utterly absorbed in her task and she did not see the look of consternation on her father's face. "Some of her early stories tried to deal with difficult subjects like the emotional role of women in revolutionary times — but they were attacked by Party activists at Yenan. Since then, as far as I can see, she's played safe and followed the Party line."

Abigail continued reading in silence for several minutes, then picked up the magazine and held it out toward her father. "There's a photograph here of her. It's a little blurred but she looks as if she might be very beautiful."

"Yes, that's right — her appearance is striking." Jakob glanced at the magazine, but turned back to his papers almost at once, pretending he was engrossed by a translation.

He was already familiar with the photograph, of a group of writers taken at a Party conference. Like the other men and women in the picture, Mei-ling wore the dark, high-collared cotton jacket and trousers which had become an almost universal official uniform in Communist China. Her short hair was scraped unflatteringly back from her face, but despite her drab clothes, the fineness in her features was still recognizable. When Jakob had first seen the photograph two or three years earlier, it had stirred his emotional memory of Mei-ling with a surprising force. In the weeks that followed he had sometimes taken out the file to look at the picture when alone in the office late at night, but eventually the sight of it had only saddened him and he had put it from his mind.

"There's a suggestion of refinement about her, Daddy. What kind of background do you think she comes from?"

Jakob found Abigail looking expectantly across the room at him and he dropped his pen and leaned back in his seat. "She was born into a rich Shanghai family. I believe her grandfather was a comprador for one of the British trading houses and her father already owned several textile factories in the thirties. She and her brother were appalled by what was happening to China and they rebelled against the family. Her father and mother fled to Formosa before the Communists took over. Her brother, Lu Chiao, has become a senior officer in the People's Liberation Army. In fact, he was made a marshal recently along with a handful of other illustrious heroes —"

A knock on the door interrupted Jakob, and his senior translator appeared holding a thin paperbound volume with a pictorial cover showing an endless column of Red Army soldiers toiling up a precipitous mountain crag under a great red flag.

"Excuse me, Mr. Kellner," said Wu, smiling apologetically. "I offered to check our cross-references for Miss Kellner, to see if we had anything to add to the file on the writer Lu Mei-ling. I've found an old volume of short articles by a dozen different contributors about the Long March." The translator advanced into the room and laid the booklet tentatively on Jakob's desk. "One of them was written by Lu Mei-ling and I thought you'd like to have it straightaway."

"Thank you, Mr. Wu." Jakob picked up the booklet and flicked through its pages with an abstracted expression until he came to the start of Mei-ling's article. He began to read the text beneath her name, then, realizing the translator had left the room, he closed it hurriedly and turned to his daughter again. "As I was saying, in the meantime, Lu Chiao has become one of the top officers in the People's Liberation Army. But not only that, he's now also a leading member of the Party's Central Committee. . . ."

Abigail's forehead crinkled in puzzlement. "How did Lu Mei-ling manage to take care of me? All you've ever told me before is that she helped your cookboy, Liang, in some way. Will you tell me the whole story?"

Jakob pulled back the cuff of his jacket and made a show of glancing at his watch. "I haven't much time right now, Abigail. There are still a lot of translations for me to check through . . . May we talk about it later?"

"Can't you just give me some idea what it was like?" There was an almost desperate, beseeching note in Abigail's voice and her face was taut as she looked across the office at her father. "It's all so tantalizing now that I can see a picture of her."

Moved by the intensity of his daughter's curiosity, Jakob relented. "I'll try," he said slowly, "but I'll have to be brief . . ." Again he hesitated, considering his words with great care before he spoke. "At dawn on the morning your mother died, we hid you in a stable where we'd slept. We were taken to a hillside outside the town — but the execution was interrupted by the arrival of Nationalist troops. That's how I survived."

Jakob closed his eyes momentarily and pinched the bridge of his nose with forefinger and thumb. "I was hurried away from that terrible place by guards but I managed to send Liang back to find you. He didn't catch up with the column of soldiers holding me prisoner for many weeks and during that time he hid you in his shoulder baskets. He fed you mainly on crushed soy milk we'd given him. His two young sons were with him and helped him look after you. . . ."

Abigail was sitting rigid in her chair, her expression tense as though she were mentally reliving the experience. "What happened when Liang caught up with you?"

"He hid near the column and smuggled a message to me. I managed to escape and we all spent a night together, sleeping in a barn. I was overjoyed. I could hardly believe you'd survived. I thought all our troubles were over then. But we were attacked by a band of wild mountain dwellers who called themselves spirit soldiers. We got away from them, still carrying you in one of the baskets. But unfortunately the Red Army soldiers pursuing us heard the commotion and we were recaptured."

"It doesn't seem possible that I went through all that without knowing anything about it," said Abigail in a half-whisper. "What did they do to us after we were recaptured?"

"My jailers separated us. Liang had to prepare my food and look after you on his own. I wasn't allowed to see you at all. Food of every kind was short, we were all close to starving, and Liang got desperate when he began to run out of soy milk." Jakob stopped and drew a deep breath. "So he approached Lu Mei-ling secretly one night and she agreed to care for you."

"Did she look after me for long?"

"For about six or seven months altogether. On the march she either carried you herself or led you on her mule in a basket. You traveled with her all across the Snow Mountains and the Great Grasslands, the wildest parts of the whole trek."

"I never imagined it was anything like that." Abigail's eyes were wide with surprise. "I had no idea."

Jakob looked uneasily at his wristwatch again, and shuffled together some of the papers on his desk. His daughter's questions had begun to make him feel on edge and he was anxious to escape further probing.

"Lu Mei-ling and your cookboy, Liang, really saved my life," she said, looking up suddenly with a wondering expression in her eyes. "I wouldn't be here now without their help, would I?"

"No, that's true."

"What became of Liang, do you know?"

Jakob shook his head quickly. "He joined the Red Army eventually. He fought heroically at the Luting bridge. But after that I've
no idea what happened to Liang, I'm afraid."

He stood up, gathering his translations together. Abigail was staring again at the magazine photograph of Mei-ling and he could see
that her mind was beginning to seethe with new questions. When
he was sure he was unobserved by her, he concealed among his
papers the old booklet on the Long March which his translator had
discovered and crossed quickly to the door.

"I have to check something in the archives," he said over his
shoulder. "I'll leave you here to browse through the rest of your
file."

Without waiting for an answer Jakob hurried through the outer
office to the institute's archive, where long rows of indexed shelves
held back copies of newspapers and folders of old translations. Seating himself at an empty desk by a window, he spread out his papers
and opened the Long March booklet. He noticed, thumbing carefully
through it, that its pages contained the kind of idealized drawings
of triumphant Red Army troops that were already familiar to him
from other Communist publications dealing with the Long March.
Its texts too were unrelieved eulogies of revolutionary heroism: cooks
described how they had braved hails of enemy fire to deliver food
to beleaguered units, peasant soldiers testified to acts of valor in
which comrades had sacrificed their lives selflessly for the revolution,
and Red Army commanders gleefully detailed the wily guerrilla
strategies with which they had repeatedly duped foolish Kuomintang
officers. The dog-eared publication, printed in Chinese on coarse,
yellowing paper, was at least a dozen years old and had obviously
been printed during the Yenan period of the revolution. It seemed
likely that it had passed into an obscure file on arrival at the institute
without having come to his desk for scrutiny. Some of the articles
he remembered reading in more recent anthologies of the revolution,
and he realized that Mei-ling's contribution had probably been dropped
from later editions.

When he came to her article, he ran his eye swiftly down the rows
of printed Chinese characters, noting that the same dutiful thread
of positive propaganda ran through all the descriptions of incidents
she had witnessed. He skimmed quickly to the last page without
discovering anything very illuminating; then, near the end, an abrupt

change to a more intimate style of writing caused him to slow down. In the final paragraph she had departed from the propaganda conventions and introduced an unusual personal note, saying how she felt strongly that her own individual experiences had "echoed the significance of the great Long March." His interest aroused, he read on more slowly, jotting down a rough translation as he went.

"From the suffering and sacrifice of thousands of brave comrades in the Central Red Army, a new revolutionary China has sprung gloriously into being," she had written.

> And after much suffering and privation, my own almost exhausted body achieved its own modest "revolutionary" successes. It was not only able to endure privations previously thought impossible for a woman, it both sustained and produced new life during the most arduous final stages of the historic trek. Because of the Long March of the Chinese Workers' and Peasants' Red Army, the oppressed masses of China came to realize for the first time that a new era lay before them — an era in which they would seize control of their own destiny! Both as a revolutionary and as a woman, I was glad to have had the privilege of playing a minor role in this great achievement.

Jakob sat and stared for a long time at the last few lines, reading the printed characters and his own translation over and over again, trying to wring the most precise English translation from the Chinese text. But try as he might, from the oblique language he could not be certain beyond all doubt of Mei-ling's final meaning. Had she, he wondered, meant to convey merely that she had borne and succored her own child, the one that had died so tragically? Or was she making an obscure reference also to the efforts she had made to save Abigail? As he wrestled with the puzzle, he remembered again those desperate, sublime moments they had shared on the blizzard-swept Snow Mountains and suddenly he found himself wondering whether Mei-ling's words could possibly be interpreted to contain another meaning.

His pulse quickened as he reread the last paragraph — but, tantalizingly, the Chinese characters continued to resist his efforts to establish a definitive meaning. Closing the booklet, he sat for a while gazing out of the window without seeing the stark, saddle-backed bulk of Victoria Peak framed beyond the glass. Gradually what he had read inspired a new feeling of resolution, and he forced himself to check and annotate the routine bulletin translations before him as rapidly as possible. As soon as he had finished and delivered them to the senior translator for printing, he hurried back to his office. Abigail was still engrossed in her reading, and he spent a few moments tidying his papers. Then he perched himself on the corner of the desk at which she sat.

"You know, Abigail, that I received an invitation to go to Peking yesterday," he said quietly. "What you don't know is that I've been wondering hour by hour ever since whether I should accept or not."

Abigail looked up, surprised by his unusual tone of voice. "And have you made up your mind at last?"

Jakob nodded. "Yes, I have. I'm going."

Abigail closed the file she had been reading and pushed it to one side. "Does that mean that you're ready to face up to what your friend Joseph Sherman called 'ghosts from the past'?"

"I don't know exactly what Joseph meant by that. Perhaps he meant that we sometimes find ghosts of our past selves when we return to places that were once important to us. If so, I think I'm ready."

"I'd like you to take me with you," said Abigail, raising her eyes to his. "Will you, please?"

Startled by the request, Jakob stood up and shook his head. "I don't think it would be at all suitable for you to come . . ."

"You might find it more painful than you think, going back to the place where you and my mother were happy together," said Abigail insistently. "And if you do, it might help if I'm there."

Jakob did not answer but she could see that he was thinking over what she had said.

"If you asked your hosts to extend the invitation to your daughter, they could hardly refuse," she added gently. "Will you do it — for my sake?"

Jakob looked perplexed. Then he turned away to look out of the window at the towering Peak again.

"I won't make any promises," he said in a subdued voice. "But I will ask."

6

From the balcony of his hotel room overlooking the gnarled gray stonework of the old Tartar Wall, Jakob stared sadly out at the plumes of smoke belching from factory chimneys in Peking's recently industrialized suburbs. Although it was still early morning and the sun was barely risen above the eastern reaches of the ancient capital, new iron and steel foundries were already creating a sooty haze in the autumn sky. This curtain of murk almost blotted out the distant azure roofs of the Temple of Heaven, and as he stood looking southward, Jakob suddenly saw the smoke as a symbol of his mood. A dark, indefinable feeling of regret, he realized, blurred his senses and obscured his past in Peking as surely as the industrial smog screened the Temple of Heaven. Since arriving five days earlier he had attempted to focus his mind unfailingly in the present in order to absorb all that was new. In the quarter of a century that had passed since he had first come to Peking, the capital of what was now the world's largest Communist nation had changed greatly and at every turn he had consciously resisted the temptation to slip into maudlin reflections on the past.

Fortunately, there had been much to distract him and for most of the time, he had succeeded in keeping his mind on the present. From the viewing stands flanking the vermilion-walled Gate of Heavenly Peace, he had stared out across the vast concrete plain that had been cleared in front of it, watching half a million Chinese — youths, workers, women, and soldiers — parade before Mao Tse-tung and the other Communist leaders on China's National Day; during a crowded program of visits to factories, schools, and agricultural cooperatives in the days that followed, he had forced himself to concentrate on the unending flow of facts and figures provided by the Communist Party cadres who were his hosts; at a succession of banquets and receptions he had listened dutifully to repetitive antiwar speeches attacking the United States, although with each passing hour he had felt increasingly at odds with the mainly Soviet and East European delegations invited to Peking by the Chinese Committee for World Peace. At first he had watched carefully for some hint of a special greeting that might explain his mysterious invitation — but the unfailingly anonymous faces of the Chinese officials who escorted the delegates had so far given nothing away.

Now, despite his previous good intentions, as he stared into the industrial smoke Jakob found himself visualizing the terraces of dazzling white marble around the Temple of Heaven and the shady groves of ancient cypress trees where he had strolled with Felicity on that spring day in 1932 when she accepted his proposal of marriage. He conjured up from memory the simple grandeur of the historic enclosure where the altars, halls, and pavilions had been erected with great precision, in accordance with the mystical beliefs of antiquity. In his mind's eye he saw the rose-pink walls of the temples, the bright cobalt blue glaze of the roof tiles, and wondered whether he would ever feel again that unique sensation of having reached out to touch the ancient past that he had first experienced at the Temple of Heaven as a carefree young man. As these thoughts drifted through his mind, Jakob suddenly felt desperately wearied by the drab, utilitarian modernity of Communist Peking and a strong desire to immerse his senses in the rich, restful atmosphere of the past welled up in him. He sighed involuntarily, jamming his hands deep into his trouser pockets, and at that moment a door to an adjoining room opened and a soft footfall sounded behind him.

"I sense you're beginning to get a little tired of all the heavy-handed propaganda and the official smiles. Am I right?"

Abigail spoke in a quietly sympathetic voice as she stepped out onto the balcony. She wore a cool frock of yellow linen and a matching woolen jacket to guard against the fresh autumn morning and she moved to the parapet beside her father to follow the direction of his gaze.

"I suppose I might be," conceded Jakob with another sigh. "I've been trying hard to see Peking as my hosts want us to see it — not as I remember it."

"Is that for their sake or yours?" asked Abigail with a little frown.

"I think I've been trying to do it for all our sakes."

"But you haven't always been successful, have you?"

"Perhaps not." Jakob looked sharply at his daughter. He had become gradually aware that closing his mind to his own past associations with Peking had induced a growing feeling of tension in him as the days passed. Abigail, who was promptly included in the peace committee's invitation as soon as he made the request from Hong Kong, had remained dutifully quiet at his side during the functions and visits, but he realized from her pointed question that she must

already have sensed something of his mood. "Has it been that obvious?"

"No. I can see you've been fascinated by everything you've heard
and seen since we've been here. But you'd hardly be human, Daddy,
if the past didn't creep up on you at times. I guessed that was the
reason you decided suddenly last night to drop out of today's program."

Jakob looked out over the balcony again toward the Temple of
Heaven. From the moment when he had first caught sight of the
gilded Summer Palace roofs at the end of their flight from Canton,
he had felt the tug of the past. The palaces, the shimmering lake
with its willow-pattern bridges, and the curved-roof teahouses had
reminded him vividly of the China of his boyhood imagination and
at that point he had consciously clamped an iron band of discipline
on his own thoughts. Once on the ground, however, he discovered
that the austere Communist present had stamped its image more
firmly on Peking than he had imagined from afar. The road into the
capital from the modern, functional airport was newly constructed
and ran straight for twenty miles past freshly planted saplings and
featureless concrete buildings that housed schools, research institutes, and factories. Unbroken cliffs of new brick-built apartment
blocks marked the outer suburbs of Peking and although the Forbidden City's golden-roofed pavilions and palaces remained undis-
turbed at the heart of the capital, the network of roads and public
buildings that had begun springing up in the Outer City gave it a
much-changed appearance.

Many old houses of the imperial courts, with their walled courtyards and moon gates, had been pulled down or modified for use as
workshops and schools. The streets of the Outer City, which had
once seethed with rowdy, rumbustious life, were, to Jakob's disappointment, filled now each day with orderly swarms of cycle-
borne Chinese dressed in standard blue cottons, and all these changes
had made it more difficult for him to recall the Peking of his own experience. But with each passing day he had felt the desire to seek out
familiar reminders of those earlier days grow stronger within him,
and the previous evening, claiming that he needed to rest, he had
excused himself from yet another factory visit that his fellow delegates were due to make to a distant town that morning. He had not
withdrawn Abigail's name from the official party, suggesting instead

that she represent them both, and he was surprised to find she had
not already departed.

"Isn't it time for the delegation to leave?" asked Jakob, glancing
at his watch.

"It's already left," replied Abigail, smiling faintly and looking at
her own wristwatch. "I decided to scratch too at the last minute.
Wherever you go, I'd like to be with you."

Jakob smiled uncertainly and nodded toward the blue-tiled temple
with its spectacular crowning orb of gold. "I'd just decided to take
another look at the Temple of Heaven. Your mother and I loved
going there together." Jakob hesitated, his expression becoming serious. "In fact, that's where I proposed to her . . ."

"I'd like very much to come with you, Daddy. What time will
you go?"

"When we've had breakfast."

Jakob left the balcony to put on his jacket and tie and when
breakfast was finished, he led Abigail outside and hailed two passing
pedicabs. As these creaking successors to Peking's old-style rickshaw
carried them through the once-familiar streets of the Outer City,
Jakob became aware that all the old gambling and drug dens had
been swept away, along with the houses famous for their "singing
girls." There was no longer any sign of curbside dentists and barbers
or itinerant food peddlers with portable charcoal stoves bouncing at
the end of their shoulder poles. All these colorful figures, he had
learned from his hosts, had been absorbed into handicraft and small
merchant cooperatives and nowhere on the street corners could he
any longer buy *chiao tzu*, the little dumplings stuffed with spiced
vegetables that he had once loved to eat. The unruly open markets
that had formerly filled the streets with the noise of haggling and
quarreling had disappeared. In the subdued silence which now cloaked
the city Jakob also missed the pigeons that had once swooped overhead, creating sweet, harplike music with tiny pipes that their owners
had bound to their pinion feathers.

As the pedicabs carried them farther from the center of the capital,
Jakob saw that swaying camels and slow-moving donkey carts were
still hauling bulging loads of vegetables and other daily food supplies
into the city, but now silent rubber tires had replaced the noisy
rumbling wheels of solid wood on which the carts of old had run.
The loud, clanking trams had given way to purring electric buses
and whenever these vehicles passed their pedicabs, the rows of yellow-

brown faces crowding the windows peered curiously out at the rare sight of white foreigners. All the other people thronging the pavements turned to stare at them as they passed, and after paying off the pedicab drivers Jakob and Abigail were glad to escape into the walled enclosure surrounding the Temple of Heaven.

It was deserted at that early hour and the moment they stepped through the Gate of the Western Sky, the deep, natural stillness of the enclosure seemed to envelop them in its welcoming embrace. A sense of peace which he had not experienced since arriving in Peking stole over Jakob as they strolled slowly along the avenue of ancient cypress trees toward the Red Stairway Bridge. At last the years seemed to have rolled away to expose his past with a perfect clarity, and on catching sight of the main triple-roofed temple in its full glory, Jakob stopped and stared, transfixed by its simple, timeless elegance.

"Chi Nien Tien!"

In a hushed whisper Jakob murmured the Chinese name of the Hall of Prayer for Good Harvests and in that instant he felt he could almost see his twenty-one-year-old self dashing headlong through the rain and up the long flights of balustraded marble steps toward Felicity.

"It's extraordinarily beautiful," said Abigail softly. "It's so uncomplicated — yet it's breathtaking."

They stood side by side in silence looking at the ancient temple, and finding himself moved in turn by Abigail's emotional reaction, Jakob took his daughter gently by the arm.

"It was April when we came here," he said in a husky voice. "From where we're standing now I could see your mother waiting for me alone on that marble terrace beneath the eaves of the temple. She was wearing a Chinese jacket of green silk, I think, embroidered with plum blossom patterns. Because it was still cold she'd tucked her hair inside a fur hat . . ."

Sensing the depth of her father's feelings, Abigail remained silent; when Jakob began walking again, she fell into step with him.

"We'd agreed to meet here at the end of our study course to tell one another about the designations we'd been given. Your mother had doubts about our future together, you see, and we'd decided it would be best to let fate decide. . . . I'd always wanted to preach in remote areas and I'd just been told I was being sent to a region of Hunan where no white missionary had been before. . . . I was bursting to tell her my news. But when I reached the terrace, she insisted that I wait and made me go into the temple with her. She was a little upset but inside it was wonderfully peaceful. . . ."

Remembering the gentle, sacred silence of the empty temple, Jakob increased his pace, impatient to savor it once more. As he walked, he glanced along the Red Stairway Bridge at the other major sanctuary, the Imperial Vault of Heaven. In doing so, a movement caught his eye and he turned his head in time to see the figure of a Chinese man slip quickly in among the cypress trees a hundred yards away. Puzzled, Jakob continued to watch for several seconds, but the man, who had appeared to be wearing a navy blue cadre's tunic, had become invisible in the shadows beneath the trees and he did not reappear.

"What's the matter?" asked Abigail. "What did you see?"

"I thought somebody might be following us," replied Jakob, shaking his head in mystification. "But perhaps I was mistaken."

Determined not to be distracted from his goal, Jakob dismissed the man from his mind, and taking his daughter's arm again, he hurried her up the white marble steps to the temple. Inside, the morning sun shining through the open-lattice walls was dappling the carved stone floor with pools of golden light just as it had done after the shower of rain twenty-five years earlier, and Jakob and Abigail entered the domed chamber in a respectful silence. Standing quietly at her father's side among the "dragon well" pillars, Abigail gazed up in awe at the colored frescoes that decorated the high roof. Her young face had an enraptured look, but as Jakob watched her, the tense, tearful image of Felicity returned suddenly with such haunting clarity that he closed his eyes and bowed his head. In his imagination he again heard her halting voice expressing apprehension at the prospect of moving to an isolated inland area, and he regretted anew the impetuosity that had led him to take her by the hand and run to the Echo Wall to ask her to marry him.

"What is it, Daddy?" asked Abigail softly, touching his arm. "Is something wrong?"

When Jakob raised his head he had an agonized expression in his eyes; although he tried to speak calmly, his unsteady voice betrayed the inner turmoil he was suffering. "Your mother wasn't physically brave by nature. Left to herself, I think she might have been happiest filling a teaching post in a missionary school in one of the bigger cities. . . ."

"What do you mean?"

"I persuaded her to go to one of the wildest parts of China against her better judgment. I was convinced I could protect her from anything. Standing here, I told her she needn't ever worry about her safety, I would protect her. But in the end I wasn't able to . . ."

Abigail looked at her father with a shocked expression. "Do you mean you blame yourself for what happened?"

Jakob nodded miserably. "I've never been able to say this to anyone before . . . but whenever I've looked back over what happened, I've felt it was my own foolishness that caused your mother's death."

"You couldn't possibly have known what would happen!" Abigail tightened her hold on her father's arm. "I'm sure she went with you because you loved her and she loved you. Isn't that right?"

Abigail moved around in front of him and looked directly into his eyes, waiting for his answer. As he considered what she had said, Jakob's face remained troubled but at last he nodded. "Yes, I suppose that's true."

"Then there's no question of you having forced her to go against her will. Don't you see, it was right for her to go with you. It can't have been your fault."

A faint look of relief softened Jakob's features, and he and Abigail drew closer to one another. Something indefinable in the stillness of the soaring, circular vault seemed to soothe them and for a long time they stood on the symbolic carved motif of dragon and phoenix, saying nothing.

"Was it here that you proposed?" asked Abigail, breaking the silence.

"No." Jakob shook his head.

"Will you show me where it happened?"

Jakob hesitated, then smiled for the first time. "All right."

They began to retrace their steps along the Red Stairway Bridge in the direction of the Imperial Vault of Heaven, walking slowly. Because he was lost in thought, Jakob failed to notice when the figure in the Chinese cadre's uniform emerged from the trees and began following them again. The new sense of companionship which his confession had engendered made both of them temporarily oblivious to their surroundings, and at the foot of the steps leading down to the Echo Wall, Jakob stopped and turned to look at Abigail.

"I'm glad that you know," he said in an emotional voice. "It doesn't seem quite so terrible now."

"You should've told me long ago," said Abigail quietly. "There was no need for you to suffer in silence all that time."

Jakob smiled sadly, then pointed toward the San Yin Shih, the Triple Sound Stone, which they were approaching, and began to explain how the Echo Wall functioned.

"I invited your mother to marry me from up there. I asked the question from the bottom step, and because she was so taken aback, I repeated it from the second. After listening to the echoes, she stood on the top step to give her reply. . . ."

Inside his head Jakob imagined he could already hear his own voice echoing his insistent proposal and this moved him to climb alone to the third step. When he stood facing the curved echo wall, Felicity's softer response seemed to come faintly alive again too: "Yes, Jakob, I will! Yes, Jakob, I will! Yes, Jakob, I will!"

When a new voice broke softly across his thoughts he assumed at first that it was as imaginary as Felicity's. Then it repeated itself more insistently and Jakob heard an echo that was unmistakably real bounce back from the curved wall of polished bricks.

"Ke Mu-shih! Ke Mu-shih! Ke Mu-shih!"

Jakob turned to find the Chinese in the dark blue cadre's tunic standing close behind him. His black hair was the color of steel at the temples, and around his eyes and mouth the creases of a delighted smile were etched deep into a dark, weathered face. He was holding out a welcoming hand, but because of the astonishment Jakob felt, he remained rooted to the spot for a moment, staring in disbelief. Then he recovered and grasped the proffered hand of his former cookboy with an exclamation of pleasure and surprise.

"Hsiao Liang!"

"Ke Mu-shih!"

In the emotion of the moment both men found themselves incapable of speech. Their hands remained locked as they looked at one another; then Jakob threw an arm around Liang's shoulders and embraced him. Jakob felt his eyes dampen, and when the two men pulled apart again, he could see there was a hint of tears in Liang's eyes too, despite the broadness of his smile.

"I can hardly believe it's you, Hsiao Liang," said Jakob, speaking in Chinese. "This seems almost like a miracle."

"It's truly wonderful to see you again too, Pastor Ke. . . ."

Remembering suddenly that Abigail was standing tensely at the foot of the steps watching them, Jakob took Liang by the arm and led him toward her. Her face was puckered with curiosity and he could see that although she had begun to study Chinese while waiting to make the journey to Peking, she had understood little or nothing of their conversation.

"Abigail, prepare yourself for a surprise," said Jakob, speaking slowly in English for Liang's benefit. "This is Hsiao Liang, the man who saved your life all those years ago."

An expression of astonished delight appeared on Abigail's face, but on glancing at Liang, Jakob saw that he had not grasped what had been said.

"Excuse please, Pastor Ke," said Liang apologetically. "I forget all English."

"This is my daughter, Abigail," said Jakob, speaking in Chinese once more. "You remember the tiny baby you hid in your basket? That was Abigail."

Liang stared in amazement at the beautiful, flaxen-haired girl before him. "Now I feel as if *I'm* dreaming, Pastor Ke," said Liang, laughing and shaking his head in wonder. "Who could have imagined . . ."

"I never thought I'd meet you, Hsiao Liang," said Abigail with a catch in her voice. "I know that if it wasn't for you I wouldn't be here today . . . So I'm very glad I can say thank you in person at last for all your kindness and courage."

"It was my duty to help your father," replied Liang with a warm smile, after hearing Jakob's translation. "Pastor Ke is a brave man. He was a wonderful friend."

Above the dark green cypress trees the blue of the autumn sky was deepening as the sun climbed higher. The rose-colored walls of the temples and pavilions were beginning to glow with a soft luminescence, some flower-bearing shrubs were still in bloom, and the beauty of the setting heightened the unexpected pleasure of the reunion for all of them.

"I didn't turn round when I first heard your voice, Hsiao Liang," said Jakob as he led the way back along the Red Stairway Bridge, "because nobody has called me Pastor Ke for so many years."

"Are you no longer a missionary, then?" Liang's face showed surprise but his smile of pleasure did not fade.

"No, I gave up missionary work many years ago."

"And what do you do now?"

"I live in Hong Kong, Hsiao Liang. I write about the politics and economy of China."

A guarded look came into Liang's eyes; then, after an awkward silence, he smiled again. "I notice you make the same mistakes as me, Pastor Ke. I'm no longer Hsiao Liang. I became a grandfather some years ago. Now you should call me *Lao* Liang — 'Old Liang.' "

Although in his mid-fifties, Liang still possessed an air of rugged self-reliance. He limped slightly, his lined face still bore traces of scar tissue from his Luting burns, and he looked a little tired as though from overwork; but the neat formal tunic of a cadre buttoned high at the throat did not entirely disguise the strength and physical self-confidence of his hard peasant upbringing.

"Grandfather or not, you'll always be Hsiao Liang to me." Jakob laughed affectionately. "Which reminds me, how are your wife and those two fine sons?"

"They're all well." Liang's smile widened again. "The boy you knew as Little Liang now has three children of his own — two small sons and a daughter. He's a cadre of the All-China Trade Union Federation in Changsha. Big Liang works with the Provincial Committee of the Party in Hunan. He has a boy and a girl. When we all meet up for the New Year festival there are grandchildren everywhere!"

"You've obviously done well for yourself, Hsiao Liang — in every way." Jakob smiled and gestured toward the cadre's tunic that he wore. "You've become a respected *kan pu*. What job do you do?"

"I hope I've done well for the Party and for China," replied Liang, speaking slowly to emphasize that he was making a correction to Jakob's statement. "I'm a cadre with the Party Agriculture Commission. Like my sons I was lucky enough to study at the Revolutionary Academy in Yenan. I visit the countryside in many provinces. I help the peasants work out their own collectivization programs and explain how our Party and government agencies can help. We're teaching them to share and help one another and they've learned to trust the government. The recent harvests have been the best for thirty years."

"You must have been working very hard."

"Yes." Liang turned to look directly at Jakob, a gleam of intense pride showing in his tired eyes. "But it's very worthwhile work. You know that my own father's land was stolen from him by rich landlords when he couldn't pay their cruel taxes. Now all that's been changed. There's a great mood of optimism in the countryside. The peasants of China are beginning to realize that they're in charge of their own destiny at last."

As they walked Liang turned frequently to smile at Abigail and he listened attentively whenever Jakob paused to translate for her. Although the language barrier separated them, Abigail could see that the bond of friendship forged between Liang and her father so many years before had survived the passage of time. She soon began to feel something approaching a sense of kinship herself for the sturdy, likable Chinese peasant striding at her side; he answered all the questions put to him with animation, his expression alive with interest, and when at last the questions dried up, he turned an inquiring expression to Jakob.

"You have an interesting job now, Pastor Ke — but may I ask what made you decide to give up your job as a missionary?"

Jakob smiled uncomfortably. "It's difficult to explain. Perhaps my time with the Red Army made me change my mind. Afterward it seemed foolish to think that a few Christian missionaries could help solve the terrible problems of China. And I don't think there's much evidence that all the work done by foreign missionaries produced any lasting effects."

"Perhaps the work had more effect than you suspect, Pastor Ke. On my travels I find a lot of people continue to worship in secret."

Jakob looked sharply at the Chinese cadre. He had spoken quietly but in a firm tone and Jakob saw that he was staring pensively toward the Hall of Prayer for Good Harvests as they walked. Above the shimmering marble terraces, the blue-glazed roof merged harmoniously with the bright autumn sky and its glittering tiles were reflecting the sunlight like wavelets on the seashore.

"I still have the signed Bible you gave me, Pastor Ke," continued Liang quietly, "and on the Luting bridge when I thought I was going to die, I found myself repeating a prayer you'd once taught me. I had to charge into shoulder-high flames and was sure I would be killed. As I ran into the fire I remembered your prayer and repeated it over and over to myself: 'O Lord God, in my hour of need, please forgive and protect me!"

Jakob stared at his former cookboy in surprise. "I had no idea, Hsiao Liang . . ."

For a moment Liang continued gazing up at the temple. Then he turned to Jakob with a mystified smile in his eyes. "I don't know why it came into my head at that instant, Pastor Ke. I can't explain it."

"I'm very glad you told me," said Jakob softly. "It's a great privilege."

"All the survivors of the Luting bridge assault were awarded the Gold Star, the highest decoration in the Red Army for bravery," continued Liang in a low voice. "Perhaps it was more than we deserved — but my comrades always make sure that when I visit the countryside, the peasants know about the Gold Star in advance. Sometimes I'm even asked to wear it. I see many of them looking at me with awe in their eyes — and then I often remember your little prayer."

Liang turned his steps in the direction of the Gate of the Western Sky, and Jakob and Abigail followed, walking comfortably on either side of him in a companionable silence. For a minute or two each of them remained submerged in their own thoughts; then, halfway along the avenue of cypress trees, Jakob stopped and laid his hand gently on the Chinese cadre's arm.

"Tell me, Hsiao Liang, how did you know we were in Peking? And how did you come to find us here this morning? Nobody knew we were coming to this place."

"Marshal Lu Chiao informed me of your visit," said Liang unhesitatingly. "He called me back urgently from the countryside."

At the mention of Chiao's name, Jakob's eyes widened in surprise. "How do you know Marshal Lu?"

"He was the commander of the special assault force at Luting."

"Was he?" Jakob reflected on the information in silence for a moment. "But why, do you think, would Marshal Lu wish you to see me?"

"Perhaps it was simply an act of friendship, Pastor Ke. He knew that if you ever came back to China I would wish to see you. He told me of your intended visit some time ago and when he heard that you'd decided to stand down from the peace delegation program today, he contacted me. He suggested I wait outside your hotel to seek a chance of talking to you alone." Liang smiled uncomfortably. "I'm afraid I followed you here in a pedicab without your noticing. . . ."

Jakob stared at the Chinese in astonishment. As he absorbed the implications of what Liang had said, his mind began to seethe with questions. Why had Chiao gone to so much trouble to ensure that he met Liang again? And why should Chiao interest himself in the details of their movements? Was Chiao in some way behind the unexpected invitation to China — and if so, what was its purpose? He searched Liang's face, trying to decide if he was in possession of further information that might throw light on the mystery. But the decent, gently smiling face of the Chinese did not suggest he was party to an intrique.

"Couldn't we have met openly, Hsiao Liang?" asked Jakob at last, watching carefully for his reaction. "Couldn't we arrange for you to have dinner with us?"

Liang looked suddenly uneasy. "It's not advisable for Party cadres of my rank to have personal friends in Western countries — especially those with Christian backgrounds."

Jakob nodded. "I think I understand. I've heard rumors that Chinese Christians as well as intellectuals are being sent to the Hundred Flowers labor camps."

Liang glanced anxiously around the enclosure, then began walking again, increasing his pace. "Perhaps it's better not to talk of these things, Pastor Ke. This is a bad time — few people are safe. . . ." Liang hesitated and looked directly at Jakob. "Even Marshal Lu's sister has gone to work in a coal yard."

Jakob felt his stomach contract instantly. Liang seemed to have been at pains to give the casual remark some significance and although he knew Abigail's grasp of Chinese was only rudimentary, he looked quickly at her to see if she had registered anything of what they were saying. He had not translated any of the exchanges about Chiao and to his relief he saw that Abigail was not paying undue attention to the conversation.

"Do you mean Lu Mei-ling?" asked Jakob in an undertone, turning away from his daughter.

Liang nodded. "Yes, Pastor Ke."

"But what has she done?"

"I don't know — and nobody asks. Perhaps they've found something in her writing — or perhaps she volunteered to go." Liang stopped and pushed back the cuff of his tunic sleeve to glance at a cheap metal wristwatch. He smiled but there was a hint of tension in his manner, and at that moment Jakob caught sight of a shiny black official limousine parked outside the Gate of the Western Sky. "It's time for me to leave now, Pastor Ke. I'm very glad we've had the chance to meet." Liang inclined his head toward Abigail. "And it's been a great honor for me to meet your lovely daughter."

"Will we be able to see one another again?" asked Abigail.

"Another meeting might be difficult to arrange," said Liang, smiling uneasily again.

"Then please know I shall never forget what you did for me." Abigail seized one of Liang's hands in both her own and held it for a long moment in a spontaneous gesture of affection. Then she stood back and watched with tears in her eyes as her father and Liang took their leave of one another, shaking hands with great warmth.

"It's been very good to see you again, Hsiao Liang," said Jakob in an emotional voice. "Please pay my respects to your wife and all your family."

"I will, I will."

Jakob and Abigail stood and watched Liang hurry toward the Gate of the Western Sky. His stride was quick and nervous, and something in his bearing increased the feeling of agitation Jakob felt upon hearing the information about Mei-ling and Chiao. A stream of brightly dressed children from a kindergarten were entering the enclosure with their teachers but they took no notice of the hurrying figure of Liang, and he disappeared through the gateway, without looking back, ignoring the official limousine parked outside.

"What were you discussing at the end, Daddy?" asked Abigail quietly at Jakob's side. "Your expression was quite worried."

"We were talking about the Hundred Flowers campaign," replied Jakob shortly, still staring toward the gateway. "Sad things are happening. Many people who don't deserve it are being sent to reform-through-labor camps."

Abigail was about to ask a further question but another Chinese cadre in a dark, high-necked tunic had climbed out of the official limousine and was hurrying in their direction. When he reached them, he was smiling politely but there was something faintly ominous in the way he gestured toward the limousine with an open-palmed hand.

"Please come with me," he said, addressing Jakob. "I have a car waiting for your convenience."

"But we have no appointments to keep," replied Jakob, without moving. "We have a free day and we came here for recreation."

The cadre smiled fixedly again. "If you will take the car, Mr.

Kellner, your daughter can be dropped off at the hotel. An extra appointment has been arranged for you."

"May I ask what it is?"

"I'm not authorized to tell you that," replied the cadre, the smile fading from his face. "Please be kind enough to accompany me to the car now."

The official gestured ahead again, indicating they should precede him, and after glancing back over his shoulder for a last look at the spectacular temple, Jakob took Abigail reluctantly by the arm and guided her toward the limousine.

7

The rear windows of the Russian-made Zil limousine were closed off, as in all official Chinese cars, with elasticized nylon curtains of a greenish hue. They admitted some light but shielded the vehicle's occupants successfully from the gaze of passersby, and in the fish-tank gloom of the backseat, Jakob and Abigail sat side by side without speaking as the uniformed driver maneuvered through crowds of identically dressed cyclists. Jakob could see they were heading back toward the center of Peking but the forbidding presence of the cadre in the front passenger seat inhibited conversation. Abigail's expression betrayed a trace of inner anxiety and when the limousine stopped to allow her to alight outside their hotel, Jakob climbed out briefly to reassure her there was no need for alarm.

From the hotel the limousine was driven rapidly to the Square of Heavenly Peace, and Jakob felt a mounting sense of excitement as it drew up at the foot of the broad terrace of steps leading up to the Great Hall of the People, the massive stone megalith which the Communists had built along the western side of the hundred-acre square. During the journey all his conjectures about who might be responsible for the mystery summons had led him to Marshal Lu Chiao. In previous weeks, when speculating about who might have been behind the unexpected invitation to China, he had sometimes considered the possibility that Chiao might in some way have been involved. But no tangible reason for such an involvement had suggested itself and eventually he had dismissed the thought. Liang's revelation that Chiao had helped arrange their emotional reunion at the Temple of Heaven seemed to prove conclusively that he was a party to the invitation, and this knowledge raised many intriguing new questions in his mind. From the moment he stepped into the official limousine Jakob had begun to suspect that the "extra appointment" must be with the Chinese marshal and when the uniformed cadre motioned him from the car and ushered him toward the twelve giant columns of marble flanking the entrances to the Great Hall, he became convinced his guess was right.

Soldiers with fixed bayonets on their rifles stood guard at the foot of the soaring pillars, and Jakob was led quickly into the building through a huge central portal where tall bronze doors stood open. Once inside, the cadre conducted him wordlessly through a succession of lofty marble vestibules and corridors to a sparely furnished reception room where armchairs had been arranged around a low table. There the cadre motioned him to be seated, then departed, leaving Jakob staring at life-size heroic murals of the Long March that decorated the walls.

Jakob was still studying the murals when a minute or two later an inner door opened and a bustling, quick-striding figure appeared, followed by a female aide. Stocky, dapper, and precise in his movements, the approaching Chinese wore a polite, formal smile as he crossed the room, but because Jakob had been so sure he was to meet Chiao, for the space of a second or two he did not recognize his host. Then with a start he realized that he was looking into a face he had last seen twenty-two years before as he rode out of the walled town of Tungwei, on the eve of his release from captivity. Then, pale and emaciated from his severe Long March illness, the man before him had worn a soiled Red Army uniform with tattered cloth sandals, and a curly beard had covered his cheeks. Now, dressed in a well-tailored cadre's tunic and carefully pressed slacks of dove gray worsted, Chou En-lai was urbanely clean-shaven, as befitted the grandson of a Manchu dynasty mandarin and the prime minister of a nation of six hundred million people. His neatly clipped hair was steel gray and from beneath dark, bushy brows his keen eyes regarded Jakob unwaveringly.

"Welcome back to Peking, Mr. Kellner," said Chou courteously in Chinese, motioning for Jakob to be seated. "The circumstances of this meeting are fortunately quite different from those existing the last time we met."

For a second the premier's gaze strayed to the Long March murals around them and he smiled ironically.

"I'm very glad they are," replied Jakob with equal politeness. "But I'm still a little puzzled as to why I've been invited to return here."

"You may interpret your invitation to Peking, if you wish, as an act of personal goodwill," said Chou, watching a second aide, who had just entered, place a tray of lidded porcelain teacups on a low table beside Jakob's chair. "It's been noted that you long ago gave up missionary work and that in a recent book you laid emphasis on the positive achievements that have been made in the eight years since the founding of the People's Republic of China. In Western countries this is still unfortunately rare."

Chou made an elegant gesture with one hand in the direction of the tray and Jakob reached out to remove the lid from his cup. He recognized the subtle fragrance of jasmine tea at once and the dry, aromatic taste was pleasantly refreshing. Chou sipped from his own cup only very briefly, then set it aside.

"I should say at this stage, Mr. Kellner, that it's not customary for ministers of the State Council, whatever their standing, to grant interviews to writers from capitalist countries. Therefore you should treat this conversation as private and entirely confidential." Chou paused, and as though to lend emphasis to his remark, he glanced around pointedly at the silent female aide, who had seated herself behind him and was making notes of the conversation. "We took considerable pains to ensure that the factories, schools, and agricultural cooperatives included in your program of visits would provide important new information about our economic development. It's a pity, therefore, that you chose not to participate in today's tour."

"I wanted to see something of the old Peking I once knew — without a guide," said Jakob, setting down his teacup. "I have many personal memories of my time here as a student. I feared I wouldn't have the opportunity to visit places that once meant a lot to me."

Chou nodded. "That's perfectly understandable. But it might have been preferable if you had informed us of your wishes in advance."

"It was a spur-of-the-moment decision," explained Jakob quietly. "I wanted to see the Temple of Heaven again. I visited it often with my wife more than twenty-five years ago."

Chou's expression became less severe and he took a reflective sip from his teacup. "Then I trust you enjoyed your meeting there with your former house servant."

"It was a great pleasure for us both," said Jakob slowly. "And it was a moving occasion for my daughter to meet the man who had cared for her in China when she was very small. But I had no idea I would meet Comrade Liang — there or anywhere else."

The premier smiled fleetingly. "Then it seems to have been a fortunate coincidence for all concerned."

"It could hardly have been just a coincidence, Mr. Premier," said Jakob, watching his host's face closely for any reaction. "Somebody must surely have given Comrade Liang a helping hand."

"It's important for personal understanding to exist between individuals from different countries." Chou smiled dryly again, his face showing no sign of surprise. "It can sometimes help promote understanding on broader political questions. . . ."

Jakob looked uncertainly at the Chinese premier, trying to decide what lay behind his oblique response. It seemed obvious that he either had prior knowledge of the meeting at the Temple of Heaven or was aware that Liang had been under surveillance. But he had given no indication of whether he had himself initiated the meeting or whether he knew of Chiao's part in it, and because he made no attempt to explain further, Jakob realized that he was unlikely to learn anything more. As he struggled to extract some meaning from what Chou had said, he suddenly remembered Liang's reference to Mei-ling and he decided he would be foolish to pass up the opportunity to find out something more about her plight.

"During the visits of our delegation to your factories and institutions, none of the officials who've addressed us have mentioned the Hundred Flowers campaign or its aftermath," said Jakob tentatively, searching even as he spoke to find a way of inquiring about Mei-ling. "You're probably aware that there's a great deal of interest in the subject in the West at present and many questions arise in my own mind . . ."

Jakob paused, noticing that Chou had become very still in his chair. There was a new alertness in his manner, and it was evident that he was now on his guard.

". . . Many of China's critics suspect a trap might have been deliberately set for intellectuals who are being punished in the 'antirightist' campaign," continued Jakob cautiously, "and like many others I'm curious to know if there's any truth in that."

"That's an erroneous assumption." Chou did not raise his voice but the firmness of his tone suggested his displeasure at the question. "Genuine attempts were made to invite constructive criticism in order to bring about greater national unity."

"But is it possible that some people might have been victimized unjustly —"

"To our great disappointment, many counterrevolutionary tendencies have emerged," interjected Chou, cutting Jakob off deliberately in midsentence. "The situation's still complicated. It's not appropriate to consider such questions here."

Chou's tone indicated unmistakably that he would countenance no further discussion of the topic, and he turned and signaled to his female aide, who immediately handed him a single sheet of paper. He glanced over its contents for a moment, then looked up at Jakob again.

"You were asked to come here today, Mr. Kellner, so that I could explain the amendments that have been made to your schedule. Yourself and one or two other chosen delegates are invited to inspect a new major hydroelectric project that's under construction in the northwest, by the Great Wall. It will produce the biggest reservoir in north China, provide us with a new power grid, and mark a great forward step in the nation's flood-control program. We shall also arrange for you to visit a new steel-making complex." Chou looked up from the paper and smiled deprecatingly. "In Hong Kong and other centers reporting on China, most writers concentrate on the negative aspects of life in the People's Republic. In *China's New Age* you reported fairly and without prejudice. To be precise, that's why an invitation was extended to you. You display a sympathetic understanding of our problems and that's why we're now offering you these new and exclusive reporting opportunities."

"Thank you, Mr. Premier," said Jakob. "Although I've long since given up missionary work, my interest in China and my sympathy for its people have never flagged. I'd be glad to visit the places you've mentioned."

Chou laid his briefing paper aside and his manner became less formal. "The last time we met, Mr. Kellner, you had just reached the end of a long journey. But I believe you've never published anything about your experiences on the Long March. Am I right?"

"Yes, that's correct," said Jakob guardedly.

"May I ask the reason for this?"

Jakob hesitated, taken by surprise. His instinct was to hedge, but seeing an opportunity to steer the conversation back in the direction he had tried to take earlier, he decided to be frank. "I've had many requests to write a detailed account, Mr. Premier," he said in a quiet tone. "But I've always declined."

"And why did you decline?" asked Chou.

Jakob looked pointedly at the female aide seated at his shoulder. "May I ask you, Mr. Premier, for the same guarantee of confidentiality that you requested earlier from me?"

Chou nodded and turned to the aide, motioning for her to cease writing and leave the room. When the door had closed behind her, he turned expectantly back to Jakob and waited.

"I've never written about that period out of respect for somebody who helped me."

The premier leaned forward in his chair. "Please explain further."

"My infant daughter was thought to have died during the march. But in fact she was cared for secretly by one of your people and survived. That same daughter, as you've probably realized, is accompanying me on this visit. I've never felt able to tell the whole story in detail in case it caused trouble for the brave woman who helped save her life."

"And who was she?"

"She was one of your close aides, Mr. Premier."

A faint look of surprise appeared on the face of the Chinese. "Which one?"

"Lu Mei-ling, the sister of Marshal Lu Chiao."

The premier's eyes widened for an instant; then his official face composed itself once more.

"I felt it best to be frank in my reply." In his turn Jakob leaned forward in his seat. "I hope nothing I've said will be detrimental to Comrade Lu Mei-ling."

"I appreciate your candor and will respect the confidence." Chou rose briskly to his feet, holding out his hand. "I trust the additional visits we've arranged will prove of value to you, Mr. Kellner. If you have any other reasonable requests we will do our best to satisfy them."

Jakob rose from his chair and shook the premier's hand. As he did so, a thought began to grow in his mind. "I do have one small request, Mr. Premier."

"Yes, what is it?"

Jakob drew in his breath slowly. "I'd very much like to see Comrade Lu Mei-ling. I understand she may have volunteered for reform through labor — but I'd still like to visit her if that's possible."

"That may not be feasible, Mr. Kellner." Chou smiled quickly. "But we shall look into your request and let you know. Good-bye."

The premier swung on his heel and walked quickly from the room. In the same moment, the cadre who had brought Jakob to the meeting entered silently through another door. Motioning for Jakob to follow, he led him out into the maze of marble corridors and a minute later they were descending the steps of the Great Hall to the Zil limousine in clear autumn sunlight.

Looking northward, Jakob became aware for the first time how completely the giant neo-Stalinist structure of colorless stone had come to dominate the heart of the capital. At the square's northern end the ancient Gate of Heavenly Peace with its crimson walls and shimmering golden tiles looked much smaller in comparison. Gazing out from the stands which flanked the gate on National Day, Jakob had been preoccupied by the vast crowds taking part in the celebrations but from the Great Hall's steps, the chief symbol of Peking's glorious past seemed dramatically shrunken and diminished. The monolith to modern Communism from which he had just emerged now dwarfed the Ming dynasty gate, robbing it of much of its former grandeur, and as the limousine moved off, awareness of the conflict between these symbols of past and present heightened the vague sense of perplexity which Jakob carried away from his surprise meeting with China's premier.

8

Jakob saw the towering mound of coal from the train long before he reached the loading yard of the mine, some ninety miles east of Peking. Rearing up like a black mountain above the surrounding flat countryside, it was the height of a twelve-story building. All around it, tiny scurrying figures were visible, toiling with baskets and bamboo shoulder poles like an army of worker ants. As the train drew nearer Jakob saw that narrow plank walks had been laid across the muddy yard around the coal stack and unending streams of workers were hobbling back and forth to a succession of trucks onto which they were emptying their baskets. All wore ragged cotton tunics and trousers which had once been blue but which were now soiled and blackened by the coal dust swirling constantly across the yard in the gusting autumn wind. Their faces and hands were black too, the shoes of many were in tatters, and some limped painfully along the boardwalks on bare, blackened feet.

As he took in the scene through the window of his carriage, Jakob slipped a hand into the inside pocket of his jacket to reassure himself that he had brought the letter which had been delivered to his hotel by messenger the previous morning. Four days had passed since his meeting with Chou En-lai and during that time he had heard nothing of his request, so he had been surprised to find on opening the letter that it contained authorization for him to visit Mei-ling "for personal reasons" at the Tangshan Number 3 Coal Yard the following day. Written above the signature of the coal yard's "Reform-through-Labor Warden," the letter instructed him to take the midday train from Peking and said he would be met at a small wayside station close to the Number 3 Coal Yard. But when he alighted from the train, the station was deserted, and after waiting for a quarter of an hour, he set out to walk.

A tall chain-link fence topped with barbed wire surrounded the yard. As he approached, Jakob could see that many of the coal carriers were frail figures who were bent almost double under the weight of their burdens. They stumbled frequently, sometimes falling, and Jakob realized with a shock that many of them were women. A sickening feeling began to grow inside him as he tried to scrutinize each distant carrier, searching vainly for some recognizable characteristic. But all wore caps pulled low over their faces and there was little to distinguish one sooty figure from another.

A loaded truck pulled away in a swirl of coal dust every two or three minutes, to be replaced by another from a long line of vehicles drawn up outside the yard gates, and a creaking automatic conveyor from the nearby mine was constantly dumping fresh coal on the heap so that the stock never diminished. Occasionally small avalanches of coal cascaded down its flanks, scattering the workers who were loading their baskets, and whenever this happened, supervisors, who stood by clutching long bamboo staves, yelled angry orders for the work to be speeded up again. If any of the workers fell, the supervisors manhandled them to their feet and pushed them back into the hurrying lines, ensuring that the tempo of the loading was never broken.

On the far side of the yard beyond the coal heap Jakob could see rows of huts that looked like barracks. A long wooden administration building had been erected inside the gates through which the loaded trucks were entering and leaving, and when he reached the entrance, Jakob showed his letter of authority to one of the two uniformed People's Liberation Army soldiers who barred his way. After eyeing him with great suspicion, the soldier led him to a shabby office at one end of the administration building and conducted him into the presence of a middle-aged cadre with a pinched, sour face who was seated behind a metal desk. The cadre read his letter slowly, casting puzzled glances at Jakob's polished leather shoes, his well-cut double-breasted suit of navy blue worsted, and the gabardine trench coat which he carried neatly folded over one arm. Then abruptly he rose and hurried from the room without any explanation, leaving Jakob standing uncertainly in the empty office.

For the next half hour Jakob waited on tenterhooks while the cadre made a succession of audible telephone calls to Peking from the adjoining office. He quoted the letter repeatedly in a querulous voice and from the exchanges Jakob eventually gathered that the coal yard's senior labor warden had been taken ill, leaving a cadre who was an inexperienced deputy in charge. But when at last the cadre returned to the office, he was followed by two soldiers carrying a pair of collapsible metal chairs, and they led him through a long corridor to a small room that contained only a rough wooden trestle table. After positioning the chairs at either end of the table and motioning for Jakob to seat himself on one of them, the soldiers went out, closing the door behind them.

As ten more minutes ticked by in the cheerless room, Jakob experienced a growing sense of desolation. The floor beneath his feet was scuffed wooden boards, the paint on the bare walls was faded and discolored, and through the grimy, uncurtained window he could see the anonymous lines of coal carriers still scurrying ceaselessly back and forth across the yard. He began to question in his own mind the wisdom of the request he had made, and when he heard the sound of footsteps coming nearer along the corridor, he watched for the door to open with a growing feeling of agitation.

"This meeting has been specially arranged on the orders of a high official in Peking," said the harsh voice of the deputy warden on the other side of the door. "You will be allowed fifteen minutes with the foreign visitor — and that is all."

Jakob found himself holding his breath as the door swung back on its hinges. At first he could see only the deputy warden; then a slighter figure appeared beside him and took a hesitant step into the room. For a moment or two Jakob stared uncomprehendingly. The newcomer was dressed in the same kind of soiled clothes as the workers in the yard outside: cap, baggy trousers, and jacket of dark blue cotton. No hair was visible under the cap that was pulled low over the newcomer's face, and only when the eyes beneath it widened suddenly with the shock of recognition did Jakob realize he was looking into the face of a woman — and that the woman was Mei-ling.

Jakob rose awkwardly to his feet, a turmoil of old and new emotions churning inside him. Mei-ling was standing as though frozen at the far end of the table and for a few moments the deputy warden continued to watch them from the corridor. Then he closed the door with a bang and they were left alone. Unable to summon any words, Jakob watched Mei-ling sink wearily onto the chair. With a tired gesture she tugged off her cap and dropped it on the table, revealing short-cropped hair, and he noticed that her hands, although recently washed, were ingrained with coal grime.

"Mei-ling, I'm sorry if my visit has come as a shock to you," said Jakob, speaking Chinese in an unsteady voice. "I just didn't realize what it would be like . . ."

His voice tailed off lamely, but Mei-ling neither replied nor looked up. She had fixed her eyes on the grimy cap lying before her and Jakob was seized by a terrible sense of inadequacy. Cursing himself inwardly for failing to anticipate how shaming Mei-ling might find such a meeting, he searched his mind desperately for consoling words.

"I've just returned to China for the first time since 1935," he said at last in an apologetic tone. "Premier Chou called me in to see him unexpectedly. On an impulse I asked for special permission to visit you . . . I suppose I hardly expected my request to be granted. . . ."

She raised her head to look directly at him and Jakob felt his heart lurch within him. Her expression was puzzled and surprised but despite her shabby clothes and the grime on her skin, to his astonishment the essence of her beauty was still visible in her wide eyes. Although she was obviously physically wearied, the high-cheekboned face that had first entranced him on board the *Tomeko Maru* still seemed hauntingly lovely to him, and in that instant he could scarcely believe that more than twenty years had passed since their last meeting.

"How did you know where I was, Jakob?" she asked haltingly.

"I met Liang, my old cookboy," said Jakob, relieved that he had broken the awful dam of silence that had stood between them. "Your brother, Chiao, had arranged it. It was Liang who told me what you were doing."

In spite of the humiliating circumstances, Mei-ling retained a quiet, dignified air which enhanced her natural beauty and all Jakob's past feelings for her welled up again suddenly with great force. A suffocating sensation constricted his chest and in that instant he realized just how thoroughly he had suppressed all emotion in himself during the intervening years. As the seconds ticked by he ached to tell her what he was feeling but the surroundings daunted him.

"Why are you here, Mei-ling?" he asked instead. "What have you done wrong?"

Through the window behind Jakob, Mei-ling watched one of the coal trucks revving across the yard in a swirl of black dust. The light in her eyes seemed to intensify as though she felt some inner pain, and he could see that answering the question was difficult for her.

"For the future of our country it's important that educated people should learn for themselves what hard physical labor is like," she said distantly. "Perhaps my crime was to forget that."

She continued to gaze out through the window and Jakob was unable to decide whether she truly believed what she was saying or was merely repeating what Party activists would expect of her. "Are all the people loading coal here from backgrounds like yours?" he asked quietly.

"Many of them are teachers, scientists, and doctors. Some are still students. For two thousand years in China people like us have believed in the Confucian concept that 'he who works with his mind rules and he who works with his hands is ruled.' It's vital that we change that."

"Did you have to come here, Mei-ling?" asked Jakob in an undertone, leaning forward on the table. "Liang said he thought you might have volunteered."

"My writing hasn't always given sufficient prominence to working people. It's up to me to set an example. Working here is helping me understand how they live. It was right for me to come."

She spoke again in the same distant voice, still avoiding Jakob's eyes, and he felt a new wave of compassion surge through him. He knew from his own conversations with refugees who escaped to Hong Kong that Communist officials often persuaded intellectuals to "volunteer" for reeducation through labor. But behind such persuasion lay the unspoken threat of force if they refused and Jakob thought he detected in Mei-ling's evasion a hint of the confusion and sense of indignity that this ambivalence created. He realized that she might not truly know whether she was there voluntarily or not, and because of this, her efforts to justify and explain her shaming circumstances seemed unbearably tragic. Determined suddenly, come what might, to break down the barriers which time had raised between them, he pulled out his wallet and extracted a photograph of Abigail taken recently in Hong Kong. Without explanation he rose and placed it on the table in front of Mei-ling and watched her study it with a mystified expression.

"That's my daughter, Abigail. She's twenty-three now."

Mei-ling looked up from the photograph, comprehension dawning in her eyes. Gradually her expression became pensive and Jakob felt a sense of relief that he had succeeded in distracting her thoughts from her present discomfort.

"Although she's never met you, she's very grateful for what you did for her," he added quietly, sitting down again. "She's come to Peking with me. So she's seeing China through grown-up eyes for the first time."

Mei-ling picked up the photograph and looked at it once more. "She's become a beautiful young woman," she murmured.

"Thanks to you."

Mei-ling raised her head from the photograph and for a long moment they looked directly into one another's eyes. Despite the bleakness of their surroundings, Jakob was profoundly moved, as he had always been, by something indefinable in the depths of her gaze. He remembered again the moment of their first meeting on the deck of the *Tomeko Maru*, the sight of her riding the mule down the luminous hillside in Kwangsi, and the intense pain of their final parting on that brilliant morning among the loess hills of Kansu. On all those occasions he had felt himself strongly drawn to her and he again experienced the same sensation with astonishing force.

"Have you ever remarried, Jakob?" asked Mei-ling softly, still looking at him.

"No, I haven't . . ." Jakob hesitated, taken aback by the directness of her question. "When we parted in Kansu, I wanted to marry you, Mei-ling, you know that. Since then I've never felt the same way about anybody else. . . ."

Mei-ling dropped her eyes and toyed again with the cap on the table.

"I suppose you've married, haven't you?" asked Jakob. "And had children."

"I married in Yenan in 1938. My husband was killed in the fighting against Japan. We had a daughter but she didn't live very long."

"And you haven't married again?"

She shook her head. "No."

Jakob absorbed the news in silence, mentally comparing what she had just said with the enigmatic closing paragraph of the article in the dog-eared Long March booklet. There seemed to be no obvious link but he saw that his questions had created a sudden new tension in Mei-ling.

"I recently came across something you wrote some years ago," he said slowly. "I was puzzled by your meaning . . . and that was one of the reasons I wanted so much to see you again."

Mei-ling lifted her head and looked at him again; there was a new wariness in her expression and Jakob felt himself become tense.

"You said that after much suffering and privation during the arduous final months of the Long March, your own body 'sustained and produced new life' — I think those were the words you used — and I couldn't help wondering what you meant. . . ."

Mei-ling was staring fixedly over Jakob's shoulder but when he turned to follow her gaze, he saw nothing unusual. Outside the work of loading the coal was going on at the same frantic pace and the automatic conveyor was still replenishing the giant coal stack without letup. When Jakob turned around again, Mei-ling was twisting the filthy cap in her hands and her face had lost its look of composure. She seemed suddenly saddened but she remained tight-lipped, saying nothing.

"I'm probably being very foolish," continued Jakob gently, "but

I've never forgotten those hours we shared in the Great Snow Mountains. They were the most precious moments of my life. . . . I felt sure at the time they were very important to you too. . . ."

"Yes, they were!" Mei-ling spoke with great vehemence as though an emotional dam had suddenly broken inside her. She was staring at him with a kind of defiant expression, but to his dismay tears started in her eyes. "I swore to myself that you would never know! But now that you're sitting here asking me . . . it's impossible . . ."

Jakob waited in an agony of suspense as she struggled to regain her self-control. He felt an overwhelming desire to take her in his arms and comfort her but the long trestle planks stretched forbiddingly between them.

"Your suspicions are correct, Jakob," she said at last in a fierce whisper. "I had another baby, a son . . . your son."

Confirmation of what he had hardly dared admit to himself as a possibility reduced Jakob to a stunned silence. At the other end of the table Mei-ling closed her eyes and covered her face with her hands. It was some time before Jakob found his voice and when he did, he had difficulty controlling it. "What's happened to him, Mei-ling? He must be quite grown up now."

"He's a graduate student at Pei-Ta University, in Peking," said Mei-ling without opening her eyes. "He's been a brilliant student. He's already a member of the Party and he has a bright future."

"Hasn't he suffered in any way?" asked Jakob in a surprised voice.

"He's been fortunate. He's completely Chinese in appearance — and Kao has always assumed that my dead husband was his father."

"His name is Kao?"

Mei-ling nodded. "Yes, Chen Kao."

"My delegation is to visit Pei-Ta before we leave," said Jakob distractedly. "It's possible I might run into him —"

"You must reveal nothing!" Mei-ling's eyes opened wide with alarm. "Nobody knows the truth but you and I. You must not speak of what you know — the truth could destroy him."

"I'd never wish to do anything to hurt him," said Jakob quickly. "But does nobody else know the truth?"

"Premier Chou must know he wasn't my husband's son. Because of my work for him in the past, the premier has always taken a sympathetic interest in Kao. He helped him get a good education. I think he imagines that his father was the German Comintern adviser — I don't know. I've never confided in him."

"And your brother, Chiao, does he know?"

She shrugged and shook her head uncertainly. "Chiao perhaps has the same suspicion . . ."

From the corridor outside the sound of approaching footsteps became audible, and glancing at his wristwatch, Jakob saw that fifteen minutes had flown by. A new feeling of desperation seized him and he half rose from his seat. "Can we try to keep in touch after I return to Hong Kong, Mei-ling?" he asked hastily in an undertone. "I could find some safe way of writing . . ."

Mei-ling looked distressed but she shook her head emphatically as she stood up. "There's nothing to be gained after all this time." She thrust the photograph of Abigail toward him along the table and turned to face the door as it opened.

The deputy warden looked suspiciously from one to the other, then motioned silently with his head for Mei-ling to leave. The soldier who had accompanied the warden fell into step behind her and Jakob stood listening to the soft scuff of their retreating footsteps with a sinking heart. When he left the administrative building a few minutes later he found he could no longer bear to look at the activity in the yard. The coal dust blowing in the wind stung his eyes, and turning sadly out of the gate, he hurried to the railway station without a backward glance.

9

Applauding groups of students waving big red silk flags greeted the peace delegation as it walked down a willow-fringed path toward the assembly hall of Pei-Ta University two days later. Over loudspeakers, the stirring strains of "The Internationale" were ringing out loudly across the campus and from their place at the rear of the moving group, Jakob and Abigail could see that a red and gold banner bearing the image of a white dove of peace had been hung above the entrance. In front of the steps, smiling Chinese girls dressed in blue denim hurried forward from among the welcoming committee of lecturers, workers, and students to thrust bouquets of red and white carnations into the arms of the delegation leaders. Inside the hall, where a big audience of several hundred students was already gathered, the whole delegation was led, amid loud applause, to a raised platform on which a lectern had been set up.

The delegates applauded the audience in response, and Jakob and Abigail joined in as they took their seats at one end of the back row. Scanning the sea of young Chinese faces that filled the hall before him, Jakob felt the tension that had been growing in him all morning increase. The delegation had toured laboratories and lecture rooms, meeting students at every turn, and had inspected the dormitory blocks of both male and female undergraduates. In the principal's office they had been given tea and shown models and plans for extensions of the university buildings while the delegation's host, the chairman of the Chinese Committee for World Peace, had explained the government's future educational aims. But all the time Jakob had found himself surreptitiously scrutinizing the face of every young male student they encountered, searching for something his mind had not defined but which he was sure he would recognize on sight. In one of the spartan dormitories a quiet-spoken student with a pale complexion had unaccountably caught his attention and he had lingered after Abigail and the other delegates had moved on in order to ask the youth his name. The young man was at first mystified, then suspicious that a foreign stranger should want to identify him. But on being pressed he had reluctantly given his name — which had proved to be of no significance — and Jakob had been forced to retreat, apologizing in embarrassment.

The incident had left him feeling more agitated than ever and by the time the delegation was ensconced on the assembly hall platform, he was making a conscious effort to conceal his unease from Abigail. It seemed certain that one of the students in the crowded body before his eyes must be the total stranger who, in the light of Mei-ling's startling revelation, was also his son. But he found it almost unbearably tantalizing to realize that, despite this near-certainty, he would probably be unable to distinguish him from the hundreds of other young men.

Because of this, he scarcely heard the peace committee chairman introduce China's minister of education. While the minister outlined the long-term objectives for China's new socialist educational system, Jakob began trying to inspect each male face in the audience in turn, moving his gaze slowly and carefully along one row after another.

But the effort of concentration required and the mounting inner tension he felt began to make his head ache, and when distant faces in the back half of the hall became little more than a blur, he reluctantly gave up and closed his eyes to concentrate more closely on the minister's address. Frequent applause interrupted the speech and for a minute or two Jakob listened intently. But then he felt the light touch of a hand on his arm and he opened his eyes to find that a uniformed People's Liberation Army soldier had come quietly up the platform steps behind him.

"Would you be kind enough to come with me for just a few minutes, Mr. Kellner," said the young soldier, whispering discreetly in Jakob's ear during a renewed burst of clapping. "Somebody wishes to speak to you urgently about an important personal matter."

Waiting only for the next round of applause, Jakob explained to Abigail that he would return soon, then moved unobtrusively off the platform. He followed the quick-striding soldier through nearby double doors into a long corridor and along a succession of other corridors to a rear fire exit. After looking back the way they had come to ensure he was not observed, the soldier unlocked the exit and pulled it open to reveal a dun-colored military Warszawa parked outside in an enclosed yard. The rear door of the Polish-built saloon stood open and the soldier motioned Jakob quickly into the shadowy, green-curtained interior, where an older Chinese wearing the uniform of a marshal of the People's Liberation Army was already seated.

"Thank you for coming so promptly, Mr. Kellner," said Lu Chiao quietly in Chinese, extending his hand. "You must be back on the platform before the speeches end, so we can't afford to waste any time on pleasantries."

While an astonished Jakob was shaking Chiao's hand, the young soldier relocked the fire exit, climbed behind the steering wheel, and started the Warszawa's engine. Driving slowly, he pulled out onto the deserted campus, and in the submarine gloom of the curtained rear seat, which gave them complete privacy, Chiao smiled apologetically. "Please forgive the secrecy, Mr. Kellner. I assure you it's necessary. Although those people who sent your invitation aren't aware of it, I was responsible for bringing you back to China."

"Why?" asked Jakob in a puzzled voice. "Was it just to give me the privilege of some exclusive economic sight-seeing?"

"No," replied Chiao slowly. "But that's a very important part of it. When you hear the whole story, you'll almost certainly be offended. I apologize in advance for that. But I hope you'll understand when I explain the reason for my actions."

Chiao removed his marshal's cap and placed it on the seat between them. In the half-light Jakob could see that his hair was now turning gray at the temples but his eyes were bright and his tunic was tailored to a body that still looked lean and hard in early middle age. From the alertness of his speech and manner, it was clear that the shrewd, forceful intelligence of his youth remained undiminished.

"Is your motive connected with the Hundred Flowers movement?" asked Jakob, studying Chiao's face closely.

"Everything in China at present is connected with the Hundred Flowers movement," said Chiao grimly. "I haven't the time nor the wish to explain fully. I've no desire to betray state secrets because this is a personal matter. . . . But there's no harm in telling you that the Party leadership is far from united on these things. Divisions are growing — hundreds of thousands of intellectuals are being sent to reform through labor. But not everybody agrees with the ferocity of the antirightist campaign."

Jakob stared hard at Chiao. "What do you mean, a personal matter? Does this involve your sister, Mei-ling, in some way?"

"Yes. Once she helped you. She saved the daughter you've just brought to Peking. Now she needs help."

"I'll do anything I can, of course — but can't you help her yourself?"

Chiao's eyes glittered with suppressed anger. "Personal loyalties are highly complex in the Chinese Communist Party, Mr. Kellner. Too complex to explain. But when passions for a new campaign are running high, it's possible even for high-ranking leaders to destroy themselves by speaking out critically at the wrong moment."

Through the windshield of the Warszawa, Jakob noticed that they were repeatedly cruising the same tree-lined streets near the university campus without attracting any attention. In the curtained rear compartment of the car, which was separated from the driver by a thick glass partition, they were perfectly cocooned from all prying eyes and ears, and Jakob realized Chiao had planned the meeting with the same thoroughness he had applied to all aspects of his visit to China.

"I don't understand what it is you want me to do," said Jakob slowly. "Please be more specific."

"You've seen my sister. Her health will break if she has to endure such conditions for very long. More important, when she returns to normal life her record must be expunged, she must be officially rehabilitated."

"But how can I influence such things?" queried Jakob.

"You have power you're not aware of," said Chiao in an undertone. "What you write and publish about your visit is more important than you think. What you haven't realized is that your experience in China and your background make your voice unique. Your publications are read with great interest by our Communist allies and others abroad with whom we need to finalize important trade and aid agreements. They see you as a valuable independent guide to what's happening in China. Also, for internal Party reasons, certain sections of the leadership need to show that they can project at least one favorable international impression at a time when almost all the world's press is unfavorably disposed toward us."

"You're suggesting I'm in a position to make demands about Mei-ling in return for writing a positive account of my visit," said Jakob incredulously.

Chiao nodded quickly. "At this delicate moment, yes."

"And you've contrived all this from beginning to end," said Jakob, shaking his head in disbelief. "You suggested in somebody's ear that I be invited back to write something to counteract the bad international press you've been getting — then you arranged for Liang to tell me that your sister had gone to a labor camp to set the ball rolling."

"I've already apologized, Mr. Kellner," said Chiao. "But my sister is very dear to me — and I'm not suggesting you write something dishonest, something that you don't believe in. You need only make a request at the highest level — to the premier himself — for Mei-ling to be assisted in the way I've suggested. Make the writing of your usual fair analysis conditional on her release. The premier knows Mei-ling helped save your daughter — it will be natural for you to make a plea on her behalf. If necessary you could hint that you would write instead about the labor camps with firsthand knowledge if the request is not met. . . ."

Jakob felt a momentary anger well up in him as the full extent of Chiao's chicanery became clear. "So it was you who obtained the authorization for my visit to Tangshan? I never expected to be allowed to go."

Chiao nodded. "I anticipated that once you knew of my sister's plight, you might ask to see her for reasons of past gratitude. But your request to Premier Chou to visit her would never have been granted in the normal course of events. I saw to it that contradictory instructions were issued at a lower level. In the confusion the coal yard labor warden himself sent the authorization direct to you, imagining that was his duty. I expect you found he was absent when you arrived — that was what I advised." Chiao paused, subjecting Jakob to a searching scrutiny. "I think it's true to say, Mr. Kellner, that most things you write reflect in some way the attachment to China you developed as a young missionary — and this never seems to have left you. I always kept this in mind when making my plans and didn't feel I was going against your true interests."

"It won't be difficult for Premier Chou to recognize your hand in all this," said Jakob. "Won't that be dangerous for you?"

"Perhaps." Chiao looked steadily at him. "But that's a risk I had to be prepared to take. I hope when all's said and done, the premier will be human enough to understand."

Despite his initial feeling of anger, Jakob realized that in fact he bore Chiao no real grudge. After the emotional trauma of his coal-yard visit he was glad and relieved to have the chance to try to help Mei-ling. The prospect of taking some decisive action again after years as a neutral bystander also fired an unexpected feeling of excitement inside him. "In spite of all you've told me, I'm glad I came back to China," said Jakob. "I've never lost my affection for this country and its people."

"Then you'll do all you can to help Mei-ling?"

"Of course."

"Thank you," said Chiao, offering Jakob his hand again. "Perhaps our meeting on that Japanese ship all those years ago was lucky for us all."

Chiao pulled one of the curtains aside to look out of the window, then rapped out instructions for the driver to return Jakob at once to the assembly hall. The Warszawa immediately accelerated; two minutes later it pulled up outside the same fire exit in the enclosed yard and the soldier helped Jakob regain entry to the building unnoticed. When he reached the assembly hall, the education minister was winding up his address, but Jakob climbed quickly onto the platform and resumed his seat in the back row in time to join in the final, prolonged swell of applause.

10

"Is everything all right?" whispered Abigail as the applause died away.

"Yes, perfectly," said Jakob without looking at her.

"Who wanted you, anybody special?"

"Just another acquaintance from the old days." Jakob deliberately gave his words a careless inflection and forced a smile. "He'd heard I was coming to the university . . . but he didn't have much time to spare."

One of the peace delegates from Albania had stood up and was launching into a ringing speech extolling socialist education as an essential stepping-stone to world peace. An interpreter at his side was rendering his address into Chinese at intervals, and loud acclamations began to greet every ritual condemnation of "Western imperialism."

"You're not worried about anything, are you?" asked Abigail in a concerned whisper. "You look a bit on edge."

"No, I'm fine," said Jakob hurriedly. "Just a little tired, perhaps."

Abigail settled down again to listen to an English translation of the Albanian delegate's speech through a pair of headphones, but she noticed that her father was paying little attention to what was being said. Whenever she turned to look at him, he was staring abstractedly into the audience, as he had done earlier, his mind apparently on other things. All morning he had seemed preoccupied, speaking in reply to her questions in little more than monosyllables, and once again she found herself struggling to subdue the all too familiar feeling that she had again been forced to take second place to other unspecified priorities in his life.

The disappointment she felt seemed doubly acute, since during the early days of the visit she had begun to believe that a much longed for intimacy was at last growing between them. Although reluctant at the outset to bring her to China, Jakob had seemed gradually to warm to the idea of her accompanying him to places that might hold painful memories. On arrival Abigail had quickly sensed the attraction that the vast, ancient country and its people held for him. Despite the all-pervasive presence of modern Communism, she found herself responding to the country's great, austere landscapes, where distant hilltop pagodas and temples often still formed enigmatic backdrops to the modern industrial plants they inspected daily. Communism had given a drab, uniform appearance to the population, but the individuals they met were energetic, engaging, and good-humored, and she was also intrigued to discover that China's imperial past, so much castigated by the nation's ideologues, remained an intangible source of pride and inspiration in the daily lives of the people.

During their official travels Jakob had delved frequently into his own memories of China to bring the past alive for her. Abigail had felt her fascination with the country grow almost daily in step with a new affection for her father, and his sudden confession at the Temple of Heaven of the unspoken agonies he had harbored for so many years had made her feel closer to him than ever before. As a result she had been at first surprised, then later baffled when he withdrew unaccountably into himself again after going off alone to visit a coal mine, which he told her was one of several extra excursions arranged specially for him by the premier's office. To her dismay, he had returned self-absorbed and uncommunicative, as if he were suddenly determined once more to keep her at arm's length, and all her efforts to reestablish their earlier rapport had come to naught.

"You weren't arranging more special excursions just now, were you?" asked Abigail with a hint of sarcasm as the Albanian delegate ended his speech. "You're not planning to go off on your own again?"

"No, of course not." Jakob was still scanning the audience and because of his distraction he failed to register her sarcasm. "We're leaving tomorrow as planned."

When the Albanian delegate sat down, the peace committee chairman announced that the leader of the university's Joint Student Organizations would give the closing address, and Abigail watched a tall Chinese student wearing a faded tunic of gray cotton rise from the middle of the hall. He had a broad, handsome face and he held himself very straight, walking to the platform in a calm, self-confident manner. Abigail noticed that all the students in the hall were watching him expectantly and it was evident from their demeanor that he was a popular, respected figure among them.

"Comrade Chen Kao," continued the chairman as the student mounted the platform steps, "is a research graduate in his final year who has excelled in both his political studies and the organizational work of the student body. He has been admitted to the Communist

Party at an unusually early age in recognition of his hard work and unflagging application."

Enthusiastic applause from the students greeted Chen Kao's arrival on the platform and he placed a single sheet of paper on the lectern in front of him before launching confidently into his speech. "While striving for world peace we must never forget that class struggle won't die away on its own," he proclaimed in a clear, passionate voice. "Class struggle will continue to exist so long as capitalism and imperialism exist anywhere in the world. Here in China in recent months we've seen that the revolution in economic ownership has so far failed to consolidate the overall revolution. Therefore we must continue to wage a class struggle fiercely in our daily lives as our contribution to world peace."

The whole of the student assembly applauded warmly, and Abigail leaned toward Jakob. "Master Chen Kao seems to be a young firebrand, doesn't he?" she said quietly. "He's the first man on the platform today with a real orator's talent."

Jakob did not reply and Abigail saw that he was staring intently at the young speaker. Assuming that he was concentrating hard on the political content of the speech, she listened more carefully to the translation coming through her headphones.

"Bourgeois rightist intellectuals everywhere in China have shown that they are unwilling to submit to the will of the Communist Party," continued Chen Kao, making an eloquent gesture with one hand. "In their hearts these people have contempt for manual labor. Such people are being unmasked every day by the Hundred Flowers campaign — and they deserve to be because they are anti-Communist and antisocialist. They're determined to have a test of strength with the Party and because of this the antirightist struggle against them may go on for ten or even fifteen years!"

A new sustained burst of applause interrupted him and Chen Kao stood back from the lectern, waiting expressionlessly for it to subside. He turned his head to survey the audience and in that moment Jakob was able to see more clearly than before that Kao had inherited his regular features from his mother. His dark hair, parted at one side, was short and neatly brushed, and it was immediately evident that what Mei-ling had said was true: although his complexion was pale, it was not unusually so, and his appearance to an unknowing eye was completely Chinese. But as Jakob watched and listened, he became gradually aware of an eerie parallel between the passionate Marxist student revolutionary and himself as a young man. A mental image of himself dressed in a traditional long-gown, preaching the Gospel in Chinese in a remote walled town, flashed into his mind and he wondered whether he had used the same gestures that Kao was now employing in his impassioned oratory.

With part of his mind, Jakob had also become aware that all the Party and government cadres on the platform were sitting very still in their seats, listening intently to the student speaker. Because he was familiar with the Hundred Flowers rhetoric from his daily researches in Hong Kong, Jakob felt sure that Kao was saying nothing that had not already been stated officially on the Party's behalf in one form or another. But the force and boldness with which he was daring to speak out for himself was remarkable at a time when differences obviously existed among the Party leaders and public caution was a universal watchword. The students in the hall were clearly aware of this too and they continued to applaud Kao with great enthusiasm.

". . . Even within the Party, bourgeois individualist tendencies are not unknown," Kao continued, raising the tone of his voice to underline his meaning. "The antirightist struggle will therefore be a severe test for every Party member. It may take fifteen years for the working class to train its own professors and teachers, its own scientists, journalists, writers, and artists. And until this huge new army of proletarian intellectuals is created, it won't be possible to consolidate the revolutionary cause. . . ." Kao paused, looking slowly around the hall, preparing to give special emphasis to his closing words. "Most of the rightists have now been exposed and criticized and some have been isolated from the masses to help them change their thinking. But we must remain vigilant if the antirightist struggle is to serve peace at home and abroad. We must not relent for a moment. The struggle must be carried through to victory both on the political and ideological fronts — until all rightists have been well and truly defeated!"

Chen Kao picked up the copy of his speech and stepped quickly down from the platform. After a moment's hesitation the Party and government officials began clapping loudly. The audience followed suit and the noise of their applause filled the hall as Kao made his way briskly back to his seat. Jakob stared after him, unable to reconcile the conflicting emotions that the fiery, uncompromising address had aroused in him. He had come back to Peking, apprehensive that he might be haunted by uncomfortable reminders of his past, only to find a living image of his young self. But although Kao was obviously as bold and courageous as his father had once been, he had become a "missionary" for Communism, and that irony seemed almost physically painful to Jakob. At the same time, Kao's very existence reaffirmed the reality of his profound love for Mei-ling, which he had come to doubt and conceal even from himself over the past twenty-two years, and this realization brought with it a con-tradictory feeling of exhilaration.

The touch of Abigail's hand on his arm rescued Jakob from these whirling thoughts and he saw that the chairman of the peace com-mittee had closed the meeting and was preparing to lead the foreign delegates off the platform. Jakob motioned for Abigail to precede him and they followed the other delegates down the steps to renewed applause. As they approached the doorway Jakob saw that the uni-versity officials who had been their hosts had formed a line to say a formal farewell to the departing delegates. To his dismay he noticed that Kao had taken the last place at the end of the line as the rep-resentative of the students, and with Abigail moving ahead of him, Jakob grasped each proffered hand as though in a dream, his mind numbed by the prospect of having to shake his son's hand as a stranger. As he neared the end of the line, he became vaguely aware that Abigail was smiling warmly and exchanging animated words with Kao but he could not look directly at them. When at last his turn came, Jakob found his face had grown stiff with tension, and to his horror, he was unable to smile or utter any word at all. Their handclasp as a result was brief and perfunctory, and Kao merely nodded his head quickly in response before hurrying away to rejoin his friends, who were still seated in the body of the hall.

In the doorway, Jakob stopped and turned to look back. As he did so, Kao rose to his feet and smilingly lifted a clenched fist above his head to bid the delegation farewell. The next moment his voice, raised in song, rang out vibrantly and at once the rest of the students rose to their feet to join him.

> *"The East is red!*
> *The sun rises high in the sky!*
> *China has brought forth*
> *A Mao Tse-tung!"*

As he turned away, Jakob carried with him the image of his son's face, alight with fervor, leading students crowding all around him in a stirring rendering of their emotional patriotic anthem.

11

"Are you glad I came with you?"

Abigail deliberately stifled her feelings of disappointment and frustration and asked the question in a quiet, neutral voice as they watched the north China plain fall rapidly away beneath them.

"Yes, of course," replied Jakob in a surprised tone. "You don't regret coming, do you?"

"No, I'm very grateful." Abigail was careful to let no hint of complaint show in her reply. "It's meant an enormous amount to me."

The blue-and-white-liveried Ilyushin 18 airliner of the Civil Aviation Administration of China was banking and turning its nose south for Shanghai and Canton, and young Chinese stewardesses in red silk jackets and red hair ribbons were preparing to serve savories and small glasses of Shao Hsing wine. Jakob had taken the window seat and as the airliner climbed toward the clouds he stared down pensively at the ancient patchwork of fields below.

"All those factory visits probably weren't your cup of tea," he said apologetically. "But there was no way of avoiding them."

"It didn't matter. Meeting Hsiao Liang made up for everything else. Knowing he really exists helped put some firm foundations into what was just a shaky, empty space before."

Jakob took a sip from a glass of Shao Hsing he had just been given and looked quickly away out the window. He was suddenly aware that he had given little consideration to his daughter's thoughts and feelings for several days. As the plane took off he had been struggling to come to terms with the rush of events in which he had been caught up. Late the previous evening he had arranged for a sealed personal letter to be delivered to the prime minister's office as a matter of urgency, couching his request about Mei-ling in terms which were diplomatic and respectful but also unmistakably firm. Overnight he had slept badly and during bouts of wakefulness he had been assailed by doubts about whether he had been wise to intervene and even whether his request might harm her further. But shortly before he had boarded the plane, one of the peace committee cadres who had accompanied departing delegates to the airport had sought him out to pass on a discreet oral message "from the premier's personal assistant." He said with careful deliberation that Jakob's communication was "being dealt with positively" and although it was obvious that the cadre was merely passing on a message without any detailed knowledge of its meaning, Jakob had felt a great sense of relief flood through him.

The knowledge that he had been able to help Mei-ling had the effect of restoring some clarity of thought and as he watched the land recede far below, he began to appreciate that in the space of a few days, the visit had radically reshaped the perspectives of his life. For the previous eight years he had been a detached observer of China but now his deepest feelings were entangled in the web of political events which absorbed the vast, troubled nation. His interest, he saw, would never again be merely professional and academic; he felt a new sense of anxiety that China should thrive around Mei-ling, Kao, and Chiao.

Seeing Mei-ling again had also made him more aware than ever before of how lonely and empty his life had become. In the dingy squalor of the reform-through-labor coal yard, long-frozen feelings had returned with astonishing intensity, giving new significance to the drab years in between, and suddenly it seemed as if part of him had known instinctively all along that someday those fierce passions of the Long March would be vindicated. Mei-ling's rejection of any future contact between them had saddened him but a feeling of exhilaration nevertheless persisted: although circumspect in what she had said, it had been obvious that Mei-ling too still had a reverence for the love they had once shared. These reflections had focused his mind obsessively inward, and he realized that he had scarcely spoken to Abigail for several days. With this realization came a strong feeling of guilt and he shifted uncomfortably under his daughter's gaze.

"I'm very glad too that you confided in me at the Temple of Heaven," said Abigail quietly, determined to persist in an explanation of what was in her mind. "That helped in another way to strengthen those shaky foundations I was talking about. . . ."

"I don't know what made me say that." Jakob sipped his wine awkwardly. "But I'm glad if it's made you happy. . . ."

"I didn't say it had made me happy." Abigail hesitated, unsure how best to express thoughts which she knew would be distressing for them both. "It didn't make me happy, because I sense there's something else . . . something important that always stands between us. Maybe you'll never want to talk about it."

Jakob turned from the window, a startled look in his eyes. "What do you mean?"

"That's the trouble — I'm not sure what I do mean. And for a long time all this has made me very unhappy. But I want to tell you now that I've made up my mind not to let it bother me any longer. After coming to China with you, I'm resigned to it, at last. It makes me sad, but for my own good I realize it would be wiser to put it all behind me and concentrate on the future."

In Abigail's lovely young face Jakob saw a calm resolution that was clearly the result of careful reflection. She had the advantage of having considered her words while he was flustered and unprepared, but although he wanted more than ever to show her the love she craved, how could he explain to her what he could scarcely understand himself? How could he speak of the overwhelming passion for Mei-ling that had filled his dreams long before he asked Felicity to marry him? How could he explain that the guilt he felt about Felicity was inextricably linked with the love he had shared with Mei-ling so soon after her death? How could he give voice to the suspicion which had nagged at him over the years that he had never really loved Felicity but had married her out of a mistaken and overzealous sense of duty? Worst of all, how could he tell her of the momentous discovery made only days before that he had a son — a half brother to her — who had been born to Mei-ling? In bringing her to China he had hoped to find some way of confiding in her, some way of breaking the emotional barriers that had grown up between them. But now events seemed to have conspired to make an already painful task impossible. Through no fault of her own, Abigail had become a living reminder of his own past regrets and confusions.

". . . You've given me the chance to catch a glimpse of my own roots and I'm very grateful for that," Abigail was saying, her voice matter-of-fact. "But I think coming to China's given me something even more important."

"What's that?" asked Jakob warily.

"I'm not sure how to define it — but I think it started when I saw your own excitement at being back here after more than twenty years. I began to understand the spell that China had cast on you when you were my age. It's something about the landscape, the people, the tantalizing fragments of the imperial past still visible here and there. I'm not sure when it started to happen — perhaps it was at the Temple of Heaven. But somehow I began to fall under the same spell."

"But there've been so many changes in the China I knew," protested Jakob, feeling a faint sense of alarm begin to grow inside him without knowing why.

"The Communists have tried to throw a blanket over the past but in a way that makes it all the more intriguing to the outsider." Abigail straightened in her seat, becoming more animated. "And I was moved by the way austerity seems to inspire the people here to greater efforts. Those students we met seemed to have a great belief in the future. They're so obviously dedicated to something greater than themselves and their own selfish needs. That student who gave the final speech was outstanding. He just radiated zeal and optimism . . . in fact, all the students had an enviable sense of purpose. That's something I missed — and I think some of it has rubbed off on me."

"What do you mean?"

"I want to come back," said Abigail simply.

Jakob stared hard at her. "To do what?"

"Don't worry. I haven't caught the Communist bug. It's not the politics that attracts me."

"What is it, then?"

"I think it's simply the people."

Jakob took another sip of wine. Beyond the window ragged clouds were beginning to envelop the aircraft and he gazed downward until the last trace of land was obscured. Then he turned to look at his daughter again, his expression strained. "Are you sure of what you're saying?"

"Yes, my mind's made up," said Abigail in a calm voice. "I'm determined to come back and work in China."

PART SIX

The Marchers
Break Ranks

1966

The explosion of anti-Communist criticism set off by Mao Tse-tung's Hundred Flowers movement of 1957 marked a historic watershed in China's revolution. In effect, it undermined his authority for the first time since he took control of the Communist Party on the Long March. In the "rectification campaign" that followed, some four hundred thousand "rightists" are believed to have been seized, and many of them remained in labor camps for the next twenty years. From that moment onward Mao and the nation's intelligentsia became deeply distrustful of one another, and Mao abandoned his efforts to involve intellectuals in China's economic transformation. Instead he put his faith in the forces that in his view were pure and uncorrupted — first the nation's half a billion peasants and later school-age and student Red Guards.

By temperament Mao was impatient and romantic; bolstered by his experiences on the Long March, he believed fervently that sheer determination and the human will could conquer seemingly impossible obstacles. This led him to introduce the catastrophic Great Leap Forward the following year, in 1958. Under this new campaign, which had no precedent anywhere in the Communist world, China's entire rural population was reorganized very rapidly into massive People's Communes, where many lived under semimilitary conditions, sleeping in large barracks and eating in communal mess halls. Husbands and wives were often segregated, and their children were cared for in impersonal crèches. In contrast to the small agricultural cooperatives that previously em-

braced about a thousand people, each of the new People's Communes had a population of around thirty thousand. The communes were designed to catapult China toward utopian
Communism and put her on a par with Western industrialized nations within a decade or two by combining in each self-sufficient
community the functions of agriculture, rural industries, education, defense, and health. Similar commune structures were set
up in some cities, and peasants and town dwellers were exhorted
to work all day and through the night to produce iron and steel in
absurd miniature blast furnaces set up in their backyards. At first
a euphoria swept the country as the peasants and town workers
endeavored to respond to Mao's inspirational exhortations. "Let
the achievements of a single night surpass those of several millennia!" he urged them — but events proved, as they had in the
wake of the Hundred Flowers, that Mao had gravely miscalcu-
lated. The economy collapsed and grain production fell; three
successive years of calamitous drought and floods in 1959–61
brought terrible famine back to China and twenty million people
are believed to have died of starvation.

Mao refused to accept responsibility for his policy failures, saying rural cadres had failed to execute his orders correctly, but he
had launched both campaigns against the wishes of the more
pragmatic leaders around him, and in 1959, under pressure from
them, he stood down as head of state, to be replaced by Liu
Shao-chi, the Party vice chairman. Mao remained chairman of
the Communist Party, but as the deeply disillusioned nation recovered from the disastrous effects of his Great Leap, he faded
into the background, taking no further direct role in the day-to-
day running of the country. The Party's united leadership, which
had been strained by the Hundred Flowers, this time began to
fragment. One of the heroic generals of the Long March, Defense
Minister Peng Teh-huai, attacked Mao openly for his rashness,
but Mao managed to rally enough support to sack him, and for a
time the widening cracks among the leaders were papered over.
In the early years of the 1960s, President Liu, Party general secretary Teng Hsiao-ping, and Premier Chou En-lai put China back
on a more rational course; the communes were reduced to
smaller units, private plots were restored, and life became normal
again for most Chinese.

Unbeknown to them and the Party leadership, however, in a golden-roofed pavilion where he lived beside the Forbidden City, Mao was brooding behind the scenes. The outside world did not realize then how completely he had been eclipsed, but it later became clear that he had spent several years intriguing and plotting to regain control of China from President Liu, Teng Hsiao-ping, and the supporters who helped them pick up the pieces after the Great Leap Forward. His political differences with them in reality were slight; all shared the same fundamental beliefs, but Mao's desire to stamp his own personal image on a rapidly transformed nation had not diminished during his enforced idleness. On the contrary, as he aged and his health faltered, a paranoid apprehension of being reviled by his successors, as Stalin had been, haunted him. His legendary ability to lead and inspire deteriorated into a fearsome megalomania, and in late 1965 the first traces of what was to be Communist China's most cataclysmic political campaign began to appear in newspapers in the form of complex literary attacks on some writers and their works. They baffled ordinary Chinese and foreign China watchers alike for many months but were eventually seen to be aimed at prominent Party leaders responsible for governing Peking.

In the summer of 1966 Mao reemerged suddenly and spectacularly from obscurity to plunge into the Yangtze River and apparently swim several miles downstream with the fast-flowing current. Propaganda photographs of this surprise feat were circulated to the world's press from Peking, and much later it was discovered that Mao had already laid meticulous plans in secret. He had quietly gained military control of the capital through his loyal henchman Marshal Lin Piao, the replacement defense minister, and he had used this military strength to take charge of the all-important Party propaganda machine and the national mass media. With his new "guerrilla base" at China's heart secure, Mao developed a unique new force of Red Guards with which to launch a nationwide assault on the majority of Party cadres loyal to men he saw as his deadly enemies. To help him organize this force of radical students, he formed his own Cultural Revolution Group of second-rank cadres, in the same way that China's emperors of old had set up inner councils to intrigue against their mandarins. His wife, Chiang Ch'ing, was prominent among them,

and in August 1966, Mao called a plenary meeting of the Communist Party's Central Committee in the intimidating presence of
a mass of Red Guards to give a veneer of Party legitimacy to his
plans to "change the mental outlook of society" and "overthrow
people in authority taking the capitalist road." It was the first
Central Committee plenum since 1962, and armed troops pa-
trolled the aisles inside the hall to underline the military stranglehold Mao and his supporters had achieved in Peking.

A few days later the mysterious movement, tantalizingly named
the Great Proletarian Cultural Revolution, burst into the open. A
million-strong army of high school and university students,
dressed in khaki uniforms, appeared out of nowhere, marching
joyfully in step past the Gate of Heavenly Peace, in the center of
Peking. They carried little red booklets of quotations from Mao's
writings and lifted them in salute toward the balcony of the gate,
where a corpulent, seventy-three-year-old Mao Tse-tung, dressed
for the first time in many years in the olive green uniform of the
People's Liberation Army, stood waving and smiling benignly.
Wearing crimson arm bands labeled with the characters *Hung
Wei Ping* — "Red Guard" — similar throngs of youths flocked to
the capital from every province in China's vast hinterland. After
traveling free on trains and buses to march in a dozen review parades, these multitudes broke up into jeering, anarchistic mobs
that ran amok in all the major cities of China, screaming a single
quotation from Mao's writings: "Rebellion is justified!" They
seized private citizens and Communist Party officials and paraded
them through the streets, forcing them to wear tall dunce caps
and signs that condemned them as "anti-Party ghosts and monsters"; they yelled slogans vowing to destroy the Four Olds — old
customs, old culture, old habits, and old ideas; and handwritten
wall posters, which would become emblems of the Cultural Revolution, began to appear in every urban street, railing against
"the black gang of capitalist roaders" who allegedly opposed
Mao Tse-tung. These were the opening shots in a furious internal
revolution that would smash the twenty-million-member Communist Party, disable the government, and drag the whole of China
into what Mao's successors would eventually term "ten calamitous years." Sympathetic outsiders at first saw these early events
as Mao's greatest and most noble attempt to transform human nature

on a grand scale; others less favorably disposed viewed it more pragmatically as an unusually complex Communist power struggle. But whatever they thought of it, the Cultural Revolution intrigued people of all political persuasions, and in the late summer of 1966 the world watched it unfold daily with bewildered fascination.

1

Drifting with the dense, excited Chinese crowds through People's Square in the heart of Shanghai, Abigail Kellner craned her neck constantly and sometimes stood on tiptoe to scan above the heads of the people pressing around her. The thud of drums and the discordant clash of cymbals and gongs filled the hot August night, and in the fading light the tall red flags and giant colored portraits of Mao Tse-tung borne by countless marching groups of Red Guards lent a dramatic, theatrical atmosphere to the center of China's greatest industrial city. All the Red Guards wore crimson cotton *Hung Wei Ping* arm bands and carried little red plastic-covered books of quotations from Mao's writings, which they flourished exultantly above their heads. Each marching column was followed by a small open truck or platformed pedicab carrying a noisy percussion group, but the Red Guards beating the drums and gongs always allowed the sound of their instruments to die away while slogans were being chanted. All the demonstrators, Abigail noticed, took their cues from student supervisors, who strode along the flanks of the marchers, consulting sheets of paper in their hands. Everybody shouted dutiful, identical versions of the same slogans, which appeared to have been written out for them by a higher authority, and none varied the wording or the order in which the chants were delivered.

"*Defend Chairman Mao!*" yelled the cheerleaders.

"Defend Chairman Mao!" chorused the marching groups.

"*We will defend Chairman Mao with our lives!*" shouted the leaders.

"We will defend Chairman Mao with our lives!" echoed the marchers.

"*Drag down all anti-Party ghosts and monsters!*" screamed the leaders.

"Drag down all anti-Party ghosts and monsters!" roared their followers in response.

In side streets through which she had walked on the way to People's Square, Abigail had passed parked trucks piled high with Four Olds booty ransacked from nearby homes. Bolts of brocade, lacquered screens, bronze incense burners, statues, and clothing were jumbled together on the trucks or piled in scattered heaps on the pavements; big-character wall posters pasted on the houses by Red Guards denounced their occupants as "black elements." Above some courtyard walls spirals of smoke were visible, rising from bonfires of books, and in the windows of craft shops, emptied of all goods, identical portraits of Mao Tse-tung had been hung, giving the streets an eerie, uniform appearance. In the square itself, nonstop revolutionary songs with titles like "Rebellion Is Justified!" and "Mao Tse-tung's Thought Glitters with Golden Light!" blared from street-corner loudspeakers, adding to the din. Other Red Guards, standing on temporary platforms set up around the square, yelled raucous demands for the city's population to "join in the Great Proletarian Cultural Revolution."

At one platform Abigail saw a group of male Red Guards lifting girls bodily from the crowd to slash off their braids with garden shears. Others were ripping open the tight-legged Western trousers worn by girls and male youths and tugging off their pointed shoes. Most of the girls screamed and wept, protesting that they were "workers," not "class enemies," but the jeering Red Guards ignored their protests, flinging their torn Western-style garments after them as they scurried back into the crowds.

"Why do you copy the bourgeois Westerners?" roared one Red Guard through a bullhorn. "Why wear tapered trousers and pointed shoes? The Great Proletarian Cultural Revolution has been launched to liberate you from the Four Olds — old bourgeois habits and customs, old bourgeois culture, and old ways of thought!"

Abigail turned her back on the speaker and moved on without haste, taking care not to draw undue attention to herself. Having seen Red Guards begin attacking Chinese people who wore Western clothes the previous day, she had deliberately dressed in a pair of dark blue baggy cotton slacks, a loose jacket-blouse, and a cone-shaped local sun hat of rice straw. Ever since coming to Shanghai to teach at the city's Foreign Languages Institute five years earlier, she had been in the habit of wearing her blond hair in a neat chignon in public, and beneath the sun hat it was scarcely visible. While she knew that she could not hope to disguise her pale, foreign skin under close scrutiny, her choice of clothes, she knew from experience, would spare her the discomfort of constant stares among Chinese crowds and make her generally less conspicuous.

In the week that had elapsed since Mao reviewed the first parade of a million Red Guards in Peking, many Red Guard groups had sprung into existence in Shanghai and they were taking to the streets daily in increasing numbers. As a result Abigail had spent more and more time each day walking in the city, trying to understand what was happening. She had mastered written and spoken Chinese during a three-year course at London University before coming to live and work in Shanghai, but the sudden proliferation of slogans and wall posters plastered on public buildings around the city provided a fascinating new challenge to her knowledge of the language. During her stay in Shanghai she had discovered, like many outsiders before her, that much of China's internal life remained tantalizingly inaccessible to foreign eyes, and the sudden visible upsurge of political activity hour by hour on the streets was so rare and compelling that she had given little thought to any personal danger she might be facing.

When she thought about it at all, she had comforted herself with the reflection that as foreign residents she and her fellow teachers at the institute stood outside the conflict, whatever its real basis might be. Furthermore, although the Red Guard groups were haranguing and molesting Chinese passersby, there seemed to be a strong suggestion of theatricality in everything they were doing. She recognized the traditional Chinese liking for powerful symbolism in the vast red flags and colored portraits of Mao carried by the marching Red Guards, and from the whispered comments of ordinary working Chinese that she had overheard in the crowds around her, she knew that she was not alone in wondering whether the scenes of youthful rebelliousness were anything more than unusually elaborate propaganda exercises.

This impression had been heightened by the fact that the Red Guards' first acts had been to wrench down old street names and replace them with bizarre new signboards. The previous day Abigail had watched a cheering crowd of middle-school Red Guards replace the signs for the Bund, the famous avenue running along the Shanghai waterfront, with nameplates reading Revolutionary Boulevard.

Bubbling Well Road had been renamed August First Street to com-memorate the anniversary of the founding of the Red Army, and the streets outside the Soviet and British consulates had become Antirevisionist Street and Anti-imperialist Street. Normally officious Public Security Bureau policemen had added to the air of unreality by standing quietly aside, watching the Red Guard activity without making any attempt to intervene; many even smiled their approval, ostentatiously respecting the Central Committee's directives for the conduct of the Great Proletarian Cultural Revolution that had been published in the *People's Daily* under red-banner headlines after the Party's plenary meeting in Peking. Abigail had heard some Red Guards arguing loudly with the police on street corners that first day, demanding that the traffic lights be changed so that traffic could go on the revolutionary color, red, and stop on green. Because no agreement could be reached, the Red Guards had introduced an element of farce by switching off the lights altogether, and ever since, the traffic flow throughout the city had become erratic and confused.

Each evening more and more of Shanghai's mystified workers, who seemingly had nothing to fear from the Cultural Revolution, had come out onto the streets. With their families they were content to watch the strange antics of the chanting youth groups and on this particular evening Abigail realized that a greater tide of humanity than ever was swamping the city center. When she reached the north side of the square she saw that one militant group of about a hundred Red Guards was adding to the chaos by boarding buses to distribute pamphlets forcibly. Some of the overexcited youths were trying to eject passengers whose clothes offended the Four Olds rules, and scuffles and fistfights began to break out around the halted vehicles.

As she watched, a line of commandeered trucks heavily laden with confiscated possessions arrived with horns blaring, attempting to force a passage through the crush. Jeering Red Guards waving red flags clung to the outsides of the trucks like conquering heroes re-turning with the spoils of war and on the leading vehicle Abigail could see an enormous gilded Buddha lolling upside down with its face split open. Its young custodians were shrieking "Making revo-lution depends on Mao Tse-tung's thought!" at the top of their voices and their leaders were waving what looked like Chien Lung vases furiously above their heads as they demanded that the way be opened for them.

When the Red Guards searching the buses refused to clear the road, a violent dispute broke out and the youths on the trucks began to curse and hurl the vases and other heavy ornaments down at them. Several Red Guards crumpled to the ground under the onslaught, with blood streaming from head wounds. On seeing this, their enraged comrades stormed the trucks in a frenzied rush. Crowbars and staves appeared in the hands of both groups and the fighting quickly became savage. The dense crowd which had been attracted to the scene of the conflict retreated suddenly in panic and Abigail was forced to her knees in the confusion. She struggled upright with difficulty and began to stumble away but the sound of an authoritative voice booming out through an electric bullhorn caused her to turn her head. A tall, youthful-looking Chinese in a cadre's tunic had clambered up onto the disfigured statue of the gilded Buddha; standing commandingly above the mass of fighting youths with the bullhorn in his right hand, he was waving a giant portrait of Mao Tse-tung aloft with his left, and Abigail stopped and turned back, staring hard at the calm face of the young cadre.

"If you want to topple the old world and build a new one based on Mao Tse-tung's thought, stop fighting your own comrades!" he roared through the bullhorn, drawing out each word sonorously for maximum effect. "Chairman Mao has launched the Great Proletarian Cultural Revolution . . . to remold the souls of all the people. Everybody can be reformed and drawn into our ranks. . . . Chairman Mao has ordered his loyal Red Guards to win victory on the spiritual front first . . . in order to gain greater victories on the material front. . . . Violence is unnecessary. . . . Use persuasion, not coercion. . . . Stop this fighting now . . . once and for all!"

As the cadre spoke, other determined-looking Red Guards who had arrived with him were flinging themselves into the fray to separate the combatants, and the fighting quickly subsided. Reassured by the official's firmness, the watching crowd also quieted. When she had regained her composure, Abigail made her way back toward the scene of the fighting, still staring uncertainly at the cadre. She stood to one side, watching while he climbed down from the truck and issued a series of crisp orders to his well-disciplined supporters, who quickly dealt with the injured and dispersed the warring Red Guard groups. Within minutes the convoy of laden trucks was able to move off without interference and the passengers were shepherded onto their waiting buses. When the jam was cleared and the traffic had resumed its slow passage through the crowds, Abigail walked over to the cadre and politely touched his arm.

"I'd like to thank you for dealing with the trouble so efficiently," she said quietly in Chinese. "Many people in the crowd were becoming alarmed — and I was among them."

A faint hint of surprise showed briefly in the cadre's eyes when he turned and saw that the face beneath Abigail's cone-shaped straw hat was not Chinese. But his expression remained composed and unsmiling and he quietly dismissed the young Red Guard leaders around him before making any reply.

"I don't think I've had the privilege of meeting you before," he said coolly when they were alone. "But I'm glad to have been of help."

"My name is Kellner," said Abigail hesitantly. "And I've been wondering if we might have met in Peking some years ago. . . ."

The Chinese cadre was looking hard at Abigail but he said nothing.

"I attended an international peace rally at Pei-Ta University in 1957 . . . I shook hands with a student leader who gave a very fine address. Could that have been you?"

"It could have been. I did study at Pei-Ta."

"May I ask your name?"

"I am Chen Kao."

"Yes," exclaimed Abigail. "Of course. I remember now."

Kao's face remained expressionless as he subjected the square to a long, careful scrutiny and Abigail noticed that his appearance had changed little in the nine years since she had heard him speak in Peking. Broad-shouldered and dressed now in a well-tailored navy blue cadre's tunic, his student slightness had gone and his assertive manner suggested he already held a post which had accustomed him to respect. Seeing him at close quarters, Abigail remembered with surprising clarity the strong impression he had made in her mind on the day that she decided she would return to China. The memory produced a faint tremor of excitement, and although Kao was obviously used to masking his feelings, something in his unwavering gaze when he turned again to look at her suggested he might also have carried a vague memory of her blond hair and blue eyes away from that meeting.

"What brings you to Shanghai, Miss Kellner?" he asked at last. "Do you have some work here?"

"I'm a lecturer at the Foreign Languages Institute. I teach English and French."

"Then many of your students will already have joined the Red Guard movement?"

"Yes. Some of them have tried to explain its aims to me — but they sometimes seem confused."

Kao glanced quickly around the square again, momentarily distracted by the noise of the demonstrations. One of the Red Guard leaders who had helped him break up the fighting approached hurriedly to seek his advice, and Kao gave him instructions in an undertone before turning back to Abigail. "The Great Proletarian Cultural Revolution will have considerable impact abroad as well as in China," he said quietly. "It will be important for other countries too. But there's some misunderstanding of its purposes among students in Shanghai. I shall be visiting your institute soon myself to help the newly formed organizations there."

"Do you live in Shanghai?" asked Abigail.

Kao hesitated, then shook his head quickly. "No. I've come from Peking to give guidance."

"I hope when you visit the Foreign Languages Institute, we might meet again," said Abigail tentatively. "I will watch for your visit."

"That's not very likely. My work is very demanding. I have little spare time." Kao inclined his head a fraction in a formal gesture of farewell. "Now I must wish you good-bye."

Kao strode rapidly away, and watching him go, Abigail became aware once more of the hubbub of noise rising all around her. The clamor of cymbals and drums was increasing as new columns of chanting Red Guards converged in People's Square, and the crowds of excited and puzzled onlookers were still swelling although it was getting dark. Automatically Abigail fell into step with the tide of people moving southward, letting its momentum carry her slowly across the square without making any conscious choice of direction herself. Instinctively she realized that the crowd was avoiding the most turbulent areas of Red Guard activity; but she was no longer paying such close attention to what was happening around her. Inside her head she was replaying the conversation she had just had with Kao and part of her mind remained distracted, wondering at the sudden clarity with which she had recognized his long-forgotten name and the strong feeling of attraction which, as before, she had experienced in his presence.

2

"**B**e resolute . . . fear no sacrifice . . . surmount every difficulty to win victory!' "

The mass chanting of one of Mao Tse-tung's most famous quotations swelling from tens of thousands of young throats all around him penetrated slowly through the fog of sleep that shrouded Liang Kung's mind. His sixteen-year-old body was stiff and shivering from lying on the cold ground in a narrow street off Chang An, the gigantic ten-lane Boulevard of Eternal Peace which bisected Peking east to west, and for a brief moment a terrible panic surged through him. He had fallen asleep and ruined the greatest day of his life! He had missed the moment for which he had been longing, it seemed, since the day he was born. He had missed seeing Chairman Mao on the Gate of Heavenly Peace!

The first thing his newly opened eyes fell on were the blurred, black-ink characters of the *People's Daily* beneath his head; like the hundreds of thousands of other Red Guards from all over China who had been marshaled into position west of the Square of Heavenly Peace during the hours of darkness, he had spread sheets of newspaper on the cold, damp ground beneath him before lying down. The heavy predawn dew had soaked the newsprint as well as his military green cotton uniform and as his vision cleared, Kung saw that in the warmth of the rising sun his own damp tunic and those of the shivering Red Guards sitting or lying all around him were beginning to give off gentle clouds of steam. But the sight of the sun's crimson disc, lifting into view above the roofs of the capital's eastern suburbs, calmed his panic in an instant. He knew that Chairman Mao would appear on the Gate of Heavenly Peace promptly at ten o'clock, as he had done at all the other Red Guard rallies in the past month — and the position of the sun indicated that dawn had only just broken! In that same moment he felt the hand on his shoulder and realized that his sister, Ai-lien, had been shaking him gently to waken him.

"Look, Kung! The east is really red this morning!" She was thumbing through the pages of her red-covered copy of Mao's *Quotations*, searching dutifully for the next extract to be chanted. "We'll never forget this day as long as we live."

Liang Ai-lien's round cheeks were aglow with excitement. Two years older than Kung, she also wore a paramilitary uniform of green cotton, and her dark hair was clipped short in revolutionary fashion beneath a peaked military cap. A plain, sturdy girl, she had espoused the Red Guard movement just as enthusiastically as her brother in the ecstatic aftermath of the first Red Guard parade in Peking, on August 18, and she seized every opportunity she could to demonstrate that her devotion to Chairman Mao was as great as that of any male Red Guard.

"Thank you for waking me," said Kung, sitting up quickly and fumbling in his tunic pocket for his book of Mao's writings. "I was afraid for a moment that I might have missed the whole parade."

He glanced apprehensively toward the nearest People's Liberation Army soldier, who was leading the chanting. The soldiers had given them firm instructions not to sleep on the cold ground after buses had brought them to their positions shortly after midnight. The troops had stayed and led them in the singing of revolutionary songs for an hour or two, but few of the Red Guards had been able to remain awake all the time. Since arriving in Peking they had spent most of their waking hours practicing drills outside their dormitories under the supervision of the soldiers. Marching and countermarching in broad files 150 strong hour after hour, they had rehearsed carrying flags and giant signboards bearing red and gold Chinese characters that would form massive moving Mao quotations in the final parade. They had caught only a tantalizing distant glimpse of the upswept golden eaves of the Gate of Heavenly Peace as open trucks transported them from the railway station to their dormitory in a middle school in the suburbs, and this had served to heighten the tension and their growing sense of expectancy.

" 'Everything reactionary is the same,' " yelled the soldier, reading another extract from Mao's works that had become a Cultural Revolution watchword. " 'Unless you hit it, it won't fall.' "

Kung repeated the quotation in unison with Ai-lien, shouting at the top of his voice and waving a clenched fist above his head. In an instant he had come wide awake; all his tiredness evaporated and suddenly he felt more alive than he had ever done before in his young life. With the dawn light flooding across Peking from the east to warm him and the Gate of Heavenly Peace only a few hundred yards away at his back, he imagined he felt a rich new strength coursing through his body. He had chanted that quotation and many others repeatedly in recent weeks but now he was squatting on the very earth of Peking in the red dawn close beside Chang An. Close too to Chung Nan Hai, the walled enclosure of Ming dynasty pavilions where Chairman Mao lived, and in sight of the towering walls of the Great Hall of the People, which heroic workers had built in ten glorious months following the triumph of the revolution in 1949! Streets and monuments that he had previously known only as remote photographic images in his Changsha schoolbooks had sprung vividly to life before his eyes. He had never expected to visit the distant capital of China as long as he lived, and as thousands of voices about him rent the early morning air in unison he felt he understood the meaning of the words in the quotation more intensely than ever before. When he raised his fist above his head, he longed for something reactionary to appear before him so that he could strike it down with all his might! Glancing sideways at his sister, he saw that her eyes were shining and he knew without asking that she shared his feelings.

"We must try to keep each minute of today bright in our memories," said Kung in an awed voice. His clothes, like those of his fellow Red Guards all around him, were still steaming and he smiled happily as he glanced again at the eastern sky. "I truly know that Chairman Mao is the reddest sun in all our hearts this morning. I can feel his presence nearby. It's warming my body, inside and out."

His sister nodded, lifting her face toward the sun, and Kung saw that tears were glistening in her eyes. "I swear I'll never be disloyal to Chairman Mao. I don't know how anybody ever could be. I understand now why Grandfather risked his life to capture the bridge of chains for Chairman Mao and the Red Army."

At their Changsha middle school, Ai-lien had helped organize one of the first Red Guard groups to be set up in the Hunanese capital. Given a melodramatic name like most groups throughout China, it was called the Red Defense Corps of Mao Tse-tung's Thought. Because their father, now a Trade Union Federation cadre, had been a Young Vanguard on the Long March and their grandfather was a Gold Star hero of the Luting bridge assault, Kung and Ai-lien were numbered among the Five Red category of candidates — the children of cadres, revolutionary martyrs, soldiers, workers, and poor peasants — who had automatically been guaranteed membership in the Red Guard movement. In Changsha, as in other provincial capitals throughout China, the appearance of newspaper pictures of Mao

Tse-tung accepting and putting on a Red Guard arm band at the August 18 rally had electrified students and middle-school pupils. Kung and Ai-lien, like all their school friends, had flung themselves with enormous enthusiasm into the local Seven Kinds of Black campaign against former landlords, rich peasants, and those who could be dubbed a counterrevolutionary, a rightist, or any other kind of "bad element." A ballot had been held to elect Changsha representatives to travel to Peking as part of *Ch'uan Lien*, the Exchange Revolutionary Experience movement, and Ai-lien and Kung had been beside themselves with excitement when they found they were included in the delegation of several hundred Hunanese Red Guards.

Their fervor had mounted during the long train journey in railway coaches crammed to overflowing with Red Guards from other cities and provinces. After studying Mao's revolutionary writings every day of their school lives, the prospect of meeting their legendary leader in the ancient heart of Peking had seemed more like a dream the closer they came to the capital. It scarcely seemed possible that they would see in the flesh the man who had previously appeared only as a remote figure in newspapers and in the pages of their history books. Wasn't Chairman Mao the greatest savior of China in all history? Hadn't he founded the Communist Party and the Red Army and led the nation twenty thousand *li* across China on the Long March? That he should suddenly want to review a parade of young Chinese with no experience of anything except school and have them serve as "a reserve force for the People's Liberation Army" — all that to Kung and Ai-lien was almost beyond belief. But they knew they weren't dreaming because they had seen overcrowded trains and buses filled with wide-eyed Red Guards like themselves converging every day on Peking from all directions.

Upon arrival in the capital they had been met by Peking Red Guard groups led by teachers and stern, tough-looking students. Loaded into open trucks, they had been taken directly to already jam-packed dormitories attached to a middle school in the suburbs. There they were supposed to sleep on straw-covered desks or on bamboo mats spread over mounds of straw on the floor, but excited discussions on how the Four Olds campaign was being conducted in different cities and provinces had gone on all night long with the other Red Guard groups billeted there. The bartering of Mao Tse-tung lapel badges and arm bands identifying Red Guard groups from different regions had quickly become an obsessive pastime, taking up many waking hours; there was also a bewildering array of big-character wall posters to be read all over the city. Overnight the Cultural Revolution seemed to have turned austere, well-ordered China into a gaudy political carnival ground and Kung and Ai-lien, like all the other Red Guards they met, had surrendered themselves wholeheartedly to the intoxicating atmosphere which held out the promise of future glory in the service of Chairman Mao. The journey to the area adjoining the Square of Heavenly Peace and their dramatic dawn awakening among a vast crowd of one million kindred souls seemed to Kung and Ai-lien to be bringing the heady carnival to a great climax and as the hour for the rally to begin drew near, they became almost breathless with impatience and excitement.

"Eat your provisions now!" shouted the soldiers at eight-thirty, and Kung and Ai-lien opened the little reticular bags which they had been given, containing eggs, fruit, and *man t'ou*, a steamed bread. Before they had eaten them, trucks arrived and began to off-load big white character signboards and the thousands of tall red standards that looked so dramatic when moving in a forest above a marching multitude. With these distributed, the vast throng of Red Guards that stretched for several miles along the western arm of Chang An began to resemble a disciplined political rally, and the suspense of waiting became almost unbearable.

Enough Red Guard formations to fill the hundred-acre square had already been moved into position in front of the Gate of Heavenly Peace and great scarlet balloons trailing red and white streamers were drifting lazily at their anchorages in the sky above. Giant colored portraits of Marx, Engels, Lenin, and Sun Yat-sen flanked the square but the biggest human image of all adorned the front of the Gate of Heavenly Peace itself. Set in a vast gold-painted frame, the unsmiling amber face of Mao stared out across the great mass of humanity, suggesting that the omnipresent Party chairman was presiding invisibly over the gathering even before his physical arrival. Helicopters had begun to sweep the sky overhead and long queues of Red Guards formed suddenly to pay last-minute visits to makeshift lavatories that lined every street in central Peking. No more than pits dug in the roadside verges and surrounded by bamboo mats, each had its own pile of earth heaped beside it. All the Red Guards scattered a handful or two of earth into the pits after using them and the reek from these rudimentary closets added a pungent odor to the morning breeze that imprinted itself on Kung's memory, along with every other detail.

A little before ten o'clock, one of the stern Peking Red Guard leaders who had supervised the Changsha group since its arrival in the capital picked his way through the squatting crowd to the area where Kung and Ai-lien were sitting on the ground. Looking about him, he held up his hand to attract attention.

"Today, comrades from Changsha," he yelled, "an important announcement will be made from the Gate of Heavenly Peace, giving a historic new direction to the Great Proletarian Cultural Revolution. A new stage in the struggle has been reached. And tonight you will join with a group of Red Guards from the capital to carry out an important mission." He paused, looking about, searching faces. "Are Liang Kung and Liang Ai-lien present?" he demanded.

"Here, comrade!" Kung leapt to his feet with a raised hand. His heart was thudding loudly with a mixture of pride and apprehension at being singled out by name, but he fixed a calm, responsible expression on his face.

"Good!" The young Peking leader motioned Kung to sit down again. "Make sure you and your sister are both at the assembly point at the school with all the other Changsha Red Guards at nine o'clock tonight."

"Certainly, comrade!"

Kung and Ai-lien gazed at one another in mystification — but before they could start speculating on the nature of the new mission, the stirring strains of "The East Is Red" blasted suddenly from loudspeakers ranged along both sides of the street and a thunderous storm of cheering rolled slowly down the Boulevard of Eternal Peace from the direction of the square. Gradually the cheering settled into regular chants of "*Mao chu hsi wan sui! Mao chu hsi wan sui! Mao chu hsi wan sui!*" — "Long live Chairman Mao! Long live Chairman Mao! Long live Chairman Mao!" — and Kung and Ai-lien held their breath. The chanting grew louder and more frantic; then, over the loudspeakers, rising high above the slow cadences of "The East Is Red," they heard a solitary female voice intervene.

"Chairman Mao has come among us!" shrilled the voice frantically, repeating the phrase over and over again. "Chairman Mao has come among us!"

Kung and Ai-lien sprang involuntarily to their feet along with all the Red Guards around them. A tidal wave of excitement swept Chang An, catching them up in its surge, and they stumbled frantically against one another as they rushed to their marching positions.

3

Standing beneath one of the giant crimson ceremonial lanterns that decorated the gallery of the Gate of Heavenly Peace, Marshal Lu Chiao looked numbly down at the multitude of Red Guards flowing endlessly across the square below. The forests of tall flags, the huge, moving character boards, the *Hung Wei Ping* arm bands, and the countless booklets of Mao's quotations borne proudly like weapons colored the great mass of humanity predominantly red as they surged excitedly through the heart of the ancient capital. The sinister implications of the rally and all the others that had been held in the past month were sufficient to churn Chiao's stomach, but despite his rising sense of anxiety, he felt himself deeply moved by the sight of China's youth so spectacularly on parade.

At the age of sixty-three Chiao had become gray-haired, but he still looked lean and strong, and something of the vigorous physical self-confidence which had led him into acts of heroism during the Long March was still recognizable in his calm demeanor. While appearing to gaze down admiringly at the passing parade, out of the corner of his eye Chiao was in fact watching the bulky, imposing figure of Mao Tse-tung. Only a few yards away from him, Mao was moving back and forth along the ornate balustrade, jerkily lifting an arm every so often to wave in the direction of the deliriously chanting throng. Despite the riot of noise washing up from the square, Mao's big, moonlike face remained expressionless but Chiao could see that the Party chairman was behaving more animatedly than he had at any of the previous rallies. His female nurse, who had always been discreetly in attendance during his public appearances in recent years, was no longer shadowing him so closely; instead she remained inside the red-pillared pavilion, standing quietly among a group of uneasy-looking Party leaders who were following Mao's movements almost as obsessively as she was.

Like everybody else on the gate, Chiao could not fail to notice that Mao was somehow drawing new physical and mental energy from the massive rallies: minute by minute he seemed to be absorbing something tangible from the waves of adoration rising up from the vast square. For a year or two it had been rumored among the leadership that he was secretly suffering from Parkinson's disease and his slow, labored movements in public had previously supported the conjecture. But each successive rally had seemed to have a cumulative, reinvigorating effect on him and Chiao noticed that he was now moving with an unexpected sprightliness, almost darting along the gallery, followed dutifully by his chief ally, the deceptively frail-looking defense minister, Lin Piao, and Premier Chou En-lai.

One of ten People's Liberation Army leaders honored with the exalted rank of marshal in 1954, Chiao himself had for the past five years served as a vice chairman of the Military Affairs Commission, taking responsibility for supervising the Operations Directorate of the PLA General Staff. He had attended all four of the Red Guard rallies held since the middle of August — but far from becoming accustomed to the emotional intensity and the near-hysteria which the occasions generated, his sense of dismay had grown with each parade. Although Chiao knew that the gallery of the Gate of Heavenly Peace was high enough above the square to reduce Mao Tse-tung and other leaders, including himself, to little more than matchstick-sized figures, he could see that female and male Red Guards alike were again in the grip of a tearful hysteria as they stumbled past the old imperial reviewing platform. Despite the constant drilling they had received, discipline was breaking down as soon as the young marchers came in sight of the gate. After advancing in good order along the Boulevard of Eternal Peace, the dense green and khaki throngs invariably disintegrated into a scramble as they approached the western borders of the square. Clearly overcome by the occasion, all the participating Red Guards were instinctively slowing their pace, ignoring the fast-tempo marching beat of "Sailing the Seas Depends on the Helmsman, Making Revolution Depends on Mao Tse-tung's Thought" that boomed from loudspeakers all over the center of the capital. In an attempt to prolong the long-awaited moment when they at last caught sight of the living legend who was reviewing them, the wavering ranks stumbled helplessly into one another, stepping on each other's heels, sometimes falling, sometimes losing their shoes. Some were trampled and hurt but somehow the seething mass of marchers continued to flow eastward, each youth gazing fixedly up toward the high balcony for as long as it was in sight.

At the first rally, on August 18, the scene below the gate had possessed an unreal, dreamlike quality. But today, Chiao realized, the occasion had taken on the overtones of a nightmare and although nobody on the gallery was voicing such thoughts, Chiao knew instinctively that he was not the only one to feel it. A few yards away along the balcony in the other direction, Liu Shao-chi, the already white-haired head of state, stood rooted to the spot. Ascetic and dour by nature, he rarely spoke unnecessarily but now he had become an ashen-faced robot whose narrowed eyes looked out over the square without seeing. At his side, the diminutive Szechuanese general secretary of the Party, Teng Hsiao-ping, was equally pale and tense, and nobody approached to speak with either of them. The two men controlled the vast nationwide network of Party cadres who had pulled the country together after the destructive excesses of the Great Leap Forward and Chiao knew that the ears of the president and the general secretary must still be ringing with the violent words of Lin Piao's speech, delivered to the rally shortly after Mao made his dramatic entrance.

"Bombard the headquarters!" the defense minister had shrieked in his curiously nasal, high-pitched voice. "That must be the new war cry of the Great Proletarian Cultural Revolution. You have done well so far in washing away all the sludge and filth left over from the Four Olds society. But now you must concentrate your fire on the principal target in the capital and at all local levels throughout the country! Bombard the bourgeois revisionists, bombard the handful of persons in power *inside the Party* who are taking the capitalist road!"

The square had erupted with great orchestrated roars of "Bombard the headquarters! Bombard the headquarters!" and Lin Piao had waved his "Little Red Book" of Mao's quotations wildly above his head in response. The emotive phrase had been coined by Mao himself several weeks earlier when he wrote his first and only big-character wall poster in praise of rebellious Peking students who had begun attacking "bourgeois" academic figures at their university — but now Lin Piao had reemployed the slogan artfully to give a chilling new direction to the whole Cultural Revolution. Chou En-lai had also spoken briefly, lending his own authority to the directive to attack "only designated individuals in the Party," and new roars of "Long live Chairman Mao! Long live Chairman Mao!" had welled up from the square after both speeches.

Chiao had seen President Liu Shao-chi and the Party general secretary exchange baffled, uneasy glances and he noticed that the only people smiling on the upper gallery were Lin Piao and members of the Cultural Revolution Group appointed by Mao to supervise the movement. Mao himself stood to one side, remote and silent, in communion with only the crowd. He was as impassive as a Buddha in his military uniform and round PLA cap and neither he nor Lin nor any member of the Cultural Revolution Group had spoken to President Liu or the general secretary or even once looked in their direction since their arrival. Every Party and army leader present knew that the two men had already been singled out as prime targets of the Cultural Revolution; although neither so far had been mentioned directly by name, ferocious Red Guard attacks in wall posters and unofficial newspapers had recently begun to condemn "China's Khrushchev" and "another top Party leader in authority taking the capitalist road." The consistency of the attacks had made it obvious that such references, though irrational, were officially inspired and could apply only to the Party's two top bureaucrats. But as he stood above the caldron of noise which the Square of Heavenly Peace had become on that September morning, Chiao realized that in the growing atmosphere of hysteria, few of the other men on the balcony around him could be certain that they themselves would not sometime come under attack.

He noticed that even Marshal Chu Teh, the old Red Army commander of the Long March, now eighty, was watching the proceedings uneasily through half-closed eyes, occasionally reaching out with an unsteady hand to support himself on one of the stout wooden pillars. A legendary military figure in his own right, Marshal Chu looked bemused and uncomprehending. His green uniform sagged now on a wasting body that had once possessed the physical strength and stamina of a horse, and the dull resignation visible in Chu's posture increased Chiao's own sense of unease.

Chiao had for some time been aware that he might himself attract the unwelcome attentions of the Red Guards. Like most of the Party leadership, he had wholeheartedly supported the logical policies of President Liu and Teng Hsiao-ping in the difficult years following the Great Leap Forward, and the irrationality of the new speeches made him aware that no member of the Politburo was safe from attack under the irresponsibly vague directive "Bombard the headquarters!" The rally was clearly designed to open the way for arbitrary Red Guard attacks on any Party leader or cadre who had incurred Mao's displeasure, and Chiao felt a dull ache intensify in his right shoulder as this realization grew in his mind. The discomfort, he knew at once, was a sure sign that tension was growing in him; the old Hsiang River wound, inflicted by Kuomintang machine gunners as he clung to his precious pontoon bridge of makeshift bamboo rafts, had troubled him off and on over the years, and intense anxiety of any kind invariably triggered pain. To take his mind off it he closed his eyes briefly, making a conscious effort to blot out the hubbub of noise around him. For half a minute he focused his mind inward in accordance with the Taoist-inspired techniques of self-cultivation which he had practiced assiduously all his life, centering and concentrating his physical and spiritual energies deep within himself. Slowly the ache in his shoulder faded and when he opened his eyes again and glanced about, he sensed from the faces around him that many of the aging men who had strode twenty thousand *li* across China together on the Long March were wrestling silently with similar fears.

All were now fully aware that their cunning guerrilla leader had outmaneuvered them all as skillfully as he had outmaneuvered the Kuomintang divisions during the Long March. The scale and logistics of the rallies themselves were an impressive display of power, and the same agonizing questions were obviously exercising the minds of all those gathered on the gallery: would formal recantations and public self-criticism by those he termed his enemies assuage the desire for vengeance that had clearly smoldered in Mao's breast since 1959? Or were the stark slogans of the rally to be taken literally? It seemed inconceivable that the ailing figure stumping awkwardly back and forth before them should want to smash the entire Party apparatus just to satisfy a personal ambition to seize back undisputed control of China for a year or two — but nobody present could deny the evidence of his eyes and ears, which unmistakably argued the reverse.

President Liu, Teng Hsiao-ping, and the tireless premier Chou had always worked assiduously in the past to restrain the extravagance of Mao's impatience; whenever they failed they had set out as quickly as possible to counteract the damage. The sheer force of personality which Mao brought to bear in the Party's inner counsels had always made it impossible to confront him head on. More than once in the fifties he had angrily threatened to take to the mountains and raise another peasant Red Army to fight the Party if they refused to go his way, and the memory of this threat had lingered in the subconscious minds of all those around him. These memories had often induced a fainthearted resistance to Mao's proposals and Chiao realized a little shamefacedly that in recent months he had been just as guilty in this respect as any other member of the leadership circle. Their efforts to stifle the Cultural Revolution during the months when it still centered on newspaper attacks on writers had not been sufficiently courageous; he and others had stood by as the mayor of Peking, the army chief of staff, and the Party's orthodox propaganda chief had been purged, hoping that the sacrifice of such prominent victims might placate Mao and bring the campaign to an early end. But now, as a result of their lack of courage, they were virtually trapped in a capital city that was garrisoned by forces personally loyal to Mao, watching an effective Red Army of China's youth screaming slogans that could presage the downfall of each and every one of them.

All normal communications at the highest Party and army levels had long since broken down, and suspicion and unease had gradually paralyzed Chiao's own relations with men who had been friends and comrades for three decades. In shadowing Mao and Lin Piao cease-lessly back and forth along the gallery, Chou En-lai still seemed to be playing his customary moderating role, but Chiao could not even be certain of that. Chou was waving his red book above his head as frequently as Lin Piao, and the premier addressed the Red Guards often through the loudspeakers, calling them *"t'ung chih men"* — "comrades" — as he urged them good-humoredly to keep in step and hurry past the stand. Chou, he knew, would normally want above all else to protect the government apparatus and limit the disruption to the economy that the Red Guard takeover of the ru-dimentary railway system was already causing. But in the atmo-sphere of growing tension and distrust, Chou, who had always been an intimate friend, was scarcely acknowledging him and nobody knew for certain what the premier really thought, since he was confiding his views to nobody.

Chiao's own greatest fear was that the People's Liberation Army might be drawn into the chaos that had spread like wildfire through the country in recent weeks. His military role was to ensure that the armed forces were always in an efficient state of readiness to meet any threat posed by America's escalation of its anti-Communist war beyond China's southern borders, in Vietnam. A different and more pressing threat existed in the presence of the half-million Soviet troops stationed along China's northern border, and Chiao resolved silently to always keep these prime factors uppermost in his mind, no matter what might happen in the coming days and weeks. This inner affirmation of his intent and the refreshment of body and mind which his brief moments of meditation had brought him helped lift his spirits, and he squared his shoulders resolutely as he continued to watch the parade. He would meet whatever challenges confronted him as boldly as possible; his conscience was clear and he promised himself he would make no public self-criticism just to satisfy the young radicals if he was subjected to wall-poster attacks. Some Party cadres who had already been maligned as "capitalist roaders" had tried to rehabilitate themselves with the Red Guard groups by immediately making public admissions of wrongdoing, but instead of accepting these attempts to regain favor, the Red Guards had demanded more and more abject confessions and the victims had brought down greater anguish and humiliation on themselves.

These uncompromising mental decisions to stand firm helped Chiao feel more optimistic, and placing his hands behind his back, he sauntered along the gallery, watching Mao idly from beneath the brim of his peaked cap. As he approached, he saw the Party chairman turn suddenly from the crowd and pass a hand across his face in a gesture of weariness. Instantly his ever-alert nurse darted forward from inside the pavilion, and Chiao saw her press something small into his hand. Mao slipped it quickly into his mouth; then, after a short rest, he set off again, walking almost as briskly as before toward the eastern corner of the gallery. As he passed Chiao, he continued to gaze straight ahead; his rheumy eyes were focused in the middle distance and with a start Chiao noticed that his stare was glassy, almost vacant. When Mao gave no sign that he had recognized or even seen him, Chiao felt a new fist of apprehension tighten slowly inside him. At the same moment he caught sight of a familiar face in the shadows of the pavilion and moved inside to greet his nephew, Chen Kao.

Kao was conversing in an undertone with the chairman's wife, Chiang Ch'ing, who, like her husband, was dressed in khaki PLA fatigues with a Red Guard arm band fixed around her left sleeve.

After leaving Pei-Ta University, Kao had become an outstanding cadre in the Third Investigative Research Office of the State Council's Security Bureau, and his zeal and efficiency in that post had brought him promotion after four years to a junior position in the offices of the Party Secretariat. He had quickly impressed senior Party figures with his ability and enthusiasm, and during his five years as a Secretariat cadre, he had astutely avoided forming any obvious personal attachments among the leadership. But since the onset of the Cultural Revolution, Chiao had noticed Kao becoming an increasingly close confidant of members of the Cultural Revolution Group, so finding him conversing intimately with Madame Mao came as no surprise. As usual, Kao's navy blue cadre suit was immaculately pressed and he radiated his customary air of confidence; but like everyone else on the gate that morning his eyes too were wary, and as Chiao approached, he pointedly ceased his murmured conversation with the chairman's wife.

"That's a fine sight down in the square," said Chiao, smiling formally at Madame Mao. "It's wonderful to see how quickly our young people respond to discipline."

Chiang Ch'ing nodded only perfunctorily in greeting. She made no pretense of cordiality and behind her half-rimmed glasses her small eyes glittered unpleasantly. "It's a scene, Comrade Marshal," she said coldly, "that should strike terror into the hearts of all those Party persons in authority taking the capitalist road!"

Chiao continued to smile, deliberately ignoring the ominous implication behind Chiang Ch'ing's words. "I agree. Any real followers of the capitalist road would be frightened half to death just looking into the square today."

Without waiting for a reply, Chiao turned to his nephew. Normally they enjoyed a friendly relationship that reflected Chiao's deep affection for his sister, but to Chiao's surprise, Kao was avoiding his gaze and his handsome face remained blank and unresponsive. "What have you been doing recently, Comrade Nephew?" asked Chiao lightly. "Did you have a hand in organizing today's festivities?"

"Comrade Chen has been doing very important work in Shanghai," said Chiang Ch'ing shortly. "And he will be returning there tomorrow to ensure that the Red Guards in the city follow the new orientation correctly." The chairman's wife swung rudely on her heel and walked away, leaving Kao looking uncomfortably at his uncle.

"So you've been in Shanghai," said Chiao in an undertone when she had gone. "Were you able to go to the Conservatory of Music to see your mother?"

"No." Kao shook his head and glanced guardedly along the gallery, checking that they were not directly overheard.

"Have the conservatory students set up their own Red Guard groups like all the other colleges?" asked Chiao quietly.

"Of course," replied Kao, "but I haven't had time to visit them yet."

Chiao's expression stiffened. "Has your mother been subjected to 'struggle'?"

"*All* the teachers and professors at the conservatory with suspect class backgrounds have been 'struggled' just as they have elsewhere," said Kao, speaking quickly and quietly as though embarrassed by what he had to say. "You must know that very well. Since she was condemned as a rightist in 1957, she's automatically suspect. She can't be exempted or given special treatment. She's facing investigation — but for her sake and for mine it's best to let it run its course."

Chiao stared hard at his nephew, feeling the nagging sense of anxiety return. "I hope you'll do everything necessary to see that she's protected," he said in a fierce whisper. "You have a duty to your family as well as the Party, remember."

"There's no need to remind me of such things," replied Kao in an almost inaudible voice. "I'll see to it — but please don't raise personal matters in public at times like this. It could be dangerous for both of us."

In his turn Kao hurried away in the wake of Madame Mao, leaving Chiao staring after him. The cacophony of slogan chanting and strident music was still rising deafeningly from the square below and as he stood alone amid the noise, Chiao wondered anxiously what criticisms the new Red Guard groups might have leveled at Mei-ling, in the Shanghai Conservatory of Music.

When at last they marched into sight of the Gate of Heavenly Peace just before eleven o'clock, Liang Kung and his sister, Ai-lien, like all those Red Guards around them, were in a dizzy state of near-hysteria. The morning had become very hot and in the great crush of moving bodies some of their comrades from Changsha had already fainted and dropped out. The sight of their friends stumbling and falling had introduced the first feelings of alarm into the carnival atmosphere, and Kung and his sister had struggled to stay close to one another as the massive throng around them gradually increased its momentum. The tempo of the march was accelerating in time with the chanting of the slogans, sweeping them rapidly toward the square, and with part of their minds they were aware that their cries, mingled with those of hundreds of thousands of others, were becoming frenzied and strained.

Looking at his sister, who was half walking, half running beside him, Kung saw that her face had turned pale. Like him she was experiencing a mixture of elation and apprehension as the artfully induced waves of mass emotion boiled up all around them, swamping their senses and engulfing their individual identities. What had begun as an exhilarating game in the familiar schools and streets of their home city had turned now into something unimaginably vast and vaguely alarming — but it never occurred to him that he, his sister, and countless others like them were being cynically manipulated by the legendary figure they revered. They seemed to be living through a dream and their vague fears evaporated in an instant when at last the Gate of Heavenly Peace came in sight. Its imperial yellow roof tiles were sparkling like gold, making the monument look like a palace of their fantasy, and the vision reduced them both momentarily to silence; then, as they drew nearer, Ai-lien shrieked aloud at the top of her voice.

"There he is! I see him! I can see Chairman Mao!"

Ai-lien pointed to the unmistakable upright figure with one raised arm who was gazing out over their heads. In front of them other girls were already shouting and sobbing and Ai-lien felt tears spurt down her own cheeks. By chance Mao was standing on the gallery directly above his giant colored portrait, and as Kung caught sight of both the vast image and the tiny reality above it, he felt a mysterious surge of pleasure rise up in him.

"Chairman Mao! You're the reddest of red suns deep in my heart!" he yelled at the top of his lungs, trying vainly to make his voice heard over the roar of the music and the slogans. "You're the red, red sun in all our hearts!"

To his astonishment, Kung felt tears of joy course down his face too and he realized vaguely that around him others were weeping. "We love you, Chairman Mao," screamed other Red Guards. "We all love the red sun in our hearts." A new round of "Sailing the Seas Depends on the Helmsman, Making Revolution Depends on Mao

Tse-tung's Thought" was bursting from the loudspeakers; above it Kung could hear Premier Chou En-lai's voice urging everyone to keep moving.

"There's Premier Chou!" yelled Kung. "And our great leader's close comrade in arms Marshal Lin Piao."

Pushed from behind, they stumbled forward again, trying all the while to gaze back over their shoulders at the red-walled gate. But the wave of carefully engineered delirium sweeping the parade seemed to catch them up and bear them forward irresistibly, tossing and tumbling them against one another. Some fell and were trampled on, others linked arms and helped each other along. Ahead of them cheerleaders were setting up a new chant of "Bombard the headquarters! Bombard the headquarters!" and as they dashed on, blinking away the tears that misted their eyes, Kung and Ai-lien and the other Changsha Red Guards began to join in, repeating over and over again in shrill, hysteria-filled voices: "Bombard the headquarters! Bombard the headquarters! Bombard the headquarters!"

4

As they raced through Peking's narrow, high-walled *hut'ungs* later that night under the cover of darkness, Kung and Ai-lien were still in the grip of the fierce euphoria they had experienced in front of the Gate of Heavenly Peace. They grasped heavy wooden staves in their right hands, running silently among an "armed force" of more than two hundred Red Guards. Others around them were carrying axes, hammers, crowbars, and whips, as well as pots of paste and black paint, brushes, rolls of prewritten wall posters, portraits of Mao Tse-tung, and a tall dunce cap labeled in thick black characters "Cow Demon and Snake Spirit!" Their cotton-soled slippers made little noise in the dust of the unpaved lanes that lay beyond the eastern battlements of the Forbidden City, and because the *hut'ung* walls were as high as the eaves of the single-story houses they enclosed, no lights showed and the fast-moving raiding party was able to pass almost unnoticed through the deserted alleyways.

The group was led by burly senior students from Pei-Ta University and the higher-education institutes of geology, aviation, and architecture. Among them were two authoritative, older men wearing *Hung Wei Ping* arm bands who Kung thought might have been teachers. Although they had not made any attempt to give orders directly at any stage, Kung noticed that the Red Guard leaders deferred to them. The fifty or so Changsha Red Guards taking part had been told nothing about their destination or the nature of the action, but before their departure one of the Peking students, who carried a long stockwhip, had taken Kung and Ai-lien aside and told them brusquely they would have "a special role" to play when the time came. The whole group had chanted several Mao quotations before leaving the school yard where they had gathered and the last one repeated itself constantly inside Kung's head as he plunged on through the darkness: "*When the enemies with guns are annihilated, the enemies without guns will remain. We must not underestimate these enemies!*"

In his mind's eye Kung kept trying to picture what the mysterious "enemy without a gun" would look like and he hoped fervently that he and his sister would prove equal to their special role, whatever it turned out to be. At last, outside a double gate in a high wall, the leaders halted and those following crowded eagerly forward. Among them Kung watched goggle-eyed as the Red Guards with axes, hammers, and mattocks hacked vigorously at the wooden planks of the gate until it splintered and fell inward with a crash.

"We are Chairman Mao's loyal Red Guards!" yelled the Peking leaders at the tops of their voices, swarming across a small courtyard inside the gate. "We have come to take revolutionary action against you!"

The dwelling was an old courtier's house consisting of single-storied studios built around a central courtyard. After 1949 such houses had been divided up to provide homes for several families, and the Red Guard leaders stormed toward the southward-facing studio, overturning potted shrubs and yelling bloodcurdlingly over and over again, "Rebellion is justified!" The axe carriers shattered the flimsy front door with a few massive blows and inside lights immediately went on. Kung, with Ai-lien at his shoulder, was pushed bodily forward as the chanting mob poured into the house, lashing out indiscriminately to smash windows, mirrors, and crockery with their staves and hammers. The Red Guards toting paint pots immediately began to daub jagged, big-character slogans on walls, curtains, and furniture, and others slapped paste on every blank surface before sticking up big colored portraits of Mao. Pictures and ornaments were being flung to the floor, books were being scattered, and

Kung saw half a dozen Red Guards corner a terrified cat and bind a thin rope tightly around the neck of the squealing animal.

Above the din Kung heard loud yells of "Bow your head, cow demon! Bow your head!" and he fought his way through the crowd into the largest room to find the shouting Red Guard leaders confronting a trembling Chinese in his mid-sixties. Shocked and white-faced, having been woken suddenly from sleep, the balding man wore crumpled pajamas of cheap cotton, and wisps of his thin gray hair hung over his face. He was staring fixedly at the yelling mob, his shoulders hunched, his mouth wide open, like a hunted animal finding itself hopelessly at bay before a pack of rabid hounds. At first Kung saw only a badly frightened, aging man, struggling to recover his nerve; behind his shoulder the terrified face of a gray-headed woman in nightclothes was visible, watching from what seemed to be a bedroom doorway. She was merely a blur, an incidental detail in the dramatic scene, until Kung looked more closely — then as she came into focus a shock like a charge of electricity ran through his body. He recognized her familiar features! Looking back at the old man, Kung realized that he knew his contorted, ashen face as well. Normally smiling and affectionate when he had seen it during New Year visits to Changsha, it was the face of his own grandfather!

"Bow before the masses!" yelled the Red Guard with the stock-whip, cracking it viciously close to the face of the man who thirty-three years earlier had worked briefly as a cookboy to a foreign missionary in Chentai. "Your crimes against Chairman Mao stink to the highest heaven! You have always followed the orders of China's Khrushchev without question. Our investigations show you have a long record of deceit and treachery!"

He made a signal and immediately a youth carrying a bucket and a large brush lunged forward and sloshed glistening black paint all over Liang. Two others darted behind him and seized his arms, forcing his head forward, and a third jammed the tall dunce hat bearing the denunciation "Cow Demon and Snake Spirit!" onto his head. Other hands draped a white stringed placard around Liang's neck on which black characters announced "A member of the filthy black gang taking the capitalist road." Two more Red Guards smeared paste thickly over his shoulders and stuck a large pink wall poster on his back. When they spun him around, Kung was able to see from the rear of the crowd that its heading read *"Ta Tao Liang Tsa Chung!"* — "Down with the bastard Liang!"

A photographer stepped forward, lifting his camera, and two or three times a flashgun bathed Liang in a glow of white light. All around him the mob of Red Guards set up a deafening chant of "*Ta Tao Liang Tsa Chung!*" and Kung turned to find his sister standing at his shoulder; her normally rosy cheeks drained of color, she was staring openmouthed at the bedraggled, hatted figure. Kung could see from his sister's expression that the conflict between her natural love for her grandfather and her devotion to Chairman Mao and the Cultural Revolution was causing an acute inner agony. He too was wrestling with similar feelings; but all around them their comrades, led by the Peking Red Guards, were beginning a new, frenzied chanting of the slogan about "enemies without guns" and with each shout a forest of fists was being shaken angrily in their grandfather's direction. The sight close before them of one of the real "bourgeois revisionist enemies" of Chairman Mao, identified so emotionally only hours before from the Gate of Heavenly Peace, was arousing a great wave of genuine anger and indignation which rose rapidly around Kung and Ai-lien like a flood. Still dazed and exhausted from the day's events and a near-sleepless night in the open, Kung again felt the same frightening ocean of hysteria engulf him. Out of the corner of his eye he saw that one of the Peking Red Guard leaders was clambering up onto a table to survey the crowd. In that instant Kung involuntarily lifted his right fist above his head and shouted with all his strength, "Down with the bastard Liang! Down with the bastard Liang!"

At his side Ai-lien followed his lead, joining in with equal frenzy. If their grandfather was a class enemy as defined by Chairman Mao, he deserved to be attacked! To defy such an order was unthinkable; if they failed to comply, they would not only be dishonoring their emotional pledges to serve Chairman Mao, they would also imme- diately become outcasts from the Red Guard movement and expose themselves to the same kind of attack. Although they were not able to rationalize these thoughts consciously in the moments available to them, they reacted instinctively, yelling denunciations of their grandfather with as much passion as any of their comrades.

"You're a bourgeois revisionist careerist, Liang," yelled the tall Red Guard with the stockwhip, snapping it dangerously close to the cadre's face once more. "That's why the masses have come to take revolutionary action against you! You wormed your way into the Party! You slavishly obeyed the instructions of China's Khrushchev to suppress the Great Proletarian Cultural Revolution in the office of the Party Agriculture Commission. You hindered Red Guard groups in your office. Like China's Khrushchev and the rest of his black gang, you want to take the capitalist road! You are all worse than dog's turds!"

Liang flinched, moving his head away from the flicking tongue of the whip's long lash. His face remained pale and he was having difficulty breathing evenly, but he was beginning to recover from the first terrible shock of the midnight invasion. Black paint and globules of yellow paste were dribbling down his arms and legs and the tall hat jammed on his head almost covered his eyes, yet despite the terrible indignity of his position, something of the steely courage that had driven him across the iron chains at Luting under fire began to reassert itself.

"I've always been loyal to the Party and Chairman Mao," grunted Liang, struggling against the arms of the Red Guards holding him. "So has President Liu, the man you call China's Khrushchev. . . . We're neither bourgeois nor revisionist . . ."

"Shut up!"

The Red Guard flourished his stockwhip again and the crack of the lash rang loudly above the hubbub of noise coming from the rest of the house. Kung saw the leading Red Guard glance inquiringly toward one of two older men who stood watchfully against one wall and when he jerked his head at the group holding the still-squealing cat, the Red Guard leader motioned for them to come forward through the crowd.

"How dare you say you aren't a bourgeois revisionist!" shouted the leader furiously at the top of his voice. "Keeping household pets is an old bourgeois habit! It will be swept away by the Cultural Revolution — and so will all members of the black gang!"

He gestured angrily toward a beam that ran across the low room, and the youths holding the gray and white cat threw the free end of the rope attached to its neck over the beam. When they pulled on it, lifting the screeching animal above their heads, the rope bit tighter into its fur, strangling it slowly. A hush fell as its struggles grew feebler, its dangling legs ceased to twitch, and the pitiful sounds died in its constricted throat. From the bedroom doorway behind Liang, his wife let out a half-stifled moan of horror.

"My husband has given his whole life to the revolution," she said in a tortured whisper. "What you're saying is insane —"

The older Red Guard standing by the wall made a quick sign and the faltering voice of Liang's wife was drowned at once in a new howl of "*Ta Tao Liang Tsa Chung!*" With the chanting rising to a crescendo, a Red Guard with a pair of domestic scissors rushed forward and plunged them repeatedly into the cat's lifeless body until blood trickled from it. Then he set it violently in motion and the Red Guards holding Liang stood fast so that the bleeding body of the animal knocked against his face as it swung back and forth at the end of the rope, adding smears of blood to the paint and paste that already disfigured him.

"Hang the bastard Liang! Hang the bastard Liang!" roared the whole crowd of Red Guards, taking their lead again from the older man. "Hang the bastard now!"

Liang's eyes widened in alarm as the Red Guards at the front of the crowd moved nearer, brandishing their staves with renewed fury. In the other rooms the crash of axes, hammers, and crowbars could be heard as the Red Guards tore up floorboards and broke open cupboards. Glass shattered, wood splintered, furniture was overturned, and through one window a squad of Red Guards in the shadowy courtyard could be seen wrenching dwarf trees and shrubs from their tubs and digging up the small vegetable patch in their search for something that might prove incriminating.

"It would be better if you confessed your stinking crimes now," yelled the Red Guard leader, cracking his whip menacingly under Liang's nose. "Nothing will save you . . ."

"Leave my husband alone! His heart is weak! He's worked so hard for so many years he's ruined his health!" Liang's wife pulled herself free from the two female Red Guards holding her and lunged toward her husband's captors. She scratched and tore at them, screaming incoherently, but fell sobbing to her knees when the Red Guard leader laid the lash of his stockwhip across her bony shoulders with all his force, raising an instant welt of blood beneath her nightclothes. The two girls in charge of her rushed forward, cursing, to drag her from the room and the Red Guard leader jabbed the end of his whip against Liang's bloodied cheek.

"Confess your bourgeois revisionist crimes, black gangster Liang — or the revolutionary masses will strike you down!"

"How should a man who risked his life daily for Chairman Mao on the Long March confess to 'taking the capitalist road'?" said Liang angrily through his gritted teeth. "What sense would that make?"

"Many people wave the red flag to oppose the red flag!" One of the older men stepped forward for the first time from his unobtrusive place by the wall. In his hand he held a sheet of paper and he glanced down at it before speaking. "Before the Long March began, did you work for a foreign imperialist spy, an English missionary who was captured by the Red Army and sentenced to death for spying for the Kuomintang clique? Weren't you baptized a Christian by him? Weren't you all along a running dog of the imperialists who sneaked into the Communist Party just to serve your foreign masters?"

The crowd fell abruptly silent, awed by the gravity of the new charges, and Liang swallowed hard before replying.

"My father's land was confiscated when there was famine in Hunan," said Liang in a hoarse voice. "To save my family from starving I took a job with foreign missionaries. I agreed to be baptized to keep the job — but that was long ago, before I became a fighter of the Red Army and a member of the Communist Party."

The adult Red Guard flourished the sheet of paper at Liang, his eyes glittering with the light of triumph. "Then why did you meet that same English missionary in secret at the Temple of Heaven when he came to Peking in 1957?"

"The meeting wasn't secret," gasped Liang. "It took place for personal reasons, with the knowledge of Premier Chou . . . and Marshal Lu Chiao."

The adult Red Guard's face stiffened at the mention of the two well-known names and he made a quick note on the paper. Then he looked up at Liang again. "You're lying —"

A loud commotion outside in the courtyard drowned his words suddenly, and all the youths who had been searching the garden burst noisily into the room. Yelling excitedly, they forced their way through the throng behind one Red Guard who was holding up a potted flowering jasmine. He had already jerked the shrub and the clod of earth clinging to its roots from the porcelain pot and he replaced it in an elaborate mime as he reached the space in front of Liang. The watching crowd fell silent and in a dramatic gesture the Red Guard pulled the shrub and its roots from the pot once more to demonstrate how he had carried out his search in the garden. When he turned the pot upside down, an oblong package wrapped in waterproof oilcloth that had been buried beneath the jasmine fell heavily to the floor. The Red Guard holding the stockwhip snatched up the bundle, unwrapped it, and grinning in triumph, held up a black leather-bound edition of the Holy Bible with gilt lettering on its cover. Flicking it open, he peered for a moment at an inscription, handwritten in Chinese characters on the flyleaf; then looking up, he read it aloud in a jeering voice.

" 'To Hsiao Liang, a brother in Christ. With affection and gratitude, Pastor Kellner.' "

Liang stared blankly at the Bible, his expression betraying his unease, and the Red Guard leader jabbed the end of his whip viciously into his face once more.

"Why does a revolutionary cadre who is endlessly loyal to Chairman Mao need to hide a foreign book in his jasmine pot?" asked the youth in a sarcastic voice.

Liang lowered his head without replying and the Red Guard leader dropped the Bible on the floor with a snort of contempt. He made a sign to a youth holding a bucket and brush and watched with satisfaction as he sloshed black paint in among its gold-edged pages. Then, kicking it aside, he turned and scanned the crowd intently until his gaze fell on Kung and Ai-lien. He gestured peremptorily toward them with the whip, and when the crowd parted, Kung advanced, still clutching his stave in front of him, followed by his sister.

Liang did not look up at their approach but continued to stand with his chin sunk against his chest. Close up, to Kung his grandfather looked more like a terrible, comic effigy of straw than a flesh-and-blood human being. The black paint, paste, and blood were drying on him and the tall dunce cap, the poster, and placard gave his body a tragically foolish appearance. Kung's heart was thudding painfully against his ribs as he gazed at his grandfather's bowed shoulders and a turmoil of emotions raged inside him, making his head ache.

" 'Everything reactionary is the same,' " yelled the Red Guard with the stockwhip, challengingly. " 'Unless you hit it, it won't fall!' "

The vehemence of his shout jolted Liang and he raised his head to find himself looking directly into the faces of Kung and Ai-lien. For a second or two he stared in disbelief at his two grandchildren — then a terrible look of despair came into his eyes and he seemed to shrink in size.

To Kung, the grotesque paint- and blood-spattered face of his grandfather was suddenly unbearable to look at. He felt both a deep

pity for Liang's terrible plight and an irrational fury that he should
have allowed himself to be singled out as a victim. Simultaneously
the roars from a million throats in the Square of Heavenly Peace
seemed to ring again in his ears, urging him on, directing him to
demonstrate his loyalty to Chairman Mao.

"Bombard the headquarters! Bombard the headquarters!" boomed
the voices, and in an unconscious reflex action Kung raised his stave
and brought it crashing down on his grandfather's head and shoulders
with sickening force. A new, unintelligible roar from the Red Guards
crowding behind him mingled with the imaginary shouts in his ears
and with Liang swaying unsteadily before him, he raised his stave
above his head once more. Ai-lien and others around him, he realized
vaguely, were also moving forward, aiming blows at the reeling
figure, and he joined them, lashing out again and again at Liang's
unprotected head.

"*O Lord God, in my hour of need, please forgive and protect me! O Lord
God, in my hour of need, please forgive and protect me!*"

As the forest of staves struck wildly down at him, Liang heard
his own voice repeating again, as though from far off, the words of
the prayer that had last leapt to his lips in the midst of the fire on
the Luting bridge. It echoed in his ears with a strange resonance;
then the floor rose up suddenly toward him like a jaw closing and
the pain flowing through his head and body became a rushing torrent.
For a split second he clearly felt the black iron chains of the Luting
bridge cold beneath his body again. Then they parted and he slipped
between them to float gently down toward the boiling white breakers
of the Tatu far below.

Kung and Ai-lien stood side by side, staring numbly at the motionless body of their grandfather lying at their feet. They lowered
their staves and the Red Guards crowding around them fell silent.
In the filthy pool of black paint and sticky paste, the aging Gold
Star hero of the Long March was a crumpled, wasted figure and
instinctively they knew he would never rise again. At the back of
the room a single voice shouted "Long live the Great Proletarian
Cultural Revolution! Long live Chairman Mao!" and gradually the
other Red Guards took up the chant until the house was filled again
with the sounds of their voices.

5

A rising tide of Chinese and Japanese newspapers, news-agency reports, radio transcripts, and sheaves of library clippings looked as though they might soon swamp Jakob's desk as he pored over a draft of his weekly analysis of events in China in the middle of October. Behind the precarious heaps of paper he was only partly visible to visitors approaching the glass-partitioned office on the top floor of the Kellner Institute and when Joseph Sherman appeared outside the open doorway, he stood on tiptoe and waved a folded Chinese newspaper exaggeratedly back and forth to request silent permission of Jakob to enter.

" 'Celebrated China Watcher Drowns in Flood of Revolutionary Newsprint' — maybe that's the first story I should file from here for the good old *Gazette*," exclaimed Sherman, advancing jovially into the office to shake Jakob's hand. "At least a few Washington readers could understand that, if they don't understand anything else about the woefully misnamed Cultural Revolution."

Jakob's face looked tired but he smiled with pleasure as he motioned Sherman into a chair beside the desk. "Welcome home, Joseph. I heard a rumor that you were heading back here to write a special China feature for your old paper — I'm glad to find that some rumors at least still turn out to be true."

"And *I'm* a bit concerned to find that a rumor buzzing around the foreign correspondents' club also turns out to be true," said Sherman with a frown of exaggerated severity. "Everybody says you're working too hard — and we can't afford to lose the services of one of the few people around here with the vaguest idea of what's going on in Red China right now."

" 'Vaguest idea' is absolutely right," grinned Jakob, leaning back in his chair and waving a hand wearily at the heaps of paper. "The more information that spills off the mainland, the more confusing the whole thing becomes."

"Well, take it easy, Jake, that's the message from your friends at the club," said Sherman, smiling broadly. "We need you to keep us straight on the facts — right now I'd like to know the precise significance of one of the many bizarre labels which are being plastered all over Mao's deadly foes. . . ." Sherman bent his head over the Chinese newspaper in his hand, peering closely at the printed characters. "Yes, this is it, 'Cow Demon and Snake Spirit.' What in heaven's name does that quaint old Chinese expression imply?"

"Perhaps Mr. Wu is better qualified for that job." Jakob smiled at his senior translator, who had entered carrying a bundle of midday mail, which he placed carefully beside Jakob's typewriter. "Mr. Wu, you remember Joseph Sherman, don't you? He'd like to know the derivation of the term 'cow demon and snake spirit.' "

The elderly translator inclined his head and shook hands diffidently with the American. "In classical Chinese literature, Mr. Sherman, cow's demon and snake spirit are evil entities from the world of darkness which disguise themselves as humans to create trouble on earth. But if real human beings see through their disguise, they're forced to assume their original appearance." Wu paused and smiled bleakly. "Chairman Mao Tse-tung employed this term for the first time after the Hundred Flowers campaign. He said intellectuals who pretended to support the Communist Party were like evil spirits taking human form. When they criticized the Party's policies they gave themselves away and reverted to their true shape. Now the expression 'cow demon and snake spirit' is used as shorthand to describe those denounced as politically dishonest."

"I'm much obliged to you, Mr. Wu," said Sherman, pulling out a notebook. "I've already managed to get the hang of the 'ghosts and monsters,' 'the black gang,' and the 'bourgeois vampires,' but I'm very pleased to add 'cow demon and snake spirit' to my lexicon of Cultural Revolution terminology."

He jotted a few lines quickly in his notebook as the Chinese left the room, then looked up thoughtfully at Jakob again. The former missionary had taken to wearing thin-rimmed reading spectacles in his mid-fifties and his once-blond hair, still thick and curly, had turned pepper-and-salt right through. But although he was obviously tired from overwork, Jakob's gaze was still keen, his face was sunburned, and his appearance was that of a man who remained active and energetic in middle age.

"Maybe you're still working too hard on China, Jake, but I guess you haven't changed that much in the last nine years or so," said Sherman warmly. "A distinguished extra touch of snow in the hair perhaps — and a light-footed crow may have left another enhancing footprint or two on your cheeks since we last met. But otherwise . . ."

"I soldier on much the same as ever, Joseph. I bought a boat a few years ago and I manage to get out among the islands most weekends with friends when the weather's good." Jakob grinned and then sighed explosively. "But you're right, I still spend too many of my waking hours at this desk."

"And how are direct relations these days between the Kellner Institute and the People's Republic of China? You were just going off to Peking when we last talked. Were lasting diplomatic ties established?"

The American's ironic tone drew a smile from Jakob but he did not reply at once. "I'll tell you about that trip over dinner soon — it's my turn to pay," he said at last. "I've applied for visas every year since but I've only been allowed in once — in 'sixty-four. I was given the usual bland milk run of carefully selected factories and communes. But I wasn't able to talk to anybody I'd ever met before . . ."

Jakob broke off, remembering the disappointment and frustration he had felt at failing to make any contact with Mei-ling or her brother after waiting so long for a visa. All his written requests for interview meetings with leading Party figures before and during the trip had been ignored, and on the ten-day tour, to his bafflement, he had been shepherded exclusively by minor cadres who had adopted a stiff-faced official manner toward him from start to finish. Before and after the visit he had written a number of cautiously worded formal letters to Marshal Lu Chiao, making clear his desire to make further return trips, but none of these letters had been acknowledged. Year in, year out, during the course of his daily work in Hong Kong, he had scrutinized most of the written and broadcast sources himself, searching for the slightest mention of the names which meant so much to him. He had a substantial file of Chiao's official appearances at Party meetings and anniversary celebrations but they indicated nothing of significance beyond confirming his continued occupation of his senior posts in the Party and army. Jakob had never sighted any references at all to Mei-ling or Kao since his 1957 visit, but the diligence he applied to the task had never faltered. With the onset of the Cultural Revolution the great avalanche of additional broadcast and printed information had forced him to spend more time than ever at the institute, and his anxious scrutiny of the campaign's trends and lists of individuals under attack accounted for many of the long, exhausting hours he had been putting in over recent months.

"I've heard from mutual friends that your daughter, Abigail, picked up a severe case of the 'China thing' from you in the end," grinned Sherman. "I heard she went to teach in Shanghai, is that right?"

Jakob nodded slowly. "Yes, she's still there. I took her with me to Peking in 1957 and she couldn't think of anything else afterward except working in China. She went back to London to do a full-scale postgraduate language course and got herself a teaching post in Shanghai about a year after she finished. She's never looked back since."

"And the Cultural Revolution isn't making life difficult for her?"

"Seemingly not. She'd have written if there was cause for alarm. If I know Abigail, she'll take a lot of budging. The institute has published a language textbook she's written and it's in use in several other centers. So she's carved out something of a niche for herself."

"What sort of life does she lead there?"

Jakob hesitated, considering how to put the best construction on what had amounted to a near-estrangement between them since their visit to Peking. "Abigail's always been very much her own person, Joseph. She hasn't confided much in me since she's been in Shanghai. She rarely writes but she did indicate a year or two ago that she'd struck up a close relationship with one of the Chinese lecturers at the Foreign Languages Institute." He shrugged his shoulders in a little gesture of resignation. "But whether that means marriage is seriously in the cards for them, I don't really know. . . ."

Recognizing that Jakob was not comfortable talking about his daughter, Sherman flipped open his notebook again and stared pointedly at the jottings he had made. Then he raised his head and smiled quizzically. "There's no point, is there, Jake, in trying to disguise my ulterior motive in coming here — as always, I'd like to pick your brains. . . ."

"No point at all," agreed Jakob, smiling in his turn. "Pick away as hard as you like — that's what friends are for."

"My ultimate brief is a thoughtful article analyzing the foreign policy implications of the Cultural Revolution, its likely effect on the outside world — but in my first piece I want to sketch the bare bones of what appears to be happening on the ground inside China right now. I've talked to all the China watchers at the U.S. Consulate and these are some of the ideas I want to check through with you."

"Fire away," said Jakob, relaxing in his chair and smiling again.

"The guesses of an old China hand like yourself should be as good as anybody's."

Sherman scanned the pages of his notebook. "Would you agree that there seem to be three distinct categories of Red Guards in existence at this moment? First, there's the ten million or so who've flooded in and out of Peking in recent weeks — the 'amateurs' — who're running wild all over the country scaring the Four Olds generation out of their wits and fouling up the rail system. Second, there's the tough, nasty shock troops from Peking, mainly radical university students who've been dispatched by Mao to overthrow specific provincial Party leaders. And third, there are the 'enemy' Red Guard groups set up by provincial Party cadres to defend themselves."

Jakob nodded. "Seems all right so far."

"The second and third groups are fighting each other with wall posters, fists, and occasionally crowbars, the ten million are ignoring orders to go home and behave themselves, and the People's Liberation Army and the police seem to be standing by doing nothing, presumably on Party orders. It's not clear whether the regional army commanders have formed their own Red Guard groups yet, but it's a good bet they will — and when they do, the confusion will probably quadruple."

"That's as near as anybody knows," said Jakob, raising his eyebrows humorously. "And of course all of them accuse their enemies of opposing Mao while pledging undying loyalty to Mao themselves. Everybody in China claims to be a Maoist, but they still seem to want to fight one another."

"Good point." Sherman scribbled in his notebook briefly. "The economy's being rocked to its foundations because the railroads have all been taken over by itinerant Red Guards . . . and Mao's least favorite people, the president and general secretary of the Party, have already been demoted in the official pecking order by the press. Refugee reports suggest a lot of intellectuals and Four Olds victims who've been roughed up by Red Guards have already committed suicide despite the Central Committee directive to avoid violence, and organized chaos in the truest sense reigns supreme. Meanwhile the basic Maoist claim is that the Cultural Revolution is an earthshaking invention to inspire revolutionary purity in every man, woman, and child in China and later the whole wide world. . . . Does that sum it up?"

"Brilliantly."

Sherman smiled his thanks. "I've got some frills I won't bother you with and I intend to add a little glossary of terms explaining who the 'ghosts and monsters' and 'the black gang' and the 'cow demons' are." Sherman stood up, snapping his book closed. "I'll write that and file it before dinner. Will you come to the Mandarin at about eight — at the *Gazette*'s expense? We can thrash out the international implications of all this over some shark's fin soup and Peking duck, if you'll be kind enough."

"I'll be glad to. It's good to see you back in your old journalistic harness again, Joseph, if only for the brief space of a guest article."

Sherman's expression became a little wistful. "Yes, I have to admit, it feels good to me too. My ivory tower at Cornell has gotten to feel a little like a prison the last year or so. Watching my own country embroiling itself deeper and deeper in Vietnam has been very unsettling. Both my sons are involved, and I've a hankering to volunteer my own modest talents and experience if the administration feels they could be of use in Saigon — but more about that over dinner."

Sherman grinned again, raising his hand snappily to his brow in a comic salute of thanks, then hurried from the office. Jakob stared thoughtfully after him for a few seconds before putting on his reading glasses and rummaging absently among his papers for the draft of the analysis he had been working on. As he did so, his eye fell on the little pile of midday mail that Mr. Wu had deposited beside his typewriter and the sight of familiar handwriting on the top envelope made him start. The letter bore a French stamp and a Paris postmark but the writing was unmistakably Abigail's. Jakob's first thought was that his daughter had been forced unexpectedly to leave Shanghai. She had sent him only two or three letters during her entire stay in China, posted from Shanghai, but as he studied the envelope he realized that in the new climate of uncertainty caused by the Cultural Revolution, Abigail might have given the letter to a Western traveler to post in Europe so as to avoid local security checks. All her previous letters had been disappointingly perfunctory and cool in content, merely serving the purpose of reassuring him of her well-being. They had also acted as painful reminders to Jakob of the dislocation of their relationship which had followed the visit to Peking, and for this reason alone the arrival of a letter from her invariably caused him some consternation. Nothing had emerged so far to suggest that foreigners faced any direct threat from the Cultural Revolution but the growing unrest had left him feeling apprehensive about her continued presence in Shanghai. Because he had not heard any news of her since the movement began, he felt an added sense of unease as he tore open the letter.

The sight at the top of the first page of her normal address — an apartment in a modern block off the Nanking Road — confirmed that the letter had in fact originated in China, and Jakob ran his eye rapidly through the pages, seeking first to reassure himself of Abigail's immediate safety. The last page bore her usual confident signature and she had taken pains to emphasize that she was in no danger, but as he sampled fragments of what she had written, an almost unbearable sense of foreboding began to grow in him. The letter was some four weeks old, dated in the middle of September, and with an effort he forced himself to go back to the beginning and read it through again very slowly.

"Dear Father," the letter began,

> I felt I ought to write and let you know that there's no need to worry on my account. The Cultural Revolution's bark is much worse than its bite, at least as far as I'm concerned. Although schools and universities here that shut down in June are remaining closed to allow students to take part in the Cultural Revolution, I'm still being paid my salary by the Foreign Languages Institute and the authorities have said it's quite in order for foreign teachers to remain in their apartments until the colleges reopen. So I'm doing my best to follow developments. Because the atmosphere is so frenetic and so much is going on in the streets day and night, I'm writing a daily log of what I see and hear. At the end of it all I hope I might have the material to write a publishable 'worm's-eye view' account of modern Shanghai in ferment. No matter what happens, the "Great Proletarian Cultural Revolution" seems certain to become an historic event of some considerable significance. (Since I'm not too sure how the authorities might react to this and other snippets of information in this letter, I'm going to ask a French colleague who's returning home in a day or two to post this "safely" from Europe.)
>
> Some Chinese professors and administrators at our institute have been "struggled" and "hatted" already and all my students, male and female, have become Red Guards. But they've remained friendly towards me because I'm an outsider and they go to considerable lengths

to try to explain what's going on. That's not to say that they understand it all very clearly themselves. The complexities are labyrinthine
and all the Red Guards tend to get terribly overexcited about what
seem like trifles to me. But there are some ominous overtones. I've
seen some very frightened people being dragged from their homes in
the Four Olds campaign and one evening I nearly ran into a very
nasty fight between Red Guard gangs who did some brutal things to
one another with staves and iron bars. Each college and school has
its own "cowshed" too — that's Red Guard slang for the semiprison
where those condemned as "cow demons" are confined for varying
periods. They're sealed off and guarded day and night and the outside
windows are painted black. The sound of noisy "struggle" meetings
can be heard from outside but nothing can be seen. So even in the
middle of it all, a foreigner like me is still paradoxically on the side-
lines. It's impossible to tell how much of the sound and fury is symbolic and how much is real. The Red Guards in my own institute
are certainly convinced that they're obeying an historic call to "change
human nature" and "touch people to their souls," as the Central Committee resolution would like them to think. But there's obviously a
strong strain of cynical exploitation from the centre running through
it all.

One casualty for me has been my friendship with a Chinese colleague that I think I may have mentioned before. Our two-year relationship came to an abrupt end when he was suddenly assigned
elsewhere on some mysterious Cultural Revolution errand in mid-
August. He told me before he left that we would never be able to
meet again. But looking back I'm not unduly upset. I don't think it
was going to work out anyway. And there have been some compen-
sations — one might be of passing interest to you. Do you remember
the very impressive young student leader who closed the peace rally
we attended at Pei-Ta University? I happened to run into him in
People's Square one night. His name is Chen Kao and he's now
holding down an important Party job of some kind in Peking. I saw
him break up that nasty Red Guard battle I've just mentioned, employing a megaphone very effectively from the top of a lorry. I introduced myself afterwards and we met again a few days later when
he came to speak to Red Guards at my institute. I contrived to offer
him dinner at my apartment and I think he was very relieved to find
a quiet spot away from all the frenzy and hullaballoo. Since then

we've become quite close friends. He pays me a discreet visit or two whenever he comes down from Peking and in the eye of the storm it's pleasant to be able to relax with somebody of Kao's calibre.

Jakob broke off from his reading and shut his eyes. He tried to close his mind to the implications of what he had just read but without any success. *Since then we've become quite close friends . . . it's pleasant to be able to relax with somebody of Kao's calibre . . .* The words reverberated tantalizingly in his head and visual images of Kao and Abigail together, unknowingly daughter and son of the same man, tumbled hauntingly through his imagination. For a long time he sat unmoving in his chair, then forced himself to continue rereading the letter.

"There's no doubt at all in my mind that the Cultural Revolution is very different from all the political campaigns of the past five years," continued Abigail.

Political activity has never been as visible and public before and never as unrestrained. I spend hours and hours every day reading the wall posters that are plastered everywhere in the city centre. The language is lurid, and the wilder the accusations, the more people read them. They attract vast crowds and it seems as if total anarchy has broken out sometimes. New posters are often pasted up by rival Red Guard squads before those beneath them have been read. It's a veritable battleground of the written word. Thousands of officials and individuals have been under attack in the city and it's become a great game identifying the victims. To my surprise a couple of weeks ago I came across a name that had remained buried for a long time in my own memory. I was outside the Conservatory of Music and stopped to read the mass of new wall posters that had just gone up there. Most of the teachers were being criticized for their devotion to "bourgeois foreign composers" such as Bach and Beethoven and as usual the name characters of those under attack were scored through with big red crosses. Among them I spotted a piano teacher named Lu Mei-ling and immediately remembered that file you showed me when I first came to Hong Kong. I made some enquiries at the conservatory and found she'd also been a writer, so the long arm of coincidence does seem to have reached out to Shanghai.

I found out her address and tried to visit her but the house was empty and closed up like several others I've noticed in the area. It had obviously been sacked by a Four Olds squad and the doors were sealed with Red Guard stickers. I've been back several times since but the doors have so far remained closed and sealed. There's a good chance that her absence is temporary; those under attack are usually allowed home after a while. Since you've never been able to bring yourself to tell me very much about Lu Mei-ling, I must confess I'm all the more determined to meet her. There's nothing I'd like more than the chance to talk to her myself.

It was this news in particular, I suppose, that really decided me to write this letter, and I trust when it reaches you, your mind will be set at rest about my welfare. I hope this great upheaval isn't over-heating the Kellner Institute's resources too greatly and I hope you're keeping well. While the unrest continues, I'll try to send a letter from time to time via Europe or elsewhere whenever a chance like this presents itself.

Your culturally revolutionised daughter,
Abigail

The ostentatious absence of any final declaration of affection and the barbed reference to his chronic reluctance to discuss Mei-ling and the past made Jakob wince inwardly. The feelings of anxiety and foreboding which the first sight of the letter had provoked continued to intensify; he reread it several times, agonizing over what might lie behind the innocent phrase "quite close friends" and wondering if he should try to intervene to warn Abigail. He felt heartsick too at the thought that Mei-ling might be suffering new indignities at that very moment, and he shook his head in dismay at the ironic innocence of the language in which so much wounding information was couched. A feeling of rage at his present helplessness and his past shortcomings seized him — then, on hearing a footstep in the doorway, he glanced up to find Mr. Wu looking at him with a concerned expression on his face.

"Is everything all right, Mr. Kellner?" asked the elderly translator hesitantly. "Have you had bad news?"

Jakob realized his feelings must have showed on his face; he was still clutching the letter tightly in both hands and he dropped it on the desk in front of him. "Somebody I know well has come under attack in Shanghai," he said in a tight voice, rising and moving across the office to stare out of a window.

"Every Chinese here in the colony has relatives and friends on the mainland they're worried about," said Wu softly. "It's not an unusual feeling for most of us."

Jakob stood abstractedly by the window for half a minute or more without speaking; then he swung around and stared hard at his chief translator. "Mr. Wu, you once told me that one of your daughters had married into the biggest shipping family in Hong Kong, didn't you?"

The translator's expression became puzzled but he nodded slowly. "Yes, that's right, Mr. Kellner."

"Then I need your help," said Jakob in an urgent undertone, crossing hurriedly to the door and closing it. "I want to travel to Shanghai at once — as a crew member on a freighter. I'll need papers for . . . say, a first mate or an assistant engineer . . . and some working clothes. I want to leave tonight or tomorrow. Will you help me?"

"I don't know if I can, Mr. Kellner." The old Chinese stared at Jakob in alarm. "Are you sure this is a wise course?"

"No, it isn't wise at all," replied Jakob in a tense voice. "You must say nothing of this to the rest of the staff. I'll never ask you to do anything like this for me again — but now it's vital."

Wu's face crinkled into a worried frown. "I'll try to help you, Mr. Kellner — if you've really made up your mind to go."

"I have," said Jakob firmly. "Please go and talk to your relatives straightaway about the arrangements."

6

A small black Public Security Bureau jeep speeding through the darkened streets of Shanghai with its siren blaring bounced and shuddered over the uneven road surfaces. From its rear seat Mei-ling stared apprehensively out at the jostling crowds of Red Guards thronging the pavements, armed with paste pots and long-handled brushes. Although an illuminated clock above them showed it was two-thirty A.M., the Red Guards were yelling and chanting boisterously as they fixed new giant slogans on the walls of offices and public buildings. Written in black characters four feet high, the slogans proclaimed "We Will Burn the Mayor of Shanghai!" "Down with Shanghai's Black Gang!" "Workers and Red Guards Must Bombard the Stinking Municipal Headquarters Together!"

Mei-ling's wrists were handcuffed in front of her and she was wedged between two silent Chinese security policemen dressed in green tunics and navy trousers. They wore soft caps with red badges bearing the symbolic images of the Gate of Heavenly Peace and beneath their peaks the expressions on the policemen's faces were grim and hostile. They had barged noisily into the Conservatory of Music only minutes before to drag Mei-ling unceremoniously from the bamboo mat on which she lay sleeping alongside a dozen other teachers who, like her, had been condemned as cow demons and confined in a Red Guard cowshed for the past month. Every day they had all been forced to write long self-criticisms of their "bourgeois class backgrounds" and face heated cross-examinations by vociferous Red Guards. All of them had been repeatedly "hatted" and "struggled" and forced to do hours of humiliating physical labor each day, scrubbing floors and cleaning student lavatories. An unbroken month of such treatment had left all the music teachers exhausted and Mei-ling's sleep-dazed mind had not at first registered any alarm when the security policemen burst in. She had been wakened before in the middle of the night by overzealous Red Guards demanding new self-criticisms or setting fresh tasks, and only when she was handcuffed and led outside to the waiting jeep did she come fully awake. In the first days of the Cultural Revolution she had often seen the ominous black vehicles dashing through the crowded streets, carrying manacled victims to prison, and when the driver switched on the jeep's siren and set off at a high speed, her heart sank.

As the jeep nosed through the noisy Red Guard crowds in the center of the city, she scrutinized the new slogans they were pasting up as best she could, searching for some clue that might link her sudden arrest to the activity in the streets. When the vehicle turned onto the Bund she saw crowds of adult workers pasting up wall posters and slogans that demanded "Unite with the Workers and Declare War on the Municipal Party Authorities" and she realized that the movement which had begun by focusing on the nation's youth was suddenly expanding and spreading. But none of the new slogans seemed to provide any clue to the reason for her arrest and she stared helplessly out of the window of the jeep as it moved along the riverside boulevard beside towering neo-Georgian edifices, which had been built long ago by Shanghai's foreign colonizers. With a squeal of tires the vehicle swung through an archway beneath one of the pillared facades, and in the cobbled courtyard where it halted, Mei-ling glimpsed a sign announcing that the building was now the

Shanghai headquarters of the Military Control Commission. Two armed sentries of the People's Liberation Army were standing guard in front of a columned doorway, and Mei-ling's police escorts hurried her past them after a muttered exchange. Inside she was led along a series of dingy, echoing corridors and up several flights of stairs. At the end of a deserted passageway she was shown into a windowless room that contained only a small wooden table and two chairs; as she stared about herself in dismay, the door closed behind her and she heard a key turn in the lock.

The bare walls of the room were painted two dull shades of green, the lower half darker than the top, and the floor was covered with fiber matting. No sound came from the passageway outside and for several minutes Mei-ling stood immobile in the center of the room, feeling thoroughly disconcerted, her heart beating fast. The hand-cuffs were beginning to chafe her wrists, and sinking down onto one of the chairs, she made a conscious effort to relax. Ten or fifteen minutes passed and then she heard the sound of a key turning in the lock; to her astonishment, when the door opened, her son, Kao, stepped quietly into the room. He was alone, and after closing and locking the door carefully behind him, he drew a small key from a pocket in his tunic and hurried to her side to unlock her handcuffs.

"I'm sorry I had to bring you here like this," he said quietly as he bent over her. "I had to do it for my own protection — it was the only way we could talk privately."

Instead of his usual neatly tailored cadre's suit, Kao was wearing a Red Guard uniform of faded khaki cotton and a cap of the same color pulled low over his face. A crimson *Hung Wei Ping* arm band was fixed to his left sleeve, and as she stared at him, Mei-ling saw that his face was smudged with dirt and there were lines of strain and tiredness around his eyes.

"I didn't know you were in Shanghai, Kao," said Mei-ling in a broken whisper, watching him unhook the handcuffs from her wrists. "Why are you here? And why are you dressed like that?"

"I've come from Peking many times recently to do special work," replied Kao guardedly. He stood up, waiting while his mother massaged her wrists; she was staring at him obsessively, still trying to come to terms with the shock of seeing him, and he became uncomfortable under her gaze. "I haven't been able to help you before because the situation in Shanghai has been very confused. But you'll be able to leave the cowshed and go home soon."

A large vacuum flask stood on the table beside two glass beakers and Kao quickly filled one of them with hot water from the flask. Handing it to his mother, he seated himself at the opposite side of the table and watched her sip the water.

"The Cultural Revolution hasn't gone well up to now in Shanghai," he said in a low voice. "The Party leaders here have been very clever. They've deflected criticism from themselves by directing all the Red Guards to attack the easiest targets — intellectuals and rightists who've been publicly criticized in the past. That's why you and a lot of your colleagues were thrown into the cowshed at the conservatory." He drew a deep breath and again an uncomfortable expression appeared in his eyes. "I'm sorry. . . . I had to let things take their course. I heard what was happening but you know how careful I have to be. It would be very easy for others to attack my own background if I gave any public cause for suspicion."

"There's no need to apologize, Kao." Mei-ling spoke almost inaudibly, dropping her gaze to stare into her glass. "Don't worry about me. Your future is more important than anything else — you're right to put your career and the Party first."

Kao gazed at his mother in consternation, wondering at her resilience. She was wearing dark blue cotton drabs and the stress of the past month showed clearly in the shadows beneath her eyes. But her hair, which was held back from her face with a single metal clip, was still lustrously dark, without any trace of gray, and the great beauty of her youth was visible in her slender figure and an almost unlined face that still remained striking in middle age.

"Has it been very hard in the cowshed?" asked Kao quietly.

Mei-ling continued to sip the hot water in silence, and when she replied she did not look at him. "Before the Cultural Revolution I was popular with my students. So I'm luckier than some teachers. But a few Red Guards are frightened of being attacked by their comrades — so they never let up on us."

"That will change now," said Kao in a vehement undertone. "The Party leadership here is the most stubborn black gang in all China. So far they've survived by confusing the Red Guards and setting them at one another's throats. But two million workers are entering the battle now to help overthrow them — they'll form a great alliance and unify all the Red Guards. They'll show the rest of China how to win victory in the Cultural Revolution."

The hard edge in Kao's voice made Mei-ling raise her head to look at him. "From the jeep I saw big crowds of workers pasting up new slogans. Did you come here to organize them?"

"It's better if you don't know what I'm doing," he said softly. "Better for both of us."

Kao took off his cap and ran a hand distractedly through his hair. Laying his cap aside, he poured himself a glass of hot water from the flask and sipped it slowly.

"You look very tired," said Mei-ling, studying her son intently. "You should try to rest more."

"My work's very important," replied Kao quickly, looking away. "I don't have much time to rest."

A silence fell between them and Mei-ling continued to look at her son. "I'm sorry we've spent so little time together in our lives, Kao," she said at last, her voice little more than a whisper. "In some ways we're like strangers. Even when you were small it was difficult. You had to grow up too much alone."

"Nonsense." Kao rose restlessly from his seat and began pacing rapidly back and forth in the small room. "In Yenan it was much more important for you to go on working for the revolution. It's nobody's fault that my father sacrificed his life fighting the Japanese. That's something to be proud of. There's nothing you need blame yourself for. . . ." Kao pulled back the sleeve of his tunic to look impatiently at his watch. "It's almost time for you to be taken back. I've arranged discreetly for your self-criticisms to be accepted now. A decision will be recorded that your attitude toward the Cultural Revolution has become 'positive.' You'll be allowed to leave the cowshed and return to your home in a day or two. I'll try to visit you soon. I'll come at night so that my visit attracts no attention."

Mei-ling nodded and smiled wearily. "Thank you for all you've done."

Kao halted awkwardly before her chair, taking the handcuffs from his pocket. "I'll have to put these on you again. The same security policemen will come to escort you back to the cowshed in about half an hour's time. Your 'arrest for interrogation' will be listed as an administrative error. . . . I'm sorry it has to be this way."

Mei-ling nodded blankly and Kao knelt to fasten the handcuffs onto her wrists once more. He had difficulty with the locking mechanism and when at last he succeeded in securing them, he sat back on his haunches, smiling uneasily. But she did not return his smile; instead she sat looking sadly back at him and suddenly he seized her manacled hands in both his own before rising to his feet and hurrying from the room. Mei-ling heard the door key scrape in the lock; then her son's footsteps faded swiftly along the corridor. No other sound broke the stillness and she sat patiently on the chair in the silent room, awaiting the return of the men in the black jeep, with tears flowing uncontrollably down her cheeks.

7

"It's a pity you decided not to stay last night, Kao," said Abigail gently in Chinese, looking at him over the rim of a glass of rice wine. "I think you really wanted to, didn't you?"

Kao set his own wineglass down on the table without taking his eyes from her face. "I had work to do after I left here last night, Abigail. But even if I hadn't, it would have been dangerous for me to stay. If anybody found out about my visits here, they would be misunderstood. They would be used to attack me."

"You can rely absolutely on my discretion, I've told you that many times," said Abigail with a quiet insistence. "Nothing will ever become known through me."

From the darkened Nanking Road outside Abigail's apartment, the chants of passing Red Guard groups became intermittently audible through the closed and curtained windows, but neither Kao nor Abigail was paying them any attention. The small room in which they sat was comfortably fitted out with modern Chinese furniture and Abigail's own small collection of blackwood antiques and scroll paintings; it was illuminated by a single beeswax candle set on the table between them and they continued looking intently at one another in its soft glow.

"I feel at a disadvantage," said Kao slowly. "You've already had a close friendship with a Chinese colleague. I've never known anybody from outside my own country."

"That friendship wasn't important to me, I can see that now." Abigail hesitated and her voice softened. "With you, Kao, I felt a very strong attraction from the moment we shook hands at Pei-Ta. The way you smiled at me stayed in my mind for a long time." She picked up the flask of rice wine that stood at her elbow to refill his glass and a hint of mischief entered her expression. "Have I shocked you by what I've just said?"

"No."

"That's a pity. I think I'd quite like to shock you just a little sometime. You're such a master at hiding your real feelings."

Kao smiled faintly but the intentness of his gaze provided silent confirmation of his own growing attraction to her. "Perhaps I try to hide my feelings because they are disturbing to me. I can't stop myself looking at you tonight."

Abigail smiled in acknowledging the first direct compliment he had paid her. She had chosen her clothes with care, tying a bandanna of sea green silk around her blond hair to match a high-collared Chinese blouse of the same color embroidered with pink cherry blossom. She also wore soft, low-heeled green slippers and matching velvet trousers bought in England that flattered her long legs, and since Kao had only ever seen her previously in drab workaday denims and cotton shirts, the impact of her appearance on him had been noticeable from the moment he arrived.

"I'm very glad to hear that, Kao," she said softly. "When I saw you again in People's Square I remembered at once the feeling I'd had nine years before at Pei-Ta. I can't really describe it but it was . . . a little disturbing." Abigail smiled and drew a long breath. "I don't think I believe in fate, but it feels a little uncanny, almost as if our friendship was meant to happen. . . ."

She watched him pick up his glass of rice wine and sip it, his eyes still intent upon her. His short-sleeved cream shirt was open at the neck and the navy high-necked tunic of his cadre's uniform hung on the back of his chair where he had flung it on arrival. He had slipped up a back staircase that led to the apartment from a side street just after midnight and although there were obvious signs of strain and weariness in his expression, in the candlelight his broad face seemed more compellingly handsome to Abigail than ever before.

"Kao, I want you to know I believe in following my instincts, not worrying about what lies ahead." She leaned across the table and brushed the back of one of his hands with her fingertips. "I'm not seeking any bargains for myself right now. In all this turmoil I want you to think of my apartment as an oasis where you can rest and relax — without any strings. Sometimes you need to get away from whatever you're doing. I'm happy to respect our 'no questions' agreement about your work. I can see that's vital — but I can also see something's taking a great toll on you. So I want you to come here whenever you like . . . and go whenever you like." She smiled warmly and her hand tightened on his. "And I hope sometimes you'll want to stay. . . ."

Kao did not move or react but sat looking down at the slender fingers which were tracing invisible patterns across his wrist. "You're very remarkable, Abigail," he said in a slightly unsteady voice. "You're a beautiful woman, you speak excellent Chinese . . ." He glanced around at the half-dozen empty dishes which had held delicacies of south China that she had prepared for them. "Even your mastery of Chinese cooking is admirable — yet you say you want no bargains for yourself." His brow crinkled into a frown. "You seem too good to be true."

Abigail drew back from him and studied his face. "I thought I sensed some reserve in you tonight, Kao," she said quietly. "And I suppose I'm not entirely surprised. By now you must have done a little private checking on me — and I suppose you've discovered the link between Abigail Kellner and the Kellner Research Institute, in Hong Kong."

She paused, giving Kao a chance to confirm her suspicion, but he said nothing.

"Well, no matter what you know, perhaps I ought to emphasize the obvious for you — I am only what I appear to be, a foreign-language teacher who loves China. You know well enough I'm not a Communist or a fellow traveler, but far from helping my father with his work in some underhand way, if that's what you might have suspected, I should perhaps tell you that in the past five years I've not seen him once. Nor have I written him anything but the briefest of letters to inform him simply that his daughter is still alive and doing well by her own efforts, thank you. You see, he didn't want me to come to China at all. But I came anyway, believing, as you and Chairman Mao do, that in certain cases 'rebellion is justified.' That's one of the chief reasons we're barely on speaking terms."

"I said nothing of any suspicion," said Kao, his face expressionless. "But your explanation is very interesting."

"I expect you're also aware by now that my father was once a missionary — and that in the thirties he became a captive of the Red Army."

Kao nodded. "And that you were born in China. I wondered why you've never spoken of that."

"Perhaps for the same reason that you don't want to discuss your work with me. I didn't want it to get in the way of our friendship. But more important, the truth is I know almost nothing about it. My father's always been tight-lipped on the subject for reasons best known to himself. That's an even larger part of the reason we're distant with one another." Abigail rose from her seat, gathering up several dishes. "But I hope I'll be able to put that right myself someday — perhaps soon."

"What do you mean?" asked Kao with a quizzical expression.

"I'll explain if and when I have something to tell you." She smiled tantalizingly. "Why don't you make yourself comfortable while I make us jasmine tea."

She carried the dishes into the small kitchen and when she returned to the room a few minutes later she was carrying a lacquered tray bearing a bamboo-handled teapot and two small decorated cups. Kao, who had stretched himself out wearily on the long sofa, watched her intently as she placed the tray on a low blackwood table and switched on a shaded table lamp. She knelt on the carpet to fill the cups and for a minute or two they sipped the fragrant tea in silence, looking at one another and listening to the occasional throb of passing Red Guard drums and the distant sound of raggedly chanted slogans.

"In case you decide you can't stay tonight," said Abigail at last, shifting closer and looking down into his face, "I'd like you to do something for me now." She took one of his hands, pressing it between her own, and unhooked two or three of the delicate silver frog fastenings that closed the high neck of her silken blouse.

"I want you to undress me, Kao," she murmured. "Now — before you go."

Kao stared up at her, his eyes burning suddenly with a new brightness; then with slow, uncertain movements he began to unhook the remaining silver clasps one by one until finally the blouse fell open from top to bottom. Abigail wore nothing beneath it and with a quick movement she shrugged the garment from her shoulders, leaving herself naked to the waist. The sensation of his first impulsive caress caused her to shiver uncontrollably and she closed her eyes, letting her head fall backward as he raised himself toward her.

"Stay here with me, Kao," she urged him in another frantic whisper and tugged open his shirt to rake her hands across his hard, lean chest. "Undress both of us."

Kao obeyed, then, catching her face in both his hands, he kissed her fiercely; when he released her they gazed into one another's eyes, awed by the breathless frenzy that had seized them.

"Kao, don't wait," Abigail gasped. "Don't wait any longer."

They encircled one another with frantic arms and she shifted beneath him, drawing him deep into herself. The profoundest feeling of union engulfed her, making her sob joyously aloud, and she forgot her separate existence for the space of several blinding seconds. Outside in the street, the sound of Red Guard drums and cymbals being beaten furiously on a moving vehicle grew louder, approaching at speed. The discordant chorus of sound reached a crescendo, drowning their ecstatic cries as the vehicle roared by outside; then the cacophony faded, melting rapidly into the distance.

Locked in their embrace, Kao and Abigail saw and heard nothing else beyond themselves. The first rage of passion began to ebb but for a long time both remained oblivious to their surroundings. Clinging tightly to each other, they had merged as one, their minds and bodies fused by an impulse of which they were both instinctively aware but which neither then could begin to understand.

8

T wo evenings later Abigail entered a narrow lane a mile or so from the Shanghai Conservatory of Music and halted before a gate set in a low wall. In the deepening darkness, washing that fluttered from bamboo poles was faintly visible above the top of the wall and Abigail guessed that several families now shared the kitchens, bathrooms, and halls of most of the dilapidated old middle-class homes. Strips of torn and faded wall posters which had been stuck on the gate and wall weeks before were flapping raggedly in the evening breeze and by the feeble glow of a nearby street lamp she could still read sections of the poster that urged "Bourgeois Reactionary Element Lu Mei-ling" to confess her "Crimes Against the Revolution." But on leaning closer she saw that symbolic Red Guard seals made of paper, which had always been pasted across the latch of the gate during her previous visits, had been freshly broken and she at once reached up and rang the bell on the gatepost.

For several minutes nobody answered but Abigail continued to ring insistently and at last she heard footsteps crossing the yard; they stopped and there was silence as if somebody inside the courtyard were having second thoughts. Then the gate opened an inch and Abigail felt herself come under the scrutiny of a shadowy figure inside.

"I'm Abigail Kellner," she said, speaking Chinese and bending toward the gate. "I'm English. I'd like to speak to Madame Lu Mei-ling in private if that's possible."

In the gloom Abigail was unable to see whether it was a man or woman who had answered her ringing but she sensed that the figure standing inside the little walled yard was uneasy. "I teach at the Foreign Languages Institute in Shanghai," she said in a reassuring tone. "I've come many times in the last few weeks but the gate's always been sealed. Madame Lu Mei-ling took care of me for a time when I was very young."

After another long moment of hesitation the gate opened just wide enough to admit her and a subdued female voice said, "I'm Lu Mei-ling. Please come in."

Abigail stepped quickly over the threshold of the gate, feeling faintly elated, but inside the small yard she found herself standing among ugly piles of debris and rubble. By the light spilling from an upper window she saw that broken furniture and porcelain lay scattered among uprooted shrubs and sodden heaps of gray ashes; stagnant pools of water lay in holes that had been dug in the flower beds. Yet the Chinese woman made no reference to the chaos as she led the way silently along a little cleared path into a tiny, shabby hall. Its walls were daubed with crude black-painted characters that said "Down with All Bourgeois Reactionary Scum!" and when Abigail followed the woman up a short flight of stairs she saw that the walls of the staircase were covered with similar slogans.

In a larger room at the top of the stairs lit by a single unshaded bulb, Abigail was dismayed to see that piles of household debris still cluttered the floor — broken lamps, torn curtains, fractured blackwood tables, and smashed fragments of ornaments, pictures, and mirrors lay jumbled together and narrow paths similar to those in the yard had been cleared to allow access to a small kitchen and a bedroom. The white walls were covered in painted slogans attacking "Stinking Bourgeois Intellectual Lu" and colored portraits of a blank-faced Mao Tse-tung had been pasted to doors and cupboards. In a cleared space beneath an uncurtained window, a cheap, mass-produced table and two chairs that looked new had been set up, and the woman, who wore a shabby tunic and trousers of blue cotton, motioned Abigail to sit down.

"Please wait, I will make some tea."

Abigail, appalled by the disorder, sat down reluctantly at the table and watched the woman walk into the tiny kitchen. Taller than average and slender in build, she carried herself with a quiet dignity, although she moved slowly as though numbed or distracted. In the shapeless blue cottons she looked curiously youthful and when she returned to the table with a small tray and sat down opposite her, Abigail saw that while she looked strained and weary, her face still possessed a beauty rare in middle age.

"I hope you'll forgive the condition of my apartment," said Mei-ling distantly as she poured tea into two small cups. "I've been detained by the Red Guards at the conservatory. I was allowed home yesterday. . . . But they haven't given me permission to clean up here yet."

Abigail gazed uncertainly at the Chinese woman. Obviously shaken by her recent experiences, she seemed dazed and disoriented and Abigail was seized by a sudden doubt. "Could I have made a mistake?" she asked in an anxious voice. "You are Lu Mei-ling the writer?"

"Yes — but that was a long, long time ago." Mei-ling peered distractedly into her teacup. "I haven't written anything for many years."

"But you did write *Women of the Revolution* . . . and you were on the Long March?"

Mei-ling nodded without looking up.

"My father is Jakob Kellner . . . he was held prisoner by the Red Army." A rush of emotion caused Abigail's voice to falter. ". . . He told me that you nursed me on part of the march . . . that you were a mother to me . . . and saved my life. Is all that true?"

Mei-ling raised her head and although the expression in her eyes was guarded, her face softened in a faint smile. "I recognize you from the photograph your father showed me. But you're even more lovely than your picture."

Abigail stared at Mei-ling, deeply moved and shocked in the same moment. "Have you kept in touch with my father?" she asked in an astonished whisper.

"No." Mei-ling's expression became pained. "He visited me for a few minutes when he came back to China in 1957. Didn't he tell you about that?"

"No. I didn't know he'd seen you." Abigail felt tears start in her eyes and she reached across the table and gripped one of Mei-ling's hands tightly. "But that doesn't matter now. I'm so glad I've found you. I've wanted all my life to meet you and say thank you."

Mei-ling stared silently into Abigail's face; then her own eyes dampened and she clasped Abigail's hands in both her own. "There's no need to thank me. I was glad to help. You were a sweet baby. . . . I became very attached to you."

For a long time the two women sat holding hands across the table, unable to summon words to express feelings that had been buried deep inside them for many years. The night outside was still and quiet and only occasionally did the sound of passing footsteps reach into the wrecked room.

"I have so many questions I want to ask you," said Abigail at last, speaking with a catch in her voice. "There's so much I'd love to know."

As Abigail waited expectantly, Mei-ling's expression became guarded again and she slowly withdrew her hands to pick up her teacup. "How much has your father told you?" she asked quietly, averting her eyes.

"Almost nothing," said Abigail with an exasperated smile. "He withdraws into an invisible shell when I ask him questions — that's why I've always longed to meet you myself."

Mei-ling passed a hand wearily across her face, brushing back a loose strand of hair, and sighed. "Perhaps your father's right," she said, rising quickly from the table and picking up the teapot. "Perhaps it's best to forget. It can do little good raking over the past."

Turning her back abruptly, Mei-ling hurried to the small kitchen, and Abigail heard her making fresh tea although very little had yet been drunk. When she came back, although she set the teapot down on the table, she did not resume her seat but began walking up and down the room between the heaps of debris. Mystified by her abrupt change of mood, Abigail sat watching her in a helpless silence.

"Is anything wrong, Mei-ling?" asked Abigail at last. "Has my coming here upset you?"

"No." Mei-ling stopped pacing, listening intently to the new sound of footsteps in the lane outside; but they passed and died away and she consulted her wristwatch with a frown. "I'm just very tired . . . and somebody else may be visiting me this evening."

"Then I'll go," said Abigail quickly, rising to her feet. "I'm sorry. I didn't mean to intrude. I would love to talk some more when you're feeling better. May I visit you again?"

"Yes, of course. Come back again in a few days' time."

The sight of Mei-ling standing wearily amid the devastation of her broken belongings moved Abigail deeply and on an impulse she picked her way across the room to her and put her arms about her shoulders in a gentle embrace.

"Please take care of yourself, Mei-ling, until I see you again," she whispered. "It will mean a great deal to me."

Abigail made her way to the top of the stairs, then turned to look back before descending. Mei-ling was still standing motionless in the center of the room, at once a courageous and forlorn figure.

"And thank you again," called Abigail softly. "Thank you for being so generous — and so brave."

9

As he strode through the noisy crowds of workers and students thronging the Shanghai waterfront, Jakob pulled the collar of a shabby reefer jacket up around his ears and hunched his shoulders, endeavoring to attract as little attention to himself as possible. He wore a navy blue seaman's cap pulled low over his eyes and he deliberately hugged the nighttime shadows cast by the solid colonial edifices that still dominated the Bund. He walked quickly, looking neither left nor right, ignoring the commotion around him. Ahead he could see the grandiose bulk of the Cathay Hotel, now renamed the Peace Hotel, opposite which he had landed from the *Tomeko Maru* more than three decades before. Externally, like all the other imposing waterfront buildings, the old hotel remained virtually unchanged and in the flare of the streetlights the Bund looked to Jakob like the immutable, classical backdrop for a living opera in which only the cast pouring across the stage in a fresh scene had changed.

Gone were the indolent white-suited Europeans who once had lounged at ease in the rickshaws, gone were the sweating, bare-chested coolies who had hauled merchandise endlessly for their foreign masters; gone too were the gleaming limousines and the sleek foreign warships at anchor on the Whangpoo which had symbolized China's subjugation. Now the Bund seethed with activity of a vastly different sort: along the whole length of the curving boulevard columns of student Red Guards and adult Revolutionary Rebels were marching and running, shouting slogans and waving giant red flags and portraits of Mao Tse-tung. At several points among the trees and gardens that flanked the river, temporary platforms decked with red banners and slogans had been set up under floodlights, and dense crowds were gathered around them, chanting and yelling in response to the amplified speeches that were booming out through loudspeakers. The visible slogans strung around the platforms and the speeches being made by students and factory workers alike called repeatedly for unity and the forging of a "great alliance," but Jakob continued walking at a fast pace, deliberately closing his ears to the details of what the banners and voices said.

To his great relief, the false seaman's card and discharge book obtained for him in Hong Kong by his chief translator had passed the scrutiny of the harbor's military guards without any difficulty when he had stepped ashore a mile from the Peace Hotel. Anxiety about inspection of these fake documents had grown steadily within him during the two days he had spent hidden on board a Dutch freighter, and although the reaction of the PLA soldiers at the foot of the ship's gangplank had given him no cause for alarm, as he hurried on he remained apprehensive that somehow discovery of his true identity might still prevent him from reaching Abigail's apartment. Nobody among the excited crowds thronging the Bund had given him a second glance, but fearing that he might accidentally become a target of interest because of his foreign appearance, Jakob turned off the main street into a side lane soon after entering the Nanking Road.

The sound of his own footsteps echoing in the gloom of the stone-paved alley immediately triggered another vivid memory of the day of his arrival in Shanghai — the sensation of sliding suddenly from the hot sunlight into a shadowy, subterranean tunnel haunted by disembodied yellow-brown faces. He wondered whether by some quirk of fate he had chosen that selfsame alleyway, and above the sound of his footsteps he seemed to hear again the rattle of the rickshaw's wheels on the slimy cobblestones and the slap of his coolie's straw-sandaled feet. It was at that moment that he had seemed to plunge headlong into Asia with the plangent music of lutes and gongs ringing in his ears. He smelled again the pungent spices, the incense, and the fetid reek of overcrowded humanity that had left such an indelible impression on his senses, and other related mind-pictures began to spill rapidly through his memory. Laurence Franklin's youthful face smiled a greeting on the teeming quayside; a Chinese courtesan in a passing rickshaw shielded her face beneath a mauve parasol; a ragged body, unmoving in death, huddled at the foot of a wall; and a legless beggar with a hole in his skull sparked off Jakob's own wild dash through the narrow lanes between the shafts of a rickshaw. The horror of those last images gave way unaccountably to a spellbinding vision of a young Mei-ling descending the gang ladder of the *Tomeko Maru* in a full-skirted dress of French muslin and a beribboned sun hat. Her golden face was radiantly beautiful and the force of the recollection jerked Jakob's mind back to his painful anxieties about Abigail and Mei-ling which had wracked him constantly since the day he received his daughter's letter.

In that moment he became fully aware that the alley down which he was hurrying was now ominously deserted. The beggars, the cripples, and the squalor had all been swept away, not, as Jakob had dreamed thirty years ago, by widespread acceptance of the Christian faith, but by other historical forces of which he had then been totally ignorant. The alleyway, a small crevice of China, had been transformed along with the rest of the country. Now garish wall posters and portraits of Mao's unsmiling face were plastered everywhere, covering doors and windows without discrimination, and in the unnatural silence that cloaked that lane and others leading into it, he suddenly sensed the unmistakable presence of fear and foreboding.

In the wider streets through which he made his way, Jakob also detected similar signs of unease; older Chinese watched warily from windows and gateways as though constantly expecting some new threat to appear and his own vague feelings of apprehension grew as he neared the area where Abigail lived. He had studied a detailed map of Shanghai while concealed in the captain's cabin on the freighter and had carefully memorized the location of her address but when he arrived outside the five-story apartment block in a dimly lit street off the Nanking Road, he lingered uncertainly in the shadows on the opposite pavement. Looking up toward the several curtained windows through which chinks of light were visible, he had to fight down a strong desire to turn away and hurry back to the ship, which was due to sail for Hong Kong again on the three A.M. tide. After so many years of near-estrangement from his daughter, bursting in on her disguised in the clothes of a seaman seemed an act of such irrationality that he wavered in his purpose. He tried to imagine what he might say in response to her shocked questions and the prospect of explaining truthfully why he had come was suddenly almost too daunting to contemplate.

Then the twin feelings of horror which Abigail's letter had provoked returned. How could he stand by idly while Mei-ling suffered so cruelly and undeservedly for a second time? How could he allow a close relationship to grow up between Kao and Abigail without telling them the truth? Jakob turned these questions over unendingly in his mind, then, unable to reconcile any of the nagging doubts and fears, he crossed the road almost at a run and pushed open the main door of the apartment building. Seeing from a row of nameplates that Abigail lived on the fourth floor, he climbed the stairs two at a time and knocked firmly on the door. It was opened almost at once by Abigail, who had started to smile, but when she caught sight of him, her expression changed to one of blank incomprehension. Realizing just how effective his disguise had been, Jakob tugged off his cap and Abigail's eyes widened in astonishment.

"Father! What in heaven's name . . . ?"

When she had recovered from her surprise, she motioned him inside and closed the door quickly behind him. At a loss for words, they both stood looking at one another in a stunned silence and Jakob saw that despite the late hour Abigail was dressed attractively in a crisp English shirtwaist dress, and her long blond hair framed her face in soft waves. The tension of the past two days made him want to reach out and embrace her now that he had reached her safely, but something stopped him and he turned and stepped uncertainly into the living room. There he noticed at once that the small dining table was set with two places and a pleasant aroma of cooking was coming from the kitchen.

"What on earth has brought you here, Daddy?" Abigail's voice was incredulous. "And why are you wearing those strange clothes?"

"I came as soon as I got your letter." Jakob stopped in the middle of the room and turned to face her. "What I read made me very worried about you. . . . I smuggled myself here on a freighter with false seaman's papers."

"But that's very dangerous!" Abigail's incredulity changed to alarm. "What on earth could I have said to make you that worried?"

Jakob drew a long breath. "It's not just what you said in your letter, Abigail. . . . From Hong Kong it's clear that the Cultural Revolution is beginning to cause terrible disruption all over China. . . . There's no telling where it will end. . . . I wanted to try to persuade you to leave now before it gets any worse. For your own safety . . ."

"Daddy, that's very thoughtful of you." She smiled in puzzlement, touched despite herself by his concern. "But I think I'm capable of judging the situation here. And I don't think I'm personally in any danger yet."

"Perhaps not directly at the moment — but I'm sure you will be soon."

Jakob's whole bearing was that of a man ill at ease and Abigail could see in his face traces of the strain that the secret journey from Hong Kong had produced. "Daddy, please sit down, " she said gently, waving him toward an armchair and crossing the room to a tray of bottles on a sideboard. "I've got some Scotch here. I can see you need something." She poured whisky into two glasses, gave Jakob one of them, and sat down opposite him on the sofa. "Please tell me what it was I said that alarmed you so much."

Jakob drank some whisky without looking at her. "You told me in your letter that you'd seen a poster attacking Lu Mei-ling, didn't you?"

"Yes, I did."

"Has it occurred to you that the Red Guards might have forced her to confess that she once cared for the child of a 'foreign imperialist spy' — and that you might be in some danger yourself if they discovered you were here in Shanghai?"

"That's hardly very likely," said Abigail with a faint sigh of exasperation. "Nobody here really knows that much about my past."

"I expect you've told somebody."

"One or two of my foreign colleagues know — but that's all."

"They might have spoken of it in the hearing of students — anything's possible." Jakob looked up suddenly from his drink. "Have you managed to see Lu Mei-ling yourself yet?"

"Yes, I have. She's just been released by the conservatory's Red Guards. I talked to her at her home two nights ago."

Jakob's shoulders hunched with tension and he shifted to the edge of his seat. "How did she seem?"

"She was still quite upset by what had been happening to her. I think she's been through some unpleasant experiences. But she's strong and resilient — and still a very remarkable woman."

"Did she tell you all you wanted to know?"

"No, she wouldn't really tell me anything of substance. You'll be glad to know she's almost as evasive as you are." Abigail put down her whisky on a side table and when she spoke again her voice was carefully controlled. "But she did mention that you'd visited her in 1957 and showed her my photograph. Why didn't you tell me about that?"

"I thought it was best at the time to say nothing to you about it. Mei-ling was undergoing reform through labor. It was very distressing for us both. . . ." Jakob stood up and began to move about the room, stopping now and then to gaze absently at the scroll paintings on the walls. "You must be expecting somebody," he said over his shoulder. "Is it Kao?"

"I'm not exactly expecting him," said Abigail, speaking slowly and deliberately. "He has a standing invitation. Sometimes he comes here to join me for a late supper."

Jakob stood still and turned to face her. "So you've become . . . very close friends?"

"I suppose you could say that," said Abigail coolly. "But I don't really see, Daddy, that it's any business of yours."

"I'm sorry, but it is some business of mine." Jakob's voice broke a little. "I wish it weren't."

"I can't imagine what you mean."

Jakob closed his eyes briefly to gather himself. "Does Mei-ling know that you and Kao are meeting?"

"I should hardly think so. What possible interest could it be to her?"

A pained expression came into Jakob's eyes. "Mei-ling is Kao's mother."

Abigail shook her head incredulously. "I can hardly believe it."

"It's true — but before I try to explain anything else I must see Mei-ling. . . ."

"You mean now?"

Jakob nodded quickly. "Yes, straightaway. The ship I came on is due to sail at three A.M. — so I don't have much time. Will you take me to where she's living?"

For a moment Abigail did not reply. Sitting motionless on the sofa, she stared perplexedly at her father. "If we're going out, I'll have to change my clothes," she said at last in a distracted voice, rising slowly to her feet. "I shan't be long."

She hurried out into the hall and Jakob began pacing agitatedly back and forth across the room again, glancing occasionally at the two place settings and the unlit candle that had been positioned between them on the small dining table.

10

The sight of the old, crudely daubed slogans attacking "Bourgeois Reactionary Vampire Lu Mei-ling" made Jakob shudder as they came in sight of the courtyard wall surrounding Mei-ling's house. It had begun to rain heavily soon after they set out from Abigail's apartment, and the painted slogans and posters along the length of the lane were being rapidly reduced to a blurred, sticky mess in the downpour. The feeble cones of light cast by the street lamps heightened the dismal, defeated atmosphere of the area and again Jakob found himself wishing desperately that he could turn around and hurry back to the docks. Outside Mei-ling's gate Abigail stopped and reached up toward the bell push, but Jakob moved forward quickly, catching at her wrist before she could ring. He had noticed that the poster-covered gate was standing slightly ajar and he leaned close to his daughter to speak in an undertone.

"I'd like to see Mei-ling alone at first. Will you wait here for two minutes, please — then come up?"

They had scarcely spoken to one another since leaving her apartment and Abigail shook her head in a little gesture of exasperation. "I suppose deep inside I knew from the time of that first visit to Hong Kong that you were hiding something to do with Mei-ling."

"You'll know everything soon," said Jakob in a hollow voice. "Just let me have a few moments alone with her."

Without waiting for Abigail's response Jakob pushed open the gate. Debris and ashes still littered the courtyard inside and he walked carefully along the path that had been cleared to the door. Acting on an impulse, he turned the handle before knocking; when it gave under his pressure he entered the shabby hall and climbed quietly up the steep flight of stairs. The walls of the staircase were still covered with slogans attacking Mei-ling. By the light of the unshaded bulb on the landing Jakob also saw that other daubings defaced the visible walls on the upper floor. His heart began thudding loudly inside his chest and when the sound of a movement reached his ears halfway up the stairs, he halted in his tracks, aware suddenly that his silent entry might be misunderstood.

"Is Madame Lu Mei-ling at home?" he called politely in Chinese.

"Who is it? Who's there?"

A faint inflection of surprise was recognizable in Mei-ling's query but the sound of the soft, educated voice stirred Jakob deeply. He began climbing again and when he reached the top of the stairs he found she was standing in an open doorway looking at him.

"It's me . . . Jakob," he said softly, removing his cap.

Mei-ling stood unmoving, as though turned to stone. A blank expression had frozen on her face and she gazed mutely at him, seemingly incapable of speech.

"Don't be alarmed," said Jakob, stepping toward her. "Abigail wrote saying she'd seen your name in a wall poster. . . . I thought perhaps I could help in some way . . ."

Although she wore a shapeless cotton tunic with baggy trousers and her hair was unkempt, Jakob found that the beauty of Mei-ling's face moved him as profoundly as it had ever done in his youth and he stared at her, transfixed.

"Jakob, you shouldn't have come," she said in a barely audible whisper. "Please go quickly."

"Mei-ling, I came secretly on a cargo ship — just seeing you again has made all the risks worthwhile." Jakob reached out a hand and touched her cheek wonderingly with his fingertips. "My feelings for you have never changed —"

"Please, Jakob!" She shrank back from him. "I'm not alone."

She half turned to look behind her and Jakob noticed for the first time that a male figure was seated at the table among the still-uncleared heaps of smashed furniture and ornaments. Pictures of Mao and slogans attacking "Stinking Bourgeois Intellectual Lu" remained splattered on all the walls and something in the stiff attitude of the seated figure echoed his ominous surroundings. As Jakob watched, the man rose from his chair and walked slowly toward them.

"This is my son, Kao." Mei-ling stepped back into the room,

struggling to keep her voice steady, and Jakob saw a fearful look come into her eyes. "Kao, this is Jakob Kellner."

Jakob felt his chest tighten as he looked at the handsome, self-possessed Chinese in his early thirties. Kao still wore his navy blue cadre suit, buttoned high at the neck, and he was staring fixedly at Jakob, his expression wary and mistrustful.

"We met briefly at Pei-Ta University in 1957," said Jakob haltingly. "My daughter, Abigail, and I were members of a peace delegation . . . We shook hands with you. . . ."

Kao nodded but his hostile expression did not soften. "How do you know my mother, Mr. Kellner?"

"We met many, many years ago. We traveled on the same passenger ship when I came to China to work as a missionary. Your mother was returning from her studies in Europe. . . . When I became a prisoner of the Red Army we met again. During the most difficult stages of the Long March she cared for Abigail . . ."

Kao's eyes narrowed but he absorbed the information without betraying any other reaction. "And now you've come back to Shanghai in secret to offer her your help?"

Jakob nodded uneasily. "That was one of my reasons for coming."

"Mr. Kellner, how can somebody like you help my mother?"

Jakob hesitated. "Some years ago I was able to request lenient treatment for her at a high level." He turned to Mei-ling, who was looking at him in surprise. "I did it with Chiao's help, Mei-ling," he added softly. "It hastened your release from the coal yard."

Kao's face betrayed his surprise briefly, then his expression hardened again. "And what are your other reasons for coming here tonight?" he asked acidly.

Jakob had not taken his eyes off Mei-ling and he addressed his answer to her. "When Abigail wrote telling me she'd seen wall posters attacking you, she mentioned that she'd met Kao again. . . . She said they'd become close friends. . . . Do you understand now, Mei-ling, why I had to come?"

As the significance of what Jakob had said dawned on her, Mei-ling's face grew taut and she turned to stare in trepidation at her son. "Is this true, Kao?"

The hostility in Kao's eyes gave way to uneasiness but at that moment Abigail entered the room quietly from the landing, where she had obviously been listening, and moved to his side.

"Yes, Mei-ling, it's true — but I don't see why it need worry you — or my father."

"Why didn't you tell me you knew my mother?" asked Kao in an undertone. "Why did you keep that from me?"

"I didn't keep it from you," said Abigail gently. "I met her for the first time two days ago. I didn't know about any of this until my father arrived tonight."

Mei-ling had been staring wide-eyed at Abigail and Kao and as comprehension dawned, the color drained slowly from her face. With a little cry she buried her face in her hands and her shoulders began to shake in a silent fit of sobbing.

"What's wrong with my mother?" exclaimed Kao, glaring at Jakob.

Mei-ling's sobbing became audible and Abigail moved quickly to put an arm around her shoulders.

"Your mother hoped you would never know the truth," said Jakob in a haunted voice.

"What 'truth' are you talking about?" snapped Kao.

"The truth about your birth. . . . You've always believed your father was killed fighting the Japanese . . . but that's not true."

"What do you mean?"

"The man your mother married wasn't your real father . . ." Jakob's voice shook. "I'm your father."

Kao stared at Jakob, thunderstruck. Abigail too was gazing at him openmouthed with shock.

"It's true, Kao," sobbed Mei-ling, uncovering her tear-stained face. "I was caring for Abigail in the Great Snow Mountains. She was just a helpless infant. . . . Her father didn't know whether she was dead or alive. He slipped away from his guards one night to come and find out. . . . There was a blizzard. He was famished and exhausted. I made him stay with us in the yurt. . . ." She closed her eyes, overcome by the memory, and Abigail, Kao, and Jakob stared at her in a tortured silence. "He asked me to marry him the day he was freed," she whispered when she had regained her composure. "But I was determined to work all my life for the revolution. . . . You were born, Kao, in March the following year."

"I knew nothing of your existence, Kao, until 1957," said Jakob urgently. "I had wanted to marry your mother more than anything else in the world . . . But there was nothing I could do when she refused. . . . When everything's explained to you, perhaps you'll understand. . . ."

"There's nothing you need explain!" Kao's voice burst from him in a shout of anger. "You've said more than enough!" He half raised his clenched fists at his sides as though to attack Jakob, then turned to glare contemptuously at his mother. "How could you do this? How could you live those terrible lies for so many years?"

"I lied for your sake, so that you wouldn't suffer," said Mei-ling in an agonized whisper. "I lied only to help you. I never wanted you to know the truth."

"You mustn't be so harsh, Kao," said Jakob desperately. "Your mother's actions were honorable and compassionate. Let us try to make some amends. . . ."

Kao's eyes glittered with an unnatural brightness and Jakob could see that he was taking in little that was being said. "You're not my father in any way that matters!" he shouted hoarsely. "You're less than nothing to me. You've come illegally to China. Unless you leave the country tonight I'll give orders for you to be arrested as a spy!"

"Kao, please . . ." Abigail left Mei-ling and laid a hand beseechingly on his arm. "Can't we talk alone for a moment?"

"There's nothing to be said." Kao ignored her, staring balefully at Jakob and Mei-ling. "I've been a terrible fool . . ."

"Kao, you're not to blame," said Abigail shakily. "Neither of us has been a fool. What we feel for each other isn't really wrong, don't you see? All this explains so much —"

"Leave me alone!" Kao snatched his arm free and took a step toward Jakob. "I'll remember you only with a feeling of disgust! In my mind the man who died fighting Japan will always be my father!"

Kao glared furiously at Jakob, then swung around toward Mei-ling. Anguish disfigured his features and when Mei-ling instinctively reached out a hand toward him, a look of loathing entered his eyes. "I'm deeply ashamed," he said in a trembling voice. "I don't want you ever again to think of me as your son."

Turning on his heel, Kao strode out of the room and down the stairs. The crash of the courtyard gate closing echoed through the silent house like a gunshot, and Mei-ling and Abigail flinched. After a moment Mei-ling began weeping quietly again and she sank onto one of the chairs, bowing her head.

"Why don't you come to the ship with me?" said Jakob in a desperate tone, moving to Mei-ling's side and touching her shoulder. "I'll find a way of getting you aboard somehow."

"No, no!" Mei-ling's voice was muffled by her hands. "You must go alone."

Jakob stared down helplessly at her, feeling a great sense of desolation engulf him. The noise of rain drumming heavily against the window was the only sound in the room and on looking up he found Abigail staring at him with a curious expression in which pain and pity were visibly mingled.

"I'm sorry, Abigail," he said chokingly. "I'm truly sorry. Will you come back to Hong Kong, please — where it's safe?"

"I don't think I want to be 'safe' according to your lights!" Tears brimmed in Abigail's eyes but she spoke with a vehemence which shocked Jakob. "I don't want the kind of safety you can arrange for me. You were an absentee father for most of my young life. You've curdled everything by clutching your awful secrets to yourself for so long. You always put me last behind your strange sense of loyalty to others. . . . I don't see the remotest point in changing things now."

"But what will you do?" Jakob gazed at her, dumbfounded. "You can't stay here."

"Can't I?" Abigail's tone was openly defiant. "I came here to teach. My life is here. You've blundered into Shanghai chasing your own selfish obsessions — but I'm not going to let that ruin everything I've been working for. I'll stay and ride out the storm. . . . Please don't ever try to interfere in my life again."

Abigail turned away and knelt beside Mei-ling's chair to put an arm around her shoulders once more. Mei-ling was still sobbing quietly and Jakob stood watching his daughter try to comfort her with a growing feeling of despair.

"I'll see that she's all right," said Abigail in an impersonal tone. "There's no more damage you can do here — it would be best if you left now."

Jakob picked his way reluctantly across the room between the piles of household debris and went down the stairs without looking back. Outside the rain was falling in torrents but he did not bother to take his cap from his jacket pocket. Stepping numbly into the deserted, ill-lit street, he turned his steps toward the waterfront, oblivious to the rain that plastered his hair against his head and soaked his clothes.

11

Marshal Lu Chiao closed his eyes with a feeling of revulsion as a scowling Red Guard swung open the creaking steel door of his underground punishment cell in an army barracks outside Peking. The Red Guard was carrying a rusty nineteenth-century torture helmet made of cast iron that had been fixed around Chiao's head for an hour each morning for the past three days, and the memory of the pain it had caused him made Chiao shudder inwardly. His hands were already handcuffed behind his back and around the ratchets his wrists were cut and painfully swollen. He was seated on a bare concrete bench with his back to the wall and he made no move to resist as the Red Guard lowered the fifty-pound helmet onto his head and began tightening the four screws that jutted through its brim.

"It's very appropriate headgear, don't you think, for a shameless counterrevolutionary servant of the comprador bourgeoisie?" The adult Red Guard who had supervised the night attack on Liang's home spat out the words with unconcealed venom from the open doorway. "It was used regularly in Peking until 1947 — by Chiang Kai-shek's jailers. His victims were real Communists loyal to Chairman Mao, not renegades and hidden traitors like you and other supporters of China's Khrushchev."

Chiao raised his head wearily on hearing the new voice. In the two weeks since he had been seized and thrown into the punishment cell, he had seen only jeering members of the Red Guard group who had ambushed him inside the camp. He had driven there alone in response to what appeared to be an invitation from the defense minister, Marshal Lin Piao, but realized too late that he had been duped. After dragging him from his car, the Red Guards had put him through a vicious round of "struggle," screaming meaningless abuse at him while drenching him with black paint which still stained his uniform. Since then he had wondered daily when more detailed accusations of misconduct might be leveled against him and the sound of the unfamiliar voice addressing him from the doorway convinced him that the time had come.

"I suppose I should have known somebody would arrive sooner or later with a list of trumped-up charges," said Chiao through gritted teeth. "I'm surprised it's taken you so long to invent something."

"Those are strange words," sneered the adult Red Guard, "for a counterrevolutionary revisionist who has conducted illicit relations with foreign countries all his life!"

"I've had no illicit contacts with foreign countries," grunted Chiao. "That's . . . purest fantasy . . . and you know it."

The young Red Guard tightened the screws steadily and Chiao felt the pressure around his skull increasing moment by moment. The agonizing weight of the grotesque iron bonnet was sending pains driving down his neck into his shoulders and Chiao strove to position his body squarely on the bench so that he could support its weight evenly.

"What about the British missionary who was a prisoner on the Long March?" said the adult Red Guard gloatingly. "Weren't you responsible for releasing him although he was a convicted spy? And didn't you later arrange for his former lackey Liang to meet him secretly at the Temple of Heaven in 1957? The traitor Liang admitted that before his death."

Chiao opened his eyes to look directly at the newcomer. He could see by the man's bearing that he was an experienced cadre and it was obvious that he had been deputed to attack him by the Cultural Revolution Group. "Everything you say . . . is twisted," he gasped. "Premier Chou and the Party leadership . . . approved the prisoner's release . . . and his return to China in 1957."

The cadre motioned peremptorily to the Red Guard to finish adjusting the iron torture clamps. "The helmet of Chiang Kai-shek's torturers will be removed in two hours' time — if you decide to make a full confession of all your heinous crimes. If not, it will remain in position for a much longer period."

Chiao felt the Red Guard twist the screws once more and at each turn a new flare of pain spread through his temples. The agony threatened to destroy his reason and at once he closed his eyes, deliberately focusing his mind on a point three or four finger-widths below his navel. Silently inside his head he allowed a phrase to form as he sought to assert the "self-preserved" strength of the ancient Taoists, as his father had first taught him to do in his early teens. "Rigid oaks may fall but supple reeds will brave the storm," he repeated to himself several times as he slowed his breathing, striving with every nerve to sense the waves of cosmic energy the Taoists called ch'i flowing softly through his limbs and torso. He visualized the pain as dead leaves floating away on the surface of a fast-running river of *ch'i*, and his body, although held firmly upright, relaxed and softened, absorbing and enduring the fire spreading from the iron bands clamped around his head.

"Confess that you plotted with the treacherous renegade who became China's president and your suffering will be at an end," said the cadre, his voice seeming to come from a long way off. "Admit that you called secret meetings to organize a counterrevolutionary coup d'état against the Party — and the iron helmet will be taken back to the evil museum from which the Red Guards fetched it when they learned of your towering crimes."

"I'll never confess . . . to any crime. I've never . . . committed any crime. Nor . . . has . . . President Liu."

"That treacherous renegade has already made a full confession," barked the cadre. "He's admitted pursuing bourgeois revisionist policies since the time of the Great Leap Forward. He's admitted in writing that he suppressed the masses at the start of the Cultural Revolution. You'll gain nothing by trying to shield him!"

"All your accusations . . . are based . . . on hysterical lies." Chiao winced and groaned as the Red Guard made his final adjustment to the screws. "You're dishonest and contemptible."

"You've called many sinister meetings of other army leaders, since the Cultural Revolution began, to hatch plots for armed insurrection," shouted the cadre angrily. "Others have already confessed!"

"I've called meetings . . . to prevent the chaos of the Cultural Revolution . . . from undermining the army's fighting effectiveness. That's my duty." Chiao paused to gather his strength. "My only concern . . . is to maintain the defenses of the motherland . . . against our outside enemies."

The cadre glowered at Chiao and motioned for the young Red Guard to leave the cell. When the youth had stepped outside, he moved closer to the marshal and stood over him threateningly.

"The Cultural Revolution Group of the Central Committee set up by Chairman Mao orders you to confess fully. If you refuse you'll be handed over to the Red Guards for public trial in the Peking Workers' Stadium. Then your crimes will become known to all."

Chiao's head was throbbing wildly; the iron clamps pressing the inner band inward seemed to stab needles of fire into his brain and the excruciating weight bearing down on the crown of his head felt as though it would break through the bone of his skull. With a supreme effort he stared straight ahead, bringing the focus of his mind sharply back to the *tan t'ien*, the Taoists' center of spiritual force in the lower abdomen. Once he had achieved the necessary sense of detachment, he slowed his breathing, concentrating his entire consciousness in this center, and gradually succeeded in achieving a state of utter calmness despite the pain. If his hands had been free he would have used them to chafe and stimulate the circulation in different areas of his body, but because his wrists were handcuffed behind him he imagined he was stroking, in turn, his face, his forehead, his thighs, and the bare soles of his feet to make the blood and other body fluids flow with increased vitality. The intensity of his imagination re-created the physical sensations which set the cosmic *ch'i* energy flowing around his body and again he imagined it sweeping away the pain in its gentle rush. Soon he could feel the *ch'i* flowing steadily back to the inner reservoir of physical and spiritual force deep within him and a profound and refreshing sense of peace began to settle over his mind, blotting out the agony.

"I shall never confess to your . . . 'crimes,' " said Chiao in a low voice. "No matter what . . . you do . . . to me."

"Then the iron helmet will remain on your head until you're taken before the Red Guards in the Workers' Stadium!"

The cadre studied the seated figure with a baffled expression; sitting with his feet together on the rough concrete bench, his arms wrenched behind him by the handcuffs, Chiao was still managing to hold his head erect. His eyes were open but they seemed to be at ease, focused unblinkingly on nothing as though turned blindly inward. Suddenly there seemed to be a stillness and composure in his body that the cadre found unnerving. Other victims on whom he had seen the device used in recent weeks had often been reduced to moaning wrecks within minutes, slumping sideways on their benches in an effort to escape the helmet's awful weight and succumbing quickly to the terrible pressure of the inner steel band.

The cadre waited for a minute or more to see if the marshal was bluffing, but he showed no sign of moving and his eyes did not even blink. Walking to the barred door, the cadre stepped outside and slammed it noisily. Through the grille he was able to see that the marshal had neither moved nor flinched at the sudden sound. He merely continued to sit motionless and erect, his eyes wide open, his head held steady in spite of its nightmarish burden.

12

"The time has come," yelled Kao, stepping up to a microphone in the center of the crowded Peking Workers' Stadium. "We're here to unmask another leading counterrevolutionary revisionist who supports China's Khrushchev and opposes Chairman Mao! You've already heard many details of his lifelong bourgeois habits — but now you'll hear how thirty years ago he shamelessly sold out his motherland to British imperialism!"

A deep howl of anger rose from the throats of eighty thousand Red Guards and adult Revolutionary Rebels packed into the circular sports arena in Peking's eastern suburbs. The terraces were filled to capacity and the crowd had also been drawn up in dense ranks across the football field to press around the raised wooden platform on which Marshal Lu Chiao had been made to stand, bent double, with his head forced down between his knees. Half a dozen muscular Red Guards under Kao's supervision were grouped closely around him; one held both his arms straight behind his back, another was pushing down his head, and a third squatted beside him, striking him viciously in the stomach with a clenched fist whenever he showed signs of trying to straighten up. Called "the jet plane" because of the resemblance of the victim's arms to the upswept wings of a modern jet fighter, the position, Chiao knew, had been universally used by Red Guards since the onset of the Cultural Revolution to humiliate and inflict pain simultaneously on their victims. During the first few minutes his back and his legs had begun to stiffen and ache, as he knew they would, but gradually the discomfort was intensifying and spreading through his upper body.

"Raising high the red flag of Mao Tse-tung's thought and with Mao Tse-tung's thought as our armament, we are presenting to you today a great number of irrefutable facts that lay bare the towering crimes of this contemptible slave of British imperialism," shouted Kao. "By plucking out this imperialist running dog and showing him to the revolutionary masses, we have won another great victory for Mao Tse-tung's thought!"

Kao turned to glare theatrically at Chiao; then, from among another group of helpers gathered on one corner of the stage, he summoned the Red Guard who had been responsible for fitting the torture helmet to Chiao's head over the past few days.

"Later you'll hear details of crimes committed by that feudalistic old swine Chu Teh," screamed the Red Guard, leaning close to the microphone. "And how 'Marshal' Ho Lung consorted with prostitutes and kept pet monkeys like a capitalist millionaire! But first listen to this catalogue of deceit and shame that has caused a great loss of dignity to the People's Republic of China and is a crime worthy of the death penalty. . . ."

Again the crowd erupted with angry roars and this time the noise subsided into orchestrated chants of "Pluck out the counterrevolutionary slave to foreigners!" Bent double beside the microphone, Chiao tried to straighten up a little to ease the excruciating pain in his back but the Red Guard crouched at his feet immediately struck him a ferocious blow in the abdomen, which doubled him over again and made him retch. Through his haze of pain, Chiao remembered seeing the ashen faces of Chu Teh, the old Central Red Army commander, and Ho Lung, who had courageously led the Second Front Army on its own tortuous Long March. He had caught sight of his two fellow marshals in one of the shadowy corridors beneath the stands of the stadium while being dragged toward the field half an hour earlier; the hands of both had seemed to be bound behind their backs, their uniforms were disheveled, and their strained faces bore silent witness to recent sufferings at the hands of their captors. Marshal Chu in particular had looked haggard and worn out, a pathetic shadow of his former self. He was still a member of the six-man Politburo Standing Committee, and the discovery that such an exalted and revered figure had also become a victim of the Cultural Revolution had increased Chiao's feelings of apprehension as he was manhandled into the seething arena to a deafening explosion of jeers and taunts.

Above the stage, big red banners had been rigged announcing in giant white characters that the rally had been arranged by the "Peking Proletarian Revolutionaries' Anti-imperialist, Anti-revisionist Liaison Station" and the moment he was dragged up onto the platform a succession of fierce-eyed Red Guard accusers had begun stepping up to the microphone. In indignant, emotional tones they yelled details from long, fabricated lists of his "bourgeois habits and crimes." Every utterance had been greeted by a new burst of outraged slogan chanting from all around the great bowl of the stadium.

Unable to discover any real grounds for criticism in his austere personal life, the Red Guards accused him shrilly of "cultivating imperial-style lotus pools as a hobby," "worshiping the feudalistic sages of Taoism," "practicing outdated, meditative martial arts," and "undermining the revolution by trying to preserve the feudal-imperial past." The "foreign slave" life histories of his father and grandfather were narrated in detail from the time of the nineteenth-century Opium Wars as though Chiao himself were directly responsible for their business activities, and he recognized the cynical technique which he knew had now become a Cultural Revolution commonplace. Into the long catalogue of accusations drawn up after the interrogation of colleagues under duress, a core of fact was skillfully interwoven with distortions, exaggerations, misrepresentations, and plain lies. The calculated intention was to produce an emotional climate of hatred and disgust, and the roars of the students and industrial workers filling Chiao's ears were a fitting testimony to the technique's effectiveness.

But as the pain produced by the jet-plane posture intensified in his back, chest, and legs, Chiao found it increasingly difficult to concentrate on what was being said. His temples were still throbbing from the constriction of the iron torture helmet, which had been removed minutes before he was taken from the army punishment cell, and he was able to catch only snatches of the accusations hurled at him. The fierce hostility of the vast crowd and the indignity of his helpless position were combining to make him tremble and sweat despite the cool December air; perspiration was pouring down his face and neck to gather in a pool on the oilcloth covering the wooden stage and he was soon able to see the agonized reflection of his own face in it. The sight of his nephew, Kao, leading his accusers had added to his sense of shock and disorientation, but although the young cadre's face contorted into a vindictive expression whenever Chiao looked in his direction, he still found it hard to decide whether Kao's hostility was genuine or an expedient pose adopted by necessity to protect himself. Occasional waves of dizziness were threatening to undermine Chiao's sense of balance, and fearing he might lose consciousness soon, he began trying desperately to focus and discipline his senses as he had done earlier in the day in enduring the agony of the iron helmet.

". . . A dragon is born a dragon, a phoenix is born a phoenix, and a rat is born with the ability to gnaw a hole in the floor," yelled the

Red Guard who had tormented him with the iron headgear, quoting a slogan commonly employed to condemn the offspring of capitalist families. "So it's not surprising, is it, that the bourgeois revisionist slave to foreigners Lu Chiao plotted and intrigued during the Long March to obtain the freedom of a British imperialist spy who had been uncovered by the masses and sentenced to death!"

Another outraged roar from the crowd engulfed the stage, followed by slow, echoing chants of "Down with the craven slave to foreigners! Down with slave to foreigners Lu!" Forests of red books were flourished in the air and Red Guards in the front rows rushed forward and spat at the painfully bent figure of the army marshal, soaking his face and uniform with spittle.

"That imperialist spy who deserved to die now publishes a slanderous 'research newssheet' in Hong Kong vilifying China and Mao Tse-tung's thought every day," screamed the Red Guard. "Doesn't that make the deeds of this slave to foreigners smell worse than dog shit?"

The stadium erupted with new howls of "Smash the dog's head of the slave to foreigners! Smash the dog's head of the slave!" and the Red Guard at the microphone made an emphatic signal to a denim-clad worker who had been crouching beside the stage. On a shoulder pole the man carried two wooden night-soil buckets that were commonly used to remove human excrement from homes in the capital's narrow *hut'ungs*, and after trotting quickly up the steps, he placed the buckets beside the microphone, then stood aside.

"The slave to foreigners should confess his towering crimes now before it's too late," yelled the Red Guard, motioning to Chiao's tormentors to allow him to straighten up. "Otherwise he must suffer the consequences!"

Chiao lifted himself slowly upright, his face a mask of pain. He began to rub his aching back with his hands as repeated roars of "Confess! Confess!" rolled down from the stands all around him. The Red Guard glowered at him a few feet away but Chiao stared straight ahead, his mouth set in a firm line.

"Confess now — or face the consequences!" shouted the Red Guard menacingly into the microphone.

As the crowd repeated the chant, the Red Guard snatched up a ladle and dipped it into one of the night-soil buckets. Chiao looked at him steadily, aware of his intention, but still made no move to speak. From the circle of stands the deafening chant of "Confess!"

continued and with a sudden movement the Red Guard stepped toward Chiao and emptied the contents of the ladle onto his head.

"The filthy slave to foreigners stinks now like his crimes!" screamed the Red Guard, hurrying back to the microphone, and at once the chanting of the crowd became more angry, changing again to "Down with the filthy slave to foreigners! Down with the filthy slave!"

Chiao could feel the sticky slop trickling down his face into his collar as he stood gazing around at the sea of wildly yelling faces. Twisting his head, he looked in Kao's direction and found the young cadre glaring at him from the side of the stage; his eyes seemed to blaze with the force of a hatred which Chiao found utterly incomprehensible and he turned back toward the baying crowd, fighting a deepening sense of despair. Closing his eyes, he listened briefly to the din of condemnation washing toward him; then he opened them again and stepped unsteadily toward the Red Guard at the microphone.

"I will confess now," he said, struggling to control himself. "Let me have the microphone."

"The slave to foreigners has decided to confess!"

The Red Guard shouted his announcement triumphantly over the relay system, and after receiving a discreet nod of approval from Kao, he stood back and motioned the jet-plane guards aside to allow Chiao to move to the microphone. Taken by surprise, the crowd quieted and an unfamiliar hush settled over the Workers' Stadium.

"I wish to confess . . . that on the Long March I commanded the party of heroes . . . who stormed the Luting bridge," said Chiao, stumbling over his words. "Afterward, the Central Red Army's commander in chief Chu Teh . . . made a memorable speech. . . . He recalled that often in China's past history, heroes who rose from among the people changed when they became emperors and generals. They forgot their beginnings and came to despise and enslave the mass of the people. . . ."

Chiao's voice was gradually growing stronger, but he was still swaying unsteadily on his legs and he put out one hand to hold on to the microphone stand. Uncertain of his meaning, the crowd listened in a rapt silence, sensing that drama lay ahead.

"At Luting, Marshal Chu said the Red Army had succeeded in creating new heroes, heroes willing to die for the revolution . . . heroes with no selfish interests . . . and he was right, it had! But standing here today I realize that's . . . no longer true!"

Chiao paused, drawing a long breath. "All those who forced you to come here today to take part in this shameful spectacle — the Cultural Revolution Group of the Central Committee and the leader behind them — are behaving like those emperors and generals of our feudal past! They're acting for selfish reasons and they've come to despise the masses. They've forgotten the ideals, the unity, and the sacrifices of the past in their lust for power. . . . That is all I have to confess!"

The guards, who had begun moving across the stage as the meaning of Chiao's words began to dawn on them, flung themselves on the aging marshal at a shouted order from Kao. Under a rain of blows they wrestled him roughly into the jet-plane posture once more. The startled crowd watched in silence, and the Red Guard who had been addressing the rally snatched up the ladle and dashed more liquid night soil from the buckets repeatedly in Chiao's face, drenching his clothes.

From his place at the side of the stage, Kao glared furiously at the helpless, doubled-up figure of his uncle, uncertain how to combat the effect of his act of defiance. Then he signaled quickly to the Red Guard at the microphone and the youth launched into a fresh tirade of abuse, picking up from the place in his notes where he had left off a few minutes before. Finding its voice, the crowd began chanting wildly in response to the promptings of its cheerleaders, and the bowl of the stadium was soon filled once more with the deafening roar of prearranged slogans.

13

Using a small piece of broken glass, Mei-ling scraped steadily at the last of a long row of latrines in the student dormitories of the Shanghai Conservatory of Music. Her arm ached and her body was stiff from crouching beside the stained latrines for more than two hours. A few yards away three female Red Guard students who made up her *kuan niu kui tui* — "monster control team" — stood guard, calling out sharply for her to continue whenever she paused for a rest. The air was fetid and the floor around her was strewn with used lavatory paper which students now threw down deliberately, knowing that occupants of the cowsheds would be forced to clean up after them. Brushes which were usually on hand had been removed and every morning for the past month the monster control team had issued Mei-ling fragments of a broken bottle so as to make the job of cleaning the inner surfaces of the latrines more arduous.

Several times she had cut herself: her left hand was already swathed in a bandage made from a torn-up sheet and her right hand bore the visible scars of older mishaps. She had been unable to get proper dressings for the injuries because she had not been allowed to return to her home at all since being dragged back to the conservatory cowshed by a mob of about a hundred Red Guards a few days after Kao returned to Peking. They had appeared unannounced at Mei-ling's house after dark and without offering any explanation had taken her forcibly by truck to the conservatory, chanting repeatedly that they had "scored another great victory for Mao Tse-tung's thought."

From the beginning, the regime they imposed on her had been much harsher than before; instead of sleeping on a bamboo mat in a communal dormitory with other victimized teachers and professors, she had been confined alone in a tiny instrument storeroom scarcely large enough to lie down in. The walls had been smothered with slogans condemning her as "Unrepentant Bourgeois Reactionary Vampire Lu" and at night she slept on a makeshift cot which had been wedged against one wall. The monster control team, led by a female Red Guard from Peking, had installed a hinged panel in the door through which they kept Mei-ling under observation day and night, and the glass of the single window high up in one wall had been covered with black paint so that little or no light could enter. Each morning her control team had ordered her to make fresh self-criticisms of both her published writing and her family background, and she had crouched forlornly on her bed to do the work, using a plain wooden chair as a desk and writing by the feeble light of a single naked electric bulb suspended from the ceiling. On her first day back in the cowshed her tormentors had written a placard bearing the announcement "Lu Mei-ling, Agent of the Bourgeois Opposition," which she had been compelled to wear around her neck constantly ever since.

A different class of Red Guards each day had taken its turn to inspect her self-criticisms and she had lost count of the times she had been drenched with paint and subjected to "struggle" because

they yellingly judged the writing "insincere." Instead of being allowed to join other teachers in a communal dining hall at midday,
she was forced to eat a sparse meal huddled alone in her storeroom
cell; each afternoon she had been made to do physically tiring work,
either cleaning latrines or shifting heaps of heavy stones pointlessly
from one part of the conservatory yard to another. Every day of
torment and ignominy had seemed to merge into the next in a dreary,
exhausting blur, and soon Mei-ling had begun to lose track of time.
Cut off from all normal contact with others, she had been struggling
daily against a mounting sense of despair, and when the jagged glass
fragment she was holding suddenly opened up a deep gash in the
palm of her hand, she sat and watched indifferently as the blood
flowed fast into the filthy water. Only when the Peking Red Guard
appeared beside her, shouting for her to stand up, did she drop the
shard of glass and rise slowly to her feet.

"You're abusing the sign prepared by the revolutionary Red Guards!"
yelled the girl, pointing to the blood that was dripping from Mei-
ling's hand onto the placard around her neck. "Wash your injury
and bind it with the bandage from your other hand — then return
immediately to the area designated by the masses!"

Mei-ling ran her hand under a tap and removed the soiled bandage
from her other hand with difficulty. When she had fixed the bandage
loosely in place around the new wound, she walked wearily back to
the storeroom between her escorts with her shoulders bowed. The
Peking girl followed her inside, pulling two sheets of paper from her
pocket, and after glaring angrily at Mei-ling she flung them contemptuously on the low cot.

"Your confession of today is inadequate! You state that after
undergoing reform through labor in 1957 you decided the best course
of action was not to participate any further in political life — and
that's why you came to Shanghai to teach music. We revolutionaries
reject that! It's evidence that you still harbored reactionary ideas.
Shanghai is your old home, where your family sucked the blood out
of the Chinese laboring classes. You returned to wallow in bourgeois
musical habits acquired when you studied in Europe as the pampered
daughter of a filthy capitalist family. You must write a new criticism
and confess all these things. We shall return to look at it in an hour!"

Mei-ling looked dully back at the girl. Slender and strong beneath
her khaki uniform, she wore a broad leather belt around her slim
waist and her pale, northern face was striking in the full bloom of

youth. No more than eighteen or nineteen, she was as beautiful as Mei-ling had been as a young woman, but the burning expression of hostility in her dark eyes disfigured her features. Behind her shoulder, the two Shanghai students who were also part of her control team were staring at her with equally ferocious expressions and Mei-ling felt her despair deepen. The two local Red Guards — formerly gentle, intelligent girls — had been among her piano students, and during her previous spell in the cowshed she had guessed from their demeanor that they had been reluctant participants in actions against her. But now in their faces she saw only a deep, irrational hatred, and suddenly a renewed sense of bafflement at the mindless persecutions of the Cultural Revolution swept over her.

The movement had engendered hatred, suspicion, and terror on an unprecedented scale in and around the Conservatory of Music; even outside the cowshed, long-standing friends and colleagues had turned against one another out of fear they scarcely understood, and all the nonpolitical practices of everyday life had long since been drowned under the flood tide of distorted rhetoric from newspapers, the radio, and wall posters. The whole population of Shanghai seemed to have become strained and tense during that long autumn, and since her second arrest the constant barrage of insults and illogical demands made by Mei-ling's jailers had taken a severe toll of her dwindling physical and mental resources. Often she had felt close to panic and because the added pain of her newly wounded hand was now making her feel dizzy, she sank unsteadily into a sitting position on her cot. For several seconds the three Red Guards continued to gaze contemptuously at her; then, with another shouted order to write a new confession, they swept out, slamming the door behind them.

Alone and exhausted in the storeroom prison, Mei-ling felt her sense of hopelessness grow. Among the daubed slogans a big colored portrait of Mao Tse-tung gazed silently down from one wall, and as she looked at it, she was seized by a terrible feeling that nothing in her life had ever made any sense. The recent image of the young Peking Red Guard's lovely face so sadly contorted by her misguided fanaticism made her think involuntarily of her own idealistic youth and she sat shaking her head slowly from side to side in silent bewilderment. Could the cold, totemlike features staring grimly at her from the wall of that wretched cell really belong to the exhilarating, heroic figure who had become the focus of so much awe and affection

on the Long March? Could this be the gangling, mop-haired bohe-
mian who had smiled engagingly at her while jogging over mountains
and rushing rivers at the head of a peasant army, composing poetry
about the greatness of China's landscape? Could that young inspirational leader have become the ailing, unstable demagogue who had
deliberately set neighbors at one another's throats, turned children
against their parents, and unleashed the tidal waves of violence that
were engulfing the country? Could she ever have shared the same
ambitions for China's future with such a man? Or were all those
early years, in fact, just a barely remembered dream? Had she truly
walked and ridden twenty thousand *li* across China at the heels of
that hero — only to end up in a filthy, improvised punishment cell
constructed for her and countless others like her on his specific orders?

Mei-ling closed her eyes in an effort to shut out the living nightmare that the present had become, but other harrowing images from
the past flashed unbidden into her tired, tormented mind. She saw
the tall, waving vegetation of the Great Grasslands with endless
columns of the Red Army snaking away into its mists and knew
again the daily fear and horror of plunging accidentally into the
morass; she felt herself falling, felt the terror of sinking unstoppably
downward, saw herself fighting a frantic battle for her life in the
black, oozing mud. She clutched a tiny, pale-skinned baby to her
breast and as she struggled the baby grew quickly in her arms and
became the beautiful flaxen-haired Englishwoman who had appeared
so suddenly amid the devastation of her Shanghai apartment only
weeks ago. The swamp and the wrecked apartment merged, and
Kao too was struggling frantically in the mire beside them — he was
shouting unintelligibly and his face was twisted but Mei-ling felt an
unbearable anguish seize her because she was unable to tell whether
he was trying to rescue them or not. Then thrashing through the
black slime came Jakob himself, youthful, bearded, and dressed in
a Chinese long-gown. As had happened in reality, she felt his arms
tighten around her and slowly but surely he bore her up out of the
swamp. In a sudden transformation of mood she felt again the deep,
peaceful silence of the yurt they had shared in the Great Snow
Mountains. The fire was crackling gently in the hearth of stones and
the infant, tiny and defenseless as before, slept safely beside it. While
the blizzard banked snow softly around the yurt walls outside, she
experienced again the profound sense of purity and rightness which

had come upon her as she gazed into Jakob's famished face. The feeling strengthened inside her until she was sure that if she had opened her eyes she would have found herself once more seated amid the furs and animal skins in that mountain yurt. She felt her arms go around his shivering body and press his face against her naked breasts, felt his searching mouth draw life from her, and she knew again the exultation of peace and love that had filled her, body and soul, during those few hours when they had lain entwined with one another on the high mountain.

Never before during the thirty intervening years had Mei-ling recalled those fleeting moments with such vividness, and a soft cry escaped her lips. Clasping her arms tightly about her own body, she rocked gently back and forth on the edge of the cot, invaded suddenly by a deep sense of remorse. It was in the pure light of that Kansu dawn, she realized now, that she had made her tragically mistaken choice. In her imagination she saw Jakob waiting in the same agony of expectation as she splashed through the shallow stream toward him, leading the pack mule with his baby on its back. During the entire jolting journey through the weird loess mountains she had been fighting and refighting a desperate emotional battle with herself; by then she sensed intuitively that she might be carrying a spark of new life within her, but although she had often been overwhelmed by the strength of her feelings for Jakob in the difficult weeks following the crossing of the Great Snow Mountains, she had never been able to rid herself of the conviction that her first duty was to her country and its revolution. Right up until the moment when they spoke and Jakob had declared his love for her, she had wrestled with her indecision — then abruptly, against the urging of her heart, she had closed her mind and deliberately turned her back on the fierce and tender passion they had shared. As her mule stepped back into the stream, Mei-ling saw now, she had set out along the path that had led her through much mental agony to the ultimate depravity of imprisonment in the barricaded instrument room. With blinding clarity she understood how she had helped shape her own fate and in the sheer vividness of the recollections she felt a powerful sense of retribution: from a lack of courage she had spurned Jakob's love, stifled her own deepest emotions, and as a result had suffered greatly. If she had obeyed her instincts on that morning in Kansu, her whole life would have changed; all the pain and horror of the confrontation with Kao and Jakob would have been avoided and Abigail would never have suffered. Suddenly her mind filled with the vision of Abigail gazing numbly at the furious Kao in her apartment while Jakob looked on helpless and white-faced. She tried to dismiss it but the scene expanded frighteningly inside her head, enveloping her totally until she felt as though part of herself were merging into the tortured expressions of all the people around her. Then something snapped and the images faded, giving way to an immense and over-powering sadness.

At that instant the door of the storeroom was flung open with a crash and Mei-ling opened her eyes to find herself looking into the angry faces of her monster control team. In her lap, her still-bleeding hand had soaked the bandage with crimson blood and she realized that an hour had passed, although she didn't know whether she had slept or not while she sat on her cot.

"You have disobeyed our instructions to write a new confession!" yelled the Peking Red Guard. "Why?"

"I was too tired," replied Mei-ling in an exhausted whisper.

"Then watch this!"

Mei-ling saw that the Red Guard carried in her hand two or three slim books. From the covers she recognized the volume of Long March recollections to which she had contributed, a book of her own short stories from the thirties, and a novel of the Yenan period she had written in Shensi. The Peking girl was shredding pages with both hands, and producing a box of matches from her pocket, she knelt and set fire to a little pyramid of crumpled paper on the dirty concrete floor. Working quickly, she tore up pages and covers to feed the fire until flames two feet high were leaping from the burning books.

"It isn't enough just to criticize and repudiate vile representatives of the reactionary bourgeoisie who have sneaked into the Party, the army, and all spheres of culture," sneered the Red Guard girl, adding more torn pages. "We must physically burn them and sweep them away!"

Other female Red Guards crowding the corridor beyond the open doorway clapped and cheered while the flames reached higher, and some began chanting "Sweep away bourgeois vampire Lu!" Mei-ling stared, mesmerized, at the fire, and even when the final pages of the books had been added and the flames burned low, she continued to gaze blankly at the pile of black ashes in the center of the floor. After chanting more slogans at her, the Red Guards withdrew, banging the door loudly behind them, and Mei-ling listened numbly to the sounds of their voices as a heated discussion developed outside the storeroom.

"Why is it necessary to be so severe on her?" asked one of her former students in a whisper. "Is she so important?"

"Her brother, Marshal Lu Chiao, was subjected to public 'struggle' before thousands of Red Guards in Peking," snapped their leader. "It was our duty to take strong action against this bourgeois vampire since she lives among us. I informed Peking of our intentions and the answer came back at once saying 'No objections.' "

The voices grew fainter as Mei-ling's tormentors moved away down the corridor and for a long time she sat motionless on her cot, staring in front of her — the words she had heard repeated themselves over and over inside her head and suddenly she rose and crossed the room to pick up the box of matches which the Red Guard leader had dropped accidentally on the floor. Opening the box, she saw it was almost full and at once she removed the metal clip from her hair. Turning her back to the door so that her body would conceal her actions if the observation flap was opened, she knelt by the chair and scraped the sulfur carefully from the head of each match. When she had finished, she crushed the little pile of chips with the bottom of her drinking mug, then brushed the heap of finely powdered sulfur into her left palm. With one quick movement of her hand she tossed the powder into her mouth and began swallowing hard, but while she was doing this, the observation flap swung open and a member of the monster control team peered in. A moment later the door flew back on its hinges and three female Red Guards dashed into the cell and began trying to wrench Mei-ling's hand away from her mouth.

"Stop her," screeched one of the Red Guards. "She's trying to kill herself."

They struggled fiercely with her and each girl in turn tried to tear away the hand which Mei-ling had clamped to her mouth. But she resisted with all her fading strength, and when at last they did succeed in freeing the hand, it was empty save for a few grains of pink powder. In the same moment Mei-ling became still, sagging unconscious in their arms, and the three Red Guards stared at one another in dismay.

"We must take her to the hospital," shouted their leader. "She has confessed her guilt by her actions and must not be allowed to escape punishment."

Dragging Mei-ling's limp body between them, they rushed out of the room.

PART SEVEN

The Long March Ends

1976

The violence and confusion that marked the early stages of the Cultural Revolution in 1966 intensified as the movement spread to factories, mines, and rural areas. Hundreds of millions of workers and peasants were drawn into the fray, spreading chaos to all parts of the country. Hard-line Red Guards from Peking, acting on the instructions of Mao and his wife's Cultural Revolution Group, spearheaded campaigns that overthrew virtually every Party secretary in each of China's twenty-nine far-flung provinces. The People's Liberation Army and police continued to stand aside, on Peking's orders, while provincial Party headquarters were ransacked and officials were humiliated, tortured, and sometimes killed. The Communist Party administration was crippled nationwide, but because Mao had devised no alternative power structures, local Military Control commissions and "Revolutionary Committees," dominated by the People's Liberation Army, eventually had to take over in almost every province. These organizations, however, only heightened the confusion; the regional military rulers set up their own new Red Guard groups, and endless disputes broke out among the innumerable factions that had been created. This led to great loss of life, and in some cities workers and Red Guards broke open military armories and fought pitched street battles with mortars and machine guns. Eventually the army had to crush the unrest by force, with the result that most regions of China came under the direct rule of the local military commander — a shadowy reminder of warlord days.

In the spring of 1969 a Communist Party congress appointed a new Central Committee and Politburo dominated by military leaders, and these same soldiers took control of the provincial Party administrations. As all Red Guard organizations were disbanded, tens of millions of young, urban Chinese were dispatched to remote rural areas to "learn from the peasants," which meant living in straw huts and caves while doing backbreaking agricultural work. In these harsh surroundings a deep sense of disenchantment set in among the former Red Guards, and this was heightened by the discovery that most peasants no longer felt any affection for the Communist leadership anyway in the wake of the Great Leap Forward disasters. Many of the exiled youths began sneaking back to the towns to live in hiding, and what had once been a regimented, well-ordered nation became deeply demoralized: crime mushroomed, corruption flourished, and back-door bribery and black markets unheard of since 1949 again became commonplace.

Externally China had become more isolated than ever during the frenzied phases of the Cultural Revolution. American support for Taiwan and Chiang Kai-shek had until then kept mainland China out of the United Nations and deprived her of diplomatic recognition by many of Washington's allies — but a series of wild incidents involving Chinese students, diplomats, and overseas Chinese in a dozen foreign countries in 1967 touched off massive demonstrations in Peking that turned China into an international pariah. The embassies of the Soviet Union, Yugoslavia, France, Italy, India, Burma, Indonesia, Mongolia, Bulgaria, and Czechoslovakia all suffered defacement; many diplomats and their families were physically abused and driven out of China. When Communists in Hong Kong began mounting violent demonstrations in support of the Cultural Revolution, they triggered a train of events that ended with the burning down of the British embassy in August 1967. This welter of xenophobia reached its climax in 1969 with a flurry of armed clashes along China's northern border with the Soviet Union, which left many dead on both sides. The conflict perhaps demonstrated how easily a devastating war might break out and helped bring China's leaders to their senses.

A change of direction toward stability and rationality was supervised by the country's pragmatic premier, Chou En-lai, who had survived the Cultural Revolution and preserved his position by dint of his legendary diplomatic talents. Although he had been closely associated with those policies condemned by Mao as revisionist, Chou also managed to protect some other moderate leaders, and most important among them was Teng Hsiao-ping, the former Party general secretary whom the Red Guards had singled out and vilified, along with President Liu Shao-chi, above all others. President Liu died of maltreatment in a prison cell, the Cultural Revolution's most prominent victim, but after succeeding almost single-handedly in restoring sanity to China's highest counsels, Chou rehabilitated Teng Hsiao-ping and in 1973 made him a vice premier, earmarking him for the succession.

Teng's dramatic comeback was made possible by events of high melodrama involving Mao's previously designated successor, Defense Minister Lin Piao. The famous Long March general who had given Mao vital military support during his early Cultural Revolution maneuverings apparently became a victim of the Party chairman's obsessive paranoia in September 1971. In that month a Chinese military airliner flying toward the Soviet Union crashed in Mongolia, killing and burning all its passengers beyond recognition, and after a long silence Peking announced that Lin Piao had been on board with his wife and supporters, fleeing to Moscow. It was said officially that Lin had tried to assassinate Mao before escaping, and although this is open to doubt, it seems certain that Lin died or was assassinated around this time for reasons that may never be fully known. Subsequently, Marshal Lin's supporters were removed from power in the Party and army, but although this massive purge loosened the military stranglehold on the country, China's fragile stability was once more undermined. With Parkinson's disease taking an increasing toll of his mental and physical energies, Mao from that time onward played an ambivalent role in ruling China. In turn and without much apparent logic he encouraged both the moderate policies of Premier Chou and the radical extremism of his wife's group, which would later be condemned as the Gang of Four. Yet despite these internal conflicts, Peking's new diplomacy began to bear fruit. Entry into the United Nations was secured at last in the autumn of 1971, and a rapprochement with the arch-imperialist American enemy began. President Richard Nixon was invited to Peking in 1972, and the United States, along with such other Western nations as Canada, Australia, and West Germany, belatedly extended diplomatic recognition to the People's Republic of China more than two decades after it came into being. Unfortunately for China, Chou En-lai became ill with cancer, and as his condition worsened, Teng Hsiao-ping became the nation's effective premier. The deterioration in Mao's health, meanwhile, had accelerated, and visiting statesmen whom he insisted on receiving encountered an increasingly pathetic, slack-jawed figure surrounded by nurses. But so long as he breathed, on the strength of his legendary past he remained the supreme ruler of eight hundred million people, and while his life ebbed away, rival factions for the succession plotted and intrigued in the pavilions bordering the Forbidden City as China's imperial courtiers had done so often in the past at the fall of a great dynasty.

Events were further complicated in January 1976 by the death of Chou En-lai; it had long been assumed that Chou, who was seventy-eight, would survive and succeed the eighty-two-year-old Mao, but his untimely death threw the question of succession wide open. Mao's wife, Chiang Ch'ing, and her radical group seized the opportunity to launch strident new press attacks against "unrepentant capitalist roaders" in the Party, and these broadsides in effect plunged China into a new, mini-Cultural Revolution. Mao once again showered the weary population with vague inspirational exhortations, urging them "to clasp the moon in the Ninth Heaven and seize turtles deep down in the Five Seas," and Teng Hsiao-ping's dominant position was further undermined in February when a little-known second-rank leader, Hua Kuo-feng, was appointed acting premier on Mao's instructions. Because Teng's continuation of Chou En-lai's pragmatic policies had been winning widespread popular approval after the years of turmoil, tension began to mount again across the nation, and in early April it exploded into the full view of the world in the Square of Heavenly Peace. In the days leading up to Ch'ing Ming, the Chinese spring festival for commemorating the dead, millions of people went to the square to lay wreaths at the Monument to the People's Heroes in honor of Chou En-lai. Many of the wreaths also carried veiled attacks against Madame Chiang Ch'ing and her radical supporters, and this conflict sparked off the first truly spontaneous political riots in Peking since 1949.

The revolution thus entered a cataclysmic six-month period, and before 1976 ended, China was to suffer a wave of death, destruction, and political upheaval as dramatic as the Götterdämmerung of European mythology — the twilight of the gods.

1

"It's almost as if the great spirits of our ancesters have suddenly become impatient with us all," said Marshal Lu Chiao, gazing grimly up at the mellow gold tiles and red columns of the Gate of Heavenly Peace. "Why else should the nation's three greatest heroes have been struck down at the same time? Premier Chou En-lai has already passed away, Marshal Chu Teh is on the verge of death in his ninetieth year, and Chairman Mao himself is sinking slowly in one of those old imperial pavilions over there."

Chiao nodded in the direction of the curved roofs visible above the walls that enclosed the Forbidden City, and at his side Jakob studied the lined face of the aging Chinese marshal. Since their last brief meeting, at Pei-Ta University, his hair had turned completely white and his face now had a sallow, unhealthy pallor. Dressed in a civilian cap and a wadded overcoat of blue cotton, Chiao looked no different from the thousands of other Peking residents thronging the center of the capital; but in the timber of his voice and the dullness of his eyes Jakob could detect something of the toll that the events of the past decade had taken on his energy and optimism.

"Your system of government doesn't allow for graceful retirement," said Jakob gently. "Premier Chou was seventy-eight, after all. And Chairman Mao's eighty-two."

"In feudal days mandarins and army generals all came to this spot on important occasions," said Chiao, ignoring Jakob and speaking in the same grim voice. "They were made to kneel here, facing the Golden Water River. Courtiers lowered the emperor's edict from the top of the gate — in the mouth of a golden phoenix carved from wood. A Board of Rites mandarin collected it on a tray ornamented with clouds and his officials copied it onto pieces of yellow paper for imperial messengers to deliver to all parts of the country. . . ."

They were standing before the moat that ran beneath the sixty-foot-high vermilion rampart of the Tien An Men, and Jakob looked around at the seven curved bridges of white sculpted marble that spanned it. Stone lions and two carved pillars decorated with clouds and dragons guarded the central entrance to the imperial palaces, and the sense of power and grandeur which the Ming dynasty monuments still possessed made it easy to imagine the awesomeness of the old ceremony which Chiao had just described.

"That ritual of the imperial despots was called 'issuing edicts by golden phoenix,' " continued Chiao quietly. "Since the Cultural Revolution began, that's how the chairman of the Communist Party of China has tried to rule. The golden phoenix today is the *People's Daily*, which reverently prints every casual remark he makes as though it contained the essence of eternal wisdom. And the people have suffered more from those edicts than they ever did under the worst emperors." Chiao turned to look directly at him and Jakob saw that even though the old marshal's eyes were faded, they still retained the steely glint of determination that had sustained him in positions of high authority in the Party and the army throughout all the trials of China's long revolution.

"So you see, it's more than our present system of government we're fighting. It goes much deeper — it's something in our blood and our very bones. Something perhaps only the spirits of our ancestors are powerful enough to change."

Jakob smiled. "I'm surprised to hear a lifelong Marxist speak of anything so unscientific as ancestral spirits intervening in China's affairs."

"Somebody who's known China as long as you shouldn't be surprised at the persistence of our ancient beliefs and customs — no matter what the rhetoric of the Cultural Revolution might have said."

Chiao turned his back on the Tien An Men to look out over the Square of Heavenly Peace and Jakob followed his gaze. Long lines of Chinese carrying colored paper wreaths were wending their way across the vast concrete plain toward the granite and marble obelisk of the Monument to the People's Heroes; some were on foot, others rode bicycles in disciplined files, ringing their bells in slow, mournful unison. On the face of the tapering hundred-foot pillar, eight gold-plated characters in the calligraphy of Mao Tse-tung were visible, proclaiming "The People's Heroes Are Immortal!" but a growing mound of wreaths laid all around its base was already threatening to cover up the lower ideograms.

"I'm sure you're aware of the Confucian traditions of the Ch'ing Ming festival," said Chiao, moving off slowly toward the memorial. "In the past, the living were required to sweep their ancestral burial sites so as to placate the spirits of the departed. But this year people of the capital are choosing to celebrate the occasion at the monument to our revolutionary heroes — by paying tribute to Comrade Chou and all that he stood for. It's a spontaneous example, you might say, of how the past can serve the present."

Jakob fell into step beside the marshal, scanning the crowds ahead of them. In the April sunshine, the pale lavender granite of the memorial, which commemorated revolutionary martyrs back to 1840, stood out sharply against a background of evergreen pines and cypresses. But although the day was bright, a cold, gusting wind was sweeping across the square and Chiao buttoned the collar of his padded topcoat closer about his throat as they walked.

"I'm honored to have the opportunity to witness the grief of the Chinese people at such an important moment in their history," said Jakob quietly, glancing at the serious-faced files of adults, students, and schoolchildren moving reverently past them, carrying wreaths decorated with beribboned poems and eulogies. "But I'd like you to tell me why I've suddenly been allowed back into China again after all these years. I wrote to you many times after our last meeting at the university and never received any acknowledgment of my letters. Even during the tour I was allowed to make in 1964, all my requests to contact you were ignored."

"I couldn't risk acknowledging even one of those requests. I think you can imagine why it would have been dangerous for me if I was suspected of having friendly relations with such a prominent foreign political commentator." Chiao increased his pace and hunched his shoulders, speaking in a low, urgent tone. "But although it's so long ago I'm still very grateful for the help you gave my sister. I arranged your visit in 1964 as a token of my gratitude, although I couldn't reveal that. And since then, to avoid suspicion I've had to ensure through secret contacts that all of your subsequent visa applications were turned down."

Jakob stared at Chiao in dismay. When the antiforeign hysteria of the Cultural Revolution subsided he had again begun submitting regular requests for entry visas to the Chinese Foreign Ministry, but although he had received no response, he had never suspected that such a direct and personal embargo had been in force. Two days earlier he had been surprised to receive a confidential telephone call at his office from one of Hong Kong's prominent Communists, who had asked if he was interested in visiting Peking "to gather some new insights at this important time." He had been directed to Lowu, the railway crossing point into China, and there he had found that all formalities had been completed for him to visit Peking immediately. Shortly after his arrival at his hotel on Chang An Boulevard, an unsigned note had been delivered to his room, inviting him to meet "an old acquaintance" in front of the Tien An Men. When he stepped out of his taxi beside one of the marble bridges spanning the Golden Water River, Chiao had materialized immediately from among the milling crowds and offered his hand before launching into his resigned soliloquy about his nation's fading heroes.

"I'm very sorry that I had to deprive you of further visits to China," said Chiao, stopping suddenly in the middle of the crowded square and turning to face Jakob. "I know how disappointing it must have been for you — for both professional and personal reasons. But perhaps I should also tell you that I was able to help your family in another way. When your daughter applied to return to China and teach here in Peking after the worst of the violence had passed, I was able to take a discreet hand and ensure that authorization was given."

Again Jakob could only stare at Chiao in surprise. Abigail had stayed on in Shanghai until the wave of anti-British hysteria had forced her to leave in the summer of 1967. Then she had returned directly to London and taught Chinese there for four years before obtaining a new post at the Foreign Languages Institute in Peking. He had not seen her since that rain-swept night in Shanghai when she had ordered him to interfere no further in her life, and she had rebuffed all his subsequent attempts to see her, ignoring every letter that he had written to her in London and Peking. He had obtained his sparse news of her through friends in the field of China studies, and his immediate response to the unexpected invitation to return to Peking had been conditioned only partly by his continuing fascination with events on the Chinese mainland. In the ten years that had passed since their angry confrontation in Shanghai, his feeling of responsibility for the rift between them had weighed ever more heavily on him, and during the journey from Hong Kong he had allowed himself to hope that his visit to the Chinese capital might present him with a chance to try to see Abigail again. He had also quietly resolved, if it became possible, to seek out Kao, of whom he had heard nothing in the intervening years. He had made no attempt to work out what he would say or do, but the instinctive desire to make some amends, which had always been with him, had grown suddenly stronger. Also, the prospect of being able to do something at long last to ease the ache of his own inner emotions had raised his spirits. As he stared at Chiao, the feeling became so pervasive that he found himself wondering illogically whether the Chinese marshal might somehow have understood intuitively what he was thinking about Abigail; then he realized he could scarcely have known anything of his dispute with his daughter and he smiled his thanks.

"I'm glad for Abigail's sake you were able to help her," he said sincerely. "But I'd still like some explanation of why you've now lifted the ban on me."

Chiao subjected Jakob to a long, silent scrutiny; it was clear to the Chinese that the former missionary was still physically robust and alert in his mid-sixties. The hair that had been so fair in his youth had now turned silver but his face had the healthy, weather-burnished color of a man who took advantage of Hong Kong's sea island climate to keep himself fit and active. Although the wind was cold, Jakob wore no hat and Chiao noticed he had not turned up the collar of his black tailored overcoat.

"We've known one another for many years. We're not close friends but invisible ties of long standing exist between us. The last time we met I enlisted your help by subterfuge. This time I can see you're suspicious that I might mislead you again — so I'll try to take you into my confidence from the start." Chiao paused, glancing left and right to check that they were not overheard; then he fixed his narrowed eyes intently on Jakob again. "Before it was a personal matter — now much wider issues are involved. China's future is hanging in the balance. Chairman Mao is no longer in full possession of his senses. A terrible struggle for the right to succeed him has begun. Nobody knows how it will end. Even civil war can't be ruled out."

"But why should you wish to talk to me about this?" asked Jakob carefully. "What do you have to gain this time?"

"Many journalists and writers trust your judgment and the information your institute distributes. You have a special understanding of our politics as a result of your earlier experiences in China. What you write influences many others . . ."

"Perhaps — but I don't think you should overestimate that influence."

"In the present climate, with so much at stake, few of us can trust even our oldest friends. The decision of every army unit commander, every police group leader, and every militia chief could prove decisive when the final moment arrives. . . .Your influence extends even to those who prepare Chinese-language broadcasts which are beamed into China from abroad. Now do you see why it's important that you are well informed at this time of crisis?"

Jakob stared hard at Chiao, wondering even now whether he was being told the full story. Then he saw a shadow of anxiety appear in his companion's expression and he noticed that some of the foreign diplomats and journalists resident in Peking were beginning to appear among the mourners; a few carried cameras and all of them were watching the spontaneous demonstration of affection for the dead premier with great interest. His conversation with Chiao was attracting no more than casual glances, but the Chinese marshal evidently decided that the discussion would be more private if they kept on the move, and he started walking quickly again toward the martyrs' memorial.

"It's important to understand that when Chairman Mao dies, few will really mourn his passing." Chiao was speaking in a clipped voice and staring down fiercely at the paving stones of the square as though he were a little ashamed of what he was saying. "Most Chinese are exhausted from the constant political campaigns. They want peace in their lives now. They've given themselves to the revolution for decades — now they need some tangible reward in return. They've no time for the empty idealism of the ultraleftists who've grouped themselves around Madame Mao. The peasants don't want their private plots to be taken away, the industrial workers don't want bonuses and wage incentives abolished. They all want a little taste of prosperity instead of endless class war against imaginary enemies. . . ."

"What does Chairman Mao want them to have?" asked Jakob. "Which group does he support?"

Chiao let out an explosive sigh of exasperation. "Neither. He detests Comrade Teng Hsiao-ping. He's convinced Comrade Teng would destroy his revolution with his 'capitalist' ideas. That's why he gave strict orders in February that Comrade Teng must never succeed to the premiership."

"From outside it looks as though Chairman Mao is supporting the leftists."

Chiao shook his head vigorously. "That's not true. He detests his wife too. He ordered her to move out of their home more than a year ago. He's very suspicious of her ambition. Calamity has always struck whenever a woman has exercised power in China. That's why Comrade Hua was appointed acting premier as a compromise. But now the chairman's mind is unstable. He's too ill to attend meetings. Sometimes he's lucid, at other times he's not. He's dying in agony because he fears death and the destruction of all his achievements."

The crowd of wreath bearers was growing thicker as they neared the martyrs' memorial, and Jakob and Chiao had to slow their pace. Among the crush of people mounting the balustraded platforms around the plinth, some individuals were declaiming their eulogies to Premier Chou before adding their wreaths to the pile, and their words were ringing loudly across the quiet square.

"It sounds as though Chairman Mao is dying a very lonely man," said Jakob, lowering his voice.

Chiao nodded. "His isolation feeds his fear. I think that's why he continues to give audiences to visiting statesmen and prominent foreign guests despite his illness. While his energy lasts he likes to discuss history and philosophical questions. I think in those subjects he finds some relief from his mental anguish."

"Doesn't he see anyone else?"

"The acting premier visits him occasionally. But only Chiang Ch'ing and members of her group have regular direct contact. She's still his wife, remember. She controls his telephones and all the working papers he receives. Sometimes he sees his nephews and nieces and their cronies — imperial blood ties and the whispered flattery of courtiers, you see, have replaced the socialist constitution. And behind everything lies the threat of the gun."

Jakob fell silent, suddenly feeling the chill of the wind through his thin wool overcoat.

"Chairman Mao knows of your presence in Peking," said Chiao, shooting a sideways glance at Jakob. "I had a message passed to him, reminding him of your last meeting at the stone fortress of Chokechi. He said he remembered you well and expressed a wish to meet you again — as I hoped he would. It will add an important legitimacy to your visit if you are received by Chairman Mao. Do you agree?"

Jakob glanced toward the memorial. Some students were beginning to clamber up onto the balustrades to make their speeches praising Chou En-lai and he became forcibly aware of the growing sense of tension in the square.

"I certainly agree," he said quietly. "I'd regard it as a great honor to meet Chairman Mao again."

2

The lower plinth of the Monument to the People's Heroes, built in the shape of a cherry-apple flower, was faced with green polished granite. On its sides, white marble bas-reliefs depicted heroic scenes from China's revolution stretching back to the anti-British Opium Wars of the mid-nineteenth century, and as Chiao led the way up one of the balustraded stairways, the crowds parted automatically to allow him passage. He neither spoke nor looked directly at those around him but Jakob saw that something in the dignified bearing of the white-haired marshal won him immediate respect, even though he was dressed inconspicuously. The wreaths were now heaped head-high around the base of the tall central column and when they reached the upper platform, Chiao bent forward to draw Jakob's attention to some of the verses written on them.

"Look, the messages are very emotional."

Jakob followed Chiao's pointing finger and read a poem that said:

> "With the death of Premier Chou, the sun has sunk from sight.
> Unhappy clouds are rising.
> Soon the nation will falter.
> Then it will feel the gap left by this great man."

Another proclaimed: "Premier Chou was our beloved father. Now there is a conspiracy in the Party to overthrow his policies."

"You see," said Chiao quietly, moving to another position. "Here's one wishing long life to Yang Kai-hui, the first wife of Chairman Mao. She was executed by the Nationalists. Another says 'Down with the Dowager Empress!' They're both subtle attacks on Chiang Ch'ing."

Jakob drew closer to read the inscriptions for himself. One said: "We swear to protect Premier Chou and his successors! We will fight a bloody battle to the end!" Another warned: "We will have no mercy with traitors inside the Communist Party who mislead the masses." A third promised: "We will fight to the death against anyone who tries to interfere with Premier Chou's legacy of modernization."

On glancing up Jakob saw that the marshal was visibly moved by some of the verses; unaware of his own reactions, he sometimes nodded his head in a little tacit gesture of approval or closed his eyes briefly after absorbing an emotional poem. Around them, the crowd continued to add new tributes respectfully to the heap and only occasionally did a shouted recitation break the silence. When Chiao turned to make his way down one of the four stairways, Jakob followed wordlessly, making no attempt to intrude on his mood. For some time they walked side by side among the crowds spilling across the square without speaking and Jakob found he had to bite back the questions which were uppermost in his mind.

"Many of us owed debts of enormous gratitude to Premier Chou," said Chiao at last. "His farsightedness and his cool nerve often saved us from chaos."

"I saw Red Guard newspaper reports of your 'trial' at the Workers' Stadium," said Jakob hesitantly. "When I read those insane accusations that you had 'helped an imperialist spy' in the thirties I feared the worst for you."

"Fortunately Premier Chou was able to intervene in the end," said Chiao, his voice cracking with emotion. "If it hadn't been for him I wouldn't be here now."

"You must have endured great hardships," said Jakob gently. "You disappeared for a long time."

"Not as long as men like Comrade Peng Teh-huai!" Chiao swung around on Jakob, his eyes suddenly burning with pent-up emotion. "You saw the heroic commander of the Third Army Corps many times on the Long March, didn't you?"

Jakob nodded.

"After eight years of torture in a damp prison cell he died in a puddle of his own blood. By then he was suffering from tuberculosis and he was denied all medical treatment. President Liu was also tormented to death in isolation. Thousands of others like them were murdered. I was held in isolation for four years and tortured frequently with old Kuomintang instruments from our own museums."

"How did you manage to survive all that time?"

Chiao smiled grimly. " 'Through ease and softness of movement there is a development of enduring strength' — you probably know that maxim. Endurance is only possible if one is in harmony with nature. If your spirit is entire and concentrated, your body becomes indifferent to pain."

Jakob stared at Chiao in surprise. "You practiced the Taoist arts?"

Chiao nodded. "My father taught me assiduously as a boy. I never dreamed I would have reason to be grateful for any legacy from my capitalist father. But the teachings of Lao-tzu had stayed with me. I found after a time I was able to summon the old disciplines from memory. 'What we truly know, we do effortlessly and know unconsciously.' Do you remember? I had more than enough time to practice — both the meditational arts and T'ai Chi Ch'uan. I learned again through much suffering that the road to enlightenment is truly an inward path leading us back to our original nature."

They walked on in silence across the great, ugly parade ground which the Communists had bulldozed from the heart of the ancient capital. To create it, all the imperial buildings which had stood on the site during Jakob's early days in Peking had been demolished, and this had seemed to him to leave a terrible, symbolic vacuum at the center of the old China he had first known. It was as if the very heart of the historic capital and all it stood for had been ripped out, but now in the act of crossing the soulless square for the first time on foot, he suddenly felt a paradoxical sense of encouragement begin to grow within him. The poetic spontaneity of the tributes to Chou En-lai seemed to spell out a message which transcended the bleak materialism of the square, and more important, amid all the horror and despair of recent years, the ancient spiritual wisdom of China had helped the man at his side prevail in the face of terrible adversity. Jakob began to feel a strong sense of companionship with the Chinese marshal he had first met forty-five years earlier, and although he had no logical reason to do so, he began to hope he might succeed in his own efforts to make peace with Abigail and even Kao.

"In case you're wondering, perhaps I should tell you that I'm aware of all the facts concerning my nephew's past," said Chiao uncomfortably, as though reading Jakob's thoughts. "But there's no need to be alarmed. I'm sure nobody else knows. Premier Chou probably suspected the truth but was never sure. That's perhaps why he did so much to help Kao when he was young."

Taken aback by the abruptness of Chiao's revelation, Jakob could only stare down in consternation at the paving stones of the square.

"It would be quite natural for you to want to see Kao while you're in Peking," continued Chiao in a faintly embarrassed tone. "But it might be better for all concerned to avoid such a meeting."

"I've spent ten years thinking about what I'd like to say to him," said Jakob in a barely audible voice. "I met him in Shanghai at Mei-ling's house in 1966. I entered China for a few hours illegally on a ship from Hong Kong. It was a stormy meeting, I'm afraid . . . and I've often wondered since what he was doing."

"Then he found out that you are his father?"

Jakob nodded miserably. "Yes. But I hope you'll never reveal your knowledge to him."

Chiao quickly nodded his assent.

"What's he doing now?"

"Kao married five years ago. He has a young son." Chiao hesitated, looking uneasy. "But I'm sorry to say he threw in his lot with Madame Mao and her supporters long ago. He's been one of their chief activists for a long time."

Jakob absorbed the information in silence. "Do you ever see him?"

"There have been many bitter moments between uncle and nephew in the past ten years." Chiao's face darkened. "If you decide to try to visit him, please be circumspect."

"How did you find out about Kao?"

"Mei-ling confided in me after she was freed from the Tangshan coal yard."

"What's happened to her?"

The question Jakob had been aching to ask for so long came out in an anxious whisper but Chiao did not answer at once. "My sister has suffered terribly," he said at last, speaking slowly. "She was subjected to very severe punishments. She was driven beyond the limits of endurance."

"Is she dead?" asked Jakob in a horrified tone.

Chiao shook his head. "She's not dead — but it might be better if she were."

"What do you mean?"

"When her anguish became unbearable, like many others she tried to take her life."

"But she didn't succeed?"

"No, she scraped all the sulfur from a box of matches and swallowed it. But that wasn't enough to kill her. . . ." The muscles of Chiao's jaw tightened. "They preserved her life — but her mind had snapped."

Jakob stared at Chiao, aghast. "Where is she now?"

"She was confined to an institution for the insane in Shanghai. When I regained my freedom and discovered what had happened, I had her transferred to a similar institution here in Peking."

A chill seemed to spread slowly through Jakob's body. "I'd like to see Mei-ling, please. Can you arrange it?"

"I can, of course." Chiao's sunken features gathered into a frown. "But she rarely speaks — and when she does, she shows no awareness of reality. She recognizes nobody. Visiting her is an ordeal."

"I'd still like to see her," said Jakob without hesitation.

3

Early that evening Jakob gingerly pushed open the courtyard gate of a small house to the east of the Forbidden City, wondering how he would cope with the ordeal that lay ahead. Chinks of light were visible behind curtains drawn across the windows of the single-storied house, and he made a conscious effort to steady himself as he crossed the empty courtyard and knocked on the screened door. Countless times since his clandestine visit to Shanghai he had tried to imagine how he might approach such a moment, but now that it had arrived, he found he was having to steel himself in preparation. The old courtier's dwelling reminded him of the similar house little more than a mile away which had been his home while he was studying in Peking forty-five years earlier, and as he waited for an answer to his knock, he remembered something of the naive sense of excitement that these ancient surroundings had then invoked in him. The tranquil atmosphere of the silent, shadowy courtyard seemed to roll back the intervening years and he remembered too the fierce, unshakable faith which had then spurred him to preach in China's remote hinterland.

The force of these recollections distracted him momentarily and he started when the door swung halfway open to reveal the unsmiling face of a young Chinese woman dressed in a blue cotton tunic and trousers. Her expression betrayed surprise at seeing a foreign face but she said nothing, waiting for him to speak. At knee level, a small boy with a fringe of black hair falling across his eyes clutched at her left hand and stared up wonderingly at Jakob. Dressed in gray trousers and a jacket of vivid red, the boy was aged about four and from his expression it was evident he had never seen a real, long-nosed "foreign devil" before. Over the woman's shoulder Jakob could see a large colored portrait of Mao Tse-tung hanging on the wall of a small, austerely furnished room, and yellow-covered volumes of Mao's collected writings stood on a shelf. Somewhere an unseen radio was broadcasting indignant extracts from the current *People's Daily* editorial, making repeated references to "rabid class enemies" who were "fabricating rumors" and "stirring up trouble among the masses," but otherwise the room betrayed no more information about its occupants.

"I'm sorry to arrive unannounced, but I'd like to speak to Comrade Chen Kao," said Jakob uncertainly. "Is he at home?"

"My husband is here. But he's busy at his desk and shouldn't be disturbed. Who are you, please?"

"My name is Jakob Kellner." Jakob offered his hand but she ignored it and after a moment he bent toward the boy. "*Ni hao,*" he said, smiling playfully. "*Ni chiao shen mo ming tzu?*" — "What's your name?"

The boy gazed, mystified, at the unfamiliar foreign face: then he murmured "*Wo chiao Ming*" before shrinking back shyly against his mother.

"*Ni hao, Hsiao Ming,*" said Jakob, taking the boy's hand and shaking it gravely. "*Kan tao ni chen kao hsing*" — "I'm very happy to meet you."

The boy giggled and flung himself behind his mother's legs to hide, and in the act of straightening up Jakob caught sight of the sharply handsome face he had last seen at Mei-ling's house in Shanghai ten years before. Wearing a dark, high-necked cadre's suit, Kao strode to the door holding a sheaf of papers in one hand and a ballpoint pen in the other. His composed, blank expression did not alter as he caught sight of Jakob and it seemed obvious that he had heard what had been said. When his wife turned to look questioningly at him, Kao asked her in a quiet voice to pay a short visit to a neighbor in the next courtyard, and he waited in silence until his wife and son disappeared through the gate into the street. Then, with a stony look, he gestured for Jakob to enter and closed the door behind him. In the middle of the small room that obviously served both as a sitting room and dining room, Kao turned to face Jakob. A scowl of displeasure distorted his features and Jakob found himself momentarily at a loss for words.

"I've rehearsed this moment many times inside my head," said Jakob haltingly in Chinese. "But face to face with you, it's difficult even to begin to say what I feel. . . ."

"I have no interest in what you feel. There was no reason for you to come here." Kao's eyes flashed with hostility. "You weren't invited. You're not welcome."

"I understand," replied Jakob shakily. "I'm very much to blame for the shock you had. I wanted to tell you how deeply sorry I was that you had to find out that way —"

"It's of no significance," snapped Kao. "You only offend me further by coming here."

"But I'm your father, Kao," persisted Jakob. "Ever since that terrible night in Shanghai I've wanted to talk to you. Until now it hasn't been possible. . . ."

"I've never had any need for a father! The Chinese Communist Party and its great leader Chairman Mao have been father and mother enough to me."

Jakob stared helplessly at his son and a sense of futility gripped him. Kao's pale features had changed little in the ten years since Jakob had last seen him but there was a fierce hardness in his manner now and his self-possession had a cold, chilling quality.

"I didn't intentionally dishonor you, Kao," said Jakob, struggling to keep his voice steady. "I told you in Shanghai I had asked your mother to marry me. We had both been through terrible experiences. But she was determined to devote herself to what she believed in . . ."

"These matters are of no importance to me." Kao's voice shook with a scarcely controlled fury. "I have no wish to hear about them."

"I'm sorry that's how you look at things. Marshal Lu told me briefly today of how your mother has suffered. I suppose I had hoped —"

"The battle between Chairman Mao's revolutionary line and the line of the Party's class enemies has been long and bloody," put in Kao quickly. "Those who fail to support the Party have to face the consequences. . . ."

Jakob stared at his son, appalled by his seeming lack of feeling. Then he took a half-pace toward him, searching desperately for words that might ease the terrible hostility between them. "A whole world divides us, Kao. Perhaps any real understanding is impossible now — but I suppose I came here to tell you that despite all the freakish tricks fate has played on us, I've never ceased to love your mother." Emotion rose suddenly within him and Jakob stumbled over his words. "I've never married again . . . and my feelings could never be separated entirely from you. . . . In a perfect world, Kao, we might have known one another as father and son. It's pained me terribly over the years that I've never been able to show you anything of these feelings . . . and if I could ever help you in any way, I hope you would ask me."

"How could you ever do anything to help me?" asked Kao scornfully. "Until I met you in Shanghai, I believed my father was a patriotic war hero. You destroyed that idea — you destroyed everything for me! Do you think I've had no thoughts or feelings about that in the last ten years? Do you think I could forget that my mother betrayed herself and the revolution with you?" Anger and contempt contorted Kao's face and his voice roughened. "You've never caused anything but harm to me. Take your selfish offers of help elsewhere."

"I've never wished to harm you, Kao. Surely you must understand that."

"Then go!" Swinging on his heel, Kao strode to the door, wrenched it open, and stood glaring angrily at his father. "If you want to help, leave China tomorrow and never return!"

For a long moment father and son stood looking mutely at one another; then Jakob shook his head slowly. "I'm sorry, Kao, I can't promise to do that."

Kao did not reply but merely opened the door wider and Jakob stepped out into the courtyard. The door slammed loudly behind him, and when he reached the street he found it full of people making their way southward toward the Square of Heavenly Peace. Many were carrying paper wreaths and small portraits of Chou En-lai, and as soon as Jakob came in sight of the Monument to the People's Heroes he saw that the tributes to Chou were now piled to a height of thirty or forty feet around the tall center column of lavender granite.

4

From the rear seat of a Tatra taxi, which had collected him from his hotel shortly after breakfast, Jakob watched the swarms of Chinese cyclists milling along the narrow, tree-lined road in the northeast corner of the old Imperial City. For some minutes he had been aware that the streets through which he was passing were vaguely familiar from his student days and he found himself subconsciously searching for the three-story European-style building standing in a leafy garden which had once housed the Joint Missionary Language School. He had begun to assume that it must have been pulled down when the taxi halted outside a pair of dun-colored double gates in a high wall of gray brick above which a sign reading "Peking Number 7 Mental Health Center" was visible. He paid off the taxi and rang a bell beside the gate. When it was opened by an elderly Chinese, he stepped through and showed him the stamped letter authorizing his visit, which he had found waiting at his hotel the previous evening on returning from Kao's house. After the Chinese grunted his approval, Jakob began walking up a short asphalt drive toward the portalled front door and because his mind was distracted by the prospect of the visit, he did not fully recognize where he was until he reached the short flight of steps leading into the building.

Then the sight of the aging panels of colored glass in the double doors and a rusted iron bell pull beside them brought him to a sudden halt and his memory vaulted backward forty-five years. The scarred paint on the doors was a different color and yellowing notices fixed to the begrimed glass marred their decorative effect, but he was in no doubt that he was standing before the entrance of the old Joint Missionary Language School through which he had passed daily as a young man. Turning to look back the way he had come, he saw then that some of the original cypress trees still flanked the drive, which had once been graveled, but the grass beneath them was rank and untended and the ornamental iron railings that had surrounded the shady garden in the thirties had been replaced by the high wall clearly designed to deter unauthorized exit or entry.

For a moment Jakob stood rooted to the spot, overwhelmed by the awful irony. A sense of foreboding had begun to grow in him as soon as he stepped into the taxi outside the hotel, but finding himself unexpectedly in surroundings which he had last inhabited as a novice missionary, he felt his agitation increase. It seemed for a moment or two as though he were caught up in a nightmarish dream; he found himself wondering how many other transformations the old language college might have passed through, and looking at the garden brought back poignant memories of Felicity hurrying earnestly in and out of the building at his side, clutching her Chinese-language books. Then the sound of the door opening behind him broke his train of thought and he turned to find a Chinese male orderly looking questioningly at him from the threshold. He mounted the steps hesitantly, and when he produced his letter of authorization the orderly directed him to a small reception window inside the entrance hall. After his credentials had been checked, the waiting orderly led Jakob away along a drab corridor that he immediately recognized; some doors that led into once-familiar classrooms stood open, but in place of the rows of desks at which he and Felicity had sat, he saw iron beds and wooden chairs on which vacant-eyed Chinese patients were slumped in attitudes of bemused idleness.

Other patients were wandering aimlessly along the corridors, shepherded by white-overalled orderlies, and behind the few closed doors they passed, Jakob could hear the sound of crazed voices babbling and shouting incoherently. As they entered a corridor where all the rooms were visibly occupied by women, his heart began to thud painfully. Young girls and gray-haired crones alike looked out numbly through the doorways, their eyes blurred and unfocused, and he was seized by an irrational fear that he might not be equal to the demands of the meeting. When the orderly finally halted before a half-open door and motioned him ahead, Jakob had to take a deep breath before stepping past him; once inside the room, his first glimpse of Mei-ling seemed to paralyze his senses and he could only stand and stare.

The loss of her reason had left Mei-ling strangely tranquil and composed. Her face was smooth, almost unlined, and her hair, still lustrously dark and long, was dressed with a girl's care in glossy braids. Slender and straight inside a tunic and baggy trousers of faded blue cotton, she sat unmoving on a chair in the middle of the sparsely furnished room, and despite her age, in her blank expression there was an unearthly beauty. She made no move and gave no sign that she had noticed his arrival but sat staring fixedly at a small window beyond which nothing was visible except a blank, white-washed wall. Even when he took a hesitant step toward her, she did not move or acknowledge his presence in any way, and after the male orderly closed the door softly on leaving, Jakob found himself listening uneasily to the man's footsteps retreating along the scuffed linoleum of the passageway.

Left alone with her, Jakob suddenly found the silence and the statuelike stillness of Mei-ling unnerving; a feeling of panic seized him but after a few moments he realized that all the agitation was inside himself. In Mei-ling's eerie, unchanging posture there was a curious peacefulness — her expressionless face possessed a rare se-renity, as though she had passed beyond all pain and anguish, and on becoming fully aware of this, Jakob felt at once calmed and soothed himself.

"Mei-ling, it's Jakob." He spoke softly in Chinese, his voice break-ing with emotion. "I'm very happy to see you again."

She gave no sign of having heard and he glanced quickly around the room. Its walls were painted a dull green and it contained a neatly made bed positioned against one wall, a small table covered with pale cloth, a locker, and a spare chair. On the table stood a large vacuum flask of hot water and a plastic beaker, but otherwise there were no signs of personal possessions.

Picking up the vacant chair, Jakob moved it to the center of the room and sat down. But Mei-ling did not move or even blink: instead, she continued to look toward the window, her dark eyes fixed steadily ahead as though seeing something that remained invisible to others. Nothing indicated that she was aware of his presence in the room and Jakob stared at her in consternation. Close up, to his astonish-ment, she looked far younger than her years. Her complexion was unblemished, and there was a curiously youthful light in her un-wavering gaze. It was as if in the absence of her reason, her soul had somehow repelled the ravages of time from her body and she radiated a startling and strangely ageless beauty. For several minutes they sat together without speaking — but although no words were uttered, an indefinable sense of communication seemed to Jakob to exist between them. The feeling intensified until it became almost unnerving and he spoke at last just to break the eerie silence.

"I expect you already know, Mei-ling, that it's the festival of Ch'ing Ming today," he said in a quiet voice. "Hundreds of thousands of people are laying wreaths in Tien An Men Square for Premier Chou. It's peaceful and very moving." He watched her face intently as he spoke, searching for a flicker of expression in her eyes, but she gave no outward sign of having heard anything. "People are laying wreaths because they want a better future. They're tired of political struggle. Chairman Mao is very ill. Changes are coming — changes for the better."

After another long silence the sudden sound of her voice startled him, although it was little more than a whisper. Her lips scarcely moved and at first he was unable to distinguish what she was saying. Then he realized she was repeating one single phrase very slowly, over and over again.

"*Tsao fan yu li! Tsao fan yu li! Tsao fan yu li!*"

She continued to stare straight ahead and the whispered words seemed to rise automatically from her throat without any conscious act of will. She repeated the unchanging words of the old Cultural Revolution slogan — "Rebellion is justified!" — a dozen or more times in the same soft, hoarse whisper; then, abruptly, she fell silent again, still without acknowledging Jakob's existence.

At her side, Jakob felt a deep sadness well up in him. Her ethereal beauty seemed to imbue the banal words with some new dimension of cruelty and he felt hot tears of compassion start in his eyes.

"I saw Kao yesterday," said Jakob on an impulse, leaning close to her again. "I told him how sorry I was for what happened in Shanghai. I said I'd never wanted to dishonor him. I told him our feelings for one another ran very deep." Again he watched her face intently but still no trace of response appeared. "I saw your grandson, Ming, too. He seems a fine boy."

"*P'ao ta si ling pu,*" said Mei-ling softly. "*P'ao ta si ling pu! P'ao ta si ling pu!*"

Her words were clearer this time but she spoke in a remote, faraway tone that seemed to echo the intonation of a voice other than her own. "*P'ao ta si ling pu!*" — "Bombard the headquarters!" she said again and continued to repeat the quotation until her voice reached a kind of crescendo. But all the time she remained motionless on her chair, her hands lying quietly in her lap, and when at last she fell silent, Jakob reached out and gently took hold of one of them.

"Mei-ling, I don't know whether you can understand anything I say. I hope you can." He gazed beseechingly at her, swept by a feeling of great helplessness and loss. "I want you to know I've never forgotten you. I've never forgotten the great love I felt for you during those terrible days on the Long March. I told Kao yesterday that I've never stopped loving you. . . . He couldn't understand and I don't blame him. It's impossible for him. But I know you felt as I did and I know why you had to turn away from me. You've been truly brave and constant. You've done nothing to deserve your terrible suffering."

Jakob felt tears overflow onto his cheeks, yet Mei-ling made no response. Her lips were moving soundlessly but he sensed that she was still attempting to utter only the meaningless slogans of the past. Lifting one of her hands, he pressed his lips despairingly against her fingers; they were cool and smooth and he held her hand against his face for a long time.

"Mei-ling, perhaps you don't know . . . but this building was once a school. I studied Chinese here when I was only twenty years old. . . ." Jakob's voice broke. "Coming back to find you here . . . has brought to life something very valuable that's been dead inside me for years. . . ."

Overcome by his anguish and complex feelings he little understood, Jakob detached his hand from hers and rose to his feet. Looking down at her, he felt as though his heart might burst, and he turned and hurried blindly to the door. Before opening it, he glanced around at Mei-ling, and to his astonishment he saw that a quiet, seraphic smile had come to her face. She was still staring toward the window but the blank expression had gone and her features were transfigured by the smile. Then, for the first time since he had entered the room, she moved, turning her head to look in his direction. Lifting the hand he had kissed, she pressed the back of it gently against her cheek, and holding it there, she continued to gaze toward him. Even then he was not sure whether she saw or recognized him, but in the same moment she was both an eerily beautiful and deeply tragic figure and Jakob could not take his eyes from her.

"May God bless you, Mei-ling," he whispered. "May God bless you always."

The words sounded strange in his own ears because he had not uttered them for so many years, and how long he stood there looking at her he could not later recall. Eventually the dazzling intensity of her expression became unbearable for him to look on, and with great reluctance he turned and left the room. After closing the door behind him, the lovely, frozen smile remained vividly in his mind's eye and he carried the memory of it away with him along the shabby passageway, knowing that it would remain etched in his heart for as long as he lived.

5

A dense pall of black smoke drifting low across the Square of Heavenly Peace obscured the weak April sun as Jakob ran toward the Monument to the People's Heroes. Orange flames were leaping from the wreck of an overturned bus on a nearby road and the air was filled by a tumult of shouting. The sudden explosion of the bus's gas tank sent flames shooting high into the air, setting several ornamental pine trees alight close to the memorial, and in the distance Jakob heard the clamorous bells of approaching fire engines.

Bewildered-looking factory militiamen wearing red arm bands and carrying long wooden staves were trying to throw a loose cordon around the southern end of the giant square, but they were overwhelmingly outnumbered and clearly lacked the discipline and experience to carry out such a demanding task successfully. As he ran, Jakob saw long columns of People's Liberation Army troops moving past the Museum of Chinese History at a fast jog-trot; they carried no arms and he guessed they were being moved to positions in adjoining buildings as a precaution. Although the militia forces of the capital were known to be under the direct control of Chiang Ch'ing and her radical supporters, new waves of students and workers converging from all directions were ignoring their shouted orders to turn back from the square and a crowd already tens of thousands strong was growing rapidly. Tussles were breaking out between the demonstrators and the outnumbered militia, and Jakob saw jeering bands of students tear off the arm bands of several militiamen and trample them derisively underfoot.

Some groups of demonstrators were chanting "Long live Chou

En-lai!" in rhythmic unison as they ran, and others yelled "Long live Yang Kai-hui! Down with the Dowager Empress!" From the tall, grape-cluster streetlights in the square, beribboned portraits of Chou En-lai swung in the stiff wind alongside many streamers that now all carried the same warning: "We swore to protect Chou En-lai and his successors and we'll fight a bloody battle to the end!" Adulatory wall posters referring to Chou En-lai as "our beloved father" had been pasted on the concrete bases of the lamps, and as he drew nearer to the memorial, Jakob could see that hundreds of Public Security Bureau police in khaki caps and jackets had linked arms around its upper plinth and were trying to hold back the yelling crowd. The central obelisk of the monument, which twenty-four hours earlier had been smothered in commemorative wreaths, was now starkly naked of all adornment, and it was clear that this was the cause of the crowd's anger.

Jakob had been taking a late breakfast in the Peking Hotel when he overheard other foreign guests speaking excitedly of demonstrations that were apparently being mounted in protest against the overnight removal of the wreaths by security police. Leaving his food unfinished, he had returned quickly to his room to fetch a camera, then hurried out into Chang An Boulevard. On catching sight of the great cloud of black smoke wafting toward the Forbidden City, he had begun to run with the streams of demonstrators that were moving urgently toward Tien An Men Square. Although the square had been the scene of many spectacular parades and rallies since 1949, political riots were unheard of there, and among the crowds Jakob again noticed groups of foreign diplomats and journalists surreptitiously carrying cameras and tape-recording machines. Because foreigners with cameras had frequently been hounded by Red Guard mobs during the Cultural Revolution, Jakob had taken the precaution of hanging his camera around his neck and buttoning the front of his overcoat over it; some of the diplomats and foreign correspondents were taking similar precautions, he saw, and all of them were behaving with discretion, noting the details of slogan signs and written wall posters without stopping ostentatiously to read them.

Above the shouts and chants of the milling crowd in the square, the voice of one student leader could be clearly heard. He had climbed to the lower plinth of the memorial and was speaking through a megaphone. His address was being interrupted by frequent bursts of cheering, and when another demonstrator clambered over the cordon of security policemen holding aloft a large colored portrait of Chou En-lai, the cheers turned to roars of approval and applause. To hear better what the youth was saying, Jakob pushed his way through the crowd until he reached the balustrades guarding the steps of the lower plinth, and there he pressed himself against the stonework, listening intently to the speech.

"Some false Marxists who follow the Dowager Empress have tried to stop us reaching this memorial today, comrades," he yelled. "They want to stop us because they're very frightened! They know that we, the people, are determined to defend Premier Chou's legacy — but *they're* conducting an underhanded conspiracy to get rid of Premier Chou's chosen successor. They're trying to burn the plans of Comrade Teng Hsiao-ping to turn China into a great industrial nation. . . . But we're not going to allow them to commit these crimes, are we, comrades?"

The crowd roared "No!" and surged forward against the security cordon again. In the melee the megaphone was wrenched away from the student speaker and new scuffles with the police and militia broke out on the steps. Jakob had to struggle to keep his feet and all around him groups of demonstrators began to fight one another, using staves they had torn from the hands of militiamen. Over their heads Jakob saw that other gangs of demonstrators had halted the approaching fire engines and that flames were still leaping from the wrecked bus and the grove of pine trees. A group of European journalists trying to get close-up pictures of the fires were set upon by the mob, and within moments their cameras and tape recorders were ripped from their hands. On the western side of the square a mob of several thousand demonstrators was converging on the tall bronze doors of the Great Hall of the People; troops with bayonets fixed to their rifles were trying to bar their way beneath the twelve massive pillars, but the racing mob swept them aside and ran up the steps to hammer on the doors. In the rush, shiny official limousines standing at the foot of the steps were rolled over onto their roofs and overexcited youths leapt up to dance on the undersides of the vehicles.

"Chou En-lai opposed Chairman Mao all his life!" yelled a new male voice and Jakob turned back, startled, toward the memorial to find that another student leader had sprung up onto the balustrade. A small group of supporters was steadying his legs as he addressed the crowd through the captured megaphone and others were fighting off hostile demonstrators who were trying to pull him down. "Chou En-lai's so-called successor is of the same stripe! He wants to take the capitalist road and make us dependent on foreign goods and foreign technology! He wants to turn the clock back to the time when China was dependent on foreign imperialism! He wants to split the Central Committee and incite people to demonstrate on the strength of rumors and lies. . . ."

A fresh howl of rage arose from the crowd and a determined rush broke the line of security police in a dozen places; the student holding the megaphone was seized and dragged bodily onto the upper plinth of the memorial, where furious supporters of Chou En-lai battered him mercilessly about the face and head with captured staves. The Public Security Bureau cordon collapsed under the assault and many of the policemen were trampled underfoot by the mob as it stormed back onto the monument. Jakob was flung against one of the revolutionary bas-reliefs and he clung there as yelling students clambered over him. Looking up, he saw demonstrators rip the shirt from the critic of Chou En-lai and bind his arms tightly behind him with a loop of wire. Others rained blows on him relentlessly until blood flowed down his face and body. Stripped to the waist, he was dragged roughly up and down the steps while other frenzied youths kicked him and struck at him with their bare fists. Some of his supporters had also been bound and stripped half-naked and they were beaten with the same terrible ferocity until they too hung limp and senseless in their captors' arms.

A new pall of smoke caught Jakob's eye and he looked up to find that a building in the southeast corner of the square was on fire. Flames were shooting from its lower windows and demonstrators with improvised battering rams were smashing down doors along its entire frontage. From the same direction Jakob saw a squad of about a hundred militiamen marching fast toward the memorial in a double column, escorting half a dozen civilian cadres in their midst. It was obvious that the officials were being sent to appeal for calm, and as the militia bodyguard forced its way through the turbulent mass of people thronging the monument, Jakob saw Kao. Grim-faced and determined, Kao was marching at the head of the cadres, and the moment they reached the foot of the steps he raised a voice amplifier of his own and shouted in the direction of the melee on the higher plinth. At first the demonstrators on the memorial took no notice, but on hearing his authoritative voice, a large part of the crowd quieted and Kao called out again, more loudly.

"Cease this struggle!" he commanded in a ringing voice. "You're being exploited by troublemakers who support those taking the capitalist road! . . .They like to divide the masses and play different groups off against one another! . . . You're helping them to sabotage production and undermine the revolution. . . . You must resolve your differences by discussion!"

The leaders of the riot hesitated, staring down uncertainly at Kao. From his unobtrusive position clinging to the side of the monument, Jakob saw a look of satisfaction appear on Kao's face and for several seconds a near-silence reigned; but then one of the leaders pointedly detached a long loop of wire from the wrists of an unconscious prisoner and raised it menacingly above his head. He held the pose for a second or two before yelling a new command at the top of his voice and flinging himself headlong down the steps toward Kao. His supporters followed in a torrent, engulfing the militia guards in a mass of struggling bodies. The militiamen tried to close around Kao and the other officials, but the furious demonstrators easily broke through their ranks. They seized Kao, pinioning his arms, and with a shout of triumph their leader flung the wire noose over his head. Using both hands, he drew the wire tight and Jakob saw Kao's eyes bulge from his head in terror as it bit deep into his neck.

Kao tried to cry out but only an animalistic choking noise escaped his lips as he was dragged up the steps of the monument. The leader of the rioters strained at the wire noose, tightening it vindictively, and the crowd went quiet, aware suddenly that an important official was being strangled to death before their eyes. Kao's arms and legs thrashed wildly for a second or two; then he went limp as his captors hauled him onto the topmost plinth and spun him around, holding him up by the wire noose like a human puppet. Noticing that his tongue had begun to protrude from his mouth and his eyes had closed, Jakob shouted out with the full force of his lungs and scrambled up onto one of the balustrades.

"This will make fine pictures for all the world to see!"

He yelled the words in Chinese and jerked his camera into view from inside his coat; holding it conspicuously in front of his face, he clicked the shutter repeatedly, taking snap after snap of Kao and the demonstrators holding him. Then, as though to get a closer shot, he raced along the top of the balustrade and focused again from a position directly beneath Kao. On seeing a white-haired European openly snatching photographs of them, the wild-eyed demonstrators on the steps abandoned their victim to turn and surge down in Jakob's direction, screaming hysterical abuse at him. Within moments arms pinned him from behind and his camera was wrenched from his hands by a burly student; a roar went up as it was broken open and the film was plucked out and stretched in loops above the student's head.

Higher up the memorial, militiamen raced to the fallen figure of Kao and unfastened the wire from his neck. He was coughing and retching, but Jakob saw them help him to his feet and begin carrying him away down the steps. The next moment a fist struck Jakob with sickening force on the left temple, spinning him around, and the Gate of Heavenly Peace, at the northern end of the square, became a somersaulting blur of red and gold as it plunged downward into the black earth. Yelling demonstrators closed around Jakob while he lay slumped on the ground, kicking him and lashing him with staves, and by the time the militia guards fought their way to him and drove off his attackers they found he had lost consciousness.

6

A tentative knock on the door of his hotel bedroom wakened Jakob from a light afternoon sleep but he made no immediate response, imagining that the resident nurse from the British embassy was paying him another visit. During the two days he had spent resting in bed, the nurse had made four or five calls to check that he was not suffering any concussive aftereffects of his beating, and he raised himself against his pillows in anticipation of seeing her enter the room. But the door did not open, and when the hesitant-sounding knock was repeated, he turned his head and called out politely, "Come in."

The sight of Abigail standing on the threshold made him start. She was wearing an elegantly tailored navy coat and high-heeled shoes, but when she stepped into the room he saw that her expression was anxious and concerned. After closing the door, she walked slowly toward the bed and stood looking down uncertainly at his bandaged right hand and the dressing that covered his left temple.

"I heard about your accident," she said stiffly. "It seemed silly not to come and see if you were all right."

Jakob was so overcome by the first sight of his daughter in ten years that he could find no reply. She was still strikingly attractive and wore her long blond hair in a fashionable chignon; maturity made her seem more poised and self-contained than ever, and perhaps because of this, words failed him.

"They told me at the embassy that you'd been pretty badly beaten. But I couldn't think what you might need, so I'm afraid I haven't brought anything."

"Please sit down," said Jakob, gesturing toward a chair. "I don't think there's anything I need. . . . The hotel staff bring me all I ask for."

Abigail sat on the edge of a straight-backed chair, looking uneasily at her father. "Are you really all right?" she asked, frowning. "After the stories I heard, I didn't know what to expect."

"I think I'm going to be fine," said Jakob, trying to smile. "My head still aches a little. But a doctor from the Swedish embassy has given me a thorough check. He can't find much wrong with me beyond this gash on my forehead and a couple of cuts on my right hand. My ribs are badly bruised and I suppose I was shaken up a bit — that's why he insisted I rest for a day or two."

An uneasy silence lengthened between them but as Jakob's feeling of surprise subsided, he realized that for the first time since her visit to Hong Kong nearly twenty years earlier, Abigail had sought him out, and his spirits began to rise.

"You're looking wonderfully well yourself, Abigail," he said quietly. "Are you still enjoying your teaching here?"

"Yes, very much." Abigail's voice was curt as though indicating that she had no wish for the conversation to become too personal. "I had a second English-language textbook published last year. Everything's going well."

"I'm very glad."

They lapsed again into silence; then Abigail looked at her father with a quizzical expression. "How did the accident in Tien An Men Square come about? I heard the crowd attacked you for taking photographs — but that didn't seem to ring true for someone with your experience of China."

"What you heard was right. I did take some pictures when it wasn't a very wise thing to do." He hesitated, apprehensive that a full explanation might destroy the fragile truce between them; then he decided he had no choice. "I let others think I'd got a bit over-excited. In fact, I went out of my way to show that I was taking pictures — because of Kao."

"Because of Kao?" Abigail's eyes widened in surprise. "What do you mean?"

"Quite by chance Kao was sent out to try to calm things down . . . The mob turned on him and it looked very ugly. I saw an opportunity to distract their attention and pulled out my camera . . ."

Abigail stared wonderingly at her father as the significance of what he had said became clear to her. "Did Kao know you were here in Peking?"

Jakob nodded. "I talked with Marshal Lu Chiao on the day I arrived. He gave me Kao's address. He lives now at 15 Nan Chihtze, and I went to see him that same night to try to apologize for what happened in Shanghai. He still wouldn't listen and I suppose I don't blame him for that." Jakob paused, feeling again the force of the emotion that had led to his rash intervention. "He's married now and has a small son, Ming. . . . I met the boy. When I saw Kao in the square all these things were very fresh in my mind. . . ."

Abigail stood up suddenly like a spring uncoiling and walked over to the window. Keeping her back turned to Jakob, she leaned on the sill and stared down into Chang An. Jakob watched her, waiting for her to speak, but she said nothing.

"Have you had any contact at all with Kao or Mei-ling since that night in Shanghai?" asked Jakob diffidently.

"None whatsoever." Abigail kept her back turned to her father and her voice sharpened again. "I thought it best to put all that behind me once and for all."

"Mei-ling was persecuted by Red Guards until she lost her mind." said Jakob quietly. "She's in an institution now. I visited her but she doesn't recognize anybody. . . ."

Abigail neither moved nor spoke but continued to stare out of the window, and Jakob sat up straighter in the bed.

"You may think, Abigail, that I'm only interested in what's going on in China — but the truth is I came here this time hoping above all else to see you. . . . Although I've never known how to put things right between us, I haven't given up hope. Perhaps you've thought

I didn't care about you because I haven't been able to say it. But
the opposite is true. I cared so much that when you came to Hong
Kong it hurt even to look at you. In a way you reminded me of all
the pain and the tragedy of the past, although it wasn't your fault. . . ."
Jakob hesitated, searching for words to express complex inner feelings. "But coming back here this time has made me think again of
many things I'd lost track of. For some reason I can't explain it's
given me new hope . . ."

Abigail swung around suddenly and walked back toward the bed.
She had a faint look of bewilderment in her eyes and her unsteady
voice belied the force of what she said. "I didn't come here to reopen old wounds, Daddy. They're better left to heal on their own.
I learned the hard way that you have to look inside yourself to find
real solace. And I made peace with myself long ago. . . . I only came
here to find out if you were all right — so I think I'd better go now."

Without waiting for his reply, Abigail walked to the door and
opened it. She hesitated, looking back at him over her shoulder,
preparing to say something further; but then she changed her mind
and went out, closing the door quietly behind her.

7

From the Pavilion of Eternal Spring on the crest of Ching Shan
Hill early the next morning, the palaces of imperial Peking still looked
like spectacular shoals of golden carp basking in a green jade lake.
Nestling below, among cypress and acacia groves, the curved golden
roofs glittered as brilliantly in the dawn sunlight as they had more
than forty years before. It had been autumn then but now it was
spring, and on the hill around the pavilion, magnolia, *yulan*, and *sal*
trees were breaking into bud. Beside the pathways, peonies were
beginning to unfold their showy flowers and the early sunlight shone
everywhere on fresh pink and white blossom quivering in the morning breeze.

Jakob could scarcely believe that forty-five years had passed since
he first climbed excitedly to the highest central point of the Inner
City with Felicity at his side. Apart from the season, nothing seemed
to have changed in the old private garden of the Ming emperors.

The same ancient pines still brushed the triple-tiered roof of the Wan Chun Ting pavilion, where, during one magical dawn, he and Felicity had practiced Chinese calligraphy with a silk-robed scholar; the glazed roofs of four smaller pavilions standing on grassy mounds of earth excavated from the Forbidden City's moat were still visible among the pines; a locust tree from which the last Ming emperor hanged himself as a peasant army broke into the city still jutted from the eastern slopes of the hill; and despite the tidal waves of destruction that had swept China in the intervening years, the panorama of halls and palaces with their ornamental gardens and courtyards was as unchanged and timeless as it had been in 1931. The mystical heart of ancient China still seemed to Jakob to be beating powerfully in the spectacular imperial enclosures, and the breathtaking sight revived the memory of that distant dawn with astonishing vividness.

He remembered suddenly the numinous, awestruck feeling that had seized him, the sense that in the lovely, antique pavilions spread out below the hill the immortal souls of China's great emperors might have been gathering in the hush of that early day to re-celebrate their solemn rituals on behalf of the nation's teeming millions. A vague, elusive conviction that somehow the sublime beauty of that dawn would live on in him in some influential way had followed, and on closing his eyes the memory of that feeling intensified. He imagined that Felicity was again sitting beside him in her peach gingham dress, her hair neatly parted, her gentle, serious face radiating its simple piety. The faint fragrance of new blossom sweetened the air and the illusion became so strong that he felt Felicity's earthly image might easily appear before him again as it had seemed to do in the blackness of the night on the rock stairway in the Taloushan Mountains.

Although Jakob's head still throbbed faintly from the beating he had received in the Square of Heavenly Peace and his body ached in a dozen different places, a curious feeling of refreshment and renewal began to steal over him as he sat quietly in the old Ming pavilion with his eyes closed. After two days in bed he had risen very early to wander aimlessly through the almost empty dawn streets in the heart of the capital. The sight of shadowy groups of Chinese men practicing graceful T'ai Chi Ch'uan movements beneath the misty willows fringing the Forbidden City moat had transported him backward in time to that first magical Peking dawn he had shared with Felicity, and on hearing the plaintive wail of panpipes from the direction of Gorgeous Prospect Hill, he had deliberately turned his footsteps in that direction.

As he reached the summit, the rising sun had suddenly fired its first shafts of yellow light low across the city from the east and he had been immediately moved by the deep sense of tranquillity which pervaded the old imperial vantage point. Tien An Men Square, which was partially visible from the hilltop, was almost deserted at that early hour, and it was hard to imagine that only days before it had been the scene of so much violence and ugliness. Jakob had heard rumors that several demonstrators had been killed in the fighting and hundreds injured, although there had been no official confirmation. The unrest had also been followed quickly by a dramatic announcement in the press that Vice Premier Teng Hsiao-ping had been removed from all his government and Party posts. The acting premier, Hua Kuo-feng, had been formally appointed premier of the State Council and, more important, deputy chairman of the Communist Party, which marked him clearly as the approved successor to Mao Tse-tung. Well-marshaled parades supporting these announcements had immediately appeared in the streets, but these demonstrations, unlike the emotional riots, had obviously been mounted in compliance with Party orders. Although wary-looking militia units had continued to guard the empty Tien An Men Square and its approaches, an uneasy atmosphere had persisted in the streets as though everybody knew that some danger was still simmering not far below the surface. Consequently it had been an added relief for Jakob to stumble again upon the haven of peace on Ching Shan Hill, and because the park was deserted at that hour, he continued to sit quietly in the Pavilion of Eternal Spring with his eyes closed.

The remembered images of Felicity which first filled his mind faded gradually to be replaced by the dazzling smile of Mei-ling as he had seen it only days before. Her eerie beauty and his enchanted surroundings seemed suddenly part of one strange, indefinable harmony, and Mei-ling's fresh, young face merged in his memory with the dizzying feelings of love that had long ago consumed him. Other visions of the past also tumbled gently one upon another through his mind as if summoned by invisible command. He saw the Red Army's standard bobbing again above the heads of Long March soldiers, furled inside the looted oil canvas, that showed him only the star of Bethlehem; he smelled the wholesome, earthy odors of the grain store where he slept beside Abigail and Liang during their escape; he saw the enigmatic, gray-robed Taoist priest standing out-side his mountainside temple; and he heard Laurence Franklin describing how Matthew Barlow had died smiling up at the soaring eagle while his Bible translations were scattered on the wind. The fragrance of winter plum blossom, sharp in the cold January air, teased his senses again; he heard his parents describing the crowded prayer meetings held for him in their local church hall; and in quick succession he saw the shocked faces of Abigail and Kao in Shanghai, saw Kao ordering him angrily from his Peking home, then struggling to free himself from the screaming mob around the Monument to the People's Heroes. The day-old image of Abigail's lovely face peering anxiously at him in the hotel bedroom lingered longest, and despite the feeling of strain that had persisted throughout their brief meeting, a promise of contentment seemed now to enhance the memory, and when Jakob finally opened his eyes again, he felt lightened and calmed.

His aching head had cleared and although he was still aware of the soreness in his limbs, a feeling of ease flowed through his body for the first time since he was dragged down from the balustrade of the monument in the riot. A strong breeze was blowing and all around him the newly opened pink and white tree blossom was shivering and dancing in the early sunlight. The scene before his eyes possessed an ethereal loveliness and in that moment past and present fused suddenly, releasing in him a gentle feeling of joy. As he gazed down through the blossom at the palaces and lake-spangled gardens flanking the Forbidden City, he was gripped by a powerful sense of having arrived at an important destination — at the selfsame spot where his journey had begun. Despite the tragedies of the past, a feeling of goodness and beauty seemed to vibrate softly in the dawn air and a new certainty about the existence of a supreme divinity swelled within him.

When he had sat in that imperial pavilion on Ching Shan Hill for the first time, his youthful mind had been guided by an untested and unknowing certainty, an unquestioning faith. In the wilderness of China, doubts had undermined that certainty, and he had eventually drifted into a vague and unsatisfactory ambiguity of belief. But even after he had encountered his crisis of faith, that first enchanted autumn dawn, he saw now, had continued to exert its invisible influence. It had surely played a part in his deciding to spend the rest of his working life untangling the threads of China's politics from Hong Kong. Every man's life, he realized suddenly, was to some degree a journey into the unknown, undertaken to understand himself. As he gazed at the new blossom trembling on the branches around him, he knew without any doubt that he had found journey's end where it had begun, that by means of a long, tortuous trail he had traveled from autumn into spring.

With these conflicting feelings of exhilaration and sadness mingling in his mind, Jakob rose and stepped out of the pavilion, letting his gaze range over the golden rooftops to the west of the hill. Somewhere below in one of those lakeside pavilions, a modern, despotic emperor who had misused his mandate to cause terrible suffering to his people lay slowly dying; his greatest and most loyal general was also sinking toward death in another anonymous old palace nearby. With the passing of the Communist "emperor" it seemed likely that much agony would pass too and perhaps hope would be reborn. Meantime, the hush of the early day enveloping the ancient capital seemed to convey that all of China was distracted with the waiting.

Turning toward the east, Jakob noticed for the first time the forests of factory chimneys in the industrial suburbs; wispy plumes of smoke spiraled weakly into the lightening sky as though even the nation's engines of production were misfiring in the uncertainty. Nearer at hand, among the gray-roofed *hut'ungs* to the northeast, he tried to pick out the building which had once been the Joint Missionary Language School and wondered sadly whether beneath its roofs Mei-ling was already awake and seated on her lonely chair. With her reason gone and all her love generously given as gifts to others, was the beauty of her soul, he wondered, still shining out of her with that same brilliance that was too dazzling to behold? The questioning thought pained him deeply and in an effort to put it from his mind, he turned to search among the trees and courtyard walls on the eastern bank of the Forbidden City's moat. He was trying to locate the old single-storied courtier's house where a four-year-old boy named Ming might soon be waking and searching for a toy. Unknowingly, Ming was carrying Mei-ling's inexpressible hopes into the future, and the boy's existence was all that made the thought of her misfortune bearable for Jakob.

The daylight was growing and he turned reluctantly away and began walking down the hill toward the Forbidden City. For as long as he could, he kept his gaze fixed on the spellbinding vision of the blossom and the golden palaces spread out below, absorbing their exquisite beauty into his soul. When he entered the shadows beneath the trees the magic, revelational moments slipped gently into the past, but Jakob knew instinctively that the memory of them would remain with him always, a clear, sweet source of certainty and hope amid the painful regrets that had marred his past.

8

"We have no yak meat to offer you this time — but there is tea!"

Mao Tse-tung tried to gesture toward a low table that bore a tea tray but his right arm could only flap ineffectually against his side. For a brief moment a vacuous smile flickered across features that were waxen and pallid but it dissolved abruptly as if it had already cost too much effort.

"That's all right — I prefer tea to yak meat anyway."

Jakob spoke his Chinese slowly and smiled as two female nurses stepped forward to assist the tottering leader of China to an armchair in the outer study of the single-storied Ming pavilion where he lived. Three official Chinese photographers had already recorded the formal greeting which the chairman of China's Communist Party had accorded Jakob on his arrival, waiting dutifully until the nurses had helped him up before taking their flash pictures. But Mao's scrawny hand had felt cold and limp in Jakob's grasp and when the nurses took him by the arms to help seat him once more, Jakob noticed that he meekly allowed them to position and maneuver him as they wished, without protesting.

"My modest home is not as spectacular as the great tower of Chokechi . . . but it's a little more comfortable." Mao sagged down into the chair with his arms hanging over its sides, looking like a giant puppet whose strings had been suddenly loosened. His gray tunic, buttoned high at his scraggy throat, hung on him like a tent, and as he mumbled his words, the vacuous smile appeared again. "We no longer need to sleep in hammocks. . . . And we won't make you cross the Great Grasslands again after you leave here."

Jakob smiled politely once more in response. Although he had already indicated he was happy to converse in Chinese, two interpreters with notebooks and pencils sat on small stools behind Mao's chair, bending forward anxiously to catch his soft, badly slurred Hunanese speech. Whenever he said anything, they anxiously jotted notes, then, in case Jakob had not understood, they read them back in slow, clear "national language." A cadre was discreetly operating a tape recorder on a small table to the rear and after Jakob had been waved to an armchair on Mao's right hand, another young, anonymous Chinese in a cadre's tunic entered unobtrusively and sat down on Mao's left.

"When we met last, didn't we discuss the difficulties of your Christian missionary work in China? . . . Those days seem long ago . . ."

Mao's head waggled on his wasted neck and his eyelids drooped with fatigue. Looking at him closely, Jakob felt sure he had only recently risen from his sickbed for the meeting. At one moment he mumbled his words toward his chest, at another his head fell weakly backward to rest against the white antimacassar on the chair behind him.

"I still have the copy of your poem 'Mountains,' which you gave me at Chokechi," said Jakob. "It hangs on my office wall in Hong Kong."

Mao looked blearily at him. "Enough time has passed since Chokechi to turn an eager Chinese revolutionary into a tired old man. . . . But hasn't the truth of our conversation at the fortress been proved by the years? . . ."

"Perhaps." Jakob turned in his chair to face the ailing Chinese leader. "But perhaps not. It wouldn't be wise to underestimate how long a seed of truth can lie hidden before sprouting."

One clawlike hand lifted briefly from the arm of the chair in a dismissive gesture. "In 1966 virtually every Bible in China was confiscated and destroyed by the proletarian revolutionaries. Everything else connected with old superstitions was also swept away. . . ."

Jakob smiled gently. "Refugees in Hong Kong still tell stories of prayer meetings held secretly in many country villages. Pages torn from the few Bibles that survived are passed round. I've heard that baptisms too are still sometimes performed in mountain streams."

Mao gave no indication that he had heard or understood Jakob; his clouded eyes were fixed vacantly on one of the long windows of the old Ming dwelling beyond which the waters of Chung Nan Hai — the Central and South lakes — sparkled in the afternoon sunshine. Known originally as the Small Pavilion of the Fragrant Concubine, the house had once been a modest dwelling set aside for a Board of Rites mandarin and its windows afforded a panoramic view of the terraces, marble balustrades, and lookout pavilions that bordered the lakes. The walls of the room itself were hung with a few scroll paintings of mountain scenes but otherwise its furnishings were austere and Jakob had immediately recognized the setting for the formal photographs that had invariably appeared on the front of the *People's Daily* whenever Mao granted an audience to an important foreign guest.

Jakob had been summoned there himself at only a few minutes' notice when an official limousine was sent to collect him from the Peking Hotel just after lunch. But although from inside the room the setting seemed timeless and peaceful, Jakob knew that at least a battalion of troops in full modern battle order was patrolling among the willows and cypresses outside. The entrance to the Chung Nan Hai compound west of the Forbidden City had been heavily guarded by troops ostentatiously armed with grenades and submachine guns, and as Jakob's limousine negotiated the winding drive that led to the house, he had spotted concentrations of soldiers and camouflaged armored personnel carriers deployed among the lakeside trees.

"I said the last time we met that there can be no Christian 'brotherly love' while different classes exist." Mao returned his distracted gaze from the glittering lake to his visitor, and his blurred eyes lingered briefly on the dressing on Jakob's forehead and the white bandage around his injured hand. "It was true then and it's true today. Class struggle is still the key link to future progress — everything else hinges on it."

"I believe exactly the opposite to be true," said Jakob. "All of us need to seek what unites us with our fellow man — not what divides us from him. Fanaticism breeds fanaticism. Virtually every revolution in the world has left behind a legacy of hatred and suffering." He paused, choosing his words carefully. "In the days when I was a missionary I would have said it more simply: 'Love God and love thy neighbor.' I'm no longer a missionary and haven't been for many years. But today I believe more strongly than ever that if those two simple commandments could be implemented, a true revolution of the spirit would sweep the whole world and change it for the better . . ."

Mao struggled upright in his chair, his face contorting with the effort. Strangled sounds devoid of any meaning came from his throat and Jakob saw that his nurses and interpreters were watching him with anxious expressions. For a moment he stared at the floor, breathing quickly as though gathering himself; then he leaned toward Jakob, resting an elbow unsteadily on his knee.

"There is struggle within the Party," he croaked. "The struggle between two lines has never ceased and will never cease. I was always in a minority — but I have always won victory in the end. . . . Even when you first marched with the Red Army, I was ignored. When the journey of twenty thousand *li* began, I was a minority of one. But the minority overcame the majority by waging a fierce class struggle. . . ." He paused, breathing erratically, and his voice sank to a near-whisper. "On the Long March the revolution burst fully into life. You were a witness. After I'm gone the struggle must continue — or all the victories of the revolution will be lost!"

Jakob stared in dismay at the dying man before him. His jowls were quivering uncontrollably and his rheumy eyes had grown dementedly wide. The crumpled, senile features bore no resemblance to that gaunt, powerful face which in the light of a rapeseed-oil lamp at Chokechi had glowed with the force and quiet inner strength of a brazen Eastern god. It was not only age, Jakob saw suddenly, that had robbed that face of its essence; the power, the stillness, the balance, had all been sacrificed to the impersonal, loveless creed which had long since become a merciless obsession. All that was left in the sagging, empty shell of a face was a profound, barely suppressed fear — a fear of death and a greater, paralyzing fear that his own life's certainties would be found wanting and reduced to nothing when he was no longer present to enforce them.

"It wasn't class struggle which brought the revolution to life on the Long March," said Jakob in an even voice. "I believe it was something more elemental. When you led the Red Army through the remote mountain regions of China, you walked back by chance into the ancient past. You reentered the primeval world where man was part of nature and still intensely aware of his creator. You fasted and starved and slept on the bare earth. You warmed your backs against great trees, ate bark and grass and small animals. The rain and the sun nourished you — body, soul, and spirit. You suffered the extreme heat of summer and the cold of winter, sometimes on successive days, and I suffered them with you. But the earth's physical and spiritual energies always sustained you through all those impossible hardships because in the wilderness you drew closer together with your fellow men than you'd ever done before — or since. Your instincts sensed that all humanity and its creator were one indivisible spirit, along with the earth and everything in it. That's why you felt exhilarated and were able day after day to live on nothing more substantial than your imagination, your optimism, and a furious hope for the future. The simple peasants of China who've never ceased to live instinctive lives followed you because they recognized a rare, inspirational spirit. They sensed the greatness of the soul in you . . ."

Mao had flopped back, exhausted, in his chair and was staring goggle-eyed at Jakob. His lower jaw had slackened and his mouth gaped open. The eyes of the interpreters and the young Chinese cadre shifted uneasily from Jakob to Mao and back again, but they made no attempt to intervene.

"At dawn today I went to Ching Shan Hill and sat in the pavilion at the top," continued Jakob, speaking slowly and clearly. "The new spring blossom and the beauty of the palaces in the dawn light made me more conscious of the divine nature of all things than I've ever been before. The feeling was beyond words, but in those moments, many things fell into place for me. On the Long March you wrote noble poems to the mountains — and kindly gave me a copy of one, which I've always retained as a prized possession. Perhaps your poetry was the nearest you came to acknowledging with your conscious mind what your instinctive nature already knew. I'm sure now that the last great journey will be a long march *inward*, into man's own soul, to seek out his own true nature and his relationship to God. . . . And only at the end of that long march will men be able to renew their links with one another . . ."

Jakob paused, considering what he was about to say with great care.

"Unfortunately, many other great leaders have been blinded by the selfish desire for power — but your instincts spoke out many times independently. You've talked often of trying to 'touch the very souls' of the Chinese people. You've tried to change human nature for the better, urging others to make unselfishness and self-sacrifice a way of life, just as it was on the Long March. But for the past forty years you've set yourself above those ideals. They were never proclaimed in the name of the profound truths of the Long March. Your exhortations have always been aimed at glorifying the destructiveness of class struggle and the material needs of the revolution.

You taught conflict, hatred, and cruelty instead of love and understanding. You created a spiritual vacuum in your people — but one
day I'm sure it will fill again with an awareness of their own spir-
ituality." Jakob paused again and drew in his breath slowly. "I believe
no lasting changes will be achieved in China or anywhere else in the
world until political leaders with some unselfish understanding of
the human spirit emerge. People everywhere long for such leaders —
in time I'm sure their waiting will be rewarded."

A hush fell in the room as Jakob finished speaking. Mao's mouth
still hung loosely open as he hunched in his chair and he gave no
sign that he had heard or understood what had been said. Then he
made a guttural sound in his throat, but no intelligible words emerged.
Making a greater effort, he shook his shoulders and a strange roaring
sound came from him. He clutched at the arms of his chair with
both hands and seemed to be trying to rise; the roaring noise continued growing louder, and the two nurses who had been standing at the back of the room hurried forward anxiously to bend over
him.

Gradually he quieted and when the nurses stepped aside, Jakob
saw that Mao was gazing blankly toward the windows again. There
was a moment or two of uneasy silence; then the young cadre on
his left rose from his chair. With a hurried gesture the cadre indicated
to Jakob that the audience was at an end and he was ushered outside.
On the way to the waiting limousine, Jakob turned to look back.
Between them the interpreters and nurses were trying to help Mao
from the room — but he was staggering and clutching at them for
support, and just before he stepped into the limousine, Jakob heard
the unintelligible roaring noise begin again.

9

Kao was sweating and an anxious frown furrowed his brow as he
closed the courtyard gate behind him and hurried into his house.
Inside, his wife, I-ping, was carrying a plate of cold vegetables to
the dining table and he greeted her distractedly before entering a small

washroom, where he splashed water onto his face. The moist, clammy heat of late July had plastered his short-sleeved shirt damply against his back and he changed it before taking his place at the table. When his son, Ming, appeared from another room and ran to greet him, he patted his head affectionately but continued to eat quickly and mechanically without taking any pleasure in the act.

"You look worried, Kao." I-ping sat down opposite him and lifted the boy onto her lap. "What's wrong?"

"Things are going from bad to worse." Kao continued to eat rapidly, speaking between mouthfuls. "Two more banks were robbed in Wuhan today. . . .Textile workers have gone on strike in Kwangtung province. . . . And the street gangs are fighting again in Tientsin."

"Have you got to return to your post straightaway?"

"Yes." Kao nodded. "On top of everything else I've had some very worrying reports from the Seismology Bureau this afternoon."

"The Seismology Bureau?" The tone of I-ping's voice betrayed her concern. "What do the reports say?"

Kao looked up at his wife with a worried expression. "It looks as though there might be a serious earthquake soon."

"Where, Kao?"

"Somewhere here in the northeast perhaps — but you must keep this strictly to yourself. In Shantung many villages have suffered plagues of rats and snakes over the past week. In Liaoning and Hopeh the lakes and rivers are full of dead fish. All these things point to the kind of chemical changes and increased temperatures underground which usually precede earthquakes."

His wife's face tightened with alarm. "Is anything being done to warn people?"

Kao shook his head grimly. "The leadership doesn't want to cause unnecessary panic. Things are bad enough already because of all the uncertainty."

I-ping watched him eat in silence for a while, biting her lip with apprehension. Then she gestured toward a square brown-paper package tied with string on a side table. "That parcel arrived this afternoon. It was brought by a pedicab driver. It's addressed to you but it's marked 'For Ming.' "

Kao nodded absently and continued eating in silence. When he had finished he got up from the table and crossed the room to pick up the parcel. After peering at the label with a puzzled expression, he tore open the outer wrapping and lifted a black and white toy panda and a sealed white envelope from the cardboard box inside. The envelope contained a single sheet of paper covered in handwritten Chinese characters, and it read:

Dear Kao,

Please accept this toy for Ming with my very best wishes. I saw my father for the first time in ten years when he came to Peking recently. He told me he'd visited you and met Ming briefly and I learned from him where you were living. I'm teaching at the Foreign Languages Institute but I haven't tried to get in touch before in case it seemed like an intrusion. Seeing my father again and learning that you were married with a young son made me realize how much time had passed since we last met. Perhaps it will be possible for me to meet little Ming and your wife when time allows. I feel now that I would like that very much. I hope you're all well.

Very sincerely,
Abigail Kellner

Kao crumpled the letter in his hand as soon as he read it and made to throw it into a nearby wastepaper basket.

"Who is the package from?" asked his wife from the table.

Kao checked himself in the act of throwing the letter away and pushed it uneasily into his trouser pocket instead. "It was sent by an Englishwoman who teaches at the Foreign Languages Institute. . . . She and her father were friends of my mother a long time ago. He visited us briefly in April, remember?"

"How kind of her to send Ming a gift."

"The gift is of no consequence," snapped Kao. "We don't need such presents from foreigners — it can be thrown away."

Kao turned to stuff the toy back into its box but Ming had leapt down from his mother's lap and run across the room. Snatching up the panda, he held it out at arm's length, whispering questions and answers back and forth between the bear and himself in an imaginary introductory conversation.

"Surely there's no need to throw the toy away," said I-ping gently. "Ming seems to like it."

Kao watched his son playing with the toy bear for a second or two; then reluctantly he nodded. Picking up his briefcase from the chair where he had dropped it, he glanced at the watch on his wrist.

"I have to get back immediately," he said apologetically. "Don't worry if I'm late returning home."

He ruffled his son's hair fondly with one hand and hurried out into the sweltering dusk. There was no breeze and because the heavy, saturated air was making the interiors of the houses stifling, Kao had to pick his way carefully among the children and families who had come out to squat and wash themselves on the dusty pavements. Several times he passed People's Liberation Army soldiers patrolling the streets in pairs, the bayonets on their rifles glinting ominously in the glow of the streetlights. The presence of the troops lent an extra dimension of tension to the steamy night and whenever they appeared, families moved aside to let them pass.

Halfway along the street Kao turned in through the gates of a small school and strode quickly to a corner of the dusty playground where a flight of railed concrete steps led downward into the earth. Taking a key from his pocket he unlocked a steel door at the bottom and stepped into a cement-lined shaft containing a further flight of steps. After locking the door carefully behind him, he descended twenty-five feet into the vast interconnecting network of underground passages which stretched for hundreds of miles beneath Peking.

Walking comfortably upright in a tunnel eight feet high and five feet wide, Kao passed under the moat and the crenellated walls of the Forbidden City and hurried on beneath the foundations of the ancient imperial palaces toward Chung Nan Hai. The air in the tunnels was much cooler than the humid night outside and his way was lit by naked light bulbs which were suspended from the tunnel roof at ten-yard intervals. As he walked he passed entrances to kitchens, grain stores, armories, ammunition dumps, and chambers housing generators and air purification plants. Occasionally he had to stop to open one of the blast-proof doors which separated the tunnel sections, and every few minutes a soldier loomed out of a shadowy niche to inspect his pass. The whole network had been excavated in the eight years since Chinese and Russian troops had clashed on the Ussuri River at the height of the Cultural Revolution; each section had been laboriously dug out by the people who lived or worked above it. Since the labyrinth had been designed both for fighting a defensive guerrilla war and evacuating the capital's population of four million safely to the countryside, machine-gun embrasures had been built into each junction to provide a line of fire in all directions.

Another thirty feet below Kao's feet, a second tunnel system had been constructed to provide bunkers for troops and militiamen. All the passages were linked to a subterranean road network that led to exit points in the hills far beyond Peking's outskirts. Signs on the walls of the maze of tunnels indicated the street names they shadowed above ground, and every large store and shop had its own entrance to the network for its employees. A separate, secure underground road broad enough for cars and trucks linked the walled Chung Nan Hai compound with the Great Hall of the People, so that Party leaders and their aides never needed to show their faces in the streets when going to and from meetings. With suspicion and mistrust increasingly rife, Kao had fallen into the habit of using that passageway and other parts of the underground complex almost daily.

But as he hurried on through the tunnels he suddenly remembered the growing list of freakish natural phenomena that were being reported to the Seismology Bureau and he looked up apprehensively at the low roof close above his head. At that moment the normally protective atmosphere of the tunnels became ominous and oppressive, and Kao broke into a run toward the checkpoint where a whole company of specially trained 8341 Security Unit soldiers stood guard around elevators that would take him up to Chiang Ch'ing's quarters in the heart of Chung Nan Hai.

10

In the Great Hall of the People, Marshal Lu Chiao glanced around the large polished table at which half a dozen of China's top military leaders were gathered. All wore badgeless People's Liberation Army uniforms of olive green cotton but their gray heads distinguished them clearly as the most senior officers in the land. Only one man among them, a round-jowled man in his mid-fifties, wore a civilian cadre's tunic: obviously ill at ease among the uniformed military officers, he puffed nervously at a cigarette and repeatedly shuffled papers on the table in front of him as he listened to what was being said.

"Criminal bank robberies, industrial strikes, and lawlessness in the streets are phenomena we've rarely experienced in the People's

Republic of China," Chiao was saying. "These are all very clear signs that our country is gripped by a feeling of crisis — and more evidence of unrest in the cities and in the countryside is arriving daily. What's more, in the last twenty-four hours, comrades, there have been indications that we might soon be threatened by a natural disaster of massive proportions." Chiao paused and glanced at a sheet of paper before him. "The Seismology Bureau attached to the Academy of Sciences has begun receiving a spate of reports from all over the northeast which suggest that a major earthquake might be imminent. These reports concern the unnatural behavior of wild and domestic animals, and such traditional methods of predicting earthquakes have proved reliable over hundreds of years. . . . Swarms of bees are stinging cattle to death, pigs are jumping from their sties and running amok, farm fowl are flying off into the forests. . . ." Chiao paused and looked around the table. "Clearly, comrades, action needs to be taken swiftly in many directions. But the bad relations which exist between certain sections of the Party leadership are having a paralyzing effect on the government's will. That's why all of us at this table have felt justified in calling this informal meeting." Chiao paused again and glanced pointedly toward the sole civilian. "Consequently, Comrade Vice Chairman, we're very grateful that you've consented to attend and hear what's in the minds of your leading generals at this time."

Hua Kuo-feng nodded a formal acknowledgment, still without raising his eyes, and Chiao waited deferentially to see if the man who had unexpectedly been appointed vice chairman of the Communist Party and premier of the State Council in April wished to volunteer any remark. When it was obvious that he chose to remain silent, Chiao continued in the same deliberately respectful tone.

"Since one issue is crucial to all other considerations, Comrade Vice Chairman, perhaps you'd care to give us some precise information about the health of Chairman Mao Tse-tung. Then we might be able to define our feelings more clearly."

When Hua Kuo-feng looked up at last, his expression was strained. Before speaking he glanced nervously toward the two armed sentries who stood on guard inside the locked door of the small anteroom, then looked quickly around the table at the array of grim-faced marshals and generals. Their ranks no longer included the venerated Red Army commander Chu Teh, who had died three weeks earlier, and Hua was aware that in past crises Marshal Chu had often maneuvered the military leadership to support Chairman Mao. Chu's absence heightened the atmosphere of uncertainty which now bedeviled all high-level discussion, and consequently, when Hua finally spoke, he directed his words at the empty center of the table, as though anxious to give the impression that he sought no personal involvement with any of those present.

"Chairman Mao is deeply fatigued with old age, comrades," said Hua. "As you all must know, he's been suffering for some years from a wasting disease of the nervous system. This has now worsened considerably and he's partially paralyzed on one side of his body. His speech is impaired and no longer intelligible. For long periods he appears to slip into a coma and he takes only the smallest amounts of nourishment. . . ."

Hua paused and looked up to scan the table once more; his own expression was troubled and he could see the same unspoken question in every face. Staring at Hua from the other end of the table, Chiao found himself wondering if the new vice chairman would have risen so far toward the pinnacle of supreme power if he had not been head of the local Communist Party organization in Mao's home county when the chairman made a nostalgic visit to Hunan in the late 1950s. Hua's promotion to the Central Committee and his later appointment as minister of agriculture had come as a surprise, although he had since proved himself an able administrator. He had an amiable, industrious face but his manner was bureaucratic and uninspiring. Because Hua appeared to lack the fundamental strength of character that Chiao sensed the growing crisis would demand in the coming days and weeks, he felt his own apprehension grow.

"Doctors attending the chairman believe that life cannot be sustained much longer," continued Hua in a low voice. "But they've thought that for some weeks. Although he's scarcely conscious, in keeping with his courageous character Chairman Mao is fighting fiercely to the last."

A deep hush fell over the room as Hua finished speaking. The somber news had reminded the dwindling band of grizzled Long March commanders only too clearly of their own mortality and for some moments they remained silent, lost in their own thoughts.

"We want to emphasize in the strongest possible terms, Comrade Vice Chairman, that no individual at this table has the slightest ambition to succeed to the highest office himself," said Chiao, looking steadily at the man who already effectively held the reins of power in his hands. "But as Chairman Mao has so memorably said, 'Political power grows out of the barrel of a gun.' And we wouldn't hesitate to use the power of the People's Liberation Army if confusion were to cloud the vital question of who is to lead China in Chairman Mao's place."

"But there's no confusion." Hua smiled anxiously and searched his papers until he found a single sheet, which he passed hurriedly across the table to Chiao. "You all heard weeks ago that Chairman Mao had declared to me, 'With you in charge, I am at ease.' In fact, he wrote that sentiment in his own distinctive calligraphy as a mark of confidence and gave it to me."

Chiao scrutinized the single sentence scrawled untidily across the white page with a felt-tipped pen. Mao Tse-tung's calligraphy was nationally recognizable from published facsimiles of his poems and other commemorative writings, and although the scrawl was much more erratic than usual the message, which included Hua's full name, had clearly been written in Mao's hand. After studying it carefully, Chiao handed the sheet of paper to his neighbor and in silence the army leaders passed it from one to another, watched by an eagerly smiling Hua.

"There's no doubt that this constitutes Chairman Mao's seal of approval, Comrade Vice Chairman," said Chiao at last, returning the paper to Hua. "And we are all aware of the sacred significance which the people of China are accustomed to attach to the written and spoken words of a great leader. But once the chairman is dead, it will take more than a piece of paper to protect you against the rabid ambitions of the chairman's wife and her ultraleft supporters."

Hua stared down the length of the table with a frown of puzzlement crinkling his big face. "What do you mean, Comrade Marshal?"

"An attempt has already been made to persuade the commander of the Peking Regional Garrison to arrest you!" The Peking commander was sitting at Chiao's elbow and he nodded silently in affirmation as Chiao spoke. "Fortunately the commander reported the approach to me — and I ordered him to do nothing until we'd had a chance to consult with you."

Hua's eyes widened in alarm and he swallowed hard, saying nothing.

"In April similar plans were laid by the ultraleftists to arrest Comrade Teng Hsiao-ping after he was removed from all his offices. But some of us around this table gave him the necessary military assistance to fly to a safe hiding place in the south."

As the significance of what the People's Liberation Army leaders were saying to Hua began to sink in, the face of the Party vice chairman clouded with anxiety. Avoiding the eyes of the men around him, he busied himself lighting another cigarette and drew several deep drafts of smoke into his lungs in quick succession.

"To avoid civil war and bloodshed, we believe it will amost certainly be necessary to act decisively after the chairman dies." Chiao spoke in a firm, clear voice, leaning forward on the table. "If the ultraleftists continue their efforts to seize the leadership, we are firmly agreed that they should all be arrested without delay. You'll have our full support if you decide to do this — and the loyalty and backing of all the major army commands. . . ."

"The people are no longer prepared to volunteer for unpaid work in the name of the revolution as the ultraleftists wish," said another marshal in a quiet voice. "They want the bonuses that should already have been paid to them in May under Comrade Teng's policies. If they don't get them, the strikes and the unrest will continue."

"I'm not sure how to respond, comrades," said Hua hesitantly, scrutinizing each of the expressionless faces around him in turn.

"All you need do, Comrade Vice Chairman, is tell us if you would refuse to make the arrests in the imaginary circumstances we've outlined," said Chiao, and he paused significantly. "If that were the case, we would have to withdraw our support from you."

For a long moment the vice chairman stared at Chiao; then, with his hands shaking slightly, he gathered his papers together, fitted them carefully into a slim briefcase, and stood up. "I would not want you or your colleagues to withdraw your support from me under any circumstances, Comrade Marshal," he said in a subdued tone. "I hope that is very clear."

Chiao smiled down the table for the first time. "Thank you, Comrade Vice Chairman. It is very clear. And that's all that needs to be said for the present."

The military leaders rose formally as a mark of respect when Hua Kuo-feng hurried toward the door. The sentries, however, did not move aside immediately; instead they looked questioningly at Chiao and only when the marshal nodded slightly in their direction did they unlock the door and allow him to leave.

As he went out, a junior aide hurried to Chiao's side and told him in a low voice that somebody had just arrived, asking to see him at once about an urgent, personal matter.

Chiao excused himself and outside in the corridor he recognized one of the male nurses from the Peking Number 7 Mental Health Center. The man's face was agitated and covered in perspiration, as if he had run a long way through the sweltering night, and he shifted impatiently from one foot to the other as Chiao approached.

"I'm sorry to interrupt you here, Comrade Marshal," gasped the man. "But it's about your sister."

Chiao's face stiffened in concern. "What about her?"

"She's suddenly become very wild in her behavior. We can't restrain her. And she seems to be calling for you."

Chiao gazed at the man in astonishment. "But she's said nothing and barely moved at all in ten years!"

"Yes — but suddenly tonight she's become very restless. She began to moan and run around in her room. She tried to escape through a barred window. She calls your name over and over again. Nothing we can do will stop her. We gave her sedatives but it has made no difference at all." The nurse was holding a grimy cap in his hands and he wrung it constantly as he spoke. "Because she's calling for you all the time, we thought we had better fetch you. She's behaving like a wild animal."

"Please return to her at once," said Chiao quickly. "I'll come as soon as I can."

11

Chiang Ch'ing's dark eyes glittered angrily behind her half-rimmed spectacles as she looked up at Kao from her desk. She had been in the act of replacing the telephone as Kao entered her study in the modern brick-built house where she lived and worked in a secluded corner of the Chung Nan Hai compound, and it was clear even before she spoke that what she had just learned had infuriated her.

"The heroic marshals have held a secret meeting with our incompetent Party vice chairman," she said with great bitterness. "And he's been flourishing the chairman's little piece of calligraphic nonsense at them."

Kao said nothing; he had entered from one of the outer offices, where he had a permanent desk, carrying a new batch of reports from the Seismology Bureau. Although it was after two o'clock in the morning, the volume of information reaching the bureau from half a dozen provinces in the north and northeast hadn't slackened, and Kao's own sense of alarm was increasing. The windows of Chiang Ch'ing's study were open and from the darkness beyond the fine gauze screens the high-pitched, metallic whine of hundreds of cicadas in the surrounding trees added an extra dimension of unease to the sweltering night.

"Do you suppose, Comrade Kao, that Hua the Incompetent is attempting to strike a deal with the army leaders? Is the 'peasants' friend' learning the habits of a street fighter late in his life?"

The once-beautiful former film actress, who for nearly forty years had been the wife of Mao Tse-tung, tapped a pencil impatiently on her desktop as she waited for Kao to answer. Slender and fine-boned, she radiated a nervous, excitable energy, but in her early sixties the lovely face that had first captivated her husband in Yenan had taken on a peevish look. Behind the thick lenses of her spectacles her eyes had grown small and pinched and their expression suggested she was ever ready to take, and give, offense.

"It's more likely the marshals were seeking information, I'd say," replied Kao guardedly. "Could the meeting have been called at the initiative of the officers?"

"That will be for you to find out," snapped Chiang irritably. "And please do it soon." Unlocking one of the desk drawers, she took out a file, peered into it, then looked up calculatingly at Kao. "Whatever took place at the meeting, Comrade Kao, it's clear that the chairman won't live much longer. The struggle for his inheritance has begun in earnest. You've been unswerving in your loyalty to the revolutionary line of Chairman Mao for ten years and it would be interesting for me to hear now from your own lips whether your loyalty to myself and other leading comrades who support me is unchanged."

"My support for Chairman Mao's line has never faltered," replied Kao stiffly. "I've always believed that the class struggle is the key to progress."

"I'm very glad to hear you say that, Kao. Your support will be invaluable when the time comes to neutralize the generals and set Hua the Incompetent aside. We must prepare contingency plans with the factory militia . . ."

Her voice trailed off and her expression became thoughtful, but after a moment of silence Kao gestured uneasily toward the papers he carried. "More reports are arriving from the Seismology Bureau. Shouldn't we warn the chairman that an earthquake might be expected? The shock could worsen his illness."

She shook her head quickly, her mind obviously distracted by other thoughts. "The chairman is barely aware of his surroundings most of the time," she said absently. "Giving such information in itself might have harmful effects . . ."

The telephone on Chiang's desk rang and she picked it up with an exclamation of exasperation. After listening for a moment, she pressed a switch on the telephone console before turning back to Kao.

"An urgent personal call for you has come in from Marshal Lu Chiao. It's being held by the switchboard operator." Her face darkened with distaste. "Your uncle was one of the prime movers of the generals' meeting, according to my information. What are your relations with him?"

"I've not exchanged one word with him since his rehabilitation," said Kao. "And I have no wish to do so."

"Marshal Lu is calling from the institution caring for your mother." She smiled ambiguously. "He says you should go there at once if possible. Your presence is urgently required."

Kao looked at his watch and saw it was almost three A.M. "I still have a lot of important work to do here. And I don't wish you to think I want to have dealings with a man with my uncle's record of betrayal."

"Don't be so hasty. Take the call and go to meet him. You might be able to discover what happened at the meeting." Chiang's eyes narrowed behind her spectacles. "You also have my authority to sound him out about the future when the right opportunity arises. You can mention that the post of minister of defense could be filled by a marshal who shows exceptional loyalty to Chairman Mao's line in a crisis."

Kao's eyes widened in surprise; then he nodded obediently.

"Go and take the call in your office. Agree to meet him as soon as possible at the asylum — don't waste any time."

12

Kao ran almost all the way from Chung Nan Hai to the asylum through the subterranean tunnels. He decided to take the risk because the temperature below ground was much lower. But when he climbed to the surface again through a trapdoor in the corner of a covered market, the dank, stagnant air seemed almost suffocating and his shirt was soon sticking to his back. Families living in the narrow *hut'ungs* through which he passed had dragged their beds out into the open, but since they still could not sleep in the clammy heat, many were squatting on the dusty ground in groups and they stared curiously at Kao as he hurried on his way. In his mouth and nostrils the saturated air seemed to have taken on a metallic taste and he wondered whether the air purifiers in the tunnels had broken down.

It was just after three-thirty A.M. when he entered the asylum. Half the lights in the dingy corridors had been switched off and he did not see Chiao until the aging marshal stepped suddenly from the shadows in the corridor leading to his mother's room. Through the open door a few yards away, an animalistic moaning noise was intermittently audible. A male nurse stood at Chiao's shoulder, watching and waiting to answer their questions or carry out orders.

"Your mother's been calling your name like this since midnight," said Chiao. "I've already spent half an hour with her — but I've been able to do nothing. If you listen carefully you'll hear she's not calling 'Chiao.' She's calling 'Kao.' "

Kao gradually began to distinguish the sound of his name being repeated incessantly on the same haunting, monotonous note. The inflection was agonized and despairing and a shudder ran through Kao despite the heat. The male nurse behind his uncle was standing close enough to hear their conversation, and on realizing this, Kao made a sign for him to retreat beyond earshot.

"I'll go in," said Kao uneasily. "But I'm not sure I'll be able to do anything."

In the half-light Chiao's expression hardened. "You might at least put some effort into the matter, Comrade Nephew. You haven't exactly sacrificed yourself in your mother's interest in the past."

Kao returned Chiao's gaze defiantly. "There's little point, Uncle, in raking over the past again and again — there are too many pressing matters to deal with. I'd like to talk to you soon about some questions of mutual interest."

Chiao did not reply immediately but looked searchingly at his nephew. In the silence, the eerie moaning from Mei-ling's room suddenly grew louder. "I didn't hear much talk of 'questions of mutual interest' the last time we met, on that platform in the Workers' Stadium. So I doubt whether what you have to say now would be of much interest to me."

"You would be most unwise to ignore this approach, Uncle," persisted Kao. "It could result in a considerable advantage to you."

"You've been living on borrowed time for many years," said Chiao in a level voice. "I think perhaps that time's nearly run out now. You were summoned here on a personal errand, to help your mother. She needs you — so go to her while you can."

Chiao turned and strode away along the shadowy corridor without another word. Kao watched him go, his own face taut with tension, then, gesturing to the nurse to follow him, he stepped into the room. Inside he found his mother struggling on her bed in the grip of a female nurse. Her face was turned from him but she continued to moan his name, and Kao stood watching for two or three minutes, a helpless feeling growing inside him.

"Tell her you're here, Comrade Kao," prompted the nurse, at his side. "She's perhaps not yet aware of your presence."

Kao moved slowly to the middle of the room and stopped. "It's Kao, Mother," he called in an uneasy voice. "What is it? What's wrong?"

At first his intervention had no effect at all. Then, without any warning, Mei-ling ceased to struggle and lay still. The nurse holding her sat back, wiping her sweating brow, and slowly Mei-ling shifted into a sitting position. When she turned toward the middle of the room her gaze was still vacant and unfocused, as if she continued to live in a world of fog, but she seemed somehow to register a new presence and she allowed the nurse to straighten her disheveled tunic and smooth her hair.

"I came because they told me you were upset," said Kao haltingly. "Please be calm now."

Mei-ling stared blankly at him without seeming to see him; meek and docile suddenly, she sat upright on the edge of the bed. Her lips moved once but no sound emerged, and Kao took a step nearer in an effort to hear what she might be saying. As he did so the floor

of the room bucked wildly beneath his feet. It seemed to rise like
an unsteady boat under which a massive wave was passing; at
the same time a terrible rumbling filled Kao's ears. The shock of the
earth tremor brought him gasping to his knees, and beyond the
uncurtained window a flash of elemental light illuminated Peking
for an instant as brightly as day.

The male nurse who had remained at Kao's side staggered sideways, clutching wildly at the wall for support, and Kao saw the
woman who had been restraining Mei-ling tumble helplessly to the
floor. The room continued to shudder as if it were a ship being
buffeted by wave after wave, and the rumbling grew louder. The
chairs and table toppled over, the vacuum flask exploded, and the
bed slid into the middle of the room with Mei-ling sitting on it,
staring open-mouthed at Kao.

Kao's own face registered the greatest extremes of human fear,
and when Mei-ling struggled off the bed and flung herself toward
him, he clutched at her like a drowning man. As they clung together,
a wide crack slowly sundered the dingy green wall before them,
creeping diagonally upward from the floor, accompanied by an awesome groaning sound. Plaster and dust burst from the fissure in great
clouds and Kao stared at the widening gap in horror, waiting for the
walls and ceiling to collapse and bury them.

13

All over Peking, modern high-rise apartment blocks were swaying
like bamboo thickets in a strong wind. The walls of ancient gates
shivered and crumbled; the lakes of Chung Nan Hai, which had
previously lain black and viscous in the oppressive heat, boiled up
with sudden turbulence; and inside the Forbidden City golden tiles
cascaded from the curved roofs of the Ming pavilions to smash deafeningly in the courtyards below. Outside its high, crenellated walls
the old dwellings of imperial courtiers were collapsing like houses
of cards and in the industrial suburbs people rushed into the streets
to stare up in terror at the black sky.

A hundred miles southeast of the capital, nightmarish chasms were
opening to swallow people, buildings, and a whole moving train.

The heavily populated coal towns of the region were being devastated, entire streets were subsiding into rubble, hospitals and public buildings were slipping into gaping canyons, and in the mines nightshift workers were dying instantly in their thousands as miles of seams collapsed and entombed them. Gushing fountains of foul liquids and sand were spouting from the ground to inundate great tracts of farmland, and all across a wide region of northeast China hundreds of thousands of people were dying and suffering injury as the earth's surface underwent a massive convulsion.

In Peking it seemed as if the tremor would never end, and on the seventh floor of the apartment building in the eastern suburbs where she lived, Abigail was awakened by the first incandescent blaze of light that flared over the city. The whole of her bedroom was rocking violently and a roaring noise filled her ears. Scrambling from the bed, she snatched up a bathrobe to cover her nightdress and swayed dizzily across the room to the window. Another blinding flash of light lit the city like a photographer's sodium flare and a frozen image of the roofs and streets of the darkened capital imprinted itself like a film negative in her mind. A power station has exploded, she told herself dazedly, and began to imagine she might be about to die.

She rushed unthinkingly into the adjoining room and stepped out onto the small balcony which overlooked the apartment gardens. There she found that the whole building was swaying crazily. Suddenly all the streetlights below went out, the rumbling of the shifting earth grew louder, and in the pitch-blackness Abigail stood holding on to the ledge of the balcony with both hands, paralyzed with fright.

After what seemed an age, the tremor ceased and calm returned. For a few seconds in the darkness there was a deathly stillness and Abigail felt suffocated and dazed as though time and her heart had stopped. A faint cry of pain from somewhere inside the building broke the unearthly stillness, releasing Abigail from her paralysis, and she stumbled back into the apartment. The air in all the rooms was filled with acrid dust, but she managed to grope blindly into the kitchen and locate a flashlight in a drawer. Although the dust was making her cough and choke, she found her way shakily back to her bedroom and struggled into a pair of trousers and some tennis shoes; while she was dressing, she saw that part of the bedroom ceiling had collapsed onto the bed where she had been sleeping.

From the hall outside she suddenly heard sounds of shouting and running feet; snatching a sweater from a drawer, she tied it around her shoulders and hurried to the door of the apartment to find that it had split and fallen open. The building was one of a cluster in the eastern suburbs reserved for foreign residents, and Abigail saw several of her fellow tenants running helter-skelter down the stairs outside, many of them barefoot and still in their nightclothes. When she directed the beam of her flashlight above their heads she discovered that wide cracks were appearing in the walls and ceilings of the stairwell; the structure of the whole building was creaking and groaning alarmingly and Abigail was about to dash down the stairs herself when she heard a faint thudding sound.

The neighboring apartment was occupied by a young, newly arrived Polish teacher and Abigail noticed then that although it was cracked, the door remained closed. On finding it locked, she drew back and kicked the damaged door hard with the sole of her foot. It collapsed inward immediately and inside the hall of the apartment she found that the thudding noise was coming from the other side of an internal door that had jammed in its frame. The sound of hysterical weeping became audible above the banging and Abigail called out loudly for her neighbor to stand clear. Then she repeatedly kicked at the flimsy door until it flew back on its hinges. When the dust-covered girl emerged, sobbing, from the darkness, Abigail led her quickly down the stairs into the forecourt, where dozens of other frightened tenants had gathered.

Dressed still in their nightclothes or hastily seized garments, all the tenants were pale-faced with shock, and only after Abigail's flashlight revealed that wide cracks were visible in the facade of the building did they move to safety in the middle of the gardens surrounding the block. There Abigail helped organize a head count, and when officials from the Public Security Bureau arrived, she was able to tell them that nobody was left in the damaged building.

Many of the tenants were clutching fearful children and when it suddenly began to rain torrentially, Abigail took the sweater from her shoulders and placed it around a little French girl who was shivering and sobbing in her mother's arms. The girl was no more than four or five years old and the gift of the sweater soon quieted her. But as Abigail looked at the child, a thought struck her. Without offering any explanation, she turned and ran to the cycle racks at the rear of the apartment block; taking the first machine she came to, she leapt into the saddle and began pedaling furiously through the downpour toward the center of the capital.

14

On seeing the first blinding flash of light outside the asylum window, Kao imagined that a long-feared Soviet nuclear attack had at last been launched against Peking. Then, as the rumbling and shaking gradually subsided and the terrible crack in the wall before their eyes ceased to climb toward the ceiling, his primal fear lessened and inside his head his rational mind began silently repeating the words *te chen* — "earthquake" — over and over again. In the same moment he heard Mei-ling speaking once more close to his ear — but she was no longer shouting his name.

They still stood together with their arms linked in the middle of the room, but her utterances were now being made in an urgent and imploring tone and she was plucking agitatedly at his sleeve. She seemed to be striving to pronounce the same word again and again, pausing for several seconds each time, but her voice was indistinct and Kao could not put any meaning to the sounds. Looking down at his mother, he saw that her eyes were still bafflingly glazed and it was impossible to judge whether the earthquake had registered on her senses.

The two nurses, white-faced with shock, stared uncertainly at Kao. If he had not been there, he was sure, they would have raced from the room in panic. But within seconds they regained their composure and, with sideways glances at him, they quickly moved the bed back to its normal position by the wall and righted the table and chairs. Although some confused shouting could be heard along the corridors, they ignored it and approached Kao politely to take charge of Mei-ling again. To his surprise she offered no resistance and allowed the nurses to lead her back to her chair. Kao realized with a feeling of embarrassment that she had not shown any signs of fear throughout the tremor; when she flung herself toward him, her arms had encircled him in a protective fashion and he had clung to her instinctively. Yet as soon as she was seated, she resumed her monotonous repetition of the single word and Kao turned to the nurses in desperation.

"What do you think she's saying?" he demanded.

At first both nurses shook their heads; after listening again the woman looked up at Kao. "Could she be saying *mao tzu* — 'hat'?" she asked diffidently. "Would that make any sense?"

Kao made a negative gesture. "It makes no sense at all."

Mei-ling had fallen silent again and he looked at her in bafflement. Then, as he watched, her lips moved once more, very slowly, as though she were making a supreme effort, and she framed a single word with near-perfect clarity.

"Ming!"

Deep sorrow and yearning seemed to combine in the strangled utterance and Kao stared at her, transfixed, scarcely able to believe his ears. His few visits to the asylum over the years had been brief and uncomfortable. Whenever he sat beside the frozen, silent figure of his mother, he had experienced deep feelings of unease, which had made him ever more reluctant to return. She had never spoken to him or looked at him with any comprehension in her eyes, and he had never been able to offer anything more than the truncated details of his austere personal life. He had spoken haltingly of his marriage and later the birth of Ming; he must also have passed isolated remarks, he realized then, about the boy's growth and progress but he had never imagined that any of his words had ever registered. To hear Ming's name on her lips now astonished him, and in the same moment the mental numbness induced by the earthquake left him.

"My wife and son are alone," he gasped, staring first at his mother, then at the nurses. "I must go."

He rushed to the door, but on the threshold he stopped and looked back. Mei-ling had slumped into an exhausted attitude in the chair and her head had fallen slackly forward.

"Don't leave her," he commanded. "One of you must stay and look after her until you're sure she's all right."

Without waiting for any acknowledgement from them, Kao ran from the room.

15

The dark, rain-drenched streets were filled with fearful crowds, and because there were no lights Abigail several times took wrong turnings in her haste. Only a few isolated hand torches and makeshift lanterns relieved the pitch-blackness, and she frequently heard cadres shouting warnings in the darkness for families to stay away from their damaged homes in case new tremors followed. Blankets and waterproof sheets were being rigged among the roadside trees to provide temporary shelter from the weather, and the shocked, frightened faces of adults and children peered out from beneath them as Abigail pedaled by. When she neared the center of the city the wheels of her bicycle began to bump over bricks and rubble that had spilled into the roads from collapsed walls and roofs, and she had to make several detours on finding that some streets had been closed. Eventually the congestion forced her to abandon the bicycle and she continued on foot, running and stumbling over heaps of rubble that blocked the pavements.

The downpour had not brought any drop in temperature, and Abigail's hair and clothes were drenched with rain and perspiration by the time she reached the old Imperial City. More than once she lost her bearings, but around the Drum Tower she found that some lights had been restored and she pushed on with new determination through the dense throng of people that had gathered there. The red walls of the ancient roofed gate had partly collapsed, its eaves were twisted and broken, and the silent crowds were staring up at the damage in disbelief. In imperial days the Drum Tower had been a popular meeting place where drums had been beaten regularly to mark the hours of the day, and Abigail could see that the disfigurement of this symbolic landmark had stunned the local people. The traditional belief that comets, earthquakes, and other natural phenomena had always foreshadowed disaster when great dynasties of the past had fallen was ingrained in the Chinese psyche, and Abigail sensed the presence of superstitious fear in the unnatural silence which had settled over the crowds around the ancient tower.

This in turn increased Abigail's own growing feelings of apprehension as she hurried on through the confusion; she frequently heard unseen women and children wailing and sobbing, and silent men on grim rescue errands pushed distractedly past her in the darkness. Her fears seemed to be confirmed when at last she turned into Nan Chihtze to find that many of the houses along that narrow street had collapsed. Gangs of desperate people were digging and clawing at the rubble by lamplight in several courtyards, and Abigail broke into a run again when she saw in the half-darkness that the outer wall of the house for which she was heading was cracked and leaning outward at a dangerous angle.

Although she had never visited Kao's home, after sending the gift
for his son she had walked down Nan Chihtze several times out of
curiosity to identify his house, and on stepping through its sagging
gateway, she found that one wall of the house had given way and
the roof had fallen in. In a corner of the courtyard a bent old woman
clutching a failing flashlight was crouched on a stool sobbing; she
made no response when Abigail asked if there was anyone in the
ruined building but continued to sob hysterically, and Abigail left
her to hurry around to the rear of the house.

She found a broken window in an undamaged section of wall that
led into the kitchen and climbed inside without difficulty. Because
the fallen roof beams had brought down internal walls and heaps of
laths and tiles, she had to crawl on her belly through a tunnel of
wet rubble no more than three feet high. She made slow, painful
progress, trying to identify rooms and passageways, and several times
she came up against impenetrable barriers of debris and had to turn
back. But in what remained of a narrow corridor her hand touched
something soft, and when she brought her flashlight to bear, its beam
illuminated a trouser-clad leg and foot. Moving closer, Abigail saw
that it belonged to a young Chinese woman who lay trapped under
a heavy rafter. Dust and congealing blood covered the woman's face,
and on noticing that she was no longer breathing, Abigail closed her
eyes and lay still for a minute. Then she crawled past her, moving
slowly and carefully so as not to bring any more of the dangerously
loose debris down on herself.

In the broken doorway of what she guessed was once a small
bedroom she heard a faint sound, and holding her breath, she pushed
some fallen bricks from her path. Moving cautiously, Abigail slithered into the wrecked room and found herself looking into the open
eyes of a small Chinese boy. He was lying on his side beneath a
tangle of splintered wood with one fist pushed into his mouth. But
he blinked quickly in the glow of her flashlight, and when Abigail
moved to his side and put an arm around him, he whimpered softly.

As she crawled back to the kitchen window with the boy in her
arms, the wreckage through which she dragged herself shifted and
settled about her, grazing her face and hands. But it did not collapse
further and after climbing out through the window, she closed her
eyes and leaned against the wall in the pouring rain, offering up a
silent prayer of thanks for her survival. The boy had begun crying

in her arms and she spoke soothingly to him in Chinese as she carried him back to the courtyard.

On her stool the bent old woman stopped weeping and stared up at Abigail in amazement. "Is Ming all right?" she asked hoarsely.

"I think so." Abigail wiped some of the dust and grime from his face with her hand. "He's probably just very badly frightened."

At that moment the figure of a man appeared in the gateway and although he was wet and disheveled, Abigail immediately recognized Kao. He ran across the courtyard and plucked the sobbing boy from her arms, staring at her in astonishment.

"I don't think he's really hurt, Kao," said Abigail gently. "But there's a woman still trapped in the house — I fear she may be dead."

16

At midmorning in Hong Kong the next day, Jakob sat at his desk, leafing agitatedly through transcripts of radio reports and agency stories about the earthquake. Although none of them contained much of substance beyond the time and duration of the tremor, he continued by force of habit to read many of the reports over and over again as though hoping that the bald, factual reports might yield new shades of meaning after prolonged study, as political editorials in China's newspapers often did.

He returned repeatedly to the official New China News Agency report, which was worryingly brief. "A strong earthquake occurred in the Tangshan-Fengnan area in east Hopeh province, north China, at 03:42 hours on July 28," said the report, adding evasively that "comparatively strong shocks were felt in Peking and Tientsin" and "damage of varying degrees was reported in the epicentral region." A more straightforward report, from the Reuters news agency in China, said that "a powerful earth tremor shook Peking early today, sending thousands of people rushing onto the streets, smashing windows, and cracking walls." The tremor, the agency said, had begun at 03:45 local time and lasted about two minutes.

From California and Colorado, American wire services were quoting scientists and geologists in the United States as saying that the earthquake, which appeared to have struck a heavily populated area near Peking, "may have been a major catastrophe." Tens of thousands of people could have died in collapsing buildings, said the scientists, and instruments in California that recorded the shock showed that it was more severe than the earthquake which destroyed San Francisco in 1906.

As Jakob was rereading the American reports, a young Chinese translator tapped on his door and entered, carrying another sheet of news-agency copy. "This one is reporting a second aftershock, Mr. Kellner," he said. "It was almost as powerful as the first and it hit the same region a few hours later. The report says there must have been 'heavy damage' throughout the whole area. The first tremor was the most powerful anywhere in the world for twelve years — and the most severe to hit China since the Middle Ages."

Jakob thanked the translator and frowned anxiously as he scanned the news story. He had telephoned the British embassy in Toyko several times in the course of the morning to speak to diplomat friends who were in touch directly with Peking. Although he had not been able to obtain any news of Abigail, a first secretary had assured him that there was no cause for him to be personally alarmed since no British residents had been reported injured or missing. The diplomat had explained that many dwellings had been cracked and damaged, but none of the homes of foreign residents had been severely affected. Gathering more detailed information about the effects of the earthquake had been difficult so far for people in Peking, he had said, because so many roads were blocked and permission to travel was being denied due to fears of new shocks.

On the desk before Jakob, a half-finished summary of events on the mainland which he had been preparing for the institute's weekly bulletin was still in his typewriter. He had started it the day before and beneath the flood of news stories about the earthquake lay other press clippings which he had been scrutinizing for his article — they gave details of rumors about Mao Tse-tung's failing health, the violence and unrest which were spreading across the country, and the political infighting that was developing around Mao's deathbed. The earthquake and the anxiety it had produced in him had suddenly overshadowed everything, and pulling the now-outdated summary from the typewriter, Jakob crumpled it and tossed it into the wastepaper basket. For a while he sat looking indecisively at the papers on his desk; among the pre-earthquake clippings was one report that said "Since the death of Chou En-lai in January, events in Peking have unfolded like a plot from a Ming dynasty court intrigue," and another quoted American intelligence sources as saying Mao was fading fast and discussed the possibility of civil war breaking out again once he died. As he ran his eye over the stories, Jakob felt his agitation grow, and when, on hearing a knock at his office door, he looked up to find the same young Chinese translator bringing him a sealed telegram, he feared suddenly that it must contain bad news.

Because of his anxiety he waited until the translator had left his office before tearing open the envelope; then a long sigh of relief escaped him. The brief message said:

> No need to worry. Am safe. Sadly Kao's wife was killed. But Kao and Ming unhurt. Could you try to come to Peking? Abigail.

As soon as he had read the telegram, Jakob snatched up the telephone and dialed the Hong Kong number of the Chinese Communist who had arranged his unexpected trip to Peking in April. When the man came on the line, Jakob asked if he could help him return to Peking again without delay.

"This is a very difficult time, as you must know, because of the earthquake," said the Chinese. "I'm not sure it will be possible."

"I'd be grateful if you would try," said Jakob in an urgent tone. "Perhaps through the same channels as before."

"I will certainly try through those same channels. But I suggest you also make a formal application for a visa."

"But that could take weeks," protested Jakob. "Or even months."

"Perhaps," said the Chinese politely. "But as I've already said, this is a very difficult time."

17

"Why did you come here on the night of the earthquake?" asked Kao in a strained voice. "Surely there must have been many other things for you to think about."

Abigail considered her reply carefully. "It was just an instinctive reaction, I think. My only flesh-and-blood ties in Peking were here."

Kao looked away, his expression uncomfortable.

"I'm very glad I came, Kao. And I'm glad I was able to help."
She bit her lip, groping for the right words. "For ten years I'd closed
my mind to what happened in Shanghai. I'd resolved never to give
it another thought. It wasn't always that easy, of course. But after
I saw my father again in April, I found I felt differently about it all.
I realized how much time had passed and I wanted to do something
to help put things right. That's why I sent the toy to Ming."

"It was very kind of you." Kao shifted uneasily on his chair. "And
I thank you for helping Ming. But you must never contact me or
come here again. . . ."

They were sitting in what had once been the kitchen, now the
only habitable section of the stricken courtyard house. Tarpaulins
had been nailed temporarily over the new roof rafters above the
room, but the remaining walls of the house were still under construction because a shortage of bricks had halted rebuilding work all
over the damaged capital. On the night of the earthquake Abigail
had retreated quickly from the crumbling courtyard when neighbors
gathered to comfort Kao and Ming; she had waited two weeks before
delivering a sealed note to the house, asking if she might pay an
arranged visit, and had suggested an early evening hour in the middle
of the following week. She had dressed herself soberly in trousers
and a cool shirt and on her arrival Kao had been waiting alone in
the dilapidated kitchen, his face pale and unsmiling. He had explained haltingly that his son was being cared for in an adjoining
house by the old amah Abigail had already met on the night of the
tremor and that his wife's funeral had been held ten days earlier.
He had poured tea for them both, but his strained, formal manner
suggested from the outset that he wished the meeting to end as soon
as possible.

"You and Ming have had a terrible shock," said Abigail softly.
"And I know that you probably still feel bitter about what happened
in Shanghai. But isn't it time for us to try to come to terms with
the past?" She paused, fighting a tearful feeling. "We share the same
father. . . . We're brother and sister, Kao. . . . Even if it's impossible to acknowledge it publicly, might it not help us all if we tried
to see things now in their true light?"

"I've always seen things in their true light," said Kao with a sudden
vehemence. "That's the trouble. Even now when I think of that
night we spent together I burn with shame at my own weakness and
foolishness."

"But there's no need to feel like that." Abigail smiled sadly at him. "No man should try to deny his emotions. My feelings for you were very strong. There was something wonderful between us. It was an awful blow to learn the truth as we did — in a way it made many inexplicable things clear. But we weren't to blame."

Kao picked up his porcelain beaker of tea, gripping it so tightly that his knuckles showed white around its rim. "I felt more angry and helpless that night at my mother's house than I've ever felt in my life! My heart turned to ice inside me. I felt betrayed and alone in the world as if I'd never had any parents. . . . Since then I've wished a million times that I'd never gone there . . . since then I've never once allowed false sentimentality to keep me from carrying out my duties!"

He gulped down several mouthfuls of hot tea and Abigail stared at him in dismay. "Kao, why are you so bitter? So much hatred is destructive. I grew up believing my father cared nothing for me and I became so obsessed with the idea that it almost destroyed me. But I came to see it was just an obsession. I found that if you spend all your time regretting the past, you forfeit the inner peace your soul needs to survive. You throw away the future."

Kao's expression became indignant. "I grew up believing in the revolution. I trusted the word of my mother. She told me my father was a hero of the Japanese war — but he turned out to be nothing more than a foreign Christian missionary!"

"Your mother showed great courage on the Long March and at every other stage of the revolution — and your father *is* a hero," said Abigail emphatically. "In April in Tien An Men Square he risked his life to save yours . . ."

Kao stared at Abigail in astonishment. "The foreigner with the camera . . . ?"

She nodded. "Yes, he took the pictures openly to draw the mob away from you. He knew the risk he was running."

Kao put down his cup, and resting his elbows on the table, he covered his face with both hands. For a long time they sat without speaking and Abigail refilled their teacups.

"When Father first saw you at Pei-Ta he must have seen himself again in his youth," she said in a pensive voice. "He saw a determined young man, passionately devoted to his cause. The cause was very different from what his own had been. It must have been a double agony for him to discover his son in those circumstances. But he still risked making the greatest sacrifice of all for you. Isn't that worth acknowledging?"

"Irrevocable choices were made long ago," said Kao, speaking dully through his fingers. "My mother made the first choice for me and Chairman Mao made another when he took the decision to carry the revolution through to the end. I made my own choice when I decided to devote myself to the class struggle and oppose those taking the capitalist road. Against all that, what are these vague notions of 'family' worth? Acknowledging them would certainly destroy me — then what would I have left?"

"In the end, Kao," said Abigail slowly, "the love of their family is the greatest gift that anyone is given in this world."

"Then I'll manage without that particular gift." Kao spoke with a mixture of weariness and resignation and uncovered his face to look at her. "Please go now, Abigail. There's nothing more to be said."

18

"For you, Comrade Kao," said Chiang Ch'ing, speaking with exaggerated emphasis from the doorway of his office, "there will be a second funeral to attend very soon."

Kao looked up sharply from his desk. The inuendo in the voice of the wife of China's dying leader was unmistakable and he felt himself grow tense. "Do you mean that the chairman —"

"No, not yet. But the end is very near." She advanced into his office, walking with short, mincing strides, and stopped by his desk. "Parkinson's disease causes a progressive rigidity in the muscles. Now there's only one stage of rigidity left to go."

She was wearing an ordinary suit of military green cotton, with her hair tucked inside a soft cap, but the tunic and trousers had been neatly tailored to her still-slender figure. From behind her spectacles she was observing him with the sharp, self-conscious eyes of a lifelong actress who had never entirely lost the habit of watching for a reaction to herself.

"Has the death of your wife affected you very deeply?" she asked in a speculative tone, still watching his face closely. "It can't have been easy with a small son to care for."

Kao rubbed a hand wearily across his face. In the six weeks since the earthquake he had worked at his desk for fifteen to eighteen hours each day, returning only occasionally at night to the half-ruined house in Nan Chihtze. Because the widespread destruction and loss of life had created administrative chaos in many areas, his Party work was unending and he had more often than not snatched a few hours' sleep in a nearby dormitory inside Chung Nan Hai. The sharpening tensions among the Party leaders had also produced endless secret meetings which often went on late into the night; signs of strain and weariness were evident in many faces.

"There hasn't been much time to think of my son," said Kao quickly. "An old lady from the neighboring courtyard is acting as his amah." He hesitated, aware that he was being subjected to close scrutiny. "My first duty is to serve the Party to the best of my ability. That way I serve my son too."

"Well spoken, Comrade Kao." Chiang Ch'ing looked at him appraisingly through narrowed eyes. "I need someone to undertake a special task — in confidence. Your words have convinced me I can entrust you with this duty. Please come with me to my private office."

Kao followed her and she locked the door of her office before opening a steel wall safe. From it she withdrew a file of documents and a box of tapes. She motioned for him to be seated, and he was able to see from the tape labels that they were sound recordings of the Party chairman's conversations with visiting heads of state and other foreign guests. Opening the file of documents, she withdrew two letters addressed to herself which, he noticed, were handwritten in the recognizable calligraphy of Chairman Mao. She held the first one toward him so that he could see it was dated earlier in the year.

"This is Chairman Mao's last letter to me," she said. "It was written while he was still in full possession of his faculties. Since you have sworn your loyalty to Chairman Mao's revolutionary line, and proved yourself by your deeds over many years, I shall read it to you." She paused and looked hard at Kao. "You've already worked loyally for several years as a junior member of the Party Secretariat, Comrade Kao. If you continue to serve me well, I see no reason why an outstanding young man of your ability should not one day become a contender for the post of general secretary of the Communist Party of China — and establish a reputation as a revolutionary leader throughout the world."

Kao considered the significance of the veiled promise in silence as he waited to hear details of the special task and was surprised to find that his reaction to the prospect of attaining high office in the Party was muted. Although he was aware that the grief caused by his wife's death, the exhaustion of overwork, and the emotional strain of his meeting with Abigail had dulled his senses, he had not realized how deeply he had been affected. He had harbored the ambition to succeed to the commanding heights of the Party since his student days, but he had to remind himself forcibly that coming in sight of his goal at last was the best possible vindication of the uncompromising course he had pursued . . .

"I'm going to read parts of the letters to you because it's important to understand one thing very clearly," said Chiang warningly. "The rewards can be high — but the risks too are great."

"I'm not afraid of risks," said Kao, forcing a note of determination into his voice.

"Good, then listen carefully. Chairman Mao said in his final letter: 'Human life is limited but revolution knows no bounds. In the struggle of the past ten years I have tried to reach the peak of revolution. But I was not successful. You, however, will have the opportunity to reach the top!' " She stopped reading and looked up at Kao, her eyes glittering. "This, Kao, is the chairman's last political will and testament, do you understand? It's a clear expression of his wish that I should lead the Party in his place." Without waiting for Kao to comment, she lifted the letter again to read from it. "But he also adds this warning: 'You could reach the top — but if you fail, you could plunge into a fathomless abyss! Your body will shatter! Your bones will break!' "

Moved by the graphic power of Mao's words, Kao remained silent; the warning seemed ominously overstated and a faint shudder of unease passed through him as he watched Chiang pick up the second sheet of paper.

"The other letter was written some years ago, and in it Chairman Mao gave explicit instructions on how we should deal with just such a crisis as the present one. He said: 'If an anti-Communist rightist coup is launched in China, I'm certain it will be short-lived because the revolutionaries represent ninety-five percent of the people. The rightists may prevail for some time *by using my words. . . .*' " She laid heavy stress on the selected phrase and looked hard at Kao to emphasize what was coming next. " *'But the leftists may also organize some of my other words to overthrow the rightists!'* " She made a sudden, contemptuous noise with her lips. "Hasn't Hua the Incompetent already fulfilled that prophecy by constantly trumpeting the written message he must have tricked the chairman into making? 'With you in charge, I am at ease,' " she chanted, mimicking a foolish voice.

"How do you suggest we counteract that?" asked Kao quietly.

Chiang responded by pushing the box of tapes across the desk. "These are recordings of the chairman discussing his political thought and philosophy with important foreign statesmen during the spring of this year. Listen to them carefully and select statements by the chairman about political matters that are helpful to our cause. Re-record them so that it is impossible to recognize the circumstances in which they were made. Then we can represent them as clear instructions by the chairman regarding the Party leadership after his death."

"But that would be misusing the context of the chairman's remarks," said Kao uneasily. "Is there no other way?"

"We would simply be following the chairman's instructions in this letter," said Chiang severely and picked up the second sheet she had read from, flourishing it in the air. "To 'organize some of my other words to overthrow the rightists.' " A calculating look came into her eyes. "This is not a task that a serious contender for the post of general secretary should refuse, is it?" she asked quietly.

Kao did not reply but looked back at her uncertainly.

"I hardly need remind you of the power which the chairman's written and spoken words can carry. The people of China have been accustomed throughout their history to revere the edicts issued by Peking. Do this work well and you will neutralize the marshals and generals politically. We will counteract them militarily by moving loyal divisions to Peking from the northeast under the command of the chairman's nephew. They're already beginning to move toward the capital, ostensibly 'to help in earthquake relief.' But we shall also need convincing political evidence to legitimize our actions." She paused and fixed him with an unwavering stare. "I take it, Comrade Kao, that you won't jeopardize your personal future by declining to carry out such a vital task?"

Kao hesitated for a second or two, avoiding her eyes; then he leaned forward to pick up the tapes. "It will be an honor to perform such an important duty," he said quietly.

"Stay in here, Comrade Kao, and work at this desk." Her smile betrayed the satisfaction she felt. "It would be unwise for secret tapes to be used in an insecure area."

She redeposited the file of letters in the safe, then hurried to the door. When she opened it, Kao saw that groups of silent, unsmiling men and women were filing into the conference room on the other side of the passageway. Every face was tense and among them Kao recognized all the important Politburo members who had grouped themselves around the chairman and his wife during the Cultural Revolution. As the door closed behind Chiang, he heard a key turn, locking him in.

He listened for a moment to the muffled murmur of voices before turning his attention to the tapes. Written transcripts had already been made and he leafed quickly through the discussions with the prime ministers of New Zealand and Singapore, marking with a pen some of the remarks made by the chairman. Then his eye fell on the transcript labeled "Chairman Mao Tse-tung receives a distinguished former China missionary, Mr. Jakob Kellner." He picked it up with a frown and, sitting very still in his seat, read right through the verbatim account of the meeting before fixing the corresponding spool of tape on the player. He spun it quickly to different sections in turn, listening carefully to the slurred voice of the chairman making fierce assertions about the importance of class struggle. When the Hunanese accent gave way to the clearer voice of his father speaking Chinese, Kao moved to switch off the machine; but at the last moment he changed his mind and, turning down the volume instead so that it wouldn't be audible outside the room, he leaned forward and bent his head close to the machine.

"At dawn today I went to Ching Shan Hill and sat in the pavilion at the top," Jakob began, and something in his manner of speech compelled Kao to continue listening as he quietly described the feeling "beyond words" he had experienced in the Pavilion of Eternal Spring. With a look of intense concentration on his face Kao followed every syllable. Jakob's recorded voice was saying, "The last great journey will be a long march inward, into man's own soul," when the door suddenly flew open and Kao looked up to see Chiang Ch'ing standing in the doorway.

There was a strange light in her eyes and in that instant, every insignificant detail in the room seemed to photograph itself on his memory: the gleaming black lacquer of the desktop, the neutral colors of the walls, the maker's name on the slowly spinning tape spool, the little rack of official signature stamps he would also one day possess if he rose to the highest office. His father's recorded voice was saying '*Only at the end of that long march will men be able to renew their links with one another,*' and Kao reached out quickly to switch off the tape machine.

"He's dead," said Chiang Ch'ing in a low voice. "He died at ten minutes past midnight. Our time has come."

19

A week later, standing on one of the ceremonial mourning platforms that had been erected around the base of the Monument to the People's Heroes, Kao did his best to hide his growing sense of anxiety. A few feet away, prominent among the crowd of Central Committee members and army leaders, he could see the stocky, determined figure of Marshal Lu Chiao. His uncle had avoided looking at him directly as they took their places, gazing instead at the great sea of human faces that filled the Square of Heavenly Peace. Like the other green-uniformed generals and marshals clustered around him, Chiao was conducting himself with an ominous aloofness that made Kao feel increasingly uneasy.

Before a bank of microphones on the top plinth of the monument, the rotund Party vice chairman, Hua Kuo-feng, was reading a sonorous eulogy from a typescript, but Kao was listening with only half his mind. His eyes strayed repeatedly to the bulkier, self-possessed figure of Marshal Yeh Chien-ying, the minister of defense, who stood at Hua's right shoulder. A white-haired, bespectacled veteran of the Long March, Marshal Yeh seemed to Kao to radiate the same quiet air of confidence as his uncle and the other military leaders, and a suspicion began to grow in Kao's mind that before a crowd of a million mourners, the military leaders might be attempting to make some kind of silent pledge about the future.

"The whole Party, the whole army, and the people of the whole country are immersed in boundless sorrow at the passing of Chairman Mao Tse-tung," intoned Hua, pausing to glance out over the vast crowd that had gathered under lowering gray skies. "It was under Chairman Mao's leadership that the disaster-plagued Chinese nation rose to its feet. That is why the Chinese people love, trust, and esteem Chairman Mao from the bottom of their hearts. . . ."

On Hua's left, with a dark veil draped over her head and shoulders, the chairman's widow stood alongside her closest supporters — an austere vice premier, the Party's chief propagandist, and the youthful Party general secretary. Dwarfed by the lavender granite memorial which reared above them, they bowed their heads in grief, and Kao noticed that all looked more frail physically than the aging soldiers ranged on Hua's right. Suddenly Kao felt a twinge of panic deep inside himself, and the words uttered by his uncle on the night of the earthquake echoed again through his mind: "You've been living on borrowed time for many years. I think perhaps that time's nearly run out now."

Above the square, red flags on all the tall public buildings drooped at half-mast in the gray light, and inside the main auditorium of the Great Hall of the People, the already embalmed corpse of Mao Tse-tung was still lying in state on a flag-draped catafalque. Hundreds of thousands of Chinese had filed past the body during the past week while the Politburo was holding heated meetings about who should succeed him, but each day when the official minutes and records of the discussions were returned to the Secretariat's offices, Kao found to his growing dismay that no satisfactory agreements about the new Party leadership had been reached. Fierce arguments had raged too about whether the chairman's body should be cremated or preserved in a public mausoleum, and even on this pressing problem no consensus had yet been achieved.

The uncertainty among the Party's leaders was reflected also in the country at large: almost daily, reports of disturbances continued to flow onto Kao's desk from provincial Party headquarters. The toll of earthquake casualties, which was still mounting, suggested that perhaps a million people had either died or been badly injured in the disaster. Beyond the Square of Heavenly Peace itself, the narrow, crumbling streets of old Peking were still littered with stacks of bricks, heaps of lime, and other building materials. Many homeless families were still camping on the pavements and roadsides beneath tarpaulins, and these makeshift arrangements were spawning more crime and other social disorders. Amid all these new strains, after many demanding months, Kao had begun to feel physically drained and worn out, and he often performed his duties like an automaton, not taking full account of what was going on around him.

". . . In honoring his great memory, we must never forget the cause of the proletarian revolution in China which Chairman Mao pioneered," said Hua, his unremarkable voice reverberating across the densely crowded square through hundreds of loudspeakers. "We must turn grief into strength, unite and not split. We must deepen the struggle to criticize Teng Hsiao-ping and repulse attempts by the right deviationists to reverse correct verdicts. We must always keep in mind Chairman Mao's warning: The bourgeoisie are still in the Communist Party. They'll never give up. They're still on the capitalist road. . . ."

Kao's spirits lightened on hearing the familiar references to themes central to the dead chairman's political philosophies. Their inclusion seemed to confirm that Vice Chairman Hua had not sold out after all to the confident-looking marshals. His fears, Kao told himself, were being magnified by the unrelenting stress of the past few weeks; the eulogy had suddenly made it quite clear that Comrade Chiang Ch'ing and her powerful supporters would win the battle for control of the Party and the nation.

When the address ended, the Party and army hierarchy led the multitude of people in an organized act of mass obeisance. Three times they bowed low in the direction of the giant thirty-foot colored portrait of Mao Tse-tung which hung permanently above the central arch in the Gate of Heavenly Peace. Kao joined in and the experience moved him deeply; a strong feeling of hope rose in him again, despite his weariness, and when a massed band of five hundred instruments accompanied the choir of a million voices in an emotional rendering of "The East Is Red," he added his voice to the mighty musical tide that engulfed the square. Singing the familiar words of the majestic anthem, Kao felt an oceanic sense of communion with the rest of the swaying throng all around him: "The East is red! The sun rises. . . . China has brought forth a Mao Tse-tung! . . . He is the people's great savior . . ."

This mystical feeling of communication with every single Chinese in the square persisted even after the ceremony ended, and Kao's mind remained dazed and distracted as he moved down from the stands toward the long line of gleaming Hung Ch'i limousines drawn up in front of the Great Hall. Feeling a light touch on his elbow, he turned in surprise to find his uncle beckoning him aside; Chiao's expression cautioned him to silence and with a gesture he indicated that Kao should follow him to his official car and join him in the rear-seat compartment.

"I wanted to give you one final warning," said Chiao bluntly, when he had closed the glass partition that isolated them from the army driver. "Soon decisive moves will be made. Force will almost certainly be used. Many people will be arrested. Because of the company you have chosen to keep, your name is among those on our list!"

The abruptness of Chiao's words startled Kao; then he gathered himself and summoned a humorless smile. "Perhaps you should be careful yourself, Uncle. Perhaps your name is on *our* list."

"I'm giving you this warning only because of my feelings for my sister," said the marshal in a hard voice. "Despite all the terrible suffering you allowed others to inflict on your mother, she still cares deeply for you and Ming in her strange, remote way. So heed this final warning."

"To do what, flee the country?"

"Fleeing the country will seem a very pleasant alternative when you discover what lies ahead for you and your friends."

"You're not in any position to threaten us, Uncle," said Kao coldly. "We're not entirely defenseless. There are forces whose loyalty we command."

"Don't be a fool," snapped Chiao. "Any support you have will crumble when the moment of decision comes. Millions of people hate and resent that man who lies dead in the Great Hall — because their loved ones were murdered and beaten and thrown into jail at his whim. But he'll never be discredited. Attacking him directly would undermine everything for which the People's Republic stands. So those who have aided and abetted him in his folly will have to bear the full force of the people's wrath. All I'm doing is giving you one last chance to save yourself from that."

"You seem to have decided against saving *yourself*, Uncle. But I can tell you in confidence that it is not too late for you even now. If you pledge your loyalty to the line of Chairman Mao and act accordingly, I'm authorized to say that the ministry of defense can be yours when new ministers are appointed."

"I'll try to give you half an hour's warning," said Chiao, ignoring the attempted bribe as though it had never been offered. "You will receive a telephone call giving the chairman's precise time of birth in astrological form, as though from an analyst of astrological charts. You'll then have thirty minutes to save your neck. It will be up to you. I wouldn't be able to face my sister again if I didn't at least offer you this small assistance."

"You seem to forget that Vice Chairman Hua attacked the 'capitalist road' clique again only a few minutes ago," said Kao sharply. "It's suddenly very clear who he's talking about."

"The vice chairman is playing for time," said Chiao dismissively and opened the door of the limousine, motioning for Kao to climb out. "That's all I have to tell you."

20

Jakob locked the door of his room on the second floor of the Peking Hotel and walked swiftly down the stairs to the lobby. A small Chinese saloon car with military markings was parked in front of the hotel entrance and he hurried outside to climb into one of its rear seats. The car, driven by a uniformed soldier, pulled out onto Chang An and turned eastward, then swung immediately into Wang Fu Ching, the capital's main shopping street. Jakob noticed that many of the buildings still had visible cracks in their facades and some were shored up by external wooden supports. Because of the late hour the street was almost deserted; the doors of the Peking Department Store, the East Wind Bazaar, and the New China Bookstore were locked and barred like those of the smaller shops, and he watched in puzzlement as the car turned into a dark, narrow lane to halt outside a grimy shop window displaying Chinese herbal remedies and traditional medicines.

The driver got out and opened the car door for Jakob without speaking, and after glancing both ways along the deserted lane, he took out a key and unlocked the door of the shop. Producing a small pocket flashlight, he ushered Jakob inside, locked the door behind them, and led the way between two narrow counters to a flight of steps leading down into a musty cellar. The mingled odors of fungus, spices, and dried roots assailed them as the soldier knelt to haul open a large ringed trapdoor in the old stone floor. Then he shone his flashlight on a flight of modern concrete steps and motioned Jakob impatiently ahead into a section of the city's underground defense network, where the air smelled stale and metallic. After unlocking a steel blast-proof door, they entered a lighted passageway, the roof and walls of which were coated with thick white plaster. As they hurried onward, they passed many side tunnels and clusters of signs pointing the way to grain stores, generating plants, armories, and medical stations, and Jakob found himself wondering at the sophistication of the tunnel complex about which he had previously heard only rumors.

Beyond a second steel door they climbed upward again, to a whitewashed, brick-lined passageway; here the driver halted outside a wooden door guarded by two army soldiers. After showing the sentries a pass, the driver opened the door, and when Jakob stepped inside he found Marshal Lu Chiao perched on the edge of a metal desk, dressed in camouflage battle fatigues. A steel helmet and a service pistol lay on the desk at his side, and the tense-faced marshal was in the act of putting down the telephone receiver into which he had been speaking.

"How can I help you?" he asked curtly, waving Jakob to a metal chair beside the desk. "Be brief, because I only have a few minutes at my disposal."

"I've been trying to find Kao," replied Jakob uncertainly, glancing from the steel helmet and pistol to the military maps fastened to the walls of what was obviously an underground command post. "I went straight to his home from the airport this evening. But his house is barely habitable and there's no sign of him or his son — that's why I took the liberty of delivering an urgent note to the Great Hall asking to see you."

"Kao hasn't lived there since the earthquake. He sleeps inside Chung Nan Hai most nights — close to his dearest political allies. Why have you come looking for him?"

Taken aback by the coldness of Chiao's manner and his unconcealed hostility toward Kao, Jakob stared at him in consternation. "I've been trying to get to Peking since the day of the earthquake. Abigail sent a cable saying Kao's wife had been killed. I was worried about them both — then later Abigail wrote saying she had seen Kao and he seemed very troubled . . ."

"Yes, Kao is certainly 'troubled.' Many other people are 'troubled' too. You can see now perhaps that you've come here at a bad time." Chiao broke off, glancing down meaningfully at the pistol on the desk. "Very serious steps are about to be taken — to put some of the trouble right. And Kao, I'm afraid, will be one of those to suffer."

"But can't you do anything to help him?" asked Jakob in a horrified voice.

"For Mei-ling's sake I've already tried to help him. I warned him his only choice was to leave China. But he refuses to listen. . . ."

"But why only for Mei-ling's sake, Chiao? He's your nephew."

Chiao stared fixedly at Jakob. "You're his father and I couldn't tell you this before. But Kao doesn't deserve any help from me — or anybody else. Kao is responsible for what happened to his mother. For reasons best known to himself he let her suffer a second time in Shanghai, just after he had ordered her to be freed. About that time he turned on me too, in Peking. I suspect he organized my 'arrest.' And he personally supervised the Red Guards at my 'trial' in the Workers' Stadium. . . ."

The shock of Chiao's revelation caused Jakob to close his eyes as though in pain. The terrible acts of betrayal against Mei-ling and Chiao had clearly followed close on his own traumatic meeting with Kao in Shanghai, and the realization that these events must have been connected seemed almost unbearable.

"Kao was not the only one who behaved that way," continued Chiao grimly. "The Cultural Revolution produced intolerable pressures for a lot of people. And it brought out the worst in some. Too many betrayed their relatives and friends in the heat of the moment for selfish personal reasons — and have lived to regret it."

"I still feel it's my duty to try to do something for Kao," said Jakob in a haunted voice. "Can't you help me in any way?"

"You must be aware that I've already accorded you far greater privileges than is wise in bringing you here at this time. It goes without saying that you must respect all confidences I've shared with you."

"I won't betray the trust you've placed in me," said Jakob quickly. "You can rely on that absolutely."

Chiao glanced at his wristwatch. "I told Kao I would try to give him half an hour's warning when the time came. I'll keep my word and call him as soon as you've gone."

"But where will he go?" asked Jakob desperately. "How will I find him?"

"Where he goes will be his choice. I've done all I can. Much greater things are at stake now." Chiao stood up impatiently and shook Jakob's hand. "The driver will take you back to where he collected you. I wish you luck in your efforts to help your son."

21

As soon as the sound of Jakob's retreating footsteps died away in the corridor outside, Chiao picked up the telephone and asked for a number. When a voice came on the line he enunciated his words with exaggerated clarity.

"Listen carefully," he said, "tell Comrade Chen Kao that Chairman Mao was born at the hour of the dragon, on the day of the scarlet cockerel, in the month of the green mouse, during the year of the black snake."

As soon as he had spoken, the marshal dropped the receiver onto its cradle and fastened the pistol into a holster on his belt. Jamming the helmet on his head, he hurried from the office and descended several flights of steps into a cavernous underground assembly point where half a dozen fully armed companies of the elite 8341 Security Unit were drawn up beside lines of waiting jeeps and armored personnel carriers. Handpicked from other PLA units for their strength and agility and given rigorous commando training from the first day of recruitment, the troops who permanently guarded the Party leadership wore steel helmets, camouflage battle dress, and rubber-soled boots. They carried either British-made Sten guns or light 9-mm Chinese assault weapons and some had ropes and grappling hooks slung about their chests. Stepping up into the back of his command jeep, Chiao pushed his own helmet back on his head and surveyed the force with a critical gaze.

"This, comrades, will be the most important operation you've ever carried out," he said, watching aides distribute packets of photographs to the company and platoon commanders. "All of you here have distinguished yourselves over many years acting as loyal bodyguards to Premier Chou. And Premier Chou would have approved heartily of today's action if he were still alive because it will open the way for the return to power of the man Premier Chou selected to carry on his policies. . . . So far the special training you've received for this task has been directed at anonymous targets. But the photographs now in your possession will enable every one of you to identify the targets clearly. Look at them!"

Chiao watched the commanders closely as they opened the packages and scrutinized the photographic portraits of the four top Party leaders who had stood at Hua Kuo-feng's left hand on the Monument to the People's Heroes nearly three weeks earlier. First among them was the familiar bespectacled countenance of the widow of Chairman Mao, but the training of the elite force stood them in good stead and no exclamations of surprise passed their lips. Additional packets of smaller photographs portrayed cadres loyal to the four leaders, who were also to be arrested, and Chiao caught a glimpse of Kao's handsome, confident face as a platoon commander standing near the command jeep shuffled through his selection.

"Your political instructors have been given strict orders, comrades, that they must try by word of mouth to persuade defending bodyguard units to surrender," continued Chiao, glancing quickly at his watch. "A bloodless victory is our aim. But if that isn't possible, although the defenders are your comrades and fellow countrymen, you must fight ruthlessly until they are overcome. Is that clearly understood?"

An instant shout of acknowledgment echoed around the underground assembly point.

"Good!" Chiao hesitated, and a pensive expression flitted across his face. "Forty years ago, comrades, I was given the honor and privilege of commanding the special assault force which attacked the Luting bridge. The troops who volunteered for that dangerous task were all fine young men like you. The future of the whole revolution was at stake then. If they'd failed, the Red Army might have been driven into the wilderness of Tibet or destroyed completely. But they didn't fail — and neither will you. In this special operation you will arrest four dangerous leaders of the Communist Party who have betrayed their trust. So this moment is as important in our history as the battle for Luting. If this gang of anti-Party traitors is not arrested, they'll undo all Premier Chou's painstaking work and drag the revolution down the path to destruction and catastrophe."

Chiao gazed pointedly around at each company in turn, looking directly into the faces of individual men. "So don't flinch from your duty, comrades! If bodyguard soldiers or other armed supporters try to protect the traitors, you'll shoot to kill. But the four main prisoners themselves must be taken alive and unharmed." Chiao raised his voice to a shout. "That's all. Good luck, comrades! Long live the revolution!"

Engines roared into life and the assembly point filled with noise as the men leapt into their vehicles. Chiao, although slightly stiff in his movements, moved quickly to the front passenger seat of the command jeep. A bright gleam had entered his tired eyes and he gave the signal to advance with a flourish of his hand. One by one the four separate convoys followed his speeding jeep up a sloping ramp into the underground labyrinth beneath Peking. Driving nose to tail behind him along the broad tunnel running beneath Chang An Boulevard, the vehicles of the special task force roared through the darkness toward the fortified Chung Nan Hai compound with their headlights blazing.

22

Kao heard the roar of the troop convoy approaching as he ran panting through the darkness of a narrow side tunnel leading down beneath the gardens of a fortified villa in Peking's western suburbs. Then the glow of the convoy's headlights probing along the main trunk tunnel began to brighten the darkness ahead of him and he stumbled to a halt, breathing raggedly. A side pocket of his cadre's tunic bulged with the unfamiliar weight of a service revolver which he had issued to himself from a secret Party armory a week earlier, and he took it in his right hand as he shone his flashlight desperately over the rocky walls of the shaft which linked the villa with the trunk tunnel.

As the sound of the engines grew louder, indecision held him rigid. He doubted whether he could reach the main tunnel without running into the arms of the approaching troops, but if he returned to the villa it seemed equally certain he would be trapped there. The side tunnel was the only underground entrance to the villa's heavily guarded garden, and although the beam of his flashlight revealed that there were some natural niches in the rock through which the tunnel had been driven, he could see they would barely afford sufficient cover if one of the advancing soldiers shone a light directly into them.

At the mouth of the side tunnel he could hear the sound of vehicles sliding to a halt on the gritty road; one by one their engines were switched off and he realized then he no longer had any choice. The quiet drum of rubber-soled boots on the ground indicated that the troops were disembarking and Kao switched off his flashlight and dropped into a crouch in the deepest niche. For a minute or more nothing happened — no lights appeared in the side tunnel and a curious silence fell in the subterranean passages, broken only by a quiet murmur of one distant voice which Kao guessed belonged to the troop commander.

As he waited, his heart thudding inside his chest, Kao tried to imagine what might be happening at the villa, which the chairman's widow had some months ago turned into her own fortified retreat. Ten minutes earlier he had been embroiled with her and half a dozen other Party aides in an acrimonious discussion on why, despite repeated promises, no military support from the northeast had yet materialized. Constant telephone calls had produced only elaborate excuses and deepening confusion, tempers had become frayed, and there had been angry exchanges around the conference table. Just after midnight one of his assistants had discreetly slipped Kao a written note of the anonymous telephone message about the hour of the dragon and the day of the scarlet cockerel, and to his astonishment he had at once experienced a great surge of relief. The assistant had jotted down the precise time of the message's arrival, and on noticing that it was already twenty minutes old, Kao had excused himself and slipped out immediately into the darkened garden, carrying a document case in which he had concealed the flashlight and the revolver. The usual platoon of armed sentries was on patrol and he had been forced to make a pretense of taking a relaxing stroll until he could reach the concealed steel door that protected the tunnel entrance. To his dismay, he found that the lock had become rusty with disuse, and by the time he wrenched it open he was sweating profusely in his anxiety; then, in trying to run too fast along the uneven tunnel floor, he had fallen heavily, and when he heard the noise of the approaching troop convoy halfway down the tunnel, it had come as little surprise.

As he crouched in the inky darkness of the niche, inhaling the damp, primal smell of the rocky earth, Kao became more forcibly aware than ever before of the desperate mental and physical weariness which he had been fighting against during the past few weeks. Having suddenly released his hold on the fading hopes and ambitions which had previously sustained him, he felt his remaining energy ebbing from him. With the suddenness of air rushing into a vacuum, his mind was filled with the sickening realization which he had been struggling to hold at bay since his last meeting with Abigail: for a long time, perhaps for most of his life, he had been living a monstrous pretense. Outwardly devoted to high-principled revolutionary ideals, he knew now that deep inside himself he had never really believed in anything. In embracing the empty rhetoric of class struggle he had turned his back brutally on his mother and uncle and helped cause untold suffering to countless others. Always the promise of future benefits had inspired him and those around him, but on seeing their ambitions founder amid an unseemly scramble for personal power, the lie had been given to their empty beliefs. Accepting these truths was intensely agonizing and when at last he heard the muffled sound of footsteps approaching and a shaded light appeared, he found his distracted mind welcoming the prospect of release from the endless tension of recent weeks.

Watching the booted feet of the first few soldiers passing within a few inches of his face, he felt a strange sense of detachment, not caring whether he was found or not. Holding their light submachine guns at the ready, the troops were moving rapidly forward, peering watchfully into the darkness. Some of them were scanning the sides of the tunnel as they advanced and Kao waited numbly for a shout or the sound of a shot to signal that he had been discovered.

A slower-moving pair of feet approached, hesitated, and finally stopped beside him. A light shone down directly onto his face and he blinked helplessly in its glare. But instead of the expected exclamation of surprise, the light was swung quickly away. The booted feet, however, did not move on; they merely turned so that the stitched heels were close before Kao's eyes instead of the toe caps. Then the legs in them pushed hard against Kao and he realized their owner was pressing his back against the tunnel wall so that the soldiers could brush past. In doing so, he was shielding Kao effectively from their sight and he stayed there without moving.

"Come on, comrades," called Marshal Lu Chiao several times in a fierce whisper. "Keep moving! Keep moving!"

Kao saw Chiao wave one arm rapidly in a circle to speed up the burly men crowding along the low-roofed tunnel, but he remained stationary himself and continued to cover the niche with his body until the last of them had hurried past. Then, without speaking or turning to look behind him, he hurried after them.

A moment or two later, Kao heard several rapid bursts of automatic-weapons fire from the head of the tunnel and confused shouts rang out from the garden above. More prolonged firing followed and after listening for a moment or two, Kao pulled himself wearily to his feet and stumbled away in the opposite direction.

23

Jakob ran up the stairs of Abigail's apartment block and knocked breathlessly on her door. No sound of movement came from inside and he glanced quickly at his wristwatch; he had made two previous visits without getting any response and now it was almost one A.M. He knocked again without much hope, gazing around the landing at the temporary steel supports which had been wedged in place to strengthen the damaged staircase. The sight of the ugly structural cracks left by the earthquake only served to heighten his growing sense of anxiety and he knocked pointlessly on the closed door once more.

"I think Miss Kellner is away," said a female voice tentatively, and Jakob turned to find that the door of the adjoining apartment had opened. The dark-haired Polish girl whom Abigail had rescued during the earthquake was wearing a dressing gown over her night-clothes and she looked as if she had been wakened by his knocking.

"Do you know where she's gone?" asked Jakob in a dismayed voice. "I'm her father. I've just arrived in Peking unexpectedly."

"She's gone to Tientsin to give a special course of instruction to Chinese teachers. I think she'll be away several days. But I'll give her a message when she returns, if you wish."

"Thank you." Jakob took out his wallet and quickly jotted the name and telephone number of his hotel on a business card. "Please ask her to call me as soon as she returns."

Jakob apologized profusely for disturbing the girl, then hurried down the stairs to his waiting taxi and asked the driver to take him again to Nan Chihtze. He had returned to Kao's address earlier only to find the partly rebuilt house as empty and deserted as on his first visit. He had no real expectation of finding anyone there in the middle of the night, but his anxiety had reached such a pitch that he felt compelled to make another effort, however futile, to locate Kao.

As the taxi headed eastward Jakob peered uneasily out through its windows, searching for signs of tension. Gray-uniformed militiamen carrying staves were patrolling visibly in pairs in the side streets where some families still slept under open-sided tarpaulin awnings, and an occasional covered army truck drove swiftly along Chang An, carrying apparently unarmed troops. Once or twice he saw military jeeps scurrying across distant intersections, but there was no other outward indication of any unseen struggle taking place and Jakob's feeling of helplessness became almost suffocating.

At Nan Chihtze, Kao's house still stood dark and unattended and there was no reply to his knocking. He wandered irresolutely around the shadowy courtyard for several minutes; then, baffled and at a loss, he returned to the hotel and stretched out fully dressed on his bed. But he could not sleep, and every time he heard a vehicle moving in Chang An, he rose and hurried to the window to look out. At about four A.M. he watched a curtained military car race westward past the hotel at high speed and he stared after it dully, listening to the sound of its engine dying away in the distance. When silence returned to the small room again, the waiting became unbearable and he snatched up his topcoat and strode toward the door, even though he had no idea of what he might do or where he might go. In that instant a tiny shutter seemed to open subliminally in his mind, revealing a fleeting image that was gone before he could fully identify it. He stopped in midstride and stared at the blank wall of the room, certain suddenly of where he must go and astonished that he had not thought of it before.

Opening his bedroom door quietly, he hurried to the rear stairs and, after descending to the ground floor, made his way silently through the darkness of the hotel grounds to a side street. Walking rapidly, he hurried to Wang Fu Ching, then turned north in the direction of the old Joint Missionary Language School.

24

"E*verything reactionary is the same*," whispered Mei-ling in her soft, faraway voice. "*If you don't hit it, it won't fall!*"

Although dawn was only just breaking outside the window, she was already fully dressed and seated on her lonely chair in the middle of the room. Her face was tranquil and composed, her hair impeccably dressed in neat twin braids, and in the half-light, with her smooth face turned toward the window as usual, she looked more than ever like a young girl.

Standing inside the closed door of her room, Kao swayed slightly on his feet as he looked at her. His hair was disheveled and there was a trickle of dried blood on his face where he had struck his head when falling in the tunnel leading down from the villa. His cadre's tunic was covered in dust and crumpled from the hour or two of sleep he had snatched hidden among the sacks of grain in one of the underground granaries — but his strange appearance had made no noticeable impression on his mother.

When he let himself quietly into her room she had not even turned her head; he had stood there, dizzy with fatigue, for two or three minutes but she had only murmured occasional meaningless quotations, as she would have done if the room had been empty.

"Mother, it's Kao," he said in a voice that was little more than a croak. "It's finished for me. It's all over."

Although there was a faint sound in the corridor outside the door, he took no notice, for he no longer cared whether anybody overheard him or not. The sense of release from lifelong pretense, which he had experienced in the tunnel, had left him with a curiously excited, light-headed feeling. On arrival at the front door, the staff had tried to prevent him from entering and he had realized vaguely that they must be alarmed by his appearance; but because of a strange new inner certainty that he no longer needed to worry about the future, he had made open threats about what wrath would fall upon the asylum from the Party headquarters if they denied him entry to see his mother, and the duty doctors had reluctantly allowed him in.

"Don't you understand what I said, Mother? It's all over. My career in the Party is finished! Many people have been arrested in the night. My name was on the list — but Uncle Chiao helped me get away." He took a tentative step toward her, then stopped when he saw her lips begin to move.

"Rebellion is justified." She said it very softly once, and repeated it in a slightly louder voice. *"Rebellion is justified!"*

"You don't need to worry anymore about Ming," whispered Kao, moving nearer and reaching out a hand toward his mother. "He'll be all right. Abigail saved him. Do you remember her?" Kao's face suddenly crumpled and he fell to his knees beside Mei-ling, burying his face in her lap. His shoulders shook with a fit of silent sobbing and he had difficulty controlling his speech. "I-ping was killed — but Ming wasn't even hurt. You really don't need to worry about him anymore. . . . I wrote notes an hour ago. . . ."

Very slowly Mei-ling lifted one hand and began gently to stroke the head of her weeping son. In his distress he seemed at first not to notice; when he did realize what was happening, he straightened up, staring at her in puzzlement. But still her eyes gazed ahead, blank and unseeing, and as he looked at her she began to speak again in the same faint, faraway voice.

"Bombard the headquarters! Bombard the headquarters! Bombard the headquarters! . . ."

In the growing light he could see her face more clearly and the terrible emptiness of her expression as she repeated the old slogans over and over again became suddenly unbearable to him.

"I'm sorry, I'm sorry," he gasped, seizing her hand and pressing it against his cheek. "I'm sorry for all the terrible suffering I've caused you. . . ."

For a long moment the only sound in the room was his sobbing. Then Mei-ling began murmuring once more.

"Rebellion is justified! . . . *Rebellion is justified!* . . ."

Kao raised his head slowly to stare at her again and a look of unendurable agony came into his eyes. "I'm going to help you!" he said in a despairing voice, and he fumbled at one of the lower pockets of his tunic. "I didn't help you before — but now I can help us both!"

The long-barreled revolver snagged in the lining of his pocket as he tried to tug it free, but Mei-ling took no notice. She continued to repeat the slogan in the same sibilant whisper, seemingly oblivious to his presence. Even when he was holding the revolver out at arm's length, pointing the muzzle waveringly at her chest, she still gave no sign she was aware of what was happening. Kao was sobbing as he squeezed the trigger, and his arm jerked wildly with the shock of the discharge, but he squirmed quickly into a new position on his knees and pressed the muzzle to his own head to fire a second time.

Jakob was running frantically along the corridor, followed by two male nurses, when the first shot rang out, and they heard the second as Jakob threw open the door. In the moment of silence that followed the deafening reports of the revolver, the voice of Mei-ling, fainter than before, repeated the simple three-word slogan.

"Rebellion is justified! . . . Rebellion is justified!"

Jakob and the two nurses watched in horror as Kao's body unfolded to stretch itself full-length on the floor. Mei-ling slipped slowly down from the chair to her knees, and for a moment she seemed to bend solicitously over her son, still whispering the slogan. Then she fell sideways onto him and lay still.

The two nurses started to push past Jakob but he stretched out an arm to stop them and moved forward a pace or two until he was standing over Kao and Mei-ling. Then, for the first time in many years, he bowed his head and raised his hands in front of him in an attitude of prayer.

"Almighty God," he whispered shakily in Chinese, "bless the souls of those who have departed this life here in anguish. . . . Let there now be an end to their suffering, forgive all of us our transgressions, and grant that we may at last find eternal peace through thy grace. . . . Amen."

The sound of running footsteps filled the corridor behind him and Jakob let his hands fall to his sides and opened his eyes. He stared down at the tangled bodies for only a moment or two, then turned away and walked blindly from the room.

25

As dusk fell a week later Jakob stood sadly at the open window of his hotel room watching long, noisy columns of Chinese demonstrators flowing along Peking's broad central avenue toward Tien An Men Square. Marching behind dense thickets of giant red flags, they were shouting slogans condemning the "Gang of Four Anti-Party Traitors" and waving adulatory color portraits of Mao Tse-tung above their heads. The familiar pictures of Mao contrasted sharply with the few insulting images the marchers carried of the wife who had survived him; here and there skillfully drawn cartoon placards bobbed above the throng, depicting Chiang Ch'ing and her supporters as poisonous serpents, spiders, and scorpions, and invariably the ugly caricatures were being crushed by the fists and boots of the Chinese masses.

The sudden appearance of demonstrators in the streets earlier that day had not surprised Jakob. He had first seen small parades of schoolchildren setting out for the city center at around midday while he was walking distractedly in the southern suburbs. During the week he had spent awaiting Abigail's return to Peking, he had nursed his grief privately in endless walks at the Summer Palace, the Temple of Heaven, and other quarters of the city. At the few embassy social gatherings he had attended, rumors about a massive purge in the Party leadership had been the sole topic of conversation, but because of the grief he concealed within himself, he had never offered any comment on the rumors; whatever the details, they seemed of little significance compared with his own overwhelming personal sense of loss.

The first groups of young marchers that he saw that morning had carried placards denouncing four unnamed leaders for "attempting to usurp state and Party power"; then, as the day wore on and the demonstrations had grown in size, new banners had appeared naming the Gang of Four. Now, with hundreds of thousands of people marching and countermarching in the streets, curbside loudspeakers were repeatedly trumpeting and vilifying the names of Chiang Ch'ing, a leading vice premier, the Party's general secretary, and its propaganda chief. Most of the marching columns passing below the hotel window were accompanied by groups beating drums, cymbals, and gongs in a cacophonous frenzy, and as he watched them, lost in his own forlorn thoughts, Jakob became aware only gradually that his telephone was ringing persistently on the table beside his bed. When he crossed the room to answer it, he had difficulty hearing above the noise of the passing demonstration, but on recognizing Abigail's voice he hurriedly closed his window.

"I'm very glad to hear you at last," he said awkwardly. "I've been here a week."

"I've just come in and seen your note," said Abigail, sounding equally awkward. "I got back from Tientsin this afternoon — because of the demonstrations it took forever to get to my office and back. . . ."

Jakob hesitated, trying to find a way of preparing her for what he was about to reveal; then he realized there was nothing he could say that would soften the blow. "I'm sorry to break it to you like this, Abigail, but I have some bad news."

"What is it?"

"I'm afraid Kao and Mei-ling are both dead. . . ."

Jakob heard Abigail draw in her breath sharply. "How did it happen?"

"It's rather complicated . . ."

There was a long silence at the other end of the telephone as Abigail struggled to come to terms with the news. "Has it anything to do with what I can see going on in the streets?" she asked at last.

"Yes, I'm afraid it has."

Another silence followed before Abigail spoke again in a puzzled voice. "Then perhaps that might help explain something else."

"What do you mean?" asked Jakob.

"There was another note waiting for me here when I got back. I don't know who it's from. It's very badly written. It just asks me to go to Kao's house as soon as I possibly can." Abigail paused again and her tone became apprehensive. "What do you think it can mean?"

"I don't know . . . ," said Jakob. "I'm rather in the dark. I'm waiting for Marshal Lu to respond to a request to see him that I made nearly a week ago. . . . What are you intending to do about the note?"

"I was thinking of going there straightaway."

"And will you?"

"Yes, I think I shall. . . . " Abigail hesitated. "Will you meet me there, Daddy?"

"Yes, of course."

"In half an hour from now?"

"Yes."

When Jakob put down the telephone he found his hand was shaking. He decided to shower and change his clothes, and because the marching throngs were jamming the traffic, on reaching the street he realized he would have to walk to Nan Chihtze. Dense crowds were strolling beneath the trees of An Chang, watching the demonstrations, and as he came in sight of Tien An Men Square, thousands of electric light bulbs outlining the curved golden roofs of the Gate of Heavenly Peace, the Great Hall of the People, and other public buildings suddenly shimmered into life. These decorative skeins of light, he knew, were usually switched on only for National Day and May Day and their unexpected illumination at once gave the political demonstrations a jamboree atmosphere. Jakob noticed too that new groups of demonstrators seemed to be spontaneously joining the marching students and school-age children who had been parading throughout the day; homeward-bound factory workers, truckloads of peasants from the countryside, hospital workers still wearing their white smocks and hats, and even uniformed cadres from government offices were pushing in among the demonstrating columns and swinging along smilingly in a relaxed, celebratory mood.

When Jakob reached Nan Chihtze, however, the scene changed abruptly — the demonstrators were avoiding the shadowy, dimly lit street because it was still partially blocked with building materials. In the growing darkness ahead of him Jakob saw a pedicab weaving between the heaps of bricks and building lime, coming from the opposite direction. When it stopped outside Kao's house he saw the unmistakable blond-haired figure of his daughter climb out and pay the driver, and she stood waiting tensely at the pavement edge for him as he approached.

"Let's find out what it's about straightaway," she said quickly, before he could greet her, and she led the way through the gateway in the newly built courtyard wall. They had to step around piles of rubble which still dotted the courtyard and they noticed in the feeble glow of the streetlights that a large part of the house was still under repair. A section of the roof remained open to the sky, but there was a light behind one curtained window and Jakob knocked gently on the closed door. Almost at once there was a sound of movement and the door swung open to reveal the old, sad-faced Chinese woman with gray hair whom Abigail had seen crouching amid the debris on the night of the earthquake.

"Are you Miss Abigail Kellner?" asked the old woman tentatively in Chinese before they could speak.

"Yes," said Abigail. "Did you send the note asking me to come?"

The woman nodded slowly. "I am Chen Ming's amah. I've been caring for him since the earthquake." As she spoke Ming appeared at her side and clutched her hand. The old amah looked down at him and Abigail saw tears well up in her tired eyes.

"He doesn't understand . . . his father and his grand-mother . . . there was a terrible accident."

"Yes, I've heard." Abigail dropped to her knees and gently took the boy's hand in hers. "Hello, Ming. I once sent you a panda. Did you like it?"

Ming stared blankly back at her without answering; then, abruptly, he tugged his hand free and turned and ran back into the house. When Abigail stood up again, silent tears were streaming down the shriveled cheeks of the amah, and Abigail saw that she was holding an envelope toward her in a shaking hand.

"This is for you — from Kao. It arrived after he died. He sent a note asking me to call you here."

Abigail glanced around at Jakob before tearing open the envelope. Because of the gathering darkness she had to move toward the light of the street lamp to decipher the few lines of Chinese characters that had been written, seemingly with haste, on a single sheet of paper. When she had finished, she turned and handed the note wordlessly to Jakob. It read:

Dear Abigail,

Please, will you care for Ming? The revolution and I have both failed him. Look after him here or take him to live with you and my father in Hong Kong, whichever you wish. My father, I've realized, is a good man. Please educate and bring up Ming between you as you both think fit. If it's wise, let him return to China sometime in the future. I know that I have greatly dishonored my mother and my true father. I'm deeply ashamed.

Thank you.

Kao

When he lifted his eyes from the letter, Jakob found the old amah gazing fixedly at them. "I'm too old now," she whispered. "Will you take the boy?"

He saw then that Ming had returned to the doorway with the toy panda Abigail had bought for him hanging from his hand. Grime and dust had discolored its fur and it was obvious that the toy too had been buried in the earthquake rubble. The boy was looking up at them, his dark eyes unblinking, and Jakob bent quickly to take him up in his arms.

"A long time ago, Kao's mother saved my daughter's life," he said quietly to the old amah. "So we would be more than happy to have the chance to care for Ming."

Turning to look at Abigail, he slipped an arm around her shoulders. "Do you agree?"

Although Abigail was smiling at him, tears appeared suddenly in her eyes. "Of course. I'm sure it's the right thing to do."

Epilogue

1978

From his seat at the table around which the reorganized Politburo of the Communist Party of China was gathered in the Great Hall of the People, Marshal Lu Chiao could see through the windows the new multipillared mausoleum of granite and marble that now dominated the Square of Heavenly Peace. A massive rectangular neoclassic structure, it covered an area the size of a small sports stadium in the heart of the square, but none of the Politburo members listening to an address by the squat, determined-looking Szechuanese who had recently been restored to his post as general secretary of the Party spared the new structure a glance.

Inside the mausoleum's lofty central chamber, the embalmed body of Mao Tse-tung lay on display in a flood-lit crystal casket; partially draped in a red flag, the body always looked to Chiao like a waxen effigy that had never enjoyed the fullness of life. The shrine had already become a place of national pilgrimage, but the millions of Chinese who had filed through the mausoleum since it was opened nine months earlier often emerged, Chiao had noticed, looking bemused rather than inspired. Those who had suffered during the last two decades of torment that the dead man had inflicted on the country clearly found it difficult to appreciate the first thirty years of his leadership, when he had ingeniously conjured peasant armies out of nothing and led them to impossible victories that had sparked the most profound change in the nation's history.

"Reform is the key to solving China's many problems now," the Szechuanese was saying, speaking in the blunt manner with which all the men around the table had been familiar off and on for many years. "Class struggle has had its day. Now it must take a backseat. . . ."

Chiao watched Teng Hsiao-ping closely as he spoke. He had been curious to know whether the man who had been purged twice from the Party's highest ranks and come back successfully three times had suffered any loss of appetite for the grueling political task of governing a nation of nine hundred million people. Little more than five feet in height, with a broad, peasant face that in his early seventies still looked as tough as old leather, Teng seemed as though he had been strengthened by his periods of exile. Although Hua Kuo-feng remained nominally chairman and head of the Party, both men knew well enough who had the whip hand, and it was evident from his demeanor that the stocky, quick-striding Szechuanese who had served as a political commissar to the Red Cadres Regiment on the Long March had lost none of his zest for life's battle.

"Now before we do anything else we must bring the people some prosperity," continued Teng, his jaw jutting pugnaciously as he spoke. "A start must be made straightaway by reorganizing our agriculture and returning to a family system of farming. Urban industry and commerce will also need to be reformed. But we must proceed cautiously and carefully. Our ignorance, poverty, and backwardness all stem from China's isolation. We must open our minds to the outside world. . . ."

Around the table there was no sign of the widow of Mao Tse-tung or any of her supporters, to whom Teng's words would have been anathema. The Gang of Four were languishing in separate cells in a military prison a few miles from the Great Hall. For two years they had been undergoing constant interrogations by hard-eyed cadres who were preparing documents for a public criminal trial. The early top-secret drafts of the indictments that had passed across Chiao's desk had showed that the Gang of Four were likely to be accused of a series of crimes that laid responsibility at their door for more than thirty thousand political murders during the Cultural Revolution. Other documents Chiao had seen gave details of the persecution inflicted on nearly three quarters of a million people, and it seemed certain that supporters of the late Marshal Lin Piao, who had died mysteriously in 1971, were also to be tried alongside the Gang. The death penalty, the documents indicated, was likely to be called for in the case of all the ringleaders.

"All this," said Teng, lighting one of the many cigarettes he smoked each day, "will require the untiring efforts of several generations if China is to become a civilized, democratic, and modern socialist country. Above all, our policies must be determined by a crystalization of collective wisdom, not by any one individual. . . ."

Teng drew hard on his cigarette and turned to gaze reflectively at the stone mausoleum that glowed in the summer sunshine beyond the windows.

"Although we've built a splendid memorial to China's revolution out there, it's my view that any form of 'personality cult' among leaders of the Party should be outlawed from now on. We must put realism at the center of our thinking."

Several other Politburo members turned to follow the general secretary's gaze but Chiao continued to watch Teng. Clouds of smoke billowed around his shoulders as he drew with relish on his cigarette, sitting at ease in his chair. There was something reassuringly earth-bound about the diminutive Szechuanese, Chiao reflected. He seemed careless of his own dignity and apparently lacked all conceit. His famous aphorism that it didn't matter whether a cat were white or black so long as it caught mice summed up his open-minded approach to problems of every stripe. It was as easy to discuss with him the ancient and abstruse tenets of Taoism as it was to argue about modern Marxist theory, and Chiao had never encountered any rigid dogmatism in his thinking. Although it was not customary to discuss such matters, Chiao found it easy to imagine that, like himself, Teng might have drawn deeply from the well of China's ancient traditions in surviving ten harsh and debilitating years of political exile. He would, Chiao knew, dismiss any inquiry about such questions with an unfathomable quip; but there was something in his calm, unruffled demeanor which suggested that he was a man at peace with his inner self.

The dazzling sunshine in the square beyond the windows and the rare feeling of ease among those around the table was creating an almost drowsy sense of well-being in Chiao, and as he listened his thoughts drifted gently backward in time like a breeze-borne butterfly, lighting here and there on disconnected images of the past. He remembered his father adjusting his young limbs in the correct Taoist posture for meditation as they sat side by side at twilight under a tree in their southern courtyard. A caged songbird had trilled sweetly above their heads in the growing dusk when for the first time he felt his body become as light as a leaf. It was in that moment that he had first known himself, and the memory induced in him a deep sense of gratitude to his long-dead father: the ancient wisdom passed down to him had enabled him to cling tenaciously to life and principle during his direst hours. Paradoxically, in the next instant he remembered too the agony of watching his father close the barred door for the last time on his magnificent array of antique bronze, jade, and porcelain. But the sadness of that recollection gave way in turn to a feeling of pleasure as he saw again in his mind's eye the slender-necked Tang ewer that he had taken reverently in his hands on that last evening in the small museum. Its narrow spout had been fashioned in the shape of a phoenix, and he remembered the passion that had seized him as he held it out, telling his father how he yearned for China to rise, phoenixlike, from the ashes of its turmoil. Nearly fifty years had passed since then, but as Chiao listened to Teng's brusque, uncomplicated discourse a feeling that had recently been growing in him became an intuitive certainty: after much suffering, a long, terrible night was ending. A new China was at last rising from the old; many great difficulties still lay ahead, but a new dawn, he was sure, was beginning to break.

Postscript

At dawn on Easter Sunday, 1936, Alfred Bosshardt, to whom this novel is affectionately dedicated, was released from captivity by China's Red Army, near Kunming, in Yunnan province. He had trudged 2,500 miles as a prisoner of General Ho Lung's Second Front Army on the Long March. I was privileged to meet him for the first time in Manchester, England, in 1983 as I began to research the historical background to my story. A largely unsung hero, still living in Manchester in his ninety-first year, Alfred Bosshardt is the only surviving Westerner with firsthand experience of the Long March, and recollections that he has shared with me during numerous meetings in England and Switzerland provided many invaluable insights and much inspiration. Without his help, *Peking* could scarcely have been written in this form. A step-by-step account of his astonishing survival, dictated from his sickbed in Kunming, was published by his missionary organization in 1936 under the title *The Restraining Hand*. An abridged version of this can be found in a wider autobiography, published by Hodder and Stoughton in England in 1973, entitled *The Guiding Hand*. Both books are a moving testament to the faith that helped him survive. For his generosity and his friendship I owe Alfred Bosshardt a very special debt of gratitude.

I am also much indebted to Mr. Ray Smith of Wheaton, Illinois, whose late father, the Reverend Howard Smith, was serving as a pioneer missionary in western China in the year the Long March began. Howard Smith was taken prisoner in Szechuan — also by Ho Lung's Second Front Army — in May 1934 and was marched more than eight hundred miles in fifty-two days before making a dramatic escape. Ray Smith, then a very young child, and his mother were also captives for a few hours, and private accounts of these experiences, in addition to letters and photographs that Ray Smith was kind enough to show me provided another wonderfully clear perspective through history's murky haze.

Two other courageous American missionaries, a young married couple, were captured and tragically beheaded by Communist troops in Anhwei province in December 1934. An account of their ordeal is given in *The Triumph of John and Betty Stam*, by Mrs. Howard Taylor, published in Philadelphia in 1935. Their very young baby miraculously survived the ordeal, and echoes of this and other real experiences reverberate in my imaginary story. But none of the fictional characters in *Peking*, it should be emphasized, is meant to portray or represent any living person. In this connection I should also add that nobody should expect to find any sign of Chentai, Paoshan, or Sanmo on genuine maps of China — at least not in the places I have indicated. All three of these settlements are make-believe and exclusive to this story.

No book, I suspect, is ever entirely the work of one single individual, and my sincere thanks are due to several friends and specialists in the China field who offered vital encouragement and assistance with the writing of this novel. Sinologist Roderick MacFarquhar, former neighbor in London, onetime broadcasting colleague, and now professor of government and director of the John King Fairbank Center for East Asian Research at Harvard University, helped enormously by providing essential historical pointers and scouring his extensive private library for Long March memorabilia at the outset to get me launched on my lengthy narrative trek. Dick Wilson, former editor of *The China Quarterly* and author of many outstanding books on the Far East — including *The Long March 1935* — kindly made essential volumes available to me from his personal library. Broadcaster Joseph Hang-tai Yen was equally generous with precious books and time given to translating Chinese documents; Dr. Jung Chang, author of *Madame Sun Yat-sen*, illuminated early drafts with perspicacious comments; and Brian and Alison Senior willingly contributed their considerable background knowledge of Hong Kong. Also, Madame Nien Cheng, the brave author of *Life and Death in Shanghai*, which describes her own terrifying Cultural Revolution ordeal, helped personally to put that great city in perspective for me during the chaos of the late 1960s, and I salute and thank her most warmly.

In London, librarians at the School of Oriental and African Studies, the Royal Institute of International Affairs (and especially the staff of the institute's Press Cuttings Library), the British Library, and the London Library unfailingly rendered patient and painstaking help. Much essential material on the Long March (which, when it is out of print, is not always easy to obtain) emanates from the Foreign Languages Press, Peking. Among such publications are: *Stories of the Long March* (1960), which I first read during an enforced stay in Peking; *The Long March — Eyewitness Accounts* (1963); *On the Long March with Chairman Mao by Chen Chang-feng* (1972); *Recalling the Long March by Liu Po-cheng and Others* (1978); and *On the Long March As Guard to Chou En-lai by Wei Kuo-lu* (1978). Otto Braun, the luckless German Comintern adviser sent to China by Moscow, added a polemical dimension to the story by publishing *A Comintern Agent in China 1932–1939*, which contains some unique detail, and in 1985 Harrison E. Salisbury threw significant new light on the epic Communist migration after retracing much of the route personally. His book *The Long March — The Untold Story* includes many riveting interviews with aging Long March veterans — but all these publications provided important color and detail of a fascinating historical episode.

Trying to draw an orderly line through the disorder of China's revolution over the past seventy years or so is not easy: among the great lexicon of China books that helped me do this, Ross Terrill's perspicacious biography *Mao* stood out. Jonathan Spence's *Gate of Heavenly Peace*, which deals with the experiences of intellectuals during China's early revolutionary upheavals, also contains unique insights. Agnes Smedley's splendid biography of Chu Teh — *The Great Road* — and her descriptions of 1930s China in such volumes as *Chinese Destinies* and *Portraits of Chinese Women in Revolution* give invaluable firsthand impressions, which bring the period brilliantly to life. Robert Payne's books, particularly *Journey to Red China*, *China Awake*, and *A Rage for China*, also convey singular glimpses of China's revolutionary leaders. Similarly, Edgar Snow's writings, especially his classic *Red Star Over China*, along with Nym Wales's vivid Yenan biographies of the men and women who led the revolution — *Red Dust* — are seminal reading for anyone wishing to understand the long march to power of Communism in China. Three other books — Paul A. Cohen's *China and Christianity*, Christopher Hibbert's *The Dragon Wakes*, and Harry A. Franck's compendious *Roving Through*

Southern China — were wonderfully informative about China in transition from imperial to modern times. For more recent events, Rod MacFarquhar's three-volume work, *The Origins of the Cultural Revolution*, details the slow-burning development of the cataclysm with unmatched authority.

In another dimension, an indefatigable but ever-youthful veteran of many long literary campaigns, my Boston editor, William D. Phillips, made as great a contribution to this novel as he did to *Saigon* — which was very considerable indeed; in London, Victoria Petrie-Hay also gave sustained and valuable editorial assistance. Susan Stewart typed and word-processed the last of three books for me with typical speed and efficiency before going off to become Susan Poulson — she is already greatly missed; Brian McVay and Kenneth Brown provided research assistance that turned out to be vital, as did Simon and Liz Woodside; and others who gave generously of their time and expertise include Ged Lavery, Senator the Reverend Peter Manton of Jersey, Christopher Manton, and Chinese friends Sun Shyi-ren, Tseng Yung-kwang, Yang Sy-kung, and Wang Chih-fa. I'm indebted in different ways also to staunch friends Vergil Berger, Ian Macdowall, Kim Davenport, David Alexander, Bob Wareham, and Geoffrey Smyth. In Peking I learned important lessons about the kinder side of human nature — which I hope are reflected in some ways in these pages — from "Hsiao" Kao, "Lao" Chiao (since deceased), "Lao" Wang, and Mrs. Hou. I take this belated opportunity to express my thanks with all sincerity. The nearest and dearest of my helpmates, Shirley Grey, again played a central and indispensable role in bringing this book to fruition, reading, advising, evaluating, and encouraging at every step taken through successive drafts of the six-thousand-mile manuscript.

Kind encouragement and guidance were also offered by Professor Chang Lit-sen, now of Lexington, Massachusetts. Professor Chang, a church minister and author of more than a hundred publications on Chinese law, politics, and religion, made me aware of one of the most intriguing minor facts to emerge from three years of research. In June 1978, in Toronto, Dr. Chang baptized as a Christian one of the cofounders with Mao Tse-tung of China's Communist Party. He was Chang Kuo-tao, the forceful general who had headed the Fourth Front Army and challenged Mao head-on for the leadership of the Communist movement at Fupien during a crucial stage of the Long March in the far west. General Chang, who defected to the Kuo-

mintang in 1938 after being worsted in the power struggle, called
Dr. Chang to Toronto specially to carry out the baptism — and died
a Christian believer in Canada a few months later.

London, Spring 1988

DAYS OF DESTINY

CROSSROADS IN AMERICAN HISTORY